# Our Choice:
## Freedom or Obedience

# Also By Eric Rice

America at the Brink series
*What Can One Man Do?*
*The Cost of Standing Up*
*Whatever it Takes to Win*

# Our Choice:
## Freedom or Obedience

America at the Brink

(Nick Turner, Book Two)


# Eric Rice

Copyright © 2024 by Eric Rice
Published by Mount Seven LLC
ISBN-13: 978-1-958706-12-1
All rights reserved, including the right to reproduce this book or portions thereof in any form whatsoever.
Cover Art Design by Milos Jevremovic
First Edition, March 2024

# Dedication

To my parents James and Elizabeth, who instilled in me and my six brothers' self-reliance. They gave us the good solid. One grounded in work ethic and curiosity. Leading by example and giving us the freedom to make our own choices. It was an idyllic American childhood. Free from want, but without frills. Importantly, we were taught how to think for ourselves and to challenge others with facts. Growing up, everything was a debate. I am sure there were times they regretted giving us both skills and opportunities we used to question everything. Thank you for giving us just what we needed and nothing we did not. Sadly, this type of childhood is a relic of the past. Never allowed to be experienced again by our society or within our country. I cherish these memories.

# Introduction

Sitting at my desk, I arranged the papers and books I'd refer to during the lecture. Nodding to the technician, I looked up into the camera. The blinking red light showed we were now recording.

"Welcome. I'm pleased you've enrolled in this series. I hope you enjoyed the first episode, which I published as *What Can One Man Do?*. Today we'll start the second, continuing to tell the saga of Nick Turner. As this is a virtual lecture, I'm unable to see your faces or guess your ages. For some of you, this is indeed a history lesson. For others, it is 'the rest of the story'. There are many things you don't know about the events that led us to where we are now, near the middle of the twenty-first century."

"I'm privileged to have played a minor role in these events. For those of you who lived through, or perhaps even had your own part in these, you'll recall there was no singular incident. No Pearl Harbor or 9/11. Decades of actions, results, and their unintended consequences served as a catalyst for what happened."

"Rather than present this as dry non-fiction, this story lends itself best to dramatic form. Like Homer's Iliad and Odyssey, this epic history is full of heroes and monsters, impossible situations, harrowing escapes, stories of love, honor, sacrifice, triumph and tragedy."

"History is both a window into the past and a telescope into the future. If only we'd been blessed with better and more humble leaders. Ones who understood this history and learned from it to avoid past mistakes. Perhaps none of this sacrifice, pain, and suffering would have been necessary. Then again, we are human. Human nature is such that we always believe we're smarter or better than those before us. Sadly, this was catastrophically wrong."

"With that, let us begin with a quick recap of book one. *What Can One Man Do?* introduced Nick Turner, the junior senator from Colorado.

Appointed to fill out the remaining term of a senator who died. A popular hero, his role in the senate was to be seen, not heard. To vote with the Party leadership without question."

"We saw how Nick struggled with the dysfunction of Washington. Seeing elected representatives promise one thing to the people and then vote the opposite. No longer fearing repercussions from the frustrated and increasingly powerless voters. Having never aspired to office, Nick could resist the siren song of Washington, neither selling out his constituents, his integrity, nor his soul."

"Having no desire to continue as a senator in this government, he dared to disobey the Party leaders, as they worked to remove the legislative filibuster. This was the last remaining Constitutional check against unrestrained Congressional majorities ruling against the people's will. By chance of fate, his vote became the deciding factor in either preserving the Constitution or removing it from relevance."

"Nick's moment of triumph is short-lived. Through nefarious deeds and utter contempt for life, the Party leaders overcame his effort, ultimately removing the filibuster. Their actions proved to Nick his instincts were correct. Because of his betrayal, Party leadership and their allies in the media relentlessly smear him, even blaming him for the death of a fellow senator."

"Nick turns their rhetoric against them, beginning to attract a following. He realizes there is an untapped group of citizens who are simply leaderless and too scared to stand up. They want to, but they don't know how. As the first book ends, Nick leaves the Party, declaring his campaign as an independent candidate for president."

"This book continues the story, as Nick seeks to find a third way. One different from the hopelessly compromised members of either of the two major political parties, referred to here as the Party and the Opposition. He begins his improbable presidential campaign, seeking to rouse the silent majority to the choice they face. As the story moves beyond our junior senator and his antics. The avalanche he started in book one picks up momentum."

"Finally, in this story, I'm refraining from getting inside the head of participants as much as possible. In almost all cases, I do not know what they were thinking. Instead, I let their actions and their own documented words provide insight into their state of mind and logical statements they might have made."

"As I worked to pull together this history, I received access to information prior historians could only have dreamed of receiving. This knowledge of the inner workings and actions within various current and former government agencies, including many previously shielded from public scrutiny, may indeed help us understand and prevent future abuses of power."

"I am shocked, appalled, disappointed, and often brought to tears by the corruption and the lengths humans will go to gain and maintain power and control. I have also been amazed, inspired, and humbled by the sacrifice and determination this same human nature enabled in individuals during these times who fought against this corruption. Those determined to bring sunlight to the darkness, exposing the dangers of limitless power being used to subjugate the common people."

"This tale exposes both the worst and the best of ourselves. I present this to you in hopes it opens your eyes, helps you recognize our darkest hours and our finest triumphs. Finally, to remember, it is only us, all of us, who can once again prevent this. It is our choice to make."

"I leave you with the immortal words of American Philosopher, George Santayana, who famously said, 'those who cannot remember the past, are condemned to repeat it'. Once more, we have a chance to heed his maxim. Let us not ignore it yet again."

Eric Rice
Undisclosed location
In the middle of the 21st Century A.D.

# Prologue

Fatmir Zota listened to talk radio in his small welding shop
in Munich, Germany. He'd arrived from Albania under Angela Merkel's
immigration wave. While driving a delivery truck, he learned to speak
German by listening to these shows. Eventually, he earned enough to rent a
room and move out of the high school gymnasium shelter.

In time, his German improved, and he learned to weld. After a few years,
Fatmir opened his own machine shop, married a German woman, and now
had a young daughter. He looked down at his phone and hit play on the
video. Once again, he watched pictures of his wife going in and out of her
office building, dropping off and picking up their daughter from her school.
His daughter on the playground, leaving a friend's house, even playing in
the park near their apartment. He listened to the message, watching the
video for the tenth time.

Running his hands through his dark hair, he stood up, went to his
toolbox, and lifted out the tray. Pulling out his well-worn Beretta Px4 army
service pistol, he ejected the magazine, checking the bullets. There were
only two. Slamming it back in and pulling the slide, one bullet was now
chambered. He looked at the front of his welding truck.

The front bumper was a monstrosity with reinforced steel tubing
wrapping around the sides. Fatmir stood staring at the front of his truck and
started sobbing. Lifting the gun, his hand shaking violently, he pressed it to
his temple. He couldn't pull the trigger. He began banging his head on the
hood, continuing to sob.

After a minute, he raised his head, looking toward his workbench. His
eyes filled with resolve. He placed his phone on the bench, picked up a
hammer and smashed it down on the phone, shattering the screen and
breaking the phone into several pieces. Fatmir got in his truck, placing
his pistol on the passenger seat. He drove the truck out onto the snowy
suburban street. As he turned up the road toward the city center, the garage
door to his shop slowly closed behind.

# Part One

## You did what?

*"Good Heavens. What have you done now?"*
Spencer Tracy, *Desk Set (1957)*

# Chapter 1

The junior senator from Colorado, Nick Turner, surveyed his new presidential campaign office in the hastily rented space in a building in Arlington, Virginia, across the Potomac from DC proper. He smiled, thinking back to the walk from the National Press Club to his Senate office after his press conference last week.

His chief of staff, Chuck Robinson, was having trouble keeping up. He finally grabbed Nick's sleeve to stop him.

"Hold on, I can't walk this fast. You're going to need a new chief of staff, besides a lobotomy," he gasped.

Nick smiled. He looked at the other, mostly younger members of his staff, who were also smiling. He told them to go on to his senate office and he and Chuck would catch up. As they continued, Nick steered Chuck to a convenient park bench.

Chuck glared at him.

"Really Nick? First you leave the Party and go Independent, which is bad enough, but not entirely unexpected after your filibuster vote. But a run for President? As an independent? Did you have a stroke?" asked Chuck, entirely serious.

"Nope."

"Nope? That's all you have to say. Nick, this is serious. You can't make a statement like that and expect people to laugh it off when you come to your senses. This has lasting consequences."

"Chuck, I *am* serious. I fully intend to run for president."

Chuck leaned forward. He put his hands together, staring down, as if praying, before looking up.

"Nick, it takes a billion dollars to run for president. You have maybe $7 million. You need a national campaign, a seasoned campaign manager, local offices in each state. Grass-roots organizations to get out the vote. Armies of professionals for communications, policies, and financial managers to make sure you don't violate campaign finance rules and end up in jail. My God, Nick, the list is endless. I don't even know if you can still get on the ballot in all 50 states at this point only a year away." Chuck was shaking his head as he just scratched the surface.

"Chuck, I get it. I stepped in it this time," said Nick, entirely serious as well. He held up his hand to stop Chuck.

"I have no idea what I don't know, and that's a good thing. This can't be like any campaign before. It has to be different. Our target is not Party or Opposition or even Independents. Our target is the people. People who are afraid and need a voice. We can't do it like everyone else has. This is how we ended up with a voiceless and fearful silent majority. They hold all the power and don't realize it. They need to wake up and realize they are strong, but only if they all stand up together."

Chuck sat listening to Nick's explanation.

"You know Margie is going to kill you. For not giving her any warning. Or working on a message."

"Maybe, maybe not. Get me on *Tommy*, and I'll try again."

"Ok. First rule. We cannot even mention the campaign in our Senate office. Not a peep. In fact, you should probably check into a hotel until we get office space rented. Then we have to figure out which staffers move over and then find you a campaign manager…" Chuck continued to rattle off all the things they needed to do.

Nick came back to the present, turning as the rest of his senior staff filed into the conference room next to his new campaign office. He wandered in as everyone took a seat on stacks of boxes and a few folding chairs.

"Boss, not to imply you haven't thought this through, but typically candidates, even third-party ones, have a platform. You know, something to stand for and rally support around. Usually, they have some points to make during the one chance they get for free exposure, the Presidential announcement press conference." This from a young, attractive black woman, shaking her head, her shoulder length curly black hair waving back and forth. "Remind me what our platform was? You know, the one you made clear *to everyone* in your speech?"

"Ok, so maybe I *should* have put a bit more thought into what we were saying and why, Margie. But when have I ever done that in the past?" asked Nick with a wry smile.

Rather than be mad, Marjorie Wilson, Senator Turner's communications director, merely smiled and shook her head again.

"I want a raise. It was bad enough cleaning up after you as a nobody senator. As a presidential candidate, I feel the messes are going to be much bigger. I'm going to need a bulldozer instead of a shovel."

"Of that I can assure you," interjected Chuck. "Nick, it is one thing to buck the party and vote against the filibuster. It is a whole different animal to change parties and then announce a run against the Vice President. In case you didn't notice, she is polling above 65% against *any* other candidate, in any party. It still isn't too late to claim temporary insanity and tell everyone you were joking."

"I think not," replied Nick.

"Precisely," agreed Chuck, getting a small laugh from the group.

Nick gave him a sideways look before continuing.

"As I was saying, before I was so rudely interrupted. I am running for President and yes, as an independent. This is not a joke, just like I said in the press conference. I believe we are at a crossroads, both politically and among our citizens. We must choose to stay a democracy based on our Constitution or cave in to the allure of the Progressive's siren song of retreating to the government womb. You want a platform. How is that?"

"Not exactly the stuff of slogans," frowned Margie. "I also think you're going to need to let up on hammering the press. Especially without a party to back you up. How you treated Bergamo at your press conference is once again going to be the story. Nick, you have to understand, they choose what gets shown. With selective editing, they can make you out to be a big bully, picking on the helpless little reporter, just doing her job."

"Margie, we've been through this before," observed a late fortyish woman seated on a folding chair in front of Nick's desk.

"I know, Jenny, but I don't think it is the right way to win hearts and minds," responded Margie.

"I disagree. I'm in an older demo than you. We are the soccer moms with kids in the school systems and we're worried. Yes, ANC and FLCN and the networks are all selectively editing the interviews, but EXN and others are not. Plus, we keep posting our videos of these conversations on our social channels. The truth is getting out and each time they do this, it backfires on them. Look at the earlier time Bergamo selectively edited her conversation with Nick. After the filibuster vote," voiced Jenny, leaning forward in her chair, talking with her hands.

"They made it look like Nick bullied her there. Look how he turned that around by going on *Tommy*. He didn't even have to show the actual footage. Why? Because people are on to the lies of the media. They are digging their own graves doing this. At least for anyone with common sense and eyes. I think Nick is right to double down on hammering the press. I believe it is the path to winning the common people. They are tired of this. I know I am, and I am a nobody."

Nick smiled at the last statement, looking at Chuck.

"Jenny, I think maybe you just created a slogan," grinned Nick.

She looked confused. "I did?"

Nick nodded. "Our campaign is about everyone who our government and our progressive friends feel is a nobody. 'I'm not nobody. I am somebody'."

Nick looked at Margie, who had her head tilted, thinking.

"I like it." This was from the blond-haired younger guy sitting on the boxes. "I'm a nobody, too."

"See, Greg likes it," said Nick with a laugh. "We can work on it. Whether we use it, I can work it into the speeches. It'll drive Lexi crazy."

"I think everything about you is already driving our wonderful Vice President crazy," laughed Chuck. He looked at Margie. "Has Lexi issued any statement regarding Nick's announcement?"

"Not a peep."

"Interesting. I would've thought she'd at least trot out the usual talking points about my being an unelected senator picked to fill out Senator

Richard's term. How I betrayed the Party cause and the majority of voters who gave them all three branches of government. My trying to thwart their plans by not going along with destroying the filibuster?"

"You are a national hero. Maybe she thinks saying nothing keeps you from getting any attention. She has fifteen primary challengers already. You're an independent, with no money and no track record," offered Greg.

"You're probably right. How about honest dialogue about our problems? Does it really matter what I said or didn't say? We all know they're going to twist it the way they want."

"True," acknowledged Chuck.

"I know, not exactly a well-oiled machine. All I know is this place sucks, and it needs to get better or start over. It's like watching a movie where you know the tsunami is coming and you are waiting to get washed away. It's not right and somebody needs to fix it," Nick said, getting up out of his seat.

"Has anyone told you what a Debbie Downer you are? You pile on about how bad things are. What solutions are we offering?" asked Margie earnestly.

"She's right. We need to make sure every time we point out something bad, we offer our view of how to fix the problem," agreed Chuck, as Jenny and Greg also nodded.

"Got it."

"You're going to be on the number one show on cable tonight. Have you thought about what Tommy is going to ask? About the points you want to make? Why you threw away a potentially promising political career? There has to be a reason," asked Chuck.

"My staff drove me to do it?" quipped Nick, looking around his office. No one laughed. "Tough crowd. OK, how about Congress is corrupt? The members are all thieves and liars taking the taxpayer money and giving it to each other, big business, Hollywood, big tech, big media, etc. and regimes that want to see us destroyed, like Iran, China, Russia, North Korea. I want to stop it," Nick paused.

Chuck made a big show of yawning.

"How is that for a position? Oh, and let's see, we can close all the departments of anything, clean out the FBI, CIA, and the other thirty so-called intelligence agencies. Fire 90% of the federal workers other than the army and the national park service. Start from scratch with the state department and, of course, we can shut down all the media companies while we are at it. What do you think?" ended Nick, somewhat frustrated, sitting back down.

"Well, your Majesty, that is nice. Somehow, I don't think that's going to help," said Chuck, in a less than accommodating tone.

"Chuck, I've been shot at, shot down, and just plain shot. Stabbed by a terrorist, confronted by angry mobs, addressed congress, and taught a room full of stoned 19-year-olds. This should be a piece of cake," announced Nick, in a sarcastic tone.

"Sounds like you're scared to me. Is it hitting home what you have signed up for? You should be scared. I know I am. Isn't that the first step? Admitting you have a problem?"

"Ok, I don't know what I'm doing and no, I don't have a platform. But I need to say something tonight. Suggestions?" said Nick, looking at the team around the table.

"Good," nodded Chuck. "Finally, you realize this is not a joke. You did this. What do you want your campaign to be about? And no, you can't say Congress is corrupt and irredeemable."

"Not for nothing, but I think I already said that part in the press conference," admitted Nick, as the others laughed.

"Try not to say it again. Nothing stings like the truth. It just riles them up," suggested Chuck.

"There is no such thing as bad publicity. Right Margie?"

"Whoever said that was not a communications director," Margie answered with a frown on her pretty face.

"For tonight, you need something short and catchy. Something people can see and touch and feel in their bones. No empty slogans and promises. The voters are getting plenty of that from the two parties," offered Jenny.

"And it can't be hokey. I really feel the problem is the bureaucracy and corruption. Our elected officials are there to set themselves up for life after government. The real problem is the departments of lifetime bureaucrats who are not subject to the voters. The Presidents come and go, but the power is really in the departments full of unelected lifers," Nick stated in a righteous tone.

"BORING. Nobody cares. And if they do care, there is nothing they can do about it. Next," said Chuck dismissively.

"That was helpful," countered Nick, giving Chuck a look. "I meant what I said about education. The voters are ignorant. They don't get facts and don't get to decide on their own."

"Double Boring. Come on Nick. You can't go out and tell a bunch of middle-aged truckers, welders, grocery clerks and teachers they need to get smarter in order to understand their life sucks and the government is no help," said Chuck as he stood up going to the whiteboard. "We gotta be different and better."

"I don't disagree, but this has to be more than sound bites. I think you are selling the people short. The Party assumes they are ignorant, but I don't think so. I think they have the capacity and the ability to think and to understand these issues and to make informed decisions."

"Nick," said Chuck, getting serious, "I get it. You are full of ideas and you know what the problems are. You want to get into a debate and convince people to change their mind or get motivated or whatever. It doesn't work that way. Their attention span is too short. They are more concerned about keeping their job, how they will pay their bills or score their next fix. We have successfully trained them to be that way. We did it. They are dumb, ignorant, and uninterested. You can't expect to undo over 100 years of indoctrination and cultural rot with words."

Nick stared at his staff from behind his desk. They all looked at him. It was in their eyes. They thought Chuck was right.

"You're saying the only way I can get through to them is to do the same thing all those other shit heads are doing? I need to pander and lie and promise more and better than the other guys? Sorry, I think they are smarter. I have to believe they are or else this is over before it begins," said Nick, unwinding his six-foot four frame from his chair and wandering the room.

"Nick, you're gonna have to toughen up. If I can make you quit this easy, get out now. You know this is going to be horrible. *If* you are even moderately successful in getting any message out there, both sides are going to come at you with everything they have. They can't afford to let you be right. They screwed up before and let the fox in the henhouse. As a result, they destroyed our election integrity to make sure it never *ever* happens again. They know what to look for and they won't let you or anyone else get away with it this time."

"You think I should just get out?"

"No. But you need to be realistic about what you can accomplish. You need to be tough, and you need to be non-emotional. They'll try to get under your skin constantly. Be a rock. Let it flow over you. Don't react. You cannot afford *any* mistakes. That is going to be damn near impossible since we have nothing right now," ended Chuck.

"Not true. We have right on our side. It is called the Constitution. We have our road map right there. They are the ones making it up as they go. Our job is simple. We have to convince people we have the blueprint. We need to go back to using it properly. Back to first principles. This is why we don't have to make empty promises. History is on our side if we choose to use it correctly. We were the greatest country the world has ever seen and there are two reasons. Our Constitution and the freedom *to be free* it provided. If this is not enough, we are doomed."

"You know, that makes perfect sense," interjected Jenny, as Greg and Margie both chimed in as well in agreement.

"See? Maybe I have a platform after all," smiled Nick.

Chuck raised his hands in surrender, waving an imaginary flag.

"We need to get a real campaign website up and running and more staff immediately. Fundraising has to be job one, or this crusade ends before we even get started. You also need a real campaign manager with a network and knowledge of what it takes to run a national campaign. I've been on them, but I have not run them," added Chuck.

"Where are we going to find anyone worthwhile? Aren't they all working on one of the other twenty-six campaigns?" asked Jenny.

"Leave it to me," said Chuck. "We still need to figure out what to say tonight. This is your second chance to make a good first impression."

"Congress sucks and is trying to sell out the country to China," proclaimed Nick.

"Perfect. There you go again. This will be the shortest campaign in history. The talking heads will love it." Chuck shook his head.

"So, I can't shoot them?" laughed Nick.

Chuck walked over to Nick, suddenly very serious. He grabbed him by the shoulders.

"I am only going to say this once. If you ever, **EVER** say something like that with others in the room, we are done. Finished. I am dead serious. You have to be *so* careful of everything you say and do, Nick. You cannot just fire off the hip. Even trying to be funny. Promise me you will think before you say *anything*. Contemplate every twisted evil way they can use what you say to imply something else. This you have to do *every* second of *every* day for the next eleven months. If you can't do this, we are done. For all of them," said Chuck, turning to look at his colleagues. "Promise all of us you understand."

Nick nodded slowly, realizing how right Chuck was.

"You're right. I use humor to break up the tension. I will try to be more careful."

"Don't try, do," said Chuck, still deadly serious.

"Ok Yoda," agreed Nick with a smile.

"Remember, it is not just you or even us. There'll be hundreds, potentially thousands, of people who rely on you to get it right. They'll be giving up careers and staking reputations and livelihoods on you. It is a lot of pressure, but you need to consider it. You can't take it lightly. Once in, no matter how bad it gets, you can't give up," said Chuck. "You owe that much to all of us who bet on you."

"Still doesn't solve what we need to say tonight," noted Nick, digesting what Chuck was saying.

"There is nothing wrong with speaking from the heart. You still need to be specific, and you need to give people a reason to get behind you," counseled Chuck, walking to the whiteboard, marker in hand.

There was a knock at the door. Carla, his aide, now on his presidential campaign staff, stuck her head in with a big smile. "Sorry to interrupt. We hit $10M raised since your presser. They're all small dollar donations. People are identifying as being from all parties."

"Thanks Carla, that is great news. Make sure I have the latest number and I'll reference it tonight on *Tommy*." Carla nodded, leaving.

"I guess calling Congress corrupt plays in the heartland," said Margie, smiling, as Chuck shrugged.

"Okay," said Nick, rolling up his sleeves, also picking up a marker at the whiteboard. "Let's figure out what we stand for."

# Chapter 2

Vice President of the United States, Alexis Smythe-Thomas, sat in her office in the Capitol, sipping tea while seated behind her desk.

"Just heard from Sherman at *America's News Channel* and some of the others. They are all going to smear Turner ten ways to Sunday as young, impertinent, inexperienced, and a flat-out traitor for his antics these last couple of months ending in this childish run for President. What do you think?" asked Lexi.

Mel Arenson, a thin, balding man with gray hair and wire-rimmed glasses, turned in his seat, looking up from his tablet. Lexi always thought he looked like a poor banker or an undertaker. He had been her chief of staff for over twenty-five years. He was also probably the most ruthless *man* in Washington. Lexi held the overall title.

"I like it. Slow news week. Get it all out there and use the sound bites sparingly now until he gives up. We need to make sure we turn it all off come January. His message resonates with a subsection of the population. Especially those who feel we don't hear them. We can't afford to give him any oxygen."

"Agree. I told Sherman as much. He understands. It's why he got the job at ANC after the last guy screwed up, giving away those billions of dollars in free coverage. We won't repeat that mistake again," growled Lexi.

"You mean the free and independent press won't make that mistake again, right?" smiled Mel in return.

"Of course," she replied with her own shrug and smile, taking another sip of tea. "Be nice if they didn't all say the same thing, though. 'Benedict Turner' references all day on a few stations should do the trick."

Mel laughed. "I agree. Look at the damage he has done to our plans. Wilhelm did his duty and then Grayson screwed us over by replacing him with Crawford from the Opposition. This ensures we get nothing passed during this election year. Even with the filibuster gone. All our planning and efforts thwarted by a boy scout. Appointed, not even elected. Who would ever have imagined it would happen this way?"

"Clearly not us," complained Lexi in an annoyed voice. "We are still on track for my landslide?"

"Yes, you'll have token opposition in the primaries. Most of the candidates are only in it for the cabinet posts. Senator Klausen is making some noise, but he is a regional candidate, not national. You should have it wrapped up by Super Tuesday in March."

"Mel, I don't like it. Too many surprises already. Too many plans upset. We were supposed to ride the filibuster's demise into the election. Like you said, Turner is a rabble rouser and there is certainly a rabble to rouse. We need to crush them as soon as we can. If we don't, they are going to destroy our democracy."

"Lexi, relax. We are still in a position of strength. We have demographics on our side. You're going to win big. We'll make sure of it. The less you know about the specifics, the better."

"I know, I know, plausible deniability and all that," she said with a small smile. "Are you *sure* we shouldn't be turning the guns on Turner full bore? Blow him out of the water before he gets started?"

Mel sighed. He understood her concern. It was his, too. Nick Turner was everything the Opposition had not had previously. Competent, young, energetic, principled, charismatic, and a dynamite speaker. And a national hero to boot. But he was also a man with little to no resources and no national party to help him organize. He was starting from nothing, trying to win the most costly and complicated job in the world. Using a process he knew nothing about, and for which he was so woefully unprepared. Mel smiled and shook his head.

"Lexi, we got this. Trust me."

"You haven't let me down yet," replied Lexi, smiling over her now lukewarm tea.

# Chapter 3

"Welcome Senator and now Presidential candidate Nick Turner. Senator, your last appearance, after your filibuster vote, was the most popular segment of the show in history. More downloads, more views, more comments," said Tommy Charles, host of *The Tommy Charles Show* on the *EXcellence in News* network, EXN. His was the most popular cable show on the most popular cable news channel.

"Thanks for having me, Tommy. I guess folks appreciate a politician who'll tell the truth. Go figure," confided Nick, grinning.

"So much has happened since we last spoke. We are going to have you on for the first half of the show without interruption. You've left the Party, become an Independent and shocked the establishment by announcing a third party run for President. Why not just run for a party nomination?" asked Tommy, a serious look on his face.

"I think you know the Party primary is already over. Outsiders may have made waves years ago, but the reality is the party machine nominates who it wants, and no one is going to unseat Lexi."

"I think there are a few other candidates who would disagree with your statement. You are saying the other thirteen candidates are just looking for cabinet posts?" asked Tommy, turning in his chair.

"They can complain all they want, but I am a realist," laughed Nick. "Aren't we up to fifteen now? I can't keep track of the number. Most are only there, so they can claim they were once a presidential candidate, when they are hawking pain relief cremes on TV later."

"Ouch. Senator, this is why we enjoy having you on. You're not afraid to tell the truth and cut through all the BS," said Tommy with a genuine laugh.

He shrugged. "You asked a question. I answered truthfully. Most of Lexi's opponents are looking for places in her administration or the odd ambassadorships and other roles. They are just there for visibility and to make her look presidential, like she had competition."

"Makes sense, so that's why you left?"

"Not really. I think Reagan said it best when he said, 'I didn't leave the Party, it left me'. Tommy, the reality is I am a true minority. I am a middle of the road Independent. I don't subscribe to either party platform."

"When did you decide to run for president? It is not usually something you just wake up and do one day," paused Tommy. "Or is it?"

Nick laughed before replying. "In my case, yes. You sound like my chief of staff. The reality is this country is dying. Economically, morally, culturally, ethically, religiously. We have lost hope, and we have lost our sense of what made us great once. Our institutions, at all levels, have decayed to a point where public confidence is so low we don't even talk about it any longer. Sort of like the debt, the border, or crime. The public hates government, yet so many have now become dependent on and beholden to that same government they hate. The people rightfully mistrust the media and are just angry at each other all the time. Egged on by that same media and Congress intentionally dividing us into warring tribes. A divided people are so much easier to control. If we are busy screaming at each other over silly things, they can shred what's left of the Constitution without us noticing and replace it with their progressive utopia."

"That's a pretty bleak picture, Senator," said Tommy, almost frowning.

"Tommy, you have paid talking head after talking head on this program, saying similar things. Is having a sitting Senator say it, somehow bleaker? What part is not accurate? Be honest."

"No thanks, I like my job," said Tommy with a laugh. "I'll ask the questions here. I'll leave career suicide to you."

"It would be great for ratings," noted Nick in a serious tone, but smiling. "Tommy, you just identified the problem. For all of us. Too many of our leaders are unwilling to say what they know is true. Instead, we kick every can down the road, making it someone else's problem. The reality is it will never get fixed. It will just lead to an ending. We are letting it happen by being afraid to stand up and stop it. Why? Because it is going to be unpopular? Last time I checked, Armageddon, depression, genocide, famine, world war, they are all pretty drastic outcomes and immensely unpopular. Why let them happen out of fear of being unpopular trying to stop them?"

"Senator, I hear you, but everyone who tries to tell the truth gets creamed by the media and social media. Then the government institutions come after them. God help you if you don't toe the line. Now we have the Ministry of Truth disguised as a Homeland misinformation discovery service, deciding what is truth and what is hate. They just erase you from society if you dare utter an opinion they don't like," argued Tommy, as Nick could hear Tommy's producers yelling in his own earpiece for Tommy to tone it down. He ignored them and continued.

"First, you had COVID police and lockdowns. Multiple times. Then turning the citizens into a bunch of angry 'Karens', yelling at everyone to conform to their mask rules. Then came the vaccine mandates along with the destruction of civil liberties in the name of science. The race riots are still going strong. Rampant crime. Small business decimated. Doubling the size of the IRS, auditing everyone who dares to speak out against this administration. You buck their agenda; you lose your job, and they make sure you never work again. How is that right? No wonder people are staying quiet. Aren't you afraid they will come after you as well?" asked Tommy, with only slightly less emotion.

"I expect it. I know they will throw everything at me. You can't do what I did and not expect retaliation. Tommy, the time to stand and defend America has come. I have no business to ruin, few assets to seize or freeze. I'm sure they will attack me, but I think I am in a better position than most to weather this storm. Plus, if they come after me, they'll make the exact point I am trying to make by standing up to them."

Tommy nodded, mesmerized by the words coming from a sitting US Senator. "You think you can somehow stop this?"

"If I do nothing else, I need to educate and inspire others to take the same risk. To stand and keep America free. To know they are not alone if they stand up together. Yes, there is risk and yes, they may cancel a few or even many. They can't cancel everyone. If we all stand up and say, 'I am not nobody, I am somebody', we can win. It is not too late."

"Nice slogan. But why are you doing this? You are throwing away a potentially lucrative and promising career? As a third-party candidate, you can't hope to win," pleaded Tommy, begging Nick to reconsider and stay in the Senate.

"Who knows? Tommy, why can't it work? We are in grave danger of following the path of other great failed civilizations. The road to ruin from internal strife, corruption, and neglect. When Rome fell, it only took a thousand years to recover."

"Senator, folks have been saying the end is coming for decades."

"Tommy, it isn't immediate. It happens slowly, but one thing is always common. In every case, the regular people suffer. I feel it is my job to point this out and stop it before it is too late."

"Senator, I can't fault your conviction. I sincerely believe you mean what you say."

"If I didn't have that conviction, I couldn't do this. Remember, I'm not a politician and am not trained to lie. I can't fake it like so many of my colleagues," laughed Nick.

"Touché, Senator," said Tommy, playing with a pen in his hands.

"So, we are about to become a police state or we are about to collapse like Rome. Is there a third choice?"

"I think there is. I believe there is a silent majority, cowed into submission by fear of speaking up, just as you said. The equity the left speaks of is not the equality of opportunity we have built this country on and, incidentally, why so many people immigrated here legally for years. If our country has been such a shit hole built on the backs of all these hardworking immigrants, my grandparents and yours, why did they keep coming? Sorry for cussing, but geez, this is such BS," said Nick, leaning back again.

"It's cable, and we're all adults. I think we can handle it," smiled Tommy, as Nick continued.

"Why do they still keep coming? Legally or illegally. This is the height of hypocrisy. I encourage everyone to look up this word and understand it. What these folks are proposing with reparations and white fragility, this equity, is pure socialism. You work, I take. It is not America, it is wrong, and it is evil. We need to stop letting them tell us to shut up every time we call them on it."

"Wow Senator, I see what you meant. I agree with you, we are in a dangerous place and if we let them get away with remaking our society, we have no one to blame but ourselves."

"It is what they are trying to change. An equal opportunity to work hard, fail, try again, but most of all to keep a majority of the fruits of the labor you created. That is equality of opportunity. That is what the Constitution enabled. What they want is *equity*," said Nick, raising his hands in quotes.

"They want people to feel guilty because they have succeeded. It is not just white people, but people of all races, blacks, Asians, Hispanics, who have worked hard and succeeded in their chosen fields. The idea any of this hard work and success was based on other's suffering, is baloney."

"That's not how they put it. To them we owe them, just because all of us had some giant advantage they did not."

"Let's put it in perspective. Tommy, let's say you get paid by the viewer. You have worked hard for years to build a brand and a message to entice viewers to tune into your show instead of your competitors. Now you get what, 2 or 3 times the viewers of your competitor."

Tommy held up his hand, and a second hand with one finger raised. "Six, sometimes seven," he explained with a giant grin.

"In their mind, you have an unfair advantage and the person on your competitor network is being treated unfairly. You need to pay him half to three quarters of what you get paid, to make it *not* equality of opportunity, but equality of outcome. How would you feel about that?"

"I'd be pissed," said Tommy. "I worked hard to get here and to keep this audience."

"Sure you would, but what can you do if they demand this? All you can do is quit and then nobody gets anything. Or you can capitulate and knuckle under while they take part of your hard work and effort and the corresponding pay and give it to your competitors. Because if you don't, you'll have pickets outside and boycotts and they'll call you a racist and a white supremacist."

"They already do that," interjected Tommy in a monotone.

"You get my meaning. This is happening everywhere in every job where corporate HR departments are telling people to shut up while creating programs to promote no longer on merit, but on quotas. It is segregation. And is anti-everything the Civil Rights Act tried to solve. We are going backwards. This is Marxism and Socialism. This is Progressivism. What it is really is *Stupidism*."

"Those are some powerful statements. You are going to make their job too easy to attack you."

"Tommy, I think I have already showed I don't give a shit what they think. What I do care about is what everyday people think. The little guy always pays the ultimate price. They die in the wars. They die in the genocides and Cultural Revolutions. They die in the real revolutions, but the elites survive and thrive. We need to look out for the little guy this time around," finished Nick.

"Couldn't agree more. What's next?"

"I'll go local, grass roots. I won't play their game, raising tons of money, making promises to big business and powerful elites. I'm going to talk to as many real people as possible. In every state, in small towns and villages, in VFWs and diners, in YMCAs and bodegas, in private homes. Wherever I can get people to tell me their stories and listen to mine. If I convince enough of them, we can be the change. They will tell their friends and neighbors and we'll build a coalition of the willing. Those willing to stand up and fight for a country they love and believe in."

"One person at a time? When you need what, 75 million votes to win. That is a lot of conversations," pointed out Tommy, shaking his head in concern.

"I am counting on a movement starting of like-minded individuals who want a return to sanity. I am not fooling myself. It won't be easy. The progressives have a 130-year head start and control most of the levers of power and culture now. I don't imagine they are going to roll over without putting up a fight," admitted Nick.

"The single-issue voter is the Party voting bloc. I have talked to many people in only the last year, most of whom agree regardless of political party on fiscal policies. Closing the border and the need for more police combined with better reform. Better education for their children and safer streets with fewer drugs, less government debt, etc."

"They all have a hot button. An issue making them vote Party because the Opposition is an all-or-nothing party. Be with us on everything or we don't want you. Many women vote Party *not* because they agree with partial birth abortion but because the Opposition wants to ban *all* abortions all the time. Even if they don't really agree on 85% of the platform, their one issue trumps common sense and the Opposition stance," finished Nick, letting it sink in.

"It does seem like many people have powerful feelings for one item that sways them to go one way," agreed Tommy.

"This is my goal, to find a third way. To build a middle ground movement. We'll see if I am right."

"Great, I hope you can do this. I agree with you it seems counter to many voters' overall wellbeing. You realize they are going to do everything they can to keep you from getting your message out?" Nick nodded as Tommy continued, "You can, of course, keep coming on this show and making your points, but they cannot let you do this. It would mean the end of all their grand plans."

"Regardless, I am going to try. Tommy, my campaign slogan is pretty simple. Wake up. Stand up. Think for yourself. Choose for yourself. I must be doing something right. I have raised $12 million since the press conference, all in small donations," said Nick.

"There you have it, an honest assessment, and an attempt to wake up the silent majority. Senator, we wish you luck and Godspeed. You are welcome on this show anytime."

As they went to commercial, Nick stood up while the producers were removing his microphone and he walked away from the stage. As he turned to go, Tommy called out.

"Man, you are crazy. But it makes for great ratings. We'll have you on anytime you want to make a big announcement. You know they are going to kill you, one way or another," said Tommy.

"We'll see. They've tried to kill me before," laughed Nick.

Off camera a producer said 20 seconds.

"Keep in touch. I love the ratings boost," said Tommy, looking back into the camera as Nick exited the studio.

# Chapter 4

Maksim Pavlovich pulled down a book from a shelf in his library and thumbed through it. The book was old, a hundred years, but not as old as many of the tomes on the shelves. This book had many pages with turned down corners.

Pavlovich 'tsk, tsk'd' at this, tempted to turn them back up, as he was every time he looked at it. To deface a book offended his sensibilities. He turned to one of these 'dog-eared' pages and looked at the underlined sentence.

'*The best defense against propaganda: more propaganda*'

He smiled at this simple explanation. He turned to another page with markings.

'*Propaganda is the executive arm of the invisible government*'

Over his long life, Pavlovich had seen this become truer. First with radio, then TV, and now ubiquitous with the internet, especially social media.

He shuffled slowly toward a leather wing-back chair and an antique table in one corner of the library, sitting carefully.

'*The whole basis of successful propaganda is to have an objective and then to endeavor to arrive at it through an exact knowledge of the public and modifying circumstances to manipulate and sway public opinion*'

Pavlovich leaned back in his chair, contemplating this quote. He spoke aloud to no one:

"The public. The public is a menace. To themselves, to their neighbors, to their family, to their country and most of all, to the entire planet. The public is the problem. Especially the public in America. With their freedoms and their misbegotten beliefs. They are neither smart enough nor educated enough to even contemplate the correct course of action, let alone have the will to make it happen."

He often gave this speech to his many World Harmony Society organizations, as he had explained to them their goals and objectives. Goals he expected them to meet. At least if *they* expected to continue to earn his trust and their part of the millions he provided in funding. He looked down, thumbing further into the book looking for a particular page.

*'As civilization has become more complex, and as the need for invisible government has been increasingly demonstrated, the technical means have been invented and developed by which opinion may be regimented'*

The first time he read this sentence, decades ago, Maksim realized weapons, money, and power were not needed to ensure change. Words and human nature would be sufficient. The advent of mass media made it possible to manipulate many with the rhetoric of change. He turned more pages.

*'People want to go, where they want to be led'*

As he finished, a bell rang in the library. He reached into a pocket and looked at a small remote device with a screen and a series of buttons. He smiled, seeing who it was, and pressed a button. A door unlocked, granting entry.

His assistant Petr entered the room. He looked toward the large ornate antique desk where his employer usually sat, momentarily confused at his absence. He turned in the cavernous room, spying Pavlovich seated in the corner.

"Ah Petr. Thank you for coming."

Petr merely bowed his head slightly.

"I presume you saw the show young Mr. Turner put on yesterday on EXN?"

"I have reviewed it, yes."

"Good. We must do all we can to prevent him from gaining momentum. I sense in him an uncanny ability to rouse the masses."

"Sir?"

Pavlovich held up his book. The title down the spine read *Propaganda*, by Edward Bernays. "This man understood how to manipulate people and get them to do exactly what you want, with words. Marx and Engels may have coined the term 'Opiate of the Masses', but even more than religion, public opinion is the true drug with which to manipulate and control them."

Petr waited, sensing his master had more wisdom to impart.

"This man, Bernays, turned propaganda from the dirty word it was, changing it to 'public relations'. The new opiate of the masses was born. He codified it in several books. Then he put it into play in America and almost single-handedly created the advertising business. Turning these principles into action. Who else could get doctors to promote cigarette smoking as healthy? Then to turn this around later, when finding out it caused cancer, to use these same doctors to explain how you need to stop this insidious habit? And get away with it!"

"One of those American lists named him one of the most influential men of the 20th century," laughed Pavlovich. "Sort of like thanking the man for the child your daughter has after he rapes her. These techniques have killed more people, willingly, than perhaps anything else, except of course blind faith in God."

Petr nodded again, still waiting.

"Petr, by now you have seen how this works. This is what we do. With all our foundations and donations to these organizations. We do not have to do anything. Merely suggest. We provide guidance and a means for them to achieve *our* ends. From eradicating the lesser races and the poor with our support of Planned Parenthood, to the destruction of education standards with our support of teachers' unions and socialist curriculum. We have radicalized their universities and professors and have taken control of their election processes. And of course, their media has long been our willing ally. It has all been too easy."

"Timothy had it correct in the bible when he documented *the love of money is the root of all evil*. He would have been more accurate to say human nature, temptation, greed, envy, and love of money are the true road to damnation. This explains all the ills of our world as we speak," finished Pavlovich, looking up at Petr.

"Indeed, sir. But in your case, as you say, you are using this very money to rein in human nature and its society destroying powers."

Maksim smiled, showing his crooked yellow teeth.

"You learn well, Petr. Look at the inscription in the book," he said, closing and handing the book to Petr.

Petr took the book carefully from him. He was unused to touching anything in the library. Some books were over a thousand years old, handwritten on various animal skins.

This book was a conventionally bound hardcover with a dust jacket. He opened the book, which was written in German, and looked at the inside page. In a clear, firm hand, in German, *'My dear Adolf, this is the secret to my success. The people are ignorant and ready to be led, Josef'*.

Petr looked up at Maksim, the question inherent in his look.

"Yes indeed. Josef Goebbels gave this book to his friend Adolf Hitler. He did indeed follow the guidance found in it. While Bernays himself, the nephew of Sigmund Freud, was an intellectual, propaganda was an exercise in clinical psychology. Understanding how to influence opinion and human nature, Goebbels saw it as the way to control and direct the masses. Both were correct. It is ironic, a book by a Jew should be used to whip up the masses into accepting and celebrating the very extermination of the author's race," finished Maksim with a shrug of his bony shoulders.

"Goebbels is famous for saying, *'A lie told once remains a lie but a lie told a thousand times becomes the truth'*. There was never a clearer understanding of manipulation than this. He prepped the German people with relentless propaganda until they believed the lie. He and Hitler used it to convince them to charge into the face of death, righteously, to make their destiny a reality. That, my dear Petr, is more power than any arsenal of nuclear weapons. This is exactly why we must stop our young Turner from using the power of words and ideas to unite those *we* have spent so much money and time disuniting, for *our own purposes*."

"How shall we do it?"

"Not in the way you would expect. I fear eliminating him will make him a martyr. There may be others who could pick up the cause or give them something to rally around. Americans are unpredictable. Turner is a perfect example. No, we must discredit him and his words. We fight his propaganda with more of our own," stated Pavlovich, using his hands to make his points.

"Use our allies in the media and our broad reach to smear his words and to pressure his allies. We show his followers how dangerous he is to *their* way of life. We make examples of not him, but them. Show them what happens when they make themselves a target. If I am right, Turner has a conscience. He will not want others hurt by following his lead. He may choose to go away, quietly, rather than lead others into pain and suffering."

"Excellent plan. I presume you would like us to have agitators at his rallies. He will hit the campaign trail now that he has announced his candidacy. We can disrupt these."

"Petr, I believe we need to tread carefully. We need to let him build some momentum. To get followers and attract others to his words and suggestions. We need to force them to show themselves and their true colors. When he has people willing to stand up and shout their support. When he has people with something to lose, exposing themselves to cancel culture, that is when we attack. We make examples of all of them. We make sure all their friends, neighbors and colleagues understand the genuine danger of following him. For now, we wait. When the time is right, we unleash our wolves."

"Antifa?" asked Petr, in a questioning tone.

"No. They served their purpose years ago. They are uncontrollable fanatics and serve no end goal other than complete anarchy. Once Ms. Smythe-Thomas is in power, we will deal with them. We need agitators we can control through money, fear, intimidation, and coercion. Our student activist, labor organizations and the anti-racist leagues we prop up should work fine. Especially the ARL. They are easy to control. It only takes money and material. We have plenty of both."

"Yes sir. I will begin the plans and we will be ready to implement when you give us the word."

"Soon Petr, soon. Turner cannot wait and he must get out there. I can see it in his eyes on that television program. He is a believer. A knight on a crusade. A fanatic. I have seen it before. It can be dangerous. It must be stopped."

Petr nodded and turned, leaving Pavlovich alone again in his giant library.

Pavlovich stood and walked back to the shelf. Before placing the book back, he turned to the back. On the last page, written in faded pencil, were several other phrases, apparently written by Goebbels himself, and not Hitler, since the writing matched the dedication. Maksim translated from German in his head as he read them:

*'Propaganda works best when those who are being manipulated are confident they are acting on their own free will'*

*'It is the absolute right of the state to supervise the formation of public opinion'*

*'The essence of propaganda consists in winning people over to an idea so sincerely, so vitally, that in the end they succumb to it utterly and can never escape from it.'*

*'This is the secret of propaganda: Those who are to be persuaded by it should be completely immersed in the ideas of the propaganda, without ever noticing they are immersed in it.'*

Pavlovich often wondered if this was the first place Goebbels had written these quotes before uttering them himself in public. The most telling ones and the most prescient were the final two:

*'There will come a day, where all the lies will collapse under their own weight, and truth will again triumph.'*

He always found this one disconcerting, especially considering who wrote it. Whose truth was he talking about? His own? The Third Reich? The west? God? The final quote summed up their bet with the German people and the world.

*'If we have power, we will never give it up again, unless we are carried out of our offices as corpses'*

Maksim closed the book and placed it back on the shelf. He pulled out his remote as he ambled back to his chair. His nurse arrived as he sat. She hooked up the IV and the steady flow entered his veins. As his body became alive again, he pondered his new, and totally unexpected adversary, Nick Turner. As a rebel senator, he was an annoyance. But as a presidential candidate, he was an unexpected wildcard. He would not allow another wildcard to delay or derail his plans this time.

# Chapter 5

Nick pulled into his driveway in Fort Collins, Colorado, carefully steering his twenty-five-year-old Toyota Land Cruiser into the second garage bay. He inched forward until his front bumper gently tapped a sensor, turning a light on the wall from green to red. The Land Cruiser would fit with about 2 inches to spare when the garage door was down. Nick retrieved his day pack from the back seat and entered the house, hitting the button to lower the garage door.

He always listened to make sure the door came down fully, before closing the door to the house. Once inside, he walked through the kitchen, grabbing a bottle of water and stretching. He had taken an aggressive hiking trail this morning in Rocky Mountain National Park, about ninety minutes from his house. The trail he wanted to take had too much snow. Nick hadn't felt like unpacking his snowshoes. He opted for a hike on lower elevation trails, longer than he intended.

Walking into his library, he noticed the flashing light on the old-fashioned message machine. He pressed the button, 'You have 19 new voice messages' said the mechanical voice. Nick pressed the play button and dug out his phone, turning it on for the first time in ten hours.

"Nick! Where the hell are you? Answer your goddamn phone," screamed Chuck into the phone as the answering machine played the latest message. Nick hit delete on the machine, dialing Chuck's number.

"Jesus Nick, where the hell have you been?" Exasperation and concern coming through in Chuck's voice.

"I went for a hike in the mountains. Phone wouldn't have worked up there, anyway. What's up?" asked Nick calmly.

"I suppose you haven't turned on the TV either? Where are you now?" asked Chuck, settling down now that he had actually found Nick.

"Home. No, I have not turned on the TV. I just walked in and saw all the messages. What happened?" Nick's antenna were now up, sensing something bad.

He could hear Chuck take a deep breath. "No one is really sure if this is coordinated or not, but there were a series of attacks on various Christmas markets around the world a few hours ago. Lots of kids are dead and lots more in awful shape. It's bad Nick, terrible," said Chuck in a sad tone.

Nick closed his eyes, pausing before he answered.

"Where? Any in the states?"

"Thankfully no. Quebec City, Madrid, Copenhagen, London, Munich, and Stockholm. There is sketchy info one was stopped in France and maybe another in Rome."

"We need to issue a statement, right?"

"You already did. When I couldn't get a hold of you, we issued one from your campaign. Tommy is calling me every 15 minutes, looking to get you on a live shot. Can you do it from your house?"

"Sure, I haven't shaved, but maybe the rugged look is the right tone, anyway."

"OK, I'll let Tommy know. Just be careful. We know very little. Don't let him goad you into making any statements on response or anything like that, OK?"

"Got it. I'm being handled again."

"Get used to it, Mr. Presidential Candidate. Welcome to your life for the next ten months."

#

"Good afternoon Senator, thanks for joining us on this sad and somber day around the world," said Tommy in a firm tone.

"Thanks for having me."

"Senator, this was obviously a coordinated attack. From all accounts, they occurred within 15 minutes of each other. Before they could spread word to local police forces to be on the lookout for any similar attacks in their own markets. What do you make of this?"

Nick sighed before answering, remembering Chuck's warning. He ignored it. "Tommy, there is a reason they call it terrorism. It is cowardly and designed to create fear among the people. They want everyone to question whether it is safe to go outside their home."

Nick could see Tommy's bobbing head on a screen on his monitor while he stared into the camera.

"The only response to these kinds of acts is to find out who did it, track them down, and deliver justice. It is key to locate the local ringleaders and follow the money back to the source," said Nick.

"I agree. Someone funded a coordinated event like this."

"Those are the real evil doers. They are the ones manipulating actions. Seeking these outcomes because it profits them. This is the real problem. They stay in the shadows using their money and influence to get others to commit these atrocities in the name of some activist cause. These organizers couldn't care less about their cause." Tommy nodded again, not wanting to keep Nick from making controversial statements.

"No Tommy," stared Nick into the camera, his dark eyes narrowing as if he were confronting his worst enemy. "These are the monsters we must find. The monsters we must stop. And the monsters we need to end collectively. If we do not, they will just pop up elsewhere to spread their evil once again."

"Senator, an excellent plan indeed. Did you not find it strange each of the assailants made sure the police killed them rather than being arrested? This speaks of fanaticism we have not experienced."

Nick did not know this, but kept on as if he did.

"Tommy, it does not surprise me. These are not the actions of the mentally ill. Rather, the actions of the sane. These are the foot soldiers of radical ideology. Sadly, the ideology of anarchy. They have no desire other than to burn it all down and rebuild from the ashes. Attacks with no rhyme or reason are the worst. They are hard to predict and hard to prevent. The public loses faith in our ability to protect them."

Nick paused, thinking about how far to go, before continuing. Tommy waited patiently.

Nick leaned closer to the camera. "We have lost the deterrence factor. Crime does indeed now pay. Or at least the fear of penalty is now diminished. We must help them find the people behind this and send a message to all. We will find you. Wherever you are, and we will punish you harshly for these deeds."

"Senator, once again, the right response."

"Tommy, people are already afraid to leave their houses in many cities. In broad daylight. They did not attack us today, but as we mourn for our fellow men and women around the world in these communities. For the children whose lives they tragically cut short, we too feel the specter of this event and wonder where will it happen next and who will stop it? These are valid questions for all citizens, everywhere."

"Senator, what should we do?" asked Tommy, with emphasis on 'we'.

"Tommy, we should do anything we can to help the injured. To help the law enforcement personnel in each of these countries. To share any intelligence, to help them any way we can. We *all* need to find out how extensive the network is and if they have plans here as well."

Tommy nodded in agreement.

"In the meantime, we should be vigilant and alert. What we shouldn't do is hunker down again. We've hunkered down too many times in the last few years. Retreat isn't working as we've seen with COVID, crime, race relations, schools, cancel culture, revisionist history and a host of other incidents," said Nick, now throwing out all restraint.

"We are only weak if we allow ourselves to believe we are. It is time to wake up, stand up, and fight back. We are not a nation of sheep and we are not a nation of victims. Let's take the fight to the enemy and not sit around waiting for them to attack us."

"Senator, those are not the words we are hearing from the administration. They are suggesting we tend to the injured, support law enforcement, and establish commissions. This includes interfering in the investigations in these countries, taking control if we have to, in order to figure out why and how this happened. They are not advocating for any kind of aggressive action to track down the perpetrators."

"Tommy, they did not directly attack us. I understand their position as one of diplomacy. However, I disagree with doing anything to undermine the credibility of local authorities. It is unwise. We should provide help but allow them to investigate in their own manner. We should instead focus on our own soil and determine if these kinds of activities are being planned here as well. Mine is a plan of action, but not interference. I choose not to sit and wait to become a victim. I advocate taking steps to make sure it will not happen here."

"Well, if it matters, Senator, I prefer your way to another commission to investigate how people were killed yet again," said Tommy.

"Today we just need to pray and help those who can be helped. I can tell you, the authorities in these countries are not likely to be satisfied with commissions, either. Or at least *their* citizens won't be. Let's hope their leaders realize they need to find the organizers quickly. We need to stay out of their way."

"Good point Senator. Thank you for your thoughts on this."

"Thank you, Tommy."

#

"He's right, you know," said CIA Director Rhett Chadwick in the situation room looking at the Vice President.

"Maybe. But we can't get away with saying we are going to go into other countries, track down the perpetrators, and kill them. Why are we even watching EXN?" answered Lexi, a look of disgust on her face.

"That's not exactly what he said," countered Rhett carefully.

"Really, that is what I heard. Actions, not words. If he were President and said that, we would already have an international crisis on our hands. What an infant. He is undermining our efforts with his rhetoric. Can't we shut him up for national security reasons?"

"We are watching EXN, because we need to know what the others are saying about our response. Including our loudest critics. Our response is being positioned as weak and insubstantial."

"I had nothing to do with it," countered Lexi, raising her hands in frustration. "The President, or more likely Sam Vincent, issued the statement before I even got to the situation room."

"Whomever it came from, it was stupid. Now we are in a bind." This came from a smallish woman with clear Indian ancestors.

"How so Susanna?" asked Lexi.

"Our statement, claiming the right to find and prosecute people when we were not even attacked, looks magnanimous on the surface. But it steps all over the law enforcement in each of these countries and makes a mockery of their rights to handle their own issues without the interference of the United States," answered Susanna Bangura.

"We've forced these countries to either denounce our statement and suffer backlash for being ungrateful, or they can accept our offer and then risk damaging their credibility with their own people in these investigative branches." Susanna got up to pace while continuing.

"In the haste to get something out and to do it without consulting either you or me as the Secretary of State, we have screwed the proverbial pooch. I suspect this was an attempt to prevent you from deciding. You notice there was no appearance from the President, only the statement delivered by Amy."

Lexi sat, shaking her head.

"Turner gets to say find them and kill them. We say we want to find them, try them, and bring them to justice, and we are the ones stepping all over our allies?" asked Lexi, frustrated.

"He is not the President or the administration. In fact, most people will never even hear what he said. Everyone, by now, has heard what we 'said'. That is the difference," answered Susanna.

Lexi looked at the others in the room, who had remained silent.

"Henry, what do we know so far?" asked Lexi of the skinny National Security Agency director.

"So far, we have confirmed the driver in Canada was an immigrant from Malaysia. No criminal record and no affiliations to any other terrorist organizations. They killed him when he got out of the truck and charged police with a gun in his hand. The gun was a fake. It was clear he was committing suicide by cop," said Henry, referring to the briefing papers in front of him.

"So why does someone without a fanatical religious affiliation do something like this? It makes no sense," said Lexi in a disbelieving tone.

"Madame Vice President, it gets more confusing. The London attack was a Syrian refugee seeking asylum. He left his vehicle once it hit a wall and started attacking bystanders with an iron pipe, forcing police to kill him. In Stockholm, it was a Turkish immigrant who had been in Sweden for years. He attacked with a machete. When the police refused to kill him, he slit his own throat."

"Munich was an Albanian male who shot once at police and when they would not shoot back, he killed himself. The funny thing was his gun only had two bullets. He saved the last one for suicide if the cops didn't kill him. That is pretty cold-blooded planning."

"The Madrid driver is unknown so far, but he, too, was killed by the local authorities. This is too much coincidence. These men have no connections, no common religion, no common country of origin. This is frankly mystifying," finished St. Cloud.

"Why not here?" asked Lexi. She looked at Rhett and then at Claude, the FBI director. "Did we know this was coming? Did we stop any of these from happening here?"

Claude glanced at Rhett before speaking.

"Lexi," replied Claude in a voice made wheezy by his declining health from his late-stage lung cancer. "We hear rumors all the time of suspected activities. We stop countless attempts to commit mass murder. Think what happened in Waukesha years ago."

Lexi looked like she was about to explode.

Claude held up a hand. "It is very difficult to stop a mentally deranged person. Yes, we have stopped similar style attacks here and even in the last few weeks."

"We knew?" asked Lexi, the anger showing on her face.

"Madame Vice President," said Rhett soothingly. "No, we did not know where, when, how, or how many attacks would occur. What we knew and what we did share with our friends in MI-5 and Interpol and others was 'chatter' about plans to make some type of attacks during the holiday season. We do this all the time."

"Unbelievable. If this gets out, we are screwed."

"The good news, as Claude said, is we prevented any of these from occurring on our soil. This is our job. We help where we can, but we cannot share everything. Sometimes our information is leaked from within our allies' *own* intelligence services. We have to be careful not to feed their own intel back to them," reassured Rhett.

Lexi turned to Susanna. "Now what? How do we fix it?"

"I suggest we refrain from issuing any more official statements other than offering to help wherever possible and leave it at that. Turner got that much right. We offer to help, but don't step on their sovereignty. If you can convince the President and Vincent from putting stuff out without consulting us, that would be a good start."

"OK, I'll see what I can do. Rhett, anything else we need to do? Up security, put local law enforcement on alert for anything specific?"

"Lexi, most of them are always on full alert. They have so many protests and smash and grabs and drug deals, overdoses, homeless incidents, and murders. There is nothing much else they *can* do."

Lexi ignored the implied issue with lack of policing.

"Lexi, we can issue a statement from the FBI if that will help?" said Claude. "We can tell folks we do not have any credible threats, but as always, to remain vigilant and alert to anything out of the ordinary."

"Thanks Claude. Go back to your families, it is almost Christmas. Thank you all, try to enjoy your holiday."

Lexi walked down the hall to her office in the White House, in the West Wing, trailed by Mel.

Mel shut the door as Lexi paced.

"What a shit show. It is bad enough he is senile and unable to do the job, but now I have to worry about his chief of staff playing president. I don't need this. Especially as we head into primary season," said Lexi, sitting on a couch in her office and kicking off her high heels.

"This might be the opening you need to shut him down."

"Which one? Vincent or the President?"

"Both," said Mel. "Vincent, because he overstepped his authority and made an international incident worse. The President, because he didn't issue the statement and let Vincent do it instead. Hell, you need nothing else on the President. The cabinet is already yours. You are already the President for all intents and purposes. None of them are going to talk because you would take them down with you. We just need to put Vincent in his place, and he just gave us the ammunition."

Lexi sat twirling a pen, thinking through what Mel said.

"You handle this?"

"My pleasure. Vincent is a hack. He doesn't have money and is counting on a book deal to make his post-White House money. He'll crumple like a disposable water bottle."

"Just get him to keep his mouth shut. Don't make him desperate. Desperate people have nothing to lose."

"I'll take care of it."

"You always do," finished Lexi, looking down at her text messages on her phone, dismissing her chief of staff.

# Chapter 6

Luc Gauthier stood in a large room with several wooden conference tables
pushed to the walls, creating a large open area. On the floor, spread out on
tarps and sheets, were pieces of debris from the explosion that had killed the
President of France, Jean Paul Gaspard, in the fall.

Luc sipped his espresso as a woman sat amongst the debris, holding up
pieces for observation. She was younger than Luc, probably early thirties,
with shoulder length pink, turquoise, and blonde hair with white streaks.
Glasses perched on the end of her nose. She periodically slid them up and
then down again as she scrutinized each piece.

"Annie?" asked Luc softly in French. She did not respond and continued
to examine a piece of debris, turning it in the room's light.

When she did not respond, Luc retreated to a chair, pushed against the
wall on one side of the room. He knew better than to distract Annie from
her focus. He sat down and reviewed the room.

Alain Chaumont, then Prime Minister, and now the new president of
France, had asked him to get involved in the investigation into why and
how their friend Gaspard had been killed. Luc had reluctantly agreed. He'd
stipulated he wouldn't return to Interpol.

Alain had kept his word. Luc was now installed in a basement conference
room a couple of blocks from the Palace of Justice, in the La Bibliotheque
du Palais de Justice, the Library of Lawyers building.

It was dark, musty, and quiet. Exactly what Luc had asked for.
Importantly, it was away from both the Paris Prefect of Police and Interpol's
meddling. Unfortunately, Luc was having little luck in tracking down leads.
No better than his former counterparts in those agencies. With the arrival of
Annie, he hoped his luck would change.

He looked once more at the woman sitting on the floor. Luc had worked with her previously when he was the chief investigator at Interpol. Her particular skills of observation and keen analytical mind had helped him crack more than one case where obvious investigative techniques failed.

He noticed she was now rocking back and forth as she reviewed the piece in her hand. She set it down and picked up another, continuing to rock back and forth in her seated position.

"Annie, what do you see?" asked Luc in a calming tone.

"Have you slept with anyone since your wife died, Luc," responded Annie, in a normal tone.

"Annie, we discussed this before. No sex talk. You should limit your questions to the evidence. What do you see?"

"You need someone to sleep with," she said, turning to look at him. "You know, the nuns tell me I sleep with God every night. It's not particularly satisfying," she said with a disappointed sigh.

"Annie, we can discuss sex later. What do you see?"

Annie kept looking at Luc and stopped rocking. "I'd rather talk about your sex life. It is easier to solve than this puzzle."

"OK Annie. I promise I will. What do you see?"

"You will what? Talk about it, or do it?" she asked.

She stood up and started rearranging the pieces on the floor. Moving the larger pieces farther away and the smaller pieces to the middle. The parts were now in a semicircle approximately 180 degrees in an arc beyond the middle. She moved one part and backed up, looking out over the pieces.

"What do you see, Annie?" asked Luc again, gently.

"No. No. No," she said over and over. She moved in again, moving pieces until there was a clear path from the center out in almost a complete circle. She stood, now looking at two distinct arcs from the center. Annie was in the center, turning her back to the debris behind her. She took a step back over a small pile of debris at her feet and turned to Luc.

"Now I see. These are the parts from your bomber," she said, pointing to a group of tiny pieces at her feet in the center.

"Are you sure Annie?"

"Yes, the bomb detonated with approximately 2.4 kilos of nails, 1.8 kilos of ball bearings and 1 kilo of broken glass. The bomber faced here, toward Gaspard. As he detonated, the force of the explosives in the center of these items blew 42% of the materials toward the President. As he was in the 15 degrees of arc directly in front, it maximized the force," she said, spreading her arms in a small arc toward the front.

"It dispersed by an order of magnitude for each 30 degrees to either side. People who were only 20 feet from the President but down and away were not killed, only maimed," said Annie, clinically as if she were explaining an algebra problem.

"Yes Annie, only the President, two bodyguards and two aides who were on either side were killed in front of the bomber. Most of the casualties were behind. How?"

Annie nodded. "Of course. 58% of the projectiles went behind the bomber. The explosives liquified his soft tissue, leaving only his spine and ribcage intact, initially after the explosion, until the projectiles pulverized these in their rearward trajectory. Most of the damage was to those on either side," she said, pointing to the two arcs of debris.

"The closeness and density would have maximized the damage as these projectiles easily entered and exited through 10 or 12 people before losing their penetrating velocity. Someone who understood the physics of explosives designed this bomb. They knew to have projectiles and explosives on the back and front of the bomber to effect all around, not just kill our president."

"Annie, how can you tell this?"

She grabbed Luc and took him by the hand, leading him to the debris field.

"See how the size changes? See how the composition of the materials changes the farther we move. We are now 15 feet away, six or maybe seven people from the detonation. We now see pieces of cell phones, cosmetic cases, even pieces of shoe heel and part of a necklace. These show the degradation of the velocity of the projectiles. They are losing their ability to break what they hit. From this, I can see the first survivors were standing here," she said as she moved 27 feet behind the center and toward the inside, next to the clear path behind the bomber.

Luc shook his head. Annie was entirely correct. The closest survivor was standing exactly where she was. They had lost their right arm but survived the blast that killed others further back.

"What else do you see?"

Annie turned back to the center and looked at the small pile of debris she had placed at the origin of the blast.

"The bomber did not have a phone. Or keys. Or a ring. These parts would have survived because only the blast pulverized them. Any hard objects on the body would not have entirely disintegrated."

She sat down, looking at the small pile. There were several small pieces of metal that looked like they might have been circular at one time. There were also a couple of chunks of other metal, also not easily recognized. Luc sat down next to Annie, who was rocking again.

He reached out to pick up a piece of mangled metal.

"Gromet. From a sneaker."

Luc nodded. He picked up another piece about an inch long and half an inch wide. It showed signs of being burned by high temperature. What might have once been stainless steel was now tarnished black. It had a slight bend to it. Luc rubbed his finger on the metal and could feel some type of etching below his finger. He rubbed harder, to no avail.

"Annie, how can I find out what is underneath this?" asked Luc.

"Lemons."

"Ah. Thank you."

Annie's phone alarm rang. Expertly switching off the alarm, she went to the table where her lunch box was sitting. She opened it, took out a peanut butter sandwich, a celery stalk, a juice box, and an apple. Sitting at the table, she placed her hands together in prayer and quickly recited her mantra, thanking God for the food. She then unwrapped her sandwich.

Luc watched, as he always did, as she took a bite of sandwich, then celery, then a sip of juice and a bite of the apple. Continuing this rotation until she finished the last bite of sandwich, celery, sip of juice, and of the apple. She placed the debris back in the lunch box.

"Do you enjoy living with the nuns?" he asked as she finished.

"Yes Luc. They talk, teach me to stay calm, and to focus. You know I need focus. And purpose. Thank you for sending me to them."

"That is good, Annie. Are you happy to work with me again?"

Annie smiled. "Yes Luc. Now, can we talk about sex?"

#

Luc was in his run-down apartment, sipping scotch and reviewing evidence files. What he did every night since agreeing to take on the case. Glancing at the lemons and bowl on the counter, he walked there pulling the blackened piece of metal from the lemon juice bath.

He scraped a fingernail on the edge. Miraculously, some of the black came off. Picking up an old toothbrush, he scrubbed at the black on the bracelet. Soon the dull silver of the stainless was revealed. Luc could see part of a symbol on the metal. He turned it back and forth, trying to see if the angle would alter his perspective. Perhaps it was a piece of artwork, a symbol from a necklace or bracelet. But why would the bomber have that, but no phone or rings?

#

Annie looked up, once again on the floor, contemplating the debris. He had never noticed her bracelet before.

"Annie, what is that?" asked Luc, pointing to her bracelet.

"It tells medical personnel of my condition."

"What does it tell them?"

"That I am autistic."

"Anything else?" asked Luc again in a calm voice.

Annie took off the bracelet. "Look on the inside."

Luc turned the bracelet. Engraved on the inside was contact information for the convent where Annie lived. It also listed her 'a high-functioning autistic savant. Responds to calm voices'. He looked closer at the bracelet. It showed four colored puzzle pieces fitting together.

Luc returned to his desk and picked up the piece of bracelet he had cleaned the night before. The part of the shape he could not figure out was a portion of a puzzle piece on the bracelet, just like the one Annie wore.

He looked on the back side, but unlike Annie's, there was nothing on this portion of the inside.

Luc handed it back to Annie, who took it, silently placing it back on her wrist. She kept looking at the debris.

Luc contemplated his discovery.

"Annie, are you sure the debris in that pile is from the bomber?"

"99.4598734 percent," she recited without changing her focus.

"Thank you, Annie."

The bomber was autistic. Luc could feel the anger building at this revelation. Suicide bombing was one of the most cowardly crimes one investigates. To use a person with limited capability to understand what they were doing was beyond heinous.

Luc knew something of the disorder, having originally rescued Annie from a syndicate using her talents to help with their money laundering and accounting schemes. He'd placed her with the nuns at the suggestion of his late wife, Marie. He always thought it ironic that someone obsessed with talking about sex would do well with an enclave of women, who had sworn off sex.

She thrived with the nuns, helping them with their finances and investments of their charitable funds. Luc and Marie had stayed in touch with the nuns to make sure Annie was OK. When his wife and child died and he quit Interpol, he had ceased checking in on Annie, just as he had withdrawn from every other aspect of his former life.

Luc pulled out his phone and dialed.

"We need to meet," he spoke to the voice that answered.

# Chapter 7

Nick sat down in a booth in a cafe just off the Colorado State University campus. He'd woken up with a dozen protesters outside his house at 6am, banging drums and chanting. After confronting them on the silliness of their calling *him* a fascist. He even used their own words and tactics to educate them, that they were the ones exhibiting fascist tactics. They gave up when it was clear he wasn't going to call the police or make the scene they had hoped for. All the same, Nick now realized his life would never be the same.

After his confrontation with the protesters, he was hungry. He hunkered down in his booth, trying to stay anonymous. Immediately, one of the wait staff appeared with a steaming mug of dark roast coffee.

"Senator, good to see you," said the pretty brunette with a big smile.

"Jess, you know it's Nick. How are things? Seems pretty quiet," said Nick, looking around the thankfully mostly empty cafe.

"Yep. It is *a* Wednesday, so it's always slow between breakfast and lunch. With school out for Christmas break, not a lot going on," explained Jessica, a long-time server at the cafe.

"You running the joint today?"

"Yep, the boss lady went to visit her mom in Michigan for the holidays. She'll be sad she missed you."

"Tell her I said hi and I'll catch her the next time I'm in town."

"You bet. You going to sit and drink your coffee a while?"

Nick nodded.

"Anyone joining you today?"

"Nope, just me."

"OK, just give a holler when you are ready to order."

"Thanks Jess, I will."

Nick sat nursing his second refill of the cafe's dark roast, glancing through news streams on his phone. Most of it was coverage of the attacks in Europe. The death count was up to eighty-four total, with sixty of them children. Many others were in the hospital with horrible injuries. The authorities still had no motive. Nick sensed someone coming up behind him. He looked up.

"Well, look what the cat dragged in."

"You're the cat lady, not me. I'm a Labrador guy," responded Nick, getting up to give the older woman standing at his booth a hug.

"Andrea, how the hell are you? It seems like forever since we've seen each other."

"Well, *Senator* Turner, you seem to have been busy this last year or so," said Andrea, a twinkle in her blue eyes and a crooked smile on her lined face. Her gray hair was styled in a fashionable above the shoulder bob, with an expensive scarf around her neck and sweater. "May I?" she asked, pointing to the empty booth.

"Of course, have a seat. You can fill me in on all the professorial gossip I've been missing," laughed Nick.

"It is mostly about you, so it should not be too surprising."

"I bet. Especially from the Philosophy and Poly-Sci departments. Surprised I'm not banned from campus," said Nick with a chuckle as Jess arrived.

"Jess, not sure if you have ever met Professor Andrea Weston."

"I've seen you in and out of the cafe through the years. A pleasure to meet you. Any friend of Nick's is a friend of ours. Can I get you something to drink?"

"Coffee would be fine, cream and sugar please," she said, looking around the table noticing Nick was drinking his black.

"Coming right up."

"So, my former colleagues are talking about me? No surprise, I guess," as Jess returned with coffee, cream, and sugar.

"Kids too. You've made quite a stir."

"I sense some disappointment."

"I'll be honest Nick. Your lack of support for the removal of the filibuster disappointed me. So were a lot of us."

"Andrea, if I may ask, exactly why?"

"Why? Look around. Society is crumbling. Crime is rising. Drugs are rampant. People are suffering. Only an institution like the Federal Government has the power to enact change at a significant enough level to have a major impact. The states can only do so much. The filibuster was being used to stop legislation from passing that would help ease these problems. Surely you can see that," she said in an almost pleading tone.

Nick paused, looking into his coffee cup before answering.

"Did you support the building of the border wall?"

"You know I did not," answered Andrea. Nick nodded.

"How about the legislation to force sanctuary cities to give up federal funding if they remained sanctuary cities? Or stripping planned parenthood of federal funding if they continued to perform elective abortions?"

Andrea shook her head 'no' at each.

"You, of course, know why none of them got made into laws?"

"Sure, the Party stopped them because they were horrible ideas."

"Actually, no, that is not how they were stopped. These were a couple of laws the previous Opposition administration tried to pass when they had majorities in the House, Senate, and the White House. Majorities, I might add, that are much bigger than the ones we, rather the Party, enjoy today."

"What is your point?"

"My point is the way the Party could stop this was with the legislative filibuster. The tool specifically put into the Constitution by the founders to ensure a simple majority would not rule over the minority. Until a month ago, it took a majority of sixty senators to pass legislation, almost always ensuring minority involvement and compromise to craft legislation with input from both parties."

Andrea crossed her arms, leaning back as Nick continued.

"Despite a majority Opposition government, the minority, our Party, could still make their voice heard and demand changes to legislation. If not, they could use the filibuster to ensure legislation brought to vote without their input would not pass. The filibuster ensured a majority of 50 to 50 does not treat the minority as if the majority is 100-0."

Not seeing a reaction, Nick kept going.

"That is why I voted to keep it. It was the last bastion to ensure the minority still has a say in the crafting of legislation. Unlike my colleagues in the Senate leadership, I am not assuming we will be in the majority forever. When this inevitably happens again, I want to squeeze concessions from the majority in order to pass less radical bills."

"Well, it is a different world now. The Opposition lost and we have an agenda to pass to save the country," said Andrea indignantly.

"Does the make-up of the federal courts and the Supreme Court bother you?"

"You know it does. *Roe* gone and now what we are trying to do to codify it in Congress is hanging by a thread because the last buffoon got to pack the court."

"Did he? He followed the rules and the processes. It was us who made it possible, and acceptable, by doing it first," explained Nick.

"Hardly. We fought tooth and nail. All of his nominees are criminals. We showed it to the world, and they still got voted in, if only barely," she huffed.

Nick looked up to see Jess approaching. He gave a subtle nod of his head and she headed back to the kitchen.

"Andrea, we did it. We gave them the ability to take those seats. We killed the judicial filibuster years before when we had a majority so *we* could get our federal judges appointed over opposition. So, we could get our judges approved with 51 votes. We blew up the safeguards the founders put in place to keep radical judges of either party from being approved over the objections of the minority. We made those three seats possible. As luck would have it, the vacancies happened under the Opposition and not our Party."

"You mean your former Party. That will all change now that it's gone. We expand the court until we get enough liberals to overturn the conservatives. It will have to wait until after the election now, thanks to your antics."

Nick shook his head. "You are missing my point, Andrea. What happens if Lexi does not win the election in November? What if Garcia from Texas does? Plus, the Senate and the House. With no filibuster, it is easy for them to pass all that stuff we stopped before using the filibuster. What happens then?"

"Revolution. Anarchy. The end of America," replied Andrea in a fierce tone.

"Really? You honestly believe another Opposition president in the office is going to be the end of America?"

"I do, don't you? Can't you see what it would mean? Women would have no rights over their body any longer, in every state. What is next? They'll destroy voting rights, implementing voter ID requirements. Disenfranchising millions of American voters. They would round up every alien in the country and immediately deport them. Tearing parents from their American-born children. Pull immigrant kids out of schools and day cares and sending them in bus loads back to Mexico or worse, putting them in camps with no rights. They would force the teachers to teach what the conservatives want. Prejudice and racism would return. Separate but *unequal* would be re-instituted. To be poor, black, brown, gay or trans, would be a death sentence under the Opposition. The Supreme Court has already assured college is no longer an option for the poor or minorities. With their racist rulings striking down student loan forgiveness and affirmative action. It is clear we need to expand the court to re-institute these and prevent further damage."

Nick sat back in his booth, stunned by what he was hearing.

"Andrea, what do you think will happen if I win?"

She laughed. "You win? Come on Nick. This is all just a publicity stunt. Are you writing a book or looking to get a gig on EXN? Nobody is taking your announcement seriously."

"Why?"

"You said so yourself. They appointed you to fill out the term of a Party Senator. To vote with the Party. To support our platform and you betrayed us with your filibuster vote. You have lost the base. The members in Colorado now despise you. All liberal and progressive Party members everywhere hate what you did and while the Opposition applauded your effort, they don't like you either. You are a candidate without a party for a reason."

"Interesting."

She looked at him for a second.

"You're serious? You really think you are running for president? Legitimately?"

Nick nodded, waving at Jess for a refill.

"I thought you were smart. Now I'm not so sure. What do you think you can say to cause enough people to look at you as a viable candidate?"

Jess showed up with coffee.

"Eating anything today?" she asked, looking at Andrea.

"Nothing for me, just came in for a coffee. I will take a cup to go, though."

"I'll have a veggie omelet with a side of fruit and toast. Thanks Jess," smiled Nick.

"How do I plan to win? Andrea, you know I respect you and I think you are a dynamite philosophy and ethics professor. I disagree almost entirely with everything you've said today." Nick held up a hand. "Hear me out please, then you can tell me I am full of shit."

Andrea shut her mouth, sat back, and crossed her arms again, clearly not inclined to listen.

"Care to hazard a guess how many times the Party used the evil filibuster in the last year of the last Opposition administration? To *stop* the 'rightfully elected majority from implementing their expected platform for which their voters elected them'. Using the words of my colleague, the Senate Majority Leader?" She stared daggers.

"*300* times. The Party used it three-hundred times. The Opposition used it once. Now imagine how much legislation would have passed that you would have loathed without the filibuster being in place to help the minority have a say? Now you are all in favor of removing this tool from the toolkit because the Opposition dare to use it occasionally. They have used it nowhere near the amount the Party. This is because we can convince the Opposition to work with us occasionally. When the shoe is on the other foot, we never work or attempt to work with Opposition. At least not since Lexi or Fontana have been the Majority/Minority Leaders these last 20 years."

"And your point is?"

"What happens when we are in the minority again, like I said?"

"Unlikely to happen. Once we pass our agenda, folks are going to be so happy with the problems we're solving, we'll never have to worry about losing the majority," answered Andrea with confidence.

"Let's say it happens. Then what?"

"Like I said before. Revolution or anarchy. It all gets burned down."

"What you're saying is it is your way or the highway? What about the people who didn't vote for the Party?" asked Nick.

"No Nick, it is the difference between enacting what is right and just and what is wrong and hurtful to people and the planet. We have one chance to reverse the wrongs done by countless mistakes of our prior leaders. Of both parties, I might add. It is now or never."

"Andrea, I disagree. I believe in the Constitution. I believe we have made mistakes, but our Constitution has helped us work through these mistakes and has provided a framework within which we can recover. To learn from, and to improve upon, our way of life because of the freedoms it gives us. The agenda of the Progressive wing of the Party seeks to replace those freedoms with blind obedience to their vision and any who cannot adhere to it, who dare to stand against it, must be overcome."

"You have to break a few eggs to make an omelet. If we have to give up a few freedoms for the good of all, so be it," she replied, righteously.

"Andrea, that is not democracy. It is tyranny. That's why I'm running. It is also why I think I'll convince people from both parties to vote for me. Common sense tells me no one wants to be a serf or slave. The progressive agenda is willingness to march into the bondage of government dependency and to turn one's back on the freedoms that have made and will once again make this the best civilization the planet has ever seen."

Jess stood nearby, listening to Nick's words. Once he finished, she set his plate down. Andrea wrapped her scarf around her neck.

"Nick, you were always good at the speeches and lectures. You do have a way with words. I can see you are getting better and more persuasive, but you are hopelessly naïve. The Constitution also allowed all the current injustices to happen. It is old and for another time. Freedom allowed all of this to occur. The freedom to breed bigotry and greed. To build fabulous wealth on the backs of the less fortunate. To collect taxes and distribute them to corporate cronies. Most egregiously, it allowed and institutionalized racism in all aspects of life. Your precious Constitution is now the problem," she finished, standing up and looking down at Nick, who did not get up.

"Andrea, it is unfortunate, a well-educated person, like yourself, cannot be swayed by common sense and facts. Your blind faith in government is unfortunate. Not only for you, but for our country. Without people like you, they could not steer us down the path to totalitarianism," stated Nick.

Andrea laughed confidently.

"Nick, I wish you luck. Luckily for you, the Vice President and her policies will restore the very freedoms you are so concerned about. She will provide hope for the less fortunate and make the uber rich return some of their ill-gotten gains to fund these changes. If a few freedoms need to be relinquished to solve these problems, then sign me up. I'll make that small sacrifice. Happy Holidays," she finished heading out.

Nick looked up and noticed the few other patrons in the cafe were pretending to not have been listening to their conversation. Jess showed up with a fresh pot of coffee and a new mug.

"I figured you were probably cold by now. Do you need me to put the food under the heater for a minute?"

"Thanks Jess, I think it will be fine."

"She's wrong you know."

"Excuse me?"

Jess set the pot down on the table and sat down opposite Nick.

"Nick, I heard the last bit you said. You're right. I can tell you I am scared about the way things are going. I'm not political, and I don't watch the news. In my gut, I know things are not good and we're going in the wrong direction. When the Party is in charge, things have only gotten worse. What they are saying they want to do sounds good, but it is not right. I just want to be left alone," she looked around the room, before continuing in a softer tone.

"The COVID stuff terrified me, but after two years of lock downs and masks and shutting down the business and then another year and a half for the second wave, we no longer think they know what they're doing. None of it mattered. I have had ten vaccine shots now, and I got a mild dose twice. Lots of folks I know still caught it, even after everything we did. I also know three people who committed suicide because they didn't want to be vaccinated. They lost their jobs and the ability to get a job unless they got the vaccine."

"There is a definite unwillingness to use common sense and admit mistakes when we have made them. Especially in how the pandemics were handled," agreed Nick.

"Nick, this is crazy. Everyone is on edge. Everyone is angry, just like your friend. Nobody is happy anymore. You have my vote and I never vote," laughed Jess. "Just keep talking truth and I think you'll have more people on your side. I see idiots like her from the college come in here all the time. They are all the same. Smarter than all the rest of us, looking down on us like we are worthless. They are not the majority. You keep fighting," said Jess as she got up.

"Thanks Jess. I guess my days of sitting down for a quiet cup of coffee are over. Just the right words to make me forget my blahs."

Jess smiled and headed back to the kitchen.

Several of the patrons stopped by to introduce themselves and to take a selfie. Those who came by had heard his debate and said they agreed with his point of view. He also overheard several tables loudly expressing disgust at him for even still claiming to be in the Party. He smiled, paid his bill and left, heading back to his house.

It was a twenty-minute walk through leafless, tree-lined streets. The weather was sunny but cold. As he walked by one of the few commercial buildings, he thought he saw a flash in the reflection of the glass windows. Quickly stepping to the side, he turned, looking behind. There was only a young couple walking in the opposite direction. Nick shook his head as he resumed walking.

Down the street behind Nick, Roland Gill cursed silently. Nick had almost spotted him. While Nick had no formal special forces training, he reminded himself he had showed remarkable capabilities in the past. He would have to be more careful. Roland looked down as his phone silently vibrated. If this was the summons he expected, his studying of Turner would have to resume in Washington, DC.

# Chapter 8

"He is making a fool out of me. I deserve to head up the investigative team doing his background," demanded Lauren Bergamo.

"Lauren, we have other researchers digging into his past. We need you to stay focused on reporting the current news and his actions, not his background," said her producer, Jeff Carter.

"I need to be involved. I need to dig something up and pay him back," said Lauren, fuming.

"Lauren don't get personally involved; it won't end well. You're on camera every day and there are too many chances for you to do or say something to make it worse. This guy is going nowhere and will be gone in another 15 minutes."

"What have they found so far? Anything?" she asked, ignoring Jeff's comments.

"Nothing yet, but they are really just getting started. As a senator, he was just another politician. Running for president is a whole different show," said Jeff, rubbing his hands together in delight at the prospect.

"Exactly. That's why I keep trying to catch him on camera," she said, leaning forward in her chair, her dark auburn hair falling forward over her shoulders. "If I can get him to say something, to make an offhand comment, something we can get him with…"

"Lauren, for your own sake, let it go. He is on to you now. He is going to take anything you say, anything you ask, and use it to embarrass you."

"I know, but I can't let him get away with treating me this way just because I'm a woman," grumbled Lauren, throwing her phone on the desk and leaning back in her chair.

"I think your being a woman has nothing to do with it. In fact, I would say he is one of the more respectful politicians when it comes to being courteous. You rubbed him wrong with the whole traitor thing," said Jeff hesitantly.

Lauren smiled, leaning forward again. "Good. Getting under his skin could be useful. I will catch him eventually. All these guys have something to hide. Teenage girlfriends, or boyfriends, drugs, dirty business deals, Chinese ties. This guy comes across as a saint. There is always something. I will find it. With or without your help," she said in a determined tone with a fire in her eye.

"Please don't," said Jeff in an almost pleading tone. "Just let it go."

"Why do you care?" asked Lauren suspiciously.

"Lauren, please. The higher ups just want you out there."

"I see. Why did you guys edit my interview with him? That really pissed him off. Now he is mad at *me* because of it. He hates me because the network, our vaunted *America's News Channel*, decided to creatively edit my interview. You guys set me up. You hoped he would confront me and make it look like the big man is attacking the poor innocent little female reporter," she accused, now standing in her cubicle, looking down at Jeff, sitting in her lone guest chair.

"That's not how it happened," replied Jeff weakly, holding out his hands.

"Really? You just confirmed it. I don't like being used as a pawn in someone's game."

"Are you kidding? How long have you been doing this? You know the game. They can use you anyway they want. Selectively edit your reporting, put you in uncomfortable situations for ratings. You name it. They own all of us. This should not surprise you," responded Jeff, almost amazed at Lauren's tone.

"So, you're saying you guys are throwing me out there like a sacrificial lamb to rile him up? Get him to go ballistic on me so you can make him look bad? Like a red flag in front of the bull," remarked Lauren, looking down at Jeff with her hands on her hips.

"I get to keep going out and have him embarrass me for ratings in the hope something good comes out of it for ANC? And if my reputation gets trashed in the interim, that is just too bad. Have you seen the memes?" Lauren held up her phone, showing a picture of her smiling face, wearing a tight blouse with a word cloud saying, 'Truth? Who cares? Just look at my boobs'. Jeff glanced at it and looked away sheepishly.

"I didn't decide; it came from higher up. Besides, we are all pawns in someone's game. That's what they pay all of us to do. To alter facts and create realities, *they* decide. Lauren, don't be naïve. We are struggling with the ratings. EXN is killing us. We need to get eyeballs on the screen. More eyeballs on the screen are more folks looking at you. They see you being aggressive and him attacking you. It is good for your reputation too. What better way to do that than put you out there waving your 'red flag in front of the bull' as you say? It worked. Ratings went up. You even got a segment on *Women's Viewpoint*. Plus, it almost worked. Turner nearly lost it," finished Jeff with a slight smile.

"What planet are *you* on? It totally backfired on us. Sure, you got a few more eyeballs, but EXN got more. What's worse, Turner got on *Tommy* and he had the best ratings in his whole fucking history," blurted Lauren, leaning forward, looming over Jeff, and raising her voice.

"Not only did you throw me out there, you made sure more people than ever got to see me get humiliated. Then you gave Turner a venue to complain about *my* journalistic integrity and the dishonesty in reporting by our network, while blaming me for it. You guys should have checked this before you did it. You should have figured he had a recording of the whole interview showing we were lying about what he said." Lauren was now speaking so loudly that people in cubes turned to check out the commotion.

"Lauren, calm down," quieted Jeff, as she paced back and forth in front of him in her small cube. He looked around and saw some heads bobbing up and down over various cubicle walls.

"You know what, I won't calm down and in fact, if you won't put me on the story, then I think maybe I'll take my 'damaged journalistic principles' elsewhere," she threatened, turning to go. "Maybe I'll go to EXN or Substack and do my own reporting. I'll start with what it means to be a female reporter at ANC. Perhaps even discuss how producers here knowingly play with the facts."

"Lauren, wait, let's talk this through," said Jeff as Lauren grabbed an empty copy paper box from under her desk and swept the contents of her desktop into it. She grabbed her lone plant and headed for the elevator. By this time, others in the forest of cubicles stood up to see what was unfolding. As she neared the elevator, Jeff came scurrying after her with his cell phone pressed to his ear.

"Lauren, wait a minute," Jeff caught her as she entered the elevator. He held the door as she gave him a look of menace. He moved his hand and let the door shut without another word.

When the elevator opened, Sherman Hallberg was waiting.

"Good day Miss Bergamo. Leaving early?" asked Sherman in a conversational tone. "May I help you with your box?"

"Mr. Hallberg, I appreciate the opportunities ANC gave me, but I think it is time for me to move on," stated Lauren, standing straight as she delivered her resignation.

"May I buy you a cup of coffee so we can chat for a minute," commanded Sherman, in a tone that left only one plausible answer.

Rather than make a scene, Lauren handed her box to Mr. Hallberg and followed him into the corporate cantina. They entered and headed to a back corner table. Several employees, seeing the network president approaching, got up from their table and moved to the other side of the cantina, leaving them alone.

One of the cantina employees showed up with tea for the Sherman and coffee for Lauren.

"Jeff called and told me you were unhappy with our coverage of the Senator," explained Sherman.

"You used me and made a fool out of me to improve ratings," accused Lauren.

"Indeed we did Lauren. How long have you been on this network?" asked Sherman, sipping his tea.

"Five years or so."

"Five years, seven months and three days to be exact, I checked. You know what else? You have three years, two months and twenty-seven days to go on your contract. Your contract also has an iron clad non-compete in it. I know because I wrote it myself. If you leave, not only will you not be paid, but we will also request you return a pro-rated amount of that ridiculous signing bonus we paid when you signed the contract extension."

Sherman took another drink of his green tea before continuing.

"Further, if you leave, you cannot join another network, appear on any network, or even be an independent investigative reporter, including blogging on Substack, as you suggested to Jeff. We own the rights to everything you write or say. So, unless you are going to turn letters on a game show, I suggest you march back upstairs, water your plant, and do the job for which we are paying you an obscene amount of money," finished Sherman with a smile.

"Maybe I'll get a lawyer and see what my options are," said Lauren defiantly, refusing to be intimidated.

"By all means, use some of your precious savings to pay some pricey lawyer to tell you if you leave, you are out of the news business. I was an entertainment contract lawyer and agent before I took over running this network. I have seen it all and know every trick they will try to play. In the end, all you'll do is spend your money, lose your fancy condo in Buckhead, and end up back in Topeka. Weren't you Miss Kansas or something?" asked Sherman.

"It was Indiana, but of course you know that. It is certainly one reason you hired me, though I stood my ground at not dyeing my hair blonde," countered Lauren.

"You said it, not me. We hired you strictly on the merits of your resume and your talent," proclaimed Sherman, in his best politically correct voice. "I guess you have a decision to make. Go back to being a weather girl in the Midwest or head back upstairs and take the assignments we give you. Gladly, and with a smile on your pretty face."

Sherman leaned back in his chair, sipped his tea while staring at Lauren to gauge her decision.

"How's your brother doing?" asked Sherman casually.

"What do you mean?" answered Lauren, stiffening slightly.

"How's his rehab going? Painkillers are a terrible addiction," said Sherman, looking down at his phone. "This time though, hasn't he graduated to dealing as well? I believe the rehab was court ordered so he could get probation rather than jail time. Pretty expensive too. Nice of you to cover that for him."

Lauren merely sat, trying not to let the shock on her face show at his knowledge of her brother's situation.

"And your mom, are you still sending her money to live on every month? Must be tough for her ever since your dad left her for that much younger woman. Didn't your dad meet your future stepmom at a party you took your parents to? That kinda sucks doesn't it? Mom's not taking it well, is she? Seems to be following in your brother's footsteps. You know what they say: marijuana is a gateway drug to bigger things. Didn't you do a story about that a year ago? Won an award if I remember right," said Sherman, trailing off.

"I'm sure they can both do fine without your help and money. At your age, a career change makes perfect sense. Well, I need to get back upstairs. You have a good day, Ms. Bergamo," nodded Sherman, smiling as he got up. "Happy Holidays, enjoy your holiday break," he added as he headed out of the cantina, back to his private elevator.

Lauren remained in the cantina, finishing her coffee. She picked up her paper box full of belongings, got in the elevator, and headed back up to her floor to put her plant back in her office.

# Chapter 9

Nick turned his Land Cruiser onto a side street and parked. As he got out, he stood in the bright sun, looking west at the snow-covered Rocky Mountains of the Colorado front range. Standing for a few seconds, watching his breath exhale in a cloud, he turned, heading into the building. In the lobby, a sign announced he was in the Weld County Colorado Sheriff's office. At the counter, he asked to see Sheriff Greene.

"I believe he is in. Let me check. Hold on a sec," said the uniformed deputy. Nick looked at her as she dialed a number. She was in full gear, pistol on one hip and Taser on another. Mic clipped high on one shoulder and other items of protection strapped in various positions on her vest and belts. When she got an answer on the phone, she looked up.

"Your name, please," she asked crisply.

"Nick Turner."

She repeated his name on the phone and then, in a moment of recognition, he could see her cheeks redden against the dark hair she had pulled back in a ponytail. She looked at him wide eyed and smiled finishing her conversation.

"He'll be right out, Senator. Sorry I didn't recognize you," she said, beaming as she stood up. Nick shook her outstretched hand.

"Nicole, if you would unhand the Senator," said a deep voice.

Nick turned, releasing the deputy's hand, and shook the outstretched hand of Sheriff Earl Greene.

"What brings you out to Greeley, Senator?" asked Earl.

"Was in the neighborhood and you said drop by anytime."

"I didn't expect you to take me up on the offer. Let's go to my office," said Earl, turning to lead the way.

Nick turned back to Deputy Nicole.

"Thank you for your help Deputy…"

"Minick, Nicole Minick," she said, still blushing.

"Thank you Deputy Minick," said Nick, turning to follow Sheriff Greene. As he did, he noticed the remaining people in the office were all staring at him. He now expected this, even if he still found it strange.

Nick followed the Sheriff down a corridor to an office in the southwest corner of the building. As Nick entered, he noticed the Sheriff had a magnificent view of the Rockies.

"Coffee?"

"That would be great. Just black," said Nick.

"I'd have been disappointed if you wanted it any other way, but then again you were Air Force," said Earl in a disapproving tone.

Nick was looking at the pictures on the wall. One caught his eye.

"Anbar?" asked Nick, looking at a picture of a team of special forces soldiers posed in front of a bridge over a river in a dry desert climate.

"Yes," said Earl, standing by Nick, handing him a cup of coffee.

He took the cup, taking a sip, sizing up the Sheriff. He was about Nick's height, a tad shorter at probably 6'2" or so, broader in the shoulders, short black hair, graying at the temples, and a tight beard and mustache. He still had the look of special forces warriors Nick had encountered a time or two in his past.

"Thanks, not bad, dark roast?"

"Can't stand the frufru stuff. I'd drink tar if I could get the machine to brew it. Can't be too strong."

"Agree, no such thing as too strong,"

Earl waved Nick to a chair and sat on the edge of his desk. "You didn't come out here to talk coffee, now did you?"

Nick, sensing Earl was a man of few words, replied, "I did not. I want you to come work for me."

Earl spit up his coffee. He held the coffee away from his chest and brushed his hand down the front of his shirt and tie.

"Surprised?" asked Nick, in a mischievous tone.

"Not at all, obviously. Shit, I just washed this shirt," commented Earl as he blotted at the coffee stains on the dark shirt.

"At least it's not a white shirt."

Earl nodded agreement. Walked around his desk and sat heavily in his chair. Nick got up after noticing the guest chair was intentionally lower than usual. Earl smiled.

"Interrogation 101. Nice try," said Nick.

"Actually, my predecessor set all this up. He was a real SOB. I didn't waste my time with redecorating."

"What do you waste your time with?" asked Nick as he continued to survey the pictures on the wall, a few more military and a few hunting. No family, wife, or children.

"The usual domestic disturbance, opioid overdose, lots of illegals, drug deals gone bad, and the occasional barroom brawl. We're a rural Opposition county after all. We don't get the protesters and looting, they get in Denver and Boulder. Or Fort Collins, since a professor announced a run for president," revealed Earl with a smile.

"Interesting," replied Nick, not taking the bait. "Sounds pretty boring. I mean, no looting or riots to handle that is."

"Senator, if they tried that shit up here, say looting Jimmy's liquor store, for instance. I'd find at least two dead looters from Jimmy's wife and probably three more from his workers. Jimmy being nearly blind from the IED he took in Fallujah. I wouldn't arrest them either and we don't have one of those Pavlovich funded DAs in this county. We believe in the rule of law around here," said Earl in a forceful tone.

Nick held up his hand with the coffee and the other palm first.

"Didn't mean to offend. Truth be told, I would think that is the right response."

After an uncomfortable pause, Nick spoke again.

"I'm serious. Turns out national campaigns need security, and some folks think I need to be more mindful of my personal security."

Earl rolled his eyes in reply. "Can't imagine why."

"You seem like a pretty capable guy, and I need someone I can trust. The way you handled the bar incident makes me think you're a good guy to have in my corner. I'll continue to piss people off. Eventually, I may go from nuisance to threat. I need someone to keep me alive while I take this journey," declared Nick, turning to look Earl in the eyes. He did not break eye contact.

"Senator, luckily the people you are pissing off are mostly in the Party. They don't have the guns or the guts for physical violence in most cases. They choose words and news cameras to make their smears and attacks. Just as deadly, though."

Nick nodded in understanding as the sheriff got up.

"We had two Capitol protesters who lived here. They both killed themselves once they finally got released after more than a year in prison with no charges. Having their pictures shown everywhere by the media and being accused of killing that poor policeman who died from the stroke, their lives were ruined."

"They couldn't find work. One became an addict. I arrested him five times for breaking into cars and houses in order to get stuff he could sell to get his fix. The last time he suicided by cop. So now I have a deputy who has to live with that guilt as fallout," said Earl, shaking his head before continuing. He looked up into Nick's face.

"The other gal took her husband's shotgun and ate it. Her son found her. I knew them. They were good people, fed up with Washington and our politicians. All they did was attend a protest, supposedly a right, according to that same media, but only as long as it is for the right cause, apparently. The media and Congress sacrificed these people to tarnish *a political candidate*. No one actually cared what happened to them."

Nick nodded as he sipped his coffee. "Before my time. If it is worth anything, the entire episode was wrong. An obvious example of the double standard the Party denies and the public is resigned too."

Earl turned to Nick, clearly worked up. "Look, I am all for arresting and prosecuting people for their actual crimes. Almost all were simple misdemeanors. Most broke nothing or hurt anyone, and they were used as props. Yet the anti-racist league protesters and rioters in Portland, Seattle, Chicago, Minneapolis, DC, you name an opposition run city, are on TV, on fucking camera, breaking into stores and walking out with thousands of dollars of someone's hard earned inventory. Yet we in law enforcement are the problem? They beat shopkeepers, kick police, try to burn them alive and other things and not one of them is ever charged. They certainly never have to pay for any of their protests, property damage or the looting." Earl paused, taking a calming breath.

"Even I've had a few smash and grabs at some of the high-end stores in Greeley. The ones that happen in Denver and Boulder are never prosecuted if they even bother to catch them. This unequal application of the law makes it really hard to enforce it."

"Sheriff, that's why I am running. I don't agree with any of that. In order to tear it down and have the rule of law applied equally and with a blind eye to race, politics or social status, I'm going to need to survive long enough to see this through. Come help me change things."

"Senator, you need professional security and an organization designed to do this. Besides, don't you get secret service protection?"

"Call me Nick, please. I wouldn't get secret service unless I become a viable candidate or a party nominee. Since I'm not going for either, I'd have to get to some threshold in the polls. No one has ever done that. It's a gray area. But even then, it is the end of December now. I doubt any of that would happen until August at the earliest. I'm not counting on ever getting it." Earl stared at Nick as he finished.

"I assume you know why I am a sheriff in a rural county in Colorado. It's a pretty good gig here. Nice people, slow life, minor issues to deal with. You're sitting in the biggest city in the county and while the drugs, illegals, and gang problems are getting more prevalent, I have the support of the community to be aggressive at keeping it under control. I'm pretty content," relayed Earl.

"Yes, I did my background on you. I know what you did and why you are hiding in Weld County," revealed Nick.

"I am not hiding."

"Right, running?" said Nick with a raised eyebrow. "Earl, a piece of advice. You can't run from your past. You need to confront it, head on, beat it, and then move on."

"I'm sure you've done just that," retorted Earl. "Senator, hero, presidential candidate. Real tough. What are you running from?"

"Same as you, Sheriff, trust me. I've been through hell. Looked the devil in the eye, spit in it, taken my medicine and come out the other side. The scars are there and the nightmares. You have to find a purpose and dive in. I did. This is my fate. I can't run from it. Lord knows I've tried, but it seems to pull me right back. If I can't escape it, then I am going to do all I can to succeed at whatever fate has in store," finished Nick, staring at the sheriff.

"I did what I did. I paid the price. It is the past. I have moved on. I live with it and do what I can to keep my people safe. You have exactly zero chance of winning. Why would I give this up for the next three, six, eleven months? After you lose, I have to find another gig like this? My people like me. I can keep this job as long as I want to," declared Earl.

"Earl, in the bar, what would you have done if I had laid those guys out?"

"I'd have arrested you."

"No, you wouldn't have. You knew they were all punks and as long as I didn't kill any of them, you'd have figured they had it coming, and I acted in self-defense. That's the kind of sheriff you are. You have a code. Fair is fair. Bullies and punks deserve to have their balls kicked in. Hide the women and children and deal with the bad guys. I've seen it before and frankly, it's my code, too."

"I guess we'll never know."

Nick stood up. "Any place around here where we can shoot?"

"Excuse me?" asked Earl, confused.

"I need to see if you can shoot. Can't have a head of security who can't hit the broad side of a barn," responded Nick skeptically.

Earl laughed. "You do know you need to be an expert marksman to be in the Special Forces unit I commanded?"

"Sure, but now you're older, fatter, slower, grayer."

"OK hotshot, what do you want to shoot? Pistols, rifles?"

"Shotguns. Sporting clays, trap, skeet, I don't care."

"Hang on." Earl picked up the phone, making a quick call while Nick went back to perusing pictures.

"OK, a buddy owns an outdoor shooting range close by," said Earl as he pulled out a shotgun case from a closet. "You need a gun?"

"No, I have mine in the car," Nick pointed to a picture on the wall showing a younger version of the sheriff, a big, muscular black guy with a big smile, standing with a tall lanky blond-haired guy in what looked like Afghanistan. "Is this him"?

"Yes," replied Earl, not even looking at the picture. "Let's go."

"OK, I'll drive. Less conspicuous than showing up at a shooting range in a sheriff cruiser."

"Suit yourself," shrugged Earl, throwing his case in the back seat of Nick's Land Cruiser. He noticed a shotgun case and a large gun bag, no doubt full of pistols and ammo.

"Planning on having to defend yourself?" asked Earl.

"This *is* Opposition territory," said Nick, not smiling.

#

They drove out of Greeley and up Colorado highway 85 toward the tiny towns of Nunn and Brush. Just outside Brush, Nick turned off the highway onto local dirt roads. A few minutes later, they arrived at an outdoor shooting range. He could see the towers used for launching sporting clays, essentially golf with shotguns. There were also a series of rifle ranges of various lengths, 50, 100, 200 and even 300 yards, carved out between giant shoulders of dirt thirty-five feet high on each side. They drove past the skeet houses to the trap ranges. Nick backed his Land Cruiser up to the second trap range.

"Trap OK with you? My skeet is rusty," asked Nick.

"Mine too. Never liked skeet, it is a bit too contrived for me, you always shoot to the same point. I like trap, unpredictable," nodded Earl.

They retrieved their shotgun cases and laid them on the picnic table outside the trap stand. Nick put on his shooting vest, shooting glasses, and dumped a box of twenty-five twelve-gauge shells into the pocket. The sun was now high in the sky and the temperature was perfect for shooting. He examined his headphones to make sure the battery powered sound suppression was working.

Earl was doing the same and opened his shotgun case. Pulling out a well-cared for shotgun with a dark walnut stock. Earl caught Nick admiring the gun and handed it to him.

"Very nice. Browning Broadway, a serious trap gun. You going to hustle me out of my money, Sheriff?"

"Hey, you asked for it. A hundred bucks?"

"Only if you let me shoot your gun as well. This is a classic. I'll use mine on the second round to get my money back," said Nick.

"Fair enough."

They proceeded to the range, working their way around the 45-degree course, shooting their 25 shots from the points of the compass. Nick and Earl made their way back to the table, emptying their pockets of their spent shotgun shells.

"It's a very sweet gun. A true beauty. Shoots like a dream and the aim is spot on," admired Nick.

"My father gave it to me and his father gave it to him. Not sure what will happen when I go. A museum, I guess," sighed Earl.

"Hey man, we're both still young enough. Maybe we'll find women who like projects?"

Earl let out a big laugh, his first true, cheerful laugh of the day.

"God help her, she'll have to be a saint. OK, you want your money now, or do I get a chance to win it back?"

"Your call."

"My call? I thought I was good. You didn't even come close to missing one. Talk about being hustled. Who taught you how to shoot? Some Olympian?" asked Earl.

"Funny you should say that. I don't think he ever shot in the Olympics, but he sure could have. You shouldn't have given me a gun with such wonderful sights," snickered Nick.

"What are you shooting? Can I see?" asked Earl, taking off his shooting glasses.

"Be my guest."

Earl went over to Nick's gun case. Inside was a beautiful work of art. A polished wooden stock in some golden brown European wood and several sets of over and under barrels in various gauges.

"Holy Shit," said Earl as he carefully lifted out the stock, examining the inlay. He set the twelve-gauge barrels into the stock, closing the breech.

"Is this what I think it is?" asked Earl.

"If you think it is a 1968 Perazzi MX8, then you are correct," said Nick with a smile.

"Where in the world did you get this?"

"It was a gift from a friend, who *was* an Olympian," smiled Nick.

"Some friend. This gun is worth a small fortune."

"And it shoots even better. Care to give it a run?"

"Really? You wouldn't mind?"

"Fair is fair. See if you can beat me with mine."

They headed back to the table after their second round. Nick broke down his gun and put it back in the felt indentation in the case.

"I guess I failed," said Earl as he handed Nick two crisp $100 bills. "You got 'em all again."

Nick took the bills from Earl and handed them back.

"You got 23 each time. That's pretty darn good. You're hired. Consider this a down payment."

"Just for grins, are you as good with other guns?" asked Earl.

"Shotguns are one of my weaker ones," laughed Nick.

"Then what the hell do you need me for?"

"I need someone to make sure no one around me is getting killed. I am not worried about me, but I have to worry about everyone else. That's why I need someone who can think through scenarios and plan. Make sure we are prepared to react on the fly," he answered.

"I thought I read you were a pilot. Last time I checked, you have to fire like six shots to pistol qualify in the Air Force?" asked Earl.

"OK, I am going to explain this, so even a dumb snake eating army grunt can understand. I was in the Navy, in Intelligence, and then the Air National Guard. Not the 'Chair Force'. I'm wondering if all that wandering around in the woods, eating snails and God knows what else, earning your merit badges for your girl scout beanie, ruined your memory," said Nick in a sarcastic tone, shaking his head while smiling.

"No shit? You were a weekend warrior and got called up? That sucks," said Earl, not taking any offence at Nick's ribbing of his Special Forces training, as they finished putting their guns back in their cases.

"Actually, I transferred to the 190th squadron of the Idaho Air National Guard since they were already deployed. I wanted to fly Warthogs to protect you guys on the ground," clarified Nick.

"You're a strange man," said Earl, shaking his head.

"I presume that is a yes," remarked Nick, pausing as Earl slowly nodded. "Good, so here is the plan and I need you to draw up a way to protect those around me as I implement it," explained Nick as they put the gun cases back in the Land Cruiser.

# Chapter 10

Nick glanced at his phone as he drove through rural New Mexico. He was two hours out of Albuquerque in a rental car headed toward Taos. As he neared the outskirts of town, his phone told him to turn onto yet another dirt road. As he drove further into the wild, he noticed small farms and ranches. His phone said it was time to turn again. This time down a driveway past a faded mailbox in the shape of a red barn.

He turned off the navigation as it announced he had arrived at his destination. He drove up to a white farmhouse with a wraparound porch. It appeared to be in the midst of being remodeled. The siding was patched in several places with unpainted wood. As he walked on to the porch, he noticed many floorboards were in the same state, patched but unpainted. He reached for the screen door to knock.

"You lost?" asked a woman walking from around the corner of the house, hand at her hip. Nick glanced to his right. Confronting him was an older, raven-haired woman, wearing jeans and a hoodie with Harvard emblazoned across the front. Her face was light brown and her dark eyes were all business as they surveyed Nick. She was turned at a slight angle. Classic defensive shooters posture. Recognizing this, Nick slowly held up his phone.

"Not unless the phone is giving bad directions, which I suppose is not out of the question out here."

"OK, if you aren't lost, what can I do for you?" asked the woman. This time she moved her hand away from her hip, revealing the butt of a holstered revolver.

"I'm just here to talk, promise," said Nick, now holding up both hands peacefully. "I assume you are Denise Rojas?"

"Shit. I assumed Chuck was messing with me. I thought I recognized you. Senator, if you don't mind my asking, what the fuck are you doing?" asked Denise, as she walked up the steps to the door.

"That is an excellent question," said Nick, drawing out each word carefully. "That's why I'm here, because I, rather, we, don't really know what we are doing. Or frankly, what we *should* be doing."

"You sure as shit have that right. I thought Chuck was smarter," she said, shaking her head, opening the door and walking inside. She led the way through a living room in various stages of remodel. "Sorry for the mess. This place was falling down when I moved in. It was supposed to be therapeutic. Now I need therapy."

"Building things is good for the soul," Nick said in a philosophical tone.

She turned and looked back at him.

"You own a house, Senator?" asked Denise as she continued to guide Nick through rooms in various states of disorder.

"I do."

As they walked into the kitchen, she pointed to a table with a couple of chairs. "Whoever said this was good for the soul was obviously the owner of a Home Depot. Coffee?" she asked.

"That would be great, thanks." He watched as she poured two cups of coffee from a pot.

"Should still be hot enough." She handed one to Nick and sat.

Nick noticed she sat down sideways on the chair, keeping access to her gun. Clearly, this was on purpose.

"Get many trespassers out here?" asked Nick, taking a sip.

Denise laughed. "Not anymore. At least not after I shot the last one. He still has a limp. Word gets around to the local vagrants. I hate these fucking things," she said, looking down at her hand on the .357 revolver on her hip. "Campaigned against them my entire life. Sheriff gave it to me and taught me how to shoot it when I came out here. Said he didn't want to do the paperwork for a 'greenhorn easterner' being killed by local drunks. Believe me, there are plenty of them."

"Drunks or greenhorn easterners?" asked Nick with a grin.

Denise sat back in her chair, contemplating Nick.

"The sheriff the one who taught you how to sit while carrying?"

Denise had a quizzical look on her face. "You don't miss much, do you, Senator? Enough of the small talk. What caused you to waste a day of your campaign to come out to rural New Mexico?"

"First, call me Nick and second, I need a campaign manager, because as you said, I don't know what I am doing."

"Admitting you have a problem is the first step, or so they told me. I am sure you know something about my past," said Denise.

"Chuck filled me in."

"You must be scraping the bottom of the barrel to make a trip out here to track me down."

"I sure as shit don't want any of those blood sucking bottom feeders the others are using," said Nick in a tone expressing exactly what he thought about the K street pirates of DC.

"That, and I am sure none of them will leave their other candidates to work with such a losing proposition."

Nick laughed in response. "That too."

"Working on your campaign is more of a kiss of death than working on Mondale or Dukakis in the old days. I can recommend a few folks I think would be good for your kind of campaign."

"So, you're not interested either?" asked Nick, looking around.

"Look, I'm damaged goods. You said it yourself: they may not be able to come after you, so it will force them to attack those around you. I have so much baggage. I need two baggage carts at the airport," said Denise in a resigned tone.

"Did you see my interview on *Tommy?*"

"I did some research after Chuck called. And no, Tommy is not someone I normally watch. I usually watch HGTV to figure out how to do all this shit around here. The web is great too for DIY videos," she said, waving her arm to encompass the house.

"Chances are we aren't going to get enough attention to warrant them even turning the big guns on me."

Denise stared at him before answering. "You're kidding right? Either you are hopelessly naïve or really stupid. I may be out of the game, but I get calls, emails, texts. You haven't poked the hornets' nest, you kicked it over, stomped on it, covered it in gas and lit it."

"Guess I must be doing something right," agreed Nick.

"Hardly. You're giving the enemy time to gather its forces against you. Doing nothing to protect yourself, let alone to go on the offensive. You claim to be a student of history. Perhaps you should reread your *Art of War*. Sun Tzu would not approve of your strategy."

"I agree. That's why I'm here. Clearly, I need your help."

"What you need is a psychiatrist and maybe a lobotomy. You are certifiable. Somebody putting you up to this? Is Lexi paying you to make a fool of yourself? That's the kind of Machiavellian shit she would pull. I could see her organizing this."

"Sorry to disappoint. Have had a few concussions in my day but I assure you this is all my idea."

"I am disappointed in Chuck. He should have stopped you from doing this, and then he should've stopped you from squandering your few opportunities to get your platform message out."

"In fairness to Chuck, I didn't tell him before I did any of this. *He* did tell me I squandered those opportunities."

"Ah. You're a loose cannon? Great. I've been there and done that. If you won't take direction and advice, then you're wasting your donor's money, your staff's careers, and my time."

"Chuck says you are the best for this type of campaign."

Denise laughed a big, hearty laugh. "You mean a losing campaign? I am good at that."

"No, I mean a nontraditional, grass roots, take it to the people kinda campaign."

"Like I said, a losing campaign. Nick, save yourself a lot of trouble and frustration. You cannot run a grass roots *presidential* campaign. It is all about money, media control, and dirty tricks. You've got no money, or at least the kind of money you'll need. You certainly have pissed off everybody in the media, though I love how you stuck it to that Bergamo bitch on national TV. Serves her right. Goddamn Barbie dolls," said Denise with a snarl. "You are way too nice and principled to take part in the shit you're going to have to do in order to win. You gotta be willing to sell your soul, sleep with your enemies, betray your friends, and promise to do things you hate. Is that you?"

Nick looked in his cup. "Refill?"

Denise shook her head no.

Nick got up and walked to the coffeepot. As he turned back to Denise, she said. "It's a dirty business, and you need to realize that."

"Is that why you are living out here, as far from politics as you can get?" asked Nick.

"I am living out here because working in politics cost me a marriage, countless jobs, and turned me into a raving alcoholic lunatic bitch," said Denise with a sad smile. "But you knew all that. I may be in exile, but at least I am honest with myself."

"Do you think the country is going in the right direction?"

"Doesn't matter what I think."

"And that is the issue. Why do you think it doesn't matter what you think?" asked Nick, leaning against the kitchen counter.

"Nice try, professor, but I am not playing your game."

"Why not? Because you don't like the answer? Or the game?"

"Because you're going to tell me it does matter and if enough of us who feel it doesn't matter, stand up, we *will* matter," said Denise. "Nice in theory, impossible in reality."

"Why?"

"Seriously? You've been in DC for a year, you know why."

"Yes, I've been in Washington for a year. In that year, I decided to buck the system, screw my party, preserve the Constitutional limits on the Federal government, and run for president. Is that the 'why' you meant?" asked Nick with a smile.

"Bet you also learned it is all about power and control. How do you get power and control? Money. I assumed they had you dialing for dollars and now you feel like a telemarketer."

"They did and yes, I felt like a late-night infomercial. Frankly, it is disgusting. Grown men and women elected to make our laws and represent us, groveling for money."

Denise laughed. "Welcome to the most powerful country in the world and to one of the 535 most influential jobs in the country. What do you spend your time doing? Not passing meaningful legislation, but dialing for dollars so you can stay in *that* job? Wonderful stuff, right?"

"Yes, it was disillusioning."

"So, you learned enough to know what congressmen and women say and what they do are two entirely different things, right?" asked Denise, continuing before Nick could answer.

"You learned promises are made, but leadership sets policies. It is rarely in line with what the masses want. You also learned that media are in cahoots with the Party and social media, print media, and most of cable news along with Hollywood, pro sports, and now thanks to the latest woke politics, even big business are now knuckling under, especially big tech," finished Denise.

"Yes, I know all that, but what is *your* point?"

"What is my point?" asked Denise in an exasperated voice. "My point is you don't control the money, you don't control the message, you don't control the culture, you don't control the delivery of the message, and these folks are lined up to support Lexi and no one else. If you can't get your message out, how do you expect to influence people enough to get out and make a stand?"

Nick looked her in the eyes.

"Answer a question. If the Party adds two states and expands the supreme court to 13 or 15 or whatever number. When they expand the Affordable Care Act to be the *only* choice for health care. When gun control moves from restriction to mandatory gun turn in, and when voting is all mail in without an ID check, with ballot harvesting available in every state, what happens then?" asked Nick.

"I agree it is not a good thing and you know I have supported progressive candidates and politics my whole life, hell I sacrificed my public life in its name," admitted Denise.

"Precisely my point. It's the classic case of 'we meant well, sorry about the consequences'. I'm sure Mao, Lenin, and Hitler all convinced themselves what they were doing was good for their people, too."

"That might be a little extreme," uttered Denise.

"Really? We call the Opposition Hitler the minute they argue against *anything*. It is one of the most effective retorts. No one wants to be accused of being Hitler. Except, exactly what we propose to support as the Party platform is *exactly* what Hitler told the Germans. Just change the Jews to Opposition or anyone else who opposes their platform, and you are witnessing a very disturbing similarity."

"Nick, Hitler hardly told them he was going to gas the Jews."

"Anarchists and anti-racist league groups are reenacting *Kristallnacht* in our liberal, Party-controlled cities nearly every night. Just because Hitler didn't *tell* them about his ultimate solution, they could see what *was* happening and they chose not to stop it."

Denise had a pensive look on her face, contemplating Nick's point as he continued.

"The only recourse eventually is going to be federal intervention. As part of that, they will *have* to remove anyone's chance to resist. This will be the justification for the gun grab. Just like Hitler in the 30s and Lenin and every socialist, totalitarian, or communist society. You take away the ability of the people to fight back before they figure out you are taking the rest of their liberties," finished Nick.

"Done with your militia recruiting speech?" asked Denise.

"What did I get wrong? Tell me this is not the way we are going? Look beyond your Ivy League, save the world bleeding heart ideals, and focus on our reality and the platform of the Progressives now running the Party. What do you see?" asked Nick angrily.

"I think the picture you paint is a bit extreme. I have to admit the little news I see, and the state of things, is one of complete decline. Progressivism was supposed to mean progress, not pure socialism. Socialism, which has failed everywhere else it was tried," said Denise as she rose to fill her coffee. "So back to my initial question, what do you hope to accomplish with none of the tools the Party or even what the Opposition has?"

"The United States and our exercise in democracy are on the brink of being another chapter in the history books on fallen empires and failed regimes. I don't want that to happen. Dismantling this in favor of socialist redistribution or communism is going to destroy us," lectured Nick.

"Nice words. I can read those in many online rags on any day. Those are the same people who are getting paid, the loyal opposition. You know most of them are funded by the same people funding the left as well. What can you do?" asked Denise.

"I can help people understand what they are allowing to happen by being disgusted, disconnected, upset, frustrated, cynical, unhappy, and therefore disengaged. They are letting them win by doing nothing. They think by protesting and not voting they're doing some noble thing. In fact, they're doing exactly what the other side wants. While we still have elections, they still need to win the votes. The fewer who take part, the fewer votes they need to win majorities," said Nick.

"Bingo. So now you have discovered the worst kept secret in Washington. Voter suppression and disenfranchisement is a *Party* effort. Even a key to victory. Exactly what they claim the other side is doing is what they are doing in spades. With much better results. But again, what can you do to change this?" asked Denise.

"You hang out at the local diner?"

"Huh? Sure, I go a couple of times a week. So what?"

"Talk to the locals?"

"Ya."

"What are they concerned about?"

"Jobs, economy, illegals, in this part of the country,"

"Right, same thing they care about in Colorado and Nebraska and Arizona and Tennessee," said Nick. "They ever talk about raising minimum wages to $25? Or $35? How about support for using tax dollars to pay for tuition for illegals or to give healthcare to them? Ever hear them talk about replacing their Ford pickup with an electric one? How about solar panels and wind turbines? They ever talk about being worried we are causing climate change, or the world is going to end in four, eight or twelve years as a result? I bet you never hear about any of this, unless they are shaking their head at the stupidity of Washington spending money, *their* money, doing all these things. Am I right?"

"Ya, but they are all Neanderthals," said Denise with a shrug.

"Really? Your Ivy League snobbery is showing again. What part of what they are complaining about is wrong?" asked Nick. "Do you blame them? If you're an American and your family has been here paying taxes and dying to preserve the ability of people to protest the national anthem and burn the flag, don't you think common sense says they would be a little pissed when the government pays for college and health care for illegals? Especially while they struggle to do both for their own family without help?" he said in an animated tone.

Denise did not respond, so Nick continued.

"Same thing for climate change. Doesn't it go against common sense that we are restricting our economy and making things more expensive in the name of solving climate change when the Chinese and Brazilians and Indians keep opening coal fired power plants? Not being held accountable for increasing their emissions while we reduce ours with voluntary conservation?" Nick now paced around in the small kitchen, using his hands to make his points, careful not to spill his coffee as he got more excited.

"All good points and each can be easily refuted with statistics making their points and claiming yours are backwards, dangerous, racist, and downright deadly if they follow your advice," responded Denise.

"Only if I am fighting with other talking heads and the Wokerati," agreed Nick. "I'm not going to play on their court. I'm going to go to local diners and into the communities where the silent majority live and try to make headway in their world. Demonstrating how these progressive policies destroy any chance of their happiness. I'm going to show them whose fault it is. *Their own.* It is their fault all of this is becoming a reality *and* they are paying for it whether or not they like it."

"Not a bad plan. If you had 50 years to campaign. You'll need 75 million votes minimum. No way you can convince that many people to vote for you if you are getting your message out 10 people at a time. Trust me. Just because they agree with you over a coffee or a beer, it doesn't mean they are going to vote. You'll make a lot of good friends and get invited to a lot of tail gates and barbecues. You'll win a few votes, but you cannot run a national campaign one diner at a time."

"Denise, are you familiar with multi-level marketing?"

"You mean Ponzi scams? Where you swindle one and they tell two and those two sell two and so on with you getting a piece of every sale? I believe it is called fraud, and is a felony."

"Exactly. That is my plan, without the scam part, of course," said Nick, smiling.

"Nick, most of those end up collapsing and the founders go to jail when the downstream sellers realize the product they are selling is shit."

"Well, since my product is knowledge and it is free, there is no investment and no risk for them except time," noted Nick.

"Interesting. Actually, that is where you are wrong. You are selling a product. Nick Turner. So, you intend to convince them of your message and then what, arm them with messages and send them forth like apostles to spread the gospel of Nick?" she asked.

"Why not? The message is really simple. Think for yourself. Choose for yourself. And you don't even have to go research facts, since they no longer exist. It's *all* propaganda. All you have to do is use common sense. Trust your gut. If it sounds like shit, it is shit. Sound too good to be true? It is and you'll pay for it. If it sounds unfair to you or someone else, it is. This is not hard," finished Nick, drinking his coffee.

"Are those people able to convince others like you do? Your entire plan is built on building an army of followers able to convince others to wake up and think for themselves," said Denise, using Nick's terms.

"Denise, you know why I think it will work?"

He continued as she stared at him, awaiting his answer.

"It's because there is nothing to learn. Nothing to subscribe to, only common sense. Because they are not trying to convince someone to change their mind. Just to ask themselves if they think things are going well and the plans being proposed are going to make their life better. Go with the gut. Common sense. There is a giant lack of it in Washington and the media, etc. They think people are too lazy to think for themselves. Too ignorant to realize the outcomes of the progressive policies. In fact, this is what they are counting on. They'll continue to use social media and the threat of publicly persecuting anybody who does not toe the party line," explained Nick.

"You're still going to need money. You'll need to send your message out and you're going to need to defend against attacks from your competitors if you ever get enough support to be a threat."

"What if we keep our support hidden? What if no one knows how much support we have?"

"How are you planning on doing that?" asked Denise. "Polling has gotten much more sophisticated. Mind you, not the public facing polls used to manipulate public opinion, but the internal polling the campaigns use."

"What if every pollster who called a supporter was told they were going to vote for Lexi or they supported positions that are 180 degrees opposite of how they feel or plan to vote?" asked Nick.

Denise laughed. Then laughed more and harder as she began to understand Nick's plan. She slapped her hands on her thighs.

"You okay?" asked Nick as Denise continued to laugh. She shook her head as she headed back to the coffeepot.

"We're going to need another pot for this," she said as she grabbed a filter and the coffee can. "That is diabolical. Using their polls against them. I love it. They gather the data and then lie to the people in the published polls. You want to get the people to lie to the pollsters. This is genius. How would you do it?" she asked.

"I would just tell them. If you get a call, lie. Tell them the opposite. Because it is what they *want* to hear, they will believe it. If they try to question it, then it will only make the other side look good and they definitely don't want that. They'll believe it is gigantic support for their policy and they'll get complacent," remarked Nick.

"But if you tell them to lie, people will attend your rallies, they'll hear you tell them. How do you figure they won't know they are getting lied to when they call for opinions?" questioned Denise.

"How do they know if it is somebody at my rally or a supporter of mine? Again, they are never quite sure who they are talking to. They will roll with it and assume, again, they are more popular than they are. Confirmation bias. I'll use their own tools against them," he said.

"That just might work. You're right. They believe what they want to hear. I take it back. Maybe you *did* read your *Art of War*. If you have all this figured out, what do you need me for?"

"We still need to build all the pieces of a national campaign. Organize local offices, fundraising, advertising, travel, logistics, press, position papers, all the usual stuff. I need someone who knows what to do and what not to do," rattled off Nick.

"Since I have made all the mistakes, you figure I won't make them again?"

"No offence, but I doubt you and I are going to get involved. So, sleeping with the candidate is a mistake you won't repeat."

"I like direct. That was a very long time ago. Are you not worried I will fall off the wagon with all the stress?"

"Denise, my campaign is all about redemption. Redemption of our country, its people, and principles. Those who join and come along for the ride will be passionate and committed. This should be enough to help you keep your demons at bay. If not, I guess I'll just have to kick your ass," said Nick in a serious tone.

Denise laughed, fingering the butt of her holstered gun while staring him in the eye.

"So, you're willing to trade all this for life on the road for the next year?" asked Nick.

"You hope it's a year. We'll see if we can raise enough money to make it through primary season," warned Denise.

"We've raised $60 million in the month since I announced. Not a single donation above $1000. We have well over a half a million donors so far. And since I am not buying expensive consultants, I think we'll be alright."

"Good start, but you'd be surprised how much it costs to run 50 state offices, plus all the things that go with running a national campaign. Just keep raising the money. Since you don't want to make any promises, you are going to need every one of your voters to donate. Alright, let's get started," said Denise as she moved a pile of paint fans and trim samples from her kitchen table and grabbed the cups to refill their coffees.

# Chapter 11

"After the unprecedented replacement of the President by the Vice President for the State of the Union, one would be right in asking just who is in charge of our government?" asked Tommy Charles. "Senator, you were there during the speech. Did you know the Vice President would give the State of the Union? What are your thoughts?"

"Thanks Tommy, good to be back," answered Nick. "I have to say, it was a shocker when the Vice President walked up to the podium rather than her traditional seat behind, next to the Speaker of the House. Nobody knew it was going to happen. In fact, sources tell me, they only decided about 5 minutes before the speech. The fact we have not seen the President since the speech leads me to believe he is not well."

"Is this even legal?" asked Tommy.

"Technically, the State of the Union is simply a speech. There is no requirement it be given by the President or even happen at all. There is no violation of any laws or rules. Plus, this President has delivered the shortest State of the Unions historically. It sure gives the VP a lot of free coverage and a chance to dry run what she would look like as President. I don't think it was her speech, though. It was not radical at all. The official statement from the press secretary about the President having a touch of the flu is concerning. Especially at his age," concluded Nick.

"We are entering the most important election in our lifetime, again. With a President who is MIA, a Vice President who appears to be staging a coup, and a congress who can't agree on any legislation. Are we supposed to just idle for the next year?" asked a frustrated Tommy.

"I'd like to think the alternative of the Vice President and the Majority Leader moving forward at full speed would be enough for the moderates among us to be happy we can keep it in neutral until November," said Nick in a genuinely concerned tone.

"Senator, I could not agree more. I agree with you about the speech. You could almost see the Vice President gritting her teeth over some passages she read from the President's address to the nation," smiled Tommy. "Clearly, she and the President do not see eye to eye on most of the issues. Do you think they will try to invoke the 25th?"

"I doubt it. There are few things people would get riled up about anymore. Trying to force somebody out who is the duly elected President, regardless of the excuse, will not sit well with a majority of both the Party and Opposition. Now, of course, if it were an Opposition President and his cabinet was forcing him out, big tech, media and the Party would fully support it. They would see to it that public opinion was manipulated in their favor. The Party isn't doing that to one of their own. Not going to happen. Now who is calling the shots in the White House? That I can't tell you with any certainty," added Nick, shrugging.

Tommy laughed and responded, "We've been saying that ever since he got elected. We believe the President was merely a puppet, since the beginning of his administration. Maybe now they finally tired of pulling his strings and benched him in favor of the Vice President."

"If we don't see him soon, you'll have your answer. Bigger worries for me are what our enemies may try? Since it is not clear we have a captain at the wheel of the ship, our enemies may be emboldened. It is not safe for us to have chaos or unclear chains of command. I, for one, hope the President makes an appearance assuring everyone he is still in command."

"Amen Senator. Thank you for your time."

"Thanks Tommy."

#

"Once again, he is right," said Mel to Lexi, sitting in a chair in her office. "We need to get the President in a photo op or throwing a ball for the dog, something to make sure the world knows he was just under the weather."

"You mean something that doesn't require him to speak?" asked Lexi with a sideways glance at Mel.

"Yes. His dementia is quickly progressing to full-blown Alzheimer's. Of course, his doctors assure us he is still physically healthy. The drugs he's taking to slow down the dementia do not appear to be having much effect any longer. They are recommending a couple of new ones, but for the next nine months, he is going to have to lie low and only make limited appearances," said Mel.

"I get to play Edith Galt to his Woodrow Wilson?"

"It appears so."

"Shit. The difference here is I loathe the man and would just as soon smother him than protect him," said Lexi menacingly.

"Just like then, we control the media and what gets out, so we need to keep the charade of him being in charge for another few months. Just like we have since his re-election," explained Mel.

"And the first election before. I get it. Thankfully, his staff agrees with us. None of them want to be out on their asses before the election. They'll do whatever we ask in the hope they can transition into mine in some manner, except Vincent, of course," said Lexi, grimacing.

"Yes. But I think I have him cowed into submission. We'll keep a closer eye on him. There are other things we could do. Maybe you don't have to smother him…." said Mel, tapering off suggestively.

"I thought about it. The problem is the Opposition would demand an autopsy, by a disinterested third party. I'm not sure we could fight that one off. We couldn't risk them finding out about any foul play. Or discovering any organ damage from the experimental drugs we've been pumping into him for the last eight years to stave off the dementia. Too many ways it could go sideways. We need to prop him up until the election is over," said Lexi in a ruthless and calculating tone.

"Got it. *Weekend at Bernie's* part three is underway," said Mel.

Lexi shook her head. "How they took one sight gag and turned it into not one, but two movies is beyond me. I don't care what you call it, just get him out there so folks can see he is alive."

# Chapter 12

"Quite the operation, isn't it?" asked Mel as he and Lexi walked through her campaign headquarters operation in Arlington, Virginia, across the Potomac from the Capitol. Coincidentally, only a few blocks from Nick's campaign office. The difference was the Vice President had the entire six floors of the much bigger office building for her campaign. They walked along the perimeter of rows and rows of cubicles and past a bullpen in the center surrounded by white boards showing various status of efforts in all fifty states.

There was the hum of voices cajoling and encouraging those on the other side of the phones to 'do more' and 'press on'. They approached a conference room at the corner of the floor. As they entered the room, Lexi's campaign manager, Harriet Jordan, an older, stately looking black woman with long iron gray hair held back in a grandmotherly bun, stood up and greeted Lexi with a hug and a smile.

"The conquering hero returns. Nice save at the State of the Union," said Harriet.

"It was step in or watch him collapse mid-sentence or worse, start reciting a speech from 30 years ago," grimaced Lexi. "How are things going here, Harry?"

"Getting right down to business, I see," said Harriet, smiling. "I'd say we are in pretty good shape, especially on the state levels. You looked very presidential during the State of the Union. I expect we'll get an even larger bump. Iowa is in a couple of weeks and New Hampshire the week after now that we bumped South Carolina back to where it belongs. You'll take both those easily," she continued.

"We have good volunteers in both states. The state leaders are solid. Most of them have been with me before in other presidential elections. There is the usual grousing about some issues, economy, crime, inflation, jobs, and immigrants mostly. We keep highlighting how we have led the economic recoveries, stabilized inflation and tackled the pandemics, both COVID1 and 2 and how important it is to keep our foot on the gas to prime the pump. The race riots have not hit either of these states too hard."

Lexi nodded. "Nevada after that?"

Harriet shook her head with a frown.

"Nevada is tough. They lost a lot of jobs and the administration's policies were not kind to the service workers. Plus, a lot of the refugees have gone to Nevada and a real underground economy of non-union, under the table labor, is taking a bunch of entry-level jobs. They passed minimum wage bills to go up to $25, but that seems to hurt more than it helps. Forcing many of these businesses to go back to off the books illegals for labor."

"We tried to get tough there and then stopped once it was clear it was doing more harm than good. We got caught between our unions demanding we do something and our immigration advocates saying they were doing jobs no union workers wanted to do," said Mel with a shrug.

Harriet nodded. "Yep, the raids the administration instigated to round up the refugee workers and punishing the owners didn't have the desired effects. The two casinos involved, who were heavily fined, declared bankruptcy and closed. Putting even more people out of work. There is a lot of Party resentment there."

"And of course, the workers' pay the price as the owner avoids the damage," said Mel in a disgusted tone.

"The local SEIU union heads begged the administration to stop once the owners threatened to shut down the casinos. On that one, you're getting tagged being part of the administration. I would say we finish 2nd, maybe even third. Nevada could be a state the Opposition picks up in the fall," said Harriet with some concern. "We just can't overcome some of the blunders made there. Lockdowns, cheap illegal labor, minimum wage hikes in a town full of low wage service workers," Harriet shook her head as Lexi contemplated the info. Harriet had worked with Lexi before, so she knew enough to move on quickly. Lexi never liked bad news, and the messenger even less.

"We're already working on ads to counter whomever the Opposition put up. You can expect to see lots of Nevada and 'I told you so' ads. Especially since Wellborn, the guy who owned the Casinos, opened new ones in Macau that are going gangbusters. He is happy to be a poster boy for the Opposition. Any chance you can speed up those investigations to shut him up? He is good on camera."

"I'll see what I can do," said Lexi. "We still have this wrapped up on Super Tuesday?"

Both Harriet and Mel replied, "Yes."

"Good. I don't want it to drag out. I want to get going on destroying the Opposition candidate, whoever it is. We need a landslide, Harry. No more squeaking out victories. Any idea yet who I'm trouncing?" asked Lexi with a laugh.

"Governor Blackbird of South Dakota, or Governor Carson of South Carolina seem to be the front runners," said Harriet.

"A Native American or a blonde half-Indian." said Lexi, tapping a finger against her lips.

"I guess you could say so, although Blackbird is five generations from any true Native American blood and Carson is only one quarter Indian and she doesn't look it at all with her blonde hair and southern drawl. In either case, we can point out their token representation and highlight it as pandering to minorities," strategized Mel.

"They'd be much better off running a white guy, as we will use any minority status against them. After all, we are the party of inclusion, right?" Harriet commented without a smile.

"What about Wilson and Garcia? After the 'COVID miracles' Wilson supposedly pulled off in Florida, I would expect him to be higher?" asked Lexi.

"So did everyone else. It appears he is a smug bastard in real life and pretty universally disliked. They exposed this in his last presidential primary campaign. He can't raise the money. Garcia is popular, but he is so staunchly conservative he can't attract any moderates in his own party, let alone independents," she said.

"Super Tuesday?" asked Lexi, getting them back on track.

"We'll be done by then. I don't see you losing any of those states, maybe Colorado and Vermont which are close but who knows if Harrington and Williams will still be in by then," said Harriet. "Our only challenge will be not having an opponent to attack for a while until they pick theirs."

"What about Turner?" asked Lexi.

"Turner who?" responded Mel with a smile.

"I agree," nodded Harriet. "We'll monitor him, but I don't expect a lot. He may stick around for a while because he is not spending lots of cash, not being in any primaries. He isn't even registering in polls so far."

"It's really too bad. He could have been useful to us. A good-looking hero type who can form a sentence is unusual in our party," said Lexi wistfully.

Harriet laughed. "That already puts him head and shoulders above most others in congress."

"We have others we can use, don't worry," countered Mel. "And they already owe us. We'll get something on him. Nobody is that clean."

"What else?"

"We have offices up in all 50 states, fully staffed. Also, auxiliary offices in all the most populous counties. We're fine on recruiting volunteers. In some places, we have more than we can handle. We have our team leads working the urban areas and moving into the suburbs in the key counties."

"Good," said Lexi, listening intently.

"They are teaching the volunteers how to target the youth in the households to get them to vote. Our social media apps are in full swing. Finally, we have our leaders out teaching seminars on ballot harvesting and how our volunteers can get their friends and family to fill out ballots for them to deliver. With the new mail in ballot rules, we should have plenty of ballots ready to dump in any place where we are surprised," explained Harriet.

"Excellent. We didn't go through all the trouble to make all this shit legal to not take advantage of it. The Opposition still behind on this front?" asked Lexi.

"Woefully, so far. Orange County is the only place they have mounted an effective operation, and they are trying to do the same in a few other.

Maricopa in Arizona and Fulton and DeKalb in Georgia. But we have moved on and around from those. They are always playing catchup. Plus, they will spend all their time, money, and scrutiny on those places. We will just shift our focus to other metro counties," replied Mel.

"No worries. Besides, it's all more or less legal now," smiled Harriet, agreeing. "I think we are good. We have tons of cash, over $400 million, and we will press for more once you are officially the nominee. Then we can also tap the Party national committee funds if we want, but we shouldn't need to. Money will not be an issue."

"Good, good," said Lexi. "Is there anything we need to be worried about?"

"Well, since you asked," said Harriet, carefully. "People are getting fed up with some of the shit coming out of Washington. We are not winning a lot of friends among those still paying taxes."

Lexi shrugged. "What are they going to do? Vote Opposition? I don't think so. There aren't enough of them anymore to make a difference, even if they leave. We have to break them down and get them used to living more like everyone else in the world. There is no reason we should have it so easy at the expense of everyone else."

"I wouldn't include that in any of your speeches please," said Harriet. "Let's keep telling them we are working to help every working family while making sure everyone has equal access to the same opportunities, health care, schooling, and jobs with dignity."

"Nice. Let's work *that* into a future speech," smiled Lexi.

"Already there," replied Mel, scribbling in a notebook. "Maybe you should moonlight as a speechwriter."

"Who the fuck do you think is writing most of them already?" asked Harriet, giving Mel a dirty look as Lexi laughed.

"Not those Ivy League clowns you hired. They are clueless about how to connect with real people," said Harriet with a snort. "Mel, really, I don't know how much you are paying them, but these guys suck. You need people who actually know what it's like to work from paycheck to paycheck. What it's like to have lost a job. All this pie in the sky crap is great for commercials. It sucks when you are in Des Moines talking to a bunch of farmers and small businesspeople trying to recover from all these lock downs we keep endorsing."

"Now, who is saying things we need to keep out of our speeches?" said Lexi with a smile. "The reality is we have to do what we can to protect folks. While also getting them used to looking at us to provide guidance and help to get through these things. We don't want them self-sufficient; we want them dependent and compliant. That's the goal. Thinking for themselves has only gotten all of us where we are now, and it is not pretty. We can fix it, but we need people to stop believing all this self-reliance crap leading to bad choices."

They both nodded in agreement, with Mel scribbling notes.

"What has that gotten them? Fat, addicted to video games and porn. Watching their phones all day. Unable to write a complete sentence, spell, or even sign their signature in cursive. It's a Great Society we've built here. It is time to tear all this shit down and rebuild it the right way. We're almost there. We need to get past this last hurdle, and we can start knocking over the dominos," finished Lexi forcefully.

Mel and Harriet both clapped as Lexi smiled and bowed.

"How are the congressional races going? We going to regain decent majorities?" asked Harriet.

"Sal says we are in good shape to win a couple of seats in the Senate, especially now that Turner imploded his career. We should still be OK in the house seats that are competitive. We need to keep the presidency and then we can finally pass all this shit, burn the fucking Constitution, and replace it with something modern," said Lexi.

"OK, one more time, don't say that in any speeches, please," laughed Harriet. "I get it, but keep it bottled up until after the election."

"Don't worry. I didn't get this far by running off my mouth at the wrong time or saying the wrong thing on camera, unlike our current puppet. He can't even read it correctly off the Goddamn prompter anymore," said Lexi in disgust.

"Any chance you just take over?" asked Harriet.

"We have discussed it. As long as he is breathing, it makes more sense to go through with the election. Unfortunately, other than his mind, he is healthy as a horse. We will just keep going the way we are. Since I gave the State of the Union, and after he made that appearance going to Marine One to confirm I hadn't murdered him, we really don't need him out there much any longer. Except for an endorsement at the convention, and we can do that by video if necessary." Harriet nodded.

"In the meantime, make no mistake we are in charge just like we have been for his entire administration, just more overtly now," said Lexi walking around the conference room, looking at the windows with their light curtains and hearing the whirring of the machines blanketing the room with white noise.

"You test this room and sweep for bugs, right?" asked Lexi, considering what she had just said.

"No worries, this is a secure SCIF, just like your offices and the situation room at the White House. No recordings, no surveillance is possible. What we say here stays here," said Mel.

"We test it every week," confirmed Harriet.

"Good," said Lexi with a tired smile. "One of these days, we'll actually be able to tell the people why we are doing this, for real. I can't wait until a year from now and the inauguration."

"Amen," said Mel with a sly smile.

# Chapter 13

"Luc, are you certain?"

"Almost positively. It appears someone loaded up an autistic person with a suicide vest and used them to kill Jean Paul," replied Luc to Alain Chaumont, now the President of France. He stood in Luc's makeshift office in the basement of the Lawyer's Library in Paris.

Chaumont stood in stunned silence, digesting the news.

"I have done some checking and no DNA at the scene was tied to anyone in the audience with a known autistic condition. I am digging deeper and can assure you I will not stop until I find the people who would do such a despicable thing."

"Thank you Luc. I don't know how we would tell our citizens. This is heart wrenching. On top of the riots in Paris, the yellow vest strikes, our energy issues, and now the farmer revolts over the new fertilizer rules in the spring," Chaumont paused, suddenly looking up at Luc.

"Do you think there could be others?"

"It is a concern, but typically, a person with autism is just enough different to stand out in a crowd. We need to tell our security forces, subtlely, to be on the lookout for people who do not act the same as the rest of the crowd. Not necessarily suspiciously, but differently. Either showing too much emotion or none when others around them are. They should stand out. Now that we know what to look for, I suspect we can pick someone out in a crowd," replied Luc.

"Good. Tell me how and what you need to spread this directive and I will make it happen."

"Alain, that is not a good idea. If I do this, Maximilian will want to know why I am here and what I am working on, and how I know."

"Well, I cannot tell them to suddenly start looking for autistic suicide bombers in the crowd at every one of my speeches without giving a reason."

Luc shrugged. "Your choice. I have told you what I have found. What you do with it is your business, or perhaps *your* life."

Alain grimaced and walked around the room, thinking.

"You could pick someone from the Prefect of Police and send them over, and I can share some information. Perhaps you could say you brought Annie in, given her experience and she 'found' the connection and could pass this on to the police. Not Interpol. I won't work with them," proclaimed Luc.

Alain nodded at the potential solution.

"Luc, I have one more request."

"Alain, I don't want to discuss it."

"Not that. I would like you and Annie to look at some of the evidence from the Christmas massacres. Much like the death of Gaspard, Interpol is coming up empty of motive or reason for these attacks. We stopped the attack in Marseille before he could get to the market. But he leaped in front of another car and was killed instantly before we could apprehend him. He was a Jewish immigrant from Russia and a father of four daughters."

"That was not reported."

"I know. We did not want to frighten people more."

"I understand," said Luc, thinking about this new information. Any others stopped?

"Yes, Rome and Vienna. Same result. The drivers both committed suicide. Interpol is investigating them as well," said Chaumont.

"Luc, these attacks *had* to be coordinated. Yet no one is taking any credit and we cannot find any financial connections, nor associations at all between the attackers. They were Christian, Jewish, and Muslim. Different ethnicities and status as immigrants or naturalized citizens. The only commonality is they were all male and not native born."

"Where is the evidence?"

"We can have the material they found from several of the workplaces and homes of the attackers in Munich, Madrid and Copenhagen sent here. Our best forensic technicians have failed to find anything useful."

"I'll have Annie review them and see if there is something different to her. I'm going to dig into the autistic angle. Check some of the autistic institutions to see if there is any record of residents leaving."

"Thank you, Luc," said Chaumont, deciding not to bring up Luc's sister, now the First Lady of France and her desire to hear from her brother for the first time in over two years.

#

"Bonjour?"

"In here," replied Luc from the inner office. He got up and headed out to the new female voice.

A woman in her mid-thirties, of medium height, with short brunette hair, walked into the larger office area, wearing slacks and a sweater. She smiled tentatively.

"Chief Inspector Gauthier?" she asked.

"Call him Luc," said Annie from her seat on the floor.

Luc laughed. "Indeed, please call me Luc. I assume you're from the Prefect of Police?"

"Yes, Gabrielle Martin. They have appointed me the investigative judge for this case."

Luc walked over, holding out his hand. "Nice to meet you, Mademoiselle Martin."

"How formal of you, Inspector. Please call me Gabi," she said with a big smile.

"Luc."

"Gabi, are you married? Boyfriend? Lesbian?" asked Annie without turning from her place on the floor.

Luc looked at Gabi, seeing the flush in her cheeks.

"This is Annie. She is rather forward and very interested in people's sex lives."

"Nice to meet you, Annie," said Gabi, regaining her composure.

"You didn't answer the question," responded Annie in a conversational tone.

"No, no, and *no*," answered Gabi emphatically.

"Luc is a widower. He has not slept with anyone since his wife died," responded Annie, turning to look at Gabi, pushing her glasses down on her nose. "You are very skinny."

"Annie, we have discussed this. What would the nuns say?" remarked Luc calmly.

Annie, frowning, turned back to her work, looking at the new piles of debris from the Christmas massacres.

"Gabi, perhaps we can talk in the other room and leave Annie to her work," suggested Luc, holding out his hand pointing to the office.

She smiled, walking into the office. It was barely functional, with a desk, chair, and a single guest chair. She glanced at the whiteboard with names and lines connecting them. Each took a seat.

"Forgive Annie. She is a savant. A high functioning one, but obsessed with talking about sex, and apparently now, finding me a new mate," remarked Luc with a wry smile.

"We are all familiar with your tragedy, inspector. My condolences. Annie is," Gabi paused, searching for the right word, "refreshing."

"Indeed, she is. Do you know why you are here?"

"No. I got a cryptic email to come here and to not let my superiors know why or where I was going."

"If I may ask, from whom?"

"The Minister of Justice."

"I bet that made you curious."

"That is not the word I would use. I am not used to getting directives from the Minister of anything, Inspector," she saw the look on Luc's face. "Sorry, Luc. Why am I here? Why are *you* here?"

"I am doing a favor for a friend. Obviously, you were brought here because someone trusts your discretion. I have been working on the assassination of President Gaspard. They asked me to take a look once Interpol came up empty."

"Ah, now it becomes clearer."

"You are quick."

"Top of my class, inspector," said Gabi sarcastically. "And Annie?"

"I have worked with Annie in the past. When I was working with Interpol. Her particular savant trait is a keen eye for mathematical inconsistencies. She has been investigating the explosion and the remaining debris. To make a long story short, we think we have discovered a link to the bomber."

"You have? That is great news," responded Gabi, sitting up in her chair.

"Yes, and no. What we have surmised is the bomber was an autistic person."

"What! How could an autistic person do this? They would not know…" Gabi paused, realizing the true cruelty of the revelation. The outrage showed on her face. "Are we sure?"

"Yes."

"Who did this?"

"That we do not know yet. I am continuing *my* investigation of this. You were not called in to help with this." Luc held up his hand as she protested. "The Minister contacted you directly, not through your own departments. We cannot publicly divulge what we have found, nor do we have evidence sufficient to announce anything definitive."

"Then why am I here?" asked Gabi, confused.

"We need someone in the department to spread the word to the security forces. They should be on the lookout for anyone in crowds who is not responding to the emotions, or not acting in the same way as the rest of the crowd. These are potential signs of autism."

"Exactly on what basis am I going to make this outrageous claim? A message from God?" asked Gabi, angrily.

"As you said, you were the top of your class. You'll figure something out. You should suggest that scrutiny be raised and security forces lookout for this type of activity in the crowd. We need not bring autism up in the suggestion. While I could not care less about our president, I love my sister, and I do not wish to see her become a widow, as my friend Gaspard's wife is now."

"Your sister is married to our president?"

Luc nodded.

"Even more reason for you to be the one talking about this and bringing the theory to the public. Your reputation is sterling and people would believe you if you suggested this theory. Why all the subterfuge? I don't understand."

"Gabi, there is a reason I am no longer involved in Interpol. And your ultimate boss, the Prefect of Police and I also do not see eye to eye, so that is why you are here. Chaumont does not want to die from another autistic bomber, and we need to raise the alert without causing panic. That is your job."

"What will you be doing?"

"Continuing to investigate. I will keep you informed of our progress. When we find anything out and hopefully track down who did this, I will include you. I cannot expose them for the reasons I just stated. This will be your job to do when the facts are known."

"I would like to go on record saying I dislike this. Nor do I enjoy waiting for you to do *my* job."

"Gabi, I am sure this isn't the first time you've received an uncomfortable order."

"I didn't like those times either," said Gabi, rising and handing Luc a card. My number is on it. Please let me know when you need me to be your *pigeon voyageur* again. I can find my way out.

Luc sighed, listening as Gabi left. He heard the door to their offices shut. He walked out to where Annie was still scrutinizing the pieces.

"Well, that didn't go well, Luc. You need to work on your seduction skills. You suck at this. She's cute. Did you get her number?"

"Annie, what do you see?" asked Luc calmly, ignoring her statement. Annie did not answer, instead rocking while looking at a piece of a smart phone in her hand.

# Chapter 14

As had been increasingly the case, the President left the cabinet meeting early. He had dozed off during most of it, and when awake, it was clear he was incapable of understanding any of the topics being discussed. Out of the blue, he announced he wanted some ice cream.

"Dismissed," he said to no one in particular as he stood with the help of the nurse and secret service agent. Everyone else stood as well. Sam Vincent, the President's chief of staff, stayed in the room as everyone sat back in their seats. Lexi gave him a look.

"Sam, I think it would be best if you accompanied the President," suggested Lexi.

"I think I will stay," answered Sam defiantly.

"And I think you will go. While the President has invited you to his cabinet meetings, as he has left me to continue the meeting, I choose not to have you stay for mine. Do I need to have Russ help you find the door?" asked Lexi in an icy tone as she glanced at her lead Secret Service agent now standing in a corner of the room.

"You think you can just take over? He's still the President, and still in charge. I won't let you get away with this," accused Sam, in open defiance.

"What exactly do you think I'm getting away with? We're all his duly appointed cabinet. We are merely continuing to oversee his policies and do his bidding. If he leaves early and takes a nap, that's certainly his prerogative," shrugged Lexi as she turned to Russ and then looked at several of the cabinet secretaries.

"Further, I would refrain from making direct threats to the sitting Vice President of the United States if I were you. Especially in front of witnesses."

Sam looked startled at *her* threat. "What are you talking about?"

"I distinctly heard you say you would not let me get away with something. That sounded threatening to me. Did it to anyone else?" asked Lexi, looking around the table at a sea of nodding heads.

"Javier, did that sound like a threat to my personal wellbeing?"

"Indeed, Madame Vice President. Perhaps the Justice Department should serve out a warrant?" answered Javier Guzman, the Attorney General of the United States.

"Sam, I think it would be best if you left, as you aren't an invited guest, and you are threatening my person with witnesses. I would think about what you said and implied. I choose not to do anything about it, *yet*. But I suggest you be more careful about who you threaten in the future," finished Lexi, turning back to the assembled cabinet secretaries to continue the meeting. Sam slumped, humiliated, and simply walked out of the room.

"Geez, you practically waived a red flag in his face. We are all in trouble if he goes public," said Henry St. Cloud, the NSA director.

"Henry, grow a pair." Lexi did not hide her disgust at the skinny NSA Director. "He's not going to spill the beans. I have this under control."

"Lexi, Henry has a point," said Susanna, less confrontationally. "What are we going to do? You already gave the State of the Union. The President doesn't even realize he didn't give it. He really can't do public events any longer. Ten minutes ago he was quoting *Schoolhouse Rock*, for God's sake. We need to assure the country he is at least alive. A walk to Marine One was nice, but it was hardly a speaking engagement or a closeup. I saw articles implying we were using a double. We can't hide his condition forever. At some point, folks are going to ask why we didn't invoke the 25th."

Lexi sighed. "We have been through this. As long as he is alive and able to do *anything*, he is the President. It is our job to execute his policies, whether he is aware. We have taken steps to ensure the nuclear codes can be used by me with the two-person rule. A majority of us agreed to allow this as a special power until the election or until the President shows complete capability again."

"I will not invoke the 25th. If the rest of you do, I will refuse to sign it. I won't be the first Vice President to institute a coup. We are managing fine. This government comprises an enormous bureaucracy, which continues to function and perform without direct involvement from the President. As long as they see us continuing to implement *his* policies, and his stances, and his platform, no one can accuse us of usurping anything. When I am elected this fall, I'll implement my agenda, but not before. Am I clear?"

Susanna, the Secretary of State, sat back in her chair.

Lexi focused her icy blue eyes around the cabinet. Several seemed uncomfortable, but no one spoke. They all knew they were complicit in the charade, and they would all sink or swim together.

"OK then, let's move on."

"Claude, Rhett, Henry, where is Europe on figuring out who caused all that mayhem before Christmas?

Rhett looked at his colleagues before answering.

"They're not getting anywhere. They raided the houses of all the men, interrogated their wives and children and co-workers. None exhibited *any* radical tendencies. All were happily married with families. It makes no sense any of them, let alone all of them, would commit such a heinous crime, especially with the number of children killed and maimed. Frankly, Interpol is baffled."

"First Gaspard and now this. And no one is claiming credit for either event. Does anyone think they are connected?" asked Lexi.

"There is nothing to connect them, but Interpol is not ruling anything out. It is still early. They're sifting through all the evidence to see if they can find any connection or a lead to follow. Nothing so far," finished Rhett.

"Claude, anything on our side of the pond?"

The FBI Director looked like a pale imitation of his former self. He had survived the holidays, but it was clear he was not long for the world. His eyes were still bright, even if his body was failing him.

"There has been some increase in chatter, but nothing specific. We seem to be experiencing a few more cyber threats than usual, but there does not seem to be any coordination between any of them. And as Rhett just commented, we are not seeing anyone trying to make hay out of the attacks. No obvious recruiting or propaganda off them. It's as if they are intentionally downplaying the after effects. It is not following the usual pattern of boasting after a successful terrorist event. Eerily similar to how the French Presidential assassination played out. I don't like it. Terrorism without a purpose or pattern is much more difficult to track and therefore to stop. We must be even more vigilant about any anomalies we see." As he finished, he began a coughing fit that had others around the table wincing at the obvious pain he was experiencing.

"Thank you for that insight, Claude," said Lexi in a soothing, almost motherly voice. Something most had not heard from her ever before. Claude nodded.

Lexi spent the next hour orchestrating discussions on several foreign and domestic initiatives, all started by the President and continuing to move forward under Lexi's management. She was very careful to not interject any of her own opinions and to stay true to her word of focusing on the President's agenda. Once the meeting adjourned, only Mel and Lexi remained in the cabinet room.

"You came down pretty hard on ole Sam, don't you think?" said Mel, leaning back in his chair.

"He's a putz. I dare him to open his mouth. I'll tear him apart ten ways to Sunday."

Mel laughed nervously. "Lexi, of that I have no doubt, but remember, you are now being scrutinized. Every move you make, every word you say or don't say, is going to be analyzed and dissected by the talking heads on every channel. We don't want to invite any extra attention. Even if you have ways to destroy him, you are backing him into a corner. He may see no way out other than blabbing."

"What does he know? He knows nothing about our nuclear code authority. Other than that, all I have done is make sure someone is in a place of command when our doddering old President sings *Schoolhouse Rock* ditties instead of reading his State of the Union speech. Imagine where we would be if we had sent him out there to make a fool of himself and show our enemies he is incapable of standing up to them."

"All true, but as you know, perception is everything. You and I know you are just keeping the wheels on the bus turning. But if Vincent goes out and says you are staging a coup, keeping the President from getting the care he needs, the story will have legs. Are you sure you don't want to do the 25th and get it done on the up and up? You'd still get to serve your own two terms, plus the last year of his."

Lexi sighed loudly. "Mel, it is the perception. I have the chance to become the first duly elected female President, by acclimation, not by Constitutional fiat. Even if I win in November, it would be with an asterisk. He is still lucid for the first hour every morning. Let's call a press conference for 6 am and have him tell everyone he is fine and just recovering from the flu or a cold. Take a couple of questions and put this to rest once and for all. Make it happen."

"OK. But let me deal with Vincent. I don't want you going all postal on him in public. He is not worth your wrath."

"Fine, but be quick about it. I know he is plotting something and there are still investigative journalists who believe these stories are legit."

"Got it."

# Chapter 15

Nick and Chuck walked into Dolly Wells-Monroe's estate for her annual Winter Ball. Seated in the ornately decorated foyer was Senator Baxter Banks, in his usual chair, greeting guests as they arrived. He had a scotch in one hand, shaking the hands of the men and kissing the hands of the women as they arrived. The Senator was now ninety-five years old. Currently, the longest serving senator and far and away the longest serving in Congressional history. He waved as Nick and Chuck entered.

"Ah Senator, dapper as always. You pull off the white dinner jacket with ease. Two times makes it a signature look, I am afraid."

Nick merely smiled at Bank's acknowledgment of his white tuxedo jacket. Truth be known, his staff practically had forced him to attend. Nick hated the Washington social scene. The ladies of his staff had picked out the tuxedo and had been delighted when Chuck regaled them with the tales of Nick's antics with the hostess at her Fall Gala.

"Mr. Robinson, how are your parents? Enjoying Florida?" asked Banks in his slow South Carolina drawl.

"They are fine, Senator. They're actually at their villa in France for the holidays. I'll give them your regards," replied Chuck.

"Senator, everyone still full of holiday cheer?" asked Nick.

"The libations will quickly solve that part," laughed Banks, holding up his drink. "They are more interested in a certain junior senator stirring up Washington. I believe your attire and dance floor antics won't be the reason for gossip this time," predicted Banks.

"They must be desperate indeed if gossip about me is the best they can do," answered Nick. He stared at the glamorous hostess as she made her way up the stairs to the foyer.

Dolly Monroe looked dazzling as she glided up the stairs to them. She wore a floor-length gown in two delightful shades of hunter green with crepe satin skirts, a velvet top with three-quarter sleeves and a sash detail at the waist. The gown edges draped slightly at her feet. Dolly's dark brunette hair fell about her shoulders in shimmering waves, displaying a bright and genuine smile upon seeing Nick.

"Well done, cousin, two in a row," praised Dolly, nodding at a laughing Chuck, who truly *was* her distant cousin.

"Senator, a pleasure to see you again." Nick took her hand, made a little bow, and brushed his lips along the back of her hand.

"Ms. Monroe, how could I refuse such an invitation?" he replied, staring into her dark eyes. Her cheeks flushed as she laughed nervously.

"Senator, you are quite the scoundrel, just as I suspected. Baxter, I'm not sure we should allow his type?" suggested Dolly in mock seriousness, trying to break eye contact with Nick. She could not.

"Well…" said Banks, drawing out the word. "I, for one, believe we could use a few more Nick Turner's in this town."

"That settles it then. Welcome to our winter ball, Senator. May I lead you to a drink? Come on cuz; Baxter, you OK?"

"I am alright my dear. Hobson keeps an eye on me. You youngsters go have your fun."

With that, Dolly, arm in arm with Chuck and Nick, made a grand entrance coming down the staircase into the packed living room. This year's theme was winter wonderland. Snow covered greenery, trees, snowflakes, and lighting simulating falling snow made the entire cavernous space seem like an outdoor snow scape.

As was always the case, Dolly spared no expense. Approaching one of the many bars in the room, the crowds parted, staring at the trio.

"The benefits of hosting, we can jump straight to the front of the line. Chuck, the usual?" she asked.

He nodded.

"Joe, we need a Manhattan and two Nolet dry martinis up with twists, please."

"Coming right up, Ms. Monroe."

They raised their glasses in a toast.

"What should we toast, gentlemen?"

"Governor Grayson?" answered Nick.

"Indeed. To courage," agreed Dolly, raising her glass to theirs.

"Kids, I think I will leave you two alone. I didn't have time to eat any lunch and the prime rib over there looks fabulous," noted Chuck, walking toward one of the carving stations.

"It's beautiful, Dolly," remarked Nick, looking around at the decorations and the hundreds of people milling about, celebrating.

"Thank you," she said, smiling at Nick over her martini glass.

"I don't know how you ladies do it. Finding dresses for all these parties," mused Nick, looking her up and down admiringly.

"That's half the fun. It's all about the reaction."

"Well, you look fabulous. The dress isn't half bad either."

Dolly blushed again. "I see you've continued making your white jacket statement?"

"Like you said, if it works for Bogart and Connery, that's pretty good company."

"Have you been out since the last party?"

"I think I went out once. I've been busy saving our democracy."

"You're doing a pretty poor job of it, I might add," replied Dolly, getting into the spirit of their banter.

Nick laughed. "That's why I'm running, so I can finish the job."

"Destroying it or saving it?" quipped Dolly in a wicked tone with a lopsided grin, her white teeth framed against the dark red lipstick.

"I guess that depends on your lens," replied Nick.

"You're learning. Good non answer."

"Hey, aren't you violating your own rules? Can you kick yourself out of your own party for talking politics? I can borrow Chuck's car and we can hit the Chick-Fil-A, though you are a tad overdressed."

"Oh? And you're not? Careful, Senator, I might just take you up on it," she warned.

"It's a date. Changing subjects. This time next year, I assume you throw the granddaddy of inaugural balls?"

"Actually, no. I don't like to compete. Mine is always before or after the swearing in. I rarely invite the President. Too much hassle with the Secret Service. We usually have a lot of either unhappy folks drowning their sorrows or happy ones thinking they're now important."

"So, the same as always," said Nick with a laugh, looking around the room at both Opposition and Party guests. The Party guests seemed to be in the more festive moods, smiling and laughing while the smaller groups of Opposition members were more low key.

"Except I don't let people complain or gloat. They have to hold it all in for a night."

"And if I win?" inquired Nick with a grin.

"I *might* make an exception. It could be worth the hassle," responded Dolly with an equally bright smile. "Senator, much as I would enjoy it, I cannot let you monopolize me like you did the last time."

"Really? I thought you were monopolizing *me*," Nick said, shaking his head. "I seem to recall it was *your* lipstick on my cheek."

"Believe what you want," she said, turning with a flirtatious smile. Nick watched her as she walked away. Admiring her curves in the form-fitting gown, he shook his head, wondering. Turning, he surveyed the room. This was his least favorite part of being in Washington, making small talk. He loathed it, preferring to spend his time on substantial topics, solving problems.

Wandering to a nearby bar, he set down his half empty martini glass and had the bartender pour him a club soda with a lime. No one would be any wiser, assuming it was vodka or gin. He retrieved his drink, thanking the bartender and looked around, trying to find a safe conversation partner. He spied Senator Garcia and his wife doing the same. They made eye contact and nodded as Nick made his way over.

"Nick, let me introduce you to my much better half, Ginny. Honey, this is Senator Nick Turner, who really needs no introduction," chuckled Freddie Garcia, the senior senator from Texas and one of the eleven Opposition presidential primary candidates.

"A pleasure to meet you, Senator," said Virginia Garcia, a petite blonde with a bright smile and honest face. Nick understood why Garcia introduced her as his better half. He immediately sensed her sincerity.

"Please call me Nick, and the pleasure is all mine. Now I understand why Senator Garcia gets so much done in Washington. I have no doubt you have things well under control at home."

"How can you possibly know that in one sentence?" asked Garcia as Ginny laughed, confirming Nick's thought.

"Am I right?"

"Freddie, I adore him," she said, looking up at her husband, smiling. "I hear he can dance as well," she said, poking him in the side.

"Way to go Turner. Now you are ruining my domestic bliss among your other antics," accused Garcia sarcastically.

Nick simply smiled and shrugged in response.

"So, you've jumped into the circus," said Freddie, now serious.

"That is my cue to go freshen our drinks. Nick, it was a pleasure to meet you. Don't let him get too riled up. I enjoy coming to these parties, and I don't want Dolly kicking us out."

"Nice to meet you as well, Ginny. I think we'll be fine."

"Seeing how Dolly looks at you, I would have to agree," chuckled Ginny with a mischievous wink as she turned.

She began greeting others as she slowly strolled away. Nick looked at Freddie. "You're lucky to have such a great partner."

"You don't know the half of it, Nick. She's raised our five kids, been a nurse practitioner for 30 years, runs the local meals on wheels, organizes the Salvation Army bell ringers at Christmas, and a host of other programs back in San Antonio. She has done more for people than I could ever do. We almost lost her during the second pandemic when she was working with the infected in the hospital. She pulled through, like she does with everything. I'd be lost without her."

Nick contemplated what Freddie said as they both looked at her, smiling and laughing, talking to a Party senator's wife.

"Look at that, Opposition talking to Party. See, it is not so hard. We should all resign and let the spouses take over," suggested Nick.

"Who'd take over for you? You have a hidden wife, or a dog?"

"I'm an unperson now, so it really wouldn't matter."

"Really? You are the most prominent unperson this town and this country may have ever seen. It took me 25 years to get to this point of even thinking I could make a credible run for President, and you've accomplished it in less than a year. Unperson, right?" scoffed Freddie.

"We'll see what happens. For what it's worth, I'd vote for you."

"My abortion stance wouldn't stop you?" queried Garcia.

"I don't agree, but I am also not a one issue voter. You have to look at all the candidate's positions. You'll never succeed in completely banishing abortion, so it doesn't worry me. I *do* agree with a majority of your fiscal stances," replied Nick, equally serious.

"Can I quote you?" asked Garcia, laughing.

"Denise would probably kick me in the crotch if she knew I even said that. I guess I'd have to deny it if you tried to repeat it. I'm slowly learning you cannot be funny, honest, or sarcastic as a candidate."

"The first rule of presidential politics is to never give a definitive answer on anything. I'm sure Denise has told you that much."

"Oh yeah. No jokes, no controversy, no promises. I got the lecture after my first snarky comment in a staff meeting."

"You're lucky to have her. She's very good. Unconventional."

"You know Denise?" asked Nick, surprised.

"She ran the campaign for my opponent three elections ago. I barely eked out the win. She took a nobody, made him into everything I was not, and almost pulled it off. Her mistake was sleeping with him. Lost him some votes when the wife found out and called a press conference," said Freddie, with a raised eyebrow.

"So that was the campaign? I knew she had some difficulties. I heard about that and some struggles with the bottle," said Nick carefully.

"Nick, Denise is like Patton. She is great on the battlefield of the election campaign, but she is self-destructive anywhere else. She'll do great things for you, but you have to help her with the rest of it. I have tremendous respect for her and her ability. I'll leave it at that."

"Thanks Freddie, I appreciate the candor."

"No problem. Listen to her. Their job is to keep us from saying something off the cuff and sticking our foot in our mouth. With today's 24-hour news outlets, the media all need content. Nothing plays better than presidential gaffes. The current president has given them a lifetime's worth in his seven years so far. They long since stopped reporting on gaffes and even when he falls down. Besides, it looks like Lexi is even more in charge now, after the State of the Union."

Nick shrugged. "Seems so. I hate to disappoint on the careful statement front, but I intend to be honest. I'll get a lot of coverage from those talking heads complaining about what I say."

"Nick, look around," said Freddie, turning his head. "You're standing here talking to me. I can guarantee you every other conversation is about what we are saying."

"What a sad statement. We have so many irrelevant things to talk about. Why would they care?"

"Because we are competing presidential candidates. This is not kosher. For us to have a civil conversation. After all, this is now a gladiator sport. They want blood. They want to see us stab each other in the heart. What does that say about our country?" asked Freddie.

"It says our media has way too much influence. What happened to us, Freddie? Where did the spirit of cooperation go? We seem to think each of us is now the only one who knows what is best for the country. It is a sad state of affairs."

"See, we are already on the right track. You and I agree. There are probably thirty or forty others who also feel the same way in the Senate. They are waiting for someone else to stand up and take the arrows by leading. The one thing they have in common is a lack of a spine and probably testicles in most cases. At least on the male senators anyway," revealed Freddie in an ironic tone.

Nick bent over, laughing. Freddie put a hand on his shoulder. Between laughs he said, "I love it. Now all these people are trying to figure out what in the hell we could laugh about."

Nick straightened up. "Well, I guess we could play it up. Who should we stare at, really hard?"

They both turned and looked at Lexi, who stared back icily.

"Now what?" said Nick out of the corner of his mouth.

"Who wins the Super Bowl, Dallas or the Chiefs?" asked Freddie while still staring at the Vice President.

Nick broke eye contact with Lexi and turned back to Freddie.

"As a Broncos fan, I could never root for the Chiefs, so I guess I have to root for the Cowboys."

"I guess we gave them plenty to speculate on tomorrow. They probably think we just made some secret pact."

"I hope not for your sake. I'm a joke, remember?"

"You and I both know that is what *they* want people to think," said Freddie as his wife headed their way.

"I fear I need my husband back, Nick," she said.

"Thanks for the loan, Ginny," he replied, smiling, taking her hand and kissing it.

"Great, now they will talk about this as well. Turner, you're a menace. Be gone," said Garcia with a smile and a flick of his hand as he took his wife's hand. They separated, laughing. Nick headed upstairs to see what the youngsters were doing this time around.

# Chapter 16

Nick continued up the grand staircase and stuck his head into the ballroom to see what the young staffers were doing. Dolly invited some to each gala to learn what it means to mingle. Eventually, they all made their way upstairs to dance. The DJ had already started playing a modern beat, and the kids were thrashing about.

He walked to the balcony and surveyed the crowds below. He saw the senate majority leader Sal Fontana, Lexi, several ambassadors, both to the US and to other countries, a Supreme Court justice, and a couple of recent Nobel prize winners he actually recognized.

Dolly loved to host an eclectic group, but she avoided inviting any actors or nouveau rich, including the billionaire tech moguls. Most of all, she detested shallow people who were more interested in themselves than in intelligent conversation.

"Senator, quite a sight, is it not?" asked an accented voice.

Nick turned toward the man, greeting him. He was of medium height and build, with distinctly middle eastern features.

"I haven't been to many, but it is quite an impressive undertaking," answered Nick in a pleasant tone.

"I have been too a few and our hostess always seems to top the previous one. Senator, I am Ammi Chaffetz, an undersecretary of the Israeli embassy here in Washington. Ms. Wells-Monroe always sends a couple of invitations to the major embassies. Her late husband was a staunch supporter of Israel. She has continued with her support as well. For which we are eternally grateful."

"Ammi, nice to meet you. Nick Turner."

"Senator, have you seen Ms. Wells-Monroe's library?"

"I have not. Please, lead the way."

They made their way down the hallway past the ballroom with the dancing young staffers. They turned down another hallway with Persian rug runners on the old wide plank hardwood floors with several doors on either side of the wall. There were various antiques perched on equally antique side tables on either side of the hall. Nick would have loved to stop and examine them, but he followed Ammi down the hallway to a set of double doors.

"Senator, these are the famous Twin Pines studies. Many treaties or brokered cease fires have started in these. This one is her library and the two on the opposite side are a true study and a smoking room. No one but Senator Banks dares to smoke in there any longer," laughed Ammi. As they entered the library, Ammi closed the door behind him.

"For an undersecretary, you know your way around."

He smiled.

"Am I correct in assuming you are perhaps Mossad or even Aman? Masquerading as a diplomat?" asked Nick.

"Straight to the point, I see Senator. I must remember you are not simply a politician, but also a warrior and an intelligence legend if the rumors are true."

"I don't know about legend, but I learned to recognize the moves and mannerisms of operatives. How they talk, how they act, frankly, how they move. You exhibit all the signs. An undersecretary of a nation representing their country abroad has a certain arrogance and ego you do not exude in the slightest. You blend in, you move in silence, you speak in short sentences and never about yourself. No undersecretary would have gone this long without asking for something or making a point of their own importance to a US Senator."

Ammi smiled and held up his hands in resignation.

"I, of course, cannot confirm any of your *assumptions*, Senator. What I can confirm and what I would like to pass on to you is a concern for your own wellbeing."

"Seriously?"

"You merely think you are asking your fellow citizens to stand up and reassert the rule of your Constitution. If I may, I would tell you that others have seen activity both in your own country and abroad. Signifying efforts to stop your candidacy before it can get established."

"Do your *sources*," said Nick, playing along with the charade, "have any specific details I can prepare against or work to mitigate?"

"Senator, unfortunately, we do not have specifics. But you must understand, you must *know*, these forces will not, cannot, allow you to succeed. To do so would be to limit their power. Power they've spent countless dollars and lives to gain. They are using this influence to establish this network of power and control to remake the United States. This effort has been underway for decades, if not a full century."

"Ammi, of course I know I'm now wearing a target. I'm not naïve. I spent a more than a decade in Navy Intelligence starting with 9/11. There are people in our country, in the world, who don't have our country's best interests at heart. Who long to see our democracy fail." Nick paused as Ammi merely stared at him silently.

"I get it. But what else can I do? Somebody has to stand up before it is too late. Someone has to have the courage to say what I believe many feel is right. Others are cowering in fear, afraid to stand up. They need leadership. I will take my chances and try to give them hope."

Ammi had walked to the mini-fridge in the library, pulling out two sparkling waters, handing one to Nick. He motioned to a pair of chairs near a fireplace, flipping a switch igniting the gas fireplace.

"Why do I feel like I am about to be seduced? You seem to know your way around this place."

Ammi ignored Nick's quip, staring at him as he took his seat.

"Senator, Israel is in the place you are, *every* day. We've been in this position each day since we declared the formation of our country in 1948. Even more so after October 7th. We, more than anyone, understand the situation you are in. Like you, we too have willingly put ourselves in the line of fire. Waving the red flag in front of all enemies who would see us not only defeated, but eradicated from the planet."

"Good point. We forget in our little bubble the struggles of others around the world," acknowledged Nick.

"We understand this. America has a unique situation where you don't face the evil we face daily on the European and Middle Eastern continents. A single breach of your bubble and your response is to destroy Afghanistan and Iraq. You wield tremendous power when focused. The problem with America is your heart is never in it. Look at your dwindling support for Ukraine and even our efforts to contain Hamas in Gaza."

Ammi took a sip of his water before continuing.

"America is the guy who stands up to the bully, punches him in the nose and walks away, assuming the bully is cured."

"At least we punch back. Europe thinks it can reason with them," interrupted Nick.

Ammi looked at Nick. "Instead, you allow the bully to plot and dwell on their humiliation, waiting for the right time to strike back. America is naïve in this manner. You carry a big punch and maybe you even break the bully's nose, but he always gets back up and eventually he strikes back. He did in Iraq, and Afghanistan, and is doing so in Mexico, Russia, China and within your own Party. Today they're electing people in not only Congress, but in every facet of your criminal justice system. In the state governments. Wherever the power is to ensure change is possible. Primarily in your voting mechanisms."

"Again, Ammi, why are you speaking in riddles? You are saying our enemies are attacking on multiple fronts. Something we know and understand. We are in a period of decay. Can we stop it before it becomes infected beyond repair? I hope so."

"Senator, your faith in your processes is inspiring. Do you really believe it is possible to still use these compromised systems to reinstate a change back? You yourself said the filibuster was the last bastion of protection for the common people. How can you use this same system to correct itself when all the tools no longer exist?"

"Sadly, Ammi, you already show a greater knowledge of our governmental system than most of my fellow citizens. I did not say it would be easy. As long as we can still vote to elect people who can be held accountable for their actions, we still have hope. Hope that we can reinstate some of these safeguards. Those against democracy are running out the clock. This may be the last chance. This election. If the Vice President wins, she can remake our systems irrevocably. The judicial, the legislative and eventually the executive branches. At that point, we have anarchy. They know this is necessary to get the population to accept authoritarian leadership, willingly, as the only alternative."

Ammi sat in his chair, looking at Nick as he made his speech.

"Senator, how much do you know about Maksim Pavlovich?"

"Pavlovich? He is the boogeyman. The conservatives have been blaming him for every liberal success for decades. He has single-handedly destroyed the schools. Defunded police, kept abortions legal, propped up labor unions, funded ARL, and changed the school curriculum to indoctrinate our children in socialist or communist principles. His WHS endorses and funds gender fluidity for underage children. Promotes the idea climate change is our single biggest challenge and advocates for open borders. What have I missed?" said Nick, laughing. "Oh yeah, he heads up QAnon too, right?"

"I take it you do not believe he's responsible for any of these things?" asked Ammi, trailing off.

"The only thing I believe is he gives a lot of money to organizations that agitate for change. Supposedly, he paid to elect every liberal district attorney and attorney general in all the states. He is not the only rich liberal funding causes by the way."

"If I told you all that and more is true. Would you believe me?"

"He gives money. Maybe he gives a lot of money. Maybe he believes he is a kingmaker and enjoys manipulating geopolitics. But people vote. These DAs and AGs are being elected in our most liberal cities, in our most liberal states. If he spends his fortune to support these efforts in states where they probably would win anyway, it is his money. He can do what he likes," said Nick, shifting in his chair.

"Let me ask you. If a candidate, or a sitting judge or secretary of state or even a sitting congressman were suddenly approached by an entity that owned their family's mortgage. Their children's student loan debt, or held some other instrument of coercion in their hands. Compromising information or proof of corruption and used it to threaten these people if they didn't vote or prosecute a crime or charge a felon the way they want. Does that change your opinion?"

"What are you saying? Are you telling me Pavlovich is using these kinds of tactics to force people into compliance?"

"Would you agree this is not fair? According to the very principles of fairness and honesty you believe still exist to allow you to win this 'last' election opportunity?" pondered Ammi.

"Do you have concrete evidence of these activities? If so, we need to investigate and expose these efforts." posed Nick, sitting up.

"Senator, you haven't been paying much attention to your colleagues on the right. They've been making these statements for years. Backed with endless amounts of concrete evidence. Your intelligence agencies have all this too and have for decades now. It compromises them as well. In all cases, your liberal media has ignored these stories. Do you know how many local newspapers and TV stations Pavlovich has a majority stake in? Or rather, his endless stream of World Harmony Society organizations, NGOs, and shell corporations. Especially in the last decade?" asked Ammi, getting up and pacing the library.

"I am not telling you this because I expect you as a senator to investigate or even stop this. I say it as a representative of my country who hopes you will be successful, Nick. We believe you are the last best hope for the country formerly known as the United States. Our most stalwart ally. I say this for entirely selfish reasons. If you cannot reverse the trajectory of America toward socialism or outright totalitarianism, we will not long survive on our own," he said, pausing his pacing to look Nick in the eyes.

"It is the idea of a strong and forceful America standing behind us that keeps our enemies at bay. Without a strong and united America, with a focus on foreign policy, the rule of law and democracy are in danger not just here, but everywhere. The European socialist states, relying on America for peace as well, and certainly Japan and Australia."

"Pardon me, but that seems dramatic. We've been through periods of unrest and uncertainty in America previously. Once we get too far right or left, we correct. We always end up in the middle again. The people vote for change. They always have in the past."

"Senator, if you believe that, why are you running? Do you *really* believe people will rise to protect their freedoms? In those previous times, were the people besieged by cancel culture and censorship? Were they surrounded by militant friends, co-workers, and neighbors? All incented to expose them if they espouse an alternate belief?"

Nick contemplated Ammi's statement. He stood up and paced the library as well, looking at random books on the shelves. As he browsed the shelves, thinking, he was drawn to one containing the works of Alexander Solzhenitsyn.

"Again, what is your point?" asked Nick, turning back to Ammi, who was standing, sipping his water, watching Nick as he paced.

"My point is your upcoming presidential election is a shift, perhaps tectonic. We will all feel the repercussions. An Opposition win merely delays the inevitable for Israel. If, by some miracle, you win, we may still avert disaster. The election of the Vice President will be more damaging to the world's wellbeing than Hitler's rise in Germany."

Nick laughed. "Ammi, I thought you were being dramatic before, but a reference to Hitler? Perhaps I should have added Kidon to your suspected affiliations? You have been watching too much American TV. Lexi is a lot of things, but she is not Hitler."

"Are you sure?"

"I doubt she will send America's Jews to the gas chambers."

"No. But do you not think she would imprison or, at a minimum, marginalize those who dare to have an alternate view? Is it not already happening? How is this different from Hitler's genocide? She may not be using Zyklon-B, but she is denying them their right to earn a living, to care for their families. She is 'killing' their ability to live as they choose. To return to normalcy, they need to swear an oath of fealty to the policies of your Progressives."

"Cancel culture is bad, but folks push back. You cannot believe everything you read and see," said Nick, less forcefully.

"The ones who have been victims of cancel culture would disagree. With Lexi in charge, do you think it will shrink? They may not kill those who refuse to be cowed, but for all purposes, they will be the modern version of the walking dead. Waiting to return to the fold or to do something in desperation. Suicide or striking out against authority to be killed. Either way, they will not be tolerated in her plans. There may not be any black armbands, but virtually there are. In some form. Look at the people forced to place signs in their yard as virtue signaling. Just to keep the mob from assuming they were white supremacist by simply *not* having an ARL yard sign present. You laugh. We do not. We *cannot*."

Nick glanced again at the bookshelf in front of him while cogitating over Ammi's statement. Besides Solzhenitsyn, Orwell's *Animal Farm* and *1984* were next to them. The shelf contained several other dystopian novels from Wells, Huxley, Bellamy, Atwood, and even arguably the worst book ever written, *Philip Dru, Administrator*.

A book written by Edward House, the architect of the modern bureaucratic state under Woodrow Wilson. The book was a horribly written novel painting the future of American success depending on rule by experts in a bureaucratic state. Experts who decided for a compliant and ultimately grateful people.

"Surely you have a retort. Perhaps an example from US history of how we are mistaken in our analysis?" asked Ammi.

"Are you saying this is not your opinion, but the view of your government?" asked Nick, carefully turning back to face him.

"Officially, I am attending a party and taking advantage of an opportunity to speak with a presidential candidate."

"So, let's *assume* everything you are saying is true. Pavlovich is buying, threatening, or otherwise influencing elected officials to manipulate results. Lexi is the next instantiation of Hitler, dooming half the population to virtual gas chambers. Why tell me? I'm already running for president. There is nothing else I can do about any of these theories. They change nothing I'm doing. I'll still go out and promote the Constitution as the solution to our troubles. To inspire the fearful to stand up for their rights. To choose the rule of law, Constitutional law, as the return to the path of prosperity for all. Nothing you have said or speculated changes any of that," finished Nick, leaning back against the bookshelves as he spoke.

"Are you sure? Senator, we have a dossier on you this thick," said Ammi, holding up his hands showing two to three inches. "If half of what we have collected is true, you analyze all the angles and then more. Coming up with solutions to problems ranging from the unexpected to the inspired. You have a proven track record of recommending unconventional missions with an exceptional ratio of success. Already you're assessing this new information and calculating what is necessary to overcome these obstacles. You appear to be doing all this on a whim. We know better. Unfortunately, there are others who also know your background or suspect. They'll not underestimate your ability to pull off the improbable or, frankly, the impossible."

"You are giving me way too much credit. I have been very lucky, yes. In the right places at the wrong times. Making the correct decisions. Those were hardly premeditated. Unfortunately, as much as you would like to accuse me of following some master plan, talk to my staff and my campaign manager. They'll tell you how woefully unprepared I am to be running for president. Further, I apologize in advance if you are counting on me to be the savior of America, Israel, or anywhere else," said Nick as he stood in front of the fireplace, soaking up the warmth.

"I am running to force people to open their eyes. To see what is happening. What will happen if they do not stand up and fight for their freedom. I'm only one person, but I'll use whatever voice I have for as long as I have it to inspire folks and to at least get them to open their eyes. They have to take ownership of what happens if they sit and do nothing. This is the one place where I agree with your Hitler analogy. They sat idle and let him do what he did. It will be the same here if nothing changes."

"Senator, I have delivered my message. There are forces lining up on both sides in this election. Unfortunately, those aligning behind the Vice President have much more power, massive organizations, and are firmly entrenched in all aspects of federal, state, and local government. I fear a belief in an honest election and a goal of simply inspiring more voters to go to the polls may not be enough."

"If that is true, then we deserve what happens. If goodness and honesty and people standing up and voting to preserve our Republic is not enough. Then we must let things get worse before a massive majority of like-minded folks rise to overcome or overthrow corrupt government," predicted Nick. "It has happened before."

"Perhaps. But usually accompanied by a massive loss of life. Senator, it has been an enlightening conversation," said Ammi, walking to Nick to shake his hand.

"I wish you luck. We will do what we can to help and to let you know if we discover anything we feel you need to know."

"Thank you Ammi. I appreciate the thoughts and I do support Israel. I understand you are paranoid. You have to be. We take for granted the freedoms we have. It has been so long since we've had to fight to preserve them."

"Senator, I hope you never have to fight to preserve, or worse, to regain, your freedoms. But if you ever have to, Israel will be there."

"Ammi, this was one of the strangest conversations I have had in a very long time."

He smiled and left the library, leaving Nick standing by the fireplace. He walked around the room, examining the volumes. Pulling a few from the shelves, turning pages in some of the more noteworthy ones, while contemplating his conversation with Ammi.

"There you are," said Chuck, popping his head into the library thirty minutes later. "It's getting late, and I'm heading home. You ready?"

"Chuck, I think I am going to spend a bit more time exploring this library. I'll get an Uber back to the office."

"You sure?" said Chuck, looking at his watch. "Could take a while for an Uber. It's already after one."

"I'm good. Thanks. I'll see you on Monday."

"Alright then, good night," said Chuck, sensing in Nick's tone his determination.

Nick went back to perusing the shelves and pulled out a book. He went to the bar in the library and found a bottle of cognac. Pouring himself a drink, he sat in the chair by the fire, and opened his book, reading, while setting his drink on a side table.

# Chapter 17

Nick heard a noise and slowly opened an eye.

"Hello sleepyhead," said Dolly, seated in the chair across from him in front of the fire.

Nick looked at the beautiful hostess, a wide smile on her face. She was still wearing her fancy green gown and sipping her own cognac.

She raised a finger to her chin, looking up.

"You know, I wasn't sure what to do. Should I call the cops and tell them a vagrant US Senator is passed out in my library? I could make quite a scene. Terrible for an aspiring presidential candidate."

"Yet, instead, you sat here, poured yourself a drink, and watched me drool all over myself. What does that say about you?" asked Nick, slowly and carefully stretching.

"Chuck mentioned you were here when he left. When I didn't see you leave, I figured I had better make sure nothing had happened. You have pissed off a lot of people lately and not a few of them were in attendance tonight. I didn't want to be the subject of a murder mystery movie on *Lifetime*."

"Guess I was more tired than I thought."

"Might be the hide-a-bed you sleep on in your office, or perhaps it was your choice of reading material?" She said, turning her head to look at the book laying in Nick's lap. "Thomas Aquinas' *Summa Theologica*? Out of all the reading material in this wondrous library, you chose a dusty old religious tome?" she asked, sipping her cognac.

"Dolly, who stocked this library?"

"It is a combination of books assembled by various Monroe's going back quite a few generations. Some of them were my late husband's relative, President James Monroe's. He collected many when he was an ambassador to France and Britain. My own parents contributed as well, given I was their only child. They had an extensive collection of their own. No one wants books any longer," lamented Dolly, shaking her head. "Why do you ask?"

"This is a printer's proof of the first English edition of Aquinas's work. Translated in 1911 and printed well after President Monroe. This is a one-of-a-kind version and it had a strange dedication in it. I was just curious about who collected it. Aquinas is the true father of modern philosophy, not Descartes. He was the first to combine the ethics of Aristotle and philosophers from other religions with the faith of the gospels. Synthesizing them into a coherent canon on which subsequent writers built most of our western philosophy. Either in agreement or in disagreement with Aquinas's view," Nick leaned forward, closing the book carefully while looking at Dolly.

"To Aquinas, faith and reason, as rational thought and natural law, are the two tools needed to interpret nature and discover the true knowledge of the divine. Of God, if you will. Amazing stuff. I hadn't looked at this in a very long time. When I saw this copy, I was drawn to it. Some thought-provoking stuff. Outside the seminary, this is not taught any more, sadly," said Nick, shaking his head before looking up at Dolly again.

"What?" he asked, smiling, seeing her reaction.

Dolly sat back with a smile on her face, wondering how a grown man could get so giddy, first at finding an old book and then at describing with such joy the thoughts from a writer dead over 800 years.

"The seminary, huh? Is that where you read it? That could explain some things. You are a strange man, Nick Turner."

He laughed. "Not strange, stupid would be a better description. Here I sit, in this lovely library, with a roaring fire, a nice glass of brandy, with a divinely beautiful woman seated across from me. And I am talking about faith and reason from a Dominican friar."

Dolly got up, walking away to hide her reaction.

Nick watched her as she glided away. He glanced at his watch.

"Good God. Is it really 5:30?"

"Past your curfew? You don't look like a pumpkin," replied Dolly devilishly, looking over her shoulder at Nick.

"Dolly, I am so sorry. You *should* have called the cops on me and had them throw me out on the stoop," apologized Nick, rising in alarm, preparing to go, while putting the book back in its place.

"Relax Nick. My last guests only left 30 minutes ago," replied Dolly, turning and leaning against a bookshelf, looking back at Nick. "There are crews arriving downstairs to begin cleaning up debris and take down the decorations. This is standard for post party activities. Well, almost. Having a senator asleep in my library at this hour is a first."

Nick calmed down and smiled. He pulled out his phone, tapped it a few times, and walked to Dolly. She gave him an inquisitive look. He took her cognac glass and set it on the table with his phone. As he walked back to her, she met him in the middle of the room. Nick took her hand as Frank Sinatra started singing *The Way You Look Tonight* on his phone.

"May I have this dance, Miss?"

"I believe my dance card is empty at the moment."

"Can you dance in that dress?"

"As long as you keep your clumsy feet off the hem."

Nick laughed as he pulled Dolly close so they could slow dance to the smooth voice of Sinatra.

"Did I mention how beautiful you are in that dress?"

"You did, but you can say it again."

They swayed back and forth. Nick looked down into her eyes, brown with a touch of hazel, more in one than the other.

"Any treaties to report?" asked Nick impishly.

"Not that I'm aware. I saw Ammi abduct you. Perhaps I should ask you?"

"Are you allowed to talk politics now that the ball is over?"

Dolly shrugged. "My party, my house, my rules," she said, looking up at Nick, smiling as the song changed to another ballad, this time by Dean Martin.

"Fair enough. Your Israeli friend merely told me to be careful."

"Ha. I know Ammi too well. He talked to you about more than your well-being. I assume you know who he really is?"

"Mossad?"

"Most likely."

"I must say, Miss Monroe, it is quite the eclectic group you draw to your events."

"I have a reputation to live up to. In fact, with the polarization of our politics, my studies are not hosting many brokered *anything*. No one wants to compromise anymore. Can we just dance?" she said, leaning her head into Nick's chest.

He could feel the tenseness leave her body as they continued to sway. Nick was content to hold her and enjoy the feeling.

"The party a success?" asked Nick after a few minutes.

"Uh hum," she murmured into his chest.

At the end of *Blue Moon*, the song switched to *Strangers in the Night*, another Sinatra ballad. Dolly put her arms around Nick's neck and looked up into his face, staring into *his* dark eyes.

"Why are you doing this?"

"I enjoy dancing with you," he answered.

Dolly raised her knee, hitting him in the thigh in response.

"Smart ass. Why are you running for president?"

Nick looked down, opened his mouth to reply and instead sighed, disentangling himself from Dolly, returning her drink.

"Killed the moment, did I?" she asked with a pout, standing alone in the middle of the library, holding her glass.

"A bit. But you also reminded me I have certain *obligations*."

"I see," she said, turning away from Nick. "You know, I have been called a lot of things, but never an obligation," murmured Dolly in a winsome tone, continuing to look away.

"Now, who is being the smart ass? You of all people should understand this dilemma," said Nick, walking back to her, gently turning her to face him again. "Trying to maintain your position above the fray. Able to keep a non-partisan reputation and invite both sides to your soirees. Sometimes we have to choose with our head and not what our heart says or wants."

"Says who?" said Dolly defiantly, eyes glistening.

The attraction was certainly mutual, but in Washington, one couldn't just act. Every action was scrutinized. Even more so when one was a presidential candidate and the other was the doyenne of Washington society. How could it be used for or against its subject? Was it a strength or a weakness? They both knew this. Nick stared back, looking deeply into her eyes, until she broke eye contact.

"It sucks to be us, now doesn't it?" she said, sighing.

Nick smiled in reply. "In the scheme of things, it is merely unfortunate. Happiness may not be on the menu of choices for me. At least not in the near term."

"Well then, you can at least answer the question."

"Dolly, all I can say is I feel as if every decision I make, every speech, every vote, is driven by fate." Nick got his drink, taking a sip.

"Look around. There are thousands of books in this library. Why in the world would I choose a book by a religious leader from the 13th century? And why in the world when I open it, am I drawn to his article discussing the combination of faith and reason as the paths to an understanding of divine knowledge?"

Dolly listened intently, sipping her drink.

"These are the twin pillars of my reason for running for president. Faith in my fellow citizens and a rational common sense approach to recognizing and solving our problems."

"So, you are saying you are being inspired by what, divine providence?" asked Dolly skeptically.

"Who knows? But look around. Surely you know in your bones we are not going in the correct direction. I spoke to several others tonight and the conversations always led back to what am I doing, why am I doing it, and am I certifiable of course," laughed Nick.

Dolly smiled. At this moment Nick's phone, which had been playing classic ballads, switched to Dean Martin singing his Christmas classic, *Baby, It's Cold Outside*. Nick and Dolly burst out laughing.

"Instead of kissing you, I'm talking about politics. What is wrong with us?" She did not resist, putting her arms around his neck again as he once again held her waist.

Nick bent down to kiss her. As their lips met, there was a tentative knock.

"Yes, Nina?" said Dolly, looking around Nick's shoulder, spying her assistant peering carefully around the doorjamb.

"I am so sorry, Ma'am, but a worker has discovered a problem that needs your attention. Sorry," she said in a timid squeak.

"I will be right there Nina, thank you," answered Dolly with a sigh. "Is this your great fate intervening again?" she asked with a twinkle in her eye and a frown as she took her arms from around his neck.

"It appears so. Thank you for a lovely evening. And for not calling the cops on the vagrant senator in your library. May I walk you down?"

"I need to change first before I go down into that mess. I owe my gown that much respect."

They exited the library, holding hands. In the hallway, Nick gave her a kiss on the cheek. He squeezed, then released her hand and headed down the grand staircase while Dolly headed the other way to the residence wing of the estate. He could not see the tears streaming from her eyes as they went their separate ways.

# Chapter 18

"Everyone getting settled in? Denver seemed as good a place as any to manage the campaign from. I appreciate those who have moved for the duration, and I also appreciate those of you who have chosen to commute. I will try to make it worth your while," promised Nick. "It's the end of January. Where are we?"

"You want the good news or the bad?" answered Denise Rojas. She sat around a large table in the main conference room. The walls of the room were covered in flip chart pages and several white boards with various statistics.

"I see you've settled right in," said Nick. "Hello to you, too."

"You didn't hire me for my personality," replied Denise, without missing a beat. "The good news is your fundraising is going well, especially considering we barely have our local offices up and running. In some states, we only have one paid staffer. Most of this is simply based on your shenanigans on cable. What is the current tally, Greg?"

"So far, about $85 million. Once we organize locally, word is spreading slowly. Your grass-roots groups are calling themselves the 'Turner Rabble'. We get more requests daily. Maybe you can go back on *Tommy*?" asked Greg.

"As long as he will have me. What about hiring?"

"That is part of the bad news," answered Denise. "We are trying to fill some of the national roles, but most of the good ones are working on other campaigns. I am trying to entice some folks to leave and a few others to come out of retirement. You may need to make some calls."

"Let me know when and where I need to go. Thankfully, with so many senators running for president, there are not a lot of votes being scheduled.

Since I am not running for re-election, if I'm absent from some minor debates, it shouldn't hurt me too bad."

"Not a good idea. We need you to be seen to be doing your job in Washington. Otherwise, they'll use it against you. You say you're for the people and then you duck votes? Not a good visual. Too many others do that already. We'll keep a jet on retainer everywhere. You can get back to Washington in a few hours for any votes," said Denise.

"Geez, how much will that cost?" remarked Nick.

"Welcome to the big leagues champ. It's the cost of running nationally," educated Denise.

"You're the expert," replied Nick.

"I am trying to get Penny Watts from Senator William's staff, but I doubt we can get her until after New Hampshire. Williams has no chance, but he wants to be Secretary of something, so he needs to stay in at least as long as New Hampshire. Penny is one of the best at coordinating local grassroots efforts. I may be able to arrange a clandestine coffee for the two of you to see if you mesh. It is an important role. Your local organizer is key to mass appeal," said Denise.

Nick nodded.

"We also need a campaign finance manager. No offence, Greg," continued Denise, turning to look at Greg across the table.

"The sooner the better. I am not ashamed to admit I am in over my head. Can't wait to take off the finance hat," he said, smiling in relief.

"Chuck, what about Jackie Alexander? I almost forgot about her. Think we can entice her out of retirement?" asked Denise.

Chuck stared at her for a second. "Guess you didn't hear. She died during the 2nd pandemic wave, a bad reaction to a vaccine."

"Shit. I am out of touch," said Denise, who then turned to Nick. "I warned you I was out of the loop."

"When do I get out on the road?" Nick ignored her admission.

"You're still set on going from town to town and walking into diners and VFWs and having conversations? No cameras, no staff, no security?" asked Denise.

"Yes, you know the plan."

"Earl, will you please explain the situation to him?"

"Do you really think that would matter?" replied Earl Greene from one corner of the table. Everyone around the table laughed.

"Hey, I *am* here, you know," said Nick, causing more laughter.

"Nick, if you are dead set on your diner tour, then you need to let us figure out where to send you. We have to recruit some locals in these cities and states quickly. You need to get them drinking the Kool-Aid so we can start spreading the gospel of Nick," pointed out Denise. "I'm sending Earl out with you at a minimum."

"How about communications, Margie? You ready to join Denise as the face of the campaign while I'm getting fat in diners?" asked Nick.

"I sat down with Denise. We have a strategy and yes, between the two of us and Chuck, when needed, we should be fine until things get crazier. We'll keep your media limited to *Tommy* and maybe a few radio shows. Brad Hudson wants you to schedule a day for a call in. That's big, because he never takes callers, and he talks to fifteen million folks daily. Your antics are quite the buzz on conservative talk radio."

"That is certainly news. Of course, there is no liberal talk radio, so let's take it with a grain of salt. Let me know when I need to do it and I'll call in. I guess I should listen to his show and see what they are saying. I'm sure Earl can find a station."

"KCOL 10am to one, in northern Colorado. Hudson is the leader on conservative radio. They like Nick better than most of the Opposition candidates," laughed Earl.

"I guess that's progress," pondered Nick.

"You're going to need to get folks from the middle of both parties to have any impact," said Denise. "The crazies on both sides will never change allegiance."

"Alright, what else?"

"I know you hate dialing for dollars, but it would really help if you could at least have some conversations with key lobbies," pleaded Denise, as Nick shook his head no.

"Hear me out. It is more than begging for money. A few key lobby endorsements could provide some much-needed visibility even if you disavow their financial support. Also, there is nothing you can do about PACs and Super PACs who want to spend money to support you. They are already airing commercials for and against you. You can't talk to them anyway, nor can any of us, speaking of which, Greg," said Denise, turning to look at Greg. "Let's get the rules of engagement finished so we can get it to everyone and have them sign."

"Rules of engagement?" asked Nick.

Denise smiled. "Nick, there are a million things we need to do you don't need to know about. This is one of those. We need a document that spells out what anyone on the campaign can and cannot say. Who they can and cannot talk to. Comments on or off the record, who they should refer questions to, etc. It is key to make sure everyone knows what is at stake. It's typically referred to as a 'kill switch'. We frighten the shit out of people, so they never consider violating the terms. Usually works," said Denise.

"Usually?" asked Nick.

"There is big money in presidential politics. Cyber bad guys trying to hack emails to leak them to the press or to WikiLeaks. Remember the Party server leak? Ask Seth Rich what happens. It isn't even leaking to the opponent so much as it is to enterprising third parties who want to make money with salacious gossip and embarrassing conversations. Of course, there is not much we can do if Lexi follows the prior Party playbook and pays for a fake dossier this go round."

"Sorry I asked," frowned Nick.

"My advice to everyone is to stay off social media and put as little in email as possible. Also, assume everything you say on a cell phone is being recorded by someone. The FBI, NSA, Homeland, and CIA for sure and we all know they are no longer non-partisan. Speaking of which, Earl, how is the security in here?" asked Denise.

"SCIF level. Secure Compartmented Information Facility for the uninitiated. In this conference room and in Nick's office. Just had it installed. Nothing is being recorded here. I've done what I can for the rest of the offices. Think about everything you say on the phone or write in an email and pretend it falls in someone else's hands. What would be the damage? Be paranoid. You'll live longer. That is a pretty good mantra for all facets of life these days," said Earl with emphasis.

"Gosh, I'm so looking forward to hitting the road with you. I can see the storm clouds getting ready to follow us," groaned Nick.

"Staying alive is important, in case you missed the memo," replied Earl, in a dry tone.

"Back to lobbies. Nick, are you at least open to conversations I can set up to talk to some of them? Obviously, I won't make you talk to the teacher's union or the other hard core progressive ones."

"If they want to talk to me, I am open to talking to any of them, including the teacher's union. They probably won't like what I have to say, but I'll talk until they hang up," said Nick. "I really can't turn down any chance to speak to an audience, even one who hates me."

"Alright, get ready to not be the master of your own schedule for the next ten months. Pretty soon, you are going to hate all of us. You may even want to immigrate to North Korea to get more freedom," said Denise as she got the expected laughter from the group.

"I had an interesting conversation with a guy named Jeremy Kwan. Any of you heard of him?" asked Nick.

"Sure, big internet security mogul. Sold his company for big bucks a year ago," replied Greg. "Why were you talking to him?"

"He's planning on using his tech expertise to start a new social media platform. He claims he can ensure all the posts and comments are from verified users, keeping the trolls and bots from posting. Says he has a new algorithm or something. Anyway, I had breakfast with him after Christmas. He wants me to be the first account and post. He talked a good game about truth and keeping the sewer out of his social platform. Not sure how he can do that given free speech allows for shit to be spewed. Look at ANC on any night," laughed Nick. "Anyway, I told him I would get back to him."

"I say do it," said Margie. "We need all the exposure we can get. Being part of his launch means he can reference you in his marketing, giving us free press. Those folks will want to check out what you are saying and check out his app."

"Denise?" asked Nick.

"I defer to Margie on the social media front. She is much more aware of what is and is not trending," said Denise, turning to Jenny. "Any legal issue with Nick taking part in a launch like this?"

Jenny shook her head. "Nope, go for it."

"Kwan has a good rep. He forced the folks buying his company to keep his people and let them work the same way before he sold it. They agreed, believe it or not. We can take whatever exposure we get. Hey, if he can keep the trolls from posting, ask for equity in the company. It will be worth a fortune," said Margie.

"Now *that* would be illegal," chimed in Jenny, as they laughed.

"Come to think of it, should we be looking to Kwan to host all of our online presence? I am going to be saying some pretty provocative things, at least as far as the progressives, and now our intel agencies are concerned. I don't want any of the big hosting companies being the ones to decide if I have an online voice or not. They will de-platform me at Lexi's request in a heartbeat. Margie, ask Jeremy if he would host our sites. If his app is a hit, we know we'll have one non-banned account."

"Sure Nick, makes sense. I'll ask," said Margie.

"Just don't post at three AM," said Denise, who then turned to Earl. "I'm counting on you to make sure he doesn't post after a few beers or some heated conversations."

"Good luck with that," replied Earl.

"Hey, don't you trust me?" said Nick in a hurtful tone.

"No," said five voices in unison.

"Traitors," said Nick. "If that is all for now, let's get out a map and figure out where I'm going."

# Chapter 19

Mel entered Lexi's office in the Capitol, holding the door for Roland.

"Welcome, welcome," said Lexi, getting up from behind her desk to shake Roland's outstretched hand.

"Alexis Smythe-Thomas, may I introduce Roland Gill, our new security consultant?" said Mel with a smile.

"A pleasure to meet you, Madame Vice President," said Roland.

"Please have a seat," motioned Lexi, looking him up and down. A little over six feet tall, wearing an expertly tailored suit. It highlighted his trim and powerful figure.

Lexi watched as he took a seat. He moved like a wildcat. She could sense raw, untamed power. This was a dangerous man.

"Roland, tell me about yourself. Where did Mel find you?"

He smiled, showing his white teeth in contrast to his black mustache and goatee.

"Madame, I believe we are not fooling anyone regarding my expertise. Nor where I have worked in the last few years, providing private services to the highest bidders for discrete situations."

Lexi laughed and looked at Mel.

"Discrete situations? Clearly, a silver tongue is one asset not listed in your dossier. Tell me Roland, why should we trust you to handle our discrete situations and keep your mouth shut?"

Roland smiled back at Lexi's directness.

"One does not live long in my profession without demonstrating both tremendous loyalty and discretion. The fact I have lived as long as I have should prove two things. One, I am very good at my job and two, I have lived this long without betraying my client's trust. Had I done so,

I can assure you, even as good as I am, I would not have survived the consequences of betraying their trust."

"True, but you have probably not been providing those services for the most powerful person in the most powerful country in the world, either," said Lexi with a questioning tone.

Roland merely shrugged in reply.

"Madame, even more reason for me to keep my word and my mouth shut. You have entire covert agencies at your beck and call and yet here I sit, recruited by you and your team. If you do not need my services, I am happy to return to Europe. As they say in your American movies, my business is a target rich environment. Human nature and corruption know no boundaries. There are always things to put right."

Lexi smiled, turning to Mel.

"Mel, I like him. He is brutally honest and not intimidated in the slightest. What do you drink, Roland? Mel, I'll have a scotch."

"Madame, I do not drink. This assists me in keeping my fidelity to my employers. If we are finished, I believe your chief of staff would like to discuss me further without my being present." Roland stood. Lexi merely smiled and looked up at him. He held her eye contact, his dark eyes boring into her own icy blue.

"Indeed, he would. Thank you, Roland. I believe you will be very valuable in our effort to save democracy."

Roland gave the slightest bow, nodded to Mel, and left the office, shutting the door behind him.

"Where did you find him? Can we trust him?"

"It's better if I don't tell you anything about his background or how I found him. Plausible deniability, and all that. I spoke to several of his prior employers, and he got glowing recommendations," lied Mel.

"He'll have a lot to use against us if he turns," said Lexi.

"Trust me, I understand, and have it covered."

"He seems ruthless enough for our needs. No remorse."

"That, I don't think we need to worry about," said Mel prophetically.

# **Chapter 20**

"Bring back any memories of spring break?" asked Nick.

"Spring Break?" responded Earl in disbelief. "This is Nebraska, not Florida, and it's February. You see that stuff? It's called snow, not sand." pointing out the windshield from his perch in the front passenger seat at the cornfields covered in snow.

"Can't say I was big on spring break either, boss," said Greg from the first bench seat in the rented Suburban. "Put myself through school so I didn't waste money going to Florida or the Gulf."

"What a bunch of killjoys, and we are only a couple hours into our first road trip," groaned Nick in disappointment as he drove.

"I figure we go to North Platte first. We can get rooms at a Hampton Inn there, should be empty mid-week. Then we can drive to Omaha tomorrow," guided Greg, looking at a map on his phone.

"You sure about this? Is this is the best use of your time? Of our time? Driving around talking to folks in small towns?" asked Earl.

"I honestly don't know. Denise is busy building out the staff and getting the state offices established. Not much any of us can do there. But I can tell you when I drove around Colorado last fall, stopping in the towns and talking to everyday folks, it was enlightening. For the first time since joining Congress, I felt like I knew what my purpose was. To help those people with their problems, to fix them. Isn't that what congressmen are supposed to be doing?" asked Nick, glancing at Earl.

"Keep your eyes on the road or I'll drive," said Earl, giving Nick a strange look. "You just now figuring out Congress doesn't care about their constituents? I wonder if I can still get my old job back."

Greg chuckled in the back seat.

"Pipe it," said Nick in mock anger. "What I am saying is, the people think little of Congress. Yet they vote them in, or some of them do. Why?"

"Don't know," shrugged Earl. "I guess they vote for the lesser of two evils, rather than not vote at all."

"Some truth to that for sure, but for a lot of them, they *want* to believe what the candidates say," said Nick, emphasizing want. "But they are always disappointed. Everything is national. Nothing is local and nothing ever seems to trickle down to help them. That's what I want to find out. Is it just Colorado or does everyone feel this way?"

"Could probably save us all a lot of time. They all feel the same."

"I agree," chimed in Greg from the back. "I see a lot of the emails we get and a lot of them say the same thing. They see Congress passing legislation that does nothing to help them and solves problems that don't exist in their community. They want to know why their taxes are being spent elsewhere."

"OK. How better to connect with the people than to sit down and have a cup of coffee, hopefully anonymously," said Nick.

"Incognito? You have some Groucho Marx glasses," asked Earl. "You're fooling yourself if you think folks won't recognize you. Like it or not, you're a celebrity. All you need now is an Instacrap account."

"Gram. Instagram," said Greg, shaking his head. Earl turned and gave him an evil eye.

"He has one. We don't let him post or they would ban him. Speaking of insta'crap," said Greg, nodding to Earl. "I'd like to film our conversations. We can use snippets for campaign ads and postings on social media. I had Jenny draw up a simple release form for folks to sign or we can get them verbally agreeing on camera. We need something that says it is OK for us to post."

"As long as it doesn't clam them up. I want them to speak freely," said Nick.

"We should get to North Platte mid-afternoon," announced Greg. "Want to do some email?"

"We might as well see if doing these in the car is going to work or if I have to stay up all night reading these things," agreed Nick.

Greg started reading Nick's emails aloud.

\#

They pulled their black rented Suburban into a gas station just off I-80 and highway 83 in North Platte, Nebraska. Greg was filling the tank as Nick and Earl entered the store. Nick walked up to the attendant to pay for a six-pack of bottled water.

"Where would you suggest we get some decent food?" he asked casually.

"What kind you looking for?" asked the attendant, a young strapping kid with blond hair and a crew cut.

"Prefer something where the local's hangout. No chains."

"Carlsberg Diner. You want real locals, go to the one in the Airport. Jamie should be there. She runs the place after her old man passed a few years back."

"Thanks," said Nick as Earl returned.

"North on 83 and right on 4th. Just drive to the airport. It's right inside the terminal," said the attendant.

"Off to a great start, I see, eating at an airport for our first meal and we didn't even fly," commented Earl, shaking his head.

Nick laughed. "We gotta go where the locals are. Don't worry, I'm sure that'll mean a lot of bars and bar fights you can break up."

"Oh great, even better, I can see the headlines now. 'Presidential pretender arrested after pissing off Nebraskans asking exactly what a cornhusker is'," quoted Earl.

"I know what a cornhusker is. Do you?"

"That's easy boss. It's the person and now machine that takes the husk off the cob of corn," answered Greg, as they arrived at the car.

"Do I look like I have been anywhere near a cornfield, Greg?" asked Earl, looking at him.

Greg stared back at Earl, who despite being well north of 50 was still an imposing 230lbs of muscle resembling the linebacker he once was in college.

"Probably not," said Greg warily, as he continued. "In case anyone wants to know, it took $130 to fill up the tank."

"Good lord, how big is the tank?" asked Nick.

"Twenty gallons and we only put in 18. It was over seven bucks and that was E85. Did you see how much diesel was? Almost nine dollars a gallon," grumbled Greg.

"So much for using all that corn to lower the price of gas. I guess the cornhusker is not doing much for gas prices?" commented Earl in a slightly disgusted tone.

"Now this is my kind of airport," announced Nick as he pulled into the parking lot across from the terminal. He could park right up against the fence leading to it. "Bet you could get through security and on your plane in 5 minutes here."

"Good, I'm hungry. Let's find this place and eat," said Earl. "Protecting you is tiring."

"Ha," responded Nick.

They were all wearing jeans and jackets. It was in the thirties and slightly overcast. There were piles of snow in the parking lot from the last big snow, but the rest of the pavement was dry.

They walked into the terminal and saw the Carlsberg Diner on the left as they entered. Heading towards the entrance, inside was a large open area inside with various sized tables. Several had couples, and one large table had three older guys. The last were definitely farmers or ranchers, in Carhart jackets, Deere, and Ford ball caps.

"Hello, three for lunch?" asked an attractive middle-aged woman with longer straight blonde hair and a twinkle in her blue eyes. "You guys waiting on a flight or arriving?" she asked as she led her way into the room.

"Neither. Just driving through. Your place was recommended. Are you Jamie?" asked Nick.

Jamie stopped to look at Nick.

"I am. Have we met?"

"No, the kid at the gas station on the interstate recommended this location for lunch. Blond hair, crew cut, probably played lineman on his football team."

She laughed. "My nephew, he's always sending people this way. I guess I owe him another free breakfast burrito."

"I'm Nick, this is Earl and Greg," intro'd Nick, shaking Jamie's hand. "We're looking to eat and maybe talk with some of your locals? Get a feel for how things are around here. Do you think those guys over there would mind some company?" asked Nick, nodding at the ranchers.

"That tribe? I have to warn you, they'll talk your head off."

"Perfect."

Jamie took them to the table, explained they were driving through and wanted to get a feel for how things were going. She warned them not to scare Nick and company off.

"Nice to meet you guys. Thanks for letting us eat with you. Nick, Earl and Greg," he said, introducing them.

"No problem." This from a guy with a weathered face with a lot of wrinkles, wearing a green John Deere cap. "I'm John, this here's Billy," he said, pointing to another old guy similar in appearance and age to John, but sporting a gray mustache and beard. "And this is Bubba, Billy's kid." Bubba did not look like a 'Bubba'. He looked like he weighed 150 pounds dripping wet. He had dark hair with a mustache and beard like his dad and was sporting a Ford cap and a missing bi-cuspid as he smiled in acknowledgment.

"Nice to meet all of you. We are on our way to Omaha from Denver and stopped here for some lunch and conversation. What do you guys recommend?" asked Nick.

"How hungry are you?" asked Bubba. "Pork chops if you have a good appetite. Breakfast is also a favorite of the locals. Chicken fried steak or fried chicken for lunch is also good. If you're looking for salads, they ain't bad, but you are missing out on some good stuff."

Jamie smiled as Bubba gave his recommendation. They gave her their orders.

"What's in Omaha?" asked Billy.

"We are on our way to some meetings. We work in government and there is a conference there," lied Nick.

"Government huh," said John. "Not the IRS, I hope," he said, getting a laugh.

"Or the CIA or FBI," said Bubba as he spit tobacco into a handy paper cup.

"Hardly. We are more in the paper pushing side. Don't get out much and wanted to see how things are in Nebraska, so we drove instead of flying. So how are things?"

Jamie showed up with two iced teas for Nick and Earl and a diet Coke for Greg.

"Now be nice to them John, they are just passing through," ordered Jamie. John held up his hands in mock surrender.

"We won't hurt'em Jamie, at least not before they pay," he said with a smile.

Earl just flashed his perfect white teeth at the final bit of John's sentence.

"Just kidding. I doubt we would want to mess with ole Earl here. Nick, you look like you can take care of yourself too," remarked John.

Nick answered him with a brief smile.

"So really, how are things around here?" he pressed.

They looked at each other. John started.

"We have our share of issues, like anyone else. Property tax is too high, driving away the young people and causing the old to sell their farms out to big companies. But that is how the state funds most of their budget. Been trying to get it reduced for years, but we can never seem to get a majority to agree. Too many urban folks in Omaha like the services *our* taxes fund. We don't see any of it out here, but we pay the lion's share of it."

"Bubba here is one of the few who has stayed on to keep a family farm going. When I'm done, my kids will sell my farm. They don't want to farm," said John as Bubba spit in his cup in response.

"It will just get sold to ConAgra or more likely Gates and they will farm my acres with more equipment and fewer people," revealed John with a sigh. "Don't get me wrong, the tech advances have been fantastic. I can farm 15,000 acres with just four guys. The machines practically drive themselves. We have specialized equipment for all aspects. We're way more efficient, using the exact amount of fertilizer and water, no waste, no runoff, and I maximize our yields."

"Wow. I suspect most folks don't realize how much farming has changed," commented Nick.

"Got that right. We use satellites to tell us exactly when to plant, water, fertilize, weed, and harvest. Something called analytics to decide what seed to use depending on the weather forecasts going back 100 years. I don't understand it, but it works. It needs to. We are growing and feeding more and more people. Our crop yields have gone up probably four to five times since I started farming, just because of technology. The prices are generally good. Everyone's gotta eat, right?" said John, pausing as Jamie showed up with their lunches.

"John's right, I have 50,000 acres. We rotate through a couple of crops, soybeans, field corn, seed corn, and popcorn. Some goes to feed, some to Monsanto. We get vouchers from the government for the ethanol, so lots of the corn goes to that as well," said Billy, shrugging. "Ethanol makes no economic sense, but hey the government is paying us to grow corn for it, so we do."

"What do you mean about ethanol?" asked Nick, already knowing the answer from sitting on the Nutrition committee.

"You know how ethanol is made?" asked Bubba. The guys shook their heads while digging into their lunches.

"Have you noticed the price of ethanol at the pumps, E90, E85? It goes by different names. It's about the same as mid-tier unleaded. Without the subsidies the government pays to us and to the refineries to make it, we figure it would cost somewhere in the $12-$13 a gallon range, maybe even $15 now with this crappy inflation. Who would buy it at that cost, right?" asked Bubba.

"Nobody. So, we get paid to cover our costs because the refineries wouldn't pay enough to buy the corn. We get paid, and the refineries get paid to refine it instead of other gas, but guess what? It costs way more to refine corn into biofuel than it does crude oil to gasoline. Even with $7-$8 gas, ethanol hasn't gotten any cheaper to refine. The government makes up the difference there too, to make it affordable."

"Doesn't seem to make much sense," said Earl, between bites.

"This is all part of their 'green new deal'. Keep the price of gas so high to get cars and trucks and trains and planes to use biofuels and electricity instead of oil. They should spend their money on how to power all these with natural gas. We have tons of it. We can collect it cheaper and we can refine and transport it much cheaper than anything else. The other dirty secret is natural gas burns clean, so emissions are low. Lower than a coal power plant providing electricity for your Tesla. Or coal plants in China where they make the batteries and pump the waste chemicals into the rivers. Do you have any idea how much water it takes to refine a gallon of ethanol? Way more than we used when fracking was allowed. And they recycled that water. It takes three to five gallons of water minimum to refine a gallon of ethanol here in Nebraska. Takes a lot more than that in states where corn is fully irrigated, like California," explained Bubba, shaking his head in disbelief.

"It takes a lot more water than regular gas refining or natural gas production. Every gallon of water used to grow and refine corn for ethanol means water not used to grow food for consumption. We tap into the Ogallala aquifer. It is showing signs of not recharging as fast as in the past. If the world population keeps growing, the additional corn is coming from here. That is assuming we have water to meet the demand and we are growing corn for food and feed versus ethanol. These decisions do not make economic sense. So much for the free market," complained Bubba, spitting in his cup to make his last point.

"You don't think we should do ethanol?" asked Nick.

"I do, but I think we should try to use the waste from the corn. The stalks, silks, leaves, cobs, etc. If they can make fuel out of algae, they can do it out of this as well. We need folks to work on these. This means grants, and it means a way to recoup that investment by motivating entrepreneurs to make a profit on doing this," answered Bubba. "They won't do this as long as the government keeps propping up an industry that would die in the free market. It sucks, but we'll still make a living selling our corn for other purposes."

"Interesting. But you are getting money from the government, right? It is probably more than you could sell it for feed?" asked Nick calmly.

Bubba stared at Nick for a second. "Most years, that is true. What folks forget is, if that gallon of ethanol is $13-$15 to produce but can only be sold for $8. Someone is making up the $6. That someone is the government. But the government does not earn a wage. They build nothing and sell nothing. Don't even offer a service someone wants to pay money for. They are simply a middleman, taking your and my taxes and then spreading that money around as they see fit, in this case, $6 or more of it per gallon of ethanol."

"If you think you are doing a favor to the environment by using E85 or E90, maybe you are, but you are paying way more for that gallon than the $8 you shell out at the pump. Part of your taxes are paying the difference. Nobody gets this. What else could that $6 incentive be used for? That is billions every year. No one asks that question."

"That's my boy. That Nebraska economics degree is showing," said Billy proudly. "Glad he came back to the farm."

Nick finished his pork chops and pushed away his plate.

"Don't think I'm gonna need dinner tonight. That was filling."

"I told you," said John. "How was the chicken fried chicken and pork chop?" said John, looking at Greg and Earl.

"Just like you said," Greg and Earl nodded as they finished their meals as well.

"You guys heading to Omaha still today?"

"Maybe. We may stay here tonight."

"Fat chance of that," laughed Billy. "Last week of hunting season. Every hotel room in town is booked. Same all the way to Omaha. Looks like you boys'll be sleeping in the car."

Earl looked at Greg, whose eyes were wide.

"Should be empty mid-week, huh?" repeated Earl, the prospect of sleeping in the suburban clearly not appealing.

Jamie was cleaning up the dishes and overheard the conversation.

"I've got room at my place. You are welcome to bunk there. My kids are all gone and since Clyde passed, I have nobody to share my evening coffee."

Nick considered the offer and was going to decline respectfully when Billy piped up.

"You have cherry pie at home? Hell, I'll come by as well," laughed Billy. "You really should take her up on it. Best pie in the state."

"Well, if you say we can't get a room anywhere else, I guess we will take you up on it," said Nick.

"Guys, mind if I ask you a question?" asked Greg, entering the conversation for the first time.

"Sure," they all said in unison.

"Do you recognize Nick?"

"You mean Senator Turner? Sure, we know who you are," said John. "Do you think we would let strangers' bunk at Jamie's?"

"So, you know Nick is running for president. We are doing this road trip to listen to regular Americans without all the hoopla and find out what folks like you feel are the genuine issues."

"Makes sense to me. I like it. About time a candidate bothered to see what it is like for the little guy," nodded Bubba.

"Guys, I have been recording this with my phone. If it is OK with you, we may want to use some of this in ads or posting on our campaign site. My legal guys need me to get an approval from you in order to use this. If you are OK with it, an affirmative is all we need. Or if you like, I can send you a document to sign via email that allows us to use this?" offered Greg.

"God, don't send me any email. I hate the stuff. I'm not ashamed of expressing my opinion. We still have a first amendment, at least until that Smythe-Thomas lady is elected. Please don't let that happen," said Billy, looking at Nick.

John and Bubba both added their approvals. They got up to leave the table, saying they needed to get back to their farms. The three of them stood with Nick, and Greg took a picture with all of their phones. Nick ordered some coffee, and he sat there speaking with Earl and Greg when he was approached by another couple. He invited them to join them.

They stayed and told Nick their concerns, and then they got up to go. Shortly, they were replaced by another family with a couple of kids. Greg got up and pulled over a new chair. This went on for the entire afternoon.

Nick was holding an impromptu town hall. Others pulled their tables and chairs closer to be part of the conversation. Throwing out questions and adding their own anecdotes. Greg had moved further away so he could set up his camera to get the entire room in his recording. Everyone was perfectly happy to be recorded and used for his promotions.

At one point, Nick realized they had been talking to folks for 6 hours and asked for a break to eat some dinner. They quickly ordered and listened to more folks telling their stories while they ate their meal. As 8 o'clock rolled around, closing time for the restaurant, Jamie shooed away the last of the patrons shortly before 8:30 so she could close. Nick took his last photo and walked over to fill his coffee from the pot before Jamie turned it off.

"Anything we can do to help you close?" asked Earl.

"Thanks honey, but we got it down to a science. We'll be done in a few," said Jamie, smiling at Earl's offer.

They sat around the table sipping coffee while Jamie and her staff finished closing. One more picture with Jamie and her crew to go on the wall and they were walking out of the terminal into the darkness of a cold February night.

"Senator, if you want to ride with me, the guys can follow us. I'm in the Ford pickup over there," said Jamie as she pointed to a Blue Ford F250 Diesel.

"Right behind you, Nick," said Earl as he caught the keys from Nick.

# Chapter 21

Jamie drove them out of town, east of the airport for a few miles, and turned onto a dirt road heading north and eventually into her driveway. She drove about half a mile down it and approached a large two-story brick house, which looked fairly new. There were lights on in the house and cars in the driveway.

Nick looked at Jamie, who smiled at him.

"I had to call the kids to give them a chance to meet you. I'm sad Clyde didn't live long enough. You two would have hit it off."

She pulled the truck into the garage and walked out with Nick to where Earl and Greg were standing with smiles as well. Earl nodded to the front window where there were several children's heads peering out from behind curtains.

"Looks like our cover is blown."

"You could say that," agreed Nick, grinning.

They walked in the front door where they were greeted by two large dogs who sniffed all three of the newcomers, eventually retreating once satisfied they did not need to be in attack mode. Jamie introduced them to her son Nathan, his wife Julie, and their two sons Caleb and Brody.

Jamie's oldest daughter, Nora, and her husband Jeff and their toddler Jane, who tottered over to Nick, grabbed his pant leg and wouldn't let go until he picked her up. Finally, Jamie's youngest daughter, Audrey, took Jane from Nick and shook his hand. They all stood around for a bit, not knowing what to say or do.

"Any chance I can get some coffee? It's what keeps me going," asked Nick. Audrey, Julie, and Nora raced over each other to get to the kitchen to start the coffee, laughing when they all collided at the doorway.

Jamie laughed, "Come on in Nick, let's sit down," she said, motioning to the large living room with a variety of sofas and chairs.

"I'll sit in a minute. Been sitting all afternoon. I need to stretch a bit. So, what do you guys do for a living?" asked Nick.

Nathan spoke first. "I take care of the farm. We have about 20,000 acres we farm and then we also have a feed lot with about 600 head of cattle. Dad got it from Granddad and it's my job to keep it in the family. Mom's always had the restaurant. Nora and Jeff manage the diner downtown and help Mom at the airport location. Julie does the books for the farm and the diners, and Audrey is working on her masters in education online from Clemson while she teaches at the local middle school."

"Sounds like an American success story," said Nick.

"It is. It hasn't always been easy, especially when Dad passed way too young. Mom kept it together, got us all through school and made sure we made it," said Nathan.

Jamie wiped a tear from her eye. Nick noticed.

"Jamie, you should be real proud." She nodded and was kept from having to talk by the girls carrying coffee mugs, a pot of coffee, and a pie with plates. Julie handed out the cups and Nora poured while Audrey started cutting pieces of cherry pie. The boys were jumping up and down at the prospect of late-night pie.

Earl and Greg sat on the floor with their coffee and pie, Nick perched on the corner of the hearth in front of the fireplace. The rest of the Carlsberg clan sat on various chairs and sofas.

"First, thank you for the coffee, the pie, and the roof over our head tonight. I guess we need to do a bit more advanced planning," laughed Nick. "You know, I kinda shoot from the hip," Nathan snorted his coffee, and Julie elbowed him.

"My husband said the same thing about you. That you appear to shoot from the hip. No focus groups, or polls before you say something. He likes that," said Julie with a smile.

"Nathan is right. My staff will tell you that may or may not be a good thing." This time it was Greg who let out an 'Amen', earning a glance from Nick as Greg shoveled some more pie in his mouth.

"Anyway, my plan is to do exactly what I did today. Go to small town America in every state and talk to folks like I did today. Learn about what concerns you guys. Your issues, what you think is good, and what needs to be fixed. We got quite an earful today. I have a much greater appreciation of where some of my food comes from," said Nick with a smile.

"It is an honest profession for sure," said Nathan. "Hard work and subject to the whims of weather and global conditions. More and more our feed goes to China and Japan, and the beef to Japan as well. We pay attention to trade treaties. Tariffs hurt us, but we understand what is happening and why. We are better off than most. We have cash reserves, and we have diversity."

"Diversity?" asked Nick, in a questioning tone.

"Of crops," said Nathan, smiling. "Some farms around here rely too much on corn and soybeans. If China changes what they buy, they go under in a season. We control what we can and hope the idiots in Washington, no offence Senator, don't make policies that hurt us."

"None taken. This is exactly the info that helps. Putting faces to industries and realizing there are families and houses and livelihoods affected by every decision we make," noted Nick.

"Have you guys recovered from the COVID lockdowns with the restaurant?" Nora and Jeff looked at each other and Nora spoke.

"To be honest, we almost lost the restaurants. If Mom hadn't mortgaged the house, we would have lost one or both of them. We were planning on opening one in Grand Island, but that obviously got crushed by the pandemic. Strangely enough, the lockdowns were bad, especially the first wave, but what really almost killed us was when we tried to open up. We couldn't find enough staff willing to work. People were coming back, but our service was suffering because we couldn't keep trained staff and we were getting killed with critical reviews. We've been a mainstay here for almost 30 years," said Nora.

Jeff took over once Nora paused.

"Senator, what almost killed us was really two things, the minimum wage raising craze and then the continuous extension of unemployment benefits and checks from the government. When you are working for minimum wage and tips, you don't need a very big unemployment or a stimulus check to stay home for another month or another or another. The young people in town didn't have any incentive to get a job to make a few dollars more than unemployment."

"The only way we solved it was to raise our wages above minimum wage and even then, we still had to restrict our capacity to get our service back to where it needed to be. We are not real happy with the geniuses in Washington who think they were helping by removing the need to work and destroying the work ethic in our youth. There is too much 'leisure' activity to distract them."

"Now, with the inflation and those additional wages not going as far, we have to raise our prices and pay our staff even more. It is a vicious cycle," added Nora.

"Drive around town mid-morning or mid-afternoon during supposed school hours and you'll be amazed at the number of school-age children out and about. This is going to cost us big time in the long run," said Jeff, a little riled up.

"What did you put in his coffee?" quipped Nick, getting a smile from around the room.

"Sorry," said Jeff, "but it really worries me what we are doing to our teenagers. It also worries me I could be at a hundred percent capacity, and the reason I can't is the government, who caused all these problems. Then continues to keep us from recovering fully. It's par for the course. You guys in Washington really have no clue."

"Jeff, I think you know I agree with you. That's why I'm doing this. We have to stand up and take back our country. It means each and everyone of us has to vote and get our friends to vote and stick together to demand common sense reform and governing. If we don't, we'll continue sliding into socialism or worse," said Nick. He looked around and found Audrey. "You're a teacher?"

"Yes. 6th graders," stated Audrey.

"That must be fun," groaned Earl sarcastically.

"Forgive my head of security. He is used to rousting Colorado rednecks out of bars in his former role as a sheriff."

"They aren't much better than a 6th grader, I suspect," said Earl.

Audrey laughed. "There are two types, those whose hormones are just kicking in and who think they are young adults and those who have not and still want to be little kids. It is an interesting time. Generally, I like it. I did a year teaching 6th graders at an elite private school in New York City. The mayor and governor's kids were there to show you how elite. It was quite the job to land, the kind most who teach would die for. Big starting salary and clear opportunity to progress into a full tenured job in four years with perks. They might as well have sent me to Riker's Island prison. It was the worst year of my life," said Audrey, her face showing her dislike of that experience.

"Really? That is supposed to be the best of the best. What happened?" asked Nick.

"The teachers were all militant liberals spewing the latest doctrines. They were all either absentee parents sending their kids to a top school to be baby sat or else they were helicopter parents involved in every one of Jimmy's assignments. All grading you on how well you were preparing him for Andover and then Yale."

"Finally, we had the activist board who signed on to every far-left theory of teaching. 1619 history, critical race theory, annual showings of *An Inconvenient Truth*, transgender documentaries, gender fluidity exercises and other sexual 'health' studies that would make an adult blush, let alone an 11 or 12-year-old. It was insane. The kids were lost, angry, conflicted and, frankly, confused. They didn't know what they should or shouldn't be doing, saying, or thinking. Sadly, those in their life they should've been looking to for this guidance were absent or were the ones feeding them this shit." Audrey cringed at this last word, looking at Julie in a panic.

"It's OK. The boys are out," Julie pointed at her four- and six-year-old asleep on the sofa on either side of Jamie.

"Is it better here in Nebraska schools?" asked Nick.

"Yes, though occasionally we get a parent from the east or west coast asking about why we are not teaching our children about various activist programs aimed at elevating the latest victim du jour," said Audrey. "Plus all the mask and ZOOM nonsense. We are a year removed from the end of the second pandemic's mandates and we still have students afraid to come back to school and many who are still opting to wear their masks out of fear. We have trained an entire generation of children to be afraid to breathe without a mask. It is frankly criminal."

"That is unfortunate," asked Nick.

"It was a pleasure to meet you Senator and we will help you and tell all our friends about your common sense approach. We have to work in the morning and we need to get our little ones to bed," said Julie, getting up and picking up one son while Nathan grabbed the other. They shook hands with everyone and made their way to the door. Nora and Jeff, carrying Jane, also said their goodbyes and headed out.

Audrey was picking up cups and plates with Earl and Greg's help and taking them to the kitchen. Jamie stood at the doorway as her kids loaded up the grandkids into the car seats and set off for their nearby homes.

"You really did well Jamie, they are great kids."

"Thanks. Clyde was a great dad and a better husband. They all keep me going," she said, turning as Audrey came up. "Now I just need to get this one married so I can have some more grandkids," said Jamie.

Audrey turned a shade of red.

"Goodnight mother. Senator, let us know if you ever need anything or plan on coming through again," she hesitated and then leaned in and gave Nick a peck on the cheek and hurried out like a schoolgirl from a first date.

Jamie shut the door once Audrey headed down the road.

"I think you made an impression on my family," she said with a little laugh. "If you have this effect on everyone you speak to, Nick, you may be onto something with this road trip idea of yours. You guys agree? You've been watching all day." noted Jamie.

"Whole-heartedly. It is amazing to watch the change that comes over people," observed Greg. "They are tense or uptight and want to get their point across and somehow you listen and turn their concern into confidence. Confidence in you. I doubt there was a single voter in the room who won't vote for you in November."

"I think you're right. Something happens, Nick. They all feel you're their best uncle, brother, father, or pastor. They put their faith in you. Whatever it is, we need to bottle it and send it out over the airwaves and hope everyone reacts the same," explained Earl.

"They will. Keep doing what you're doing. You don't need to change a thing. Just keep being you," added Jamie presciently.

"I have three bedrooms upstairs. Let me show you guys the way. I get up at dawn. If you do, I can whip up some breakfast. I don't have to be in until 8 tomorrow."

"You don't know how much I appreciate all you've done," thanked Nick.

# Chapter 22

The next morning, Nick came down to the kitchen in Jamie's house to find Earl, Greg, and Jamie already there drinking coffee. He could smell the bacon cooking and smiled.

"I guess you snooze you lose."

"You did do all the talking yesterday," pointed out Earl.

"Jamie, we stripped the sheets and put them in the basket in one bedroom. You want us to do a load of laundry?" asked Nick.

Jamie looked at him with a sideways glance.

"I wanted to offer, anyway. My mother wouldn't be happy if I didn't."

"Is you mother still alive?" asked Jamie.

"No. I lost them both a long time ago, but that doesn't keep me from using the manners they taught me."

"I'm sure she is smiling right now."

"That's nice of you to say. I haven't thought about them in a long time."

"They don't mind, just keep the faith," said Jamie.

Nick poured a cup of coffee while Jamie worked on a large skillet of scrambled eggs and popped the toaster down with 4 slices of sourdough.

"Faith, what got you through everything?" asked Nick quietly, leaning against the doorjamb, sipping his hot coffee.

Jamie looked up from the skillet.

"It did. Without faith, I would have given up. Nick, I believe we have a purpose. I believe in fate as well. I could have sold the property and the land and the mineral rights. Oil company has been after me for rights to drill for years, offering stupid money. I was sitting on the rocker on the front porch looking over the land, with one of their offers in my hand, thinking about selling and moving to Arizona. Winters up here can be tough," said Jamie as she plated the scrambled eggs for the three boys, setting another plate of bacon, toast, and butter in the center of the table they all now sat around.

"So why did you stay?" asked Earl. "Sounds like you had the perfect opportunity to leave it all behind for warm Arizona."

"Clyde and his Daddy. I swear while I was sitting there, I heard a voice in my heart. This is Carlsberg land. It anchors us to the world. It is our purpose. To grow the food, to feed the communities, to be a steward of this property and do good. Nathan went through a rough patch after college. Tried to work in Omaha and got into booze and pain killers. I got him home and put him to work on the farm. Way better than rehab. Working from dawn to dusk, and he found faith again, too. He bonded with the land and realized he had a purpose as well. His was to be the third generation Carlsberg to run this farm."

They all nodded, listening and digging into the breakfast.

"He reconnected with Julie, his sweetheart from High School. They got married and took over the farm. That let me focus on the restaurants. That gave Nora and Jeff a purpose as well. If I had sold all of this, where would they all be? I have faith. I believe we are what we do and eventually there may be a reckoning. Even if there isn't, what does it hurt to do good, as if there could be a day of reckoning? What does it hurt to lead a wholesome life? That is how I lead my life. I have faith and I believe things happen for a reason. Call it fate, but we are the sum of our actions, good and bad," said Jamie with a shrug.

Nick sat watching her as she delivered her statement on purpose and faith. He shook his head as she finished.

"Jamie, you are a joy," said Nick, smiling while he looked her in the eyes.

"And a helluva cook," added Earl.

Jamie laughed. "It's only eggs, pretty hard to screw them up."

Earl looked up. "My wife always found a way. I think it was her way of making *me* cook breakfast."

"I didn't know you're married," said Nick and Greg at almost the same time.

"Was. I lost her to cancer. Listening to Jamie made me remember how faith got me out of my dark place. And having a purpose," said Earl in a somber tone.

Jamie reached out and touched Earl's face.

"We have the memories, and we have a purpose. You have found yours as well. Keep him safe," said Jamie. "It is going to be important to all of us." Earl smiled, meeting Jamie's gaze.

Nick and Greg ate in silence.

"Thank you, and make sure you thank your nephew for sending us your way," said Earl.

"You're headed to Omaha? I'll give my cousin a call. She runs a B&B with a restaurant as well. Lots of locals come by there. There is also an interesting pub downtown you might want to try for some local color. Folks from the air force base hang out there. They'll have plenty to say. About how things have changed. My daddy was in the military. Thankfully, he passed before it went to hell with all this PC crap," said Jamie, making a face.

"Thanks, we'll help you with the dishes and then be on our way. I can't thank you enough. It proves our idea to road trip is exactly what I need to get in touch with America," said Nick.

"If you think I am going to let any of you load the dishwasher, you are crazy. Men never load it right. You can barely unload it," complained Jamie.

"I like her," laughed Earl.

They all gave Jamie hugs. Earl's lasting longer than the rest. Jamie gave Nick and Earl her numbers in case they ever needed to contact her. She also gave Nick the address of her cousin Natalie's B&B in Omaha and her phone number.

Nick was driving again, headed east on I-80 toward Omaha.

"Earl, I'm sorry to hear about your wife. I didn't even think to ask about a family before offering you the job," remarked Nick.

"It was a long time ago, when I was still in the Army."

"How about you, Greg? Got a family I need to know about?"

"No worries, boss," laughed Greg. "No hidden wife or kids or even a dog."

"How's the rest of the world today?" asked Nick.

"Well, they have officially kicked you off the last of your committees."

"Great, more time for me to be on the road. When is the next vote I need to fly back for?"

"Two weeks. There is an appropriations bill and a bill to renew FISA for another 3 years," reported Greg.

"Okay, we need to figure out where we will be then and arrange so I can be back and at least lodge a protest vote against renewing FISA. It will pass anyway, since it also has opposition support."

"I'll work through the logistics," commented Greg.

# Chapter 23

They drove for hours on I-80, eventually making it to Omaha. They headed toward the south end near Offutt Air Force Base. Stopping at Stella's bar and grill as Jamie recommended. They had a repeat of the same conversations they'd had in North Platte.

Some different points but the same outcomes. Jobs, crime, homelessness, protests, and lack of common sense local government, compounded by the lack of common sense state and federal government decisions. Nick was sensing Earl and Greg were right when they said he would hear the same story everywhere.

They talked to a variety of folks, including some from the nearby Air Force base, stopping in for lunch. This also included a story of retaliation against a whistleblower who had exposed hypocrisy in the implementation of ESG and DEI rules within the state government agencies.

Rather than being protected, as federal law demanded, the whistleblower had instead faced the full wrath of the media, even garnering national attention. Eventually, fired from their job, they had to move out of state. What was more interesting was the treatment of the reporter trying to report the story and the whistleblowers' allegations honestly.

He had witnessed protesters being bused in and handed signs as they got off the bus to protest. He also witnessed them receiving cash as they reboarded the buses to be driven back to Chicago, St. Louis, and Minneapolis. Once he tried to broadcast this story with the video and interviews, his local affiliate of the RBS network would not play it.

Eventually, he published it in an underground newspaper and was promptly fired for broadcasting misinformation by his network affiliate. The video evidence and acknowledgement by the interviewees of being paid to protest was ignored. These and similar stories now sounded all too familiar to Nick who'd heard them in committees.

He was looking at the GPS as he drove out of the restaurant headed to the B&B Jamie had recommended. "Let's drive around a bit." He made a circuit past the gate of Offutt Air Force Base and swung around to the west until he spotted the Willow Lakes golf course. He then continued north into Omaha and the market district. It appeared to be mostly trendy coffee shops and boutiques, many in old houses. They found a large Victorian house with a small parking lot announcing the Williams Bed & Breakfast.

Entering the foyer, which doubled as the check-in, they saw a few tables in the room off to the right, with folks sitting, having cocktails. An attractive younger woman with red hair pulled back in a ponytail, wearing jeans and a sweater, approached with a smile when she took in the three visitors.

"Ah, our esteemed road warriors, I presume," she said with a chuckle and a smile.

Nick smiled back, intrigued by the striking green eyes and lopsided smile of the woman, turning to Earl and Greg.

"We might as well be driving around with a neon sign. You'd think we are on *America's Most Wanted* for the attention we seem to get."

"I'm Natalie Williams, and yes, Jamie called to warn me you were coming. Good thing too or I would have rented out the rooms, but lucky for you, I blocked them. Come on in, I'll get you a drink." Natalie turned and led them back through the house. Passing through several other rooms with tables occupied by either couples or men having business dinners. She waved or responded to many of the folks seated. Eventually they came to a breakfast area off the kitchen with a large wooden table.

"Have a seat, gents. Can I get you a beer?"

"Sure, sounds good. Something local maybe?" asked Nick.

While Natalie was getting the beers, several wait staff moved back and forth with food and drinks and appetizers for the tables spread throughout the main floor of the house. Natalie came back with three local beers.

"Here's an ale, a stout, and a lager. I'll be right back, gotta make sure all the tables are seated," she said.

"Guys, any preference? I'll drink any of them," said Nick.

"I'll take the lager, I'm not much of a beer guy," said Greg.

"Ale for me then, don't like the dark beers," picked Earl.

"I will gladly drink the stout." Nick took a sip of the very cold beer. "This is pretty good."

"I agree," admitted Greg. "I don't normally care for beer, but this is good."

"What did the Major pass you?" asked Earl.

"Excuse me?"

Earl stared at Nick in response.

"You don't miss much, do you?"

"First, you never have to pee. I've noticed. You made a beeline as soon as you shook his hand and you kept your hand closed the whole time. Not a very good dead drop," said Earl.

"Ah, am I missing something?" said Greg, looking confused.

"Major Jenkins, the Air Force officer we met at Stella's pub, wants to meet me at the Willow Lakes golf course tomorrow at 7 am. The piece of paper he passed to me when we shook hands says he has info I need."

"What does he think this is, a spy movie?" asked Greg.

"If he wants to tell me something negative about the military, he isn't exactly going to do it in a restaurant with you recording," said Nick. "I'll meet him in the morning and see what he has to say."

"I'll go with you," stated Earl.

"No, I can do this myself while you guys get the second B, in B&B. I don't think I have to worry about an Air Force major."

"I don't like it. Something smells here," replied Earl.

"Could be the fish special. You guys are close to the kitchen," stated Natalie, her boot heels clicking on the hardwood, announcing her arrival.

"I'm sorry. I wasn't talking about that *smell*," said Earl, flustered by Natalie's quip.

"Good," replied Natalie with a big smile. She sat down at the table across from Nick and Earl, next to Greg.

"Jamie sure gave me an earful on you guys. You made quite the impression."

"So did she," said Nick. "Quite the house you have here."

"It's pretty big, isn't it? It was my husband Patrick's family's house. He grew up here. His grandfather was a colonel in the army and his father was a one star in the Air Force at Offutt. They have a lot of roots here. When I came back, I decided it was way too much house for just me and Grace, so I did some work on it and turned it into a B&B. The guests liked the food so much, I opened the restaurant as well. That was almost five years ago," said Natalie.

A pretty brunette teenager flew by on her way to the kitchen.

"Mom, table six needs a couple more glasses of Pinot."

"That's Grace. She's fifteen now and plays by all the rules, following her father's side. I need to serve the alcohol. Be right back," said Natalie as she got up to pour two glasses of Pinot Noir.

"I'm liking Nebraska. Good people. Good women. What say we just chuck all this politics crap and settle here? I could be a farmer."

"Or a bouncer," suggested Nick.

Earl shrugged as Natalie went by with two glasses of red wine.

"I wonder where the husband is?" mused Greg.

"Me too," agreed Nick, watching Natalie deliver the wine to a couple out for a romantic dinner. Natalie came back and sat back down, sipping a club soda.

"On the clock," she said. "Gotta set a good example."

"Natalie, you from here as well?" asked Nick.

"Really Senator, you better learn to recognize a Texas accent if you intend to win many votes down there," said Natalie with an exaggerated drawl. "I grew up west of Dallas in a little town called Grapevine. It is not so little anymore. Went to UT and then to Culinary School in Austin after I discovered my liberal arts degree didn't include the ability to make enough money to actually rent a place in Austin."

"I went to work in a barbecue joint outside Austin. I was the head chef at a place that served its food on butcher paper with sawdust on the floor. But it was the best damn French/Texas barbecue in the state," laughed Natalie.

"I bet. I can smell your fish now, and it smells pretty darn good," said Earl.

"Geez, sorry guys, let me get you some menus. You mind eating here? I'm all booked up on reservations for the evening. You usually need to book about a month in advance for dinner. Only have 10 tables," said Natalie, getting up to grab some menus. She returned and handed them out.

"Today's special you smell is a 6 oz piece of butter roasted halibut with asparagus and olives. I have enough for two more servings tonight. It's flown in fresh every morning. The beef is locally raised Nebraska Angus, aged 21 days, served as a filet or a NY strip. We also have locally raised pork chops, which are a fan favorite and we have seared salmon Caesar salad and a couple of pastas on the menu. Everything is wonderful and I recommend it all. We also have a pretty good wine list on the back. Take a look and I'll be back to take the order in a minute. Need to make my rounds and say hello to the guests."

"My god, I'd weigh 300 pounds if I lived here. This food looks and smells better than anything in Washington."

"Boss, you get takeout every night. Chinese, burgers, sushi, pizza, and pasta. Always from the same places and always the same thing. Your bar on good food is pretty low," said Greg, holding out his hand and lowering it as he spoke.

"What is wrong with Fat Wong's Chinese? For your information, I get salads at least twice a week," replied Nick, in a lecturing tone.

"What do you think?" inquired Earl. "Had the pork chop last night, so I am inclined to try the halibut, but who can pass up a nice steak when in beef country? Filet for me, especially since Nick is paying."

"Greg?" asked Nick.

"I can't pass up the special. It smells too good."

"I agree," said Nick. He flipped over the menu to look at the wine list.

"I know you're supposed to have white wine with fish, but I don't like it. Greg you OK if we get a bottle of red?" asked Nick.

"Sure. You know much about wine?" asked Greg.

"Maybe," said Nick suspiciously. "Why? Are you an expert?"

"I am out of my element with beer, but I have spent some time in vineyards," explained Greg.

"Fire away."

While Greg looked over the wine list, Natalie showed back up at the table, laughing.

"News travels fast. If you would be so kind as to make the rounds in the restaurant, folks would love to get pictures with you. I might have to start a celebrity wall."

Nick smiled, looking at Natalie standing with her hands on her hips. She looked more like a college co-ed than someone old enough to have a teenage daughter. "That's why I'm here. Should we order? I'm going to have the special."

"Good choice," said Natalie as she looked at Earl.

"Filet, medium rare, with mashers and another ale."

Greg ordered the special and the wine. "Do you still have the 2018 Gary Farrell Hallberg Pinot? That's gotta be getting pretty rare?"

"It is," said Natalie. "It was my favorite when they released it and I was just starting the restaurant, so I bought a bunch of cases and laid it down in the cellar. We are down to the last few bottles. Good choice. I may have to have a sip myself. Let me get your order in while you shake some hands, Senator."

"Fair enough," said Nick as he got up. "And please call me Nick." He toured the rooms, and met a couple from Texas, a local couple celebrating their 10-year anniversary, another celebrating their first, five local couples including one pair of guys out for a nice dinner and two other tables filled with businessmen in town who came in because of the reputation. He spent a few minutes with each, learning names and key concerns, listened and asked each a question in response to their question. He took pictures with each group and was chatting with one couple when Natalie showed up.

"Bob, Jerry, I need to steal the Senator back. His halibut is getting cold, and I have a reputation to uphold. Don't want a bad online review for serving cold fish," said Natalie. Bob and Jerry stood up, shook Nick's hand, and posed for a picture that Natalie took. As the Senator turned to head back toward the kitchen, the patrons all started clapping.

Those nearby shouted 'Good luck Senator,' and 'we support you Senator', the last from a table he couldn't even see. Nick smiled, mouthed a thank you, and shook his head as he went back to the table.

Natalie brought out his special.

"Should still be good."

Nick wasted no time and dug right in. The first bite of the halibut melted in his mouth, and he savored the wonderful flavor.

"Perfect."

"Let me know what you think of the wine as well," said Natalie.

The guys dug into their dinners with gusto. Soon they were pushing back empty plates. Nick sipped his Pinot. Natalie came back and stood at the head of the table. "Well, what's the verdict?"

"Better than advertised," said Nick. "The halibut was the best I've ever had. I am afraid you'll need to open another bottle if you want any wine. It was too good."

"Get you guys some coffee or dessert?" asked Natalie. "I'll also get your room keys. One room has two beds, and the other is a single." Greg and Earl looked at each other.

"Hey roomie, how about we go get the bags? No coffee for me," said Greg.

"Me neither," added Earl.

"I'll have a cup. Caffeine never keeps me up."

"OK, once I get things cleaned up, I'll join you," said Natalie.

She brought Nick a cup and handed the keys to Earl and Greg. They took their bags and Nick's upstairs and then came back down and gave Nick his key.

"See you guys in the morning. Remember, I'm gonna meet with Major Jenkins, then I'll come get you. Where are we headed tomorrow?"

"North," answered Greg.

"Good night guys, see you tomorrow."

He sat drinking his coffee and thinking through what information Major Jenkins could have that he needed to pass on. As his cup emptied, he got up and walked back into the cooking and prep area of the kitchen. Natalie was finishing up and her last staff were leaving. Nick leaned against the wall, smiling. Her daughter shook Nick's hand, gave her mother a quick kiss, threw Nick a smile, and headed upstairs to her bedroom.

"Any coffee left?" asked Nick.

"Should be enough for a couple," she answered, grabbing a cup and filling it before filling Nick's and turning off the machine.

"Follow me."

She led Nick to the front door, which she locked, and then through a hallway to a door in one wing that opened into an office, with a worn couch and an office chair. She gestured for Nick to have a seat in the chair. Natalie kicked off her cowboy boots and sat on the couch, tucking her legs under her. She sipped her coffee and stared at him.

"Mind if I ask you a personal question?" she asked in a questioning tone.

"Only if you are game as well?"

Natalie nodded. "Why are you doing this? You obviously could do whatever you want and be successful at it. You exude confidence and capability, just like my husband did. Why waste your time driving around the country, talking to folks? Washington is hopelessly screwed up. Surely, you know that?"

"Where's your husband, if you don't mind me asking?"

"You didn't answer my question. But I'll still answer yours," said Natalie. "I was working at the barbeque joint outside Austin and in walked a group of CBP trainees for lunch one day. They were carrying on and being a general pain, like your average twelve-year-olds." Natalie shook her head with a smile, remembering.

"They said they could handle the hottest sauce we had. I, of course, told them I would have them crying and they should just be good little boys and eat their brisket. One of them stood up and said, and I still remember it. 'Ma'am, there is nothing you can dish out that the border patrol can't handle'. 30 minutes later, we were in the ER. He had rubbed his eyes after I gave them the Carolina Reaper sauce and he was having a reaction. It swelled up huge. We were married less than a year later. Had Grace a year after that. Patrick was a great dad and a great husband," said Natalie. She paused and Nick leaned forward and touched her knee, eliciting a shiver.

"I'm sorry. I didn't mean to pry."

"You know, I haven't told anyone this story in a long time. Five years ago, He was on a patrol along the Texas border where he was ambushed. They found three dead cartel members. No Patrick. They demanded ransom. The

US does not negotiate with terrorists. They sent a finger as proof of life. Later, another group went into Mexico, where they found evidence of a fight, including part of a border patrol uniform and his severed hand, minus the finger they had sent previously. They found a few bodies, but the entire building had burned to the ground."

Nick sat listening, not wanting to interrupt.

"Apparently, the heat was so intense because of the chemicals in the building. Something to do with meth. Anyway, Patrick was declared dead. I got a medal and widows' benefits and I moved Grace up here. His dad had passed a few months before they killed him. His mom was still alive and the life went out of her after losing both of them. She died six months after we moved back. I moped around for a bit, feeling sorry for myself and then I pulled up my big girl pants. I still had a daughter to raise, and I refused to be a victim. It was the least I could do for Patrick. Make sure Grace turned out alright. I started turning this big old house into a business and used my cooking skills to start the restaurant. We do just fine," finished Natalie.

"I'd say you are doing more than fine," praised Nick.

"As for your question," Nick leaned forward in the seat, cradling the coffee cup in his hands. "I'm doing this because someone has to. I don't say that out of ego. In fact, I am probably the least qualified, at least in the traditional way, but no one else is stepping up. After a year in Washington, in the belly of the beast, so to speak, I can see what the problem is. What folks in Washington lack is *perspective*. They have no clue of the consequences of their actions on the regular people. That's why I'm here. Why I was in North Platte yesterday and why I'll be in Sioux Falls, Fargo, Bismarck, Minot, Billings, and on and on."

Natalie sat and listened, sipping her coffee.

"I need to reinforce what I think is right with what others are experiencing. I need to know what I do and what I say is in line with what the *real* people need. If I don't, I won't be able to convince people to stand up and fight. Just like *Rocky*, it is easy to stay down. But we have to get up. If we stay down and end the fight, give up, and admit defeat, we are done. We'll never get a shot at freedom again." Nick paused and looked at Natalie, who had a smile on her face, watching Nick get worked up giving his speech.

"I know nothing about boxing, but I saw *Rocky*," said Natalie in a deadpan voice. "I understand about being knocked down and getting back up. It is easy to stay down and hard to get up. I get it."

"Well, what do you think of my answer?" asked Nick.

"Like I said, I get it, but you have to go *faster*. You can see the people are desperate for leadership and they know a lot of what is being done is wrong. Now they are afraid to say anything for fear of losing a job, or a chance at a scholarship for a kid, or a promotion. Or getting kicked out of some club, or worse, being branded a racist by their neighbors. Everyone is scared. Scared to think differently and terrified to say anything against the status quo. We have become a nation of sheep," finished Natalie in disgust as she leaned forward.

"What pisses me off most is people like my husband gave his life to preserve this. People like you almost gave yours for the same reasons. Pretty soon, what happens when these people stop risking their lives for us? It is already happening. Even in Omaha, they are afraid to arrest minority criminals for fear of riots or showing up on ANC."

Nick sat silently, letting her vent. He noticed her cheeks were getting red as she got worked up, highlighting her freckles, making her green eyes even brighter.

"Crime is rampant. People stay away from downtown. It is only a matter of time before it makes its way into this part of town. Some people here are big donors, so that'll keep the cops patrolling for a while, but eventually, unless things change, the protesters will be here too. My clientele will also disappear. But hey, I can't complain or raise this issue with the town council, or my restaurant will be picketed and I'll have protesters outside. This is the problem. Speaking *any* truth now makes you a racist, if not worse."

Nick nodded, encouraging Natalie to continue.

"I can survive because of Patrick's life insurance. I've paid everything off. At some point, it comes down to personal safety. I am not so worried about me, but Grace is a concern. Patrick taught me how to shoot. Grace is a mean shot with a rifle, too. She hunts every year with her uncles. Got her first buck this year. Dressed it herself too. But school is becoming a woke cesspool of liberal crap ideas. Thankfully, she comes home and tells me what they taught, so I can deprogram her. I fear for others who are not so fortunate," said Natalie, finishing and leaning back.

Nick paused, sipping his coffee and digesting Natalie's speech. "Not that it matters, but I am hearing this everywhere I go. I'm going to do all I can. The odds are against me. I'll educate those willing to listen and, hopefully, make sure they are engaged and aware of what is being done to remove their freedoms before it becomes permanent."

"Nick," said Natalie, moving to the edge of the couch and looking him in the eye.

"You have something, I am not sure what, but it works. You walked into that room tonight and when you finished, they broke out clapping. Bob and Jerry have been partners for years and have never voted Opposition in their life. They won't this time either, but they won't vote for the Vice President either. I can almost guarantee they'll both vote for you. That happened in a 90 second conversation. You connect with people, and you exude honesty and common sense. People get this. It is almost a religious experience. You convert people to your way of thinking wherever you go, whatever you say." Natalie paused, looking at him with those piercing green eyes.

"Don't disappoint us," she said this last bit with more feeling.

Suddenly Nick realized how attractive Natalie was, sitting on the couch in jeans and a sweater, her red hair pushed back. She exuded wholesomeness. Nick found it intoxicating in its simplicity. The opposite of everything he saw in DC. Fresh and honest. He could see light freckles across her nose and under her green eyes. Her smile was lopsided and curled up on one side. She had on only the barest hint of makeup. Nick stood up and helped her to her feet. He towered over her in her bare feet. Reaching up, he put his hand tenderly on her cheek. She shivered but maintained eye contact.

"This is probably a bad idea," whispered Nick, tilting his head. Natalie hesitated, and then, rather than accepting the kiss, she drew him into a tight embrace. They could feel each other's hearts beating. Natalie pushed him away gently.

"Definitely a bad idea. You know where I live. Call me if you lose. Now, off to bed with you."

As she turned to go, Nick, still holding on to one hand, pulled her back into his arms and kissed her. She melted into them, putting her hands around his neck, kissing him back hungrily. When they broke off the kiss, both were breathing heavily.

"Something to think about, if I lose," said Nick, smiling down at her. "Good night, Natalie." With that, Nick turned and left the room. She could hear the steps creaking as he made his way upstairs.

She stood in the center of her office, confused by the feelings she hadn't felt in years and unsure of what to do next. With a gigantic sigh, she picked up her boots, turned off the office light, and made her way to her bedroom, alone again. It would be a while before she slept.

# Chapter 24

Nick steered the Suburban into the Willow Lakes golf course parking lot a couple minutes before seven. Being February, the parking lot was nearly empty, and Nick had no trouble spotting the Blue F150 parked under a tree. Major Jenkins climbed into the Suburban.

"Thank you for meeting me Senator, I know this is James Bond and all that, but I needed to speak to you alone."

"I have to admit, I am a bit intrigued."

"Sir, I work in SIGINT, with the 55th Reconnaissance Wing."

"Intelligence? Foreign or Domestic?" asked Nick.

"Both sir. I manage a team of enlisted and junior officers testing our worldwide surveillance technology. Mostly at night around the world, we test some of our latest stuff to see what we can pick up. As you know, cyber threats are getting more and more prevalent. We are constantly fighting off attacks by both foreign regimes and sophisticated private parties. My specialty is counter threat. We try to piggyback on attacks and follow them back to points of origin."

"Interesting, but I don't get your point, Major."

"Sir, we have some Caltech guys who installed some bleeding edge software for us to experiment with. It is untested and frankly unsanctioned. I'm not married, so I stayed late one evening listening to random pieces of surveillance we had picked up during the day."

"OK," said Nick, encouraging Jenkins to continue.

"We are focusing on encrypted and blocked lines we normally cannot penetrate. I don't even understand much about how it works, but apparently it uses Artificial Intelligence. The program uses the encryption algorithms against itself. By doing this, it recognizes the patterns being used to mask the communications and unscramble them. The problem is, if the call is short, it does not have enough time to analyze it, decode and then capture part of the conversation. Here is what I heard. I wrote it down so I would remember. When I heard you were coming, I thought I should let you know, as you are the topic."

"Really? Do you have any idea where it came from or who the conversation is with?"

"No, the origin was too well masked, but I think one part of the conversation was overseas," said Jenkins.

"How did you get the software if it wasn't sanctioned?"

"Senator, the reality is all of us who thought we were tech savvy when we joined have nothing on the average enlistee now. Between gaming, social media, and underground forums, these guys are all hackers, especially the ones we assign to intel. Airman Lin's cousin is the computer genius at Caltech who sent the code to him."

"Why?"

"He wrote the code. We have limitless power, data, and servers on which to test it. Perfect match."

"Can you trust the cousin?" asked Nick.

"The cousin's name is Ben Wong. Apparently, he is a rising star in the white hat community while working on his second PhD. Already has DoD clearance. Anyway, these guys are always loading crap on the systems, usually games, but occasionally something like this. Lin is not a risk. His grandparents were Falun Gong killed by the Chinese and his mother and father fled Hong Kong to avoid capture. If it were any other person, I would suspect it," said Jenkins.

"You're taking a tremendous risk, Major."

"Sir, I am a black man in the Air Force. I worked my ass off to get to where I am. Now I see unqualified junior officers being promoted based solely on race. My grandparents marched for Civil Rights with MLK. My parents both worked their way through school and built careers with no affirmative action and yet they had to fight the perception they only got ahead because the government helped them."

"All this so-called help hurt the middle-class blacks who had the drive, the capability, and the ambition to succeed on merit. The ones it should have helped, the working poor and urban families, were destroyed by it. I have cousins who never knew their fathers, who never had to take any responsibility for parenting. None."

"My parents wouldn't let them visit us and we rarely saw them except at our grandparents' reunions. Mainly, because they were all such good examples of everything our parents fought to prevent us from becoming. Drug pushers and dealers, lay abouts and disrespectful thugs whose response to everything was violence. Is this the legacy of MLK?"

"Well, Major, you are certainly full of surprises. Why don't you tell me how you really feel?" laughed Nick.

"I stopped by Stella's yesterday to see if you were for real. I listened to you for a while and realized you actually mean what you say. Folks were right when they said you were different. I figure you need all the help you can get," said Jenkins.

"How would you like to join my campaign?" cajoled Nick.

Jenkins laughed, lightening the mood, "Trust me, an uppity black who thinks for himself and does not spend his time kissing the black and white ass above him will not make colonel or probably even lieutenant colonel. However, I owe Uncle Sam my twenty or until he tires of me."

"The offer stands. You'd fit right in. My campaign is the island of misfit toys, malcontents, and dreamers. Just let me know."

"It is really weird," said Jenkins.

"What?"

"I mean, what are the odds? Lin gets the code and installs it. I stay late one night and hear a transmission referencing you, and then you are here yesterday."

"Major, I have ceased to question anything anymore. None of this makes sense."

"I need to get to my shift. I am not sure what that info means, but it seems pretty clear someone is not happy with you, and they will not let you mess up their plans. Senator, someone is following you. It sounds to me like they don't intend to just watch," warned Jenkins.

"How do I get a hold of you?"

"My cell is on the card I gave you."

"Thank you Major, what is your first name?" asked Nick, turning over the card in his hand.

"Laurence, nice to meet you, Senator," shaking Nick's hand.

"I think you can call me Nick."

Laurence got out of the car and into his pickup and drove away. Nick opened the folded 3x5 card and read the information it contained.

*'I am inside now. Surveillance of Turner underway. Yes, they believe me. Affirmative. We have the resources ready to disrupt any progress he makes. Affirmative. Will report any concerns in the campaign as we observe.'*

It was clear he was only looking at one side of a conversation. He contemplated the message, wondering if this side was the overseas part or the domestic. It did not surprise him his campaign was under surveillance. The question was who was doing it. Homeland, FBI, CIA, or someone else.

He put the card in his wallet and drove back to Natalie's B&B for his breakfast.

#

Earl pushed away his plate, finishing a second stack of pancakes.

"Nick, we're going to have to start each morning with a five-mile run, or else start eating salads."

"I haven't eaten this well, or this much in years," agreed Nick. "Maybe we should jog to Sioux Falls?"

"Enjoy yourself, I'll take the keys," said Greg. "I'm blessed with a high metabolism, and I have willpower. Yogurt, berries, and a Bran muffin. You guys should try it sometime."

"We should hit the road. Where's Natalie?" asked Nick.

"She had to go to town for some supplies. She sends her regards," said an older gal, coming in to clear their plates and handing a small envelope to Nick.

"Please let her know we appreciate all the hospitality and we'll let her know the next time we are in Omaha," said Nick, keeping his voice light and the disappointment at not seeing Natalie again hidden.

He took out his business card and wrote on the back.

"Can you please make sure Natalie gets this?"

"You bet sweetie, good luck with your campaigning."

"Alright boys, daylights burning," said Earl, humming "on the road again" as he headed for the front door.

Nick turned over the envelope from Natalie and put it in his back pocket to read later.

# Chapter 25

Through early February, Nick continued his diner campaign. Traveling throughout the Plains, as he left each town, those who attended called everyone they knew in the next town. Soon his crowds went from tens of people to hundreds and eventually outgrew his ability to hold his impromptu town halls in restaurants.

He also started drawing the attention of his opponents. Not all the locals agreed with Nick's message or his giving their friends and neighbors a chance to voice their grievances about how things were going. They were more than happy to call the local authorities, asking what they could do to stop Nick from gathering crowds.

Soon Nick's team's attempts to reserve sections of restaurants were being denied. When he showed up, and as crowds piled into restaurants, local sheriffs or code enforcers would show up to threaten either Nick or the restaurant with fines.

In one case, they ended up in the restaurant parking lot, a hundred folks in their winter coats standing around chatting for an hour. The frustrated city code enforcer on the phone, unsuccessfully trying to find a way to break up the group.

Besides these petty efforts to thwart his gatherings, Nick eventually also drew the attention of the FBI. Monitoring the police scanners, two agents attended one of Nick's rallies in Sioux Falls. They dutifully reported on what they heard. Lots of complaining about the economy and the administration. They were told to continue following and monitoring his speeches.

Nick moved through Nebraska, up into South Dakota, dipped into Minnesota, avoiding Iowa and the other twenty-six candidates of both parties crisscrossing that state, making their promises before the Iowa caucuses the next week. As he headed through the Dakotas, Nick continued to hear the same stories.

As in other states, Nick heard a lot about the economy, out-of-control inflation, children's education, defunding the police, gun control, and concerns about the racial tensions being amplified by the media. Along with a consistent lack of faith in Washington. One particular conversation stood out between Nick and a mid-level manager, Tom, who worked in a major banking conglomerate's processing center.

Tom spoke of the laser focus of his company, not on delivering the best product and service to maximize their profits for shareholders, but instead a focus almost entirely on achieving an ever higher ESG score. He was concerned at the increasingly intolerant work environments, where merit no longer mattered. Only conformity to these new rules defined by faceless elites in some overseas organizations. Nick had listened to Tom and others describe their concerns with the very fabric of their communities coming undone.

Continuing through North Dakota, Nick sat in the passenger seat, staring out the window as the snow-covered miles flew by.

"Boss, you OK?" asked Greg as Earl glanced toward Nick from his driver's seat.

"Yep. Just thinking."

"About the Buffalo Spear reservation?" asked Earl

"That and other conversations. The reservation didn't surprise me. It is pretty much par for the course. Paid protest camps with bussed in activists for photo ops. It is really more about the consequences of the actions. They stopped the pipeline all those years ago. It didn't matter. Now the trucks run 24/7 from one end of the pipeline to the other end across the river. Nothing changed. Facts don't matter. I did some research. Did you know the place where they wanted to cross the river wasn't even on the reservation? And the right of way is owned by the Feds. There are already two pipelines, which are much shallower, older and less safe in the *same* location."

"The kicker is, this was all done to protect the water for the tribe. Their intake is seventy-five miles downstream. Any leak could be contained, or the water intake shut off long before it ever contaminated their drinking water. It is all just hypocrisy." Nick had been counting facts off on his fingers.

"Nick, you knew this. You knew we would run into opposition and people who would not want to change. Common sense is not as common as you think it is," said Earl with a bit of regret.

"Anything else I can help with?" asked Greg quietly, as Nick once again looked out the window.

"Not yet. I am really worried about some things that guy Tom had to say about what it is like in big corporations now."

Greg laughed. "We have a request from him to charter a Turner Rabble group in Sioux Falls."

"Good. We had some hearings about ESG and the shift by corporations to strive to get higher scores. Many big investment funds are basing their stakes in companies on how well they comply with these and the Diversity, Equity and Inclusion guidelines. Our economy is becoming less and less about innovation and more about compliance with *their* ideology. Did you hear what he said?"

"Which part?" asked Greg.

"The part about the voluntary pronoun on their badges. Then, when some chose not to do it, those who did felt uncomfortable. Their solution wasn't to remove them, but to force everyone to conform. They were willing to fire their top data scientists and engineers for not complying. Imagine if you were working on the Manhattan Project and General Groves gave Oppenheimer, Teller, and Fermi a directive to put pronouns on their badges? And they chose not to comply and quit. Next thing you know, Germany gets the bomb first and history changes. This is a very dangerous and slippery slope. Innovation and capitalism are the twin pillars of our success as a country. We are taking a sledgehammer to both and now we have corporations slitting their own throats willingly. Why?" finished Nick.

No one answered. They drove on until Nick spoke again.

"I keep going over what we have heard so far. We've been at it for less than two weeks. I'm really concerned. It is even worse than I expected. And this is the heartland. Not some decaying urban hell hole in the rust belt. You've heard it. You see the looks on their faces. People are scared. They don't know what to do or how it will get fixed. Or if it even can be. They have little to no faith we in Washington are the answer."

"Nick, you're on the right path. Giving them a chance to vocalize what they are worried about is good for all of them," said Earl.

"And listening and showing them you *are* listening. This is huge. I can see that too. Remember, I review all the video," added Greg.

"I listen, but I don't have the answers they want," worried Nick.

"Sure you do. Nick, when I look at the videos, you know what the most amazing part is?" asked Greg.

"What?"

"It is the other people watching and their reactions. I look out at the crowd. They are all listening to everything you say. Every answer you give to each question. Every time when you tell them they are the only ones who can fix things. How no promise you could make would make as much difference as the *actions* they can take in their own community," explained Greg, getting more excited. Nick turned in his chair to look at Greg in the back seat.

"They are nodding their heads and turning to their neighbors who are also nodding. Nick, they get it. They don't want promises. Just reassurance that their gut feeling is right. To see others feel the same way. They need someone to tell them to act on that instinct. That's what you are doing."

"I hope you are right."

"He is," chimed in Earl as Greg smiled.

"Nick, after *every* town hall, we get requests to sanction Turner Rabble and other grassroot support groups. Something is working," assured Greg.

"What did you think of my other advice?" asked Nick, smiling.

"Again, which part?" smiled Greg back. "The part where you tell them to lie to pollsters? Or the part where you tell them to send you no more than $100? The part where you told them to boycott American corporations or the part where you told them to tell five people to go to our website?"

"All of it."

"I can tell you Denise already hates the lying to pollsters and limiting donations to $100. The tell five people part was nice and I guess the boycott suggestions are fine, but it is unlikely anyone is going to turn off social or stop shopping online, or even buying goods made in China, just because you ask," said Greg in a skeptical tone.

"Hey, they asked what to do, and I told them. If they choose to follow it, so be it. If not, I will keep trying. I believe that is the way to win. If enough people follow my advice, even those companies will notice and change. It's not a boycott. It is about supporting companies who support your values and choosing to ignore those that don't. There is a difference," said Nick. "It has already worked several times in as diverse a set of companies as beer, cable channels and retail. Voting with your pocketbook is the most effective weapon in a free market society, trust me."

"Ok, if you say so," said Greg, shaking his head.

# Chapter 26

"Senator Nick Turner visited the protest camps at the Buffalo Spear Reservation south of Bismarck, North Dakota, this afternoon. As you can see, he got an earful from the Native American protesters who did not appreciate him supporting the oil companies' attempts to continue the pipeline, risking the tribes drinking water," said the talking head on the local news.

They then showed a clip of Nick, selectively edited to show him telling the protesters none of their efforts were successful and the oil companies were still shipping the oil. The clip took everything Nick had said out of context. Making it look like he was praising the oil companies' success and the gloating at the activists failing to stop fossil fuel usage.

"You can see from the response of the crowd they needed to have the local sheriff come remove the Senator from the protests for his own safety. The protesters will continue to fight the corporate interests trying to ram through the pipeline regardless of the damage or risk to the tribe. Clearly, Senator Turner and his nascent campaign for president are trying to get whatever coverage they can. Coming to the Dakotas to support the fossil fuel companies is not likely to win him votes from the Party or Independents. We suggest he try something else to become relevant," finished the newscaster.

"Crap," said Denise as she watched the clip.

"You, of course, know that is not what I said," said Nick on the ZOOM call with Denise, Margie, Jer, and Jenny back in Denver.

"Of course. We will get all of Greg's footage up on our social channels, but that clip is being picked up by all the networks," said Margie.

"Nick. I know you like to use your professorial Socratic Method to get folks to answer your questions and make the points themselves. This is making it easy for them to cut your words into the exact opposite of the points you are eventually getting the audience to see. No one knows this, if all they see is you in the beginning."

"Your point is what?" Nick could see Denise's face getting red in frustration.

"My point is, make *your* point instead of weaving the story to get them to agree with your point of view. That way you aren't on camera saying the negative position."

"Denise, do you agree, no matter what I say, they are going to cut it negatively, if they cover it at all?"

"Of course."

"Do you also agree we are putting up the complete dialogue on our social sites for those inclined to find the truth?"

"Yes."

"Did you look at the footage?"

"Yes."

"Do you not agree, my so-called Socratic Method eventually worked? Many of the activists and their out-of-town agitators now have some food for thought to question what they are doing and why?"

"Nick, yes, but that was to what, one hundred people? Even if they all vote for you, the clip is now going to be seen by hundreds of thousands, if not millions, of people. Many of them won't see you in person. They're going to look at this and assume you are just another politician schilling for corporate donations. Ridiculing activists for their principled stances. All I am saying is there are things we can do to not make it *so* easy for them to use your own words against you."

Nick sat in a hotel room with Earl and Greg sitting on the periphery, listening to Denise's head on the laptop lecturing their boss.

"Denise, I appreciate the sentiment. But I don't think we can do anything about folks who are not open-minded. I have to believe there are others who are hearing about what we *do* say. From their friends and family. From co-workers. What they read and research on their own. I really don't think sounding like every other politician, making promises, thinking about every word I say, to make sure it *can't* be twisted, is going to accomplish what I need to do."

They could see and hear Denise sighing on the camera.

"Denise, I warned you," said Nick with a smile. "I have to do it my way, even if it means I give the enemy ammunition to use against me. I have to trust those who care about America will see through the bullshit. If not, we can't win them over, anyway."

Denise shook her head. "You also hired me to help you win. I am telling you what you need to do to win and what you need to do to not make it easier to lose. As you know, I have plenty of experience with what not to do. You can keep ignoring my advice, but don't be surprised when it comes true," counseled Denise, not taking offence at Nick ignoring her advice.

"Denise, don't worry, I won't blame you. Let's hope you're wrong and my gut is right. With that, are we in any polling yet?"

Before Jer could answer, Denise laughed loudly.

"Really? When you tell everyone to lie to pollsters, you are now going to ask poor Jer to tell you where we are in the polls? Not a chance. You know where we are. Low single digits, where I assume you want us, Mr. Sun Tzu. No picking on Jer. What else do you want to know?"

"Fair enough Denise. How about fundraising?"

"Sure, that *is* going well," smiled Denise.

"Boss, the money is still coming in strong. Lots of small donations, still from mostly first-time donors. We are now over $80 million in our coffers," said Jer.

"Great news Jer," said Nick.

"Don't get too excited, Nick. We now have campaign offices open in all 50 states and we will start spending money quickly. Would help if we could do some fund-raising events," suggested Denise.

"Sure, as long as we keep the donations to no more than $1000 a person," said Nick, knowing full well that was not what Denise wanted.

Denise sighed. "You enjoy tormenting me, don't you? This must be penance for all my misdeeds in this life and others. Karma is a bitch."

"Aw come on Denise, conventional is so boring. Bet you haven't been this far back in the polls before, right?"

"How would I know where we are in the polls?" she replied as they finished their update call with a few other housekeeping items on schedules and speaking engagements they were lining up for Nick, including an opportunity at the spring Florida state fair Denise was working.

"Where to folks?" asked Margie.

Greg answered from off camera. "Rapid City, South Dakota."

"OK, just keep getting the footage so we can counter any negative press on the networks. Be careful and maybe stay away from protest sites in the future, please?" finished Denise.

# Chapter 27

Lexi sat in the back of the suburban with Mel and Harriet, traveling from a campaign event in Des Moines to Air Force Two. Harriet was talking about the attendance and the amount of money raised.

"Talk to me about Klausen," said Lexi, interrupting Harriet.

"What about him?" asked Mel first.

"Why is he so close? What is he doing or saying that has him so high in Iowa?" said Lexi with a snarl.

"Lexi, he has been coming to Iowa for almost two years. He is from Wisconsin. This is his territory. He's built up an excellent ground organization and has been planning on running for president for years. This gives him an advantage your other opponents don't have. He has to finish second to stay relevant," answered Mel.

"Two points behind me is a bit too close to first for my liking."

"Lexi, Mel is right. Look at your crowds today. You drew 12,000 to the fairgrounds, while Klausen was talking to 400 in Dubuque. You had 200 people attending a $10,000 a plate fund raiser, in *Iowa*. Who else can do that? Relax, we have this under control," said Harriet.

"Lexi, look at all the other competitors. Most of them are barely registering. Harrington is the only other polling in low double digits besides Klausen. The rest are all single digits. Twelve of them. After Iowa and New Hampshire, where you are up by 25, I might add, the field is going to shrink quickly."

"You're right, but we are stage managing this movie. Let's not give them more lines than we have to, please," quipped Lexi.

"Was that a joke? Harriet, did you hear that? Our boss made a joke," said Mel as Harriet laughed nervously.

Lexi looked at Mel and then at Harriet.

"Harry, do you have a number for a proctologist and a cobbler?"
Harriet looked confused.

"Mel is going to need the first to get my shoe out of his ass and I am
going to need the second to get my shoe fixed," said Lexi in a normal tone.

Mel smiled. "Two jokes, a new record. Lexi, leave this part to us. You
keep kicking ass in the debates like last week and whipping up the base."

Lexi nodded. "Too bad we only got a million people to watch."

Mel shrugged in his seat. "No surprise. There is very little drama on our
side. And with thirteen candidates on stage, everyone got what, five minutes
total? They don't even bother attacking you anymore and simply go after
each other. Everyone knows you are the nominee. On the Opposition side,
it was good they got a much bigger audience. Gives their voters a chance to
watch each of them tear off their competitor's arm and beat them with it."

Lexi laughed at Mel's analogy.

"Nice one. It was nice to see Garcia get pummeled for a change. I tire of
his holier than thou attitude on everything. They really let him have it. Are
we sure he will not win the nomination?"

Harriet jumped in. "Unlikely. That debate didn't help him. A few more
like that and he's done. He alienates the moderates and independents with
his staunch pro-life stance and continues favoring outright bans on all
abortion. With *Roe* overturned for now, most of the state laws with the
most restrictive clauses are being held up or even overturned by local courts
until their states can put measures on the ballot. Our polling reveals even
a majority of the opposition favor some level of permissible abortion and
independents feel the same. Garcia is out of touch with a major issue for
most of his constituents."

"Good. I don't like him. Re-codifying *Roe* in Congress will remove the
Supreme court from this decision entirely, as it should be."

"Did you see the story on Turner's visit to the reservation?" laughed
Mel. "Denise has to be going out of her mind trying to control him. He is
handing the news media negative statements on a silver platter. My god, he
is naïve. He has to know they are going to edit what he says. He has seen it
before. Why does he continue to do it?"

"Slow learner?" asked Harriet.

"Maybe. But you also notice he posted the entire video on his social channel. For those who saw it, it further provides concrete proof of the obvious manipulation of his words by the local news station. It reinforces his points. I thought we put out the word to keep him off TV," said Lexi, looking at Mel.

"Geez, Lexi, we told the national outlets. We can't get to every local affiliate. Some enterprising supporter of yours took it upon themselves to embarrass Turner."

Lexi had been looking at her phone while Mel was talking.

"And yet, he now has five million views of his full conversation at the reservation. That is hardly local," said Lexi, showing Mel the phone with Nick's video.

Mel handed the phone back.

"I want his social channels shut down, and these videos banned at a minimum. I want the nationals to pass the words to their affiliates. No Turner on TV. Period. The bastard should be a voice in the wilderness. Literally."

"Got it," said Mel, seeing they had arrived at Air Force Two.

Mel stood on the tarmac with Harriet as Lexi boarded with her secret service team and then Felicia DeNovia, the Secretary of the Interior. One of the cabinet members had to accompany the Vice President on every trip to be the second person in the two-man rule, in case Lexi had to exercise the emergency powers act. The cabinet had agreed to this precaution in the fall when it was clear the President was not capable of issuing the order to launch nuclear weapons. Secretary DeNovia drew the short straw for this trip.

"I'm worried about Klausen," said Harriet.

"He is polling stronger than we expected. With the economy, inflation, gas, crime, and everything else, Klausen is playing to the middle. He is getting some support the Opposition should've been getting," said Mel.

"Aren't you worried?"

"Harriet, I am always worried. It's my job. It's also my job to handle my candidate and keep her focused on the prize. Klausen may last longer, but he won't win. I'll see to it. He has skeletons in his closet, like everyone in DC."

"Except Turner, apparently," said Harriet with a tinge of regret.

"We'll find something. We always do. Time to board or they will leave us. Trust me, I know Lexi," said Mel.

# Chapter 28

Nick, Earl and Greg were once again traveling through the inter-mountain west. They had stopped in Rapid City and Spearfish in South Dakota, in an American Legion Hall in one and an Elks lodge in another. Always careful to keep the crowds within the occupancy levels. In both cases, the local sheriff and mayor came by to watch and count heads. At one point, they exceeded the count by one and the mayor threatened to arrest everyone if they did not immediately vacate the premises. Nick jokingly asked him if he counted himself as an attendee?

Nick led the group outdoors into the parking lot. He continued speaking for another hour before another code inspector showed up. With the same sheriff once more in tow, handing Nick a citation for holding a public rally without a permit. A local lawyer walked up and lectured the code inspector. He said Nick would have needed to have advertised the event and to have requested people show up for a 'rally' before he would have violated any laws by not requesting a permit.

Since everyone had spontaneously showed up at the parking lot and the Elks club. When they heard Nick was in town, it was not a violation. He turned to Nick and told him he had a right to sue the city for harassment and potentially defamation of character. He would be happy to litigate the case pro bono. The code inspector was fuming, while the sheriff was trying to hide a smile.

"If you all want to stand out here and freeze your asses off, so be it. There had better not be one speck of trash in this parking lot when you're done. I know I can cite you for that and even Mr. Penrose here can't lawyer his way out of that one," said the inspector as he snatched the citation out of Nick's hand and marched away in a huff.

"Sorry Senator. I don't make the rules, you understand?" said the sheriff as he too made to leave.

"Indeed, I do Sheriff," said Nick. He turned to the lawyer. "Penrose is it? Nick Turner," he said, holding out his hand.

"Copeland Penrose, but everyone just calls me Penrose or even Pen," he said, shaking Nick's hand.

"Pen, I believe you just became the leader of the local Turner Rabble, whether or not you wanted to," said Nick as those around them laughed.

"I'd be honored Nick. Don't worry about old Stu. He is a stick in the mud, basically harmless. Not used to folks standing up to him, since he has the government at his back. But like so many bullies, you push a little, and their house of cards collapses."

"Pen, I wish it were that easy with the federal bureaucracy. You push on them, and they show up in the middle of the night with SWAT teams, and frogmen, to arrest and frog march sixty-eight-year-old pundits out in leg irons, while ANC cameras film it. Just be careful."

"Wouldn't have it any other way. I listened to what you had to say. Folks around these parts have a good dose of common sense. The farther you get from the city and the capital, it is amazing what you can get done without the help of big brother."

"Amen to that. Thanks again for the help. With my luck, I would have had to make another trip back here to answer the summons for the $20 fine and when I didn't, they would have issued an arrest warrant. I bet your governor, who has his own presidential aspirations, would have loved to issue that warrant," laughed Nick.

"Blackbird? I sure hope he isn't the nominee, or better yet, maybe I should hope. You would have no trouble beating him. He is just blah. Never met a policy he couldn't agree with. Sort of reminds me of how our current President used to be until the Progressives started pulling his puppet strings. Oh well, you don't need to listen to me bitch. Keep fighting the fight. We have your back here. We'll rouse the rabble for Turner," Pen finished as those standing around let out a cheer and yelled Turner a few times as Nick, Earl, and Greg started shaking hands, heading toward their rented Suburban.

#

They continued heading west to Gillette, Wyoming, where they had no trouble speaking at a restaurant truck stop for most of the day. Wyoming was one of the most independent minded states in the country. Here it was mostly ranching and the oil and gas industry. These operators were struggling to stay relevant as more and more regulations were being forced upon them, preventing them from opening up new oil and gas wells.

With gas prices at all time-highs, for years now, the government was still piling more and more regulations on anyone looking to drill new wells. Instead, they were imposing fines for not pumping enough out of existing older, more expensive, and lower producing wells.

Nick listened, shaking his head at the stupidity of his former Party's lack of understanding. Nick offered his usual common sense proposals. Keep pumping the oil, more in fact, and direct a portion of this profit to *fund* investment in new renewable energy innovation. This seemed pragmatic to those listening.

Actions, not words, not promises and most of all, the need to get the government out of their way and out of their lives. Each visit, he became more confident what he was doing was right. After each meeting, the attendees refused to leave, insisting on standing around, drinking coffee, and talking to him about life.

Like a pro athlete who stays long after the game, signing autographs for everyone who wants one, Nick was quickly earning a reputation as someone who cared. Not someone who flew in, made a speech for the cameras, and then immediately left with an entourage, afraid to congregate with the rabble. Nick preferred the rabble. He was at his best in these small groups. Greg and Earl sat on the perimeter, recording, smiling, and watching as their boss gestured with his hands to make his points. The word of mouth, the experience itself, and the converts to spread it, with passion, was more than any amount of advertising spend of TV spots could accomplish.

They continued up into Montana. Stopping in Billings, Bozeman, and Butte, deciding to skip the capital Helena, owing to the Party Governor, a rancher with his own higher office aspirations. They'd heard he was itching to make a scene if Nick stopped. Everywhere they stopped, they no longer said where they were going, beyond reserving the venue under aliases. Greg had learned early on to not make a big deal about it being for Senator Turner.

There was no planning. They simply showed up. The crowds would assemble, having been primed by word of mouth from the converts in prior cities. They came to hear the 'common sense Senator'. The low tech 'pass the word', below the radar strategy, was working.

At each stop, they heard variations on the same themes. Greg would dutifully record each session and send the footage back to Margie and Denise. It was grueling but satisfying. Nick felt recharged after each day's meetings. But deep inside, he knew there was a sense of urgency he was not meeting, just as Natalie had predicted. Driving around from town to town, speaking to hundreds at a time. He looked out the passenger window of the suburban at the falling snow as they made their way up I-90 between Butte and Missoula, Montana.

"Coming down heavier," said Nick to no one in particular.

"I noticed. Don't worry, Nelly, I've driven through a lot worse. Plus, *I* was a boy scout. We are covered," said Earl, who watched the road ahead as he gripped the steering wheel.

"Prepared? Looks to me like you are expecting us to go camping for a week. We have enough food, water, blankets and other things in the back. I hardly had room for the luggage," said Greg from the first bench row.

"As a sheriff in rural Colorado, I can assure you guys you can never be too prepared for sudden snowstorms. I once rescued a trapped motorist who had crashed down in a ravine. She had been there three days before we found her. She survived because she had access to a stash of granola bars in the glove box and a few bottles of water. And because she didn't panic. You never know what you need until you need it. Since our fearless leader refuses to travel with any support, I have to think of everything," said Earl with a grunt.

"And the winch on the front?" inquired Greg.

"Greg, where'd you grow up?" asked Earl.

"Southern California, baby," replied Greg, with emphasis.

"Trust me, if we slide off the road, you'll be happy I have a winch. Made sure all our sheriff's cars had them. You have no idea how many people think four-wheel drive also means four-wheel stop. They drive fast, slide, hit the brakes, and spin off the road into the ditch. Happens all the time. They don't teach folks how to drive anymore. Especially not in the snow. It's worse when there is only a little. Everyone slows down when there are a few inches on the road, but not when it is just a skiff," said Earl.

"You mean like now," said Nick.

"Nah, we're good. There is barely an inch, and it is probably just a squall. Weather report said there would be patches of heavier snow. We're only an hour to Missoula. It'll be close to dark, though, by the time we arrive."

"You know I live in Colorado too, right? The safest job in Colorado is weather caster. They never get it right and no one ever expects them to. I suspect it is the same in Montana. This doesn't look like a squall to me," finished Nick as Earl smiled. The snow continued to fall, heavier, and the wind picked up, blowing it across the road as the light disappeared. Earl slowed down, turned on his lights, and gave plenty of room to the cars ahead.

"At this rate, it is going to get dark long before we get there. I was just looking at the weather. They just issued a blizzard warning for western Montana. So much for light snow," said Greg.

"What did I tell you? Nowhere to go but on. We are more than halfway there, so on we go. Are we going up?" asked Nick.

"Actually, no, we are descending gently. I've been through here before. It goes up aggressively from Missoula into Idaho. We don't have to worry about it getting worse because of elevation."

"We just passed Drummond, that's the last stop before Missoula, but my phone service dropped so I can't tell you how far," said Greg.

"What the fuck?" shouted Earl as he pressed the brakes with even pressure and put the Suburban into a controlled slide to the shoulder of the Interstate. A man had been standing on the shoulder waving frantically. He ran up to Nick's side of the Suburban.

Nick glanced at Earl, who was freeing his pistol from the holster under the steering column.

"I doubt he's an assassin, Earl," said Nick as he opened the window. The snow immediately started swirling in.

The guy came up to the window out of breath.

"I need help. Our van is down in the trees and my wife is pregnant," said the man.

"Is she hurt?" asked Nick, unbuckling his seat belt.

"Just shaken up, but she's nine months pregnant," said the man.

"Okay. What's your name?" asked Nick.

"Joseph, Joe. Can you guys help me? I don't think she can make it up the embankment. Shit, shit, shit. We were driving too fast, trying to get to Missoula. It's all my fault," said Joe, panicking.

"Calm down, Joe. We'll get you guys to safety," assured Nick.

Earl had already gotten out of the car and opened the back of the suburban. He broke out parkas, handing one to each. "Greg, you know how to set some flares?" asked Earl, as Greg nodded.

"Okay, put a couple down the road and stay with the car. Keep an eye out for other traffic. Maybe we get lucky and a state trooper or a plow will come by," said Earl.

Nick and Earl made their way carefully down the embankment. About 65 feet down the embankment was a silver minivan with its headlights facing up the side of the embankment. Earl and Nick were moving slowly while Joe was leaping, falling, and getting up, hurrying to the side of the van.

"Honey, I brought help. It'll be OK," said Joe, out of breath.

Nick and Earl surveyed the minivan. It seemed to be intact. The snow was about eight to twelve inches deep down the embankment. Earl knew there was no way his winch was going to pull the van up the steep embankment through the snow for 60 feet. Nick came around to the passenger side and found a very pregnant woman smiling at him from the passenger seat.

"You OK ma'am?" he asked.

"Vanessa. No. I am now in labor. It's all my fault. I made Joe take us to Missoula so I could visit my parents." She turned to look at him. "I'm so sorry," she said, crying.

"Vanessa, you need to stay calm. Do you know how far apart the contractions are?" asked Earl from the open driver's side door.

"Couple minutes, but it is getting shorter. We stopped pretty hard. I think it woke him up," laughed Vanessa through her tears.

"Vanessa, we need to figure out a way to get you up the hill and to our car so we can get you to Missoula," said Earl. At that moment, Vanessa grabbed Nick's forearm and tensed up in pain as the contraction hit her. Earl started his stopwatch.

"Nick, I don't think we can pull the van out with the winch we have. And none of us can carry her up the embankment without falling. Can you go up, turn the Suburban and we'll see what we can jury rig to get her up the hill? We can't risk dropping her, or we'll break her water for sure," said Earl.

"Joe, come over here and let Vanessa break your arm instead of mine," said Nick.

"Sorry, sorry," laughed Vanessa through her tears as Joe came around to take Nick's place outside the window by his wife.

Earl met Nick at the front.

"Her contractions are way more than a minute. No way we are going to make it to Missoula."

"Let's get her up to the Suburban first. Be right back," said Nick.

He headed up the embankment. When he reached the top, there were now three cars stopped behind the Suburban. A couple of young guys and two couples were all standing with Greg at the back.

"Greg, we need to get the Suburban turned with the winch facing down. The van is too heavy to winch up, but we need to get the pregnant wife up here. Nick looked at the parked cars. Hey guys, can we use your snowboards and the skis from the Volvo back there and make a sort of stretcher we can put her on? Then we can attach the winch and use them as a sled," said Nick. "Anyone got bungees?"

One couple responded. As the bystanders mobilized, Greg turned the Suburban and Nick directed him to the edge.

The others arrived with the snowboards, skis, and bungees. Nick quickly set the boards down and used the skis as cross pieces. He used the bungees tightening the corners. It was not soapbox derby worthy, but would do in a pinch. "Alright Greg, we'll flash hand signals too?" Nick looked at one guy.

"Carlo."

"We'll flash hand signals to Carlo. Let the winch play out and I will take it down," said Nick.

Nick navigated the sled down the embankment, pulling the winch hook as he went. Two of the other guys followed. At the bottom, he pulled a little more on the winch and then flashed a fist to Carlo, who relayed 'stop' to Greg.

Earl surveyed the makeshift sled and Nick's helpers.

"Great idea. I assume we have more folks up top?" asked Earl.

"We do. How is the patient?"

"Not good. She is going to have this baby soon. We need to get her up there and get on the road," said Earl.

Nick and Earl helped Vanessa out of the car and, with two others, carried her to the sled. Joe got the bags she needed from the van. The guys helped Joe empty the car and shut it up to be towed later. They set Vanessa down on the skis set between the snowboards, covering her with blankets. Nick attached the winch hook to one ski cross brace and then made a signal to Carlo at the top of the embankment.

The snow continued to blow, swirling around them, but Carlo could still see Nick, and the winch dragged the sled up the hill. With everyone helping push and pull the sled and Joe and Earl supporting Vanessa on both sides, they directed it up the hill. When they got to the top, they lifted Vanessa from the sled, carrying her to the back of the Suburban. Greg had moved the luggage to the second bench seat to make room for Vanessa to lie down. He also laid out more of the blankets Earl had packed. They rolled up some other blankets to make a pillow for her head.

"Anyone have a phone signal?" everyone shook their head, but one guy spoke up.

"You'll get a signal 20 miles up the road once you're about 20 miles from Missoula."

While they were loading Vanessa into the Suburban, the bystanders put their boards and skis back on their ski racks.

"OK, let's caravan into Missoula," said Nick. "Earl, you drive. I'll try to keep Vanessa comfortable."

"Nick, not for nothing, but have you ever delivered a baby?" asked Earl. "I have, so maybe you should drive?"

"Actually, I did some EMT training in the service and yes, I delivered a baby in an Afghan village once. You're the better driver in this shit. I trust you to get us there as fast as possible," he said. As if on cue, Vanessa let out a groan as another contraction hit her.

"Let's get going. Greg, you and Joe get in the back seat and look over in case I need any help. Let's go," commanded Nick to the others, as everyone hurried to their cars.

Nick climbed into the back of the Suburban. Luckily, it was a full-size SUV, so there was enough room for Vanessa to stretch out. Nick held Vanessa's hand and Earl got them back on the road. She grabbed Nick's hand again as another contraction happened. Nick glanced at Greg, who started his phone stopwatch. As Earl headed down the road, Nick called out, "how's the snow?"

"We're fine. I can still see the road," laughed Earl.

"You have any gloves in here?"

"No, but there is a big bottle of sanitizer," replied Earl.

"Got it," said Nick, who rolled up his sleeves and lathered his hands and forearms in sanitizer for 30 seconds.

Vanessa's contraction ended. But less than three minutes later, she had another. And it lasted for 90 seconds. Then she looked at Nick, startled. "Uh oh, I think my water just broke."

"OK, take deep breaths. Joe, can you give Vanessa some water?" asked Nick.

Joe leaned over the seat and gave his wife some water while Nick removed her underwear and pushed the skirt of her dress up to her hips.

"Vanessa you are doing fine, you're dilating but you still have a bit to go, so just keep breathing. Deep breaths. Just like you practiced."

"I have a signal," shouted Greg, as he dialed 911.

"Tell them we need a plow and an escort to the nearest hospital," said Nick.

He continued to talk to Vanessa as Greg told the 911 operator Senator Nick Turner was 20 miles out of Missoula, leading a caravan of cars into town, including a pregnant woman in labor. He was requesting a snowplow and highway patrol escort to the nearest hospital.

Joe was looking at Greg and then at Nick.

"Holy crap, you're him. Hon, it's Senator Turner," said Joe, in an excited voice.

"Honey, I know," said Vanessa through gritted teeth.

Nick smiled.

"Let's focus on you," said Nick, checking. Still no baby head. So far, so good.

Vanessa was in one constant contraction now and Nick could tell she was close to having the baby.

"State trooper," said Earl, flashing his lights, as he saw a trooper crossing the median in front of them, taking the lead.

"Move it Earl, this baby's coming," said Nick.

"Vanessa, looks like you're going to have your baby right here. I can see the top of the head. I need you to push and count to five. OK good, now deep breaths. Let's do it again. One, two, three, four, five, breath. Good, good. Again," Vanessa leaned up and screamed, pushing.

"Alright, I can see the head. A couple more good pushes."

"Snowplows," said Earl, "we should be there soon. I can see the lights of the city. Hang on Vanessa."

"Alright, give me one more hard push and hold it," said Nick as Vanessa let out a howl.

Nick smiled as he lifted a baby boy who immediately let out a wail.

"Congratulations, you have a new baby boy with a healthy set of lungs. Way to go guys," Nick pulled a towel and blanket out of Earl's emergency bags. He pulled down Vanessa's dress to lay the baby on her skin to keep him warm, and then he wrapped a blanket around both of them.

"Keep him low on your side. The umbilical cord is still attached. I want the hospital to take care of that," said Nick.

"Thank you so much, look at him, he's beautiful," said Vanessa through her tears of joy. Joe was crying and Greg was trying to comfort him as he said, "Thank you," through his sobs.

"Almost there," said Earl as they exited the highway, following the plow and police escort. He drove under the interstate to Missoula's St. Patrick Hospital and pulled into the covered Emergency Room ambulance entrance and the waiting doctors and nurses. As they opened the door, Nick climbed out first.

"She had the boy about five minutes ago," Nick told the doctor. "The umbilical is still attached, and I think the placenta is still inside."

The doctor gave him a quick glance.

"Okay, best to get her out on the blanket. Come on guys," said the Doctor as four other orderlies grabbed the corners and loaded her onto the gurney.

"Good job. Glad you didn't cut the umbilical. We'll take it from here," said the Doctor.

"Thank you Senator, for everything," said Vanessa as they wheeled her in. Joe gave Nick a hug and followed his wife inside.

Nick turned to Greg, Earl, and some others who had helped.

"Come on folks, I'll buy you a cup of crappy hospital coffee," said Nick with a laugh.

He noticed Greg was filming. "Please tell me you didn't film all of that," said Nick, laughing.

"Every bit," smiled Greg.

"Not so crappy after all, Senator," said Carlo, pointing, as they piled into the hospital cantina. It served Starbucks.

They sat around a couple of tables pulled together, talked about the current situations and the events of the day. Nick took a lot of pictures with folks and even more with hospital staff that came in and out, having heard the Senator and presidential candidate had just delivered a baby on the road.

Eventually, they gathered in the room with Vanessa, Joe, and the baby. Everyone from the road rescue hunched around the family for pictures.

# Chapter 29

The newscaster from NWN read the latest news from the TV, droning on as Lexi and Mel were strategizing in her campaign office.

"Last night on Interstate 90 outside of Missoula, Montana, Senator Nick Turner and his team stopped to help a motorist who slid off the road and down a snow-covered embankment. It turned out the couple was nine months pregnant. With the help of several other motorists, they were able to get the pregnant couple out of the car and into their own, where they drove through the blizzard to Missoula."

"During the ride, the woman went into labor, and the Senator delivered a healthy baby boy. As you can see from the picture, the couple and the baby boy are fine as the Senator posed with them and the other helpers from the road rescue. Senator Turner is once again the Hero. Well done, Senator," finished the talking head from the venerable *New World News* network.

"Are you kidding me? That had to be staged. Please, tell me it was staged?" groaned Mel.

Lexi laughed.

"He is a lucky SOB, isn't he? Always in the right place at the right time. Stop a terrorist, stop the filibuster, deliver a baby. What's next, hit a grand slam at the all-star game? Sub for the QB and win the Super Bowl?"

"These feel-good stories have legs, and no one tires of seeing or hearing about them," remarked Mel in a worrisome tone.

"There is nothing we can do about it. Besides, they didn't even call him a presidential candidate. While he's out saving babies, we are preparing to remake the world."

"True. But I hate free press, especially when it is something we can't counterattack."

"Keep track of the kid. We'll put pressure on him in a few years to change his gender. That'll teach'em," commented Lexi, laughing.

"I really wish you wouldn't say things like that, even between us," said Mel. "One of these days someone is going to record it and then we'll be in real trouble."

"And you would take care of it, right?" suggested Lexi, looking at Mel seriously.

"Of course. That's why we hired Roland. He is an expert at stopping leaks and cleaning things up, among his other talents. But you are missing my point."

Lexi looked at Mel before answering.

"Where would they go? We set the media agenda, we fund their efforts, we drive all their progress. Same for anarchists. And our other 'spontaneous' protesters and our schools and universities graduating woketivist snowflakes dependent on us to tell them what to think or do. Hollywood is told what to say and film. The media are told what to report. We tell the teacher's unions what to teach. The other unions do what we need them to do. Except for a few mistakes, like Turner's appointment, we control the message. So, we control the masses. Our new religion, progressivism, is the new opiate of the masses, and all the groups that matter are now converts," finished Lexi.

"Or hostages," added Mel. Lexi shrugged in response.

"Still, we shouldn't get overconfident," reminded Mel. "We still have to win elections."

"For a little while," agreed Lexi with her perfect smile. "I hope your cleaner is as good as advertised. I suspect we are going to need his talents in the months ahead."

#

"Oh my god, Greg. This is incredible footage. Thank you. We can cut this into a spot showing Nick in action. This will go viral in a heartbeat. 'Just like he would work to preserve the life of our country,' or something like that. This is great," said Margie, looking down at her laptop reviewing the footage Greg had sent of their escapades.

"You should have been there. The footage doesn't do it justice. Nick and Earl really took charge," crowed Greg from the ZOOM screen projected on the big screen in the conference room.

"Okay, you get paid this week," grinned Nick, seated next to Greg in the hotel room.

"Haha," said Greg, "It really was pretty incredible."

Denise entered the conference room and turned on NWN news, who were playing the same footage Lexi had seen earlier.

"Look at that, even NWN saying nice things about you," commented Margie.

"Really? We can't see it," said Nick.

"Would have been nice if they actually referred to you as a presidential candidate," groused Denise. "I'll put a call in to them and see if we can get them to edit it, or at least refer to you as senator and presidential candidate."

"Baby steps Denise. At least they acknowledged I exist. The mother and baby are fine in case anyone wants to know."

"That was our next question, of course," said Denise, in an exasperated tone.

"Care to guess what they named him?" asked Nick with a smile.

"No, that would be too much," laughed Margie.

"Yep, Nicholas Joseph," replied Greg, grinning.

"I guess that's gratitude for you," said Denise. "Just tell me they are going to vote for you too."

"Denise, has anyone called you a killjoy?" asked Nick.

"Not yet today, but it's early," she responded.

# Chapter 30

Sam Vincent, the President's chief of staff, finished his plate of eggs and bacon from the hotel breakfast buffet. As he spread his jam over his toast, he took a sip of coffee and fumed. He was still smarting from his public humiliation at Lexi's hand during the last cabinet meeting.

Chief of staff to the President was one of the most powerful roles in the government. Sam held the role these last three years and enjoyed the power it gave him. But as the President became less capable, Lexi took on more and more of the roles and responsibilities of leading the country. The final straw was the State of the Union speech. Sipping his coffee, he replayed that evening in his head.

Prior to the speech, Sam was in the green room at the Capitol with the President, the First Lady, the VP, Mel and the Attorney General. The President's physician was also there. Lexi and the First Lady were arguing over the ability of the President to deliver the speech.

"He could recite the five words. He's fine," said the First Lady.

"Not in the order they were given," said Lexi, turning to the White House physician. "That's not good, right? Since you only told them to him thirty seconds ago."

"It is troublesome, Madame Vice President," said the White House doctor carefully.

"Ha, how much did *she* pay you?" smirked the First Lady.

"If you send him out there, it's on you," said Lexi.

"It'll be fine. He's been reading teleprompters for over fifty years. He can do it this last time," said the First Lady as the others in the room tried to make themselves smaller.

Lexi smiled in reply.

"And if he can't? If he suddenly messes up or makes an offhand comment or an off-color joke? Or worse, makes it clear he is not as clearheaded as we are still projecting through our allies in the media. What then?"

The First Lady stared back at Lexi, her hatred on obvious display. Lexi turned to the White House physician.

"Well? What is your medical opinion?" she asked in a terse tone, looking at her watch.

The Physician looked from the Vice President to the First Lady and then back to Lexi.

"Madame Vice President, in my strictly medical opinion, the President is fairly lucid for the first couple hours each day. The drugs he is taking for the various illnesses and his advancing dementia require frequent rest. By this time in the evening, I would say it is quite possible he cannot read and understand the flow of the teleprompter."

Lexi turned to the First Lady, then she turned to the President, who sat in a chair in the room staring absently at a painting on the wall.

"How long has it been?" she asked the doctor.

He looked at his watch. "About five minutes."

Lexi walked to the President. "Sir, are you ready?"

The President looked up at Lexi, finally recognizing her.

"Hi Lexi. What are you doing in the residence?"

"Is that where we are?" asked Lexi, glancing at the First Lady.

"Of course. Are you here for dinner?"

"Dear," said the First Lady, "We are in the Capitol for your State of the Union."

The President looked confused. Looking from Lexi to his wife.

"Doctor?" said Lexi in a commanding tone.

"Mr. President, I gave you five words a few minutes ago. Do you remember them and can you tell them to me in the order I gave them to you?" asked the doctor.

"Sure Doc, I'll play along. Four score and seven years ago," said the President as his wife broke in.

"Dear, you remember, chair, pipe?"

"Ma'am," said the doctor.

"Flower, nail, shoe," said the President, like a nursery rhyme.

"See," glared the First Lady.

"If you send him out there, he will make a mistake. He will ruin his reputation. It will embolden our enemies and will force his cabinet to invoke the 25th. It will be because of his actions, *and yours*, not mine," said Lexi prophetically.

"Now hold on," Sam said, entering the conversation for the first time. "That sounded like you are threatening to invoke the 25th if the President goes forward with the State of the Union. What does it say if he does not? Not speaking makes everyone question his ability to lead."

"Sam, you are in the cabinet meetings. Javier," said Lexi, looking at the Attorney General, "you are there too. Have I not made it clear I do not and have never supported invoking the 25th? I want to be president, but I don't want the job this way. You may not believe me, but I am sincere. If you send him out, I cannot stop the cabinet from invoking it. We all know he won't make it through the speech."

"What do you propose we do?" asked Sam.

"Cancel," said Lexi. "There is no law saying he has to do a State of the Union."

"That is just as bad and sends a message of inaction and concern," said Sam, looking at the First Lady.

"You could give it," suggested Javier.

"Excuse me," said Sam and the First Lady simultaneously.

"The Vice President could go out and deliver the President's speech. She could say he came down with a touch of the stomach flu and asked the Vice President to deliver *his* speech. Then in a day or two we have a press conference early in the morning to show the President is indeed fine and lucid," finished the Attorney General.

Lexi stood looking from the Chief of Staff to the First Lady, who both realized they were boxed into a corner.

"Very well," said the First Lady with a look of pure hatred for the Vice President. "Come on dear, we are heading back to the White House." The president dutifully stood and follow the First Lady out the side door, followed by their secret service team.

It was at that point, as Mel and Lexi turned to him, smiles on their faces, that Sam knew his time in power was over. The humiliation at the cabinet meeting was Lexi showing she had won. They thought he'd just take it. They were wrong. He wouldn't go down quietly.

Sam didn't appreciate her dictating to him or the President when and what they could do. After the State of the Union debacle, the Vice President, had orchestrated the 7 am photo op with the President and First Lady as he had his coffee and morning muffin. They had no choice but to take part. Lexi held all the cards. The invited reporters dutifully asked the President fluff questions he answered lucidly.

The President played his role, perhaps unwittingly, but he was even convincing regarding the fight with the flu he had supposedly had. He showed the country he was in command of his faculties and physically capable, even passing around a full pitcher of orange juice. He gave a bit of an update on how the administration was helping the foreign governments with *their* investigations into the Christmas attacks, letting them take the respective leads with the US merely working in the background to assist.

This helped fix the 'statement' the White House had issued on the day of the attack, implying only the US could find the perpetrators. He finished with a self-deprecating joke, showing what endeared him to his base most, his folksy sense of humor. From the VP's point of view, they had proved the President was fine and there was no coup underway. Talk of the 25th died down in the press.

Vincent remembered standing off camera fuming as the President looked foolish, contradicting his 'own' statement from the day of the tragedy. A statement Vincent had put out himself. He glanced over at Lexi and Mel, also standing off camera. Both had smirks on their face, having told the President to bring this up. It was true the statement had caused some international consternation. Sam felt at the time they needed to respond quickly. He hadn't wanted to wait for Lexi to decide.

Now he really had no play. At least within the White House. He needed the money his post-White House opportunities would provide. With a new wife with expensive taste and no family money to fall back on, Sam was borrowing heavily to lead a lifestyle well beyond his means. If he played his cards right, he'd have an explosive bestseller on his hands, making the rounds of pay for play on the networks.

He felt a pang of guilt. His bombshell could hurt the Party, but his hatred for Mel and especially Lexi was outweighing his years of liberal support. In desperation, he'd contacted a young investigative reporter making a name for himself, ferreting out corruption in both parties. He'd traveled to New York last night to discuss how much his story would be worth to the reporter this morning.

While in the city, he was also planning on meeting with a publishing house. He'd show Lexi. Sam started collecting damaging information after the State of the Union. He kept this info on a secure device hidden in his house, besides the encrypted copy on his phone and laptop. He was getting paranoid, waking up from nightmares of the FBI storming his house, marching him out in leg irons, ruining his life and career. Just as *they* had used the FBI and media themselves to do repeatedly to the enemies of their administration.

Sam left his hotel in midtown Manhattan. He was meeting the reporter at a Starbucks near Rockefeller Center on 48th. As he prepared to head east on 50th, his phone buzzed with a text.

'Change of plan. Let's meet near Times Square, Starbucks on 43rd'. The text came from an unfamiliar number, but they had his number, so he figured the reporter was using another 'burn' phone.

Out of habit, Sam texted the old number he'd used with the reporter.

'OK, be there in 10'. He changed direction and headed south on Seventh Avenue, dodging folks on the sidewalk. He was midway between 49th and 48th avenue, glancing at texts on his phone, when what sounded like a shot rang out. It startled him and those around him. The other people on the sidewalk looked around in a panic and scattered, jostling him, causing him to drop his phone near the curb.

He bent over to pick up it up. Something shoved him hard enough to propel him off the curb, directly in front of a New York City Transit bus, speeding up to make the green light at the next corner. Sam had no time to even glance up before the bus struck him. The impact propelled him 25 feet down the road, where his body struck another car.

As was usually the case in New York City, most folks carried on with their routine as if nothing had happened. A few tourists rushed to Sam's side while they could hear sirens in the distance.

#

Further east, sitting in the Starbucks near Rockefeller Center, Dan Baker sat sipping his usual venti chai with skim milk. He looked down at his phone as it buzzed. It was a text from Sam Vincent.

`'Ok see you in 10.'`

Dan was puzzled. He hadn't texted Sam. He didn't like leaving digital fingerprints. Dan was mistrustful of everyone. It was his nature as an investigative journalist, to assume everyone was out to get you.

He replied with two '??'. He sat and drank his chai as their meeting time came and went. It was over 10 minutes and then it was 30 minutes past. Dan looked at his phone again. No more texts. He checked his social feeds, stiffening.

'Presidential Chief of Staff, Sam Vincent struck by bus on New York City's Seventh Avenue.'

Dan turned off the burn phone, removed the battery and threw it in the trash on his way out the door. Maybe he had seen one too many spy movies. The phone was an anonymous one, not registered in his name, so they couldn't trace the text he received or sent earlier.

He headed back to his apartment, looking over his shoulder occasionally and taking a roundabout route. Vincent hadn't provided him with much information, just enough to whet his appetite and get his attention about what he wanted to talk about. But it was a start. He'd certainly started on other stories with less info. He'd see where this one went.

#

Mel Arenson was in a meeting with Harriet and several of Lexi's other senior election staff, working through polls and 'get out the vote' plans for the upcoming primaries. An aide knocked on the conference room door and popped their head in. "I think you may want to turn on ANC." As a staffer turned on the TV, Mel looked down at his phone at a text from Lexi. Meanwhile, an ANC news reporter was speaking.

"I am on scene in midtown Manhattan where in a horrific accident, the President's chief of staff Sam Vincent appears to have stumbled into traffic following a mini panic caused by a truck backfire. Mistakenly thought to be shots fired. Apparently, according to witnesses, in the ensuing panic, everyone was scrambling, and it appears Vincent stumbled off the curb just as a Transit bus was coming up the bus lane. It struck him and hurled his body further up the street, striking another vehicle."

"The EMTs pronounced him dead on scene from the massive head trauma. There is no comment as yet why the chief of staff was in New York. We are awaiting official comment from the White House," finished the reporter.

Mel glanced at Harriet, who was looking at him with a strange look on her face. He looked down at his phone to answer Lexi's text that yes; he had just seen the news on ANC. A tragedy. Yes, he would work with Ana to get a statement out for the Vice President expressing their shock at the tragedy and heartfelt loss for the administration.

# Part Two

## The Impossible Dream

*"If your actions inspire others to dream more, learn more, do more, and become more, you are a leader."*

John Quincy Adams

# Chapter 31

Shaking his head in disgust, Nick put his beer down on a coaster amidst the empty Chinese takeout containers on his desk. He leaned back in his chair in his Senate office for a change. His feet up on one corner of the desk, his reaction was in response to reading the latest attempted power grab from his former Party colleagues in the Senate. Hearing a light knock at his open office door, he looked up.

"Senator, do you mind if I come in?"

He looked up at the tentatively smiling face of Lauren Bergamo.

"Honestly, I would prefer you weren't here at 9pm on a school night. Especially when no one else is around to referee," he replied, looking at his watch while taking his feet off the desk and standing up.

"I just finished a live segment in our Washington bureau across the street. I swung by on the off chance you might still be awake. Since you are the only senator sleeping in their office. I saw a light on at the front door to the suite and it *was* unlocked. Plus, I have credentials to be in the building this late," she said, holding up her badge on a lanyard hung around her neck.

"What can I do for you, Ms. Bergamo? If you're looking for an interview, I suggest you give Margie a call to see what we can set up, say after the election," responded Nick with a fake smile.

"I get it. You don't like me."

"Whatever gave you that idea?" asked Nick sarcastically.

Lauren smiled. "I think you've made it pretty clear to me and to the world you don't appreciate my attempts at tough questions."

"I think I have proved to everyone, especially you, it is not tough questions I don't like. It is dishonest playback of my answers framed to deceive the viewing public and manipulate their opinions."

"Senator, you need to toughen up," countered Lauren, wandering around Nick's office, taking in the spartan surroundings.

"Do I?" responded Nick, trying to stay civil, watching her roam.

"Would it matter if I said I have no control over what my producer and my network do with the footage?" When Nick did not answer, she continued.

"Or if I told them I didn't like it and you made a fool of me because of the decisions *they* made? Would it matter that I threatened to quit over it? Does any of that make a difference?"

Lauren stood in front of Nick, looking up at him defiantly.

"It might, but it looks like they didn't accept your resignation," he said, looking down at her, still a head taller, even in her high heels.

"But then again, you are a reporter, and I am a story," he continued, walking away toward the kitchen area. "You could just be telling me all this to get in my good graces. Where are my manners? Coffee?" asked Nick with his back turned working the coffee machine.

"Are you just being polite?" asked Lauren, picking up Nick's notebook in its purple sleeve from his desk.

"Yes."

"In that case, I will," she said, with a small laugh, as she flipped through pages. Only the first dozen had any notes.

"And yes, let's just say they talked me out of leaving, showing me the consequences if I left. However, I wanted to say my piece, off camera, and let you know I fought to make it right. To have them give you a fair shake. You can choose to believe me or not."

"I doubt you care if I believe you," retorted Nick, setting the second cup under the machine.

"Not that it matters since you have Tommy eating out of your palm," she said, making a face. "You turned our little game into a huge PR win, so you came out smelling like a rose," she finished, looking up at Nick as he stood in his kitchen area. She quickly flipped more pages.

Nick waited for his machine to finish brewing both cups, turning back to face Lauren. He noticed she had his notebook and walked over to her, setting his cup down while taking it out of her hands. He handed her a mug and put his notebook back on the desk.

"Thank you for the coffee."

"You're welcome. I suppose this is the time you tell me you have suffered indignities and lost sleep over being berated by a US Senator?"

Lauren shrugged at him as she sipped her coffee.

"Nice try. I know you got to headline a segment on the *Women's Viewpoint* show. What was the title?" said Nick, tilting his head. "If I recall, it was on 'misogynist patriarchal white males in power'. I believe that was it and my treatment of you featured heavily. I think you made out fine as well," he finished ironically with a half-smile, now perched on the edge of his desk, keeping his distance.

"Oh, so you watched? You don't strike me as the *Viewpoint* type," she said with a big smile, still standing in the middle of his office, sipping her coffee.

Nick saw she had a dimple on one side when she smiled for real.

"No, but some of my staff do. They told me I was being vilified by the hosts. I figured that had to be worth a few sympathy votes from suburban moms."

"No doubt. Is that just a prop?" she said, pointing to his ever-present purple notebook.

"No, I just started a new one, after I filled up the last. Not much for you to snoop in this one. See anything interesting?"

"You have horrible penmanship. Can you blame a girl?" she said, smiling and shrugging in response.

"Usually takes a few months to fill it. May take longer this time, with fewer committee meetings and an election year. That's why I bought the cover. It's too hard to find matching notebooks. This way, I don't have to remember what it looks like. Why do you care if it's a prop?"

"Just curious. Anytime you appear, you always have it with you. I figured it was a security blanket or something, like your Binky," said Lauren, smiling devilishly this time, showing her dimple again.

Nick grinned in return. "I use it to capture my thoughts and to make a list of who said what and when. You never know when the documented truth is necessary to prove when people are lying."

"Interesting. Since you were just being polite and this is your bedroom, it is probably best if I leave. Before some enterprising investigative journalist gets the wrong idea about my spending time, late at night, with a senator who hates me," remarked Lauren, setting the coffee on a table and turning to leave.

"Hate is a strong word. How about professional disdain for your profession, rather than you personally?" suggested Nick, watching her as she approached the office door.

Lauren paused in the entryway, the light from the hallway silhouetting her shapely figure and legs in her tailored business suit. Lauren turned to look at Nick.

"Senator, no greater than the disdain I feel for a majority of your colleagues in Congress. Yet I still have a smile on my face, listening to them jabber while they leer at my chest or legs." This last delivered with a smile and the slight turn of one high heel clad leg toward Nick.

"Maybe I'll give Margie a call for an interview. Somehow, I think there is more to you than the Mr. Smith persona you project. Good night, Senator," she finished, turning to leave.

"Good night Ms. Bergamo."

Nick couldn't help but admire her for the first time as the beautiful woman she was, rather than just the pain in the ass obnoxious Washington reporter. He paused for a minute to make sure she was out of the office. Going to the front door of his office suite, he locked the door, turning off the light before returning and dropping the Murphy bed from the wall.

"Dodged a bullet there. Gotta remember to tell Chuck to lock the front door when he leaves," he said to himself, shaking his head.

# Chapter 32

Nick looked around the conference room in his campaign office in Denver. Margie, Jer, Greg, Jenny, and others were closely collaborating with a host of other young people in a wide variety of attire. They wore jeans and t-shirts, cargo pants and even one wearing shorts. In February. In Colorado. Tattoos and body piercings distinguished the guests from his staff, who were all smartly attired in business casual.

Nick couldn't help but grin at the contrast between Washington business and West Coast business, though Jeremy Kwan had wisely moved his company to Texas from California. The interlopers were people Jeremy brought with him to work through the launch of his social media platform, now named Hibiscus.

The two teams were standing and seated working on white boards and laptops, strategizing what to say and how to say it via posts and videos. Nick smiled at the excited nature of the mostly 20 somethings plotting to take the world by storm. He caught Jeremy's eye and motioned toward the door.

"Are you ready for the shit storm headed your way?"

Jeremy Kwan smiled. He was quickly balding with wire-rim glasses and Korean features. His Asian heritage made him look no older than most of his co-workers. No one would have guessed his age in his late thirties, nor was there any outward sign showing he was one of the world's youngest self-made billionaires.

"Hey, any publicity is good publicity in this age," replied Jeremy, smiling. "What I'm really liking is the hype. The minute we started promoting the new app, folks were going crazy. When we announced you would be the first poster, we got roasted on cable news. It was fabulous. We already have over 25 million downloads to prepare for going live tomorrow. I think you're going to be a big hit."

"Thanks for hosting all our campaign websites as well. We couldn't risk them deplatforming us. As you can see, I am not exactly holding back on my thoughts and have already been suspended a few times from some of them."

Jeremy laughed. "Glad I could help. I own my servers. I also own the company that does the hosting, so it is an entirely closed loop system. Nothing they can do to stop me, short of shutting down the internet."

Nick looked at the confident young man in front of him.

"Jeremy, trust me, there are things you are not considering. You shouldn't be too confident. The government has endless supplies of your tax money. The Party is not afraid to do whatever they think they need to in order to win. Remember what they did to Senator Wilhelm? If they will sacrifice a United States Senator for their cause, they can marshal all kinds of forces to thwart your plans if you get any traction. I know Faceplant, Instacrap, and BirdBrain are all hemorrhaging subscribers to alternatives," said Nick.

Jeremy laughed, "Faceplant, Instacrap and BirdBrain? I love it."

"I hate to give them any free press," laughed Nick. "You know how I feel about all of this social media. Any good it does has been far outweighed by the bad habits it is breeding in our youth. Maybe you can tackle online porn next," suggested Nick. "Over 60% of the web is porn."

"Already thinking about it. My girlfriend just announced she is pregnant," beamed Jeremy.

"Congratulations," responded Nick, smiling and patting Jeremy on the shoulder. "What do you need me to do for the launch?"

"I think the teams are working well together, putting a content plan and posting strategy in place. You have some amazing content already. I watched some of Greg's recordings of your talks with real Americans. It is amazing and super authentic. People are eating it up. It'll give you access to an entirely new demographic."

"I hope so. I don't feel old, but man, watching those guys work in the conference room, I realize I am nowhere near as savvy as I thought I was."

"Sad truth is, neither am I. Given the proper tools and leadership, these guys can solve any problem. Everything is moving so fast now. It's scary, especially the acceleration of AI," shared Jeremy.

"I agree. AI is becoming an immense problem. I'm glad to hear you say it. If you feel it, then I don't feel so bad."

"Oh, I feel it. Trust me. We need you to record a short post to intro the app, talk about what you are doing and why you think it is important for young people to get involved."

"Sounds pretty boring. Don't I need to jump off a building or set myself on fire to get the attention of young people these days? Isn't that what that KooKoo app demands?" asked Nick, semi-seriously.

"KooKoo?" laughed Jeremy. "I love your names. As for antics, maybe that works on 'KooKoo', but for an app like mine, I am hoping to actually appeal to people who want to use their brain. To discuss issues and work collaboratively to resolve them. We'll see if they reward my faith in humanity."

"Alright. I think me just talking is going to put folks to sleep."

"Talk, make your points, and we'll figure it out," replied Jeremy.

"Sounds good," agreed Nick, skeptically.

"Nick, they need to wake up and realize what they are squandering. You can explain it so they can understand it. I have seen it. Just be yourself," suggested Jeremy as Nick nodded.

# Chapter 33

"Hello, for those of you who don't know me, I'm Nick Turner."

"I'm a senator from Colorado and an independent presidential candidate," said Nick as he walked around the table in his conference room and sat on the edge while they filmed.

"More importantly, I think I'm a lot like you," Nick paused for effect.

"I'm worried. Worried about what is happening in our communities, in our schools, at our workplaces, on social media, and in our country. I am concerned how the conversations on social media, on TV, in our school board meetings, and even on our streets are now always Us versus Them."

"I know I'm probably speaking to people who are a lot younger than I am. When I was your age, I remember I had all the answers too. Everyone who tried to teach or show or tell me differently was full of shit. Well, you know what, they *were* full of shit." Nick paused again.

Off camera, someone could not stifle their laugh.

"But they were also right," he said with a little laugh, too. He took a sip of his coffee and continued. "Like you will one day find out the hard way. You don't have all the answers and folks who have already fallen on their face, and stood back up, really do know something about not falling down again."

"I'm not going to tell you what to do. You'll ignore it anyway. Instead, I'm going to ask you questions and challenge you to think for yourself. My first request is for you to think about who is benefiting from all this divisiveness? Who benefits by telling you to hate yourself? To hate your classmates, your family, your employer, or anyone else?"

"When we can't come together and find common ground, we are apart. And we are alone. We have to face our anxieties and try to survive by ourselves." Nick used his hands to emphasize his points.

"No family, no friends, no one we can trust, no one to confide in, and no one to lean on when times get tough. Is that how you want to live your life? It's like we came out of the pandemics, and we are afraid of everyone around us. Here we are years later, and we are still alone. Is that how you want everyone else to lead their life?" Nick paused, taking another sip of his coffee. "That's not how I want to live mine."

"*They* stacked the odds against you. There are two reasons *they* have done this." Nick held up one hand, a single finger extended, emphasizing 'they' at each mention.

"First, if you are ignorant and are taught to believe and trust everything they tell you, it will be easy to manipulate you. People who have no support system. Who are afraid are easier to manipulate. It is easier to manipulate you into believing you are a racist, homophobe, or just a shitty person because you question something they tell you is fact. You'll do what they tell you because you don't want to be called out publicly, bullied on social media or, worse, *excluded* from their tent."

"Like donating money to their cause or putting a sign in your yard. Using pronouns to promote diversity, or some other virtue signaling to show you don't think for yourself but do what others *tell* you to do. You conform, because the alternative, to stand up for what you believe, is too painful. They have made it that way on purpose. You thinking for yourself is their worst possible nightmare," Nick raised a second finger on his outstretched hand.

"The second reason is the most important. It is called *money*," said Nick with extra emphasis. "With money comes power. The power to manipulate the school curriculum into what they feel is right. Left *or* right. To manipulate the media into reporting only the stories they want you to see. Power to pay hackers to disrupt your life, steal your identity or ransom your pictures. To fund AI to manipulate reality to what they want you to see and convince you it is a fact. The power to stifle the actual truth," emphasized Nick, stopping to drink coffee again.

"*Money leads to power and power leads to control.* Remember that. In one sentence, it explains **everything**. You, me, all of us are in a war. Right now. A war for the hearts and minds of American souls. Your souls. And it is a no holds barred conflict. There are no rules of engagement. If people's lives need to be ruined for standing up to something, for simply disagreeing. Or expressing support for one candidate or one idea, so be it. To them, your wellbeing is of no consequence. This is not only wrong, but morally reprehensible. Make no mistake, they seek not only to control government forever, but to force you to live the way only *they* know you need to live," said Nick with increasing passion.

"This is happening and trust me, we need to stand up to it *now*. We need to demand sources that tell the actual truth. To have honest and open dialog about tough subjects like race, class, and gender. About why we need sovereign borders or need to stop runaway government spending. To talk pragmatically about conservation and climate change mitigation, not as the apocalypse, but how we adapt to the changing planet. About the influence of foreign governments in our media and, critically, all of us, have to pull up our big boy and big girl pants and start taking responsibility for our own actions. You own your actions."

Nick stared into the camera, his honesty and concern clear.

"We need to seek truth. And we need to understand big media is not truth. The so-called papers of record in New York, Washington, and London do not write the truth. Nor do the major online search and social media outlets. They are printing and saying things, not to inform you of facts to let you form your own opinion. Oh no, can't have that. Instead, they are slanting stories to ensure you form the opinion they want. So, you vote the way they want, on the issues they want passed, and against those they don't want passed. Like limits on their power. Or limits on their ability to shape public opinion through state approved censorship," he said, shaking his head.

"They have duped you. It's not too late. Yet. Shortly it'll be too late to turn around this experiment in self-government and freedom. Soon, they'll no longer have to manipulate you into thinking the way they want. Soon, they'll no longer need your approval. No longer need your vote to keep them in power. When that happens, *it is over*. They will tell you what you can and can't do. What you can and cannot drive, or eat, where you can live, what school you can attend, what job they need you to do. What temperature to set your thermostat. When you can and cannot charge your mandatory electric car. What kind of dishwasher, stove, light bulbs, and if you are even allowed to have air conditioning. Personal freedom will be gone." Nick stared into the camera.

"You are the future. The choices are in *your* hands. It is your responsibility. If you don't mind doing what others tell you to do. If you don't want to do any research. Don't want to make up your own mind. Then just stop watching now. If you think all this is fine, then you won't like what else I have to say. My way is not easy. Thinking is hard. Doing is even harder. Being a mindless drone is easy. Giving up, even easier."

"So many other societies ask themselves afterwards, 'why didn't I do more, when I could have, to stop this'? I'm sounding this warning now. This is why I'm running for President. To help open eyes, your eyes. To get you to think for yourself. To implore you to be curious. Don't believe what you see or read, and question *everything*. Including what I say. Ask who benefits. Follow the money. If you find they lead back to big government, big media, or China, please do the opposite of what they suggest. Only you can find this out. Only *you* can convince yourself, your friends and family, helping them on the journey to self-discovery.

"The reason I'm here talking to you on this first post on Hibiscus is I believe in what Jeremy Kwan is attempting to do. Hibiscus is going to be a place where you can have open debate, where you can talk about issues. Ask questions without fear. Debate these issues and discuss reasons and solutions. Two principles that made this country possible. Where you can have an opinion and ask and talk about the tough questions without being shut down for voicing an opinion. Where you can find common ground and where you can interact with others civilly. Compromise for the greater good is only achieved through dialogue. We have to have this open dialogue to come together."

"Hibiscus is a place where no trolls and bots are allowed. Importantly, no violence is tolerated. We can disagree civilly. Without debate, there can be no genuine progress. Censoring differing opinions is not progress."

"It is a tall order. Frankly, the rest of social media is a sewer. This is another sign of the divisive times. We are better than this. We are in the freest country and society the world has ever seen. With freedom comes responsibility. Freedom is difficult. It takes work to get it and even more to preserve it. Like putting up with all kinds of crap you don't agree with. It also means you have to *tolerate* their right to say and do what they do. This is where we have gone off the rails. Dissenting opinion is no longer tolerated. Anyone who dissents must be silenced, no matter what."

"I leave you with one more thought. Who is afraid of dissent? People who know their positions are indefensible, that's who. People who would prefer to not allow open discussion. Who fears alternate opinion or opposing facts and points of view? They fear this discussion may make more sense and change people's minds. When someone says the science is settled, they do this because they do not want you to question their authority. Or their conclusions."

"Science is never settled. How can it be? We are always striving to learn more, to do more, to solve more, to cure more. They are obviously lying to you, because they do NOT want you to question what they are saying. When other social media outlets ban contrary opinion, they say they do so to protect you from misinformation. What they really mean is they protect you from alternate opinions. They try to prevent you from studying different views and perhaps, in thinking for yourself, reaching a conclusion contrary to their desired narrative," Nick oozed passion and credibility as he gave his speech to the camera.

"Keep your eyes and ears open. Seek alternate opinion. Use services allowing you to see these competing theories and to reach your own conclusions. In fact, when you discover, and each of you must do this on your own, stop using the services who seek to tell you what to think. They do not deserve your money. Once enough of you wake up, they will feel the pain. In a capitalist society, this is called supply and demand. When folks stop watching your channel, consuming your beverage, buying your product, or using your service, if you want to regain your profitability, you change your service to once again attract those you drove away. There is no way to force them to use your product or service. You have to convince them. This is the *only* way things should work. In a free society, you earn people's trust by what you say and do," said Nick, now standing closer to the camera.

"Sadly, in our world today, those with the power seek to limit you to *only* their approved products and services. To *their* truth. Do not succumb. Do not give in. You hold the power. They need your eyeballs, clicks, and money. Do not reward them for being the propaganda arms of government."

"Enjoy the troll free life on Hibiscus. We will do a test and post this on our other accounts as well. Ask yourself if what I have said is something others shouldn't be allowed to hear? See how quickly Hibiscus is the only place this post remains. This will be proof of exactly what I have told you. They are afraid to let anyone question *their* truth."

"We will continue to post here, and you can follow my road to the White House as I travel the country speaking to people like you. I don't take corporate donations, and I don't seek endorsements. I'm not beholden to anyone but myself and my conscience. Join my effort to retake America and get Big Government and Big Media out of your life. Wake up, Take Charge, find the facts, form your own opinions and Think for Yourself," finished Nick. He stared into the screen for a few extra seconds until they said cut.

Nick removed his microphone; took the bottle of water he was offered and drank half of it.

"How'd I do?"

Those who had been watching started clapping, and Jeremy approached Nick with a big smile. "That is a very compelling monologue. I'm sold. We will see if people agree," said Jeremy.

"Not too long?" asked Nick.

"Oh yeah. The average attention span of someone on social media is about 30 seconds for listening and maybe a minute for viewing."

"Uh oh," lamented Nick, thinking how he could possibly get his point across in 30 seconds.

"But *your* message is compelling *and* interesting. Many folks are lost. You're throwing them a lifeline. I suspect many will stay and listen," concluded Jeremy.

"We'll post it, monitor the comments and curate them to ensure we don't get any trolls getting through the algorithms," said one of Jeremy's techs.

"But you allow people to dissent as long as it is civil, right?" asked Nick.

"Yes, healthy debate is welcomed. We review every post to determine if the poster is registered and traced to a legitimate IP address. If they are, we review the content of the post to ensure it is also legitimate and not violent or threatening. We are not trying to censor actual opinion, only those from illegitimate sources," replied Jeremy.

"Ok, we'll see how it works. Let me know what else I can do to help," offered Nick.

"One thing is for sure, your post is unlikely to be shared on other platforms. You were pretty harsh," laughed Jeremy.

"The media keeps trying to suppress the truth. Just as murder will out, so will truth, eventually. They have been lying to America and the world for so long their credibility is eroding by the day. I just hope enough folks wake up by November."

"I agree with that, Nick. But hope is a lousy strategy."

Nick smiled in response. "But common sense is not."

# Chapter 34

Lexi and Mel were sipping tea, watching the coverage of the launch of Hibiscus. Lexi made a face when EXN showed excerpts of Nick extolling the virtues of an 'unbiased' social media channel where trolls and hate wouldn't be allowed.

"Can he do it?" she asked.

Mel shrugged. "Others have tried. I doubt it is possible. From what I have read, this Kwan guy is super smart. But so were the others who tried. Many of them had more money and brand than Kwan and they all failed. Seems unlikely."

"Watch it Mel. If he is successful at all, we need to do something. Besides, between Kwan and Turner, they are going on record admitting to outright censorship."

"You mean like we do it all the time?" smiled Mel.

Lexi turned her icy gaze on Mel. "Ours is in the name of restraining hate speech. We're duty bound to protect our citizens."

Mel nodded. "Of course. Talk about putting a target on yourself. He is just daring every troll and government on the planet to test what he says. I can't imagine it stays up for a week. Once it becomes clear, he can't stop the trolls, they'll be no reason to use his platform. He'll get a few from the fringe and it'll fizzle when they can't reach critical mass."

"Find out who is hosting things, whose networks he is using. We can pressure them to shut him down if he gets any traction," said Lexi.

"He is."

"Huh? How can he do that? Don't we own the licenses and all the other stuff you need? How did he get them?"

"TV and cable work that way. The internet does not. Section 230 also provides certain protections. Bottom line, we can't stop him from using the internet. At least not without endangering all the others who are our allies," answered Mel.

"Why?" contended Lexi in all seriousness.

"Really?" replied Mel.

Lexi glared at Mel in response. "We make the rules, we pass the regulations. Why can't we pass a regulation giving us the power to determine the 'nature and result' of a product or business on the internet? We passed a Patriot Act to give us all kinds of leeway in determining what and who is and is not dangerous to our Republic? Why is preaching insurrection or preventing other patriots from identifying and stopping misinformation any different?" finished Lexi.

Mel grinned in return. "It will be a brave new world shortly."

"Indeed, it will. Soon no more split Supreme Court to overrule our opinions on what is and is not good for the country. Those who would do us harm now use the Bill of Rights as a weapon, betraying the protections it once provided. Progress cannot occur when we still allow the few to stop the many. Mel, for too long we have played by their rules. Always working on the margins, incrementally. A little here, a little there. Always being bought off by some small protection or benefit for a small group of the poor, weak, infirm, persecuted, or discriminated. No more. We will use the power of the majority and stop talking about helping. Instead, we will *show* what we can accomplish once we no longer have to compromise."

Lexi was in full on evangelical mode. Mel smiled. This was Lexi at her best. When like this, she could harness the power of their one issue constituents. Most of whom could not care less about each other or their issue, but who still gathered under the big tent of the Party.

By themselves, they were voices in the wilderness and inconsequential. But together, rallied, and unified by someone like Lexi, they represented a majority of voices. When wielded properly, they gave her a power that was unstoppable. A mighty roar of approval.

The Party made promises in return for fanatical loyalty. Even when not completely delivered, where else could they go? They stayed loyal because Lexi always tried to keep her promises. This time, she meant to fulfill her end of the bargain. Completely.

# Chapter 35

Senator Nick Turner stood offstage as the opening band was finishing on the last night of Florida's Spring State Fair. Denise had convinced the promoters to let Nick speak to the crowd as they were switching out the band's equipment from the warm-up band to the last group, one of the most popular country western acts in the world.

He'd have five minutes to say his piece and then he'd have to leave to let the band take the stage. Denise had agreed. She figured Nick would last about two minutes before the crowd booed him off the stage. These state fair revelers were not there to hear a political speech. They were there to get drunk and listen to music. She told Nick as much, as she and Earl, Chuck, and Greg stood offstage with him.

As the emcee on stage introduced Nick, Denise turned to him.

"Now remember, when they boo, say good night and exit gracefully. And if they throw things, leave sooner, OK?" she said in complete seriousness. Chuck and Earl looked worried as well.

"Don't worry. I got this. I used to teach college freshmen."

#

"Hey Florida, we having a good time?" asked the emcee, a local TV personality. The crowd dutifully hooted and hollered to his encouragement. "Well, we have a treat for you while the band's equipment is switched out. Senator Nick Turner's been down here meeting with folks. He asked if he could say a few words. He promised to be brief. Let's give me a good ole' Florida welcome," he finished as Nick walked out. The crowd clapped politely. As the emcee handed Nick the microphone, his eyes were skeptical.

"Good luck, buddy."

Nick stood on the stage and looked out over the twenty-five thousand revelers in attendance for this last show of the state fair.

"I appreciate the welcome. Lucky for all of us, I won't sing, and I won't try to tell a joke either." The crowd laughed. "You know what else I'm not going to do? I'm not going to ask you for *anything*. No money, no vote. I'm also not going to promise I'll do anything for you either. Not a very good politician, am I?" asked Nick, as he got a few more laughs from the crowd.

"I do have a couple of questions. In case some of you don't know it, Hell, maybe most of you don't know," laughed Nick, "I *am* running for President." This too got a few laughs.

"My first question," said Nick, holding up one finger. "How are you handling all those Californians, New Yorkers, New Jerseyites and even my fellow Coloradans moving to Florida?" Jeers and boos were his answer.

"You guys must be doing something right? Because they are leaving their states and coming here. Why do you figure that is?" There were a few cheers and a couple of 'go home' shouts. "Well, we all know why they are doing it, because they F'ed up their own states, right?" This got the first real cheer from the crowd.

"My advice to you is do not let them take over your school boards. Don't let them win your city council or mayor elections. Don't let them do anything to change what you have been doing." There were a few more cheers, but he could also see folks were now paying attention to his words.

"Remember, they screwed up their own states. Now they want to do the same to yours. Maybe some of them, most of them, are Opposition like many of you. Fleeing the tyranny of their Party run blue state. If that is true, good for them, good for you. But do all you can to make sure they don't ruin what you have going for you here. You know how you do that? Pay attention. And use your vote to make sure they don't make your state the next California or New York hell hole."

Nick's honesty was getting people's attention. This was *not* what they expected. He continued down this path, highlighting the differences between blue state economy destroying policies and red state opportunity driven ones. As he detailed bad move after bad move and how Florida had avoided most of these, the crowd got more and more animated, agreeing with his statements as he showed his knowledge of why so many headed to Florida to reap the benefits of their state's politics.

"You know, this is why I am running for President. Yes, I was in the Party and technically, my old Party has been responsible for some pretty boneheaded moves these last few years, decades, centuries," said Nick, getting another laugh as he drew out the timelines of Party rule and Party policy mistakes.

"Seriously though, we *have* gotten lazy. All of us. We have our iPhones and our Tesla's or Ford F150's and our big TVs and fast internet. We are the perfect example of fat, dumb, and happy. I would add one more. Ignorant. The problem with this is we allow them to make wholesale changes while we are too interested in all our gadgets."

The crowd was now paying attention to everything Nick was saying as he wove his tale, even if for some, it was difficult through their alcohol induced haze.

"Meanwhile, the progressives are quickly legislating away our freedoms. A little bit with each law they pass. Let me ask you a question. Did you enjoy wearing your masks everywhere during the pandemics? Were you pissed when you learned unless you were wearing an industrial respirator, it did not make a damn bit of difference?"

There were shouts of yes from a majority of the crowd.

Nick shook his head and took a few breaths to calm down. He didn't want to incite a riot.

"But then, what choice did you have? If you didn't, you couldn't eat out, or go to your office or perhaps even keep your job. Before anyone says anything, I am not anti-vaccine. But I am anti coercion. And I am anti-cancel culture. You should not lose your job because you won't follow a dictate claiming to 'follow the science'. When in fact they didn't have a clue if what they were saying was indeed correct. In fact, in almost all cases, it was *not* correct. People were fired, quit their jobs, or committed suicide because the government created a web of lies, fear, and uncertainty in the name of public health. Then their willing dupes in corporate America helped them enforce it," accused Nick. The crowd was enthralled, listening to his very undiplomatic speech. They had never heard a politician speak this way before. They cheered and shouted agreement at various points in his statement, especially in the last sentence.

"So again, I ask you, how did this happen? It happened because we are lazy. We're not engaged, don't seek our own facts and why our elected officials were allowing this to happen. We did not hold them accountable to do the right thing, even if it was hard. What other freedoms do they get to take away before you say 'enough'?"

"We have done this to ourselves. Only we can stop it. Only YOU can stop it. So, get off your butt, seek the truth, hold your candidates accountable. Let them know you do not appreciate them taking away your freedoms," said Nick with finality as the crowd cheered. Many started standing up and cheering and shouting.

"Sorry, I get carried away when I get going. I am just trying to get Americans to wake up and make sure they are taking part. Voting based on their own research and not on how someone else tells them to vote. I just did a post for a new troll free social media platform, Hibiscus. You should look there to have an honest debate of ideas. It is time for all of us to look around and vote for an America we want our children to experience. Right now, I am not happy the way we are trending. Are you?" asked Nick, to a resounding 'No' from the crowd. "Only we," Nick spread his arms out to include the entire audience. "Only we can make this happen. Please do not punt on this responsibility. I don't care who you vote for. But do it from an informed position. I want each of you to take responsibility for how you vote and understand you own *your* part of what happens."

"It is the greatest gift the founding fathers ever gave us. The chance to make a difference. To have a say in how we are ruled. No matter what you think, if enough of you band together, you make a difference. You can keep Florida from turning into the next California. Together with the other states, you can keep the entire country from turning into a progressive socialist shit hole. And on that note, I thank you for letting me bore you with my words. Let's hear some music."

Nick looked off stage where the band members were cheering and clapping as well, waiting for him to finish. The lead singer of the band walked out to where Nick was standing, his hand extended.

"Wow, and we follow that?" The crowd laughed and cheered. "Senator, I have to say, I have never had a warm-up act like this. How about you guys, ever heard a politician, let alone a presidential candidate, speak like that? Pretty freaking amazing if you ask me," said the singer, as the crowd cheered more.

"Are you all done, Senator? I think these folks would probably like to hear us sing," he said, smiling. Nick walked offstage. As the band took their places, the lead singer once again spoke to the crowd.

"I don't know about ya'll, but that was some pretty impressive stuff from the Senator. Total common sense." The crowd, which was still standing, started cheering and yelling, Turner, Turner, Turner, while holding up their phones with the flashlights on as Nick came back on stage to even louder cheers. He bowed and waved to them and then bowed to the singer before again exiting.

#

"I guess I didn't get booed off, did I?" said Nick with a smile, looking at Greg, Chuck, Denise, and Earl. They all stared at Nick.

"What?"

"I don't know what we just saw," said Denise, shaking her head.

"Nick, that was incredible," said Greg. "Do you know how long you talked?"

"Sure, 10 minutes, give or take.?"

"Uh, thirty-six," said Chuck, looking at his watch.

"What? Why didn't I get the hook?"

"Because the crowd would have come unglued. I have seen nothing like this in my career," said Denise, shaking her head.

"I should apologize to the band," said Nick, looking around for the band manager.

"Hardly," laughed Earl. "The emcee asked them if they wanted him to pull you off stage. They said they didn't want to be the reason you left the stage. They agreed with what you were saying as well. Can't say the emcee agreed, but he *is* from the media."

"Well, we have learned one thing for sure. You are going to speak to as many State Fairs as I can book," said Denise earnestly.

"Fine by me," smiled Nick. "My kind of people, working folks."

The band manager walked up carrying some jackets with the Band's logos on them. Nick figured they were for them.

"Senator, if you don't mind, Mick asked if I could get you to sign some of their jackets before you left?"

Nick laughed. Here was a band used to selling millions of albums and downloads, with dozens of hit singles, asking for *his* autograph.

"Sure, not a problem." Nick took a Sharpie and started signing.

"Senator, I booked us at a dozen state fairs throughout the summer. You are welcome to speak between the opening act and the band's act if you like," said the manager.

"Thanks, I think we will take you up on that. You sure this isn't going to hurt the group if they are associated with me? It will make them a target of the other candidates?"

"To be honest, none of the Opposition are very impressive and most of our listeners are in the center, or lean opposition. The way you are speaking, it is right in their sweet spot. You keep talking like you did tonight and there won't be anything for the boys to worry about. Don't change a thing."

"Thanks for the honesty."

"No Senator, it is us who should thank *you* for the honesty," said the manager.

#

As Nick was wrapping up his speech, a guy in the crowd wearing a Tampa Bay Buccaneers ball cap looked around from the middle of the crowd. He watched as the mostly tipsy crowd suddenly sobered up as Nick continued to weave his tale. When Nick was being especially strident about government overreach and restrictions on freedom of choice, he watched the crowd eat up the anti-government rhetoric.

Once Nick finished his speech, the man made his way out of the concert to the parking lot and into a nondescript black Chevy Malibu. He pulled out a laptop from under the seat, opening it and began entering notes before eventually driving out of the parking lot.

# Chapter 36

"Holy shit, he's preaching insurrection. We can't let him do this," said Cheryl Thompson, undersecretary of anti-terrorism in the Department of Homeland Security.

"Come on Cheryl. Other politicians do this on cable every night," responded Karen Coleman, representing the FBI in this hastily called meeting of the intelligence agencies. The meeting was called at the behest of Roger Brody, former acting and now recently confirmed, Secretary of Homeland Security.

"Maybe Karen, but they aren't doing it to twenty-five thousand rednecks, most of whom own guns and already hate the government. It is one thing to spout off on EXN and another to do it to folks drinking beer and eating corn dogs," said Cheryl in a snide voice.

"What do you want us to do? Go arrest a Senator who is already accusing us of playing on one side. Help make his point?"

"Ok ladies. Let's tone it down a bit," said Henry St. Cloud, the oily director of the NSA. This earned him an evil glance from both. He continued, oblivious to their ire at his sexist tone.

"The genuine concern is the response. Both to his speech and to what we do to keep him from starting a civil war. He should have had beer bottles thrown at him going on stage between acts at a state fair to give a political speech. Instead, for 30 minutes he kept their attention and got *cheered*."

"He is good. I'll give him that," said Karen, with admiration in her tone. "No way anyone else in Washington could do that."

"Which gets back to my point. This guy is good. The longer we wait to shut him down or discredit him or at least get him off the stage, the riskier it gets for us and our agenda," said Cheryl.

"And what, pray tell, is our agenda?"

This came in a calm voice from Rhett Chadwick, who was sitting in a chair against a wall, observing the conversation around the conference table. As the director of the CIA, he had little to no role in anything domestic, unless it affected relations outside the US.

"Come on Rhett, you know what Cheryl means," answered Henry, turning in his chair to look at Rhett. "We all have a vested interest in keeping Lexi in power. While we may be impartial, the truth is the radical nature of the Opposition, and now Turner, is a threat to the well-being and security of our nation."

Rhett shook his head before responding.

"Seriously Henry? Show trials that go on for years? Arresting and perp walking 65- and 70-year-old Opposition staffers out in full leg irons. While ANC is conveniently there, in the pre-dawn, to film the entire operation. What kind of threat are they? The actual damage is to *our* credibility. We continue to allow the administration to use us to enforce their banana republic strong-arm tactics instead of simply enforcing subpoenas," finished Rhett. His tone clearly showing he did not agree with the heavy-handed nature of these tactics.

"Rhett, we needed to send a message to the very people Cheryl is talking about," answered Roger before Henry could respond.

"Roger, you are new to this game. Your predecessor couldn't take the pressure all this deception caused. In fact, he keeled over in the very chair you are sitting in," retorted Rhett.

"Director!" blurted Cheryl. "Have a little respect for Frank. He led the charge against these insurrectionists and gave his life for our cause of liberty and justice. I think a little respect for the dead is warranted."

Rhett shrugged. "I'm saying, we have been through more than a decade of vilifying the other side for doing far less, then we ourselves have done, and still continue to do. The clown circus of the congressional show trials and their inability to accomplish anything all proved this by exposing their own ineptness." Rhett stood up.

"In fact, we have allowed far worse *crimes* to be perpetrated and even supported by our same agencies simply because they advance our cause and shore up this administration's voting blocs. We are supposed to be above partisan politics. Perhaps a more subtle approach to supporting the administration's goals is needed this go round?"

"Such as?" asked Karen.

"Turner is a third-party candidate. He goes on one show at EXN and speaks to five million viewers a couple times a month. He talks for 30 minutes to a crowd of mostly drunk rednecks, a majority of whom do not even vote. Before we trash our collective reputations more in public, perhaps a bit of restraint is in order. Let him have his fifteen minutes of fame. Visit a few state fairs, bloviate on *Tommy*. He has zero chance of being relevant. If he is still preaching sedition after Lexi is elected, we can arrest him then and hold him without charges or a trial like we did all those other 'dangerous' insurrectionists years ago," finished Rhett.

No one answered immediately. Finally, Javier Guzman, the Attorney General, spoke.

"Rhett, I would take some issue with your characterizations of exactly what happened back then. I was not the AG during those times, and I believe you were not in your current position, either. So, it really is a moot point. Like Cheryl, I agree Turner is a menace and a potential catalyst for trouble. However, as a presidential candidate, even an insignificant one, we are duty bound to give him leeway we wouldn't afford a common citizen."

Rhett walked toward the door, shaking his head.

"I am merely offering my advice. As was correctly pointed out, I don't have a role in domestic issues. My concern with Turner is his effect on our allies and enemies abroad. I'll limit my future involvement to those theaters. Good luck to all of you." Rhett left the room.

"Sanctimonious SOB," cursed Cheryl as the door closed.

"He makes a good point," admitted Karen as Roger, Javier, and Henry all sat quietly, reflecting on Rhett's statement.

"What? That Turner is untouchable because he is a hero presidential wannabe?" asked Cheryl.

"No," said Javier. "Anything we do just gives him free attention. Which, frankly, may be exactly what he is hoping. Only *we* can make him relevant. Rhett is right."

"I have to agree," agreed Henry.

"OK. We'll leave him alone and if he keeps it up, we can take care of him after the election in November. Cheryl, keep building a file on him of statements and encouragement of rebellion. When the time's right, we'll take him down," ordered Roger.

"With pleasure," snarled Cheryl.

Javier noticed a look on Karen's face. "You disagree Karen?"

She shook her head. "No. But doesn't it bother anyone else how the crowd reacted?"

"Not following?" questioned Cheryl.

"Think about it. Like we said earlier. A bunch of drunk rednecks waiting to hear music from a band they paid 100 bucks a head to see. Out trots a *politician*. Instead of booing him off the stage or throwing things, he avoids this response and then talks for thirty minutes. Then gets a standing ovation and an encore."

"So, he is a talented speaker," shrugged Henry. "We already saw that with his filibuster speech."

"And unlike other independents, he has huge brand recognition because of New York. These common folks see him as a hero for what he did in that subway and then even more because he didn't cash in on his popularity," added Roger.

"I am just saying, if he can do this, he may not stay irrelevant for long," agreed Karen in a worried voice.

"Keep folks shadowing his campaign and his rallies, like we do for every suspect organization. We need to get someone into his campaign," said Roger.

"That would be prudent. We are trying," nodded Karen.

"Good. Let us know when you get any actionable intel from inside his campaign. You know, Lexi is asking all our organizations for information about Turner. I want to share the pain," smiled St. Cloud.

Everyone smiled uneasily at this. No one wanted to be on the bad side of Alexis Smythe-Thomas.

# Chapter 37

Lexi sat at her table, her husband Pete sitting next to her in his tuxedo. They were listening to the keynote speech on the first evening at a global summit of major economies in Zurich, Switzerland.

The current chairman of the organization was droning on about their priorities to combat climate change and adhere to the Paris Accords. To ensure all corporations paid a fair amount of taxes, ending corruption, and ensuring human rights were a priority.

With the last statement, Lexi glanced a couple of tables over to where the Minister of Finance of China sat at his own table. His face remained impassive. It was clear many of the chairman's statements were aimed primarily at China, the biggest violator in each case.

She stole a quick glance at the others at her table. Sherman Hallberg, the head of ANC, and his dowdy wife, Beth. Her chief of staff, Mel, and his much younger wife, Ann. With her long black hair in a ponytail over one shoulder, she looked more like a teenager than her actual thirty-three. Harper Tait, the media and TV station mogul, a delightful Scot with his equally delightful wife, Fay. Finally, Rhett Chadwick, and his wife, Virginia Congresswoman Melanie Murphy. They had all made the trip over to Zurich on Air Force Two, as Lexi was officially representing the United States at the conference.

These public conferences of global elites were always disappointing to Lexi. The words were there and possibly even the intent, but countries like China and Russia and to a certain extent India and Brazil would never give up their progress voluntarily.

They'd continue to build their economies on the backs of their people, regardless of public opinion in western Europe, Japan, and America. They all saw this as a way for western countries to keep them from joining the exclusive club of the richest economies in the world.

To her, these forums were an expensive waste of time, money, and resources. Being primarily concerned with excessive virtue signaling. They all wanted points for intent, but no report for actual achievement against what they promised. All that came out was hypocrisy. The results merely armed the skeptics back home with more fodder. Pointing out the rich elites of the world concerned with stopping climate change once again jetting to Switzerland. As they each emitted more carbon per attendee in a single trip, than a family of four in a year.

What frosted Lexi was the inactivity. She had spent a lifetime working her way up from the bottom of the political ladder. Putting herself through Cal Berkeley modeling. She'd earned degrees in economics and international government, graduating magna cum laude, while also traveling the world as a model during and after school.

This had enabled her to create a network of allies to help with her plans. Choosing from an endless stream of partners to find the pick of the litter. The one offering the most power and fastest rise to power. Pete Thomas was the eventual victor.

Heir to a Wall Street fortune and real estate portfolio with few rivals. Grandson of a Senator. She used his connections to get involved in local politics in California. She fought constantly to prove she was more than a pretty face. A trail of vanquished foes, who'd underestimated her, were a testament to her political acumen.

Lexi and Pete had an arrangement. Lexi slept with important men who could advance her career. She collected favors and markers she would use to blackmail and cajole both willing and unwilling former paramours to help her remove obstacles and advance.

Always advancing, never settling, never staying in one role for long. She eventually won a seat in Congress, toiling at the bottom of the Party caucus in the House. She was loud and proud, using her voice and activism to make a name in DC and back in California. Then a Senator retired, supposedly for health reasons. The reality had been her team threatening to expose his dalliance with an underage girl. She used her notoriety and her husband's money to win the special election.

She fought 'the boy's club' in the Senate, championing progressive causes when they were unpopular, and continued to build her network of rich and powerful to support her efforts to rise. After three terms in the senate, she became the first female Majority Leader. She ruled with an iron fist going back and forth from Minority leader and back to Majority as the whims of the voters fluctuated before being picked to serve as Vice President.

She looked back on the thirty-five years of service in government. All the firsts she had accomplished, and she looked forward to putting these sniveling little elitist snobs in their place.

Her legacy would not be one of working on the margins. She would make her agenda reality. There would be no more formal complaints lodged at WTO, the UN, or any other world organization.

No more sanctions with loopholes big enough to sail an oil tanker through. She had waited, even toiled in the shit job of Vice President, watching as the President bungled policy after policy. A compromise candidate to stop a revolt, he failed to follow simple instructions. Putting the entire progressive platform at risk. She'd done what she could, taking over larger and larger portions of the agenda as the President's mind retreated to confusion. It was her time now.

It could not happen fast enough. Now she was acting president since he didn't even remember his name half the time. He could no longer even read the teleprompter. On top of everything else, she now had to perform the role of a lifetime.

Continue in public as the loyal Vice President, while also serving as the clandestine president, preserving the country, keeping it all together, until her election in another nine months. She looked up as everyone began clapping at the conclusion of the speech. She joined in, having tuned out the chairman's entire feckless speech.

As the dinner was served and toasts made, the conversation turned to the election and the first primaries in Iowa and New Hampshire. Sherman lifted his glass.

"Here's to success in the upcoming primaries, Madame Vice President."

"Here, here," said everyone.

"You look to be unbeatable if the polls are correct," stated Harper Tait, in a pleasant Scottish Brogue.

"Well, they are your papers and TV stations, Harper," retorted Lexi. "You tell me how accurate they are."

"The problem with polling is finding people who are actually going to vote and people who do not take pleasure in lying to pollsters. With this many candidates on each side, who knows? Your only real challenge is Senator Klausen. On the opposition side, does it really matter?" said Harper with a wonderful laugh. He sounded and looked like a grandfatherly Santa.

"Too bad we can't prosecute voters for lying," said Rhett dryly.

"Coming from our CIA director, that sounds ominous," commented Mel, joining the conversation.

"I'm an American enjoying a nice dinner with friends at the moment, Mel," replied Rhett, with a small laugh. "Besides, at the CIA we are focused on preventing our 'friends' overseas here and elsewhere from being too interested in the outcomes of our elections."

"A worthy duty," said Sherman.

"Indeed," added Harper. He looked up at Lexi.

"Madame Vice President, what did you think of the speech?"

"Harper, how many times have I told you to call me Lexi?"

"Madame, the Queen was always the Queen. I would never have considered calling her Elizabeth," responded Harper, grinning.

Lexi sighed with a smile, "The Chairman's speech could be the same as the one last year and the year prior. It is always a variation of the same theme. Grand goals, but little progress and no consequence for failure to achieve the goals," she replied in an earnest tone.

"At least there is a recognition of the problem," said Sherman.

"Really? Sherman, let's say your doctor comes to you and tells you there is cancer. Do you go around to two or three or twelve doctors seeking their advice, having them confirm you have a problem? Do you sit around and hold meetings to discuss the different ways to attack your cancer? Do you ask for studies and proposals to review these different treatment options? All the while, the cancer is spreading, perhaps to a point where you can no longer operate and remove it permanently?" explained Lexi as Sherman looked uncomfortable.

"Of course, you don't. You decide on a treatment quickly, and you hit it with everything you have. You either eradicate the cancer from your body or you die trying. It is that black and white. It is the same with so many of the problems we face today. We talk, we study, we plan, and we strategize. Meanwhile, the cancer of white supremacy, or economic inequality, or climate change consequences, keep relentlessly advancing while we dither. The time for talk is past. It is time for action."

Mel, sitting on the other side of Lexi, had reached beneath the table and gently squeezed her arm to signal to her to tone down her answer. She gave him one of her looks, usually a precursor to one of her classic 'off with his head' verbal tirades for which she was famous.

Harper broke the tension with a hearty Santa laugh. "Well, my dear, I can see you intend to be forceful when you are the leader of the free world. I wonder if our Chinese friend over there understands the tsunami headed his way."

Lexi simply smiled, realizing she *did* need to dial it down, as Mel had suggested. She was still only number two in the administration, to the outside world anyway. There would be a time and a place for her to disclose her plans to stop dithering. This was neither.

"Perhaps it is time to bring the spouses into the conversation. What plans do you have while they lock all of us in the meetings? I know Pete here," she said, putting her hand on her husband's arm, "is planning to ski for the next two days."

"Indeed, I am. The snow is fabulous this year," responded Pete in a friendly tone, dutifully playing his part of being seen and not heard.

The other spouses then told of shopping and sightseeing plans, most of which entered and exited Lexi's stream of consciousness with nary a thought. She had long since mastered the art of appearing to listen to the droning speeches of her colleagues in Congress while spending the time processing her own plans and thoughts in her mind.

She had taught herself to listen for keywords during this "zone out" sessions so she wouldn't be caught unaware, or if a topic or question required attention. Vaguely following their conversation, she scanned the room to see if she could detect anything out of the ordinary.

The Chinese minister, Wu Xin, wasn't engaging in conversation. She knew he spoke perfect English, having attended both Oxford and Harvard in his youth. Rumor had it he was on the short list of potential succession to be chairman of the Chinese Communist Party.

His lovely wife Isabel sat next to him. She was half Chinese, half English, born and raised in Hong Kong and a western business executive prior to Wu rising in the party. It was thought having a half Caucasian wife might hold Wu back from the chairmanship. Now, it was increasingly seen as a potential advantage in appealing to the younger generations embracing some of the western culture.

Lexi noticed Wu did not appear to be having a good time. He was at a table with other Asian leaders, new money oligarchs in internet, telecom and ride sharing services in China. The Chinese were still trying to come to grips with having an economy so tied to the global world, something totally against their insular culture. Like everyone else, the global economic malaise caused by near annual COVID outbreaks were still gripping China after the failure of their policy of 'zero COVID', led to millions of Chinese deaths.

With over leveraged real estate companies collapsing at a regular interval, the CCP was having to implement extraordinary measures to ensure their currency did not devalue precipitously. They continued to report to the world modest growth while others were shrinking, but those in the analyst community knew these to be manipulated.

China's economy was in fact contracting and resistance to CCP rule was brewing. China now had ninety million unoccupied apartments in gigantic ghost cities. The camps in western China were no longer filled with only ethnic Uyghurs and Falun Gong practitioners. More and more, political dissidents found themselves sent to these camps.

As she continued to scan the attendees, she saw the usual crowd of sycophants. Moguls, newscasters, a few Hollywood actors and directors, the odd professor or scientist and government service types of all flavors looking to rub elbows with the rich and famous.

What depressed Lexi was the preponderance of bimbos hanging on the arms of so many of the men who frequented these extravaganzas. They were looking to cash in, trading their dignity for money. There were few women present who'd worked their way to success. It always pissed her off how few had been willing to make the sacrifices she had. To strive to outdo the men to achieve what she had. Sure, it was unladylike, but who set the standards of what was ladylike? These men.

While she despised the men, she despised the women even more. All the Botox and boobs for what? They had all the power and yet they only used it to set themselves up with credit cards with no limits. Dependent on their men continuing to pay the bills. Younger versions would eventually replace them. They did not use their position and youthful looks to build power for themselves while they could. Fools. Lexi shifted back into the conversation as she heard her name.

"No comment on Carlton's new young lady," asked Harper.

Lexi turned to look at Carlton Alexander, the head of the largest energy consortium in the world. The lovely woman seated next to him was at least 40 years his junior.

"Oh, you mean his niece? Really, all of you must get your minds out of the gutter," accused Lexi with a smile.

"Seriously, that is his niece?" asked Fay in a Scottish accent every bit as pronounced as her husband.

"Of course not dear, the Vice President is making a joke at our expense," explained Harper.

"Actually, it *is* his niece. His wife had a knee replaced last week and decided not to navigate the streets with a walker," answered Mel.

Lexi smiled in triumph as Harper's face reddened.

"Well, I'll be. My apologies indeed," he said.

"None needed. He is still a cad Harper, but his niece wanted to network. So, he brought her with him on this trip," said Lexi. "She did an internship in my office in Washington years ago."

The evening progressed with endless small talk. Lexi hated making conversation. She hated sitting in idle. She wanted to get up and go talk about shipping concessions with Count Gabriel. Or ask Sir Percival Lowry to stop mining and selling so much Australian coal to the Chinese without also forcing them to curb their emissions. She longed to talk to Maksim Pavlovich about how his network of World Harmony Society NGOs were ensuring the right people were elected in the US state and local elections.

There was so much she could get done in a place like this to advance her platform. She was bound by the constraints of knowing any meeting, any statement, gesture, or action would be scrutinized and acted upon because she was representing the President and the country.

To Lexi, this was like being allowed in the shoe store, but not being allowed to try any on or make any purchases. She could not get home soon enough.

Even in a place like this, private meetings were impossible. Too many reporters, too many people willing to leak a story or start a rumor to advance a career or hurt a rival. She laughed inside at the idea of anything of substance happening at these global gatherings.

It was simply a see and be seen pissing contest from people in love with themselves. From now on, she would refer to it as the World Narcissist Forum. This eased her pain, but only slightly as she resigned herself to another lost weekend. Inauguration day couldn't come soon enough.

# Chapter 38

"Nick, you ready for this?" asked Chuck as Denise watched with a concerned look on her face.

"Guys, I need everyone I can get. This is a chance to hit an audience who may not know me or understand what I am about. You said it yourself; I have one job. To talk to as many folks as possible."

Chuck shook his head. "True, but if you go out and rile them up, like you did in Florida, you may force Lexi to respond. Or in the case today, they may boo you off the stage. Is that what we want, especially when we are starting out? Florida was great, but now you are talking to the true enemies of the Party, Lexi, and the administration."

"Why? Speaking truth is the key to victory. Conservatives are voters too. Voters who disagree vehemently with Lexi. I need as many moderates from *both* parties to have even the slimmest chance. What I have to say should be true for either party," said Nick, putting a hand on Chuck's shoulder. Denise shook her head, looking Nick in the eye.

"Try not to start a riot, and please, please stay away from abortion. There is a right time and place. This is neither."

"No promises," answered Nick, heading out onto the stage.

#

Nick walked onstage at the Conservatives Standing Together conference. He looked out over fifteen thousand attendees in the main ballroom, the fire marshals preventing more from entering. The leader of CST was standing next to Nick, introducing him to the rabidly conservative audience.

"Our next speaker used to be in the Party," lots of boos from the crowd, "and is now an independent candidate for President." A few cheers from the crowd. "As all of you know, his selfless act to prevent the filibuster from being canceled cost him his career in the Senate, and any chance of being re-elected. For this, Senator, we thank you and welcome you to our gathering."

Some in the crowd stood up and clapped for Nick, who, standing on the stage next to the host, waved in acknowledgment of the praise.

The crowd sat back in their seats as Nick approached the podium. "Do you guys' mind if I walk while I talk?" asked Nick, taking the microphone from the podium and walking in front. "I also assume all of you are smart enough to know I used 'guys' as a non-gender specific greeting." The audience dutifully laughed. "See, how hard was that? Common sense still exists." The crowd laughed louder this time as Nick broke the ice, setting a casual tone.

"Thanks for that great intro. I only did what I felt was right. What our founders felt was right. To protect why they put the filibuster in place, regardless of political party," the crowd clapped.

"I don't consider myself a conservative, in the way most of you do. Though I believe we share *many* of the same concerns and beliefs. I believe in conserving the Constitution and the Bill of Rights," folks dutifully clapped again among a smattering of boos at his admission to not being a conservative.

"I have been on the inside, and I can tell you this is not just a difference of opinions or interpretations. Both sides could not be more opposite. The Party leadership sees the Constitution as an impediment. This is not simply a power move. This is a scorched earth, take no prisoners policy. They do not intend to work on the margins any longer. Only the full removal of the Constitution will satisfy their desire. They seek to replace the Bill of Rights with what they believe you should and should not be allowed to do," said Nick, as the audience listened with rapt attention.

"I hate to say this, but you in the Opposition are too fragmented. You can't mount a credible defense. Sorry, I tell the truth." A few in the audience hooted in agreement. There were boos too.

"The best way I can explain this are the stories you hear of people who escape cults. How they were brainwashed with daily dogma into believing the cult's message was the word of God. It was only their message, only their way of life, that was righteous and true. Any who dared differ, who tried to convince you otherwise, were the devil's spawn. Trying to convince those in the cult to recant and follow these non-believers straight to hell. This is what you hear from those who escape the cult. The programming they received and how when their eyes are miraculously opened once again, they see how truly wrong and misguided the cult's message really was. How far from the truth it had strayed." Nick paused, letting his analogy sink in. The crowd was not used to having to think, only to listen and respond to candidate sound bites and promises.

"I was there. Not a full-blown cult member, but in the compound. I got to see their cult in action. You see it every day on TV. In protests outside Supreme Court justice's houses, and on university campuses. In our schools and school boards, in our TV shows and movies, in our public offices and now increasingly, our corporations. The sad news I have to deliver is this is no fringe cult. It is a full-blown religion. In the Progressive Secularism religion, there is a portion of the flock who are true believers, fanatics, who cannot be reasoned with."

"I know you have had a stream of Opposition candidates on this stage, explaining all the problems and how, if they are elected, they will stop this or do that. I get it. That is the game of American politics. Or rather, that is how the game of politics used to be played. My friends, it is no longer a game. One side does not agree there are a set of rules," said Nick, shaking his head, pacing back and forth on stage, varying his tone, volume, and delivery.

"Because you don't understand this, you keep playing along and thinking if you just execute better. Or get 4% more of the black vote, or do better with suburban women, you can get enough to win. Sorry, it doesn't work that way any longer. I have a theory of why that is. You are an educated audience. I don't have to tell you how or why the Constitution works. The bedrock of this is the phrase, 'by the people, for the people'. How does that come about?" asked Nick, leaning to the audience with a hand to his ear.

"Voting," shouted many in the crowd.

"Exactly. Which is why I want to ask you a couple of questions. The answers are common sense, and therefore totally ignored by our media and the Party." The crowd laughed as Nick continued.

"First, why would you not want voter IDs? Especially when every other nation on the planet requires them. Because you are planning on counting ballots of people who a) do not have the right to vote, or b) you are voting *for* people, without their knowledge. That is the *only* logical answer." As Nick finished this, the crowd cheered loudly, many turning to their seat mates surprised a candidate would make such a claim.

He smiled. "Since the Progressive secular religion has successfully weaponized the words racist, people of color, minority, disadvantaged, poor, white privilege, and a host of other terms, they merely need to utter these to stop you from questioning these efforts. For fear of wearing this label like a scarlet letter. Just as you would hold up a clove of garlic to ward off the vampire in the movie, they use their 'words' against anyone who suggests we demand proof of a right to vote." The crowd laughed nervously.

"The effect is the same. You cringe in fear and pain and stop whatever you are doing. Like suggesting voters prove they're eligible to vote. To ensure they only vote once. The fight to stop this is simply about one thing. Counting votes of voters who should not or increasingly, did not vote themselves. Why else fight this? It makes no sense whatsoever. Fighting voter ID use is admitting there is something illegal to stop. If you win fair and square, what do you have to hide?" Nick let this sink in. "What are you afraid of? **The truth!** It is simple as that," finished Nick, his voice rising.

"The idea we cannot get every eligible citizen a valid ID is ridiculous. We manage to get them all social security cards? Why is this a left vs. right question? Why is this not something *all* citizens want?" asked Nick rhetorically as the crowd cheered in agreement.

"Next question. Why the push for mail in voting? Why the push for longer voting periods? Our population is not that much larger than when we all voted on election day for all those other elections, for *two-hundred* years. Both Opposition and Party won those elections. Why suddenly is it such a hardship to get to the voting booth? What changed? Did we all become disabled? Or simply too lazy to choose our leaders?" More laughter.

"No, the push for mail-in ballots is the same reasoning as voter ID. There is less scrutiny on a mail-in ballot. I am sure most of you know this. If you care about our governing principles, that is. Did you know an absentee ballot used to require a reason and a notary to witness the actual signature of the person casting the vote to prove eligibility? We used to take this seriously. Verification of our greatest franchise. There wasn't even a concept of mail in voting. Now it is the norm. Why do you think that is?" said Nick, holding a finger to his chin as if contemplating the question.

"The signature on the mail-in ballot cannot be scrutinized *that* carefully, now can it? We expect every poll worker to process ballots as fast as possible. Look up a name, confirm they exist, next. Then the ballot is opened. They separate the envelope with the signature from the ballot, itself containing no identification, and never the twain shall meet again."

"Mail in votes are *not* secure. There is no validation of our greatest franchise. Remove this single option and your elections suddenly get a lot more secure and more honest. Like they used to be. I am not saying folks who vote by mail are fraudulent. But relying on mail in balloting *does* allow those who would cheat to do so more easily. Don't believe me. Look up the report by no less than Jimmy Carter, who came to the same conclusion in a bipartisan report on third world voting corruption. And we are not even third world, at least not yet."

This time, people cheered and yelled in agreement. They were getting it and the truth of Nick's statements were making sense too many. This was simply common sense for anyone considering the actual words.

"Next up, voting machines. If a voting machine is connected to the internet, doesn't that mean someone with skills could manipulate votes or change tallies or do many things that only a handful of smart people could figure out? How many TV shows do you see where the computer genius hacks the world's most secure computers, magically, within the hour of the show?" The crowd laughed.

"I guarantee you it is not that easy. It might take two hours," said Nick, deadpan, as the audience roared.

"A voting machine is not a Pentagon supercomputer and is, in fact, much easier to hack. Plus, humans program them. To claim they are tamper proof is an insult to *your* intelligence. They are, in fact, *so* tamper proof, no one is ever allowed to examine any of them after an election. How would anyone know if someone tampered with them? There really isn't anything left to be said on this. It is so obviously a risk to free, fair, and honest elections.

Anytime someone says trust us, it is secure and fair, do exactly the opposite." The crowd laughed loudly.

Nick drank from his water bottle, looking out over the crowd. He saw a surprising diversity of faces, ages, and genders. It was not a lily-white, older crowd the media loved to portray when discussing conservative gatherings. They all patiently waited for him to continue.

"As I tell everyone I talk to, we must always ask, who stands to gain from this? There is a lot of money in these contracts and elected officials decide whose machines to use. Reliance on voting machines is even more suspect than reliance on mail in ballots. There is simply too much you never see. Yes, checking off your name in a book is so *old-fashioned*. As is voting on a paper ballot. Voting machines are modern and fast. An improvement. Really? Exactly what is happening in that machine?" Nick paused, looking out over the enthralled crowd.

"When Mrs. Kleinschmidt checks my name off in the voter book, she knows who I am and I know her. Since she was also my third-grade teacher. There is no doubt about my eligibility and who I am. This may be old-fashioned, but it is effective. Could this be exactly why they hate it so? Replace my paper ballot with an impersonal machine, where they can control what comes out of it. And the paper record of the actual vote? No longer needed. Trust us. Why are we interjecting complications into what is a simple process? All it is doing is letting me check a box on a machine instead of a piece of paper. We have had tabulating machines to count paper ballots for decades. Mark here, add to count for this person," said Nick, making imaginary motions for stacking ballots in two piles.

"Abacuses have been around for millennia. Some things we do not need to improve. Where the mark is and who it is for is a binary decision best confirmed by humans. We are spending *billions* on machines to automate a process that does not need automation. I can hire a bunch of temporary workers with that money to count paper ballots, with billions to spare." Nick paced the stage, waiting for this last bit to sink in.

"How about audits? I am not talking about recounts, which are only meant to give the appearance of transparency. But real audits, to not *count*, but *confirm* eligibility. I'm not worried about the count. I know we are good at recounting ballots. My concern is with who cast the vote for that person. If you won and, as you say, you won by an overwhelming majority, why would you fight tooth and nail to prevent ballots from being examined? From having ballot signatures matched against rolls of eligible voters? Preferably live voter rolls. Maybe even going as far as checking a few mail in ballots at random to verify the person whose name is on it actually cast a ballot. You know, by maybe asking them? Did you vote? Not even for whom, just whether you cast a ballot like the machine or mail in ballot, says you did. I am sure there would be no shortage of funding to verify with Bob in Prescott, Arizona, or Valerie in south central LA or Jamal in Minneapolis if they indeed did cast a vote *themselves*. Because we show you voted."

"Again, I ask. What the hell are you afraid of if everything was on the up and up? If you won fair and square, why not let independent parties review the actual data? The votes cast, confirming they are by eligible and living voters. Put aside all those questions and conspiracy theories about each vote for one candidate being tallied at 0.75 and the other at 1.25? Why oh why would you allow electronic voting but have no paper trail to cross reference to make sure the data matches the votes cast? These simple solutions would put an end to that conspiracy theory in a heartbeat. Why does everyone not want this? Right?" 'Yes' was the thunderous reply.

"How about the logs to see what IP addresses were logged into the machine and when? Oh, and those last-minute software changes, just before election, how about we have some independent software coders, maybe some white hat hackers, determine what changes they loaded into what machines right before the election?" The crowd was getting enthusiastic and shouted their approval and agreement at each of Nick's suggestions.

Nick threw his hands in the air in frustration. "Hey if you won by a landslide, by millions, I repeat, why the *fuck* would you not want to support any efforts to prove once and for all that none of these claims are true?" The crowd went crazy at Nick's language and question.

"Finally, why is it so important to wipe all the data in these voting machines so quickly? Before anyone can examine them. I think you know the answer to this. Their own answers, their behavior, the frantic posturing against any oversight, demonstrate a need to hide *something*. The same as IDs and mail in balloting. I'm sure many, if not most, are completely legitimate, but when elections are decided by 10,000 votes in a handful of counties, widespread fraud is unnecessary. What is necessary is to restore faith in the integrity of these new systems. Me walking in and voting on a paper ballot in my local precinct is not subject to fraud," said Nick to thunderous applause and another standing ovation.

Nick waited for everyone to sit down again. "Last question: why in the world would you stop counting ballots on election night? What plausible reason could you have to stop, unless of course you were running out of ballots to count and the outcome you wanted is not occurring? Why is it this is only happening in the same key counties in the same key states that swing the election one way or the other? Pretty convenient, isn't it?" said Nick with a smile and a shake of his head as the crowd broke out again in enthusiastic agreement.

"Seems a bit too convenient to me. Then when they count again, the remaining ballots go 99% for one candidate. That in the statistical world is an impossibility and you know what?" said Nick, pausing for effect. "The science of statistics *is* settled." The crowd laughed loudly.

"There are common sense answers to each of these questions. Therefore, none of the networks cover any of these possibilities. These stories are never written. This is why the Party squashes every investigation. Or sues anyone who tries to seek the truth. Voting IDs stop ineligible voters from voting. Absentee and mail-in voting are votes cast out of sight and out of oversight. Voting machines run on software. Humans write software. We can code it to do whatever someone wants. A machine attached to an internet connection on election night can be altered. Audits reveal who and how cheating was done and cannot be allowed under any circumstances. We have an election one night every 4 years. We have over 3000 counties. All of them except ten, in four or five states, count without having to stop. Many of these are much larger than the ones having problems. There is no reason to stop, ever. Unless you are either serially incompetent, election after election, or you are trying to *alter* the outcome. Call in the national guard and have them count votes. Manpower is not an issue," said Nick, his voice rising.

"I say this as a concerned citizen, not as Party or Opposition. Most of this seems to favor one side. Sadly, the Opposition does not seem interested in stopping this either, even when they are potentially the victims. Why is that?" asked Nick, throwing up his hands again in disbelief.

"This is what it looks like when one side no longer cares about the rules, or about being caught, and is only concerned with completing their goal of total control. I said it before. They've gone beyond a cult. It is now a full-fledged religion. Not an open-minded one."

"This is Progressive Sharia. It is restrictive and rigid. You dare to vary from the doctrine. They excommunicate you. If you are lucky, maybe you can keep leading a life in hiding. If not, you are broken and destroyed and ultimately you become a non-person in their eyes and in their society," said Nick, drinking from his bottle. The crowd was listening intently. Amazed at the lack of concern of a sitting US Senator being so brutally honest regarding the state of American elections.

"Then each of you needs to ask a question, a deep soul-searching question. Does the Party, no scratch that, the Progressive Sharia religion in charge of the Party, really have my best interests at heart? Does that sound like a party or a religion that believes in an honest difference of opinion? In adherence to the tenets of the Bill of Rights? Is this the same party that always claimed to be the party of tolerance? The party with the big tent welcoming everyone? Now maybe it's because I was in the tent, but I didn't see or experience anything remotely resembling tolerance. Maybe I was looking tolerance up in the wrong dictionary," admitted Nick, getting laughs from the crowd.

"Totalitarianism, Communism, Socialism, Fascism, call it what you will. Progressivism is simply a new name for an old ideology. The result is the same. Prepare to give up what freedom you have. I will finish with this one admonishment. Please remember, I am not Opposition, but I once was a moderate Party member. I have been behind the curtain and have seen the wizards of Oz at work."

"They really don't *care* about any of your issues, they only say they do to get your vote. To get you in their tent. To tell you they care about you. In fact, before I finish this speech, the Progressive media machine will blast out reports about my 'hateful' rhetoric and my advocation of conspiracy theories around voter fraud and insane pronouncements of the Progressive agenda bringing Armageddon. How I am the problem for even daring to ask for transparency in our voting processes. How I am the one causing this doubt, because I dare to question it. Mark my words." Folks cheered and laughed as Nick described how he was now public enemy number one. Some held up phones.

Nick noticed the phones. "See, I told you so," he said, laughing. He held up his hands to calm the crowd.

"Listen, this last bit is really important to your survival and your sanity. I have come up with two tools to use to help you survive in today's crazy world. Using common sense to expose lies. The Flip and the Mirror. The Flip is a way to find the true facts. Flip anything you see, read, or hear 180 degrees. Since the Progressive Sharia mob controls most media, what you hear will be what they want you to hear, what they want you to see, and what they want you to read unless you work hard to find verifiable facts."

"If you use the Flip," Nick held up his arm in front, palm down, and flipped it to palm up. "If they say the vote was fair, it was not, if they say Russia changed votes, they did not, if they say you are a racist, you are not, if they say COVID came from a pangolin, it didn't, if they say China is cooperating, they are not, if they say AI is not a threat, it is. Flip everything you hear from the mainstream media around and you are much closer to the truth they don't want you to know." As Nick made each example, he flipped his hand from palm down to palm up, as he 'flipped' each lie to truth. By the time he got to the last few examples, members of the audience were emulating the Flip as he referenced a lie and countered it with the probable truth. He smiled as he saw the attendees nodding and talking to each other as they flipped their hands.

"Next is the Mirror, when you have a conversation with someone and it does not add up, hold up your hand palm out, against your chest. Reflect the hate and their rhetoric back on them. If they call you a racist, they are more likely the racist. If they say you are the sexist, they are more likely the sexist. When they say you are climate denier, because you don't believe man is *entirely* responsible for climate change, they are the denier because they have fallen for the narrative and false statements about settled science." The crowd cheered loudly at this statement.

"You get the idea. Make them think about why they are saying it. What they are saying. Reflect it back on them and let it roll right off your back. I can sum the Mirror up in one word. Hypocrisy. Think about it. You are fine with them having their beliefs, but they cannot allow you to not agree with them. That is Progressive Sharia. Change or be persecuted until you do," said Nick as he noticed half the audience holding up their Mirror and others practicing the Flip.

"To really finish, I am running for President because I am afraid of what happens to our country if the Progressives win. I know what they want to accomplish. Now so do you. You saw the votes a few weeks ago. Gun control, supreme court packing, expanded blue statehood, amnesty, industry destroying green New Deals and unlimited debt ceilings. Luckily, we stopped them this year. If we lose in November, this time next year all those bills will be passed."

"I don't want to live in that country, and I don't think you do either. We have to stop them at the ballot box *this* time. If we don't, the next election will be 98% for the Party candidate ala Saddam Hussein or Robert Mugabe style elections. I like our Constitution. I think our government is too big and I would do everything I can to shrink it. Stop the insanity of the voluntary return of segregation. Put decision making back into the hands of the individuals. Return governing to locals as much as possible. We have to stand up to tyranny, think for ourselves, and address this while we still have our freedom. I thank you for your time," finished Nick as the crowd stayed on their feet and gave him cheers and loud clapping. The head of CST came back on stage.

"My friends, Senator Nick Turner. A truly brave and honest man. Thank you for articulating your stances so clearly, Senator."

Nick nodded and acknowledged the crowd, who continued to clap for a minute before Nick headed off stage.

# Chapter 39

"Senator, so you are in favor of enforcing Voter IDs as a barrier to voting? Knowing it will disenfranchise primarily poor black voters," asked the AP reporter, standing outside the ballroom after Nick's speech at CST.

Nick shook his head, smiling. "You know I can't remember which black commentator said it, but I will paraphrase their reply to this idiocy. He said, 'when did blacks suddenly become unable to drive, or fly, or enter a baseball stadium or a football stadium to enjoy a game beside their fellow able-bodied citizens? When did blacks suddenly become unable to find a way to the grocery store, or the doctor, or the corner drugstore? Why all the sudden have blacks become a nation of shut-ins and children unable to figure out how to vote on their own without the help of Party ballot harvesters'? I'm paraphrasing, but I'm sure you know of whom I am speaking and can cite the proper source."

"But Senator, it is a fact, large numbers of poor blacks, primarily in urban areas, do not have IDs," continued the AP reporter.

"The reality is this. If fraud was not happening. If our populace was not losing confidence in the integrity of our elections. Because of the rampant use of unverifiable ballots sent to every resident of the country, including 45 million illegal aliens. We would not need to enforce voter ID as a way of ensuring only citizens with a right to vote were indeed the ones voting."

"Senator, there is no proof of voter fraud on such a wide scale."

"If the Party had not passed ballot harvesting and expanded the mail in voting period to three weeks and sometimes a month or more before elections. If the Party did *not* pass laws to not allow states to purge dead people from the registered voter rolls. To not even check to see if voters were registered and to allow votes to count two weeks after an election, we would not need voter IDs."

"Senator, there is no proof that any of these led to illegal votes. This is all conspiracy theory that has been debunked."

"Really. By whom? If it was all debunked, why do so many on both sides believe our voting systems are now compromised? These are your polls, not mine. Could it be what they see happen in each election? Then there is the final straw, like I said in my speech, where after the count stops and restarts all the ballots break for one candidate."

"Senator, it is because you keep talking about it," replied AP.

"Come on. Do you really think we are all that stupid? If the shoe had been on the other foot and the candidate from my former party had been on the losing end of these shenanigans, do you honestly think we would not have demanded to see the paper trail? If it could not be delivered or didn't exist, do you think we wouldn't have demanded the vote be invalidated by a judge? Forcing that state to go again until we won?" The reporters began shouting questions. Nick held up a hand.

"Let me finish my answer to the Voter ID question."

The AP reporter ignored Nick's request and shouted his follow up, "Again, Senator, everything you say is conspiracy, fear mongering. None of these accusations have ever been proved. This is stuff the losers use to damage the integrity of our elections and the process."

Nick looked at the reporter before answering.

"While I blame the Party for their deeds and actions regarding manipulation of the vote, the real felon in all of this is *you*," said Nick, waving his arm around the room. "I called you big media, but I think I'll start calling you American *Pravda*. You're the propaganda wing of the Progressive Party. The right is no better, just not as effective."

"Your role, and the reason the First Amendment exists, is not to protect *you*, it is to allow you to help us learn facts and help us form our own opinions. To count on you to dig for facts and demand for transparency, as I have advocated today. Instead, you hide behind the First Amendment. Do the bidding of one party, spewing out their propaganda, hoping to manipulate the masses into supporting their agenda. Then you attack any who dare to point out your hypocrisy."

Nick looked again to his left to make sure Greg was filming the entire encounter. He knew theirs would be the only footage posted in its entirety.

"American *Pravda* is to blame for this state of affairs. Journalism has become a cancer in society. You feed on the host and provide no benefit. Yours used to be a noble profession. Ferreting out the facts. Doggedly following leads and exposing hypocrisy. Informing the public to allow them to form their own opinion. Now you bludgeon people into thinking your way or persecute them when they dissent. You are hypocrisy in action. Do as I say, because I tell you too."

"Senator, that is a mass generalization and unfairly attacks journalism," replied Reuters.

"Cancel culture only works with a willing set of goons and hit squads in the American *Pravda* media. You should look in the mirror and realize you are the black shirts of the Progressives and one of the genuine problems in America. Stop trying to stop us from ensuring only eligible citizens vote in our elections," said Nick in a fiery tone. He then shifted to a mock light tone and called on the next reporter.

"Ms. Bergamo, what is your *question?*"

"Senator, I take issue with you painting with such a broad brush in blaming the press for all the ills of the world. I'll still ask my original question. You claim the Progressive agenda is a form of Sharia. Do you care to explain further? I don't believe the Party are enforcing child marriages, stoning anyone, or mutilating female genitalia?" she asked.

"Ms. Bergamo, thankfully, you are correct. The Progressive Sharia party is not espousing those horrible activities, at least not directly. However, Sharia is more than just its more brutal actions, it is a state of mind. One of total control over choices. Choices about what to learn, who can learn, what to say, who can get away with saying what and what you can and cannot do. Please remember I have seen this myself in the Middle East, so I am speaking with first-hand knowledge."

Lauren held her phone toward Nick, recording his words.

"In this manner, the Progressives are achieving more and more dominance using their allies in the *Pravda* media, big tech and now woke corporations to enforce their restrictive ways. Look around at the things you can no longer say or do, the words, the phrases. To be a moderate or centrist like I am is the same as right winger in their eyes. If you dare to disobey, the mob comes after you, in effect stoning you in the public square until you grovel in absolution or until they effectively kill you. If not physically, then in every other way that matters. Limiting your ability to function in society. This does not differ from Islamic Sharia. Toe the line or pay the penalty for deviating from the rules. Progressive Sharia functions in the same manner."

"Come on Senator. While you talk about stoning, it is not happening. We are not practicing honor killing. I am not wearing a burka. More than half of those in college are women. You are cherry picking the worst examples of Sharia to make your points," finished Lauren, as other reporters smiled at her counterattack.

"If the Party wins, the result will trend more like Islamic Sharia and away from our Bill of Rights. We have already seen what they plan if they win. You saw the bills they tried to pass. Choice will be diminished, certainly if you are in the opposition. The destruction of your will to resist. They are already dictating what we must teach to our children, regardless of what the parents think is right or wrong. We had an example of what it will be like, during the lockdowns in the Party led states during the pandemics. Just like the Taliban destroyed thousands of years of history in Afghanistan. We are doing the same with our own history. 1619, CRT, removing statues and monuments, destroying Mt. Rushmore, changing the names of schools, even suggesting cities change their names. This is exactly what the Taliban, practicing Sharia, did."

Before anyone could interrupt, Nick continued.

"This is my stand. I will educate and I will strive to make people open their eyes and realize Progressivism is the next genocidal movement if it is not checked. It is already well on the way to killing our Constitutional Republic. If we don't recognize it and stand up against it, we too will fall. You may not like the truth, but you need to face it with open eyes and ears and ignore what American *Pravda* is telling you is *not* happening," said Nick in an almost pleading tone, urging people to wake up and do some research. "You can also choose to ignore me and call me a conspiracy nut job. That is your *right*. Just as it is mine to question the current narrative."

Lauren was scribbling in her notebook with her recorder going as Margie cut in to end the press questions.

"Sorry, that is all the time we have," said Margie, moving Nick from the group as they continued to shout questions, one of which caused Nick to turn.

"Did someone ask if I don't think black lives matter? Who was that?" A hand went up and a young black woman came forward.

"Yes, I asked the question. Clearly you think the ARL is not a worthy cause," she said.

"May I ask what your news organization is?" asked Nick politely.

"NPR," she answered flippantly. Nick glanced at her Che Guevara emblazoned T-shirt.

"Really? While I think the veracity of your claim is questionable, I'll be happy to answer the question. Black lives do matter. So does every life. Trying to elevate one race above another or an ethnicity or a gender provokes division and disharmony. By trying to overemphasize one, you are creating a divided society."

"You mean like the white race has enjoyed for a couple thousand years?" asked the 'NPR' reporter.

"Miss, ARL does one thing. Not help blacks, but put people into tribes. To promote segregation and undue all the progress we have made since 1965 to ensure equality of opportunity."

"Ya right. Easy for a white man to say," she replied, dropping the facade of being a 'journalist'.

Nick continued. "Only now, it is not even separate but equal, it is separate, split, and pit each against the other, claiming equality is not the goal, only equity. That is straight out of Alinsky, but I am sure you already know that, don't you, as an admirer of Che? I support equality of race, sex, culture, and opportunity. I unequivocally denounce equity. ARL is about equity. It is wrong, and it is undemocratic," said Nick, turning again and leaving this time.

"Whitey, your time is coming. Mark my words," said the woman as she hurled an object at Nick. It hit him in the back. It appeared to be a small balloon full of white paint. She turned, retreating into the crowd, making it to the hallway before Earl could find her and take a picture.

Nick stopped, calmly taking off his jacket and held it out as it dripped paint onto the floor of the convention center carpet. He turned to look at Earl, who shook his head.

Turning to the media, all dutifully filming. "I don't suppose any of you are going to report this as an activist attacking a US Senator with their back turned, nor that she ruined my favorite sport coat," asked Nick, dryly.

Someone in the crowd said, "Too bad it wasn't your face."

Earl looked around, trying to find who made the statement.

Nick laughed. "Forget it Earl. This is how journalists now work. Hide in the crowd and insult you, afraid to say it to your face. Insult you on social media, where they cannot be held accountable," said Nick, looking through the crowd. No one owned up to the statement while he stared.

"They throw balloons when your back is turned. And hate online. This is the tactic of the coward and American *Pravda*. Of the person and party who knows their stance is neither noble nor right and will never gather a majority of legitimate support," said Nick as they finally turned to go.

Earl shook his head, catching up and looking behind as they walked. Nick was not making his job easy.

# Chapter 40

"Today, Senator Nick Turner, independent candidate for president, got on stage at the Conservatives Standing Together gathering in Dallas. He all but accused the current president of having won by cheating in the prior elections. His inflammatory rhetoric, reminiscent of prior Opposition candidates, has returned once again to 'The Big Lie'."

"He claims that somehow efforts to ensure voters of all socio-economic means, people of color, and those in urban environments who do not have easy access to polls or hours to take off jobs to stand in lines are not entitled to vote. Making voting accessible for these folks through absentee and mail in balloting is now evidence of out-and-out fraud by the Party, according to the Senator."

"This is obviously a desperate attempt to gain coverage while he is barely registering in any national polls. Frankly, this kind of talk is dangerous to our democracy. The authorities should look into shutting it down before he inflames the white supremacists who still believe this fallacy. I hope the administration, FBI and Homeland Security are all monitoring the fallout from speeches like this to ensure we continue to have safe, fair, and honest elections. We refuse to encourage this behavior by reporting on his conspiracy theories."

Greg turned off the TV in their conference room in Denver.

"God damn it Nick," said Denise, angrily stalking around the conference room. "You've got to tone it down. You are the example of the angry white male. Every time you answer a question, you are so righteously indignant. You're scaring people,"

"They're making fun of you on the late-night shows. They're calling you 'the Hulk' because you go ballistic on reporters. 'Turner, SMASH'," said Margie. "Now we have networks calling for FBI investigations and censorship."

"I notice they conveniently left out the part about a US Senator being assaulted by a black ARL activist," pointed out Nick.

"No blood, no foul," shrugged Denise. "And all your Sharia nonsense. Good God, Nick, now you are making this about religion?"

"She's right. You need to dial it back a notch. You don't want to be the butt of every late-night joke, and we certainly do not want the FBI making itself a nuisance to our campaign," noted Chuck seriously. "American *Pravda*? It is absolutely brilliant, but man, are they going to come unglued if it sticks."

Nick looked around the conference room at his team. Margie seemed to be with Chuck and Denise. Greg and Earl looked like they disagreed, and Jenny and Jer were both looking away.

"I understand your concerns," acknowledged Nick.

Denise jumped in, raising her hands in resignation. "Here comes the 'but'."

"But," said Nick, smiling. "We all know this entire campaign is unorthodox," Denise snorted in agreement.

"I speak from the heart. You know what? I am angry. And concerned. If the FBI and Homeland want to come after me, we'll just go up in the polls. I welcome their attention. I am disappointed, and frankly, I am disgusted. This needs to come out in my statements to the press and in my speeches."

"Oh yeah, it comes across loud and clear. I'm sure Homeland is paying attention even if the audience you want is not," vented Denise.

"I don't think the silent majority hear this enough. Who else is having this discussion? Saying what they *think* out loud? I care. The only way I can get them off their lazy asses is to challenge them to get angry. To let them know if they stay a blob, someone will eventually eradicate them like the pests the Progressives think they are. This reaction," said Nick, waving at the blank monitor, "means we are over the target."

"I wanted to answer Bergamo's question differently, but believe it or not, I showed amazing restraint. Genital mutilation is here, it is called encouraging our children to contemplate transgenderism as a gender choice in junior high or even earlier. By all means, when they are adults, go for it. But leave the children alone. Voluntary castration of young boys and fifteen-year-old girls cutting off their healthy breasts. Puberty blockers being handed out no questions asked to ten-year-olds. It is not the government telling them to do this, true, but it is Progressive Sharia when they tell the parents, they have no right to tell their children 'no' or to even complain this is being offered as a choice to impressionable and incredibly naïve children. By so-called doctors! This is just wrong."

"Nick, I get you are upset. This is a subject that doesn't sell. People don't want to hear this. It's too disturbing," advised Denise.

"Jenny, you're the only one with kids. As a parent, would you want your children doing this without your knowledge?" asked Nick, not noticing Denise stiffen at the statement.

Jenny did not hesitate. "No." Nick nodded his agreement.

He looked at Denise. "I think you're wrong. My god, what a degenerate cesspool we have allowed to thrive. This is much worse than the hedonism that brought down Greece and Rome. Caligula has nothing on what kids these days are doing or watching others do. Now with KooKoo you have all these teenagers filming themselves doing all kinds of crap and posting it for money. They are destroying their futures and they don't even know it." Nick took a couple of calming breaths.

"Mom's care about this. So do Dads. If this is news to them, it is only because they don't want to admit it is happening. Avoiding the subject won't solve it. Unless I bring it up and make sure everyone knows where this is coming from. From the progressives represented by Lexi. They are going to make this a reality for all. Removing the parent from everything after conception. I also want the moderate Party voters to wake up too."

"Come on Nick. Sex, Social Security, and religion. These are the third rails of politics. A focus on sex makes people uncomfortable, no matter how true. Talk about crime, illegals, guns, hell, even abortion, but leave these alone. It is a no-win strategy," argued Denise.

Chuck held up a hand as Nick prepared to answer.

"Nick, I agree with Denise on this one. I don't disagree with anything you're saying. We have to win voters. This ain't gonna do it."

"Guys, you are thinking like campaign managers for a politician who cares. Yes, I'm angry. I'll continue to be in the face of those who ask me to clarify my positions. I will challenge America to wake up from their opioid and marijuana induced comas to make one last stand. Because I will NOT be one of those people getting off a train car asking what I could have done to stop all of this from happening," announced Nick, now thoroughly worked up.

"You see," said Denise, throwing her hands up and turning to look at the others. "This is exactly what I am talking about. How the hell do you expect to keep this up for the next 8 months? You are going to stroke out or get shot by some lunatic you piss off. It could easily have been a knife in your back today. You can't keep this up."

"Why not? You worried about me physically? Don't. Worried about me mentally? You shouldn't have taken the job. You had to know I was already mental," said Nick. Everyone stared at him.

He stared back, opening his hands. "Sorry, I guess I need to use Harry Potter's accent when I say 'mental', right?" tried Nick, in a horrible attempt at a British accent.

"Oh my God, please stop it," said Margie, holding her ears as the others laughed.

"In the words of Hermione, 'you're saying it wrong'," intoned Chuck in a perfect British accent. "If you are going to try, please do it right. You'll just end up pissing everybody off if you do that overseas. Like JFK did with his 'Ich bin ein Berliner'. When he tried to say he was a Berliner and instead said he was a jelly donut," said Chuck dead serious as the rest of the staff laughed, harder.

"You know, that was an urban myth. JFK said it correctly. Another example of journalistic malpractice," said Nick.

"Really?" asked Chuck, crushed. "But it was such a good story. Now it is ruined by the truth."

"Always the killjoy, huh Nick?" said Denise with a smile.

"There is a cliche that does work, 'the truth hurts'. I hope to hit everyone upside the head with a metaphorical 2x4. If that makes them uncomfortable," shrugged Nick, "maybe they need to hurt to understand what they have to lose."

"Please don't say that out loud, OK?" begged Margie.

"I understand all of your concerns. Anything else would come across as fake because my heart wouldn't be in it. As I have said previously, if folks are concerned or get other offers, I wouldn't stop anyone from shifting to other campaigns. I am Don Quixote; except I know those are windmills and not giants. It is *my* crusade."

"Not for nothing, but our fundraising keeps going up. I think it is Hibi to be honest," said Jenny. "Our postings there are getting millions of views and some of them have millions of likes and forwards. Hibi is taking off like fire. They are well over 100 million app downloads now and they have only been out a few weeks."

"Hibi?" asked Nick.

"Hibi is what folks are calling Hibiscus online," answered Margie. "Jeremy was right. The people love the clean conversations and the lack of trolls. I know he is already facing a couple of first amendment-based lawsuits. He's going to use the same defense as the other social media outlets used to censor the Opposition. If they rule against him, it will be a terrible precedent to set for the other guys to face, so I don't think it will get anywhere."

"Do I need to do anymore spots?"

"Maybe," said Margie, turning to Jer and Jenny. "How many views does that first post have now?" asked Margie.

"Give me a sec," said Jer, looking at his laptop. "Wow, we're up to 104 million views."

"Is that a lot?" asked Nick.

"For a political ad, it's huge. For a Taylor Swift song or video, she gets that on the first day," said Jer, laughing.

"OK. Who is Taylor Swift?" said Nick in a deadpan voice. Jer started to reply with a shocked look on his face when Earl couldn't hold it back any longer and started laughing.

"Hilarious guys," said Jer, shaking his head.

"Sorry Jer, even I know who Taylor Swift is. Hell, she's probably closer to my age than yours. How bad have I made your polling life?"

"Jeez, let's not open that can of worms," groaned Denise, a look of disgust on her face.

"Hey, you know why I am doing it. You, of all people."

"I do, but I don't necessarily agree. If people don't think you are relevant, they are going to tune out," warned Denise.

"If I start showing up in the polls, Lexi is going to smash us like a bug. I need her focused on the Opposition and her primary opponents and leaving me alone."

"Accusing her of implementing Sharia will not piss her off, I'm sure," pointed out Denise, in a sarcastic tone.

"Ah, come on Denise, she does the same every day to much larger audiences. Jer, what about the polling?"

"Well, I am trying to figure out how to poll without triggering the Turner effect. I understand why you tell your supporters to lie, but boy, it is skewing the samples. No one I've talked to knows how to take this into account in the modeling. We don't know how many people are doing as you ask, and we don't know who they say they are for when they do lie. It is creating worthless samples," explained Jer.

"I am truly sorry, Jer. We have to gauge our support in other ways. Crowd sizes, donations, etc. I want the polls to be hopelessly flawed this time around and I want them to be even more overconfident. Any ballot updates?" asked Nick, looking at Chuck.

"Well, I'd say we are in pretty good shape for most of them. As you remember, when you announced you were running, we only had a month to get on Alabama, Arkansas, and New Hampshire ballots. It was close, but we made it on all of them. Offices and staff are up and running in each state. We continue to recruit paid and volunteer staff," said Chuck. "Jenny, what do you think, any concerns?"

"There are a few Upper Midwest states and surprisingly Texas is becoming a bit of a pain as well. Because you are not in the primaries, some of them are questioning your eligibility, citing 'Sore Loser' laws. None of these should apply, but we are watching them closely. I suspect once they choose the candidates, they may come after you if you are eroding their support in any state. Probably from both parties, unfortunately. I have some lawyers lined up to fight any lawsuits if they come up," said Jenny.

"This is one place where your polling trick may benefit you. As long as they think you are not relevant, they may not fight your ballot inclusion. No one cares about the libertarian or the communist party candidate, but popular third parties like Nader and Perot turned elections against candidates. They will be on the lookout for you making any kind of move," explained Denise.

"Hopefully Nick is pulling from both sides, so it won't impact only one candidate and trigger them to go after us," remarked Chuck.

"What happens if I don't make it on a state ballot? When do they print these?" asked Nick.

"They print most 6 weeks before the election, maybe more this time with all the new mail-in rules on some state books. If you don't get on, and we lose any appeals, we would have to resort to write-in votes. Realistically, you would never win a state relying on write-ins. The only time it ever worked was a race in Alaska and that was a Senate vote and she only needed 100,000 write-in votes to win," said Jenny.

"We need to be ready. I have a feeling we may need these votes and I am still not confident we'll be on every ballot. As you say all the time, I piss off a lot of people. Plus, we can't forget Pavlovich and his World Harmony Society organizations. His WHS has funded all these radical leftists Attorney General and Secretaries of State and other state election officials." As Nick finished, Jenny's phone started buzzing, and she got up to take the call.

"Nice, Nick. Nothing like being on Pavlovich's radar," said Chuck, shaking his head.

"You have to hand it to him. He's taken control of a lot of processes defining how the voting process operates and is adjudicated. All those lawsuits would have to get through his people, and I know I would be enemy number one to all of them because of the filibuster vote."

"You can't underestimate Pavlovich and his reach. I have seen it in action through the years. Thankfully, always on my side," said Denise. "You have to know Lexi is his preferred candidate, so he is doing everything he can to make sure she wins. Like he did for the current President and all the Party presidents for the last 40, maybe even 50 years. If we become relevant, we can expect all manner of dirty tricks."

"Way to go boss, let's make this as hard as we can," said Greg from one corner, where he was staring into a laptop.

"Ah Greg, you know you love it," grinned Nick.

"Like a root canal," answered Greg in a serious tone, still looking down at his laptop while holding up a hand, thumbs up.

"Look at mild mannered Greg. and what this campaign has done to him. Now he is sarcastic and mean," said Nick in a hurtful tone.

"It comes from hanging around with you and Earl. I take no credit for my 'change'," said Greg, eliciting a laugh from the others.

"Don't blame me. All the credit goes to Nick. But while we are at it, can we talk security for a minute?" asked Earl.

"Sure, what about it?"

"Ignoring your paint balloon incident, we are getting more and more folks on the payroll. Strategy documents are being produced and sent around. With cyber espionage and ransomware becoming so prevalent, I suggest we get a couple of white hat guys on the payroll to protect our info. Last thing we need is a ransomware attack costing us precious funds to regain access to your road videos," noted Earl.

"I'm cool with that. Denise?" asked Nick.

"Makes sense."

"Ok, now let's talk about *your* security," said Earl. "As we saw today, they are getting a bit more aggressive. You're making a lot of people mad. I talked to the Secret Service, and you would only qualify for a secret service detail if you hit 12% minimum in the polling. As this is not likely with the lie to the pollsters plan, we need to be thinking about your personal security as we move along through the spring and summer and closer to the election. I am proposing we hire a couple of folks to be our advance team. To go ahead of where we are planning. To be your eyes and ears and do some of what the secret service would do."

"Not yet Earl, let's wait and see what happens with the crowds. I am fine with you taking care of this for now. If it becomes a problem, we can look into more security, but for now, I prefer to keep it low profile," said Nick, holding up a hand as Earl protested.

"Earl, I know, one crazy with a knife or a gun and a desire to get 15 minutes of fame. A water balloon filled with paint does not count. First, I have to get famous enough for it to matter and when that happens, I promise I will let you beef it up. You and I both know nothing will stop a sniper or someone willing to trade their life for mine. It is a risk I have to take. I have been there before. Sometimes you have to trust fate," admitted Nick with a shrug of his shoulders.

"Hindsight says trusting fate is often a poor strategy," said Earl.

Jenny came back into the room, looking pale.

"What?" asked Nick and Denise at the same time.

"Apparently, the Office of Disinformation Governance in Homeland is requesting you to be permanently banned from all social media channels. I don't think Jeremy will comply, but all the others probably will. Plus, I just heard from a friend at DOJ. They are thinking about bringing you up on hate speech charges for the claims you are making about voter fraud and specifically the comparisons of the Party to Islamic Sharia."

"Shit," said Denise. "We can't lose access to the media."

"What do we do?" asked Chuck, flustered.

"Guys," said Margie looking down at her phone. "The Majority Leader is saying he will bring Nick up on a Censure vote for conduct unbecoming from a US Senator. Citing your 'hateful rhetoric and dangerous accusations'," finished Margie, looking up in a panic.

Before anyone could answer, Nick started.

"Greg, Jer, I would like you two to start compiling every statement made by other senators inciting hateful actions and violence against Supreme Court justices, former Opposition Presidents, staffers, and people merely trying to have dinner with their families. I know there are plenty of examples. You can focus on the Party Senators and Congresspeople because they have been the only ones getting away with preaching violence for years. Make this priority one please. I want to have this available. Margie, get ready to put it in a TV spot if necessary."

Greg, Jer, and Margie all nodded, taking notes.

"I want it juxtaposed with what I have told people to do. To ask, no demand for transparency, real audits and facts, not rhetoric. I want it to be clear I am not advocating violence, nor am I saying the election has ever been fraudulent. Use clips from the speech. All I am asking is the need to verify once and for all, with complete transparency with audits and examination of voting machines and ballots, the eligibility and verification of voters that they did indeed cast the ballot. I did not mention any specific election nor make any statement accusing any candidate of cheating specifically." Nick paused, pacing in the room.

"On the Sharia thing, bring it on. Let's call their bluff. Once we have this in the can. Let's make sure they are aware we have this ready to go. As for Fontana, bring the Censure charge on. There is no way Lexi will give me a chance to stand in the well of the Senate and defend myself against accusations of my fellow senators, while millions of viewers are watching," smiled Nick.

As he had explained the plan, he could see his team exhale and start to calm, realizing his plan was exactly the correct way to respond to the perceived threat.

"What about social?" asked Margie.

"Go all in with Hibi. I want all of our social advertising spend there. Cancel our other social accounts before they can ban us. Issue a statement doubling down on American *Pravda*. How these kinds of threats prove my point. We choose to no longer support state sponsored propaganda outlets. Let's play offense. Cut my speech up, especially the Flip and the Mirror bits, and get them out there on Hibi."

"Got it. You sure you want to cancel all of them except Hibi? We have millions of followers on some of these?" cautioned Margie.

"Yep, put a post up, telling them we are going to rely on Hibi. See how they react. They will take it down, but it will get out. If they don't, maybe we considering keeping accounts on those who don't remove it. Anything else? If not, we are off to the border to see what is going on down there." Everyone began to breath again.

"Stay on the right side, please," advised Denise.

"Don't worry. Mexico has border laws *they* enforce. They won't allow any illegal immigration into *their* country," laughed Nick.

# Chapter 41

"Welcome to McAllen Texas, Senator. I'm Jose Acevedo, Customs and Border Protection. I'm assigned to show you around."

"Thanks Jose, please call me Nick. This is Earl Greene, my chief of security, and Greg Simmons, one of my campaign managers. We're all here to see for ourselves exactly what is going on. Do you mind if we film what we see?" asked Nick as the guys shook hands.

"Senator, I mean Nick, film all you want. Everyone else does. Doesn't seem to make a difference," said Jose with a laugh. "There was a time when the administration didn't want any footage of what is happening. Then it leaked and guess what? Nobody cared."

"How long you been down here, Jose?" asked Nick as they all piled into a CBP extended cab pickup.

"Born and raised. Did a couple of tours in Iraq with the army and joined CBP when I got home. I've been stationed on the border in Texas for the last twelve years. I've seen a variety of border policies."

"Jose, I'm counting on you to be frank with me. I'm not going to quote you or get you in trouble. Since I am neither party, trash away," noted Nick with a smile. "Mainly I want to know what we are doing wrong and if we are doing anything right. Plus, any thoughts you have on solutions."

"The easiest solution is to give us the ability to shoot smugglers. That would solve our problems. It might cause an issue with the Mexican government," said Jose, without humor.

"Advice short of starting a war," replied Nick, laughing.

"Is it as bad as we hear?" asked Earl.

"Worse," replied Jose, still serious. "Depends on your definition of bad," he said, looking at Earl in the rear-view mirror. "As you'll see, it is a very smooth operation now. They bring them across and hand them off to us. We escort them to waiting transportation, and they go to a processing center.

Once there, they get a hot meal, some clothes if they need it, maybe some first aid and then within a day they're on a bus. The bus either takes them to a bus terminal where they board a long-haul bus to a neighboring city or they go to the McAllen airport and fly to another city. The government provides all of this and some cash. We help them fill out paperwork to get their government assistance process started. All they have to do is check into a welfare office at their destination."

"Wow, that sure is efficient," said Greg, from the back seat.

"Oh, I almost forgot. We issue them a court summons date. From what I hear now, the current hearings are now three to four years out. Relatives pick some of them up wherever they end up. Others by waiting agencies who'll get them shelter and housing and meals until they get into something more permanent," concluded Jose.

"There are around fifty official points of entry on the border with Mexico. Of course, the smugglers are not using these. It means we have to monitor hundreds of crossing points. We now have it down to science. We don't want to find dead migrants in the desert. Believe it or not, the smugglers don't want them to die either. Most of them owe cartel debt," explained Jose.

"Cartel debt?" asked Greg.

"Most of the migrants can't pay the smuggling fees. They agree to 'work' off the debt once they are in the US," said Jose, watching the dirt road as he drove toward the border.

"How do they make sure of that?" asked Earl.

"You'll see when we get to the border. Don't want to spoil the story. It's going to be a warm night for this early in March. The smugglers may bring a load across. The other day, we were on a patrol and found four dead. They got dumped on this side and left to fend for themselves. It was a frosty night, and they died of exposure."

"This happen often?" asked Greg.

"If the smugglers don't use a normal spot and just cross and dump, many of those migrants have a 50/50 shot of getting apprehended or dying. The land out here is very inhospitable. The houses and ranches are very far apart. At least for those who are still living in them. There is very little water and no food to forage. Unless you have food, which most don't, you're going to be in trouble in a hurry," said Jose, as he pulled the truck up to a spot off the dirt road.

It was dusk. They got out and put on their jackets. Jose handed out flashlights. Greg declined so he could film. Nick and Earl were both carrying holstered 45 caliber pistols on their right hips. Jose glanced at Nick and Earl's weapons.

"Keep 'em holstered guys. Any trouble, I'll handle. Nobody wants violence. It's bad for their business and we're under strict rules of engagement," ordered Jose. "Besides, if you shoot someone, or worse, get shot, I'll be doing paperwork for a month."

"Have you seen anything?" asked Earl.

"I've seen *everything*."

"Do you ever try to send them back?" asked Greg.

"Nope, not here. I know some of them get processed and if there are existing warrants, we send them back, but that is about the only time Mexico ever takes anyone back. Title 42 is no longer enforced either. Been that way ever since the current administration took power, despite what they say. The border doesn't exist. We don't stop anyone. If the river wasn't here, I know half of Guatemala would march into the US. In fact, we should thank the cartels for stopping them."

"How so?" asked Greg, confused.

"They won't let anyone cross without paying them. They are in effect the Mexican customs and border patrol. If you don't pay, they won't let you cross. If they catch you trying, they just shoot you."

"The wild west," commented Nick, shaking his head.

"That's for sure, Nick," said Jose as they made their way from the truck down a path to another area, which had beaten down weeds and grasses, as if trampled by thousands of feet. As they entered the clearing, several more border patrol agents were already there, scanning the Mexican shore with binoculars in the failing light.

"What do you think, Bob?" asked Jose, looking at the older agent with the binoculars.

"I think we should call the buses out. We're going to see a few tonight," said Bob, looking at Jose and his group.

"Senator. Bob Ruiz," said CBP agent Ruiz as he held his hand out and got introduced to Earl and Greg.

"You hunting bear?" he asked, eyeing the cannons on their hips.

"Better to have and not need than to need and not have," responded Nick.

"Good mantra. Jose. Take'm down to the water before we lose all our light so they can see the boats on the other side."

He led the guys down near the water. They could see several large rubber boats docked on the other side of the river. Jose pointed over the trees.

"If we had a drone, you could look about a 1/4 mile in and you would see a camp built to stage the migrants before they ship them across. There've been no crossings the last couple of days because of the cold. We expect them to run soon and to have a big night. We've ordered buses to come down. They'll bring down another 25 agents and another 25 or more volunteers from local NGOs who help get the folks and the children up to the buses. What you'll see is most of them are just wearing jeans and t-shirts. They're not prepared for winter at all."

As if on cue, as the darkness descended, several people walked down to the boats and prepared them.

"Smugglers," said Jose.

Suddenly, they heard screaming. Several people appeared running toward the water. Nick, Earl, and Jose all had binoculars, while Greg was filming with his phone. It appeared two men and two women were running toward the water, being chased by a couple of other men.

As they approached the river, the pursuers shot both of the men in the back several times. One fell half in the water and the other on the bank. A woman tried to make a break for the water and was grabbed by her long hair and flung back on the riverbank. One shooter stood over the two women as the other one simply threw both the men into the river. The current pulled their floating bodies out into the center, now slowly on their way to the Gulf of Mexico.

The men stood with the women while another man approached from the brush. He was taller than the other two, wearing tactical gear. Nick trained the binoculars on him. He saw a man with obvious Latin features, dark hair, and a mustache. He had a birthmark on his left cheek that looked like a giant inkblot covering half of the left side of his face.

Nick's initial thought was a childhood with a mark like that could not have been easy. This thought was quickly replaced by one of disgust as the man approached the women and hit both with the butt of his rifle, knocking them to the ground in pain.

He said something to the men. They drug the women up the riverbank by their hair until they regained their feet. Nick clenched his hands around the binoculars.

"That happen a lot?" asked Earl.

"Unfortunately, yes," replied Jose. "Much as we would like to intervene, we aren't allowed to. As if to underscore this, throughout the entire episode, the other smugglers continued to prepare the boats as if nothing out of the ordinary was happening."

"Who is that?" asked Nick in a terse tone.

"La Marca."

"The Mark? Seems to fit," replied Nick.

"He is the Peligroso cartel boss. He killed the last one with his bare hands. Ruthless as they come. He appears from time to time to check on operations. Uh oh," said Jose as he noticed La Marca now had his own binoculars scanning where the three of them were observing.

"Senator, we need to go," said Jose.

At that moment, La Marca shouldered his rifle, firing a quick burst well over their heads. Clearly not intending to hit anything, but just to show he could. Greg hit the ground. Earl and Jose merely ducked slightly, having been under fire before. Nick continued staring, standing upright as La Marca laughed.

"Nick, we should go," said Earl, helping Greg up, as Jose agreed. Several more CBP officers came trotting down the path carrying their rifles, wearing tactical gear as well.

"No worries, just nuisance shots," explained Jose quickly.

Nick hadn't felt this kind of anger since New York. The disregard for life and the absolute lack of any authority. He dropped the binoculars on his chest and reached for his holster.

Earl was watching Nick and sensed what he was thinking. He shook his head. "Wrong time, wrong place."

Nick removed his hand from his weapon. There was just enough light left for La Marca to see the US side of the river. Nick stepped forward out of the brush into the open. Jose and Earl started swearing as Nick exposed himself to the view of those on the Mexican side. He stood and looked across the water at the cartel leader, arms crossed.

Across the river, La Marca stared as a lone figure emerged. Not wearing a CBP uniform. He let his rifle fall to his side and pickup his binoculars to see who this crazy gringo was. As he stared, several more heavily armed and uniformed CBP officers came out and stood in front of the man standing there. La Marca threw back his head and laughed, causing his other cartel minions to stop what they were doing, confused. He lifted a hand and gave Nick the finger.

"Nick, what the fuck are you doing?" yelled Earl as he pulled Nick back into the shelter of the underbrush and started up the trail."

"Sending a message."

"Like what? Shoot me? Jesus Nick," replied Earl, clearly pissed.

"Let's go back up to Bob," said a rattled Jose, just glad he hadn't gotten a presidential candidate killed on the shores of the Rio Grande.

# **Chapter 42**

Nick, Earl, and Greg stood amongst the now crowded staging area, with more agents and volunteers having arrived. Over the course of the next 4 hours, Nick counted 340 illegals crossing, including 120 children. He noticed many wore colored wrist bands and tore these off once they were on US soil. Bob picked up a couple of them and showed the guys.

"Cartels have this down to a science now. Different colored bands show what cartel owns them. The other bands identify the country they are from. What is interesting today is we have had several Russians and a couple of Chinese cross. The cartel made some serious money tonight."

"Russians, Chinese? I figured they were all from Guatemala, Honduras, and Mexico. How the hell does a Russian or a Chinese get here?" asked Greg.

"Boats and planes to most likely Guatemala, but possibly Mexico if they have the funds," explained Bob to the group. "The Russians and Chinese get VIP treatment. They are paying upwards of $15,000 a head. The other day, we had a group of Venezuelans fleeing their wonderful socialist Mecca. They most likely ran out of money on the way and will have to work off significant cartel debt once they get to the states. It's about $8,000 for someone from Venezuela. Central Americans and Mexicans pay from $3000 to $4000, but most of them don't have the money either when you consider they charge it per head in the family. The white band means they have collected the information on the wearer's family back in their home country."

"That sounds ominous," said Greg, bewildered at the precision of the operation of illegal immigration.

"It is," confirmed Bob.

"We are letting in people who then have to steal or deal drugs to keep their family back home safe? How come nobody knows this?" asked Greg, the anger clear in his tone.

"I saw it in my county in Colorado. They have no choice, or the next letter is their grandmother or parent is now dead," said Earl.

Bob continued. "The administration knows this. I suspect Nick knows some of this too, by his silence."

Nick nodded. "Earl has it right. They are afraid of what will happen to their loved ones back home if they disobey. Most of these people who came today will spend the next couple of years paying the debt. To local cartel bosses in the cities they end up in. A cut of their wages, or they force them to join the local gang. Transporting or dealing drugs. Stealing, or doing worse things, for the cartel."

"Very good Senator," remarked Bob, looking at Nick.

"I paid attention. We had several former CBP section chiefs testify last year. They did an excellent job of explaining cartel debt and how we were doing for the cartel what they could not do themselves. Namely, spreading their gangs and reach to every state in the union," explained Nick as Bob nodded in agreement.

"They are also paying interest on this debt. So even if many of these want to go legit, it is unlikely they will be able to. The United States government is a willing accomplish in human and child trafficking. Then our own NGOs ensure they get set up with some basic minimal necessities, places to stay, food, clothes, all at the expense of," he said, pausing for effect, "the American taxpayer. So not only are we not stopping human rights abuses in China and North Korea, we have state sponsored abuses right here in all 48 states thanks to our administration," finished Bob in obvious frustration.

"What about the ones who have the funds? I assume they are allowed to go with no allegiance to the cartels?" asked Nick.

"Hardly Senator. If you pay, you still have to provide all the data they ask for or you don't get in. The ones who can pay are actually even worse off. While they have money, they are still illegal. The cartels use this information to blackmail their families back home. Extorting money from them or they will disclose their locations in the US. Or expose their families back home for sending their loved ones from repressive regimes to the US. Most of their families would face repercussions back home if it were known they sent members into asylum in the US."

"No wonder the cartels are shifting to human smuggling. The gift that keeps on giving," observed Earl.

"Once they get here, they are unlikely to talk about this treatment either. The consequences are too great. The idea all of these are legitimate asylum seekers is disingenuous. Living in a poor country is not grounds for seeking asylum. Of course, you would leave a country like Guatemala or El Salvador if you could go to the US where just about any job is a better one from your point of view. We could make 99% of these asylum decisions right here on the bank of the river. No hearing required. Even better, let them know there is no such thing as asylum for economic reasons. Instead, the administration encourages them to risk life and limb to get here while enslaving their futures to the cartels." It was clear Bob was reaching his limit based on what he'd seen.

"The question is, do they understand what they are doing, becoming pawns of the cartel in the United States, and not able to take advantage of the freedoms the US would offer? Most importantly," continued Bob, taking off his hat, "and I am now speaking as a human and not a government employee." He turned to Greg, who turned off the camera.

"Guys, something is rotten down here. This is way too organized. I have seen other boats moving in the darkness further down river when we are all busy with the cartel boats. What we are allowing, no, what we are sanctioning and encouraging, is human bondage. It is modern day slavery. These people have no choice but to commit crimes when they get to the US."

"This of course puts them at odds with law enforcement and may well lead to them being deported later or, at a minimum, losing their chance at asylum if they truly fled tyranny. They have to do whatever the cartel tells them to, or their families back home are toast." Bob was now speaking on raw emotion, having seen this day after day for too long.

"We claim to be humane and how all of this is to help people impoverished by corruption in their home countries. Where they are subject to rape and sexual trafficking, and much worse like you just saw. They choose to leave and are subjected to all of this on their trip *here*. Encouraged by us. Then they are trafficked by the cartel, now slaves to both the cartel in Mexico and the cartel in the US. If the cartel scum wants to sell someone's daughter into sexual slavery, they have no choice, or their grandmothers will be killed here or back home. They're told to meet someone at a cartel distribution center and they get caught carrying fentanyl for the cartel. It is no big deal to them, as this is just another pawn. If they go to jail, they will use them in jail as well. We, the United States, are making all of this possible."

Nick, Greg, and Earl stood listening to Bob tell his tale as the darkness deepened around them.

"Senator, these poor people have no hope of becoming useful Americans. Even if they pay off the debt and get into normal society, they have to worry about the information being used against them. Forever. The best thing we could do is to shut down all immigration. We need to break the hold of the cartels on these poor souls."

"Would that work? Really?" asked Nick.

"Senator, we need to do something. We swore an oath to protect our border against foreign invasion. Thanks to this administration's policies, they have invaded our shores." Bob finished and put his hat back on.

Nick stood, digesting what Bob had described. It all made perfect sense. "The real question is whether they know exactly what they are doing," said Nick to no one in particular.

"If they do and it is the truth, Senator, we're in a world of hurt," commented Bob.

# Chapter 43

They spent another day in McAllen, visiting the processing center, talking to volunteers and other CBP agents, getting the same story about the organizational skills of the cartels.

The major networks no longer bothered to cover any activity on the border. Morale was low and there didn't appear to be any end in sight. Nick left McAllen disturbed by what he saw, questioning the point of having a border if there was unrestricted access.

They spent the next day driving five hours from McAllen to Del Rio for their next visit. Once again, they spent their evening watching hundreds of illegals cross to be met by the CBP and volunteers. Nick talked to agents and tried to talk to the illegals, but they were having none of it once they saw Greg was filming.

After a couple hours of chatting with agents and observing the same processes as McAllen, Nick stood to one side contemplating the decline of American sovereignty. He didn't notice the CBP agent who came up with a cup of coffee.

"Senator, interested in a cup of coffee?"

Nick turned and looked down at the agent. She couldn't have been much over 5 feet tall and didn't weigh 100 pounds. But as he took the cup of coffee, he looked into her eyes, realizing she was not someone to mess with.

"Agent Helen Garcia," she said, holding out a hand. Nick noticed her handshake was as firm as her intro.

"So, what do you think?" she asked.

"I am not sure I can share what I actually think. My level of concern, disgust and, frankly, disbelief is off the charts. How do you do this night after night?"

"It's my job. I hope these kids will get a chance. It's not their fault they're here. Taking out my frustration on them won't change policy. I focus on the kids to get me through the days."

"How long have you been on the border?" asked Nick.

"Over 20 years now."

Nick looked at her. He would not have thought she was a day over 30. She laughed when he didn't respond. "I know. I don't look my age and I appreciate the thought. It's my Mexican heritage."

"So how bad is it?" asked Nick, echoing a statement he seemed to ask to every agent he spoke too.

"Let me tell you a couple of quick stories. Harry Johnson is a fifth-generation rancher about 20 miles up along the river. He sold land to the government to build walls on his property because it was across from one of the favored crossing spots. They build 99% of the wall except for one 50 foot section, which was directly across from the crossing."

"Of course they did. Nothing surprises me anymore," said Nick, shaking his head at the stupidity of the US government.

Don't ask me why. It channels them right to his property and onto a path that leads right up to his house and the buildings containing his livestock. They broke into his house multiple times. He moved his wife and daughters to Dallas because he caught migrants trying to break into one of his daughter's windows.

"His livestock has been stolen and killed. Each time he files complaints, sometimes arrests are made, but they're always released. He took matters into his own hands. He got a bulldozer and plowed a sheer embankment into the gap in the wall and then put a fence on top of it to close the gap."

"Because he sold the land, *he* was arrested for trespassing and forced to tear down what he built *and* pay a large fine. The very next night, the cartel came across and burned down his house. Of course, they did not apprehend them. He sold his livestock and moved to Dallas to be with his family. Where is the justice in that result?" Helen took a sip of her coffee before continuing. Nick could tell she was emotional.

"That one had a good ending. At least Harry got to leave. Joe Wilkins is rotting in a federal jail. Unlike Harry, the migrants got into his daughter's room and by the time he got to the *three of them*, they had already raped his 10-year-old daughter. He lost it. He killed one of them in the house, which was his right. The other two bolted out the window and into the dark. He tracked them down and shot'em both in the stomach and left'em in the desert to die."

"Somehow one of them survived the night and told his story to authorities, who promptly arrested Joe. Turns out all three were hardened criminals with murder and rape convictions. Released from Venezuelan prisons and shipped to the border by their government to become our problem. Joe is now sitting in prison waiting for his trial to start and the illegal is being represented by high priced ACLU lawyers doing pro-bono work."

"Joe's daughter killed herself a month ago, hung herself. His wife had a nervous breakdown and is in the mental ward in San Antonio. He has nobody. I went to see him in prison. He's lost 60 pounds. I don't think he cares about what happens to him. His life is ruined."

Nick sipped his coffee, listening.

"Despite what the media has to say about the people crossing the border, over 70% of the males coming across have criminal records. We have no choice but to catch and release them into the interior. They are not seeking asylum. If I were Joe, I would have done the same thing. Except I would have made sure they were dead. Our society is collapsing, and our administration is speeding up the demise. Worse, they don't seem to even care," said Helen. "My coffee is cold. Sorry for talking your ear off, but if the Progressives stay in office, I think I'll look to change jobs. I am nothing more than a glorified babysitter and travel agent here."

"Helen, thank you for sharing those stories. They are heartbreaking and both were preventable. If you were president, how would you solve this?"

"I would send in the Marines. I would track down and kill every cartel leader. I'd make it clear that anyone who takes their place will get a drone missile up their ass. This is a war and only one side is fielding an army. Then I'd work with the Mexican authorities to employ the former cartel members in a meaningful way to improve the Mexican economy," she continued after a second, on a roll.

"I would relentlessly track down and kill every drug dealer, distributor, or worker in the drug business until it is clear if you are involved in drugs, your life is forfeit. Simultaneously, I'd make drug distribution in the US a deportable crime. Strip them of their citizenship and deport them back to the country where their drugs came from. We would stop focusing on the users and focus on the dealers and the networks and I would not be afraid to show them we mean business," she paused and laughed. "Of course, I guess they'd impeach me after I ordered the first drone strike. But you asked."

"I did. You feel the only way to really fight this effectively is with force?"

"Senator, I am part Mexican. First generation on my father's side. The machismo is real. These guys are all about honor and reputation. They are like the old wild west. Diplomacy will not work. They will happily take any money, promise to make changes, and keep on doing what they are doing. They only respect power."

"I agree with you. On *most* of your suggestions," he said, smiling.

Helen laughed. "Now that I think about it, reminds me of the Chinese as well. If you don't punch them in the nose, they won't respect you and if you don't kick them in the crotch when they get up, they won't think you mean business. If you aren't willing to kill the heads of these cartels and keep killing them, they'll keep replacing them with the next guy in line. These guys do not fear prison. Doing time is like a badge of honor that you got away with something and only got sent to prison. In their culture, you screw up or cross them and you end up dead. You cannot show weakness. If you hesitate, they know you don't have resolve. If you start, you can't stop until they know you'll track them down if they step up to lead a cartel," she finished.

"Thank you, Helen. It is very enlightening. I agree focusing on the drug users is not working. We have to win this election and secure the border before it doesn't matter any longer. I have to say, I like your drug cartel eradication plan as well. The Mexican government would probably not approve, but at some point, if they will not stop it, we are entitled to do it ourselves."

"I agree," said Helen. "They are bringing it on themselves and with the fentanyl from China coming in through Mexico, it is a matter of life or death, and they are complicit."

"Thanks for the coffee and the conversation. We have to drive to El Paso tomorrow. Why does it take so long to get between cities in Texas?"

"It's a big country and none bigger than Texas," said Helen with a smile. "When you get to El Paso, look up Henry Burket. Tell him I said Hi."

"Will do, good luck Helen."

# Chapter 44

"Man, it takes forever to get anywhere in this state," said Nick as Earl pulled the Suburban into the El Paso office of the CBP the next day after driving six hours from Del Rio.

"Sure does," agreed Earl.

"We should probably check in and get some dinner before our next field trip."

After grabbing some dinner, they returned to the El Paso CBP office and met up with their guide agent, Robert Vega.

"Hi Rob, we're ready for our next dose of reality," greeted Nick.

Rob laughed. "Good to hear Senator. Let's get in my truck and I'll take us down to the site where most of the folks are crossing. Gonna be a chilly night so they may or may not cross tonight," said Rob as they piled into his CBP pickup. He drove for 15 minutes to the outskirts of El Paso and down to the river outside the city. He parked by several other CBP trucks, and they all exited and put on their heavier jackets, as the temperature was already dipping close to freezing.

They stopped and got some hot coffee from the mobile command center. Rob introduced Nick to an older agent who was studying a map inside. He held out a hand.

"Henry Burket, supervisor for this region." Nick shook his hand. "Nick Turner. That's Earl Greene and Greg Simmons. We've been seeing the sights Texas has to offer," said Nick with a smile. Henry glanced at Nick and shook his head.

"Well, if you chose the border instead of the Alamo, then your priorities are misplaced. What do you think so far?"

Nick paused for a second.

"Honestly, Henry, this is fucked up."

Henry snorted in surprise at Nick's response. They all laughed.

"I'd appreciate it if you would describe it this way in your next committee meeting in DC. It is fucked up and frankly has been for the entire duration of this administration. I thought they were just incompetent originally, but year after year of this has changed my mind."

"It is a diabolical plan. This is a way to rot us from the inside out. An influx of cheap labor with none of the embedded DNA of what it means to be an American, is bound to destroy communities. They don't care about the same things we do. The morals and ethics are entirely different. Combine this with the race wars and wokeness in our schools. You get a very volatile and explosive mixture."

"We would agree, and we've only been here a week," said Nick. "Oh, Helen Garcia said to say hello."

"Really? How is that ball of fire? She spits nails. People always underestimate her because of her size. I've seen her put 250 pound dealers on their knees crying. She's one of the best I have in this region."

"I know, it impressed me," said Nick. "I assume you have been doing this for a while?"

"Thirty years. It goes up and down, but we get a million through every year, except for a couple of years when we really attempted to turn stop them and threatened Mexico to take them back. Unfortunately, the current regime got rid of the policies that were working and now we are close to averaging 2 million or more a year. It is changing our country and not for the good. I am sure you realize we are the only major country *in the world* that is not enforcing our federal border laws. The only one! What I can't figure is why the Opposition aren't making more of a stink about it," said Henry.

"I can answer that one," said Nick. "Money and optics. None of them want to risk these to make a stand. It's all about getting reelected. Not about doing what is right."

"That is a sad commentary, but I believe you," said Henry. "I want you to talk to someone. He is about to be transferred out and deported, but we have a few minutes. Follow me."

Henry led him to a holding cell in the command center, where he was introduced to Herman. He was 5'9", slightly overweight, heavily tattooed, balding, with a black mustache and beard.

"You a government man?" asked Herman.

"More or less," said Nick.

"I want to thank you for arranging for my travel back," said Herman with a laugh. He was not worried about being in custody.

"How many times have you made the trip across the Rio Grande?" asked Nick.

Herman paused for a second.

"54 times in the last 5 years."

"Excuse me," blurted out Earl from the side of the room where he was standing with Greg.

Herman smiled at Earl.

"How many times have we caught you?" asked Nick.

"20," replied Herman, still smiling.

"20?" confirmed Nick, turning to Henry.

"Wait, it gets better," nodded Henry. "Herman, tell him how we help."

"Aye Agent Burket. I bring up groups of migrants, from Guatemala and Honduras, through Mexico and across the border. If I get notified there is no group ready again there, I cross back and help move the ones from the camps. When I get word there is a sizeable group ready, I let CBP capture me. They process me, arrest me, and then put me on a plane back to wherever I want. Then I pick up my group and make the journey again," explained Herman with a grin. "We call it Air America."

"Wait a minute. You turn yourself in because you know we'll deport you instead of throwing you in jail," asked Nick.

Herman nodded while still smiling.

Nick looked at Henry. "He's right. He knows it is not our policy to put anyone in jail. If they have records or arrest warrants, we deport them back to the country of origin. Good ole Uncle Sam runs a travel agency for these guys and pays to fly them back to the start so they can do it all again. We've seen ole Herman here four times each of the last 5 years."

Nick turned back to Herman. "How much to lead a group from Honduras or Guatemala?"

"Depends on size. 50-100 about $50,000 US. If it is 200, then over $75,000 per trip."

"You are making 250-300 thousand dollars a year smuggling?" asked Earl.

Herman just smiled. "More."

"We are in the wrong business," remarked Earl.

"Clearly," agreed Greg.

Herman laughed at their conversation. "I lead them along the path, cars, trains, buses. I lose a few along the way from fights. Guys take other's wives, and they kill each other. I try to stop the killing but not the rape, not my problem, but I get paid per head," said Herman, almost proud of his ability to move people and flaunt the lack of American willpower to enforce the border laws.

"How can you do this? Did you not have a mother?" asked Earl.

Herman lost his smile, but it returned quickly.

"Mother? Sure, she left me at 8. Life is tough. Mexico is tough. Honduras and Guatemala life is tougher. America is soft. You let me use you and help me move my cargo. Then you capture me, feed me, give me new clothes, and then send me back. You are stupid and deserve what happens to you. There are hundreds of groups like mine. And you are helping us do this." Herman spat on the ground near their feet.

"America is weak, America is soft, America is causing this problem," he laughed. "If I tried to go from here to Panama, or to Columbia or Canada, I would be stopped and immediately deported. If I tried again, I would end up in jail. Any way you look at it, I would not be allowed to stay. They would not put me on a bus, take me anywhere in America, and let me stay indefinitely."

"But please do not change. They have not shot at me in years. I make more money and am much safer moving people than moving drugs. By now, I would be dead instead of rich. I now own Amazon, Microsoft, Tesla, Apple stock and even bitcoin. Thank you, America," praised Herman as a

Border Patrol agent came up to take him away for processing. "Time to get ready for my trip back. See you again in a couple of months, Agent Burket."

As the CBP agent left with Herman, Nick refilled his coffee and sat at a table. He motioned for Henry to have a seat.

"I think we'll take a walk," said Earl, leading Greg out.

After they were alone, Nick looked at Henry.

"What the hell is going on down here?"

"Senator, I wish I knew, and could tell you, but I don't know what the endgame is. By my count, we have processed roughly fourteen million migrants during this administration. The dirty secret is there are probably another 5-10 million who made it past us. So realistically, we now have 40 million or more illegal citizens spread out amongst the 50 states. Well, 48 anyway, haven't heard of any trips to Alaska or Hawaii."

"A majority of the fourteen million have been transported to red states by the federal government. Some of these get redirected to large urban, Party controlled sanctuary cities by red state governors when they can get away with it. Those going to red states are not going to the cities, but to the small municipalities. Overwhelming local sheriffs and raising crime rates in these previously peaceful communities. There is a method to the madness," explained Henry.

"What is your theory?" asked Nick.

"I have two. You're not going to like either," paused Henry, drinking. "Hell, you may not even believe either."

"Well, after what I have seen these last few days, I don't know what to believe," admitted Nick.

"Here is some food for thought. Theory one is the cartel is flooding the states with millions of sleeper agents, which we send all over the heartland. They are destabilizing the rural fabric of America, driving down wages and driving up crime. This is straining resources and infrastructure in places where neither of these are in abundance."

"My guess is most of these people have cartel debt and are just waiting to be activated. That activation could be to distribute drugs. We all know the rural populations are the most prone to opioid abuse and are easy marks as the Chinese flood Mexico with cheap fentanyl. The cartels bring it into the US. Lord knows it is easy enough to do since we are distracted by the children they send across the river. They can easily smuggle tons of fentanyl in and spread it out to the hinterlands."

Nick leaned back, looking at Henry. "You know what? That plan makes total sense. It is diabolical. Is this by design or are we just useful idiots helping with the plan by our own stupidity? I wonder if it was indeed an intentional plan and not simply the misguided policies and unintended consequences of trying to be compassionate."

"I hope we are useful idiots and not complicit. Which leads me to theory two. This is where things go off the rails," said Henry.

"What if there were a plan, a plan to ensure a permanent majority for one party in perpetuity? We've all heard the conservative rhetoric from guys like Tommy and Rush Limbaugh for years when he was still alive and now Brad Hudson as well. Replacement migration. But what if they have sped it up under the current administration? What if this is an unholy alliance between the administration, or worse, some other faction? To flood the states with 'replacements' with cartel debt hanging over their head. Waiting to be activated to perform whatever deed is necessary to ensure a particular outcome?" said Henry.

"You tried to stop the filibuster, but you only delayed the inevitable. What if the next move is to naturalize a portion of the migrants? We have to do something with them. Forty to fifty million people won't stay in the shadows forever. What if that portion has cartel debt, or someone in the family has it? They are told to vote a certain way, or to even attempt to vote even if they are not eligible. To march in certain protests, to commit particular crimes, or to do particular society destroying deeds. They'd have no choice except to obey or they would lose benefits or sacrifice a family member back home."

"Chaos. Anarchy. It would not be pretty. We would be woefully unprepared to handle this kind of organized movement," agreed Nick.

"A scarier thought is some arrests we are making where we capture smugglers with fentanyl pills. Enough to kill millions. What happens when one of these gets through and they are told to hand these out in schools instead of dealing them? You are talking about mass casualty events on our most vulnerable citizens," suggested Henry.

Nick shuddered at the thought of this happening. "That is some theory. The stuff that gets you branded a QAnon nutjob," laughed Nick.

"Yep, I would agree. Pretty convenient, isn't it? You bring up something like this and they have a built-in way to shut you up. To keep us from preparing for or even stopping this. Nick, I tell you there is something going on. It is too organized and there is a plan. I don't know who is pulling the ultimate strings, but the potential for destruction is there. The fabric of society is tearing."

"Who would benefit most? China being top of the list. Russia is close behind. Iran and North Korea. Also, some big multi-nationals. And a certain political party looking to solidify a permanent majority. America has been the sole bulwark against Communism ever since the second world war," said Nick.

"Bingo," agreed Henry.

"We have also been the major roadblock for totalitarian regimes expanding their influence in various geographic zones. If we were to be focused on internal unrest, first our role as a global stabilizing force would be gone. China could take Taiwan; Russia could take the rest of Ukraine and Belarus, maybe even the Baltic states again. We would be too concerned with our own issues to offer anything more than token opposition. The same thing happened when Russia took over the Crimea and part of Ukraine. With the current woke culture, anyone who tries to bring this up, or discuss it, is immediately silenced. It is truly devious. If it is true and not just a giant coincidence," said Nick.

"Rule 39," stated Henry.

Nick laughed. "I was in a navy hospital once and the only thing they had to watch was a set of *NCIS* DVDs. I watched them during my rehab. But you're right, Gibb's rule 39, 'there is no such thing as a coincidence' is absolutely right. The challenge is, now that we know, what can we do about it?"

"Me? Nothing. You? I suggest you win the election to start. If you don't, I suspect this plan goes operational on Jan 20th next year. I have a place in

West Texas. I have been stock piling ammo and food. This is going to go bad and when it does, anarchy is going to rule. Mark my words, when they use the military to do what cops and sheriffs used to do, it is as sure a sign as any, the endgame has arrived," he finished.

"This is certainly uplifting."

Henry shrugged. "You asked."

Nick nodded. "Before I go, Henry, can I ask a personal question?"

"Fire away Senator."

"Did you know Patrick Williams?"

"Pat? Sure. How did you know him?" asked Henry with a questioning look.

"I didn't. But I met his widow on a trip through Omaha," answered Nick. "She told me the story of his disappearance. I figure since you are a lifer and a supervisor for the CBP in this region, you must have known him or what happened."

Henry sighed and paused before responding, "I remember it like it was yesterday. It is rare that we lose folks in the Border Patrol. To have one captured, tortured, and then killed is really rare. In fact, there have only been a couple of incidents. Pat's was unusual because he had a couple of chances to flee and he stayed to help others."

"That sounds like the person his widow described," agreed Nick.

"The cartel ambushed them when they stumbled on a large smuggling operation. When they tried to apprehend the cartel members, they opened fire. Most times they try to run, but apparently this shipment was too big to leave behind. Pat's partner went down and he called in for support. He continued to engage them, waiting for help. His partner died instantly, shot in the head. Pat *should* have left, but he stayed. Maybe he thought Ben was still alive. He even dragged him back to the truck. He got five of the cartel members, but eventually they must have overwhelmed him."

"By the time we get to the site, we find Ben, their truck, and five dead cartel members. We also found Pat's hat and a blood trail. We got a posse together and followed the trail back to the river. It was clear they went back into Mexico. Since we didn't find Pat, we assumed they took him. We contacted HQ to see what we could do to mount a rescue operation in

Mexico. Unfortunately, this administration had no desire to do a military incursion into Mexico with no confirmation Pat was alive," said Henry, pausing. "I trained Pat. He was always gung ho. A great guy. Someone who would do anything for anyone any time. He and Natalie were an impressive pair and their daughter was a hoot."

"They still are. She's running a B&B. They're doing OK."

"Good to know. Anyway, we finally get a ransom, a ridiculous amount, like ten million bucks. There is no way that is going to happen. Next thing we get a severed finger and a video of Pat looking pretty beat up. We validated it was his from fingerprints. We blew a lot of money, but we finally got an informant to give us an idea of where he was being held. The administration finally agreed to mount a rescue mission."

"Using drones, we followed the courier back to a giant meth lab. A Delta unit went in, but just as they were getting ready to breach, the building blew up and burned. We got permission from the Mexican government to search the ruins and found Pat's severed hand minus a finger in the remains of a metal cooler blown out of the building. Nothing else survived. They were cutting meth. The chemicals blew up, and the fire burned so hot the six bodies they found were cremated. We assumed he was there because of the hand. The bodies we found were melted beyond any chance of identification. Since there were no additional ransom requests and none of our informants said he was still alive, it was determined Pat had to be one of the bodies. They declared him dead," said Henry, shaking his head.

"The sacrifices you guys make down here remind me of my last tour in Afghanistan. You wake up every day and do your job, fly your mission, shoot more bad guys, bomb a building or a road. You get back to base and ask yourself, what did we accomplish today? Why are we here? After this visit, I realize it is the same for you. You are not securing a border; you are running a taxi service and day care center."

"Morale sucks. No one wants to work in the CBP. Why would you? I should have retired two years ago, but they begged me to stay because they have no one to replace me. Frankly, and I hate to say it, but I think we should remove all of us from the border, let them come across and eventually the states will call up the National Guard. People will get killed, but at least we will make it clear the border is not open."

"I know the Texas Governor has tried to build the wall himself and I know he tried to deploy the national guard already, but the Feds stopped him each time. They then turned around and did nothing to improve our situation. Take what I said to heart. Think about it and look at the actions, not the words. I think it makes sense. It is a scary proposition," said Henry.

"Where is your property? I may visit when the zombie apocalypse happens," laughed Nick.

"West Texas, near Big Spring. I will give you the GPS coordinates if you promise not to share," said Henry, smiling.

"Good to know. Henry, I appreciate the talk and I will think about what you said. If it's true, I don't know how we turn it around even if I get elected," admitted Nick.

"I only know the problem. Don't have the solution. Sorry," said Henry, getting up to shake Nick's hand.

"I hope you are wrong, but I suspect you're not," said Nick.

# Chapter 45

Luc sipped his espresso. He glanced at the people wandering up and down the street. He sat at a small table on a street in the former artist colony of Montmartre, in Paris. Today in March, it was mostly locals, not yet tourist season. Still, he lamented how the area had changed.

He was getting old. He remembered many days and evenings wandering the streets of Montmartre with his then girlfriend and later, wife, Marie. How happy they had been, having a coffee and baguette as a meal. Often, all they could afford in their early days.

He waited. Glancing at the watch he still wore, refusing to dispense with it and join those who relied on their smart phone for everything, including telling them the time. He took another sip of his fast disappearing and cooling espresso. It was a brisk but sunny day in late March. Luc had on a jacket and a scarf around his neck.

He spied his target, walking down the street toward him. She wore a red wool coat, beige scarf, and a knit cap. The woman halted for a moment, recognizing Luc, who had raised a hand in greeting. He motioned to the chair on the opposite side of the small cafe table. She hesitated. Stopping as the pedestrians continued flowing around her. Stepping forward, she looked down at Luc.

"Inspector," she said in French.

"No longer," replied Luc, shaking his head.

"A strange place for you to have a coffee."

Luc shrugged. "Please sit Ms. Basset. I only require a few moments of your time."

"Fontaine now. I married."

"Congratulations," said Luc as she sat. "Coffee?"

"Yes, please, since you insist on sitting outdoors."

Luc waved at a server, who nodded.

"To what do I owe the pleasure of your company? I did not expect to see you again after our last encounter," replied Mrs. Fontaine.

Luc laughed chillingly. "On that, we can agree."

"How is Ms. Roche?"

"Annie? She is well. Very happy."

"Then it appears you were correct, and I was amiss. May I go now?" asked Mrs. Fontaine in an annoyed tone.

"I am not holding you here. But your coffee has not even arrived," replied Luc, when, as if by magic, the server arrived.

"One noisette," which he placed in front of Mrs. Fontaine. "One cafe," finished the waiter. Luc thanked him.

"Ah, it should not surprise me you remembered," she said, taking a sip of her espresso with steamed milk.

"I remembered, Caroline. May I call you Caroline?" asked Luc, as she nodded. "My visit is not about Annie directly. I need to know more about autism and how it is now handled in France. I know they have proposed improvements, but I need to understand where and how adult autism is treated."

Caroline sipped, staring at Luc.

"You are no longer an inspector for Interpol?"

"You know I am not."

She nodded. "My condolences on the loss of your wife and child. A national tragedy."

Luc merely nodded, having long since come to grips with an entire nation knowing of his personal loss.

"I am not speaking in an official capacity, correct?"

Luc nodded again.

"In that case, we have made little progress. We speak the words, we spend money, we make changes. We are still not addressing the root of the problems. It is hard to shake decades of teaching families and others that autism is a learning disability and something that can be untaught. Until the generation of psychoanalysts perpetuating these horrendous myths are dead and buried, we cannot force the changes the United States, Britain, and others have done to give their autistic citizens a chance at a normal life. They focus on continuing education opportunities from childhood throughout their entire adult lives. We believed incorrectly in the 'settled science' of psychoanalysis. This has set us back half a century and embarrasses our entire nation to this day."

"So, little has changed? Institutions are still the primary methods?" asked Luc.

"Yes. A lifetime in hospital care. As you know, many who can send their children across the border to Belgium, where they can be educated. But the separation from their families brings additional burden and trauma. Much like our immigration problem, we choose to ignore it and simply refuse to admit it even exists."

Luc sat back, drinking the last of his second espresso of the morning. He pondered Caroline's words.

"Why do you ask? If you are no longer an inspector, why the sudden interest in autism again? Has something happened to Annie?"

Luc smiled, leaning forward. "No, she really is fine. She lives in the convent. It was a good match for everyone involved."

It was Caroline's time to smile, for the first time. "Somehow, I doubt Annie agrees. She is unlikely to find someone in a convent with whom to consummate her obsession with sex."

"Which is precisely why it is a good thing," laughed Luc.

"So, I ask again, why the interest?"

"Caroline, I have some hypothetical questions. Could an autistic person, a high functioning one, be 'trained' to do something?"

"Trained? You mean like standing on their head and rubbing their stomach?"

"No," scowled Luc at Caroline's sarcasm. "More like running drugs, being a courier, delivering a package to a place and time."

"It depends," said Caroline with a shrug. "On the person. On their mannerisms and fixations. Some are more challenged than others. Many are too focused, others not enough. In theory, yes, you can find autistic people who you could 'teach' to do a task, especially if it is repetitive. And not requiring them to make judgment decisions."

Luc sat for a few seconds to frame his next question.

"Would they know if the task is right or wrong? Or harmful?"

Caroline tilted her head in response. "I am not sure I am following. Obviously, if you taught them to fire a gun at someone, some could do it and others would not. It is a very subjective process, just as it is with a normal adult. Right and wrong are usually taught and experienced." She paused, sipping her noisette and staring at Luc.

"They would lack reinforcement from teachers and peers. *So*, it is entirely possible, they would not know something they are doing is bad. Or on the opposite spectrum, they would know it is bad and they would become agitated and despondent over the prospect of them doing something wrong. Sorry, but you asked," said Caroline with a small shrug and brief smile as Luc looked bewildered.

"Let's shift gears. How are the institutions funded?"

"Luc, as with everything related to health care, not enough. Many hospitals have facilities to house and care for the autistic. Frankly, we are catching up. We *are* trying. What is your specific question?"

"You know how we found Annie. Her talents being used by a criminal organization to help their money laundering. They 'bought' her from a small private institution once they found out about her particular capabilities. As you know, we put the institution out of business, jailed the owners, and took down the criminal syndicate."

"Yes, I remember Inspector, you forget how we met. What is your point?"

"I believe they used an autistic person in this manner to detonate the suicide bomb that killed Gaspard," said Luc.

Caroline stiffened at the revelation, stunned. "Luc, that is a horrible accusation. And if true, it would be incredibly damaging on so many levels. Are you certain?"

Luc studied her for a second before he replied.

"Do you think there are others like the one who 'sold' Annie? Other private institutions, where autistic patients with particular talents could be found, and like Annie, their capabilities advertised to unscrupulous buyers?"

Rather than looking shocked, Caroline did not hesitate. "Yes."

Luc leaned back in his chair.

"Do you know of any? Unofficially, of course."

"You understand the magnitude of our problems? We have upwards of seven hundred thousand children and adults we are trying to help. We cannot report and investigate every situation we uncover."

"Of course. It is no different in law enforcement. I meant no accusation. I know your agency is trying. Simply knowledge."

Caroline nodded, digging in her handbag for a piece of paper and a pen. She wrote for half a minute and handed an envelope to Luc, with the names and addresses written on the back.

"These are the ones most likely to be candidates for your recruitment. Sadly, they review other institutions' care notes and select 'candidates' whose families have abandoned them. They offer to take the person into private care, relieving the hospital of the burden, freeing up a bed for another patient. To the hospital, it is the same amount of funding. They rarely ask questions. If they do, donations typically silence these," said Caroline, in a slight tone of exasperation at the situation.

Luc looked over the list. "Thank you."

"I must get to work. Thank you for the coffee."

"My pleasure. Congratulations again on your marriage."

Caroline smiled, wrapping her scarf around her neck.

"I am happy I was wrong about Annie. Good luck on your investigation, *Inspector*." she said, turning up the street toward her office.

Luc sat reviewing the names on the envelope. He caught the waiter's attention to settle the bill.

# Chapter 46

Nick, Earl, and Greg started their morning in the crisp March air of Santa Monica, California. They had spent the last week traveling across New Mexico and Arizona. Visiting both small and large cities. As with everywhere else, they tried to keep the crowds small and avoid the inevitable sheriffs and code enforcers.

In Phoenix, they met the Arizona Secretary of State, who assured them they were working to make sure the voting process would be much smoother this time around. Nick left behind new Turner Rabble groups wherever he stopped in all these cities and towns.

He was especially encouraged by conversations in the various retirement communities. These folks were living on fixed incomes and understood the economically damaging policies of the administration much better than the economists appearing on the various DC committees. Because they lived with the consequences of these decisions and the inflation they had created, they understood Nick's stances.

Nick also met with the elders of the San Carlos Apache Indian reservation in south central Arizona. As was always the case where poverty was rampant, it came down to education and lack of employment opportunities, especially for the youth. The reservation had been in litigation with the various Party administrations these last two decades fighting against a copper mine proposed on their sacred land.

This was balanced against other concerns when the government restricted the oil and gas drilling on tribal lands. Stopping drilling cost them millions. Land leases to oil and gas companies were their principal sources of income outside government assistance. No one was happy.

Nick empathized with the tribal leaders and their desire to preserve their heritage, but he also saw the need to provide something other than the noose of government assistance slowly strangling the life out of the tribe. More than half of the residents lived well below the national poverty line. Nick left, not sure what the answer was, but he knew what it wasn't. Anything but more of the same.

They made their way into southern California after a stop at the border in Yuma. They held a couple of small rallies in San Diego and some suburbs as they made their way to Los Angeles.

As they walked down to Venice Beach to see the homeless encampment, it was worse than they could have imagined. As far as the eye could see, it was a sea of tents. The path, made famous in many films and TV shows, could barely be seen amongst the tents. The beach was nowhere to be seen in either direction. When the breeze came in from the ocean, it brought with it the smell of ocean breeze, along with urine and feces.

It was hard to believe this iconic section of beach, symbolic of the ability to enjoy leisure time in America, had instead turned into a validation of the failed policies of social welfare and government aid. These programs made it possible for these people to squat and subsist on this beach. The local police and sheriff feared the optics of forcibly removing the homeless from the beach.

As Nick walked among the tents on the path, at least when it was visible. He noticed a lot of American flags. Assuming these were the veterans who could not find jobs. There was another guy walking around between the tents. He had a red, white, and blue bandana around his head and wore faded combat pants and a windbreaker missing the right sleeve. He was putting ointment on an open sore on another person's arm. Wrapping it with gauze, he noticed the three of them watching him. He finished up, shook the guy's hand, and came over to Nick.

"Reporter or from the city?" asked the bandana guy.

"Neither. Nick Turner," he said, holding out a hand.

"Well, this is a first. Politicians avoid this place like the plague," he said, reaching out to shake Nick's hand. "They call me Trapper."

"Trapper, this is Earl and Greg. I'm not here as a politician. I am here listening and seeing what life is like in America today,"

"Well, Nick, do you like what you see? Whadiya think about America now?" asked Trapper, waving an arm in a broad arc.

"How long you been here, Trapper?" asked Earl.

"Got evicted during COVID when I lost my job. Pitched a tent here because I could. I actually got kicked out from under bridges in Orange County, but no one kicked me off the beach in LA county. I've been here for years now," shrugged Trapper.

"I want to understand why this community is here," asked Nick.

"Sure, I got nothing to hide. Nobody seems to care anyway."

"What were you doing when we came up?" asked Earl.

"I was a medic in the Army. I try to take care of people's issues, best I can anyway. That's why they call me Trapper. You know, like Trapper John from M.A.S.H."

"How busy are you?" asked Nick.

"Mostly infected cuts, blisters, and other minor items. The occasional knife wound, if I get there in time to help. It helps now that we have a local volunteer clinic. They give me the supplies and I roam the camp. People trust me more than them, so I help where I can."

"Is everyone here out of work and can't find a job?" asked Nick.

"Most lost something. Job, wife, house. Lots during the COVID lockdowns, and many more after, when eviction moratoriums expired. The landlords started kicking people out. Can't say I blame them. They still had to pay their mortgage and their tenants didn't. Sort of creates a problem. Fair warning, a lot of others don't feel that way," Trapper laughed before continuing.

"This *is* California. Some of these people feel like they should have been able to stay forever. It really pissed them off the people who owned the buildings could even kick them out. Remember, I warned you. Some folks here are clearly cuckoo. They need to be in a mental ward. There are no beds for them, but we have toilets. Go figure. They take care of their guilt by emptying the toilets every other day."

"Trapper, at this point, nothing surprises me," said Nick.

"Then there are a lot, like me, who would probably like to have a house and a job and a purpose. But we get our government aid, we have our toilets, and now we have rudimentary medical care. Unlike CHAZ in Seattle, if we need the cops or an ambulance, they come here. We're not violent, just pathetic. Life has beaten any remaining *life* out of most of us. We're resigned," explained Trapper.

"What percentage do you think are like you, resigned to your situation but willing to change if given the opportunity?" asked Nick.

"50, maybe 60%. About 25% are mental basket cases and need help, mostly to protect them from themselves. Then you have another 15-20% who are freeloading. Smoking dope and mooching off the government. They are also the ones who buy the drugs and OD. Most of us are really pretty harmless and look out for each other and the tourists who are still brave enough to come down here. We protect them from the crazies. I do feel sorry for them. I would be somewhere else, but as things go, this is the best place to not have a job or a house," said Trapper, holding his hands up and looking around at the sunny sky.

"What kind of job did you lose?" asked Earl.

"I worked for an airline at LAX. When the pandemic happened, they furloughed everyone and when the flights started again, they only brought back based on seniority. I had only been back from Iraq for 2 years then, so I was low on the totem pole. I tried to work construction, but I was competing with illegals. They were paying $10 an hour, working 10 to 12-hour days and I could make enough money on unemployment, so I gave up trying. As long as California keeps paying me enough for food…," Trapper shrugged.

"You sound like a smart guy. Surely there is something out there," asked Greg, speaking for the first time.

"Probably is. Where do I start? If you don't have an address and you can't show that you have held a job in the last few years, or you don't have the right clothes or haircut, you can't get past the first interview. It is depressing. Look, I want to work. I could probably be a damn good EMT or something, somewhere, to somebody, but there is no way to connect me with the people who need me."

"The city and county are worthless. They aren't trying to help. They're only trying to keep us out of the news and make sure we stay calm. Believe me, they have bigger issues with MS13 downtown. Those guys tried to come in here once. Sent six of them to the hospital, so they gave up and went down to Huntington Beach, where they terrorize the tourists. We got some big dudes in here and when we need to, we can help each other out," said Trapper. Earl smiled at this.

"We pool our resources. When someone needed a new oxygen tank, we moved his tent closer to the power. We have a community here and we look out for each other, because no one else gives a damn."

Nick had listened intently to Trapper's descriptions and explanations of the community.

"Trapper, if I could find you work and shelter and a decent wage, would you work?" asked Nick.

"No offence, Nick, but I don't want you to feel sorry for me and give me a job. Someone needs to figure out how to help all of us. Not just giving a few of us jobs. We need solutions for all."

"Do you know what people can do? The skills they have and their willingness to work and leave this beach?" asked Nick.

"What are you thinking?" responded Trapper, confused.

"What I am thinking is you are correct. There is untapped potential in many of you, and you only need some help to get back on your feet. What I am thinking is you need a chance at redemption. You need to get a job, build up your self-esteem and self-worth, and contribute to society." Trapper had a strange look on his face as Nick continued.

"I need to talk to some more people to see what we can do. In the meantime, can you assess how many people would take me up on the offer to work? Not charity but work. A chance to contribute and take control of their own livelihood again. Now that work to start might be on my campaign, but it could be in other things. Depends on how much I can get folks to rally to my idea," cautioned Nick.

"Sir, I have nothing else to do, and we can't be picky. But work, good work we could do to give us a chance to leave this beach is all most want. We need a helping hand, not more handouts."

Nick held out his hand and told Trapper, "Give me some time and I promise I'll be back in touch soon, probably take a few weeks, maybe a month."

"You know where to find me, Senator," laughed Trapper.

They continued walking down the path and looked at the tents. It was a sad sight as they saw entire families with children playing outside the tents in the sand. "Have you noticed anything?" asked Nick.

"You mean the fact that most of them are white?" said Earl.

"And peaceful. They just seem to have no hope. They don't seem to care and they move like zombies," commented Greg.

"Exactly, I think we may be onto something. Redemption is important, and with such high unemployment and high numbers of unemployed, we simply need to put the two together."

"It could work. It'll take a bunch of money," remarked Earl.

"Am I missing something?" asked Greg. "Are you not in the middle of a presidential campaign? How are you going to find time to help all these people?"

"Greg, I think they work hand in hand. To your point Earl, more than money, it will take logistics. We have to find shelter to rent and jobs to place people in. Money is important, but people who buy into the concept will find the money. We have army bases all over the country that are falling into disarray. I have often wondered why we could not turn these into subsidized housing instead of watching the buildings fall into ruin. Something we need to look into. We'll add it to the list. Denise will be thrilled," remarked Nick, as Greg and Earl shook their heads, smiling in disbelief at Nick taking on another cause.

# Chapter 47

Nick pulled off California highway 29, turning north onto a dirt driveway leading up to the foothills. He was between Napa and Yountville, in the heart of California wine country. Nick glanced at his GPS, assuring him he was on the right road. He continued about a mile up the driveway before a large 1920s craftsman style house showed up.

Nick parked his rental next to a vintage Mercedes four-door sedan. He exited the car and started up the path to the front steps when a screen door opened. A spry, gray-haired man approached, wearing khaki pants and a sweater. "Welcome, Senator, come on up and save me the trip down on my poor aching knees," said the man in a friendly tone.

Nick walked up the steps and took the offered hand.

"Nice to meet you, Mr. Patterson," greeted Nick.

"Please call me Howard," Mr. Patterson said, putting his arm around Nick and leading him in.

"And you can call me Nick."

"I shall," smiled Howard. "Come on in. My wife made some lemonade, and we have homemade muffins fresh out of the oven."

They passed through a picturesque foyer and into a cavernous living room with vaulted ceilings and exposed timber frame beams. Centered along one wall was a stone fireplace and chimney extending two stories through the vaulted room. Midway up another wall was a massive painting, fully six feet across, showing a fantastic landscape of mountain ranges and towering clouds colored in a setting sun.

"Is that a Wilson Hurley?" asked Nick, standing to admire it.

"It is indeed. I see you know your art."

"There is a fabulous piece down in the museum in Santa Fe. That's where I first fell in love with his art. His landscapes are breathtaking," said Nick, making conversation.

"They are indeed. But I didn't invite you here to discuss my art collection," commented Howard.

"I presume not. Wonderful home as well. 1920s?"

"This time I stumped you. It is made to look like they built it in the 20s. They actually built it in the 1980s for a movie studio president who wanted a 1920s craftsman style house but couldn't find one to buy, so he had one built. Then he got canned for not making any movies worth a damn, and I bought it," said Howard, laughing.

"Well, when you look at movies these days, it's a wonder any studio head still has a job. It's all crap," stated Nick. "There hasn't been an original idea in 50 years. Of course, most kids these days can't sit still for two hours to watch a movie unless it is a comic book. *Casablanca* or *Rear Window* would be wasted on them. Just sad."

"That is for sure," agreed Howard, continuing to lead Nick through the living room and a dining room area to a screened-in porch off one room. They took their seats in a pair of comfortable wicker cushioned chairs. Howard poured a couple of glasses of lemonade.

"Muffin?" he asked, handing a glass to Nick.

"Not right now, thanks," said Nick, who could tell Howard was working up to his reason for asking him to stop by.

"Nick, I have five kids, fifteen grand kids and now at last count seven great grand kids. I've come a long way from the streets of Brooklyn. Fortunes made, lost and made again. I achieved this through hard work, determination, sacrifice, perseverance, and no small amount of hope and luck. With all this money, and some say, power, I am, in fact, powerless to make sure my grandkids survive and thrive. Nick, I'm terrified. I look around and I see disasters of biblical proportion approaching on the horizon," pausing as he took a sip. Nick waited patiently, sipping his own lemonade.

"I've endowed countless schools, scholarships at Stanford and USC, supported the arts and sciences, with buildings at both named after me. All of this means nothing if our society collapses. I have donated so much money to the Party political campaigns and PACs, they have me on speed dial. They've gotten so used to it they just ask how much to put me down for. Not even bothering to ask anymore."

"They seem to be a bit presumptuous that way. Not exactly stellar customer service," agreed Nick.

"You've run a business, consulting services. I checked," said Howard, again pausing for a drink.

Nick laughed. "Howard, at its largest, I had 5 employees, so I think we are talking about the difference between the neighborhood lemonade stand and Walmart. I was also a college professor, the antithesis of doing."

"Doesn't matter. You know what it is like to make payroll and to look for and compete to win business. Most of your colleagues would starve in a day if they had to fend for themselves. We are a nation of builders and problem solvers. Of big thinkers and entrepreneurs, and until recently, patriots and good neighbors. We've been infected with European malaise. A lack of will to *do*. We are simply becoming a nation of followers. We do what we are told. By the government, our newspapers, TV, and the little apps on our phones."

"Now I know it is easy for me to sit here and say the world is going to hell in a handbasket. I did my part to help by funding some of these entities. And clearly, I do not want for anything. But now I am seriously worried. I have been reading history lately, looking to the past for answers. For hints on what is coming and how to turn this around."

Nick looked at Howard's concerned face. "Howard, history is a window into the future. Everything happening now has happened before. All we need to do is look and we can find out what the future holds. How to speed up or stop it, if we are only willing to look."

"You taught history. Trying to educate our youth *does* count as doing," said Howard, smiling. "You see the same things I see. Probably with much more clarity."

"Yes, I do. We are following the path of every affluent society. We have achieved the point where we no longer do the work ourselves. Instead, just like Rome, we farm it out to 'lesser' tribes we have imported into our civilization, or more often, overseas. We have turned inward, more concerned with pleasure than with the preservation of what we've built. We sit idly by, becoming softer and softer. Reveling in our own inventions to make our life more leisurely," finished Nick, taking a sip of his lemonade and looking at Howard for a reaction.

"You know Nick, my father fought in World War II. The last of the buddies from his platoon died a few years back, well over 100. In my last conversation with him, he took my hand. His mind was still sharp, and he said, 'we need to preserve America, because it still is the only thing holding back evil'."

"He meant evil in the good vs evil, not bad government, or anything else. God vs Satan, biblical good vs evil. My dad's units were some of the first to arrive at the concentration camps. They saw the walking cadavers. They saw the outcome of 'evil'. The outcome of totalitarian rule, where morals and ethics are what the rulers want them to be."

"Howard, answer this question. Because in my mind, it is the classic determiner of where a society is in its evolution. Our finest moment was World War II and the immediate decades after. A society able to send its young men to die willingly on foreign soil. For the freedoms of others, to whom they owe no direct allegiance, is a society whose core principles are noble, righteous, and sustainable. D-day personified this," asserted Nick.

"Our young men did not question their duty. The duty to freedom as they bled on the beaches of France. They understood if this evil was not confronted and stopped there, it would have to be stopped on the beaches of California and New Jersey. Our leaders knew what they were asking. They also knew we would respond as we did. We willingly sacrificed our youth. They risked this and gave what Lincoln called the 'last full measure of devotion', to leave behind a society able to evolve and achieve where we are today."

"Nick, my dad said the same thing. He believed he was doing this for me and you and all my kids and grandkids. To him and his buddies, we were all worth the sacrifice. So we wouldn't have to do what they did." Nick looked at Howard as he spoke with passion.

"Does anyone still believe we would have that same resolve? That same willingness to storm the beaches of Normandy again? Or Taiwan, Ukraine, or Vera Cruz, if that is what it took to restore freedom?" asked Nick rhetorically. "I believe we both know the answer. Even our response to 9/11 was a momentary burst of unity. It was followed quickly by the inevitable separation back into tribes. Each trying to figure out how to use the tragedy to consolidate or expand influence and power at home."

Howard listened to Nick, making no attempt to interrupt.

"We are a fading civilization. On the downside of our influence, power and, unfortunately, our mission of spreading democracy and freedom and all it can accomplish."

Howard smiled. "You don't believe that. This is the reason I asked you to come by. You are the only person with the nerve and the passion to speak the truth. Your message is getting out, despite their efforts to keep it from spreading. It still is. But not fast enough. Jeremy is helping, but he has the problem of trying to build a business in a niche already dominated by 800lb gorillas."

"You know Jeremy?" asked Nick with a wry smile.

"Oh yes. I was his initial investor in his security company when he was a PhD grad student with an idea. I am also an investor in his latest venture. In fact, he is the one who told me to do some research and sent me some links to some of your speeches. I have to admit, I didn't know who you were. Never watch the news," shrugged Howard.

"I thought he was in college when I met him for breakfast."

"You aren't the only one," laughed Howard. "Nick, what I hear you say is exactly what I think we are missing. I've been watching you and I believe you can be the leader we need to salvage our country. To wake up the country and see if we still care enough to stand up. I want to help you get your message out farther and faster."

He held up his hand as Nick made to interrupt.

"We have little time. If Lexi wins, I think we are done. She scares me. I know her too well. Also, some of the people in the shadows supporting her. I also think they are directing her, at least as much as she can be directed. They are powerful and don't care about the people, only the outcome, by expanding their power and control."

"Howard, I am doing my part. I am telling things the way they are, as I see them. Trying to get people to stand up and fight for their futures. I can't order them. I can only inspire and hope they care enough about their future to fight. This is our D-day. People are going to have to risk their livelihood, safety, and cushy existence to repel the enemy. There will be casualties. The alternative is to not fight. To give up and give in and the next question will be, are we going to end up like the people in Dachau and Auschwitz? Who is going to free us if we are no longer around to rise up against this evil?"

"Exactly. I want to help you, Nick. I *need* to help you. How do we do this? I know you don't want my money. How else can I help? All this money and influence and yet I feel powerless to stop this. I don't sleep at night, don't eat, and my wife is concerned because all I do is read and worry. I need to do something, or it is going to consume me. Please, let me help," pleaded Howard sincerely.

Nick looked at the billionaire. Amazed that a man with everything, who could do *anything*, command legions of workers to do what he wanted, was in front of him, begging to let him help.

"Howard, I am flattered. More than you can know. I can't take your money. That makes me as bad as them. Trading influence for money. I have a couple of ideas about how you can help, indirectly."

"I'm listening."

"First, I was down on Venice Beach a few days ago. What I saw was both sad and depressing. I saw a large slice of humanity in need of hope. Many were capable and willing to work, but were unable to be matched to an opportunity. I talked to one guy, a former army medic. He told me up to two-thirds of the folks there have sound minds and skills. I asked him what the problem was, why they were there. He told me about them, about the lack of opportunity."

Howard, listening intently, lifted the lemonade pitcher, refilling their glasses, as Nick continued.

"I thought, how could I give these people hope and employment? Use their skills and give them honest work, self-esteem, and confidence to come back into society and off the government dole. Most are merely unfortunate victims of circumstances. I can employ them in my campaign, going door to door, calling folks, spreading the word, but I can't find housing for them. Or feed them until they earn enough to get back on their feet.

This is an untapped knowledge base. A capable force of humans willing to contribute but forgotten and cast aside by our affluent society. Bought off by an uncaring government, giving them enough to subsist but not recover," finished Nick.

"Hmm, what do you have in mind?"

Nick could see Howard already thinking. Solving the problem, running through scenarios in his mind.

"We would need to set up programs in major locations where the homeless enclaves are the most prevalent. Then we need to send in volunteers to convince the leaders of the encampments to talk to their community and recruit those willing to work. Then help move them into some form of communal housing."

"We need to find housing, old hotels or dorms. Maybe we put those with skills in charge of running and maintaining the housing. Then we provide some form of community food services, like a cafeteria," stated Nick as he paced around in the sunroom. It was clear he had already given this some serious thought.

"Maybe we keep a portion of the earnings to fund these or we charge them rent and use the proceeds from those to fund the services. The idea would be to get them working and building confidence. Then letting them work until they can find other jobs within the org or outside so they can move to their own housing and out of the program."

Howard smiled as Nick continued.

"This will take money, but it has to be built so people cannot stay forever. It needs to be like means tested welfare and run down to no help in a pre-determined time, so folks don't abuse it. In the meantime, I can use the help and we can get them off the beaches and out of the city centers. We can improve these locations, while helping our campaign and getting them back on their feet."

"You realize they are going to say you are taking advantage of people with no other choices?" remarked Howard.

"I would love for them to do it. It will give me a chance to point out all they have not done. We also need to recruit companies willing to take a chance on these people and match their skills to the needs they have.

It is almost like the Peace Corps, but more like Jobs Corp. I see it as redemption," said Nick. "What do you think of the idea?"

Howard smiled. "Nick, this is exactly why I called you. You don't look at how to help yourself, you are looking at ways to help the people and the country, regardless of whether it helps you. This might work. What do you need?"

"The org needs funding. We need to find and lock down housing. We need to hire organizers who can help kick start things and they need to be patriots, not liberal activists. Our mantra is 'Think for Yourself', not get brainwashed to fight climate change or racial injustice. You interested in helping?" asked Nick.

"Yes, and not only am I willing to help, I think I can recruit some others who feel the same, betrayed by our faith in their words. I can arrange for you to talk to them. I believe they'll be happy to help contribute money, housing, and leaders in various cities to help. If we can be seen to help ease the homeless problems, it will help your campaign and solve a societal ill the local governments have been unable or unwilling to solve as well," explained Howard, excited at the prospect.

"I don't care if it helps me or not. All I care about is getting these people back on their feet. We also need to provide some mental health counselors. We need to get them off the drugs and get folks who need it into programs to help their mental issues. Can we also work with clinics or hospitals to fund some additional beds to get these people help? This seems like a better endowment than scholarships to university activist mills. But hey, it is your money," shrugged Nick.

"It is my money, and I can think of no better way to give back than to redirect the funds to these activities," said Howard, leaning forward and becoming more animated as the conversation continued.

"Fair warning, the minute you do this, any of your businesses are going to come under fire. The same for anyone you recruit who offers jobs. The woke mob will target your companies and put the pressure on them to disavow you and force you to change your plans and stop your efforts. I don't know how many boards you have, but if you don't control them, they will kick you out and try to ostracize you. They have tons of resources. And they are ruthless because *they* know it *is* a war, and it is win or die." Howard did not flinch. He smiled in reply.

"Our side doesn't even know it is a war. The other side is trying to make elections irrelevant and simply seize power through so-called popular mandates," exposed Nick.

Howard leaned back in his chair and opened his hands, palm up.

"I get it, but you know what? If I lost everything, so what? At least I'll do it trying to help. It does not differ from the guy sitting in the landing craft approaching the beach. He knew there was a good chance he'd die the minute they dropped the front ramp. But he didn't stop. He waited and prepared just like his buddy on each side. His buddy who might have been Jewish and from California or a Lutheran farmer from Iowa or an Irish Catholic welder from Chicago or a Baptist oil worker from Texas. All were worried about the same thing, believed in the almighty and were prepared to sacrifice themselves for each other, their country, their family, and sweethearts. They did this because it was good versus evil. They didn't shirk their duty. How could I live with myself if I didn't do my part?"

Nick smiled. "I see you spent some time talking to your father's platoon mates. Only someone who was there could have given you that kind of insight. I am glad you got to hear it from them before they were all gone. We are betraying their sacrifice. It is our job to make sure we don't squander their gift."

"You said two things?" prompted Howard.

"The second is more troublesome. In my conversations across the country, I am trying to only talk to the common people. One thing is loud and clear. People are against many of the policies being forced on their communities and schools," said Nick in a serious tone.

Howard looked down and then up into Nick's face. "Nick, this is my main reason for asking to meet with you. My wife and several of my children have asked me what they can do? They don't agree with many things. They also know being my children makes both them *and* me a target if they stand up to debate, let alone stand against the policies. Even at a school board meeting."

"Howard, I see it everywhere I go. Fear. It is their greatest weapon. It is a disease, worse than any pandemic, and equally deadly to a society built on freedom of expression and discussion. If we can't debate new or even old ideas and freely disagree, we cannot continue to evolve. There will come a time when a critical mass will finally have had enough. The question is, what happens? Will it be in time to stop the destruction of our society, or will it be after and the longer road of trying to rebuild?" declared Nick with passion and conviction.

"You think armed conflict is inevitable?"

"No, I do not. This is *my* reason for running. I have seen more mindless murder and mayhem for multiple lifetimes. Nothing gained and only lives lost in Afghanistan, Iraq, Syria and other places, for no gain. We cannot allow that to occur here. We are better than this and we have the freedom to choose to not allow it."

"Howard," continued Nick, looking him in the eyes. "I need protection. No, not for me," said Nick quickly, seeing the concern on Howard's face. "For my followers. For anyone I convince to stand up and make themselves a target by daring to differ with the establishment. There are some now who risk this and pay the price. Too many see this result and then rightfully choose to not stand up."

"That is how they are winning," said Howard in a resigned tone. "Make you lose everything. A fate worse than being killed. They make you *useless*. To your family, to your community, to yourself."

"Yes. I have an idea to combat this. But I need your help and the help of others who feel the way you do. People willing to take the same risk as those standing up to the progressive utopia being promised by the Vice President."

"I spoke at a VFW in Idaho. During the conversation, we talked about how the colonists formed Sons of Liberty organizations. Banding together to fight the most powerful empire in the world. We are doing the same thing with my Turner Rabble groups. We spoke about creating a community, where we would band together and support those who get canceled for standing up. Help pay mortgages, provide jobs, build the Turner Rabble Defense Fund. They can cancel some or even many of us, but if enough stand up and stand together, supporting each other, they cannot cancel all of us."

Howard sat for a few seconds, contemplating Nick's request.

"I am in. All the way. Tell me what you need. I will make it happen. Nick, it is now or never. I agree that this is our D-Day moment. We need to show the same courage our fathers and grandfathers did to save freedom from Hitler. This is our fight."

They both looked up to see Howard's wife, standing in the doorway, blowing her nose with a tissue and wiping tears. She came down into the room to Nick, who stood, holding out a hand. She ignored the hand and gave Nick a tight hug.

"I cannot thank you enough. You have saved his life. By giving him a purpose. I don't know what I would have done. Thank you so much," professed Claire, as Howard came up and put a hand around her shoulders.

"Nick, my wife Claire, she's a bit of a worrier," frowned Howard as she gave him an annoying look and a poke in the ribs, causing him to yelp in pain.

"Ouch" exclaimed Howard, returning a mock annoyed look.

"What is the next step?" asked Nick.

"Let me make a few calls and see if I can recruit some like-minded people. Believe it or not, we are not all bleeding heart types who want to force one world socialism on everyone. There are others who will risk it all to give our kids and society a chance to return to a way of living, which allowed all of us to succeed. I'll call you soon. I may need you to talk to a few more to convince them you are real and not just saying it for votes or donations," commented Howard.

"Let's do it. I'll get the org founded and then we can work on getting it staffed and plans and strategies to implement it. We need military precision, almost a campaign, and I think I may have the right guy to pull it off," said Nick.

"Great, let's talk in a week and get this ball rolling," said Howard, shaking Nick's hand.

"I think I'll have that muffin now. All this talk has made me hungry," replied Nick, smiling at Claire and at Howard, who laughed.

# Chapter 48

"Would someone please explain to me what is going on?" asked Lexi to her assembled senior staff with an icy glare.

They were in her campaign office conference room, reviewing the information coming in from the various Super Tuesday primaries. Several of the screens in the room announced the surprising victories of Senator Herb Klausen of Wisconsin, most notably in Texas.

"Are you kidding me?" said Lexi, her voice rising one more octave, turning to Mel and her pollster, Merri Wilcox. "Are they right?"

"We are crunching numbers as well, but it appears Senator Klausen is going to beat you slightly in Texas and Oklahoma," confirmed Merri in an analytical tone, looking at several laptops perched on the conference table in front of her.

"Georgia and the rest of the southern states, Tennessee, Arkansas, North Carolina, and Alabama. We didn't lose all of them, did we?" asked Lexi, her voice rising even higher.

No one immediately answered her, so she turned on Mel.

"I thought our organizations in all these states 'were the best money could buy'," said Lexi, raising her hands sarcastically. "This is embarrassing."

Mel moved out of range of Lexi before answering.

"We may need to rethink some of your positions, clearly. Exit polling shows people are not in favor of amnesty for migrants under any circumstances or timeframes and some of your plans on guns are hurting you in the South. Even some of *our* voters like their guns and don't appreciate all the migrants. Klausen took the moderate position. Slowing immigration, working on a compassionate situation. Putting low-income American's needs ahead of migrants. He put out that spot shooting geese, implying he isn't against guns, or at least not as much as you," finished Mel.

"I am happy to do a spot shooting some of my staff if you think that will help us," answered Lexi, glaring at Mel. "Or maybe my state campaign managers. Who dropped the ball? Why didn't we have more get out the vote? Did we take it for granted? I want the resignation of each of those campaign managers by tomorrow morning, for every state we lost. I want to send a message to the rest of the state chairman. Step up or else," threatened Lexi.

"Lexi, that is probably not a good idea. Our Texas chairman has been the head of the Party in Texas for twenty-five years and is responsible for us winning more seats in Congress there for the Party than ever," placated Mel.

"Really? How many times has the Party carried Texas since he has been in charge? I can tell you. Zero. I want him out, make it happen. Same for the other southern states. We need some fresh blood."

"Lexi, it is all about good ole boy networks, especially in the south. These Party chairmen are essential to raising money and for getting the vote out for us," responded Mel.

"Merri, how far off were our projections versus what happened?" asked Lexi, ignoring Mel.

"We had you up 10 in Texas and over 15 in most of the others," she answered. "Clearly something happened. Either a lot of folks switched their votes after our last phone polls, or we called the wrong people. I will start digging into this."

"So, what is the count?" asked Lexi.

No one answered immediately.

"What is the fucking count? Mel?" yelled Lexi, eyes flashing.

"Might be a good time for me to give you two some private time," said Merri, picking up her laptops and leaving the conference room, along with the few others who had not fled already. Mel walked to the door, flipped the switch on the light curtain, blocking all the windows to the conference room. He hit a second button and put the room into SCIF mode to make sure nothing could be recorded.

"If our math is right and Klausen wins Virginia as big as we projected, we put him ahead of you by about 80 delegates. Around 475 for us and 560 for Klausen. Remember, we are going to take California big. There goes his lead. Then we have Oregon, Washington, Illinois, New York, and Pennsylvania. He'll win Wisconsin and probably barely beat you in Kentucky, Ohio, Indiana, and Florida. But remember, unlike the Opposition, all our primaries are proportional. Even when Klausen wins a state, you are still picking up close to the same number of delegates. It'll just take a little longer, but we have this under control."

"It looks bad, Mel. This has to be a landslide to remove resistance to my policies."

"Lexi, we are victims of our own success. Too many of our voters live in urban areas and assume we, *you*, are going to waltz to the nomination. They're not going to spend their time voting in the primary. The only people motivated to vote in the primary are those who *don't* like your policies. You are getting a lopsided view. Also, look at our turnout numbers. They are way below normal. Why? Because it is a foregone conclusion, you'll win. As long as they come out in November, we'll get our landslide."

"They had better. Now I have to listen to the pundits questioning my ability to rouse the base," groused Lexi, thinking through the repercussions of not closing out the nomination on Super Tuesday.

"We didn't count on everybody else dropping out so quickly. All of their supporters are jumping to Klausen instead of you. Four dropped out after South Carolina and from my count, the other nine will drop out today or tomorrow, so it is just you and Klausen. Trust me, the Party is finally ready to accept the progressive agenda. We've been laying the groundwork for years and the pandemics helped us show folks how only the federal government can help at the scale necessary."

"Think about all the people we helped by stopping evictions, extending unemployment, and raising minimum wages. The entire economic turnaround is because of our progressive policies. The student debt payment moratorium, the forgiveness we have gotten through, and our pledge to wipe out the rest. This locks the young people into supporting us. We need to do a better job of getting these folks to vote in the primaries. Klausen is not playing well on the west coast, which only makes sense, since we know those are the most progressive states who support our policies wholeheartedly. Don't panic," said Mel.

"I am not panicking, I am pissed. I count on all of you. This is just like before. I don't want to win. I want to win in a landslide. We need a mandate. If I have to duke it out through the primaries, it means I have to defend the positions. The more I have to talk about them versus another Party member, the worse it is going to look. The more it will energize the moderates to get off their butts and vote for Klausen. No more debates. Got it?"

"Yes," answered Mel.

"We need to get the primaries over and keep the talking heads from discussing why I have a challenger in the party. We have to be unified. Look at the Opposition. There are four of them with the same number of delegates and it is going to stay that way unless someone screws up. This gives the idiots on TV plenty to talk about. How fragmented the Opposition is and how they are hopelessly fractured between defense, migrants, healthcare, jobs, abortion, crime, China and Russia. We don't have that problem, or at least I was told we didn't," she finished with a glare at Mel.

"We are executing the game plan. It will work. We need to let it play out," said Mel.

"Can't we just offer Klausen something and get him to drop out? He has to know he won't be in the lead after next week. Now he has bargaining power. After next week, his position just gets weaker."

"Exactly, which is why we wait until he knows he has lost before we talk about a cabinet position. We need to pick the right VP, to help us the most. It is *not* Klausen. We may need a moderate, and most likely a minority or a woman, but it will all depend on the Opposition."

"Mel, get it over with. I am tired of standing up in front of the press, smiling and telling the cameras competition is healthy for a democracy," admitted Lexi. "My teeth hurt from grinding them while I say this shit. If we need to spend more time giving speeches or money on ads or hire more people to get out the vote, let's do it. Spare no expense. We need to get this part done and into the election."

"Got it, leave this to me and go back to running the country."

"Good job with Vincent, by the way."

"Excuse me?" remarked Mel. "Sam Vincent died in an unfortunate accident in New York City. Tragic."

"Right." grinned Lexi, drawing out the word. "Apparently, your new head of security is already paying dividends. He struck me as extremely competent when we spoke. Where did you say he came from?"

"I didn't. He came highly recommended. Let's leave it at that."

Lexi nodded. "I am worried about some cabinet members."

"Who?" asked Mel.

"The ones who voted against me having the nuclear codes. They are the ones who think this is going to bite us in the ass."

"They're political appointees. All they care about is not stepping in shit. This situation has shit written all over it if somebody blabs or the truth gets out. Weak links. We'll handle it," promised Mel.

"For now, they are more afraid of me than what could happen. Keep an eye on them and make sure our media assets let us know if anyone tries to go public," ordered Lexi.

Mel nodded. "I will make sure we step up our monitoring of stories so we can *kill* any leaks," replied Mel, smiling.

"No more surprises. I want to start my *official* presidency and accomplish the mission."

"Yes Madame President," said Mel saluting. Lexi smiled.

# Chapter 49

"Have you figured out how to track him yet?" asked a tall black man standing in the office's doorway.

The man behind the desk, another black man, much smaller, with round rim glasses, looked up.

"I think so. Your source was right. We are now getting information sent to our account on where he is planning to be. This will give us the ability to gather our teams and either bus them in or use local resources."

"Good job Bobby. I want to earn the additional incentives. It'll be good to focus on a new target."

Bobby nodded from behind his desk. "We need the dough. Donations have been pretty sparse the last few years. Only our continued efforts to squeeze the corporations and, of course, our World Harmony Society grants have kept us going."

Napoleon Bello walked from the doorway to a chair and sat down heavily. "We did too good a job of scaring the pigs," he said with a small laugh. "They're afraid to even pull a gun anymore. They don't arrest folks for doing anything. Good for reparations, but bad for the outrage business. This could be just what we're looking for."

"Bone, you may be right. Have you seen some of the stuff this Turner guy is saying? Geez, he had better watch his ass. If he says that in the wrong place, even the cops are going to have to do their jobs and arrest the guys who eventually give this guy his beat down," said Bobby, laughing.

Bone, whose nickname was Bonaparte, was a natural moniker to go with Napoleon. It was eventually shortened to just 'Bone' on the streets of St. Louis. He'd made his reputation during the Ferguson and St. Louis riots, leading and recruiting people to the Anti-Racist League banners. Bone was not laughing. He was worried.

"Bobby, anybody talking about *what* he is saying?"

"Huh? Turner?" asked Bobby, confused.

"Yes. Have you listened to what he is saying?" asked Bone.

"Sure. He says we are shaking down corporations for money and the ARL is a shill for the communist party. How we don't care for blacks or making things better," shrugged Bobby. "What else is new? He ain't the first to figure this out. Why?"

"It is not what he says, it is how he says it. He doesn't tell people or even directly accuse anyone of doing anything. He just tells people to think about what the result is, not the action itself. It worries me," said Bone.

"Nah, you are reading way more into it than you should. Who is hearing it? Who is listening? We have way too much success for his words to make a difference. Now, if I was a stupid white woman paying $2500 for a Louis Vuitton purse and watched someone walking out of the store with ten of them for free, *she* might be pissed. But I doubt someone like that is going to show up and say they should lock up our brothers and sisters. Especially for stealing something that costs more than they make in a month because some rich white Botox bitch is mad. She is not exactly a sympathetic complainer," smiled Bobby.

Bone smiled as well. "Good point. What is our plan?"

"Simple. Follow the same playbook we were all taught. We'll show up, agitate, interrupt, shout down the speakers and hope we get a response. We have someone filming and we send the footage to all our allies in the media. Just like they have asked us to do, we target the individuals supporting Turner and go after the locals who try to hold rallies for him. We make the so called Turner Rabble feel the pain of standing up and making themselves targets. They should be easy to rile up. Most are really fed up with all the lack of law and order. We'll focus on white speakers, of course." Bobby shrugged again, leaning back in his chair. "Should be simple. They are easy targets."

Bone sat quietly, listening. He looked down at his wrist and the Rolex he wore. It was worth at least $15,000. He remembered the jewelry store he had 'liberated' the watch from in downtown Chicago during one of the many smash and grab activities during the summer of George Floyd. The corporation he took it from could afford it. He took what they owed him and faced the consequences. It surprised him when it became clear nobody cared. He was on video and yet the cops never even made any attempt to recover any of the stolen goods. The stores didn't either.

Over the years, he watched as more and more of the urban areas of major cities were becoming war zones. Crime and drugs were rampant. Laws were rarely enforced. Cops usually only showing up to clean up after mass gang shootings and the collateral damage from innocent bystanders, injured or killed. Bone now had children, and he was thinking what they had accomplished was not what they had intended. The results were not what they had been promised. It had not changed the landscape for blacks positively. He listened to what Turner had to say, and it disturbed him. What if Turner was right?

Bobby noticed Bone was quieter than usual.

"What's up Bone? Something wrong?"

Bone looked up, smiling. "Nope, let's earn our money. These bills don't pay themselves," he said, getting up. "Where does it start?"

"We will just follow where he goes. As he leaves, groups supporting him start up and try to gather followers at local rallies. We use our local assets where we have them and if we have enough notice, we will bus them in. We'll make them regret sticking their necks out," finished Bobby ominously.

Bone nodded as he left the office. He had a nagging feeling about this assignment.

# Chapter 50

Roland Gill looked down at the vibrating satellite phone. Pulling out another phone, he typed a random appearing set of numbers and letters. He received another equally random set of codes in return on his phone.

Reaching into his desk, he removed a small silver box. It was three inches high, three inches wide, and close to six inches long. It did not seem to have any seams.

He tapped the codes into the phone. The silver box made a series of noises. Finally, a metallic voice projected.

"Secure?"

"Yes," replied Roland, knowing his own voice was masked on the receiver's side of the call.

"Settled in?"

"Yes. I am managing security for the campaign efforts. I am involved in every aspect other than personal security, which the Secret Service handles, of course."

"Good. What do you see?"

"It is an impressive operation. Very organized. The campaign leaders and staff seem very competent and seasoned. It is a well-oiled machine."

"I sense some hesitation?"

"Turner."

"What of him? Remember, I told you to put personal feelings aside and focus on the mission. Your existence depends on this. Never forget that."

Roland laughed. "No need to worry. I fully understand my position. You should, however, not underestimate him. He is out maneuvering them. He manipulates them into uncharacteristic mistakes and then he capitalizes on them. They are good at the politics of personal destruction. They are not used to their enemies fighting back. I fear they are in love with this weapon and have cultivated no others if it fails. They have become complacent. You asked. That is what I see."

"It is still early. It is a balancing act. They cannot attack too overtly, or they risk a repeat of past mistakes. Providing free publicity and awakening their low information voters. Allowing them to be easily influenced by nationalist rhetoric. This is not why I called."

Roland waited for his employer to continue.

"Our friend Inspector Gauthier is making trouble again."

"Luc? I would have thought after our last encounter he would know better. Shall we make good on our threat?"

"Perhaps. First though, can you get away or contact associates you trust to investigate and perhaps discretely follow him?"

"Of course. Either. What is the mission?"

"I got a call from the 'Doctor'," his benefactor explained.

"How?" asked Roland, stiffening in concern. "Surely Luc has not tracked this back to him. That is impossible. We left no clues."

"Calm down. No, he has not. But you know the Inspector. He is worse than a dog with a bone. He visited some institutions where the Doctor ultimately got the recruits."

"How did he even know about the autistic bomber? Sabah designed the bomb so there would be no trace of the bomber left to link to anyone."

"It seems Luc is up to his old tricks. Somehow, he made the connection and started asking questions. Hence the visits. At one of these homes, the proprietor made the mistake of fabricating a story. Our good inspector will investigate and discover this error. Once he does, it will lead him further along the trail. It is possible this could ultimately lead him to the Doctor."

Roland swore in Hebrew, and the voice in the box emitted a metallic chuckle.

"Indeed, you are correct, *Daboia*. I need you to discover how he has gathered this information and to whom he has spoken. We need to plug the leaks. Eliminating the Inspector with his ties to the current President, is out of the question. We cannot be too obvious and risk a united backlash. Clearly, we cannot use more of your unwilling soldiers now that they are on to that tactic."

"I will handle this. It is my operation. Mistakes are mine to own. And clean up," said Roland with finality.

"Good. As I expected. Strike and end this. We do not need more uncertainty. Turner is enough. I do not need Gauthier on the prowl delaying or discovering our further destabilization plans."

"Yes, sir," answered Roland, already contemplating how he would remove this threat.

"It appears Chaumont has also asked Luc to review the Christmas market attacks," said the voice.

"Why? They stopped the one in France. They have no reason to pursue or involve themselves in other countries' investigations."

"That I cannot answer. Perhaps the Canadian prime minister asked. Or, more likely, the fop of a chancellor in Germany. It matters not. Just be aware. Roland, do not let him catch you."

Roland laughed a menacing laugh.

"He does not even know it was me and my look was entirely different from then. He will not see me or even know why, but he must pay a price for meddling. That was the promise we made. He broke his side of the bargain," he finished in a firm tone.

"Careful. Again, as with Turner, do not let personal feelings enter the equation. Just stop the investigation and put Gauthier back into his scotch bottle. Do not give him a reason to care again."

"Understood."

# Chapter 51

"Nick, I am not sure this is such a good idea," said Earl, looking at Nick, hoping for a no.

"How else am I going to get a sense of what it is like?" answered Nick, giving Earl a look of determination.

"Will you at least wear a vest under your jacket?"

"Do the nine-year-olds? Does your cousin? I know the risk, Earl. I have to see for myself."

"Alright, but I don't like it and it *is* my job to keep you alive. We're going to meet my cousin in North Lawndale, one of the worst neighborhoods in Chicago."

"Hey if I don't see it firsthand, then I am no better than every other politician, including the mayor, who claims to understand the problem without ever going there," declared Nick.

They walked into a Denny's, just outside North Lawndale. Earl walked up to a booth, where his cousin Ray Coleman got up. He gave Earl a hug and shook Nick's hand. They sat down in the booth.

"Earl told me you played pro ball. He left out your size. How tall are you 6'6?" asked Nick with a smile. At 6'4" he rarely had to look up.

"Senator, more like 6'5" now and about 30 lbs. heavier than when I played for the Raiders. No time for workouts anymore," laughed Ray.

"Ray runs a youth ministry now. Tries to help keep the young kids in school and arbitrates between the various gangs to stop some of the turf wars," explained Earl.

"A noble cause, Ray. Please call me Nick. How bad is it?"

"Bad is a relative term, Nick. Believe it or not, most of the deaths are not drug related, despite what the media wants you to think. Unfortunately, it is even dumber." Ray shook his head. "Most of the killings are about honor. Stupid social media. Used to be you had to insult someone to their face and you would fight with knives or fists and occasionally guns, but you had to have the courage to tell someone something to their face. Not anymore."

"Now it is all about social media apps and instant messages and videos they post. The crap these kids are all glued to all the time. They call each other out. Talk about their mothers or sisters. Insult their integrity and everyone on social media sees it. They feel they have no choice but to defend their honor. So the drive-bys happen," Nick nodded in understanding but did not interrupt.

"It is sad and hard to fight. How do you make teenagers with 4th grade educations and no other life choices understand this is really not that big a deal in the scheme of things? But it is *their* entire world. They only have their rep and their honor." The frustration was apparent in Ray's voice.

"I'd like to see whatever I can and talk to whomever you can get me access to. I really want to understand and see what is happening," responded Nick.

"Nick, I would hate to be the guy who took you into the hood and got you killed. I have already seen how popular you are on social media. I also like most of what you have to say, or I wouldn't have agreed to even talk to you. Like I told Earl, I think it is important for politicians to see the results of their 'help'. I'm game to get you in, but if I say we go, we go, understood?" ordered Ray forcefully.

"You're running the show," agreed Nick, nodding again.

"I presume you are armed and know how to protect yourself?" asked Ray, looking at them. Both nodded.

"I can vouch for him. He can take care of himself," smiled Earl.

Ray laughed. "Him, I'm not worried about. I saw the New York footage. I was talking about you, old man."

"Bet I can still beat your 40 time," challenged Earl.

"Of that, I am sure. I've had one too many good meals. Just so you know, I stand out like a sore thumb, and everyone knows me. They know I mean well. I am almost like the UN or the closest thing to it. My suggestion is you keep your hate low. These guys may not watch the news, but I'm sure some of them have seen some of your videos on social media. There is a good chance you'll get recognized. I am not sure what would happen if they do?" noted Ray.

"Got it, but if I somehow become president, these are my people, too. I need them to know their voice matters just as much as those in Virginia, Colorado, or Florida. I need to hear what they have to say."

"Let's get going," sighed Ray.

They paid the bill. Ray chatted with the manager, and Nick took a photo with the staff. They got into Ray's sedan and drove into North Lawndale. As the sedan pulled out, another sedan slowly followed them into North Lawndale.

Their first stop was Ray's community center. It looked like it had been a YMCA at one time. There were a couple of basketball courts with net-less rims and several groups of black youths of various ages going at it with vigor and lots of smack talking. As they walked up, several looked up, and a few threw out some 'Hey Rev', or 'Hey Rev Ray' or even a 'Ray Ray', as Ray waved, leading them into the building.

It surprised Nick to see a common area with tables and desks and young black boys from 8 to 16 or so. Some were doing homework and others were using a couple of computers to look up information.

"It is a safe space. I have a few computers. Old stuff. Good enough for these guys to use to search Wikipedia and Britannica, but not new enough to be worth stealing. Lots of these guys don't have internet at home. This is their best way to keep up at school. COVID killed us. So many of these kids couldn't do ZOOM. We try to get federal funding for laptops. Some came through, but lots of them ended up being pawned for food for their families. It's that desperate in some of these households."

Nick stood, taking it all in, listening to Ray explain.

"Most don't have a male in the house and if they do, he is a retired or disabled grandfather. The fathers, if they even know who they are, are in prison for either drugs, gangs, or both. Many are dead. There are no jobs. This part of town used to be a middle-class black neighborhood. This is where upward mobility for blacks was working."

Nick had taken his purple notebook out of his small backpack and was busily scribbling notes as Ray explained.

"We had factories. My daddy worked in an Oscar Meyer factory nearby. But they all left in the sixties and seventies, either going overseas or further out into the suburbs. There is nothing for them to do. The men all have records and that makes it impossible to get work. Generation after generation of our youth are following right in their footsteps. It is a problem without a solution," noted Ray as they stood looking at the kids working.

"Or rather, a problem without the will required to implement the correct solution," corrected Nick. "Do the kids know this?"

Ray called out. "Darius, can you come over here for a minute?" A young, tall black kid who looked to be around 15 got up from the table where he was working on something in a notebook and came over.

"Yes sir, what can I do for you?" asked Darius in a polite and respectful tone.

"Darius, this is my cousin Earl and our friend Nick," said Ray.

"Very nice to meet you sirs," answered Darius as he shook hands with Earl and Nick.

"Darius, Nick has a question for you. Speak freely. I understand if you don't want to answer everything, but you can trust Nick and Earl."

"Thanks Ray," replied Nick. "Darius, first let me commend you on your manners. Your mother has taught you well."

"Grandmother. My mother died when I was three. Drug overdose. My father, or at least who I was told my father was, has been in and out of prison my entire life. I have never spoken to him, but yes, my grandmother would be disappointed if I did not treat others with respect. I owe her everything."

"Darius, I see you are studying. Mind if I ask what you are working on?" asked Nick.

"Not at all, sir. I have been studying *To Kill a Mockingbird*. Our school does not teach it, but I asked Reverend Ray what other schools teach. He said the other Chicago high schools teach this, or used to until a couple of years ago when it was banned. I've also read *Animal Farm*, *Fahrenheit 451*, Sophocles, and Steinbeck's *Grapes of Wrath*. I want to be a teacher. I'm studying all of this and advanced math as well to prepare for my SATs. My school is not interested in preparing any of us for a life outside North

Lawndale. My grandmother makes me go. I do all my learning here, on my own and with the Reverend and other volunteers. I can also access Khan Academy and other courses on the computers when it is my turn."

"Darius, your determination is impressive. This can't be easy. I assume your friends are not doing the same thing?" asked Nick.

"Sir, I don't blame them. They don't have a good family like my grandmother and the temptations are out there. It is much easier to steal or deal drugs or hang out in the gangs. I don't have a phone and I don't do social media. My grandmother won't let me. Sometimes I wish I had them, but I understand why she doesn't let me get distracted. She is keeping me focused. I don't want to let her down," he ended in a serious tone.

"Darius, I don't want to keep you from your work. I wish you luck in your efforts," praised Nick.

"Thank you, sir. If I work hard, I don't need luck, or so Reverend Ray tells all of us," disclosed Darius with a smile, retreating as Ray made a playful swing at him.

As Darius walked back to his table to continue his work, Nick turned to Ray with a look.

"Darius is the exception. As you see, we have another dozen kids in here. Darius doesn't know it, but he is inspiring the younger kids and if you stood in here long enough, you would hear he's already teaching them and helping them. Sadly, this is more than they are getting from their schools," lamented Ray.

"You saw how many were out there playing ball, a couple dozen. Many more than in here. I'm happy about that. They aren't on the streets. They aren't dealing drugs or just being thugs, so that is an improvement, but none of these guys are going to make the NBA. Several of them have already fathered children, with women they never married. They have no role or responsibility in the upbringing. Either monetary or trying to be a father figure."

Earl chimed in. "I see little has changed." Ray shook his head.

"The really sad thing, Earl, is they see nothing wrong with it? They blame the mother for not being on birth control."

"Ray, do you get any federal or state funds?" asked Nick.

"A little. We get grants occasionally and we have a couple of wealthy donors who give money, computers, and stuff. Money won't solve the problem. The schools suck. Our teachers mean well, but they are not good. Beat down by the system, going through the motions."

Nick nodded. "As much as we blame the teachers, even if you have a brilliant teacher, kids have to want to learn and put in the effort. Here we have the perfect storm of poor teachers with kids who don't see a reason to try."

Ray looked at Nick for a second. "True, but don't let the teachers off the hook too easily. They should inspire the kids to learn. They're all protected by the union. The parents are not united enough to force them to make sure their kids learn the basics. Plus, lots of the parents can't explain to their kids the importance of schooling. The teachers are just putting in time and cashing their checks. The school district administrators pull down two hundred thousand dollars and live in the wealthy suburbs. They don't live here, but they love to tell us how they are getting more money to spend on our children."

Nick shook his head, looking around at the sad state of the tables and chairs Ray had in the room. He also noticed the paint peeling on the walls.

"Those who can, take their kids out and send them to Catholic schools. Where they still get an education and discipline. You'll hear later from one, another grandmother, who had a slight inheritance and is spending it all to send her two grandkids to Catholic school. I want you to talk to her about her grandson and understand what he has to do to get to his school. It is surreal. In fact, let's head there now," said Ray, leading them out.

"Nick, we are going to walk. It is only a few blocks, and I don't want any potshots at my car or have my tires slashed. Few have cars in this neighborhood, so driving one makes you a target. Since it is daylight, we should be fine."

Ray looked at Earl and Nick. "Anything happens, or we get approached. You let me do the talking. Do not reach for any weapons."

Nick, Earl, and Ray walked a couple of blocks from his community center. The further they got from his center, the worse the appearance of the houses. Grass was nowhere to be found. Front yards were a mass of weeds and rocks. The houses were built in the 30s, 40s and 50s, mostly made of brick. Many had roofs that were in disrepair. Several of the street corners they passed had groups of four or five black youths. Some shouted out a few slurs once they saw Ray and Earl were accompanied by a white guy. At one point, a group of four of them started crossing the street to confront the group.

"Stay cool," said Ray.

"Yo Rev, you giving tours now? asked a black man who looked to be in his early 20s. He had on designer jeans and tennis shoes, some jewelry around his neck and an expensive hoodie with a Nike swoosh and LeBron James' face on the front.

"Anthony, what can I do for you?" asked Ray politely.

"You know I don't use that name. I told you to call me A-Tone," complained Anthony.

"Sorry, but I know your grandmother and she would not be happy if I addressed you by that name," responded Ray.

"Whatever. Who's the ghost?" asked Anthony.

"Just someone visiting who wanted to see the neighborhood."

"You a reporter? Cop?" he asked, trying to stare threateningly at Nick. All three of them were each at least 8 inches taller than 'A-Tone'.

"I wanted to see what it is like in your neighborhood."

"My neighborhood," said Anthony, drawing out neighborhood in a square with his hands and turning to his crew. "Well, as you can see, it ain't much, but it is mine. You need my permission to cross my turf."

"Anthony, I think this side of the street is not on your turf. In fact, isn't that Calvin coming up the street now?" asked Ray.

Anthony glanced up the street where Ray was looking, and he did indeed see a couple of people heading toward them.

"Rev, I guess you should continue your tour of the 'hood'. Let's roll," motioned Anthony as he and his guys quickly crossed back over to their former corner and down the street, out of sight.

"Well, what do you think, Nick?" asked Ray.

"I was in Fallujah after an Al Qaeda surge. This reminds me of that. A scary way to live," mused Nick.

"Welcome to Chicago Senator. Let's move on before Calvin gets down here. I don't want another encounter if we can avoid it."

Ray led them down a side street, through a back alley and then into another street where the houses were a little better tended. Some of the front yards even had fences, and a few had flower boxes. Ray stopped at one of these houses, where the owner obviously tried to keep it in decent repair. They walked up a short walk, shutting the gate behind them and up to a door where Ray knocked.

"Bert, it is Reverend Ray," he called out. The door was opened by a young girl, probably younger than six.

"Well hello Laila, can we come in and talk to your Gram?" asked Ray in a small voice.

"Ah huh Reverend," said Laila, opening the door. They entered the living room of a small house. The room was clean, and the furniture was in good shape. Laila led them down the hall and into the kitchen.

"Reverend, welcome. Can I get some coffee for you and your friends? Have a seat. Gentlemen, please call me Bert," said Roberta.

Nick looked at Bert. She was a large black woman of indeterminate age. She moved around her kitchen, which was spotless. Bert grabbed clean coffee cups from her cupboard and poured out three cups while refilling her own.

"Well Rev, what brings you to our part of paradise," she delivered in a sarcastic tone.

"Bert, I want you to meet my cousin Earl and Nick," said Ray.

"Pleased to meet you, ma'am," responded Nick, taking the offered coffee cup. Earl did the same.

"I see your mothers raised you two right. Senator, what can I do for you?" asked Bert.

"So much for incognito. Did you rat me out, Ray?"

"Honey, I have a TV and cable. No offence, but a good-looking white guy does not show up in my kitchen by chance."

"I guess I stand out a bit," laughed Nick.

"Ya think? If it makes you feel better, ole' Earl here ain't much better. He's not from here either. At least not anymore."

"Ray said he wants us to hear your story. What I am trying to do is listen and learn. Tell me your story. Tell me what is wrong and what you or we could do to make it better?" Nick asked, sitting as Bert took a seat around her kitchen table.

"Do you mind if I take some notes so I can remember exactly what you say?" Nick reached into the small backpack and pulled out his purple notebook and a pen.

"Senator, alright, Nick," after Nick opened his mouth. "It would take a week to tell you all that is wrong. I know Ray wants me to keep it short. Let me give you a bit of backstory." She looked at Ray. "How did you get here? Did you use the A train or the D?"

"We used the D," said Ray.

Nick was confused. "We walked, there was no train."

Bert smiled. "The A train and the D train are routes between the community center and this street. They are routes between streets, houses, alleys and sometimes backyards. They allow someone to cross over various 'turf' of certain gangs to minimize confrontation."

Nick nodded in understanding now.

"If you live here, you have to plan out your routes. My grandson goes to Catholic school. I'm lucky, I got some inheritance. I can pay for him to get his education from the nuns. The school is literally three blocks from here. It takes him 20-30 minutes to get to school. He has to go 4 blocks out of his way in order to avoid neighborhoods where they will harass or shoot at him because of where he is going."

"He has to do this 5 days a week. Jacob is 10 years old. He's been shot at and has even been wounded from a ricocheting bullet. He is determined to get an education. You met my granddaughter, Laila. She is supposed to be in kindergarten. I am holding her out until first grade. She is smart. We have a computer, so she has been learning online. I don't want her to have to make that same journey Jacob makes every day. I am considering home schooling, but I'm not sure I can do this for the next 12 years," worried Bert.

"That is quite a story. How do you handle the worry, knowing Jacob is running this gauntlet?" asked Nick, writing notes as he spoke.

"Senator, it is our life. Every day is like that here. It isn't just trying to get to school, it is every aspect. Getting to a grocery store, which now requires a bus ride because the local businesses have all closed. You have to leave the neighborhood for everything now. Everybody left. Every activity means planning your routes and making sure you are not in the wrong place at the wrong time. And always in daylight. No honest person is out after dark."

"So yes, Senator. I worry about Jacob every day, but I also worry about my neighbors and cousins who live here. I worry I'll make a mistake or let my guard down and pay the price. These kids depend on me. Their mother, my daughter, is gone. Without me, they have nothing. They have no other relatives. I only hope to get my grandkids educated so they can go to college, leave here and never come back. That is my job, and frankly, my reason for living at this point."

"That is a depressing thought," acknowledged Nick.

"Nick, why the Hell would you stay here if you didn't have to? You took the D route; you saw what it looks like here. It will not get better. Our street is one of the best and we work hard to keep it that way, but it is a losing battle. Eventually, our street will fall into the same decay as the rest," finished Bert in a defeated voice, fighting tears.

"What would fix this?"

"That is a good question. I don't think it is more money. I know there's lots of money spent, but I think most of it goes to corruption. To political figures and payoffs. The money never gets to those who need it most. We really don't need more government handouts. There is already too much of that. It hurts, it doesn't help."

"I assume there are no police?" asked Earl.

Bert laughed, and Ray smiled. Earl merely nodded in understanding.

Bert continued. "We need two things: safe schools with better teachers and a way to keep the kids in school and off the streets. Maybe we need to send everyone to the Catholic school. But our school's priest went to jail for molesting boys years ago, so many don't trust them. I send Jacob to the nuns to be taught. We don't go there to worship. The public schools are worse than useless," paused Bert, taking a breath.

"The most important thing we need is jobs. We need businesses for the young people, to keep them off the streets and out of juvenile detention and jail. Once they have a record, they can't get a job. All they can do is steal, deal drugs or join a gang and wait to be shot in a turf war. We need investment in business. Instead, we pay people not to work and watch as the criminal element destroys the few businesses brave enough to open. We lucked out during the Antifa and ARL riots after George Floyd. We didn't have any businesses to loot or burn down, so it spared our neighborhood that damage," she said in an ironic tone.

"Jobs and better education," said Nick.

"That would go a long way. Obviously getting drugs off the street, but that is asking too much. There is just too much money. They have no other options to get that kind of money. I don't know what you do to stop that. Nobody cares about North Lawndale," she finished.

"You know who you should talk to is Josephine up the street. She has lived on this street for 90 years and is still sharp as a tack. She can tell you what it used to be like. Maybe she has some answers, or at least recommendations."

"We'll go call on Josie," sighed Ray in an almost reluctant tone. "Thank you for the coffee and God bless, Roberta."

"Ray, you know I hate being called Roberta," she said with a smile, walking them to the door. "I'll give Josephine a quick call and let her know you are coming. She's hard of hearing and may not hear the knocker."

# Chapter 52

As they left Bert's house and started walking up the sidewalk, Nick turned to Ray.

"Do you know Josephine? You seemed reluctant back there."

"I do. She is a pistol. Gotta be in her mid-nineties. Doesn't get around much, but the folks around here take care of her. Fact is, most of the reason the street is in such good shape is because of Josephine. Her husband used to be an alderman in North Lawndale when it was in its heyday. He also supported the Daleys."

"Got it," nodded Nick, understanding the implication.

"She uses this influence to make sure the city fixes the street and the cops patrol here every once in a while," He looked at Earl. "They only patrol during the day, Earl. That was why we laughed before when you mentioned it. They will come if Josephine calls, but she is the only one. Anything else, it waits until daylight. This street is sort of a haven because of her. The drug dealers stay away, partly out of respect and partly because they know the cops respond to her," explained Ray.

They stopped at a larger brick house on the corner, with a porch versus the stoops on the other houses. Seated on a swing on the porch was a stately old woman. She had gray hair pulled back in a bun and a weathered face, wrinkled with age. Her dark eyes sparkled behind her glasses as she saw Ray climbing the steps.

"Raymond, it has been a long time since you've been by," noted Josephine with a mostly toothless grin. Her voice was high, but strong.

An attractive younger black woman exited the front door with a pitcher of lemonade and some glasses. She looked at Ray.

"Hello Ray," she said, while setting down the pitcher and glasses.

"Hi Kayla, you look well," said Ray politely, but with reserve.

Kayla looked at Ray and then stuck out her hand.

"Hello, I'm Kayla and this is my grandmother Josephine. I see you already met my soon to be ex-husband."

"Nice to meet you, Kayla," said Earl carefully.

Nick shook her hand as well.

"Pleased to meet both of you. We were down the street talking with Bert and she suggested we come up here and visit with your grandmother."

Josie cackled. "Bert sent you. Now I know why Ray is here."

"Josie, I've been meaning to come by," responded Ray weakly.

Kayla gave Ray a look and turned to Nick.

"Senator, what can we do for you?" asked Kayla in a not too friendly tone, hands on hips.

Nick held up his hands in mock defense.

"Peace. We just want to talk, I promise."

Kayla looked at him, then smiled, relieving the tension.

"I'm sorry, I shouldn't judge by the company you keep. Nana, I'll be inside if you need anything," said Kayla, re-entering the house.

Ray gestured at Nick and mouthed an "I'm sorry."

"Do you mind if I call you Josie?" asked Nick.

"All my friends do, Senator, please, ask your questions."

"As you may or may not know, I am traveling around the country, trying to get a feel for the issues and concerns of different folks from as many places as I can. I figure I should have some idea of what the people are facing if I intend to be the leader of the *entire* nation."

"You know, Senator, I have lived in this neighborhood for over 90 years. My parents had a place a couple of blocks away. My husband and I bought this place in the 50s or at least we thought we did. Have you ever heard of 'contract' buying?" she asked as Nick shook his head while scribbling in his notebook.

"Well, in the 30s, 40s and 50s during the two waves of the Great Migration of blacks fleeing the so called 'freedom' of the south, the fortunate ones went to California. The unfortunate ones came to Chicago." Josie reached for a glass, which Ray took and filled with lemonade. She took a sip before continuing as the others got their own.

"My family came here. We did all right. We had more freedom here than in Mississippi. My parents had good jobs and purchased a small house. When I graduated, I worked in a factory in Chicago as a seamstress. I met my husband at a dance in 1951. I was nineteen, and he'd just returned from Europe, recently discharged from the army. We had a whirlwind romance. He had a good job at Sears and Roebuck. Used the GI bill and got a degree at night school. We saved our money for a down payment and bought a house, this house in North Lawndale. 'Contract Buying' was a process where real estate investors bought up property at a discount, in this case mostly from white Jews who they scared out of the neighborhood with horror stories of dropping property values with the arrival of the southern blacks."

Josie let Nick catch up on his notes and took a sip.

"Anyway, these 'brokers' owned the houses. No banks would lend to blacks in North Lawndale. You worked with these middlemen who would sell you the property at an inflated rate. Their intent was to take your down payment. Charge you monthly payments, and hope you did something that would cause you to miss a payment. Then they could evict you and keep all the payments you made to that point and sell the house again. You got none of your money or equity back."

Nick sat back to look at Josie.

"It was a racket, and the government sanctioned it. We almost lost this house, but my parents sold their house so we could pay off the whole loan on this one and they moved in with us. Others were not as lucky. They sold some houses on this block four or five times because of this practice," said Josie, her eyes unfocused as she searched her memory of these events so long ago.

"How did you stop it?" asked Nick softly.

"We banded together as a neighborhood, formed a group 'The Contract Buyers League' and stopped paying payments directly to the owners. We got some smart people who helped us figure out how to take them to court and eventually the practice was stopped. Nobody ever got their money back. Millions in payments and billions in house value stolen from us, by the Party, our Party. Just like what we fled in the south. Southern Party senators who treated us the same as slaves. We came north to escape, and what did we find? More of the same. People trying to keep us down with the help of the government. They said good things, but deeds speak louder than words. Senator, I am more afraid now than at any time in my life. I worry about Kayla and the kids she may still have," this last delivered with a side eye to Ray, who looked away uncomfortably.

"Could I have some more lemonade? I usually sit here and watch the world. I rarely talk," observed Josie. Ray filled her glass and watched as she took a long sip.

"It's sugar free, right Josie?" asked Ray.

"Yes dear. Kayla is helping me keep my diabetes under control," confirmed Josie with a frown as she continued.

"I've seen a lot from this porch. I've also heard a lot. Mostly from the Daleys about how they cared about us and how they were going to help. Have you walked around the neighborhood with Ray?"

"I have. Some anyway," replied Nick.

"See all the empty lots? The buildings falling down and the burned-out buildings? You know when that happened?" Nick shook his head no.

"1968."

"That long ago?" answered Nick, stunned.

"That's right, 1968. There were riots and mobs marching through here when King was killed. They torched the businesses and drove away what little business we still had. Like you see with the ARL in Minneapolis, Oakland, Portland, and downtown Chicago. Just like in 68, they don't get it. Nothing got rebuilt. People who could, left. No businessmen came back. Who would?"

"We didn't stop them, and they destroyed our neighborhood. The same thing is going to happen because of ARL. They will drive business from their poor neighborhood. Why would Walgreens, Walmart, or even a Dollar Store come back if the people they served stood by and let their businesses be destroyed?"

"I watched TV. It was the people from the neighborhood who walked out of those stores with handfuls of goods. What is wrong with our people?"

Josie stopped. She had been getting worked up and started coughing. Kayla came out the door with an inhaler.

"You guys are getting her too worked up. It's not good for her," said Kayla, giving Josie the inhaler to steady her breathing while scowling at Ray and Nick.

"It's OK Kayla. The Senator needs to get a good dose of the truth of what life is like down here. Dear, get my box from the end table by the couch please," asked Josie, breathing easier now.

"We are told each new law, by each new mayor, each new governor, each new president, things will get better if we keep putting our faith in them. But we don't need words or faith, we need vision and action. We need someone who cares enough about what is right and wrong and not about what is cheap or expensive." Kayla came back in with a cardboard shoe box and handed it to Josie.

"Ah, here we go, a box full of empty promises and lies. Here is the first. Found this in my parents' stuff when they died," said Josie. She handed Nick a very brown and curled piece of paper.

"That's from FDR's campaign in 1932 against Hoover. Notice the top. *'Give government back to the People.'* I was a little kid during the depression, but I remember a little. By the time I got to school, we were just getting into World War Two. I still have my ration book in here somewhere. Ah, here it is. Still has stamps for milk and sugar in it. I remember rubber drives and scrap drives. I didn't even understand what war meant."

"Uncle Isiah went to war and didn't come back. I remember a funeral and a flag and shots. That was it. By the time the war ended, I had a much better appreciation. Folks came back and work started up again. You could get sugar and gas again. Daddy had a car, and we could actually drive to see relatives," said Josie, digging in the box.

"You know Roosevelt promised us all this stuff. It never made any difference to us. We were already poor, so the depression made everyone else more like us. The programs helped them get back on their feet, but we were still at the back of any line for food, or clothes, or anything else. The New Deal was the same old Deal," laughed Josie.

"Here is one. This is from 1944. I have vague memories of this and conversations with my parents and their friends. People were tired of the war, but we were used to Roosevelt. It seemed for sure he would win. Then we landed in Europe, and everyone assumed the war would be over. Then he died. Some people cried and others were sad. Nobody knew who this Truman guy was," remarked Josie, handing them another curled piece of paper from the 1944 campaign, exhorting people to stay winning with the Party.

"This is some great memorabilia. It is wonderful to talk to someone who was there. Did anything change under Truman?" asked Nick, already knowing the answer and making notes in his book.

"Not here, not really. The economy started roaring and as someone said, the rising tide lifts all boats, it did the same for us. I got married just before Truman left and Eisenhower came in. That was a big deal. Eisenhower got us out of Korea, which was good, since I had a brother there. The cold war was a scary time, not knowing if we were all going to get bombed by the Russians. Eisenhower was the only politician who didn't promise us the world. He was more like a business manager, not really of any party. I think he chose the Opposition because he didn't want General MacArthur to become the Opposition candidate. It felt like we were in neutral, coasting along, waiting for something. I heard Adlai Stevenson talk during the campaign. He was an Illinois favorite son and our Governor you know," said Josie, pausing.

Nick could see her going back in time in her mind, reliving that campaign so long ago.

"Stevenson seemed like a kind man, but he had no idea what life was like for a black person, or even a working person. Eisenhower, on the other hand, connected because he treated us like we were in his army, in the trenches together. Stevenson campaigned on more of the same New Deal politics and claiming Eisenhower would send us back to the unemployment and breadlines."

"The economy was roaring, people were buying houses, no one thought this was going to happen. Then the Party ran him again in 56, that's when we were saving to buy our house. Folks were pushing back against segregation, especially up north. Stevenson was a politician tied to the machine of Illinois politics. They were afraid of civil rights and Eisenhower sent in the troops to enforce *Brown*. That won him a lot of black votes, including mine," smiled Josie.

"Then came the sixties. Everything changed. We went from being segregated and discriminated against to become wards of the state. I can't even say I think they meant well. Because I don't think they did. Remember, my family came from the south. My great grandparents worked in fields as free men and women, just like their parents did when they were slaves. Not much had changed. The black man and woman could vote, but they kept him from being able to take advantage of it in the South."

"Then came Kennedy. He seemed so charismatic and charming, saying the right things and making us believe things could change. And then he was killed," remarked Josie with a big sigh. Kayla broke in.

"Nana, please don't talk about who killed Kennedy. I am sure the Senator doesn't need to hear your theories," pleaded Kayla.

Josie smiled big, showing her few remaining teeth.

"My granddaughter doesn't appreciate my research. Kennedy was not killed by the CIA or the Cubans." shared Josie with a twinkle.

"Nana please," begged Kayla.

"Well now, I have to know," said Nick with a smile.

"Senator, you know when Eisenhower left, he said to beware of the military industrial complex, he was on to something. There is a ruling class in the world. Made up of international bankers, aristocrats, and intellectuals. They killed Kennedy because he wouldn't follow their guidance. He wouldn't be their puppet. Which makes no sense since the Mafia and the Daley machine cheated to get him into office in the first place, stuffing ballot boxes, right here in Chicago. Something they do really, really well, even today, I might add," grinned Josie, knowing she was setting Kayla off.

"Okay Nana, it might be time for you to take your afternoon nap," said Kayla apologetically.

"Kayla, my dear, I love you dearly, but you are so naïve. That is the way you were raised. To trust the government without question and to do whatever they recommend you do, for your own good. My dear, I have lived nine and a half decades. I have seen human nature at its worst. Our Democracy makes it worse because we hide our corruption."

Kayla sighed loudly, in disagreement, as her Nana continued.

"At least in a dictatorship, the tyrant does it out front and you can see it plain and simple. Here, in our democracy, they direct our tyranny under the guise of publicly elected officials supposedly working for you, on your behalf. I have one question, Senator, and I would appreciate a straight yes or no. Does Congress do what they do to help us?" asked Josie, her eyes piercing Nick's, who held her gaze.

Nick paused, then said emphatically, "No".

"Ha," said Josie in triumph. "An honest politician. Senator, if I live until November, you have my vote. But let me give you some advice. Promise nothing. Tell them it will not be easy and it is going to be hard. They have to work for everything they get. Try this. I think it will surprise you at the reaction. LBJ came after Kennedy and pushed through civil rights and created welfare and Medicare and a host of programs to help the blacks."

"He would have been an ideal plantation owner if he had been born a century earlier. Maybe he would have treated his slaves as good as his dogs, but then again, he picked them up by their ears, so who knows?" said Josie with a slight shrug and an accompanying grin from Earl, Nick, and Ray. Kayla simply sat with a scowl on her face at her grandmother's opinions.

"As soon as Kennedy died, we became the ultimate victims. We were much better off in the 40s and 50s. We were educated, we were self-sufficient. Yes, there was prejudice, but we were making progress. When Kennedy died, so did any hope we had of ever achieving equality, much like our hope for integration into the common Union died with Lincoln."

Nick marveled at the knowledge and clarity of thought and speech he was hearing from a ninety-five-year-old black woman sitting on her porch in South Chicago.

"Instead, urban blacks are now being treated as infants. Too stupid to think for ourselves, to get our own jobs, or to be held accountable for anything. Unable to challenge someone on the merits of our accomplishments for jobs or promotions. Instead, we are being damned to be forever considered as lesser humans, all because of LBJ, and all the others since. People who had the best chance of changing the course instead put us into a death spiral. Now we believe we are victims and 'we' are owed something for nothing, *because* we are African-Americans," said Josie with a shake of her head. "Not for nothing. I've never been to Africa. We are Americans, the same as everyone else who has not immigrated from Africa in their lifetime."

Nick, Ray, and Earl all sat, not wanting to interrupt her.

"When the government made it a crusade to fix the black problem, they ensured the problem would only get worse. Now, so many blacks in the urban cities can't do anything for themselves. Without the government's lifeline, they would wither and die, unable to stand on their own feet. This is the way they want it. A permanent dependent class. Dependent on the Party to keep the money rolling. It is flat out bribery. The Government machine has replaced the Chicago and New York City political machines," said Josie, getting worked up again.

Kayla rose and walked to Josie. "Nana."

"I will stop now, Senator. But I ask, no I beg you, please win and then kick our asses. Cut off all the help. Redirect the money to building businesses or putting us to work rebuilding our buildings and then opening up grocery stores and five and dimes. Whatever you do, please save our youth from themselves. Put them all in the army and destroy social media. Our young people have no hope and because they have no hope, they have no faith. They are lost. We have entire generations of good human beings wasting away. They need someone to lead them out of government bondage and into a better land. Teach them faith in themselves and their community, their country and make them take responsibility for themselves. Give them something to believe in. Give them a purpose. Please," she delivered the last as almost a prayer to the almighty. Nick nodded, getting up to help Kayla.

"Now I think I will take that nap," said Josie. Kayla moved forward and helped Josie get up, leading her into the house and pushing her walker.

"All I can say is wow," said Nick to Ray and Earl.

"That is one amazing woman. I have trouble speaking that well today and she's got forty years on me," said Earl.

"Josey is a treasure. A professor trapped in a 95-year-old body," stated Ray "What she did not tell you is she also has a Master's and PhD in Education, both of which she earned after her husband died when she was in her sixties. She taught classes as a visiting professor for over twenty years at the University of Chicago. She is not shy about sharing her opinions. Like Bert said, she is a pistol."

"I'll say. I'm certainly getting to know North Lawndale."

"We are just scratching the surface, Nick," replied Ray.

# Chapter 53

Kayla walked onto the porch, having gotten Nana settled.

"Would you like to stay for dinner, Senator? I have plenty of spaghetti. I apologize for Nana. She comes from a different world. She thinks all the problems with our community are because we are lazy and rely on the government too much," explained Kayla.

"Thank you," accepted Nick.

"I should probably get back to the youth center," mumbled Ray. "Kayla, can you give Nick a lift back to the hotel after dinner?"

"Sure, Ray. You can stay too," offered Kayla with a wink at Nick.

"Thanks, but I really should be going. Senator, I can pick you up in the morning again."

"Thanks Ray, see you then."

He left quickly as Nick and Earl followed Kayla into the house.

"Ray hates confrontation," announced Kayla with a laugh.

"What's the story between you two?" asked Earl.

"He wants to help folks who want to help themselves. I want to change the system. To him, I'm an uppity feminist black woman who thinks for herself," said Kayla with a snort.

"So, you were married?" probed Nick.

"Still are. We are both too stubborn to divorce the other. But we haven't lived together in a while now. Senator, I'll be honest, when I heard you were coming, I wouldn't have answered the door except Nana wanted to talk to you. I consider you a traitor to our cause."

"Well Kayla, I *love* confrontation," smiled Nick, rubbing his hands together. "Exactly what cause would that be? I have made a lot of people mad. Which ones are you pissed about?"

"When you voted against getting rid of the filibuster, you voted to keep promoting the oppression of blacks through the obstructionist Opposition policies."

"OK, I respect your opinion. Which ones exactly?" asked Nick.

"Voter ID laws, support for police funding and militarization of local police forces. Non-livable minimum wages, limited access to health care for the poor, and disproportionate incarceration of black men. Should I continue?" asked Kayla with a raised eyebrow.

"Please do. That's why I am here," said Nick encouragingly.

"Food and housing are too expensive. We force LGBTQ blacks to lives of desperation because we deny the services they need to support their lifestyle choices. Jobs are limited, and education to get out of here is too expensive. Better access to women's health care, and now abortion, with *Roe's* future uncertain, plus birth control options. The Opposition would prefer to deny us all of that. The only way to overturn this is to get rid of the Opposition once and for all," finished Kayla, warming up to her task.

"I didn't keep the filibuster for the Opposition. I fought to keep it for anyone in a minority party in Congress," replied Nick.

"Think what you will, Senator. To those of us paying attention, it supported the Opposition's continued oppression," disagreed Kayla.

"You seem to do alright," said Earl, looking around.

Kayla gave Earl a disapproving look.

"I was lucky. Nana made sure my mother got an education from the priests. She got to college and got married. Of course, my dad ended up leaving her for a younger woman, but at least Mom soaked him for half his money. He is a doctor. Ran away with some blonde, white nurse. Anyway, Mom had the money and sent me to school at Berkeley."

"On a whim, I tried out for the Raider's cheerleading squad when they were still in Oakland and made the team. That's where I met Ray. When I graduated, I got a job with the ACLU. Ray and I got married and then he got hurt. When it was clear he wouldn't make it back into pro ball, he turned to the ministry. The ministry and progressive activism do not mix well. We fought like cats and dogs. Then Nana needed full-time care. I moved in here. I keep my toe in the local politics. Attend ARL meetings to keep fighting the good fight," said Kayla. "So yeah, between Mom and Nana, I do alright and have enough to let me do what needs to be done."

"Do you feel you are making progress?" asked Nick.

"Except for the fact we have a comatose president who promised us change, we seem to be crawling in the right direction. No offence, Senator, but Lexi is going to be the next president. Honestly, that is what we need. Your noble sacrifice was for nothing. The filibuster is now gone. Good riddance," she said, clearly disgusted.

"Do you have any coffee? I need some caffeine to prepare for my upcoming debate."

"I can make some. Bring it," Kayla smiled. "We can move to the kitchen table. Dinner will be ready soon."

"Earl can be our moderator," laughed Nick.

"Hardly unbiased," scoffed Kayla, "He's got cop written all over him, but hey I am used to the odds being stacked against me."

"I'm not a cop," responded Earl.

"But I bet you were."

"County Sheriff and Army."

"Oppressor by any other name is still an oppressor," proclaimed Kayla.

"Do you know how silly you sound saying that?" asked Earl in an irritated tone.

Kayla turned, somewhat startled at the pushback.

"I've been called a few things, but silly is not one I have heard in a while. OK, why am I silly?"

Nick watched Earl, prepared to keep things from escalating.

"Kayla, let me ask you a question. When did you realize you were oppressed? I mean really being held back by the government, or the Opposition. When did you know you had to stand up and fight?"

"My sophomore year at Berkeley. My first Black Studies course. That's where I learned about the systemic oppression of blacks in America and how the government of white men has made sure we never achieved any semblance of equality in America," she revealed defiantly.

"From that point on, I took every class I could to further cement my knowledge of the injustice of America to blacks. When you bother to open your eyes, you can see it all around us. You walked here from Ray's. All you saw were results from white rulers in Chicago and Washington, keeping us down. We protested MLK's assassination, and the government did nothing to rebuild North Lawndale. They left it, like East Berlin, as a reminder of our second-class status."

"Do you take responsibility for your actions?" asked Earl.

"Of course, I'm proud of every protest I've attended."

"Were you downtown in Chicago when the George Floyd riots happened?" asked Earl.

"I was, and I went to Washington to protest that prick of a president too," said Kayla proudly.

"What do you think when your fellow protesters are breaking down the windows and doors of shops and walking out with armloads of loot? When they are stealing cars and driving them through storefronts. When they are setting businesses on fire over there?" asked Earl, pointing east.

"I see what you are doing. I refuse to be blamed for the actions of the entire group. Some people have a different method to get their point across," she replied with a fierce glare.

"And what exactly did you accomplish with these riots and acts of destruction?" asked Earl.

"We got people to wake up and agree that black lives *do* matter. We formed all these ARL chapters to raise awareness that systemic police brutality is real. That unarmed black men are being targeted and killed by white police. We got lots of corporations to donate gobs of money to causes to support our efforts," admitted Kayla.

"You consider it victory when you extort corporations with threats of violence or protest?" broke in Nick.

"Of course. They are the reason we have so many problems. All they care about are profits and they can afford to give some of that money to our causes," said Kayla.

"You heard your Nana, right? It was blacks from your neighborhood that rioted in 1968 when Martin Luther King was assassinated. They burned down all those businesses. In that day, Black Panthers and other groups led those riots. You know what? They said the same things you do, about the 'man' keeping you down."

"That was a long time ago, Senator. They were stupid. It was still the government's job to help them rebuild. If they had tried to burn down a white neighborhood, they'd have been shot, so there was nowhere else to make their voice heard."

Nick looked at Kayla, not surprised by her answer.

"You're going to use that cliche? I set my house on fire to protest the fire department not getting here fast enough. Now I want the insurance company to rebuild my house while I stand here with the Molotov cocktail in my hand? Do you really wonder why they don't want to rebuild your house?"

Kayla laughed. "I pay my taxes or insurance in your analogy. They don't have a choice."

"Oh yes, they do. The insurance company and the government both. The major difference is they are insuring against accidents, not willful destruction. It is the same for the government. Why rebuild a business with tax dollars when ARL is going to burn it down again?"

"If a few have to lose to help the many, that is the way it has always been. Sacrifices have to be made," shrugged Kayla indifferently, not swayed by Nick's argument.

"Really? What else did you learn at Berkeley? That statement is worthy of my colleagues in the Progressive Women for Change caucus. Empty words and rhetoric. Yeah, sacrifices need to be made. By others. This is the whole defund the police movement in a microcosm. Make everyone think the people who keep crime down, who make it possible for you to walk the streets safely day and night, are the enemy."

"The same people who run into the bullets to save you, your mother, friend, or your neighbor. Who keeps your car or your tires from being stolen in broad daylight. The ones who arrest the pedophile before he abuses your child. Or steals them to sell them to a sex slave ring. These horrible cops who work long shifts, knowing every traffic stop could be a gang banger with an illegal gun. Ready to shoot them in the face when they come up to the side of the car." Earl smiled as Nick started 'teaching'.

"These are the same people you and the PW4C want to get rid of because 1 out of every 100,000 of them are rotten apples. One of whom murdered a black man resisting arrest. How many murders were there in Chicago last week? How many *kids* were killed? Who killed them?" Nick was delivering all of this in a calm voice, refusing to get worked up as he normally would on stage.

Kayla shrugged. "Senator, life is tough. Especially in Chicago. We look at the bigger picture. Do you know the incarceration rates of blacks…" Nick stopped her with a raised hand.

"Kayla, you bet I do. Do you also realize the percentage of blacks in prison is only slightly higher than whites and the gap has been closing annually? Right now it is about 33% black to 32% whites in prison. I bet no one is making that point. Thanks to your efforts and those of your benefactors like Pavlovich, of those arrests that *are* made, nearly all of them get out without bail and become repeat offenders. Congratulations. Yes, you have lowered the black incarceration rate, and that is good. Especially when so many of those were multiple minimal drug offenders. But you have also allowed rapists, serial wife and child abusers, and violent criminals to avoid paying for their crimes as well. This combined with fewer beat cops, and you now have a war zone. Who do you call when you need help? Your ARL leaders all live up in Forest Glen and Lincoln Park. They are not coming to your rescue in North Lawndale," finished Nick, still calm.

"People have to look out for themselves. They can't trust the cops; they'd just as soon kill us as help us," accused Kayla. Nick looked at Earl as he was about to explode. He shook his head.

"Kayla. How many *unarmed* blacks were killed by cops this year in Chicago? Do you know?" asked Nick.

"Twenty?"

"Zero. Do you know how many in the entire country? Twelve. Including 8 of them by black or Hispanic cops. Of these twelve unarmed blacks, one was trying to put a cop in a headlock. Another tried to run them over with their car. One tried to throw an officer's female partner off a bridge before he shot him."

"In all these cases, these black victims were resisting arrest. Why? Because they all broke the law or had outstanding warrants. In one case, 27 of them, including attempted murder and multiple domestic abuse. All out on no-bail clauses. These are not innocent victims standing on a curb when a white cop comes up and guns them down. That happens *nowhere*, despite your uninformed rhetoric."

"It doesn't matter Senator. It has happened before and if we do not keep up the protests, it will happen again," replied Kayla.

"Kayla, surely you learned about cause and effect, right? No cops equal lots of crime. Lots of crime means higher prices. Higher prices hurt who the most? Those with the least money. The very people you claim to want to protect. You can blame the man, the president, the Opposition, and God almighty, but you have freewill, and you exercised it. *You* turned your town into a hellhole. That is why you have 43% unemployment and 70% of your men with drug, gang, theft, and murder records. Because they have no alternatives to crime. There are no jobs in North Lawndale because *you* made a statement and burned it down. Any business that was here left. Why? Because they did not want the same thing to happen again if they rebuilt," said Nick. "Can you blame them?"

Kayla, not used to anyone directly responding to her rhetoric with facts, was struggling with the idea defunding the police was making things worse, not better.

"Senator, you may think we were achieving equality of opportunity, but it was anything but that. Look around you. If this is equality of opportunity, it sucks. The time of calmly taking the crumbs handed to us is over. We need equity, not equality. If they won't give it to us, we will take it. Smash and grab, shaking down white corporations, burning down toney stores on the magnificent mile and the gold coast. This is just the beginning. We will have what we are owed."

"What do they owe *you*? Good god, look in the freaking mirror. Your grandmother fought the actual fight. Even your mother did her part. Yet you sit here all righteous, claiming to be a victim when you are the recipient of all their hard work. Going to a top liberal college on the back of your mother and grandmother's hard work. A cheerleader; who married a professional football player. You live here taking care of your grandmother, living off the money earned in her lifetime of blood, sweat, and sacrifice."

"Look in that mirror and tell me what Kayla stands for. Who is Kayla? What are Kayla's dreams? What does Kayla want to accomplish in life? How does Kayla want to be remembered? Because right now, all I see is a mindless, indoctrinated drone, spewing out the hatred of everything you claim to be fighting against. They are using you. Not to change the world, but to accumulate wealth and power so they can be like all the people you claim to be fighting against," finished Nick, intentionally challenging Kayla.

"I don't have to take this shit from you," retorted Kayla, "especially in my house. Privileged white senator from Washington who comes into our neighborhood telling us how our problems are our own. How we made this neighborhood what it is. You have some nerve. You get to go home after this, to your lily-white neighborhood. Back to your Senate office surrounded by your cops protecting you. I don't need you lecturing me on my beliefs."

"What do you believe, Kayla?" asked Nick in a softer tone.

"I believe something needs to change. The way things were going was not working. We need to try something new. At least ARL is trying to force uncomfortable conversations."

"Kayla, ARL and other organizations just like it are not forcing conversations. They are preventing them. Seeking to divide us, not give us common cause. Only with common cause and shared goals can we continue efforts to achieve equality. Equality is the answer, not equity."

"It is a good start. We can make the 'white American'," said Kayla, holding her hands in quotes, "understand what it means to live like a black. To live in fear and have things taken from them."

Earl started to respond, but Nick held up his hand again.

"Kayla, you have a lot of anger. Can I ask you a couple of hypothetical questions?"

"Sure Professor, ask away," she replied in a tone suggesting she was unpersuadable. Nick was determined to try.

"Let's assume you are successful. You destroy downtown Chicago and drive away all the businesses. Successful in destroying businesses, looting, smash and grab mobs, destroying inventory and burning businesses. Driving away the police and forcing the local politicians to instruct their police to not arrest anyone who commits these crimes, what is the result?"

"The result?" asked Kayla in disbelief. "The result is we have made the man feel our pain. We have inflicted harm on their corporatist allies. Louis Vuitton and Cartier make a little less money this quarter. We have shown the power we have when we band together in a righteous cause," said Kayla.

"So, you believe, the best way to get this point across is to turn all these cities into North Lawndale?"

"NO, it is exactly the opposite," said Kayla, now fully engaged using her hands to make her points. "It is to make them feel the pain and change their policies so those inner cities *don't* turn into North Lawndale. You don't get it. Politicians say they will fix the problems and yet nothing changes. Rich white corporation leaders get richer and richer, and politicians let them do whatever they want. Look at the big online retailers. They open warehouses and fill them full of poor people being paid low wages and not even allowed to take pee breaks."

"Nobody cares, they click to order more designer skin cream. Do you know they won't even deliver in this neighborhood? They are too concerned about being shot or robbed. They're getting rich using our people for labor, but they are too good to let us use their service," said Kayla, disgusted.

"You think you are punishing these businesses?" asked Nick.

"It's working. We have them scared. They are all donating tons of money to our causes. We use that to spread the word."

"You sure about that?" asked Nick.

"Sure about what?" asked Kayla, confused.

"About how the money is being spent. Many of these organizations you refer to are just fronts. Take one of your own ARL founders. If you remember your Marxism from school, it is supposedly about class struggle, right? Taking from the elites, getting rid of rich and poor. Normalizing all in a common equal society, where no one is above the other, textbook Marx and Engels, right?" said Nick.

"If you say so," she replied carefully.

"If I say so? That is what you just said your entire movement is about. Sticking it to the man. Tearing down his corporatist elite castle and taking away the fruits of his labor and giving it to the oppressed. Your ARL leader makes no bones about being a trained Marxist. Their entire goal is to destroy capitalist society, families, education, and churches. Any organizations that unite people in common goals and outcomes, or at least ones they are against."

"All to be replaced by the benevolent Marxist state, the commune, from those who can to those who can't. Don't run from it now. You are succeeding, you should be proud. Look around and embrace the society you are making with each Molotov cocktail you throw. With each black-owned business, you burn in your *own* neighborhoods. Your teachers cheer you from their gated communities where they live in their million-dollar houses. While you destroy what little livelihood you have achieved *away* from government handouts. Congratulations." said Nick, no longer calm but in an impassioned tone.

"Your leader has purchased multiple multi-million-dollar houses with the funds being raised in the name of poor dead black youths. Does that sound fair to you? Does that sound like a goal? If you had studied Soviet history or any other history that actually happened, instead of Zinn and 1619, you would find out that Lenin and Stalin and the chosen few of the Soviet Communist leadership lived like kings. Just like your ARL leaders. They did not suffer in bread lines or wait hours to get a tube of toothpaste. Live without heat or running water. Watch their families expire from hunger. Only their people suffered. Because their policies destroyed their ability to think and do for themselves."

Kayla now sat listening to Nick, paying more attention now.

"Capitalism is not perfect, and people are certainly exploited, but at least they have the right and the ability to tell Amazon to go fuck themselves, quit their warehouse job, and go do something else. Your average Soviet Marxist 'comrade' worked where they were told to work. If they complained, they were sent to work in the gulag in Siberia, never to be heard from again. Surely you have paid some attention to China and what they have been doing to Uyghurs and Falun Gong practitioners.

Communism cannot allow dissent. It only works if the 'comrades' follow the doctrine. Dissent is infectious and cannot be tolerated," said Nick, walking around the kitchen.

Kayla, checking the spaghetti at the stove, watched Nick.

"You either have small locally owned business run by people who live in the neighborhood and want to help their neighbors or by corporations who put a store there because there was a need and the police and rule of law outweighed the risk of theft, burglary and other unlawful activities. It is simple math in a free capitalist society. You have choices. They simply open stores where the police protect their property and their employees. Life goes on for them," said Nick, now in full on evangelical mode, making his points with rising cadence.

"You know who it does not go on for? It doesn't go on for the poor blacks, Latinos and yes, poor whites who worked in those stores during the day and cleaned and restocked them during the night. They make it much more inconvenient for the poor families, who now have to travel farther to get basic goods like groceries and see doctors. It is less safe for them to be out and about because you have made sure the police are no longer in these poor neighborhoods. There is now a much greater likelihood that these people now become victims. How has this helped *anyone*? Please answer me?" asked Nick, staring at Kayla.

She glared at Nick for a few seconds, straining the spaghetti.

"Look Kayla, I really am not trying to preach, but I am trying to get you to understand that actions have consequences and if the goals and objectives do not align with the actions, then why do them? ARL slogans and directives will do nothing to change the lives of the average poor person living in an inner city. While it *might* prevent a few shootings of blacks by police officers. What it *will* do is ensure that many, many more young black people will continue to get killed by other young black people. Over stupid things like social media posts and turf wars. Because there are no police around to stop it or show them these actions have negative consequences."

"The parents of these kids will see their lives wasted. They will never arrest the people who shot them because the cops aren't allowed to. The city *leaders and politicians* won't let them do their job for fear they will be called out by ARL and others. What does this lead to? Anarchy and hell in poor neighborhoods. Defunding the police is the worst possible thing that could happen to poor black neighborhoods. EVER."

"He's right, he is not just saying this," said Earl quietly. "Take it from someone who was once in law enforcement. Our political leaders are making it harder and harder to protect people in poor neighborhoods. You know what is not happening?" asked Earl.

"What?" asked Kayla, frustrated, checking the bread in the oven.

"There is no reduction in police patrolling rich neighborhoods. Celebrities and sports stars still have their armed protection, all while they are still calling for police to be prosecuted for enforcing the laws. All the people you blame for your status and the status of the poor blacks and Hispanics are oblivious to your plight. They live in their pleasant suburbs and go to their jobs. What you may or may not know, and Nick can back me up on this, is these white people pay a majority of the taxes that fund all the government help that gets provided to the people who live in the projects," explained Earl.

"Maybe that is true, but all those cushy suburban neighborhoods now have 'We support ARL' signs on their lawns. Their corporations are all teaching them about diversity and how their white privilege is evil," said Kayla, once again defiant. "We are making progress."

"What do you think that is accomplishing? You are forcing people to take sides. To hide their true opinions and say whatever the management wants in order to keep their job. You know what, these are the same people who did not have a racist bone in their body. At least before all this started," retorted Earl.

"They were all for everybody to be considered on merit regardless of where they came from or what race or language they speak. Live and let live. Believe it or not, most Americans are not prejudiced. You would realize this if you had bothered to look around instead of wasting your college education in communist propaganda courses and then graduating to full-blown hate pandering. How did you win a spot on the cheerleading team? How did Ray make it to the NFL? No one gave either of you that. You worked for it," continued Earl. Kayla was getting more indignant hearing this same rationale from a fellow black.

"But hey, now you have really succeeded. Since *our* former president made race relations his primary goal, we have set race relations back to a time before Martin Luther King gave his life to advance the cause. He sure helped us. He sure as shit is not living in Chicago any more now is he? Now you and your ARLs and others have managed, with your communist first principles, to divide the country into race tribes, something we had spent the last 60 plus years eradicating." Earl was now also speaking with feeling as *a black man*.

"Now, what are you asking for? You are demanding segregation again. Separate dorms in college, separate graduations for blacks, Hispanics, gays, bi, trans. Pretty soon you will want separate restaurants and bathrooms. This is exactly all the stuff people fought against and both blacks and whites died to destroy. For the evil it all represented. What is wrong with this picture?" said Earl, shaking his head in disgust.

"Done with the lecture, professors?" asked Kayla.

"I am. I have done what I can and if you can't or won't see reason, there is not much I can do to change your mind or the direction of your life. It could be so wonderful and fulfilling, but you choose to squander it, pushing policies and a way of life that does nothing but cause harm and disaster," remarked Nick.

"Senator, we have to do *something*," responded Kayla. Confusion and frustration clear in her voice. "And don't tell me to vote. I voted. It does not make a difference. Nothing changes, it just keeps getting worse. No one has any hope. You talked to Ray. He tries to help a few, but what difference does that make? You said it yourself. Every black man around here has been arrested. Most of them multiple times."

She pulled plates from an upper cabinet as she continued.

"Who is going to hire them? Their only choice is to deal drugs, join a gang, shake down honest folks, or become a gangsta rapper. Thanks to social media, everyone is offended by anything and everything. That gives them a reason to track each other down and get in a gunfight or a drive by. Life expectancy around here keeps falling. What can stop all this? How is a vote going to make a difference?" asked Kayla while dishing out healthy platefuls of spaghetti and handing them to Earl and Nick. She dished a smaller plate for herself and set down a basket of garlic bread from the oven on the table.

Nick and Earl ate in silence.

"Well?" asked Kayla.

"It's very good," said Nick.

"That's not what I meant. How are you going to fix it?"

"Kayla, I'm not. This is the same expectation many have. They look at others to solve their problems. The bigger question is, how are *you* going to fix North Lawndale?" answered Nick pointedly.

"Me? I already told you. Nothing changes when I vote. I voted for *him* with my first vote, and he did not help race relations at all. We had such high hopes, but white Opposition congresses stopped him. I joined ARL because at least they fight. Nobody else cares," said Kayla.

"Ray cares. Josie cares. Bert cares. Darius will care if he lives long enough. The first thing to understand is ARL is not the answer. They are the *problem*. They're going to turn Chicago and every other inner city into a larger version of North Lawndale. Their goal of turning this country into a socialist or communist society will never happen."

"Why is that?" asked Kayla, still defiant. "We need to try something different. Why not socialism? Seems a lot more equal, taking it from the rich and giving it to the poor."

"Kayla, there are two reasons this won't work. First, you need workers and people earning money to *redistribute* their money and give it to less fortunate and those who are too lazy. Naturally, the people doing the work will eventually do one of two things: stop working so they can get stuff for free too. Or they will move somewhere where they can keep what they earn. We already see that in migration from California, Illinois, and New York, where these policies are in place, to Texas, Florida and Tennessee, where they are not."

"The second reason we will never go socialist or communist is simple. To oppress people, you need to beat them down, mentally and physically. Make them afraid of you so you can bully them into submission. That will never work in the middle of this country. They are free, love this freedom, and dislike any government that tries to take these freedoms away. Plus, they own guns. Know how to use them, know how to work together as a community and are not afraid to defend what is theirs from those who would try to take it unlawfully," finished Nick.

Kayla laughed unexpectedly. "You're probably right about the last bit. There are plenty of guns in this neighborhood too, but none of them would ever agree to follow any of the others. They would all end up shooting each other at the first community meeting. Their 'honor' would be disrespected if a K street boy tried to tell a Disciple to do x or y and a Marauder would shoot anyone else for even trying to tell any of them what to do. You're saying ARL is not the answer. And we can expect no one else to help us. That's a rosy picture you are painting, Senator. Sure makes me want to vote for you. At least Lexi is promising to spend tons of money to support our ARL efforts," offered Kayla.

"I can tell you how to fix it, but I am not sure people will do what needs to be done to fix it. It is not simple, it is difficult, and it is not quick. It also means throwing out a lot of what is now generational here," said Nick between bites. Earl smiled.

Kayla noticed. "What are you smiling at? You like my spaghetti too?"

"I do, but I am smiling because you are about to be converted. I have seen it before," said Earl, looking at Kayla with her hands on her hips and a dish towel over one shoulder, the picture of domesticity.

"Really, I have heard nothing. No promises, no solutions, so you are right, you're already better than a normal Chicago politician," said Kayla. "Wipe that smile off your face and eat your food."

"I can see why Ray likes you," admitted Earl. Kayla glared.

"Only you can save North Lawndale. And Ray and your Nana and others like you who live here and want it to be better, to be different," said Nick, holding up his hand as Kayla prepared to retort.

"Just hear me out. I am not talking Neighborhood Watch. I am talking about a complete change of fortunes. The only way it stops is building from the ground up, locally, led by locals and without outside influences like the City or ARL or the Federal Government. It is called self-sufficiency. You need to pool your resources and build your own support network. To look out for each other. Put aside petty differences and build a community. A community that looks out for itself, that protects itself, not just from gang turf wars but from outside organizations telling you they can help."

"This means building your own grocery store, your own clinic, your own department store and building services that help your neighbors. Spending your time policing your neighborhood and making sure others don't mess with it. It doesn't mean you shoot anyone who messes with you. Instead, you build up deterrence so no one would mess with you or your neighborhood and then you can stop shooting each other. Then people like Nana have what they need, and can sleep safely at night without bars on their windows. It means you can rebuild your schools and get teachers from the community who want their sons and daughters to get a proper education and go to college."

"Maybe it means your schools are not federally run or funded. Instead, create charter schools. With locals sitting on school boards who want their children to learn about reading, writing, math and actual history, not revisionist history. We need truth, and facts, good and bad, because if we don't know what we did wrong and we don't study it, then we're doomed to repeat it. We should learn not to do the same thing again." Nick looked up as Kayla ate her spaghetti. She was paying attention.

"That is exactly what we are doing right now by breaking into tribes and segregation. It will not end well. Finally, and this will be the hardest, especially for a place like North Lawndale, you have absolutely got to get off government assistance. It is state sponsored slavery."

Kayla put down her fork. "You were making some sense until the end. That's unrealistic Senator. Do you know how many people are getting help from the government? Even if you throw out Social Security, I bet 70% of the people in North Lawndale are on Medicaid, Food Stamps, childcare benefits, disability. Most have housing stipends and flat-out welfare. Without that, none would survive."

"I understand. I am not advocating cold turkey. But I am saying you have to instill in people the desire to be on their own two feet. To contribute to your own wellbeing and ideally, to the wellbeing of those around you. The best way to do this is to work. Working with your hands and your mind, building things and making products and goods others need. Delivering services people need and desire."

"This is missing in many of the inner cities. I know you are too young to remember, but there was a president once. His name was Reagan. He once quipped, the worst words in the English language were, 'I'm from the Government and I'm here to help.' He was correct."

"Look around you. Where is the desire to work? There is no spirit in North Lawndale, except to be a hooligan; or a victim. It is the wild west and there is no sheriff and there are no communities to stand up to the hooligans and kick them out of town," said Nick. "You have to get together as a group, decide what is needed and start there."

"Put your kids to honest work, planting lawns, mowing, painting houses, learning skills. Pool the money. I am sure there are some grants you can get and use to fund some of these. Others will donate time, money, resources once they see your intent. With a little effort, you can probably convince some of these stores fleeing because of ARL to open stores here. You need to make sure groups like ARL are not welcome either. If they try to come in, you do not welcome them. Not by force, but by standing up and exposing their lies with the truth."

"The police will be on your side if you stand up to the ARL thugs. The police are not bad. I bet if you walk up and down this street, every mother and grandmother in these houses wouldn't want the police to disappear. They want them to police and protect. In case people don't know, the police forces are overwhelmingly black and brown."

"These are good jobs for minorities. It is a calling for them to help protect and defend their neighborhoods from the drugs, gangs and race hustlers like ARL. Groups whose only goal is to rile up folks and get them to destroy their own communities," said Nick.

"It all sounds good, but I can't see having time to convince the gangs to stop. Or the drug dealers. You know how much they make dealing drugs?" said Kayla. "Way more than a job at 7-11."

"I get it. I didn't say it would be easy. But as you said, the problem is they don't have alternatives. You need to create these alternatives. Imagine if you can. A neighborhood does this. Builds home grown businesses, vows to ensure no one in the group will suffer. Anyone in need will get the help they need from their neighbors. Everyone looks out for each other. People are not afraid to ask for help. You choose to be drug free and show what life can be like if you work together. You build community businesses to provide what others won't. If you need it, then you as the community can build it, fund it, and reap the benefits. As the owners, you can reinvest the profits back into the community to improve. This is not socialism, because socialism ensures people are lazy. This is capitalism. You do things because you'll keep the benefits of your hard work and share it with others as investment in other business and things that help the community."

"We need a new Mayflower Compact for the country, to get people to pull their weight. This is the American Dream. Immigrants came here before there was welfare or social security or any other government lifeline. They relied on family, church, community, and they worked. And worked. And worked some more to make sure their children could go to school and learn a trade or go to college and have a better life. We don't have to look far to see how this has worked. There are countless examples of parents sacrificing to make a better life for their children. That has disappeared in places like North Lawndale. We need to bring it back," said Nick.

"We?" asked Kayla, "Nice words, but you are gone tomorrow. You don't have to take the risks and stand up to the gangs and convince people to risk their lives to stand up and try to take back their neighborhood. There is a lot of support for ARL here," said Kayla.

"No, there isn't. There is a lot of fear. To stand up and say you don't approve of ARL tactics makes you a target in a black community. As much as it makes you a target in a white community or in a woke company or now in the military. I'll give the movement and its backers credit; they have used their monopoly of the media to amplify every story of someone standing up and being fired to make it look like everyone who thinks for themselves is being fired in droves."

"People are catching on. Trust me. Where they need to catch on the most is where they are doing the most damage, the inner cities and minority suburbs of these cities. Guys like Ray get this, but they need help and support. They need to know when they come out and say this, others are going to stand up next to them and support them. There is safety in numbers and there is power. Drug dealers and gangs are bullies. They don't do well when people stand up to them, they go find easier prey. I have seen it firsthand in the Middle East. It is no different here. Life may be cheap, but you still only have one and no one wants to give it up too soon," concluded Nick.

"What did I say?" noted Earl, the smile returning to his face as Kayla gave him a look.

"Alright, I'll give you that. He is persuasive, if totally looney. And relentless," said Kayla, shaking her head.

"I think he is exactly right," said Nana from the hallway.

"Nana," called Kayla, getting up and grabbing Nana's arm to lead her to the kitchen table. "Would you like some dinner?"

"Please honey, thank you," replied Nana, looking strangely at Nick. He stared back.

"How long were you there, Nana? You should have said something," worried Kayla.

"I heard you debating from the bedroom and decided I wanted to hear better, so I used my walker and sat on it in the hallway. I didn't want you to stop," said Josie, still looking at Nick.

"Well, I hope you didn't hear all of it," said Kayla, putting down a plate for Nana. Earl got up and took a stool so Kayla could sit.

"Honey, if you don't think I know what you are doing when you go out at night, you are young and naïve. I have contacts everywhere and now with the fancy phone you got me, I have gotten pretty good at texting," smiled Josie as she dug into her spaghetti with gusto.

"Dear, could I have a bit of wine too?"

Kayla got up to pour a small glass of wine from a box in the fridge.

"Thank you dear," she looked at Nick. "I need it to soften the bread. You know I have fancy teeth, but I figure why bother? Most of what I eat is soft anyway, so I don't need teeth for that," she said, flashing her gap-toothed grin and taking a sip of wine.

"What exactly do you know?" asked Kayla, startled. "Why have you not brought it up before?"

"Honey, you have to lead your own life and make your own choices. I have given you plenty of advice. If you follow it or not, it really isn't going to matter whether I nag you. Besides, that was Ray's job," said Nana with a sly grin.

"Leave him out of it. I take it from your tone you don't agree with my activism?" said Kayla.

"That is not activism. Did you know I marched in Washington with Martin Luther King in '63? Your granddaddy and I went and so did his dad, your great granddaddy. We peacefully marched, and we listened to what he had to say, and we followed his philosophy of non-violence. And it worked. You may not think it worked, but it did. Those who wanted to progress, did."

"Those who wanted more, faster and to make others pay, did not. They turned into politicians and preyed on those who believed their words. They promised us more and help. Instead, they gave us a Great Society."

"I used to think they meant well, and failed to deliver, but now I question if this wasn't the plan of the southern wing of the Party all along. The revenge on us uppity blacks for daring to think we could be the same as whites. They saddled us with all these 'benefits' and promised to take care of us because of all the evil they had done. Instead, they made sure we lived in slums, became addicted to their programs, and drove the self-esteem and self-reliance out of us."

"Then they continued their systematic effort to destroy our families, turn our men into thugs and felons, ensuring our children were raised by their grandparents. For those lucky enough to be born, that is. The worst thing the Party did was institutionalize abortion. They have been aborting us out of existence. I almost died a few years ago when I saw our black First Lady getting that white devil Margaret Sanger's award. I was in such a rage," said Josie in between bites and sips of her wine. They sat patiently as she ate and told her tale.

"Thank goodness for Tommy and some of those other cable news people for finally exposing Planned Parenthood and their founder for the ghoul she was. They created the entire organization for one purpose: to eradicate the poor whites, blacks, mentally challenged, and Catholics from the planet.

Plain and simple. They didn't even try to hide it until eugenics got a bad name because of Hitler. Now they stand up their claiming to be these leaders in women's health?" Josie snorted.

"It is all lies. The whole thing. But honey, you have to figure all this out for yourself. I can't do it for you. It has to come from your heart. One thing I can tell you," said Josie, turning to look at Nick. "Until King, I had never heard anyone speak the truth the way he did. Since then, I have heard no one else speak that way again. Until today."

"Wow, how do I accept that? I am just a guy who is not afraid to tell people his opinion and how to fix the world. You know, it is really just common sense," said Nick with a smile.

"Senator, if it is so common, how come no one else has said it?" asked Josie with a smile.

Kayla sat at the table contemplating what her Nana had said. "How come you never mentioned you marched? You are an amazing woman and I feel like I really don't even know you," said Kayla with a shake of her head and a big smile. She got up and hugged Nana.

"Honey, you have no idea," said Nana with a smile. "I think I am probably ready to head to bed. I didn't get much of a nap today with all the talking."

"Let me help Nana and then I will get you guys back to your hotel," said Kayla.

"Josie, it has been a genuine pleasure. It is always wonderful to hear stories from people who have lived them. Thank you for all your insight," said Nick, gently hugging Josie.

"Senator, be careful. Speaking the truth will make you public enemy number one. Hoover may be dead, but the FBI is once again corrupt. That Lexi woman is the spawn of Satan. She will stop at nothing to win. Please do not let them do to you what they did to King."

"That is why I have Earl," smiled Nick.

Josie did not smile. She turned to Earl. "Then God bless you, it is all on you then. Don't fail us." With that, she pushed her walker into the hallway to the bedroom, followed by Kayla.

Nick turned and looked at Earl, who was also not smiling.

"No pressure."

"For either of us, right?" answered Earl, as Nick nodded.

# Chapter 54

Nick and Earl looked at the pictures on the wall in the living room while waiting for Kayla to return from helping Josie. One of them showed Kayla and Ray on their wedding day.

"Oil and water," she said, entering the room. "We butted heads from day one. That should've been our first clue. Oh well, time marches on."

"It's getting dark, Senator. Would you care to see what the neighborhood looks like at night? It could be dangerous, but I know you are both armed, Ray told me before he left."

"We may be armed, but I'd rather not get into a gun battle in North Lawndale. That wouldn't be good for my campaign," laughed Nick as Earl nodded.

"Hang on. She left the room and came back with a couple of plain dark hoodies. Ray's, but they should fit you two. You're both big. You need to keep the hood low over your face, Senator. We get white folks here in the evening, mostly buying, so it won't be a total surprise. I don't intend to get too close to any deals, but I want you to see what happens here at night."

"People will leave me alone, because of Nana. Most everyone knows me and my ARL connections. If anyone comes up, let me do the talking. You need to leave your backpack, though. They'll think you're dealing and either see you as a rival or a mark. We can swing by after to get it."

"And don't make eye contact," nodded Earl. "I know the drill."

"Ok, then let's walk. We won't have to go far. A block or two should be good enough for you to see what you need to see. To understand how tough it'll be to implement your little plan."

It was dusk as they exited the house and walked down the street before crossing and heading over a block, retracing some of the route they took from Ray's earlier in the day. Nick saw groups of kids of various ages hanging out on some of the street corners. Kayla walked with her head uncovered, with Earl and Nick on either side of her. She walked with a cool confidence, like a popstar with her security detail.

As they got further from Josie's house, there was music blaring from cars parked with groups hanging around or sitting on the cars. Several of them called out to Kayla. She nodded or waved back. No one approached them. On one street corner, with a dim light, there appeared to be several young men standing lookout while a small group congregated around the stoop to a house. There was music blaring from a nearby car.

Kayla slowed down a bit as they walked on the opposite side of the street. A BMW pulled up to the house and a man wearing a ball cap and gold chains got off the stoop and headed to the car. He bent down to the driver's window. Kayla stopped a few houses away, still on the opposite side of the street. She leaned against a railing. Nick and Earl stood next to her.

"Now what?" asked Earl.

"Be cool. That's his dealer, probably delivering drugs and taking the cash from the day's haul. He's most likely dealing meth and maybe some crack cocaine. Meth is easiest. Sometimes it's pills, oxy and X, but you don't get many kids looking to score down here. It's mostly locals and the occasional tourist looking for a quick hit who gets directed here by underground texts."

As if on cue, the BMW pulled out, and another car pulled onto the street, driving slowly, as if reading the addresses. Kayla laughed. "Drug tourist, reading addresses to find the dealer when all he has to do is look up." The car pulled up, money changed hands, and the car drove away as quickly as it arrived. The dealer noticed Kayla, Nick, and Earl. He called out to one of his lookouts, who crossed the street to Kayla.

"Down boys, relax," eased Kayla as Nick and Earl both tensed up, expecting a confrontation.

"Yo, K, what you doin', film'n a documentary?" he asked.

"Chill Big D, just showing some of my padres how we do it in the hood. They're from outta town," said Kayla.

"Is cool. EZee wants to say hi."

"K."

They all walked up the street to the stoop where the dealer, EZee sat. He was short with his hair in braids and flashed a gold tooth when he smiled at Kayla. He had tattoos on his arms and neck and one up high on the side of his cheek.

"Hey Kayla, you slumming? Looking for anything? Who are these guys, bodyguards?" leered EZee, looking Kayla up and down.

"Na, guys from LA visiting. They want to see how we do it in Chicago. Gonna educate LeBron on how it is down here, you know," said Kayla, laughing.

One guy behind EZee took his hand out of his pocket, showing a small packet of white powder.

"Go tell LeBron, LA got nothing on us. The finest China," EZee turned around and swung his arm into his henchman, hitting him in the gut, causing him to drop the packet on the ground,

"Put that away."

Nick bent over to pick up the packet. It looked like the contents of a sugar packet.

EZee laughed. "Better give me that, dog." Before he could continue, a black impala pulled up, clearly another amateur.

"Hey, I'm looking to score. What you guys got," said the driver, a white guy wearing dark glasses. The passenger in the car was wearing a hoodie, leaning forward, not paying any attention to the conversation.

"Who sent you? I don't know what you talkin bout?" said EZee.

"Hey, I was told I could score some smack down here. They gave me your address," said the driver.

"Who told you? Smack? What are you, a narc? There is no smack here, unless you are talking it," said EZee getting laughs from his crew. "Quit wasting my time and go get some doughnuts,"

As EZee turned, he snatched the packet from Nick's hands while moving back up the steps. Before Earl could tell Kayla they needed to go, another car came from the opposite side of the street. It knew exactly where it was going. It headed toward the corner. The passenger and rear windows were down.

"Disciples" yelled one lookout. EZee and his crew raced up the stairs and dove through the door of the house. Guns in the car fired at them. The car with the idiot buyers peeled out as the bullets flew over and through it, shattering the passenger window. Earl and Nick threw Kayla down behind a concrete planter on the sidewalk and covered her with their bodies while they both drew their weapons.

The car sped on by as EZee's crew returned fire from the windows of the house. As Nick and Earl got up and helped Kayla up, they surveyed the damage. Big D was lying on the steps with multiple bullet holes in his torso. Nick and Earl both ran up to him. They moved him from the stairs and laid him on the sidewalk. Earl took off his hoodie and tore the arms into strips. One he pressed into a bleeding wound in Big D's torso. The wound in his shoulder appeared to be non-life threatening. Not so the one in his stomach that was pulsing out blood with each beat. Nick turned to Kayla.

"He needs an ambulance."

Kayla looked at Nick in disbelief.

"Huh? Sorry, but 911 ain't gonna show up in this neighborhood for a gunshot wound," said Kayla, her voice dripping with sarcasm at Nick's request.

"He's going to bleed out if we don't get him to the hospital."

By this time, others of the crew had come out and looked down at Big D. No one seemed to be concerned.

"Kayla, we need to get him to a hospital," yelled Nick.

"Seriously?"

"We can't let him die."

"People die every day in this neighborhood. Why is today any different?" asked Kayla, her voice rising from the adrenaline.

"We're here," said Nick with conviction.

"It will take me about 5 minutes to run home and then get back. If he is still alive, then I'll get him to a hospital," she said.

"GO" yelled Earl. Kayla got up and took off in a sprinter's run.

"What you guys doing? It's Big D's time," shrugged EZee, while observing their efforts.

"No, it is not," retorted Nick. He pulled out his knife, flicked it open, and cut away the clothes from around the wound. He felt around Big D's back while Earl held him up.

"No exit wound," said Nick.

They laid him back down. Nick looked up. Get me a pillow or something to roll up. When nobody moved, Nick barked out, "Now," and two of the guys ran up the stairs. Nick noticed EZee was filming with his phone. He said nothing. Nick used his knife and cut an X across the wound to make the entry bigger. He stuck his finger in the wound and probed around until he felt the gush of blood with each heartbeat.

EZee watched. "Why are you doing this?"

Nick pushed his finger against the pulse, and it seemed to slow.

"OK, I found a leak and plugged it," he told Earl. "I'd do the same for you. Does he deserve to lay here and bleed out with nobody trying to help? Is that how it goes down in this neighborhood?" EZee's crew looked away uncomfortably, but not EZee,

"Dude, not sure what hood you are from, but looking at you, it ain't no hood where people are dealing. This is the way it goes. People shoot, people die, we will get some of theirs next time to avenge Big D."

"You keep shooting and someone else just steps in to replace you?"

"That's how it works," said EZee, shrugging again.

"Who was in the Beemer?" asked Nick, continuing to hold his finger against the pulsing artery in the wound while waiting for Kayla.

EZee smiled. About then a car came tearing around the corner. EZee and his crew drew their guns and retreated up the stairs to the house. It was Kayla. Earl and Nick picked up Big D, putting him in the back seat of Kayla's Honda Accord when one guy came running down the steps with an old blanket. He opened the other side passenger door and laid the blanket out on the seat so Big D wouldn't bleed all over Kayla's back seat.

Nick looked at the boy, who couldn't have been much over sixteen. Nick climbed into the back seat with Big D and continued to hold his finger in the wound as Earl and Kayla got into the front seats. The boy shut the other door but leaned into the car.

"He's my big brother," said the boy, obviously scared.

"He's going to be alright," assured Nick, with more hope than he felt. "Where are we going, Kayla?"

"Community North," she said answered. The boy nodded and Kayla drove off with a screech of tires.

# Chapter 55

"This coffee sucks," said Nick. Earl and Kayla laughed.

They'd been sitting in the waiting room at the Community North hospital for almost two hours waiting on word. Ray came walking through the emergency room door and walked up to them. He was not happy. He headed straight for Kayla, who stood up.

"What the hell were you thinking, taking a United States Senator to a street corner drug deal? Are you insane?" asked Ray, in a loud baritone, standing more than a foot taller than his wife. Kayla looked like she was about to unload both barrels when Nick reached out.

"Ray, it's OK. It's not Kayla's fault. It just happened. To be honest, I need to see this and experience it firsthand. Which is exactly what I did," said Nick, looking down at the bloodstains on his hoodie.

Before anyone could reply, an ER doctor showed up.

"Exactly what you did was save that boy's life. A bit unorthodox, but making the wound bigger to get your finger in there allowed you to hold the nicked artery. Not sure where you learned that, but it worked, and he is alive because of you."

"And your ambulance driving, Kayla," added Nick.

"All of you did a good deed tonight," said the ER Doc. "Let's hope it changes his life. He owes it to you."

They were all standing around the ER when a commotion started at the entrance. EZee and Big D's little brother and some of the crew were trying to get inside to see Big D. A couple of cops were preventing them from entering. Nick walked up to the cops.

"Officer, I'll vouch for them. The guy we brought in is this one's brother. Maybe you let him and EZee here, in. No one wants any trouble right," said Nick, looking at EZee.

EZee puffed up. "If these pigs would get out of the way and let us in, there ain't gonna be no trouble." The officers did not budge.

Nick stood in front of EZee, looking down.

"Give it a rest. No one to impress here. Apologize for the pig reference and agree to play nice and you can see Big D," said Nick.

EZee looked around and saw it was just him and Big D's brother.

He looked at the cop; the bravado gone. "Hey man, sorry, you know how it is. Gotta represent for my people otherwise they think I'm soft," he said.

At first the officer resisted but Nick turned to him, a tall bald-headed black officer.

"Now it is your turn to accept his apology and let him see his guy," requested Nick in his best diplomatic voice.

"Alright ambassador," said the cop, turning from Nick to EZee.

"Give your guns to your homies," said the officer.

They gave their pistols to their guys who waited outside smoking while they saw Big D. He was sitting up in his bed in the recovery room and smiled weakly as EZee and his brother came in. Nick and Big D made eye contact and nodded at each other. Then Nick left the room and rejoined Earl, Ray, and Kayla.

"Well, I'd say I got a full day of what life is like in North Lawndale," remarked Nick with a sigh.

Kayla nodded. "Senator, I want to apologize. Ray is right. I put you in unnecessary danger and did not even consider what could have happened. That could easily have been you laying on those steps," she said and almost broke down crying. Nick grabbed her shoulders.

"Kayla, I now have a better understanding than the other ninety-nine senators, our President, and most members of congress. I now see exactly the damage we've wrought with our so-called help. Because of the experiences today, I can work to help others in places like North Lawndale build a better life, with this firsthand understanding. But you, Ray, Josie, and Bert have what it takes to do the same. People like EZee, Big D, and his little brother aren't unsalvageable."

Kayla used the tissue Ray conveniently handed her to wipe her tears. Nick looked at her before continuing.

"They can still turn things around instead of waiting to be shot. They just need to see the vision and start on the path. You can do this, and Ray can help. Only people who live here and know the neighborhood can fix it. Ones who know the people. Which ones will stand up and work together, if given the chance? Those who just need a leader to follow. Only you can do that. Not someone in Chicago or Springfield or Washington. Only you," said Nick.

EZee had walked up to the group at the end of the conversation. He looked more normal out of his neighborhood and, with his facade of bravado, dropped.

"Little D is in there now. Figured I would give them some time. It really is you? That crazy senator from TV who pisses everyone off?" asked EZee, having heard the end of the conversation.

"He seems to have that effect often," said Earl, laughing as Nick gave him a look.

"Can you do me a favor, EZee?" asked Nick.

He walked a little further away with EZee talking to him. EZee nodded a few times and smiled before shaking Nick's hand.

They walked back to the group.

"Thanks," said Nick. "Well, I don't know about you guys, but old guys like me need sleep. And since I am covered in blood," said Nick, looking down at the hoodie he still wore, "It's probably best we are getting back to the hotel this late. Fewer questions."

"I'll drop you guys," said Ray. "You get home alright Kayla?"

"Sure. Come by for dinner tomorrow. Nana and I would like to chat about some things Nick talked about tonight," said Kayla, now looking at EZee.

"Are you interested?" she asked him.

"Ain't no harm in listening. Josie is the coolest old lady around, no disrespect intended," said EZee to Kayla as she gave him a glare.

"Well folks, that's it for me. Ray, get us back to our hotel. I need some sleep. All of you stay safe and keep the faith." He took the bloodstained hoodie off and gave it back to Kayla. She smiled as she took it.

"Nick, hang on. Your backpack is in the car. I grabbed it when I got my keys. I figured you guys might need to leave quickly. Let me get it."

"Thanks Kayla. Totally forgot about it. I would hate to lose all the notes I took listening to Bert and Josie today."

Earl motioned a nurse over and asked her to take a photo of the strange group huddled in the emergency room atrium. A US Senator, a former sheriff, a former pro football player now community youth minister, a former Raiders cheerleader, activist and ARL member, and a known drug dealing felon. One white and five blacks.

As they turned to leave, Little D came out of the hospital room, walked to Nick and gave him a hug, the child inside the man coming out for a moment.

"Thank you. For me and for my mama," said Little D.

Nick stuck out his hand and shook Little D's.

"Son, turn away from this life. You can be anything. You're not destined to be a dealer. Don't let them stop you. Do you see them?" he said, pointing to the group. "Be somebody. Don't be a victim. Follow Ray or Kayla or even EZee once he gets things figured out. Be a leader that inspires folks to do good, not to start a countdown clock to being shot and killed at a young age. You can make this happen, only you. Do it. Promise me you will try."

Little D squeezed Nick's hand harder, looked into his face and said, "I promise". Nick nodded, smiled, and patted him on the shoulder, turning to rejoin the group.

#

"Son of a bitch, that was close. You said nothing about getting shot for this story," whined Paul Cochrane, as Lauren got out of the passenger seat of the black impala back at their hotel, down the street from Nick and Earl's. She pulled down the hood on her sweatshirt, and shook out her long hair, laughing as bits of car window glass fell to the pavement. Looking down at the footage on her phone, she smiled. It wasn't often you got a chance to film a US Senator making a drug deal.

"Quit whining. You should figure out how to tell the rental car company why their car has bullet holes in it and no passenger window glass."

"Shit. You have to explain this to accounting when they get the bill," complained Paul in despair at the thought.

"Smack?" said Lauren, giving Paul a disgusted look. "I mean really? What did you do? Watch *The French Connection* last night? No one calls heroin smack any more. Unless they're a cop. You gave us away before it even started," said Lauren in a disbelieving tone.

"Lauren, I'm a God damn cameraman, not an undercover cop. You're lucky we aren't dead. Geez, I hate Chicago. What a shit hole. I hope it was worth it? Did you get what you wanted? You doing a story on drug dealers? There are probably safer ways to get your info and some footage. Can we try those first next time?" He didn't know who was in the footage.

"Sure, Paul," reassured Lauren, smiling at her luck in tracking Nick down and getting the footage. Pulitzer, here I come, she thought as they headed into the hotel.

# Chapter 56

Maximilian de Montfort stormed into the office of the Minister of Justice in Paris.

"What the fuck is Gauthier doing investigating *anything*?

Leon Thibault, the Minister of Justice, put down the report he was reviewing. He nodded at his aide, who had followed the Paris Prefect of Police into the office, shutting the office door as he left.

"Maximilian, please have a seat," said Leon, standing up and moving to a bar in the office.

"Scotch?" he asked as Maximilian sat.

He handed him the scotch and took a seat across from him.

"Why was I not told Gauthier is back? What is his assignment?" asked Maximilian in an anxious tone.

"He is doing a favor for Chaumont. He is not 'back'. With Interpol or in any other official capacity. In fact, how did you find out he was even working on anything?"

It was Maximilian's time to sit back and hesitate.

"I too have my sources. One of them called me asking why a former Interpol agent is asking questions."

"And what exactly were those questions, if I might inquire?"

"I am not at liberty to discuss my source," said Maximilian, holding up a hand to stop the expected outburst.

"It is really irrelevant. The more important question is why is that bastard anywhere near law enforcement? After he accused us of causing the death of his wife and child," said Maximilian, deflecting the conversation back.

"I believe you are misremembering the facts. While he took the Paris police to task for their role in the death of his wife, I believe the primary allegation was aimed at you specifically. And if I recall, this ministry, and its former leader, now our president, backed you against his own brother-in-law. Saying you were not complicit in the tragedy," finished Thibault.

"Because it was true. It is also why he should not be involved. How can Chaumont go to *him* for anything? What is he working on and why is he assigned at all?"

"I am not at liberty to discuss missions our president sees fit to assign. Nor to whom he assigns them. My suggestion to you is to ignore this information and leave the subject alone. This will not end well for you if you do not."

"Is that a threat?" asked Maximilian, standing up to look down on the diminutive Minister of Justice, who now also stood.

"Perhaps it is a warning. Tread lightly. There is no public knowledge that Gauthier is investigating anything. Your preciously cultivated public persona as the angel of justice is still intact. If you wish it to stay so, I suggest you forget this conversation. I am, however, ordering you to tell me who told you that Gauthier was back."

"And if I refuse?"

Leon looked at Maximilian. He shrugged. "It will be duly noted. Clearly, we have a leak we need to plug. There is no telling what we could expose during *that* investigation."

Maximilian contemplated his poorly planned tirade. This was not working out as he had expected, and he had allowed himself to be backed into a corner.

"Chaumont. He let it slip. He will no doubt deny it, but as you know, our president is always scheming. Just as he has by assigning Gauthier. I would watch your own back, Thibault."

"I will take it under advisement. Good day Prefect," finished Leon, turning back to his desk and sitting once again, picking up the report he had been reviewing.

Maximilian hesitated, then turned and left the office, pulling out a phone before he even got out of the office suite.

#

"As I suspected. Maximilian knows, which means someone else knows too," said Leon into the phone.

"No surprise he would react the way he did at the news. Nor that he would try to lie his way out of it. Who tipped him? Any chance it is your Inspector Martin? Luc seemed to imply she was none too happy at being a bystander on the investigation," asked Alain.

"I doubt it. Inspector Martin has no love for Maximilian. In fact, no one in the Paris Prefect has any love for de Montfort. You of all people should know this, having saved him before."

"I know, I know," replied Chaumont, sheepishly. "Believe me, not a day goes by where I am not reminded of this mistake. Watch him. He will know you will check with me, and we will both know he is lying. We need to find out how he found out Luc was on the case."

"Should we tell Gauthier?"

Alain paused for a second, thinking.

"No. If we do, he is liable to confront him. Keep digging."

"Okay, but I don't like this."

"There are many things right now I don't like, Leon," noted Chaumont.

"Understood," he replied, ending the conversation.

Chaumont leaned back in his chair. He laced his fingers behind his head, staring at the ceiling, closing his eyes, and sighing.

#

"Yes. I confirmed Chaumont assigned him," said Maximilian into the phone.

"No, of course I did not tell them where I got the information about Gauthier," he lied.

"What do you want me to do?" he said, listening intently.

"Nothing?" he asked, incredulously.

"And if I refuse?" he said indignantly, his face reddening. As he listened, the color quickly left his face. The voice on the other side continued to deliver directions to de Montfort.

A much meeker Maximilian answered in a somber tone.

"Yes, I understand fully. I will await further requests or instructions."

He reached into his desk drawer and pulled out a flask of scotch. Removing the cap, he took a long pull. Letting the warmth permeate, he gazed at the cap. He took another long pull before replacing the cap.

#

Dr. Caroline Fontaine walked to the front door of her Paris apartment. As she entered, it was strangely quiet.

"Louie," she called out, wondering where her husband Louis was. She set down her purse and walked down the hallway toward the kitchen, unbuttoning her coat.

As she entered the kitchen, her hands flew to her mouth to scream. Louis was on the floor, blood streaming from his head. Before she could scream, a black gloved hand covered her mouth, while another held a blade to her throat.

A ski-masked figure came into view. Ms. Basset, or should I say, Mrs. Fontaine. Your husband was not much help. We have some questions for you. I would suggest you be a bit more helpful, for both of your sakes…

# Chapter 57

Nick walked into the office building on the south side of Chicago. It had seen better days, with several attempts to remove graffiti on the sandblasted surfaces. He and Earl walked up two flights of steps to the third floor. They entered the foyer of the 'Office of the Reverend Elijah Powell'. A young black woman greeted them with a smile.

"Welcome Senator, I'm Latisha Coleman, the Reverend's aide. I'll take you to him. Can I get you two coffee, tea, water?"

"A couple cups of black coffee would be wonderful. Thank you Latisha," responded Nick with a friendly smile as Earl nodded.

Latisha led them into the office in the corner of the third floor. There was a desk in one corner, a couple of bookcases, an easy chair and sofa in the opposite corner. Reverend Powell waved them in.

"Come in, come in," said the Reverend. "I hope you don't mind if I don't get up. I don't get around well much anymore," he said, gesturing at the walker by his side. Nick and Earl walked over and shook the Reverend's hand before taking a seat on the comfortable sofa opposite the Reverend's easy chair.

"Thank you for coming. When Ray told me you were in town, I asked him to see if you would meet. He's a good boy, Ray."

"Ray is doing good. We spent the last couple of days with him in the neighborhood and visited his community center. It's a tough job, but he is giving it his all," admired Nick.

"Did you also meet Kayla?" asked Latisha with a laugh.

"We did," replied Nick, smiling.

Eli let out a big laugh as Latisha handed them their coffees.

"Forgive my niece; Ray is her big brother and my nephew, and she doesn't exactly see eye to eye with Kayla."

"Oh, I saw eye to eye with her just fine, just before my fist hits, putting her on her sanctimonious rear," said Latisha, posing like Rocky.

Nick and Earl looked at each other and smiled.

"I take it you are not a big supporter of ARL then?"

"Look, our youth die every day, some self-inflicted and some because of cultural and societal bias. ARL is a celebrity driven ATM."

Nick and Earl did their best to hide smiles as Latisha continued.

"Their initial goals were admirable, but it quickly became about money. It's just another scam, no different from Madoff. It is pure Alinsky. Threaten their precious status quo and agitate. Then take their money to not do it. Several of these 'Reverends' have done this for decades now. They all betrayed the message of King, sold out for a cushy lifestyle and TV appearances," finished Latisha righteously.

Reverend Eli smiled. "Well, I guess that about sums it up, Counselor. See what a University of Chicago law degree does for you?"

"Thank you, Uncle. I had a brilliant teacher," smiled Latisha.

Eli nodded. "As you can see, we have gone another way. My office is simple. I spend my money and my time trying to help. Trying to lead our brothers and sisters back to the right and honorable road. It has been a lonely journey and our success has been limited. We have little to offer our youth. Drugs and crime offer easy money and the gangsta lifestyle is very appealing with the social media apps. Makes them feel like they make a difference. Until they die at 16 or 18 or 20."

"Reverend Powell, we saw it ourselves. It's one reason I came to Ray. I wanted to see it firsthand, without cameras or an entourage. Frankly, I wanted to see how bad it was," said Nick.

"First call me Eli, I haven't had a flock to tend in many years and, unlike some of my contemporaries, I don't need to be honored with a title I don't use."

"More tea Uncle?" asked Latisha.

"Please dear, thank you."

As Latisha left the room, Eli leaned forward.

"So, what did you think of Kayla? She's a spitfire, isn't she?" asked Eli in a conspiratorial whisper. "You should see Latisha debate her. It almost always comes to a fistfight," laughed Eli. "So far it is Latisha three, Kayla one. She cheated by tripping Latisha to win hers."

"Got that right. If I hadn't been knocked out when I hit my head, I would have gotten up and kicked her ass," said Latisha, returning with Eli's tea, having heard him despite his attempt at a whisper.

"We spent some time with Kayla. We talked a lot. I think you may find she is not so pro-ARL now," said Nick. "I could be wrong, but I think maybe she is reconsidering their motives."

"Really, that would be remarkable. She's been unwilling to listen to anything either of us has to say. We've had plenty of examples of their thuggery," said Latisha. "Uncle refuses to support them, and they routinely attack him in the community, saying he is a whitey and supports continued black oppression. Those are just some of the nicer comments. It is a travesty. They obviously know nothing about the struggle and what Uncle has done these last 70 years," said Latisha, adding milk and honey to her uncle's tea.

"Sit-ins, hunger strikes, marches, defending wrongfully accused black men, working with city leaders to help direct funds to fix our neighborhoods. More police, better schools, more jobs. Most of the time it falls on deaf ears," said Latisha. "Uncle, ring me if you need anything," as she got up to return to her office.

"She seems very dedicated to you," remarked Earl.

"You have no idea. Ever since my dear Evelyn passed, Latisha has become my caretaker. She gets me to and from my meetings and makes sure I get to my doctors and get all the pills. She helps me write my speeches and maintains my social media accounts. I wouldn't be able to do any of this without her. Latisha keeps me going. She believes there are still some who prefer my message of collaboration versus one of violence. I'm not so sure. That's why I asked you to come by."

"I agree with Latisha, Eli. I think there are many folks who do not agree violence is the answer. Even in my little time here in Chicago, I have met quite a few who dislike the direction. I think there is still hope for your approach," said Nick.

Eli sighed. "You know, Nick, I have been following some of what you are saying, or rather, Latisha has. She shows me what you say and how you say it. I understand the courage it takes to make a stand and risk everything when the power of government is used against you. I was with Mike back in the sixties. When the government is against you, they have endless resources to make your life miserable, right or wrong. I saw it up close."

"Mike?" asked Nick.

Eli smiled, "Mike is what those of us who really knew him well called him. The rest of the world called him Martin Luther King Jr. To us, he was Mike. Trust me, if he were here right now, he would shake his head. First, he'd shake it at how people in power have used and abused him and his legacy. Mike was a flawed man and no saint. But he was also not the ogre the FBI made him out to be. He was a philanderer, as were many others, including the Kennedys. It was the times."

"But his message was still his message. I don't think he was a communist. He was a crusader. If communist sympathizers could help him move his cause forward, he was not against using them, like they used him. He really was trying to make life better, and maybe his message was flawed and maybe he was guilty of 'borrowing' from others, but does that matter? In the end, he did what he could. He rallied us to stand up and fight for what we deserved. An equal chance at the American dream," explained Eli, drinking some tea.

"When Mike was killed, I was not surprised. He was upsetting too many groups. Not violent enough for some. He was too cozy with the communists for the FBI and LBJ. He pissed off too many people in power by leading the blacks to ask for better treatment. Southern Party politicians were hanging on by their fingertips after fighting against civil rights legislation."

"The Opposition was making inroads in the south since they were the ones who made civil rights legislation possible. LBJ was a ruthless son of a bitch, but he was a skilled politician. He saw the power of supporting the blacks. He could see it was inevitable. That blacks would not stop until they were better represented in society. He turned the Party 180 degrees and made it look like progressives in the Party were the friend of the black man and the conservatives in the Party from the south were really just closet Opposition. He used us and he used the Opposition to set up the progressive wing of the Party as the champion of the downtrodden. It was brilliant political manipulation," said Eli, shaking his head. "Sorry, I meander sometimes. I bet you're wondering why any of this matters?"

"Sir, I don't mind hearing from people who were actually there. Remember, I was a history professor. I love it and I love when I can hear it from original sources instead of a book."

"Well then, I'll request your patience for a few more minutes while I set the table for my reason for asking you here. Mike died, and we had a void. We were riled up and had to choose the path of violent revolt, or the path of the peaceful protest Mike championed. In the end, we simply fragmented. Some advocating for violence joined the Panthers and other para-military groups, who simply fed into the stereotype of the FBI. Uppity blacks wanting to unleash widespread mayhem and murder in the white suburbs."

"A few others tried to take over for Mike, but the infighting was too much, and they splintered. The movement lost its momentum and its way. It fell apart. Jesse tried, but he was not Mike. He wanted to be Mike, but he liked the limelight a little too much. He wanted the credit, but didn't want to do the non-glamorous work. Never liked Sharpton, he was always a hustler. We tried to move forward as best we could. We got some anti-discrimination housing bills passed because of Mike's death. Three major civil rights foundations, housing, voting and equality, were established. These were three solid legs of the stool. We needed to capitalize on them. Sadly, we didn't," said Eli with a sigh.

"It couldn't have been worse timing. We had Vietnam, we had women's liberation and labor, we had riots and we had TV blasting all of this out into the suburbs. While people may have been sympathetic to our cause, broadcasting riots and violent protests did not win us votes or public opinion. Mike's death faded and the escalations in Vietnam reduced the funding for anti-poverty programs."

"The economy suffered, and the seventies were not good for anyone. We went back to making small incremental progress, working on jobs and job training. I will give Jesse credit for helping blacks understand the value of voting and making change happen by being part of the process. But he just kind of faded away after his runs for the presidency failed. The same blacks he helped to register didn't buy into his policy positions, preferring Reagan's instead," laughed Eli.

Eli pressed a buzzer next to his chair.

"What do you need, Uncle?" asked Latisha as she entered the office. "Can you get our friends some more coffee? I think they need caffeine to stay awake for my story," observed Eli.

"Hardly," responded Earl and Nick simultaneously.

"Eli, we can certainly get our own coffee," said Nick, getting up.

"Senator, I don't mind," said Latisha with a smile, "It is good for Uncle to talk about this. It keeps his memory sharp. I can only hear the stories so many times," she smiled.

"Sit, Senator, I promise to get to the point. Indulge an old man."

"Eli, it is fascinating. Please carry on."

"We continued to advocate for changing things through the vote. Getting folks elected to alderman positions and helping revitalize the neighborhoods. We thought we were making some progress, but the reality is it was a fool's errand. For every step we progressed in winning elections and getting people in positions of power, we were constantly set back. Sometimes by ourselves, but always by the government dumping money into organizations and programs designed to help. They all failed to achieve their goals, causing more harm than good. This is the legacy of LBJ and the Great Society."

Latisha returned with full cups for Nick and Earl.

"After ninety years of seeing this unfold, I now fully realize the problem. It isn't that we didn't want to change. Or that we couldn't. It was how we went about changing. We put our faith in the wrong place. If Mike hadn't died, maybe things would have been different. Maybe he could have led us, but much like many of the leaders of the sixties, they were simply there to be martyred for the cause. Two Kennedys, Medgar, Malcolm, Mike, and others. Change is hard. Out of sympathy, Johnson focused on helping us. He meant well. I really believe this. He felt guilty. He was not a nice man, but I think he had a change of heart and felt a need to help the oppressed blacks." Eli shifted in his chair as Nick and Earl sipped their coffee, waiting for the story to continue.

"I don't know if it was a religious epiphany or if it was the weight of the office, but he decided to help, and that's been our downfall. You see, LBJ never saw us as equals. He felt we were inferior and not equal to the white race. He made it his job to take care of us, like a parent does a child. The problem was he didn't realize the parent's job was to nurture the child, let them grow up, and leave the nest to fly on their own. LBJ did what he could to nurture the black race, but he failed to enable us to grow up and leave the nest." Eli paused, drinking his tea.

"Did you ever meet him?" asked Nick.

"Yes, a few times. I was even there with Mike when LBJ signed the Voting Rights Act and gave Mike a pen. In fact, don't tell anyone, but I have the pen in my desk over there. Mike gave it to me for safekeeping once. He knew he wasn't destined to live a long life; kind of like Kennedy supposedly knew his would be short as well," revealed Eli.

"Wow, that must have been monumental," said Earl, in awe.

"It was. While I think LBJ was sincere, his advisors and especially J. Edgar Hoover never trusted Mike or blacks. Unfortunately, LBJ's misguided attempts made it impossible for us to achieve equal status."

"Had Mike lived and been able to keep advising LBJ after his reelection in 68, or even Nixon, we might not now be saddled with program after program to 'help' us achieve equality and normalcy. Instead, these programs ensure all but the most determined would forever depend on them to survive. Lincoln freed the slaves, and they killed him for it. Had he lived, things would have been different, too. We were free, but the white southern Party members made sure we did not reap the benefits of freedom."

Nick nodded, enthralled by the story Eli was weaving.

"Fast forward one hundred years and one of the last of those southern Party senators, now president by assassin, put us back into slavery because of unintended consequences. Just as the first president Johnson, Andrew, came to the presidency after an assassination and stopped the blacks from achieving equality by preventing Lincoln's reconstruction plans. This Johnson stopped those last steps to full equality too."

Eli paused for a moment, staring off into the distance, remembering, before he sighed and continued.

"Nick, we accepted it willingly. Massive government help rather than the path of continued hard work. We put the invisible shackles on ourselves. Inner cities of overcrowded government housing replaced the southern cotton plantation. There we continued the inevitable poverty cycle and exercised our hard-fought civil right to vote and what did we do?"

Eli spoke faster and leaned forward in his chair as he continued.

"We voted each time to keep the shackles on, to stay in the government housing and to continue to elect politicians who continued to lavish us with more and more government programs to 'help'. We drove away fathers from their children and put mothers into Cabrini Greens public housing, government sponsored Hell on Earth."

"After aborting so many, we started paying young black women to have more babies while refusing to hold fathers accountable. With nothing else to do between making babies, they did what we trained them to do. Nothing!" revealed Eli in an exaggerated pause, throwing a hand in the air. "They weren't educated or trained to do anything. The schools declined. Education standards were reduced because it was not fair for blacks to be judged against whites in good schools with outstanding teachers. So, we graduated illiterates. Young men with little to no chance of progressing in a career or going to college on anything other than athletic scholarship."

"But affirmative action fixed all that, insisting we be allowed to go to top schools and fail. And when we failed, they conveniently changed the grading standards. Because those were racist too. No one worried about these poorly educated blacks who couldn't keep up with the better trained and educated classmates who got into the school on merit. The solution wasn't to help them be better prepared. No, it was to lower the standards. It was and is a vicious cycle. They get in and fail or worse, they get in and graduate with a degree they did not earn and then get a job in a firm to represent quotas," finished Eli. Nick watched, concerned Eli was working himself up into a lather.

"Eli," interrupted Nick, "I fully understand the plight of the black, the Hispanic, the poor white, and anyone else subjected to the enslavement of government help. I get it."

"Son, I know you do. I have seen your speeches. I also know what you are doing now, trying to calm down an old man." He smiled. "No need to worry. My *heart* is not my problem. Back to my story. I'm almost done." He sipped his tea.

"I am painting with a broad brush and generalizing in a way I would call out in any of my students. But I need to in order to make my point."

Nick nodded in reply.

"All this affirmative action is the worst help of all. It prevents the blacks who do study, who are as smart or smarter, who really deserve their roles in business and the promotions. Those who can rise on merit are always fighting the specter of those who achieve not through their efforts, but because the system lets them, encourages them to achieve success through affirmative action. Have you read Justice Moore's biography?"

"Yes, I have," said Earl as Nick nodded.

"He was a perfect example of someone who did everything the hard way, fought constant perception that he only got where he got because he was black and not because he was smart, driven and committed. He should have been celebrated and used as an example to every poor black child. Instead, he was vilified because he dared to suggest we be accountable for our own actions. Personal responsibility, not victimhood. This was not acceptable. Thank you, American government. Your help has set us back, potentially irretrievably."

"That is certainly not the story others tell. It is not the position of the Congressional Black Caucus or the NAACP," responded Nick.

"Of course not. This is the problem with the black progressive leadership today. If you aren't a victim, you aren't black. They make tons of money from these programs. That is all they care about, money," said Eli. "Nick, it is important for us to get whites on our side. They were there in the sixties, and then their priorities shifted as their *own* communities rotted in the seventies. When things got better in the eighties and nineties, it was better for the blacks in the suburbs."

"They intermarried, and this is all progress. It is great that we have had generations of interracial children growing up in mixed race households, going to school with other mixed-race children and Hispanics and Asians, but this is in the suburbs. Our world, in the inner city, might as well be Mongolia to these people."

Eli paused again, taking a breath, and sitting back in his chair.

"We are a news story on the TV. Our last great hope was our half black President, but I knew him. I knew who he made deals with to get to power. While everyone else hoped he would be the great unifier, I knew what was coming. You don't grow up with communist influence where your only job is a community organizer and suddenly become a democratic reformer."

"He was a disappointment because we had such high hopes. He could have done so much, and yet all he did was set back race relations. His support for or at least his ambivalence to the tactics of ARL and Antifa have taken us back to the fifties. We have to fight to get it all back once again," he sighed, pushing his button to call Latisha.

"Dear," he said as she dutifully arrived. "May I have some more tea, please? I have not exercised my voice this much in years. But the Senator needs to hear this and, as he said, firsthand, not secondhand."

Latisha boiled some more water and brought the Reverend a new pot. She sat in another part of the office, where she could look busy but still hear their conversation. Eli merely smiled before continuing.

"The blacks are just pawns of the communists, whether it is a former president or the corrupt minions of this administration, ARL, Antifa or any of those great NGOs Pavlovich is so fond of funding," continued Eli, sipping his new tea.

"They are all looking for only one thing, the destruction of democracy and the establishment of a totalitarian regime where they are part of the elite ruling structure. Whether Soviet style or a hybrid of their own making. Make no mistake, they couldn't care less about blacks."

Nick started to ask a question, but Eli continued quickly.

"What have they *all* done since they left power? What have they done for us? Headed to ultra-white, ultra-rich neighborhoods where their money shields them from any discrimination for being black. Meanwhile, we continue to kill each other, abort our babies, and send generations of our young men to prison. What kind of life is that? Where is the hope? Where is the change or at least change for the better? They betrayed us."

"Reverend, what can I do for you?" asked Nick as he continued to write notes in his purple notebook while Eli spoke.

"My apologies, Senator. I needed to tell you this story. And I needed you to hear it from a black man who has seen and lived it. You need to understand why and how I have come to the position I have. I am old. I have made many mistakes. But I am not done, and I want to spend what time I have left trying to help make things better. What concerns me most now is all of this I have described, now married to the twin evils of wokeism and cancel culture."

"I can agree with you on the last two, for sure," agreed Nick.

"There are a class of people who have figured out how to use both to get their way for all the wrong reasons. They merely need to complain about anything, claim racism, sexism, and the culprit, be they a co-worker, a boss, or a company, are all pilloried in the public square at the simplest accusation. No defense is allowed. No apology accepted whether or not warranted. People, my people, are being taught how to use these *tools* to get stuff. To destroy others because they *can*," said Eli, pausing to calm down.

"If you talked to Kayla, you already heard a lot of this. This is being couched as some sort of revenge or reparation for past injustices. This is simply evil, and it must be stopped. I fear if it is not, we are in for a civil war. A civil war of race, culture, and ideas and one which will hopelessly fracture us beyond repair. How do you build trust in humanity when everything you read, see, or are taught is nothing but mistrust and skepticism? If not outright hatred for your fellow human, based solely on ideology?" Eli looked at Nick and Earl, who both clearly understood his point.

"Progressivism is not secular, it is religious. It is a cult of ideas the likes of which makes Islamic Sharia look tame. Senator, just as you alluded to in your speech. It must be stopped. We need to give my people a better chance. We need to unify all people once again around common goals. I think you are that chance," pronounced Eli.

"Eli, I am not Mike. But I appreciate the support and the story. I would like to tell you that you are wrong. That your interpretation of society today is needlessly cynical. To point out the errors in your summation, especially around the characterization of the Progressives as a religious cult rather than a political ideology. But I fear you are more right than wrong. I have seen religious fanaticism up close, in the eyes of the suicide bomber. I have witnessed the hatred between Iraqi Sunni and Iranian Shiites. All driven to suicidal madness, willing to throw away their lives because of the words of unscrupulous imams and religious fanaticism."

Earl nodded in agreement, also having experienced this as well.

"I have studied the origins of totalitarian regimes and I see it manifesting itself once again in our own society, starting with our youth and the schools. What is worse, I fear the leadership of our Progressive party has moved beyond mere power and control for *money*, to power and control to remake society no longer for their own material gain, but to change our way of life from one of democracy to one of worship at the altar of their ideas. And they are winning the hearts and minds."

Now it was Eli's turn to listen in rapt attention to Nick's 'sermon'.

"We are losing the battle because our path is the difficult one. It is the path of hard work. Of the moral and ethical way. Hedonism is easy. The Progressives started this in the sixties with the destruction of the moral code. If they could destroy the family, and replace their role in the raising children, with the state, they would eventually win. If it feels good, just do it. They have now made their mantra a way of life for generations. This is the path of submission. If it feels right, do it, is the ultimate destruction of the morals and ethics, right and wrong. The credo of scrimp, save and wait is replaced with, if you want it, you can have it now. Why wait? Zero down mortgage, now you have a house. No job, no worries. Not giving you a loan is racist. No matter that you won't be able to pay the mortgage and we'll foreclose on you. Or that this will hang around your neck for your life."

Now Nick was speaking faster and louder.

"Same with sex. Morality is for losers. Remember, if it feels right, just do it. Intimacy, love, relationship stability? Who needs that? STDs? Well, the pills are getting better and better and remember, no means no, unless your date is drugged. Eli sat and listened as Nick worked *himself* into his own frenzy describing the decay of modern society."

"And work? Work is for losers. Why work when you can get this little Visa card from the government? Hey, you can even buy weed with it. That really makes things painless."

"Nick," said Eli calmly, reaching out a hand. "Easy. I get it. It is a colossal task. But it is noble. You are being called. I can see it in your passion."

Nick shook his head.

"Eli, I will tell you what I would tell all my supporters. My efforts are for everyone, equally. I don't play favorites. I agree with you and Reagan that government assistance is insidious. Just like drugs. The first hit is great, but then you lose everything, your job, your family and eventually your soul. It consumes you. Your people need help. But you know what? Everyone needs help. That help is not free stuff, it is self-reliance. Give you the tools, give you the chance, get out of the way, and let you loose to save yourselves," said Nick.

"The real problem with changing *anything* is the media. Their near total control of information. The propaganda and disinformation. And the definition of what each of these is. While everything I say is true, too many of the common people are now conditioned to see any 'truth' as a lie. As a conspiracy theory. It can't possibly be as bad as I say or the 'government' would have done something about it. They have done a wonderful job of converting their congregation. Convincing them change is not only unnecessary, but frankly is wrong and destructive, *to them.*"

Eli nodded in agreement. "Senator, that is precisely why I am asking you to do this. I don't believe we are unsalvagable. I can't. It goes against my faith. I've seen it all. The only solution is for you to make the government leave us alone. Let us figure it out on our own. Cut us off from the suppliers. I am not talking drugs. I am talking about the government. If we don't quit cold turkey, we'll never be free. Then be there to help. But help us through education and job training. Give us equal opportunity, but don't give us an easy way. If you make it clear the safety net is gone, people will change their habits. They always do when faced with no alternative. Stop providing the alternatives," said Eli.

"Eli, that may be easier said than done. I am sure there are many who would disagree with the end of their government assistance. I don't disagree, but it would have to be phased in until folks can stand on their own two feet. Josie gave the same advice," said Nick with a laugh and smile.

"She is a wise woman," said Eli, smiling before turning serious again. "The longer you stretch it out, the longer it will take to end it. Trust me, better to have a lot of pain in one dose and help people temporarily. Any continuation of government help will ensure it eventually returns. My people will never be free unless all the invisible shackles are gone from all of us," said Eli. "Until we are *forced* to take responsibility, the same as everyone else, and stand on our own, unencumbered by help or barriers."

Nick pondered his words and the implications of stopping all assistance in one action. The chaos would be huge and widespread. But could it be managed? He made a few more notes in his purple notebook.

"Senator, I will do what I can. When I come out to support you, I'll be attacked and marginalized. I don't care. But I am worried about Latisha," he said, looking at Latisha.

"Don't worry about me, Uncle, I will be fine," she said. "Senator, I think there are a lot of young blacks, in fact young people of all races, who are looking for leadership and who are looking for a way out of the world of drugs, gangs, and crime. As Uncle says, we really haven't had good leadership since the 60s. Don't just assume we are all welfare babies who love the Party. They want us to think we have no choice except to keep voting them in, so we can continue to live on their programs."

"ARL is not nearly as popular as it appears to be on TV. Many of us in the community don't agree with the goals. We do not want the police out either. What we want are choices. Adding ARL or Antifa to dealing drugs or dying in a gang is not our idea of more *good* choices."

Eli reached out and put his hand on Latisha's arm, as she stood by his chair.

"Latisha, you give me hope every day that things *can* get better."

"Uncle, you have given so much, sacrificed so much. It is time the rest of us stand up and take up the fight for *ourselves*."

"Senator, I will leave you with one last thought," said Eli. "People talk about the return of the cold war, with Russia and China and maybe Iran. We are already and have been in a cold war. Just not one predicated on

MADD or nuclear proliferation or even force of arms of any type. No, the enemy is now much smarter. Even in our weakened state, a war of arms against the United States is doomed to fail. They cannot beat us with guns. Instead, they have to beat us with ideology and words. They have to destroy our culture of freedom."

"To do this, they are convincing us our freedoms are the cause of our failure. That our very freedom has caused injustice against blacks and other minorities, against gays and trans, against the earth, the climate, and our ability to sustain life here. According to them, it is freedom that must be eradicated or else we all die."

Nick looked at Eli as he made this statement. "You are right." Agreed Nick. Contemplating Eli's words as he made more notes.

"It is beyond sovereign borders. This is beyond people and personalities. It's a fundamental shift in the way of human life for the entire planet. Freedom stands a lone sentry post against this. Please think of it from this perspective or they will consume you as well. The inability to see the grand scheme has been the undoing of many a crusader. Do not make this mistake."

Nick nodded and stood, sensing Eli had spent a day's worth of energy in their brief talk.

"Eli, I think I speak for Earl and many of the people of this country. That was one of the most enlightening and honest assessments of the plight of blacks I have ever heard. It is unfortunate that you cannot bottle it and force feed it to my colleagues in the Senate. Who continually pass bills to perpetuate this misery in the name of help."

Eli nodded, smiling. "Son, they have heard it before. I am a lone whisper of freedom and action in a wilderness of megaphones shouting dependency and complacency as the answer."

They both shook his hand and Latisha walked them out of the office and stood with them at the top of the stairwell.

"He doesn't have much time. Cancer. Inoperable," she said, as Nick and Earl both looked back at the office.

"In that case, I feel honored to have gotten the chance to speak with him face to face."

"I have never seen him deliver his message in a more forceful way than he just did with you, Senator. I believe he has been looking to pass the baton Mike gave to him. To find a worthy successor," said Latisha, looking Nick in the face.

Nick shook his head.

"Latisha, it is not for one person to accomplish, but for each to own their own destiny. Leadership and waiting to be led is a maxim of tyrants and egomaniacs. No one should want to be led."

To this Earl, who had been mostly silent, interjected.

"Give me a flipping break. What kind of Zen mumbo jumbo is that? Latisha, you see what I have to put up with day and night. He is our leader and yet he keeps claiming he is the Force or something. Well, I am not Yoda," he turned back to Nick. "If you are the Last Jedi, you don't get a choice. Man up and take the job," finished Earl, venting his frustration.

Latisha laughed. "He is right, you know. Whether or not you want it. You are the leader. Now if you choose to tell your followers to Think for Yourself, Wake Up, Stand up, Flip or Mirror," said Latisha, throwing off Nick's catch phrases and then using her hand to show the Flip and Mirror. "That is fine, but reality is what it is. Perhaps you need to look in *my* mirror and see what we see," she finished, holding her palm up against her chest so Nick could see his 'reflection'.

"Touché," said Nick, in an almost resigned tone. "Please keep us informed of how the Reverend does and let us know if he faces any serious backlash."

"I will Senator. Thank you for indulging Eli. It made his day, and I am happy to meet you. I halfway hope what you say about Kayla is wrong. I would miss kicking her butt," finished Latisha with a smile.

Nick and Earl made their way out of the building to the street. It had been an interesting visit to Chicago.

As Nick and Earl headed to their rental car. Nick had the uncomfortable feeling of being watched. But by whom? As they pulled away in the rental, Nick looked around to see if any cars followed them. None did. Earl noticed him looking around.

"You feel it too?"

"Yep," said Nick, looking at Earl.

"I am guessing Feds, maybe private, but someone has been tailing us off and on. I will buy some tech to help us sweep the cars for bugs after every stop. Not much we can do about old school except keep an eye out for the same make and model on the same day behind us. It's not like we are being super secretive," finished Earl, looking at Nick.

"I know, but I also don't like anyone knowing who I am talking to or seeing either. Mostly for their wellbeing. Good idea on the sweep. No reason to make it too easy on them. Let's get back to Denver. I have a lot to process, and I need to see what Denise and Chuck have me doing next. I feel like a trained monkey."

"If it helps, you are only partially trained," laughed Earl.

"Gee thanks. That helps tremendously. You should at least ask for half the tips," said Nick as they headed to Midway and their chartered jet to Denver. After much argument, Denise had convinced Nick speed was more important than perception. She could not risk him being stranded somewhere, always flying commercial. They had the jet ready and on standby. Whether it flew, it cost them the same, so he might as well use it. He finally relented. He did most of his sleeping on the plane.

# Chapter 58

Nick and his senior staff sat in their conference room on an upper floor in a high rise building in downtown Denver. Their view of the Rockies was obscured by the current late spring snowstorm so common in April. They forecast this one to drop 8 to12 inches in Denver and closer to two feet in the foothills. It would be slough for anyone commuting later in the day.

"Since it may snow us in, I hope we already ordered the pizza," said Nick in a pleasant tone.

"Enough for the entire staff. We have cases of Red Bull. We'll work all night if we get snowed in," said Jenny with a smile.

"Thanks Jenny. Well, here I am. How are we doing? What else do you need me to do?"

Chuck, Margie, Greg, Jer, Denise and Jenny all looked at each other for a second. Nick glanced around and made to get up.

"Well, if there is nothing, with fresh powder, I'm going skiing."

"Sit down," ordered Denise. "Where do we start?"

"That bad, huh?"

"With no infrastructure and no planning, we are actually not doing *too* bad. But we need to do more and faster. That is going to be a recurring theme," said Denise.

"Jer or Greg, if you could project the map, please," said Denise.

A map showed up on the big screen at one end of the room. Jer used a remote to drop the shades over the windows, hiding the little light from the gray and snowy late afternoon daylight.

"What am I looking at?" asked Nick, walking to the screen.

"The green lines show where you have traveled on your 'listening' tour. The footage Greg shot has been priceless, in more ways than one. It has kept us from having to stage and shoot the typical campaign spots and man on the street stuff. It is authentic and shows you in action. We've been able to combine various comments and statements to form our own online campaign position videos. We post these on the social media channels who haven't obeyed the Homeland request and, of course, on our own website and now Hibi," finished Denise, as Nick nodded.

"By the way, great job Greg," said Denise, nodding at him.

"Thanks. Nick made it easy. He kept everyone he talked to at ease," said Greg from the other end of the table.

"How is it being received?" asked Nick.

"We've cut a bunch of those videos up. We're trending and word is getting out. More folks are watching, and we're getting more and more shares. Good news is your platform is getting out there. But we are probably only hitting those 35 or under. We need to find better ways to target the older voters."

"How is Jeremy doing? Is his troll free idea working?"

"It is. He is catching a lot of flak. From both sides of the spectrum because they are claiming he is suppressing free speech. His system simply deletes users who violate the agreement. No questions asked. His algorithm is very good. It is driving the troll's crazy," said Margie with a laugh as she continued.

"Now the hackers are attacking, constantly trying to bring his systems down. He must spend a fortune to fight back against them. But it's working. He only had one outage for like 15 minutes. People can have a civil conversation in the comments sections of posts on Hibi. He is using AI, not people, to monitor all the conversations, so there is no question of bias."

"It's catching on and his base keeps growing. Mostly people are defecting from older social media apps which have been censoring commentary for years. Lots of these older users who are fed up with the leftward lurch, the cesspool comments, banning politicians, including the threats against you. Right after that, Hibi doubled in users," smiled Margie.

"Glad to help," laughed Nick.

"Nick, I think it is working because folks are tired of not being able to question anything online or even discuss it. ARL, Antifa, critical race theory, gender fluidity, lockdowns, mandates, open borders and now the actions of the FBI, DOJ or IRS, you name it," said Margie.

"Not for nothing, but I am against all those things. I am pretty sure a lot of the footage you shot Greg shows me talking to common folks who are also against it. So why is it I am not banned?" asked Nick.

"Because we don't post any of the more controversial clips on the legacy social apps where we didn't cancel our accounts. When folks do share from Hibi to these platforms, lots of them get banned. Now it is a badge of honor. Hibi has even created an 'I got Canceled' badge you can display to show they banned you from those other platforms. Drives the other social media channels crazy," said Margie, laughing again.

"Care to guess what it looks like?" asked Jer, joining the conversation.

"Don't have a clue," replied Nick as Margie quickly showed him the badge on her Hibi app on her phone. In the corner of her profile was the palm of a hand with a circle and slash.

"Folks call it the Mirror," said Margie proudly. "They say it is the other apps looking in *their* Mirror, seeing the truth, and banning them. Nick, you're catching on."

"At last count, I think Hibi had over 15 million users who were banned elsewhere. We are betting our social life on it to be honest. We promote Hibi and they advertise on our site as well," said Margie.

"Anything we need from Jeremy? I can ask?" asked Nick.

"No, you can't. Be really careful. Any favors or preferential treatment could be considered a violation of FEC rules," said Jenny, sitting next to Nick. "You can bet Lexi has the intelligence agencies monitoring everything we do. We may not be showing up in the polls, but what you are preaching is pretty radical."

"Ok. Got it, keep me on the straight and narrow," said Nick sheepishly at the sharp rebuke. "How is the fund raising going?"

"Pretty good. Of course, we raised a ton after your Montana escapades, but it has slowed down a bit, but we aren't spending much either. We have about $150 million in the bank," responded Jer.

Denise broke in. "We need to raise more so we can get you out more. I know you don't condone it, but several PACs have raised another $150 million in your name and are spending on ads to support you. Thankfully, they are following your mantra. No attack ads against any of your competitors. Just spreading your words and positions. Your road trip tours are nice, but we can't win this one conversation at a time. We need to get you in front of bigger crowds."

"What do you suggest?"

"As much as you hate it, go on some other networks if they will book you. You can be sure they will try to embarrass you by helping Lexi. You drew a good crowd to the Florida State fair in February. If you look at the map, the green stars are the state fair locations we have booked you into so far."

"Let's not fool ourselves. I think the two popular bands were the draw, not me," laughed Nick.

"Well, doesn't matter who or how. It worked. All the speeches will be on the last day between the opening and the main act to close the fair. After the response we saw in Florida, this may be the best bet to get you in front of sizeable crowds. Louisiana is next. We've also booked some commencement speeches for graduations," listed Denise.

"How are you doing on the book?" asked Margie.

"It's all in here, I just need to organize it," said Nick, padding his ever-present purple notebook.

"So, no farther than the last time?" commented Denise in a disappointing voice. "Do you want me to hire a ghostwriter to go through your notebooks and pull it together into book form?"

"No, I promise I will work on it. Give me two more weeks."

"Okay. Two weeks and then I need a draft. We are already pushing it. They're waving all the usual lead times," said Denise. "They know it will sell. We'll do a book tour to promote the book after the conventions."

"How about more VFWs and American Legion?" asked Nick.

"We can look into those as well. Good idea. We should take advantage of your support in the military community," agreed Denise.

"How are we doing at the state level, or should I ask?"

"You see that map, Nick?" this time from Greg. who got up to point at spots on the map. "Everywhere you went, everywhere you stopped as soon as you left, we got requests to charter all kinds of Turner themed election teams. Vets for Turner, Canceled Workers for Turner, Welders for Turner, you name it every trade for Turner. And of course, the usual, Turner Rabble, Women for Turner and of our paid Turner Victory Teams in each state."

"Everywhere you go, these start and they grow fast. Every state where you haven't been, it is more a struggle. As Denise said, we need you out there inspiring folks to take the lead and stand up for what they are losing. See the yellow lines on the map crossing the rest of the states? That is your itinerary for the next couple of weeks. By June, we need to have the Turner effect in full mode in each of the states," said Greg.

Nick smiled. "Interesting," he said, looking at the map. "I think there are a few lines missing. What about Hawaii?"

"No. You're not going when it's snowing here," said Denise.

"You sure? There has to be a high school graduation I can speak at next month," replied Nick. "Always wanted to learn how to surf. I sense a 'Surfers for Turner' group waiting to be chartered."

"I hear it is balmy in Alaska this time of year, though. I'm sure the Nome high school could use a guest speaker," retorted Denise.

Nick smiled in reply.

"How did Chicago go? No footage since our cinematographer Greg was not in tow. You and Earl meet up with his cousin?" asked Chuck.

Earl and Nick glanced at each other.

"Yes, we did. Let's just say Chicago is not in a good way. I had some wonderful conversations."

"Record any of them by chance," asked Margie hopefully.

"Sorry Margie. I did not. I took some good notes for the book, so it was not all for naught."

"At least you didn't get shot at," said Denise, as Earl grunted.

"Please tell me you didn't get shot at," said Denise and Chuck in unison as the rest of the team stared at Nick and Earl.

"Directly no. But it is Chicago. It is not a safe place. We made it back in one piece, so all is good. We also spent an afternoon talking to Reverend Elijah Powell, who regaled us with tales of Martin Luther King Jr. Now that was enlightening," said Nick, changing the subject.

Denise looked over at Earl, who held up his hands.

"You try talking to him," he said with a shrug.

Denise shook her head. She had wrangled philandering and drunken candidates, even ones who could not talk their way out of a box, but she had never experienced one who loved danger like Nick. She made a mental note to move up her next hair coloring appointment. Nick was giving her gray hair faster than she could color it out.

# Chapter 59

"Luc," said a soft female voice in French.

"Yes Annie? Did you find something?" asked Luc, looking down at his assistant. She sat on the floor, surrounded by what looked like random pieces of debris.

"Have you slept with Gabi yet?"

"Annie, did you find anything?" asked Luc calmly, ignoring Annie's prying questions.

Annie rocked back and forth, not answering. Luc waited.

"You should sleep with her. You are not getting any younger. Take her out to eat first. Make her eat two desserts. She is too skinny."

Luc sighed. "Annie, tell me what you have found?"

She rose from her seated position in one fluid movement, hurrying to Luc with pieces of a cell phone. She held them out to him.

"What am I looking at, Annie?"

"Luc, before you lost me my last job, I remember one of them broke their phone. It had codes on it they needed. I watched when the boy fixed the phone enough to get some data from it. You see here," she said, pointing to a section of the insides of the mangled phone. "This is the logic board and these are the NAND memory chips. The NAND is broken, but you may get someone to connect this part to this part and download whatever the last thing this person viewed."

Luc looked at the excited face of his savant assistant.

"Annie, how did Interpol and the other authorities miss this?"

Annie looked at Nick. "This phone and the rest of them are broken. The odds of this working is 1.458765%, maybe less. They make them tougher and tougher to withstand this kind of damage. You know, like being run over by a car or falling from a balcony. Will you call Gabi now?" asked Annie with a straight face and no emotion.

Luc smiled. He leaned over and kissed Annie on the forehead. She blushed and went back to her pile of debris, sitting again and gently rocking as she picked up more pieces to study.

Luc looked down at her, marveling once again at her ability to see things others missed or could never see.

He walked to a corner, pulled out his phone, and dialed.

"Say hi to Gabi for me," said Annie from the room.

Luc ignored her. "Alain, I need a discrete electrical engineer."

#

Luc looked over the shoulder of the gray-haired man wearing jeweler's glasses. He looked up at Luc, removing them.

"She could be right. The logic board is intact enough and the solder to the memory modules is broken. I could build a bridge with micro solder and if we can apply the right current, it might work. It has to boot up though, and that could be the tricky part," he said, pointing to another mangled part of the phone. "What I would suggest instead is we try to by-pass this with a different phone and have it try to access the memory of this phone. A tandem connection. We may only get one chance to transfer the memory before this all fails."

Luc looked at the mess on the worktable in front of him. He had no leads, and his only chance at getting one could end up in a pile of melted circuits.

"Proceed please. Where will the information in memory end up?" asked Luc.

"Over here on this disposable phone," he answered. "Ready?"

Luc nodded.

The man powered on the disposable smart phone, putting his jewelers' glasses back on as he used a tiny instrument to apply a small amount of solder connecting the broken pieces of the motherboard and memory on the broken cell phone. He checked his equipment.

"It is working. We have power to the old phone. There is something there, and it is transferring."

After 45 seconds, the old phone popped, and a small cloud of smoke accompanied by the smell of burning silicon announced the ultimate demise of the broken phone.

"Did it work?" asked Luc anxiously.

The man removed his glasses and looked at the disposable phone. Yes, you have 652 megabytes of data transferred to the new phone. That could be 5-6 minutes of video, a fair number of photos, or a lot of documents. No telling until you look. Do you want to look now?

"Better for you if I do this alone. Thank you for your time. Please send your bill to this address."

Luc gave him a card.

"I see," said the man, looking down at the card listing the Office of the President of France. "You are right. I do not want to know."

#

Luc lifted his head from his toilet bowl. There was nothing left to throw up. Continuing to kneel, he reached to flush the toilet. He hung his head, trying to calm his breathing and clear his mind from what he had seen and heard. Slowly he stood, going to the sink and splashing his face with water. Now he knew the connection between the random attackers in the Christmas markets. Men, all fathers of young daughters. Each had driven their large trucks into crowds of men, women, and children, only to commit suicide by their own hand or at the hands of authorities rather than be captured. He understood their motivation. And their Sophie's choice.

#

"You have found something, haven't you?" asked Alain.

"I have," replied Luc.

"Jean Paul or Christmas?"

"The markets."

"Really? You could find something none of the others could?"

"Yes. The phone from the Munich driver. Annie came up with a theory, and your engineer was able to use it to extract some information. I called you here to see it for yourself. It is a video. It will explain the connection between all the drivers," revealed Luc.

"They were connected, after all? How? They had no religious affiliation, nothing in common. No one took credit for any of these deeds," said Alain, getting up from the guest chair in Luc's apartment.

"Watch."

He handed the phone and an earphone to Alain. He looked on as the President watched the almost 5 minutes of video the engineer had salvaged from the phone.

About the four-minute mark, Alain looked up at Luc, handed him the phone, and ran to the restroom. Luc could hear him throwing up. A minute later, he heard the water and Alain reappeared.

"God in Heaven. No wonder they did what they did. What father would not? When faced with the consequences for their wives and daughters threatened on that video. Do I need to watch the rest?" asked Alain, clearly hoping Luc would say no.

"Instructions on how to carry out the task. And orders to destroy all evidence. If they failed to complete the mission or destroy the evidence, their family would receive the same fate as shown in the video. It must never get out that it exists, or they'll kill this man's family. We must move them with new identities," ordered Luc.

"I agree. I will try to figure out how to do this without endangering them. If they were French, this would be easy. But they are German and that makes it problematic. Who else knows?" asked Alain.

"No one. Just us."

Alain sat back down. "I believe I need a drink."

Luc poured scotch in his cup and Perrier over ice for Alain.

"I will not be the reason you break your promise to my sister," said Luc, handing the Perrier to Alain.

He stared at Luc for a second, taking the sparkling water.

"Thank you. Now what do we do?"

"I don't know. We are no closer to finding who would force fathers to do such a heinous deed. But at least we now know why."

"Once again, you give me information I cannot disclose."

"Alain, I would be more worried about what is next. They claimed neither of these deeds. This tells me they were not designed to recruit fanatics. They were intended to cause fear. Here is a scary thought. What if it is the same organization? Have you received any calls like Gaspard had before they killed him?"

"Why would you ask that? There is no connection other than no credit. I have received no calls," lied Alain.

"It is the complete lack of concern for the people involved, both those doing the deed and the victims. That is the other parallel. I wish we knew what they told Jean Paul."

"Luc, keep digging. We must get to resolution on both."

"How has inspector Martin done in getting word out to watch for autistic people in the crowds?" asked Luc.

Alain smiled. "She is a resourceful young woman. She created a storyline about a group of fictitious and now dead psychoanalysts using role playing as part of their therapy for a group of autistic adults. They designed the therapy to get them more included in society by acting as heroic characters. She warned the various police agencies to be on the lookout for any suspicious people who were not reacting as others in the crowds. Suggesting it could be these poor autistic citizens, pretending to be James Bond, Superman, Wonder Woman or some other hero. People who might be a danger to themselves or others thinking they could do superhero deeds."

Luc laughed. "I knew she would come up with something."

"Any movement on that front?"

"I have some leads. Alain, I fear this will not end well. People who would use the autistic to kill. Who would force fathers to choose between killing innocents or have what they described and showed happen to their wives and children, are monsters. We are not dealing with people with a shred of decency. They are soul-less."

"Indeed Luc. What do you need? Only you have the drive to see this through."

"I will let you know."

"Thank you for finding this. I am not sure I will ever forget what I saw and heard on that video," declared Alain.

"Good. It will give us purpose."

"True," he admitted, getting up to go. He turned back to Luc as his bodyguards stood in the open doorway.

"Luc, do not let your animosity toward me prevent you from talking to Madeline. Or seeing your niece and nephews. They all miss you terribly." Luc nodded, but did not reply.

His men closed the door behind him, leaving Luc alone in his apartment.

#

As the President of France left Luc's apartment, a man down the street took pictures. Just as he had of him arriving earlier. He would upload these to a site and let his employer know of the visit.

#

Luc leaned back from his window, viewing the man taking pictures of Alain leaving. He lowered his own camera's telephoto lens. Luc had sensed he was being watched and followed these last few weeks, if not longer. He now knew his tail was not from his 'friend' Alain, but from someone else. Perhaps watching both of them. Yet another twist to investigate. He retrieved his scotch and wondered how he could convince Inspector Martin to run the picture through the Interpol database. She had rebuffed any effort to talk since their first and only meeting.

# Chapter 60

"The polls have closed in New York and Pennsylvania and the Liberty News One election desk is calling both states for Vice President Lexi Smythe-Thomas. With these two states, we can confirm she'll be the Party nominee for president in the upcoming November election," said David Johansson, LN1's lead evening anchor.

"This, of course, brings to a close the surprisingly vigorous campaign of Senator Klausen of Wisconsin. He fought a good fight but will fall short of upsetting the Vice President. The question now is, will the Vice President be able to woo back into the Party fold the moderates who supported Klausen?"

#

"Finally," said Lexi as Mel handed her a drink in her campaign HQ office. The rest of the office was cheering, and champagne was being poured in celebration.

"You should say a few words to the staff," suggested Mel.

Lexi nodded, took a sip of her champagne, wrinkling her nose a bit. She walked out of the office into the sea of cubicles. She stood at one end of the room and raised her glass.

"Here is to the hardest working and most dedicated staff anyone could ask for," everyone in the room cheered in celebration. "It took us a bit longer than we thought, but challenges only make us stronger. We need to unite behind our common goal of keeping the Opposition at bay. Removing their obstacles to the changes, we know the people support," explained Lexi.

She thanked her staff for the long hours, lousy food and late nights spent dialing the phones and emailing constituents. She revved them up with talk of how they were going to change the world for the better, making it more inclusive and fairer for all, regardless of age, race, gender, or orientation.

By the end of her speech, they were cheering raucously, shouting 'Lexi for President'.

Mel held up his glass announcing, "Let's hear it for the Party nominee and the next *President* of the United States," finished Mel, lifting his glass. The room broke out into cheers of 'Lexi, Lexi', and 'LST', as she smiled and held her glass up.

"We need to finish working on your speech for later," said Mel, leaning close to Lexi to be heard above the noise. They both waved at the crowds as they retreated to the conference room, flipping on the light curtain.

"OK, so what is the plan now?" asked Lexi, sitting down and kicking off her heels and rubbing a foot, groaning.

"Why do you wear those, if they hurt so bad," asked Mel.

Lexi looked at the middle-aged balding man with round glasses who probably weighed 140 lbs. She raised an eyebrow.

"No pain, no gain, Mel. You know exactly why I wear them. I have even caught you looking at my legs from time to time. If you ever catch me wearing a pantsuit, kill me please," she said. "I find my appearance still has a certain effect on a subset of powerful men and I intend to use every weapon I have, my legs still being one of my best."

"That and your threat to castrate any man who crosses you," said Mel in a deadpan voice.

Lexi laughed, "That reputation does help, I admit."

"Speaking of castration, we have to shut down these idiots on the news channels. Now that the primaries are done, we need to clamp down on all this talk of a fractured party. These guys have air-time to fill and they love making up conflict," warned Mel.

"We could poison their teeth whiteners. Don't they realize 60-year-old men are not supposed to have whiter teeth than 3-year-olds? It looks so silly. They must use gallons of it. We should look into it. I can see it now, 'David Johansson found dead on the floor of his bathroom with his bleaching tray still in his mouth. There is speculation he died from hydrogen peroxide overdose trying to match the pearly whites of his lovely co-host Molly Kirchner'," commented Lexi in a mock serious tone.

Mel smiled, "You know, these are the first jokes you have cracked in months."

Lexi looked at him with a half-smile, half frown.

"You know, you're right. Maybe it's been getting to me. Being President without being President, while running for President and then having to fight off that traitor Klausen. You know, that bastard said he fully supported me before the primaries started. Then he did this to me. Do I have to offer him a cabinet post?

"Yes, you do. We need him fully behind us and telling the moderates to not worry. How we are not going to remake the United States despite what he and the Opposition have been saying," said Mel again in a mocking, serious tone, which made Lexi smile.

"We have to bribe him to lie? Will he?"

"Of course, even he never thought he would do this good. You'll just have to give him a bigger post now. Maybe Energy or Transportation," said Mel.

"Unfortunately, my esteemed opponents can't even figure out who to run against me, so we can't turn the press on any of them," said Lexi pacing around the room "Besides they don't need any help from us to talk about them. Those guys are even more fucked up than I imagined. Not that I am complaining, mind you, but I would like to know who I am going to be beating come November."

"They are even more split than we were, and they never come together after, anyway. Garcia is their best candidate," said Mel, as Lexi made a rude noise across the room. "He would be the hardest for you to debate against, but he is a distant second to Blackbird," he remarked.

"Blackbird is a total squish. I think he takes a poll on which side of bed to get out of in the morning. We would be so lucky to run against him, but even the Opposition isn't that dumb, are they?" asked Lexi.

"Unless Garcia steps back from some of his conservative positions, he's not going to get any of the other candidates to drop out and support him. Blackbird is leading, but I don't think he is going to get enough, so they are going to go to the convention without a candidate. It couldn't be better for us."

"We have dirt on him?"

"Oh Ya. Our good friend, Governor Blackbird, has some skeletons in his closet. I am amazed no one dug them up, but we had to work pretty hard to get our info. Garcia has lots of sketchy stuff, too. No real bombshells but enough family issues we can use to tarnish his holier than though persona. Carson from South Carolina is a lightweight. She wants the VP spot and is probably more likely to get it from Blackbird than Garcia. Wilson from Florida is pissed he is not doing better, so he probably won't accept a VP offer and no way Garcia and Blackbird work it out. They *hate* each other. There hasn't been a weaker field in years," said Mel.

"Good. This summer can't go fast enough. Let's get this done and get me in the White House officially before something happens," said Lexi.

"You worried about China?" asked Mel.

"Yes. They really, really, want Taiwan. Despite what they say publicly about being buds with Russia, all those resources are sitting just to their north, in Siberia, ripe for the taking. Russia wants the rest of Ukraine and Belarus and the Baltic states back to rebuild their buffer from Europe. Then you have the mess we left in Afghanistan and Iraq."

"Thank you, Mr. President," said Mel, sarcastically.

Lexi shook her head. "We keep trying to buy off Iran, but the new Ayatollah is a real ball-buster. I'm not sure if he hates us more than Israel, but I think it is only a matter of time before Iraq and Afghanistan are both official puppets. Then we have to figure out what to do with Saudi Arabia. That will be the next target. I don't think Iran will mess with Israel because they will fight back and they will use their nukes if faced with annihilation. Even a zealot like Ayatollah Bashir knows that. He doesn't want to rule from a hut in the hinterlands," finished Lexi.

"Just a few things on your mind, I see," said Mel.

She laughed and went to a fridge in the corner, looking up at Mel, who shook his head. She grabbed an Evian and took a long sip. "The world is going to hell in a handbasket because we haven't been able to lead in years. We need to get our house in order and then we can work with China and Russia to get them back on the right track. All this conflict is unnecessary. We *all* need to get Iran to stop agitating. I figured once we lifted the sanctions, they would go back to saber rattling, but their election ended that. It really looked bad when we let them kill all those pro-democracy protesters with no pushback. We may have to do something about him, eventually," said Lexi half to herself.

"That wasn't your fault. Again, our President did that. And we can't even claim he was out of it when he did," said Mel.

Lexi sat sipping her water. She contemplated all the millions of things she was trying to keep track of. Without the staffing the Presidency afforded, she was having to do so much of the job in the background while keeping up appearances of still being the second in command. It was wearing her out and she knew she needed to conserve her strength for the run up to the election.

She turned to look at Mel, who stood patiently waiting. Lexi suddenly saw Mel wearing one of the long-beaked masks favored by doctors when visiting those succumbing to the black plague in the 1400s. She gave a shiver, and he was back to just Mel.

# Chapter 61

Lexi stood off stage at the Greek Theatre on the Berkeley campus of the University of California, her alma mater. The crowd exceeded the 8500-person capacity with overflow crowds standing around the perimeter. The fire marshals made no move to limit *her* overflow crowd.

With a big smile, she walked out onto the stage as the crowd stood cheering and chanting variations of 'Lexi' and 'LST'. The weather was perfect and Lexi, knowing this, had chosen her outfit for maximum effect. She was wearing a cream-colored dress with a pleated skirt and beige heels. Wearing fashionable sunglasses, her shoulder-length blonde curls blew in the wind and bounced on her shoulders as she approached the podium. She looked vibrant, exuding confidence as she acknowledged the adulation with a wave of her hand.

Unlike previous female presidential candidates who lacked the complete package, Lexi was the first with all three. Smart, beautiful, and ruthless. She worked hard to maintain her appearance, her Nordic ancestors having blessed her with great skin and a high metabolism. In a business where how you looked was a significant advantage, or disadvantage, she maximized what she still could and used it. Someone meeting her for the first time would have guessed her age at mid-forties, rather than her actual sixty.

She stood tall behind the podium, looking out over a sea of mostly women and young people of all races. Many were holding up rainbow banners and others with placards, Women for LST, Trans for Lexi, a smattering of peace signs, and ARL signs. These were her people, and she was proud to lead them. The enormity of the moment momentarily overwhelmed her. She was one step from being elected as the first female President of the United States.

Holding up her hands to quiet the crowd, she thanked them for their support and their perseverance. She thanked her primary opponents and promised to be the President for all of them and all Americans. She also thanked Senator Klausen for putting up such a spirited fight. Admitting she did not always feel that way in a conspiratorial whisper. The crowd laughed accordingly.

She reviewed all the accomplishments they had achieved. Both in the present administration and the challenges they still had to overcome in her upcoming one. She touched on the racial persecution still running rampant. The resistance to change, demonstrated by the continued blocking of groundbreaking legislature. She promised to pass a host of bills, removing prejudice, and expanding help for all in the first one hundred days of her new administration. She was working the crowd up into a frenzy as she closed.

Lexi paused for the cheering to die down.

"America is broken. And that is a good thing. We have finally risen to throw off the burden laid upon us by all the crap the Opposition has passed and continue to support. We pay the price for their short-sided policies. Their continued dogmatic support for rules no longer reflecting the society we live in. They continue to support easing gun laws to allow more and more access to guns and weapons of war. These have enabled enormous numbers of our youth, our poor, and disadvantaged, to die needlessly. This has fueled crime waves in our cities and towns. These laws were passed when folks had a musket to hunt dinner. I don't know about you, but I get my dinner at the grocery store, or my local restaurant. I sure don't need a semi-automatic rifle with a 100-round magazine. Do you?" The resounding no from the crowd quickly turned to a chant of *no more guns.*

Lexi once again raised her hands for quiet. "As we all know, when we took office, we were in the most devastating pandemic in centuries with high unemployment and an economy in a free fall. This, combined with the divisive prior administrations' poor policies, isolated the United States from the rest of the world and left us a country in pitiful shape. We have worked tirelessly to undo their mistakes. Focusing on achieving full employment, through stimulus and protections against evictions. Continuing to provide unemployment and health insurance benefits to prevent greedy capitalist corporations from fattening their profits at a time of societal need."

"We've raised minimum wages and ensured all who worked received a living wage. Forcing corporations to pay what people are worth. Giving dignity back to those who toil for a pittance to fatten the pocket of their employer. We're working to tame inflation, caused by the poor decisions of the prior administration. Those same greedy capitalist corporations take advantage of this inflation to price gouge and profit off supply chain issues. There is still much to do. We fought off the second pandemic wave. Protecting even those who chose not to follow the science. Those conspiracy theorists who made this pandemic last longer, from their ignorance, grandstanding, and refusal to get vaccinated."

"There are loads of misinformation, designed to scare you online and on the airwaves. We have worked with those companies who agree this is a danger to our society and dangerous to each of you. We will continue to work with responsible social media leaders to make sure we protect you from these people. I promise you; we will not stop until we silence all these people who are peddling their half-truths and outright falsehoods to make money off making you afraid." The crowd roared.

"You know, and I know, the struggle to achieve equality has been ongoing for hundreds of years. For blacks and Hispanics, for women, for gays and trans in this country. This results from a society founded by OLD, WHITE, MEN." Boos from the crowd as Lexi smiled.

"These same men, represented by the modern Opposition party, seek to keep this going. They claim because they have women and a few blacks and Hispanics in their ranks, they are racially diverse and fighting the same fight." Lexi paused for more boos from the crowd.

"We know it is not true. They seek to prevent true equality. They fight us tooth and nail as we seek equality for all. But worse than that, when we seek equity, for similar outcomes for all, they cry foul and say this is not fair. What is fair about building fortunes on the back of cheap labor? What is fair about being the ones in charge for hundreds of years and making laws to allow the concentration of wealth in the hands of a few white men? And now, when we are leading a movement to change all this, they scream it is not fair? Ha!" Lexi paused again as the crowd responded with cheers in a loud voice.

"We will build a better society, one based on equality and fairness regardless of socio-economic standing. It's time for an American Rebirth, not one based on prejudice and white supremacy. Rather, a blended and diverse community bringing together the best of all cultures, creeds, races, sexes, and orientations to forge a new American Ideal. One founded in equity and equality, looking forward instead of back. One offering people the opportunity to define themselves and to avoid the stigma of boundaries and rules imposed by white men." Lexi beamed as the cheering continued. After a minute of cheering, she resumed.

"Now is the time to stand together. To look around and realize we are all humans and our differences are our strengths. The time to embrace these differences and to stamp out any who would stand in the way of progress. America can no longer afford to tread water. We need to lead ourselves and the world. To progress into a global community focused on the core values of humanity, embracing who we are, who we want to be, and how we achieve these goals. Barriers used by our enemies to stop this progress need to be removed. We need to seek others who believe the way we do and push aside any who would stop progress solely out of fear." She paused again.

"There are those who say to slow down, to give it time. These are the same ones who are claiming to help, out of one side of their mouth. While passing and endorsing law after law, or blocking and stopping changes to laws that would have made *your* life better out of the other side of it."

"I am here to tell you, when I am elected president, this stops now. We will no longer allow these members in the minority of congress to dictate to us, the majority, what we can and cannot accomplish. We have spoken and we are many, we are strong, and we are committed. When I get to Washington, I promise you, we will make progress. No one will stop us from remaking America into our vision of what it *should have been and what it will become.* ONWARD," yelled Lexi in climax, raising her arms high as the crowd surged to their feet, cheering, clapping, and shouting her name. The commotion continued for ten minutes as Lexi stood on stage, soaking in the love from her rabid supporters.

#

"Nice speech," said the mechanical Voice.

"Thanks," I wrote it said Mel Arenson.

"Just the right amount of truth and the right amount of laying blame everywhere else. It always amazes me how the Party can blame others for their policies and the poor results," it seemed the person on the other side was laughing, but it was difficult to know with the voice masking software.

"Well, if they failed previously, it is out of lack of commitment and willpower, something else our Party is known for. Plus, the filibuster gives the Opposition the ability to block their implementation or funding. We will not have that issue this time," finished Mel.

"I see. We have heard that before as well," the Voice replied.

"True, but we have primed the pump, as we say. Most of the populace is ready to be led. To be taken care of and have some ills of capitalism removed in return for support from the Government. There are some who'll resist, but we know they are the minority. Once we are in power, we will use the tools of government and the rabid nature of the mobs, to expose and destroy dissent. Once these folks realize they'll lose their government 'help' if these dissenters are allowed to agitate or retake power, we'll have our army to help us root out those who resist our change," finished Mel.

"Nice words. You have a way with them. To convince these people to give up freedom for the greater good. Just make it reality. We're tired of failure and of waiting," ended the Voice.

# Chapter 62

As April turned to May, Nick continued crisscrossing the US, speaking at American Legion and VFW halls, to parent's groups gathered in elementary school gyms, restaurants and even a parking garage depending on the location and the attempts by local governments to restrict his ability to gather a large crowd. These crowds continued to grow. Word of mouth and his Hibi posts reached more and more folks. Some of his more unique visits included a woman's book club in Iowa and a quilting bee in Kansas. Nick didn't turn down any chance to speak to groups who would have him.

As he did more and more of these and even as they grew in size and frequency, sometimes six appearances a day, Nick still knew it was not enough. It was physics. There simply was not enough time for him to talk to all the people he'd need to in order to reach critical mass at a grassroots level. He'd even skipped Dolly's Spring Gala, talking instead to a group of Shriners at a regional conference in West Virginia.

While they gave him a standing ovation and let him drive one of their miniature cars, it was no substitute for an evening with Ms. Wells-Monroe. Nick reluctantly informed Dolly of his absence. When he told her why he couldn't attend and then followed up with a picture of him in the small car, she merely laughed at him choosing this over her. He promised to make it up to her at the fall one. He was sure he would be otherwise occupied on the road for the Summer Gala as well.

As Greg had expected, everywhere he went, the 'Turner Effect' left behind a slew of volunteers looking to start up the various Turner organizations. He was still staying under the radar, exhorting each audience to continue to mislead pollsters while he taught them the 'Flip' and the 'Mirror'. There was one popular video on KooKoo, from a fan showing how to do it that had over twenty-five million views.

The press hardly paid attention to Nick and his grassroot popularity. Even the local stations rarely reported unless it was to highlight Nick being evicted from restaurants or parking lots for not having the proper permits. Eventually, Nick talked with Martha Summers, getting her permission to hold rallies in her store parking lots. After laughing, she had instructed her store owners to paint in far corners of their parking lots, specific areas designated as Turner Rally 'spots'. After the press complained she was supporting Nick, she made the same offer to any candidates. Offering them the same space in her parking lots for rallies as well. No other candidates responded. He was drawing much larger crowds than any of his opponents, from either side.

Nick continued to hold his rallies and gatherings in these store parking lots. In predominantly blue states or Party controlled larger cities, there were always code enforcement or sheriffs present, ready to fine or disperse the crowds the minute they exceeded the size or grew beyond the boundaries of the store's private property. Nick and his team worked hard to have many small rallies in these places rather than fewer big ones.

Martha's refusal to stop allowing these got her cross ways with local authorities. In many of these small towns, they could not afford to alienate what was usually the largest employer for the locals and also the largest sales tax generator. Most attempts to stop her from giving Nick permission quickly died with little fanfare.

The lone holdout was Oregon, who refused to drop their lawsuits. With a Pavlovich supported Attorney General and law firms aligned with his WHS foundations, Martha found her stores in litigation. The other blue states waited to see how it would turn out before trying the same tactics.

Nick had offered to stop having the rallies in Oregon, since he knew it was a forlorn hope to even consider winning this deep blue state. Martha laughed.

"You never met my husband, Norman. This is exactly the fight he would have loved. The people are on our side. Regardless of the outcome, we won't lose. You keep doing what you are doing, Nick." He had thanked her for her support and willingness to fight for the people's right to hear views other than those broadcast by the media.

The local media in Pittsburgh had tried to paint the Turner Rabble as law-breaking rednecks with a propensity to drink and litter. The reality was Nick was drawing from the center of both parties. Tradesmen and office workers, moms and dads, small business owners, students and people of all ages disillusioned with all the promises made. People now facing the reality of sky-high housing, health care, utilities, and general cost of living on wages being eroded by inflation.

These were not the dregs of society the media said Nick was attracting. They showed footage of piles of trash and refuse in a parking lot, supposedly after Nick had spoken to 500 at one of Summer's stores.

ANC, FLCN, and the networks all ran with the story. Only to find out shortly thereafter, the parking lot being filmed was in fact not one of Summer's. It was an abandoned parking lot of a big-name clothing store in a mall shut down by too many unresolved thefts. Successful defund the police movements had allowed anarchy to triumph there.

The corporate headquarters for the chain had given up and opted to close the store after losing millions. It decimated the mall when its anchor store left, and they subsequently cut back on both security and cleanup crews around the property.

EXN picked up the story and made a huge point of showing Turner supporters picking up the trash at all their rallies. They showed the before and after pictures of each where they left it better than when they had arrived. This story had legs and allowed EXN to bring up stories from the past, showing the desolation and trash left behind by various liberal activist marches and rallies compared to Turner's orderly, polite, and clean ones.

Nick couldn't help but smile as he looked out the window of the Uber as it navigated the downtown area of Baton Rouge. It was the morning rush hour, so his progress to his destination was slow. As he reviewed these items in his head, he knew he'd been lucky. So far, everything they'd try to tag him with ended up back firing when the truth became known. In their desperation, they were sloppy with the accusations.

He knew in his heart this wouldn't last. He'd spoken the prior evening at the closing night of the Louisiana spring State Fair. Just like Florida, they slated for him to speak for ten minutes between acts. The crowd had responded well to his message. Here he talked about getting American energy independence back and the crowd enthusiastically listened.

The unemployment rate in Louisiana was still above the national average, primarily because of moratoriums on additional drilling in the gulf. Many of the attendees of the state fair were working-class parents and their families whose livelihood was tied to the oil and gas business.

The Party governor had taken a hardline on lockdowns and mandates during both pandemics. His state was still paying for these mistakes. Louisiana lost workers, to primarily Texas. This had caused a shortage of labor when things opened back up. These workers now had to compete with large numbers of illegals. Illegals who were willing to do many of the backbreaking jobs in the oil fields at much lower wages.

To return America to energy independence, a lot of it would occur in Louisiana. How we needed to return America to the short time where we were a net exporter. To build more port and refining capabilities, including the ability to convert and ship Liquefied Natural Gas. The cleanest burning of the fossil fuels.

Natural Gas was an energy source in which the United States led the world in reserves. This alone would ensure full employment. Not just unskilled labor, but good paying jobs requiring specialized skills. It would help Louisiana climb out of the bottom five economies in the country. Rejuvenate the public services and expenditures to fix the nation's worst roads and improve some of the nation's worst schools.

He appealed to their patriotism, telling the worked-up crowd an energy independent America was a strong America. It would also cut the leverage Russia and Iran had on the world, selling oil for weapons and influence over countries with no other choice. The US could easily be an exporter of energy and offer European countries the opportunity to use US LNG to cut their dependency on Russian oil and gas.

Finally, he'd explained how energy independence and reinvestment of these profits in sustainable energy research would allow responsible transitions to support climate change initiatives. Improvements in overall diversity of energy were the real path to combating any man-made climate damage without destroying the economy of the country. He got the loudest cheers of the night with these statements. Common sense resonated with the common people.

"Ok, let me finish up then. I hope I have opened a few eyes. These politicians say they do these things to help you. Do you feel like they have helped you? I didn't think so. Turn and talk to your neighbor. Talk to your friends. Talk to your family. Work together. Start local. Elect someone from your group with common sense and hold them accountable."

"So," said Nick with a pause, "Get together and vote. Now I know this is God loving country, so if I could, I would like to end this with a quick prayer if you would let me," said Nick to a crowd who cheered and yelled 'Yes' and 'Amen'.

He bowed his head, as did most in the crowd. "Father, please give us the wisdom to see the truth. Give us the strength to pursue what is right. Give us the perseverance to prevail and the faith to do all that is good for our children and ourselves. Amen," finished Nick to a resounding 'Amen' and cheers from the crowd. He handed the microphone to the emcee and walked off the stage.

"That was certainly well worth the time," said the organizer off stage. "Who'd have thought a bunch of beer guzzling rednecks would put up with, let alone demand more time for a politician at a state fair? Right before the main act? That they *paid* to see? For forty-five minutes," he said, looking at his watch, while shaking Nick's hand.

"I told them what they already knew deep inside. Most folks just need some encouragement. You are right, if I were a politician, they would have booed me off the stage in 30 seconds. But I am not a politician. I am their neighbor, coworker, son, or friend. You know what else? Every word I say is believable because I believe it."

"Son, you are right about that," said the organizer.

"They need help to wake up and realize they *do* matter. That's all I'm doing, waking people up and telling them to decide to be responsible for their own actions and lives. It is a simple choice and one with only one answer. You'll also notice I didn't ask them to vote for me or promise them a single thing. No free stuff. People really aren't looking for a handout. They're looking for a way to get by on their own without the government stopping them. Most of all, they want to be left alone to live their life as they see fit," said Nick with a shrug.

"Well Senator, any way I see it, that was a genuine miracle. Then to get them to say a prayer and to do so wholeheartedly. Geez, you got some kind of magic touch. Worked on me. I wish you all the luck in the world for all our sakes," said the organizer. "Oh, almost forgot, here," he said, handing over an envelope. "I was told to deliver this to you."

"Thanks again for letting us get on stage with such short notice."

"You let me know if any of the other fairs push back. I know most of their leaders and I can tell them what you did here, although I suspect it is already up on social media."

"Not for long. The censors at Big Tech love me. They'll take'em down as fast as we post them. Go to Hibi if you want them to stay up."

Nick joined Earl, Denise, and Greg further off stage.

Denise had a funny, almost scared look on her face.

"What?" said Nick.

"This was just like Florida. I thought that was just a fluke. I don't get it," she said, shaking her head.

"Haha," said Nick. "Any of you stop to think maybe the masses aren't as dumb, stupid, and ignorant as the media made them out to be?"

"I don't know about that, but the footage was great, especially the prayer at the end. That was magnificent," said Greg. "Shows people still have faith, even if they are afraid to express it."

"Any posts yet?" asked Denise.

"Hundreds and GFI&T are taking them down as fast as they can, but even they can't keep up. The last one got 150,000 views before it got removed. They are staying up on Hibi, but its base isn't nearly as big. As long as folks keep posting, they will see it," commented Greg.

"GFI&T? I love it. Sounds like a clothing store," laughed Nick.

"Or a drink," said Earl, laughing as well.

"Easier than saying their names each time," shrugged Greg.

"Mind if I use it?"

"Not at all, boss, happy to help," offered Greg.

"What's in the envelope?" asked Earl.

"An invitation from Everett Spalding."

"Really?" said Denise, lighting up at the thought. "Man, if you could get him on our side. He is a Party mega donor. He made a killing in the oil field equipment business. Next to Halliburton, his company is the place to go for rigs and pipelines."

"Well, I'll see what he has to say. Maybe I can get him on board with my redemption project as well," said Nick.

"Hey, that's a great idea," agreed Denise sarcastically, shaking her head. "And maybe you can also ask him to help, I don't know, contribute to your campaign? You know, your actual job, trying to be president, instead of building a giant homeless shelter?"

"And they say you're heartless, Denise," smiled Nick.

"Just focused. Please see if you can at least get him on your side. Then his PAC can spend some of their money on you instead of Lexi," suggested Denise.

#

A honking horn drew Nick back to the early morning traffic in Baton Rouge. He did not know why Everett Spalding would want to talk to him, but at this point in his campaign, he talked to anyone who stood still long enough for a conversation.

# Chapter 63

Nick looked out the window from the backseat of the Uber as it circled the Louisiana State Capitol building on the way to One American Plaza. He got out and thanked his Uber driver.

"Pleasure Senator, I was at the concert last night. Great speech. Really made me think. We are already organizing our own Turner Rabble brigade. You can count on us," said the driver.

"Thanks. Remember, keep it focused on changing your local politics and keep it peaceful, OK?"

"Aye aye, Captain," said the driver, throwing Nick a salute as he closed the door. Nick entered the modern glass building, walking to a reception desk where an older black man greeted him.

"Hello," he said, "May I help you?"

"I sure hope so. I have a meeting with Mr. Spalding. Name's Turner," said Nick casually.

The man grinned bigger.

"Senator, I recognize you from last night."

"Geez, did everyone go to that concert?" asked Nick, smiling.

"No sir, I had to be at work early, but I saw the posting of your speech before they took it down. I had to watch three different posts of it to see the whole thing. They kept deleting it when I was in the middle of watching," laughed the man.

Nick shook his head.

"What is the world coming to? What did I say that was so bad? Guess they don't like the facts. You should try Hibi, they don't censor," suggested Nick.

"I just heard about them. I downloaded the app last night and I will use it from now on. Don't like the other guys anyway," he said.

Nick held out his hand. "Nick Turner." The man looked flustered for a second. Then stood and shook Nick's outstretched hand.

"Malcolm Turner, no relation, I think," he said with a laugh.

"You never know," Nick answered with a laugh of his own. "A pleasure to meet you, Malcolm."

He smiled, showing his teeth in a big grin, then he looked around as if to see if anyone was watching and said, "Senator, we are with you. You're right, even though they try to tell us you're not. I'm not listening to them anymore. I think it is the same with a lot of other folks. What you say makes sense. About time we started thinking for ourselves." Malcom had his hand out and was 'Flipping' it as he spoke.

"Thanks Malcolm. Guess I shouldn't be late for my meeting," said Nick with a wink.

"Right, go to the elevator on the far right. It goes to the 25th floor. They'll meet you at the top. Nice to meet you," said Malcolm.

"You too." Nick walked to the elevator. He pushed the only button, and the door opened to reveal an elegantly paneled elevator carriage. He got in, looking for a button to push, when the elevator started moving. After 15 seconds it stopped, the doors opened, and he was looking at a pair of large gentlemen. One black and the other white. They both looked to be starting linemen for the New Orleans Saints. Nick stepped out.

"Welcome Senator, are you armed? We have to ask."

"I am, small of my back," answered Nick.

"Would you be so kind as to hand over your weapon," said the large black man holding out a meat cleaver sized hand.

"Nope," said Nick.

"Sir, Mr. Spalding does not allow any weapons in his presence," said the large white guard.

"Then I guess it was a waste of my time and Mr. Spalding's," said Nick, turning back to the elevator.

Both guards looked at each other, not sure what to do.

"Traditionally, I would push a button? Not sure how this works here?" said Nick, glancing up at the eye in the sky.

"I assure you, I mean Mr. Spalding no harm, but there is no way I am willingly surrendering my gun. We seem to be at an impasse," said Nick, opening his palms.

The white guard cocked his head, listening to orders in his ear.

"Senator, this way please," he said, leading Nick down a long hallway with what looked like several conference rooms on either side. There was no other person in any of the rooms as they turned toward the west side of the floor.

"Does Mr. Spalding have the entire floor?" asked Nick.

"Yes, he does, sir. He also owns the entire building," said the guard as they came up to a pair of ornate solid wood carved doors. He pressed a button on the side and the doors opened inward. The guard motioned him forward to a desk where an attractive brunette sat behind a desk. She rose as he approached.

"Thanks, Walter," she said to the guard and held out a hand to Nick. "Michelle Kolzak, Senator."

"Please call me Nick," he said in reply.

"This way, Senator," she said, not missing a beat. Nick followed her to what he figured was the Southwest corner of the floor and yet another ornately carved door. She pressed a code into the pad on the side and the door opened with a single chime.

"Please enter Senator. Mr. Spalding will be with you in a minute. There are beverages and some pastries on the table inside. Please feel free and make yourself at home. Nice to meet you," said Michelle, retreating through the now closing doors.

Nick surveyed the room. It had floor to ceiling windows to the south and west, providing a view of the Mississippi River as it meandered through Baton Rouge. The room itself had a service center to his right with coffee, juice, danish, and muffins. The massive room was furnished simply. Only a pair of couches, a few leather-bound chairs, a coffee table here and there, and a single large round wooden table with three chairs. In one corner was a magnificent wooden desk with ornate carvings on the legs. It looked ancient. The floor was a rich mahogany hardwood with no carpets anywhere. Nick helped himself to a cup of dark, rich coffee. He had just taken a sip when he heard a noise.

"What do you think of the coffee?" boomed a deep voice.

Nick turned to reply and paused.

"Not what you expected?" came the deep voice once more, but the body it came from sat in a motorized wheelchair. The man couldn't have weighed over 125 lbs. He was a shrunken version of what must have once been a strapping six foot tall man. The voice did not match the body.

"About the only thing I have left is my voice. The rest of me has just wasted away. So how is the coffee?" asked Everett Spalding.

"Excellent. I like strong coffee and this more than fits the bill. Can I get you anything?" asked Nick.

Everett smiled and lifted one emaciated arm showing a hot cup of his own, retrieved from a place in his wheelchair.

"I have my own. Let's take a seat. Well, you anyway" he laughed a deep booming laugh again, surprising Nick with its strength.

Nick followed Everett and stopped when he did. As he turned, he held out a spindly fist.

"Can't shake hands any longer, but I can gently bump fists. Everett Spalding," he said as Nick gently touched his own fist to Everett's. "Nick Turner."

"Very nice to meet you, Senator. Sorry about before. My guards have very strict rules for visitors. They didn't know what to do when you refused," acknowledged Everett with a small laugh.

"Well Everett, I am a big believer in taking care of myself and please call me Nick,"

"From what I have seen, heard, and read, you are quite good at it," he said, still smiling.

"Unfortunately, I have had to a few times."

"What do you know about me?"

"Frankly, not much. I'm not courting any big donors. Only accepting small dollar donations from individuals. I haven't studied up on mega donors. For either party. I know you are big in the oil equipment business, aside from that, not much else."

Everett smiled a genuine smile and shook his head.

"I should be crushed. You are the strangest politician I have ever met. Usually, they are groveling within the first 30 seconds. Telling me how wonderful I am, how this and that philanthropic effort have been the greatest thing, and how my money is being put to such good use."

"That's nice, but not really my style."

"I can see that. Nick, it intrigues me. I have a question though. Do you have a death wish?" asked Everett.

"Excuse me?"

"Like I said, I have been doing research on you, even if you didn't on me. I have lots of access, and from what I can tell, you're really unlucky or you have a death wish. It is the only rational explanation for how you always seem to be in the wrong place at the right time, when life and limb must be risked to save the day. You have a Superman complex?" asked Everett earnestly.

"I guess I never saw it like that. I saw it as duty. If something happens in that duty, it is one's obligation to do all they can to fix it, right?" asked Nick with a shrug.

"No, it isn't. Clearly. This is not Pearl Harbor, or D-Day or even 9/11. What you fight for may not be worth the effort and the risk to life and limb," pointed out Everett in a somber tone.

"I must humbly disagree. Right is always worth defending. Wrong is always worth fighting against. It is a simple code," said Nick with a shrug. "Or put more prosaically, fight for good, fight against evil."

"Whose definition of right and wrong, good and evil? Lots of good boys have risked and lost their lives, supposedly doing right, for all the wrong reasons. How do you square that circle? Following those orders almost got you killed, frequently, if my info is correct," said Spalding.

"Everett, I believe the United States serves a purpose. It is not without flaws. However, our Constitution has planted, fertilized, watered, and grown a society of innovative free thinkers who have accomplished more in our brief history than most other civilizations combined. I believe it has been a force for good more often than not. By good, I mean 'love thy neighbor, golden rule good'. These deeds far outweigh the negatives we have created, supported, or not fully eradicated from our society as yet."

"Interesting defense," answered Everett, listening.

"As a soldier, I swore an oath to uphold that Constitution and to obey the orders of my superiors. I had to trust they were more often than not, working towards this same goodness. I had to believe it. Just as the marines who charged into Belleau Wood in World War I to free Europe. And those who stormed the beaches of Guadalcanal and Normandy to save the world in the second one. What nation of free peoples could marshal their sons and daughters to march willingly into the hail of bullets if they did not believe their cause was freedom and, therefore, on the side of right?" asked Nick.

"The Nazis believed they were freeing the world from Jews. Communists feel they are freeing the world of the evils of capitalism. The examples of fanatical troops marching into death are limitless throughout history," replied Everett, not giving an inch.

"Indeed, but the ones we remember and celebrate are the ones who did so of their freewill. Not out of coercion. Or religious fanaticism. Not out of forced or false loyalty gained only through threat to themselves or their family. Those fighting for freedom do not flinch. They willingly sacrifice themselves so others may yet again pick up and carry the flag of freedom to victory. That flag is the stars and stripes representing our Constitution, our way of life, and the freedom to choose. There is and has been no better symbol of what a free society can build and maintain than that flag. So no, I do not have a death wish. But I am also not afraid to die for my country, for its ideals, and most of all, to preserve for others the ability to be ruled by our Constitution."

Everett stared at Nick for a few seconds.

"Strange indeed."

Nick got up to refill his coffee.

"I assume you asked me here for a reason, not just to question me about my patriotism," said Nick, returning to the chair.

Everett looked at Nick. "Would you die for this country, as it is today, with the current administration?"

"Isn't that a rhetorical question? I already said my oath to the country was to the Constitution, not to any administration. I went where I was told to go. That is the soldier's covenant," replied Nick.

"That is not what I asked. Do you think the policies and leaders of the current Party administration, and the future administration of Ms. Smythe-Thomas, are worth fighting for and potentially dying for?" asked Everett.

"Again, not a fair question. Most times, my answer would still be yes. In the service of right, you don't get to stop and review the life of the potential victim to see if they are worthy of saving."

"Do you know how I ended up in this chair?" asked Everett.

"No."

"Early in my career, I had a diving company. We did a lot of deep-sea salvage and underwater demolition, stuff like that. Being the owner, I did more than most and led many of the missions. I had several brushes with death. Have had the bends a few times, because of emergency ascents or carelessness on my part or others, rushing our decompression stops, etc."

"We were young, strong, and fearless. Soon I branched out to lay underwater pipeline from the rigs to shore. I even have a few patents for the technology and processes. Lots of boring technical stuff. I started buying other companies, even married the daughter of a Halliburton exec. This led me to acquire companies they jettisoned through poor management."

"I turned these around. Selling them back at a huge profit. I had it all: a beautiful wife, and a thriving business. Life was good. Then I started falling down. I went to the best doctors in the world. I got poked, prodded, and shot full of experimental drugs, all for naught. Soon I couldn't walk without a cane. I was determined to not let it stop me."

"Then, against all hope, my wife got pregnant. I thought the one thing we'd never been able to have would help me. But things kept getting worse. Pretty soon, I was in a wheelchair. Can you imagine the indignity of being pushed around in a wheelchair by your 6 months pregnant wife? Outwardly, I was still this big strapping guy, but inside, my central nervous system was going haywire. Actually, I could use a bit more coffee," he said, handing his hot cup to Nick. Nick walked over and refilled it before returning to Everett.

He sat down, waiting patiently for Everett to finish the story.

"One day we are getting out of the car in the driveway. Donna is getting the wheelchair from the trunk, and I am sitting on the front seat of the car, waiting to lift myself into the chair. Out of the blue, a van pulls up and three men approach, all wearing ski masks."

"There is nothing I can do. I try, but I end up lying in the driveway as they take away my pregnant wife. They wanted $10 million in ransom. I was happy to pay, but the government got involved. Specifically, the FBI, saying they needed to get these guys, or we'd be encouraging similar activities. I just wanted my wife back."

"Needless to say, it went bad. They killed several of the kidnappers. My wife and unborn child died in the gunfight, most likely from the HRT team crossfire. I found out it was a girl later. They took one kidnapper alive. Again, I trusted the system. Because of shoddy paperwork and inept, elected prosecutors, he got off on technicalities."

Everett was shaking as he recounted his worst memory. He paused before continuing. A tear trailing down one cheek unnoticed by him, but not Nick.

"Nick, do you know what that does to your psyche?"

He did understand this kind of gut wrenching loss, but he gently shook his head no, not wanting to stop the story.

"It is not good. Here I was, a powerful man with limitless resources, helplessly trapped in a wheelchair, who had allowed his wife and daughter to be killed while he did nothing. My symptoms progressed to where I was paralyzed from the waist down. I found a doctor who correctly diagnosed my illness as an acute set of degenerative central nervous system decay. Most likely a result of too many cases of the bends. He could stop the paralysis from spreading further, but eventually, my body ate all my muscle mass. I am now literally skin and bones. The kicker is my organs are healthy as horses. I am destined to live this life, in this shriveled body, lashed to this chair, in atonement for my sins," said Everett.

"What sins? There was nothing you could do to stop them. HRT did their job. You were unlucky. It could have happened if it were SEAL Team Six, Deltas, or the 101st Airborne," said Nick.

Everett's laugh had a haunting tone.

"Oh no Nick, that part I reconciled myself to. In fact, I rewarded every member of that HRT team who tried to save them. What I also did was find out the identity of each kidnapper and then I systematically hunted down each of their families. When I found out some of them worked for syndicates whose specialty was kidnapping for ransom, I hunted down those leaders and had their families killed before I killed them. I wanted them to hurt like I hurt. I wanted them to know they did evil. Mostly, I wanted them to know I was coming. I was the avenging angel, wreaking my vengeance on those who had enabled this."

"So why are you telling me this?" asked Nick in a solemn voice.

"I want you to recognize evil when you see it," stated Everett. "Sometimes it is cloaked in a veil of good. Sometimes it hides behind billions donated to charity or to endow a building at a university. Or the public library system. But all this is masking the guilt of evil doers. Beware those who endow, for they are atoning for something."

"I think maybe you are being too hard on yourself. You did what you did. In your mind, they were justified. You have to live with your deeds, just as we all do," offered Nick.

"She is evil Nick. I tell you, malevolent evil. I know. She sat in the same chair as you. Begging for my money and my support. Guaranteeing me government contracts and everlasting support from *her* administration. When I hesitated, she made a point of letting me know she *knew* what I just told you. She will do anything to win. Promise anything. Destroy, or burn down anything. Eliminate any obstacle or *person*. To her, this is not an election, this is a crusade. You will either convert or die. This is why I asked you to come here. I won't support her. She is most likely going to destroy me as retribution. Frankly, I welcome it. I deserve it." he laughed again, this time joyously.

"Can you imagine a more sympathetic defendant than me, in my chair, defending my actions to avenge my family?"

"Not a jury in the world votes to convict."

"Exactly, so she will attack in some other manner. Turn my board against me, get me declared unfit, something like that. But I have a plan," said Everett with a twinkle in his shriveled blue eyes.

"And that is?"

"In a minute. You know I have given billions of dollars through the years to various campaigns, mostly Party, I am now ashamed to say. I let the do gooder slogans and intentions blind me to the businessman's results-oriented focus, for which they were failing miserably, on all fronts. But it was the 'right' thing to do," he said, raising his emaciated hands. "I kept putting good money after bad, hoping against hope their intentions would eventually prevail given enough money and time."

"At least you figured it out, unlike so many others who keep hoping and contributing," said Nick.

Everett nodded. "I was wrong on both counts. In fact, it is something else for which I must face a reckoning. The money and time have only allowed mental atrophy and systemic dependence on a system with no goal of cure, but simply one of addiction. I realized this far too late. Lexi coming here to extol the virtues of what she could do when she no longer had to win elections. Her platitudes about my place in the new world order and my influence. How I could put into practice what I had only supported financially in the past. This told me I was dealing with the spokesperson for an evil machine. Not simply an ambitious candidate hell bent on winning at all costs," said Everett passionately.

"Should you not be telling this to a priest?" asked Nick.

"I'm way past salvation. My fate is sealed. I'm at peace with that. But I cannot in good conscience sit by and do nothing," he said.

"Now I get it, all the questions of my deeds and why. What do you propose to stop it?" queried Nick.

"Simple. You," announced Everett, looking Nick in the eye.

"I appreciate the support, Everett, and fully intend to give it all I can. I'd be happy to take a $100 donation off your hands, but other than that, I am not sure there is much else you can do to help. That I would approve of that is," responded Nick with an ironic smile.

"You'd make a lousy priest and are an even worse politician," declared Everett, shaking his head, smiling.

"I've been told so by everyone on my staff, the politician bit anyway. Never contemplated the priesthood. Became too interested in girls when I was a teen," admitted Nick, smiling bigger.

Everett laughed. "There is much more I can do to help, legally, of course," he said, seeing the look on Nick's face.

"My days of intervening in life and death are behind me. That's one reason I've not allowed anyone who is armed in this office for over ten years. You are the first and will be the last. I made an exception because I could not let you leave before we talked," he said.

"Thank you, but I cannot accept your money."

"I know, but I can still help. Howard called me. He told me what you are trying to do with your redemption idea and the TRDF. I can't imagine the effort you are putting into this instead of the most consequential election for the free peoples of the world. Then again, you are a bit strange," he smiled.

"You been talking to my campaign manager?" asked Nick with a laugh. "Don't worry. I have energy for both 'worthy' causes."

"Denise Rojas?" asked Everett.

"It seems everyone knows Denise."

"You should do your own research."

"That sounds ominous."

"Nick, remember what I said about Lexi? This is a battle of Old Testament dimensions. Never forget that."

Nick acknowledged his advice with a slight nod.

"Howie told me what you were up to and the basic idea. I have lots of vacant property in various places around the country. Acquired in case we ever needed to build man-camps for oil field worker accommodations. Plus, thousands of portable housing units for these man camps. I took most of my assets private, leaving the public company with only the government leases and some of the shipping assets for laying pipeline and rig maintenance. What I am saying is a lot of these assets are mine and not part of Spalding Enterprises Inc."

"This includes the land, the buildings, and a ton of cash. I am going to endow your Turner Rabble Defense Fund with cash and your redemption project with all this land and the buildings to help you with your effort. This will get you started on your efforts to get homeless folks' temporary housing and to protect your supporters until they can get back on their feet. I also own a lot of fiber optic laying contracts, boring being similar to pipelining," said Everett, getting more excited as he described his plans.

"Musk is my major competitor, but there is plenty to go around. It is not a technically demanding job, just takes time, people, and equipment, heavy on people. And it is a mobile job. I would like to offer to your redemption org and TRDF a lot of these jobs to help folks get back on their feet. These contracts are also owned directly by me. Pretty much everything on land is mine personally," finished Everett.

"I don't know what to say. Obviously, thank you and, of course, we would want you to be on our board of trustees to help supervise the use of your donations," responded Nick.

"That is the last thing you want from me. Remember, I am flawed and easily attacked. It would give Lexi leverage to use against you and make your org look illegitimate. Can't have any of that. I am creating a trust, putting the assets in it. The trust will transfer to the org for management. I am also endowing $2 billion a year for as long as the money holds out. You are doing good and can continue to do good if Lexi ultimately wins."

Nick nodded. "I don't know how to thank you."

Everett smiled. "You could do me a favor. Have you picked a name for your organization yet?"

Nick shook his head. "Most of the names describing what we are doing are already taken. Mostly by various militia and anti-government groups," deadpanned Nick with a smile.

"If I could make a suggestion? Donna was a wonderful woman, with a love of butterflies, among many other talents. She once told me of the Blue Morpho butterfly, famous for its vibrant blue color." Spalding pointed to a painting on the wall showing a giant butterfly with cobalt blue translucent wings. "It was also symbolic of redemption, rebirth, and good fortune. She would not agree with what I have done in retribution for her murder. She would, however, agree with my attempts at redemption and atonement," said Everett in a solemn voice.

Nick looked at Everett and stood. He held out his hand.

"The Blue Morpho Redemption Project starts today," said Nick.

Everett slowly uncurled his bony fingers and gently placed it in Nick's hand.

"I doubt any militia groups have taken that name," said Everett with a small laugh. "Thank you. Somewhere Donna is smiling."

"A small return, considering the good you are enabling."

Everett carefully withdrew his hand from Nick's.

"Finally, I have a PAC. I am not allowed to coordinate with you or your campaign, but our spend and our effort is going to be redirected to other, non-Party candidates," smiled Everett.

"I am sure those candidates will rejoice at the additional support they'll receive," said Nick in a neutral tone. "And their campaign managers, in particular."

Everett grinned. "One last thing."

"Haven't you done enough yet?"

"Actually, no, I don't believe I can, but I'll try with the time I have. When I die, I want you to take this key. It unlocks a safe deposit box in the basement of the Chase building across the street. Follow the directions in the document you find there. Consider it my final atonement," said Everett, handing a key to Nick.

"I will," said Nick, staring at the key.

"It has been a pleasure getting to know you, Nick. I have more hope now than I ever have had since my Donna and unborn daughter were still here," said Everett with another tear streaking down his wrinkled face.

"Sir, I will do all I can to ensure your faith in me is justified."

Everett looked up at Nick standing tall and strong, the lights of his office casting a halo above Nick's head through his teary eyes.

"Of that I am certain."

# Chapter 64

"Nick, get in here, quick," shouted Greg, ducking his head into Nick's office and turning back on the run to the conference room.

Nick entered the room, where his senior staff were all watching the big screen TV at the end of the room. An ANC anchor was talking while scenes of chaos and police were being shown on the screen.

"What we are seeing is a riot underway at a local event hosted by a group of supporters of independent presidential candidate Nick Turner. Senator Turner wasn't at this rally, but apparently things turned violent between Turner's followers, who we are told call themselves the 'Turner Rabble', and a group of minority and LGBTQ protesters complaining about the hateful rhetoric the speakers were using."

"From what we are being told by eyewitnesses, they started shouting insults at each other and eventually the speaker jumped down from the stage and the larger crowd of Turner supporters attacked the protesters. We have some footage of the Turner supporters being arrested."

The team could see pictures of a chaotic scene, where the mostly white Turner supporters seemed to fight with mostly black and black clad protesters with rainbow and other LGBTQ signs and various ARL type banners. The footage cut to a man, with blood streaming from a cut in his forehead, being led away by police in handcuffs.

"Shit," said Denise and Margie, at almost the same time. They both turned to Nick.

"This is bad," stated Margie. Nick held up a hand to stop her.

"No word yet on any other injuries, but we are told there were about a hundred Turner supporters at the rally and only a handful of brave protesters. Clearly, it was not a fair fight when Turner's supporters silenced the protesters. Back to you in the studio," finished the reporter.

"Thank you, Julie. Let's go to our guest. Asaad Okonjo, a former founder of a prominent ARL group and now an ANC contributor," said Martin Nash, the ANC prime time news anchor.

"Marty, thank you. Clearly, what we are seeing here is a cry for relevance. Senator Turner is out preaching his message of hate and divisiveness, the only place it will play. The so called 'heartland' of America. These are white neighborhoods and towns who are ignorant and afraid. It is easy to prey on them and say minorities and LGBTQ people, people who look like me, are a threat to their way of life. To their schools and their children."

"Opening their minds and teaching them about white supremacy and a white patriarchal ruling class. How they have systematically kept women, minorities and now LGBTQ citizens from having an equal chance at keeping the fruits of their labor. An equal chance at the opportunities and pay the white elites have enjoyed for so many hundreds of years now. It is no surprise their response to my fellow protesters is violence. This is the way of the white supremacist. 'Benedict Turner' betrayed the Party cause. By voting to keep the filibuster, the Opposition's tool for stopping progress, his true colors came out. His followers are no different."

"Assad, why attack protesters at a rally like this? Where they know folks are filming, as they do everywhere? They had to know this would be shown," asked Marty, in a concerned tone.

"Marty, they are ignorant and stupid. Their actions show this. They cannot allow a society where all of us have equal opportunity. They view all minorities as the enemy. We are trying to take back what they have stolen from us. It is all there in my book," said Asaad, pointing to the book in front of Marty on the set.

"Indeed, it is, 'White America', 400 years of wealth built on the backs of minorities. Thank you for your commentary, Asaad," finished Marty, holding up the book, as they cut to commercial.

"What do we do?" asked Greg and Jenny at the same time, looking at the others in the room.

"Shit, shit, shit," said Margie looking at her phone.

"The other stations are picking it up and playing the footage. Even EXN is talking about it."

"Nick, we have to get out there and counter the narrative," said Denise.

"With what? More words? I want facts. Greg, find out who was running the rally. Find out if they have any footage of the entire episode. Earl, see if you can find someone up there in law enforcement who will share what really happened. Jenny, I want you to contact someone named Copeland Penrose. He is on the other side of South Dakota, but he may be able to help with anyone arrested. Greg, Chuck," said Nick, looking around.

"Here," replied Chuck from behind Nick, where he was making a list on a whiteboard of things they needed to do.

"Chuck, get the word out to all of our sanctioned chapters. Under no circumstances are they to react to or instigate any violence. If they do, we will publicly pull their charter and totally disassociate ourselves with them. Make it strong and forceful. Publish it on the website." Nick looked around the conference room at his staff. He saw fear and concern.

"This is their plan, guys. While we are small, they figure a few of these episodes and folks will be afraid to announce their support for us. We need to defend these guys. I hope we have footage that shows we did not start the violence," remarked Nick.

"And if the protesters were able to goad the people into responding?" asked Denise.

"Then we need to make sure we hold them accountable and double down on our stance of peaceful gatherings. We have to take a few lumps and show we are the bigger people. Film and record everything. The best defense is showing we are the ones under attack."

"And Okonjo? And others like him going on TV, denouncing you?" asked Margie.

"You mean David Jackson Jefferson? Who got kicked out of his own ARL org and sued for siphoning off $10 million from the donors. Who is now a paid contributor to ANC? Sticks and stones, as they say. I think that about sums it up. Tweet that out," said Nick in a voice dripping with sarcasm.

"Nick, best not to let them get to you," cautioned Margie quietly.

"Did anyone read his book? It makes CRT and 1619 look tame compared to the claims he is making. And ANC is up their shilling for him. This, my friends, is what is wrong in our country. It is also what we have to put up with and fight against. Expose and educate people to see and understand it for the fraud and influence peddling it is. If the common person watching this can't see it for the crap it is, then we are too far gone to save. We have to trust a majority of people don't believe this. We have no choice but to continue to believe this is true. To hope it is. If it is not, the outcome isn't pretty," declared Nick, looking over his team. He put his hands together, then rolled up the sleeves of his shirt. "All right, let's get to work."

# Chapter 65

"Jesus, that must have hurt," winced Chuck. He grimaced as they watched footage from the riot at the Turner rally in Sioux Falls, South Dakota. They were watching video taken on attendee phones at the rally. This clip revealed a frozen water bottle hitting Tom Olsen, the local Turner Rabble leader, square in the forehead, as he stood on a picnic table talking to the crowd.

"Pen, is all of this in the hands of the police?" asked Jenny.

"It is Jenny. I finally got copies from the cops," replied Copeland 'Pen' Penrose. "They confiscated all the phones from all the attendees. Violating their 4th amendment rights, I might add. Once we threatened a lawsuit, the phones were all returned. All the footage you see on ANC and others was most likely leaked from someone in the DA's office. They've had them for a couple of days now."

"Or the FBI," chimed in Earl.

"Pen, thank you again for being willing to help defend Tom from these charges. When did they up them to hate crime status?" asked Nick. The team was sitting around the table in Denver, looking at the big screen showing Pen's head in one corner and the video footage in another.

"When the state AG got involved rather than the local DA, who was only looking at assault charges," replied Pen. "Plus, as Earl said, once it becomes a hate crime, DOJ and the FBI get involved."

"And the obvious assault of Tom? I assume someone is being charged with that?" asked Jenny, upset at what she was seeing.

"Nope. Conveniently, whoever threw the water bottle was nowhere near anyone filming. Or at least that is what they're saying. We have no idea if we have all the footage."

"I see nothing more than pushing and shoving after Tom got hit. Surely there is a self-defense case at a minimum?" asked Nick.

Pen laughed. "Nick, I don't know you well, but your faith in humans and the law is refreshing."

This drew a laugh from the rest of the campaign staff, helping to lighten the mood in the room before he continued.

"Yes, under normal circumstances, Tom would be looking at a fine and probably a few others on both sides of the scuffle. Tom was the only one bleeding, and coincidentally, the only one arrested. I have tried to get the local sheriff to explain this, but he is too busy appearing on cable shows to meet with me. His deputy was not at the rally, so he was no help."

"Frame up?" asked Nick.

"Seems so. Poor Tom is going to pay the price. They have already suspended him at work. Rumor is he'll be fired, 'for cause', because of the hate crime charge. That means no severance and no unemployment. Kids are getting harassed at school too. His wife is moving them back to Illinois with her parents," finished Pen, worriedly.

Nick leaned back in his chair with his eyes closed.

"Anyone from the crowd press charges?" asked Nick.

"Nope. No one can seem to find any of the supposed 'victims'. Just melted away after. No record of who called the cops either. Nor how they arrived only after the scuffle and not before."

Nick leaned forward and nodded. "If there are no victims, how can there be any charges?" asked Nick, who quickly held up his hand as both Pen and Jenny made to answer.

"I know. Our lovely DOJ has taken it upon themselves to protect the downtrodden," observed Nick with disgust as his staff nodded. Nick looked up at Chuck.

"I want cameras provided for every Turner group we charter. Enough to cover 360 degrees of every rally. I want folks taught how to set them up and how to film *everything*. I want the footage uploaded to the cloud thingy so we don't have to wait for cops to give us access to our own footage anymore."

"It'll cost a pretty penny, but we'll make it happen," replied Chuck, as he made notes.

"Just the cloud, boss. Not a thingy."

"Whatever Jer. Just make it happen."

"I can help with that," replied Jer, as Chuck smiled.

"Chuck, you spread the word right, about no violence?"

"Yep, right after this happened."

"Good. We see what they're going to do now. They aren't going after me, they're going to go after them. Anyone like Tom who stands up. They'll ruin people's lives to prove a point. Pen, get him out of jail, get the charges dismissed. Chuck, get him on the payroll. Make him a paid staffer. No supporter of mine, who sticks their neck out, who stands for their rights under our Constitution, is going to pay a price for standing up for it."

"Got it Nick."

"You're on the payroll now too, Pen. I figure you're finished as a practicing attorney now that you took this case," commented Nick with a sad smile.

"We'll see. My clients are pretty loyal. Hate crime charges may take some time. Think about helping Tom, but not putting him on the payroll until we get this cleared up."

"He's right," said Denise. "Isn't this the whole point of your Turner Rabble Defense Fund, right?"

"It is Denise. But I want to send a message."

"To whom? The media? They'll love it and paint you as the next fascist dictator, surrounded by racist stormtroopers. To your people? Just showing them you are helping is enough. They'll understand."

Nick looked at Denise. She held his stare, not looking away.

"Nick, use your head and not your heart."

"I have to use them both, Denise."

"Like you always say, actions have consequences. Think about the consequences of this action, that's all," said Denise.

He turned to Chuck.

"Use the TRDF to help his wife and pay the bills until he is cleared of the hate crimes. Then put him on the payroll."

"Thank you," said Denise.

"I don't agree, but the optics cause more issues than we already have. Pen, is there a specific reason for the hate crime charge? Stated in writing somewhere?"

"Intentionally vague Nick. 'Inflammatory rhetoric, including denigration of ethnicity, sexual orientation, and gender, followed by intimidation and finally physical confrontation. By a predominantly white group of political supporters assembled without a permit, on city property, against a smaller group of racial minorities and LGBTQ protesters, leading to physical blows'," said Pen, reading from his phone.

Nick laughed.

"Who at ANC wrote that? Pen, I may not be a lawyer, but we have been watching how many hours of footage from various cameras? Not once did I hear or see anything resembling *any* of those statements. In fact, the only racial slurs and denigration of orientation or gender were coming from the mouths of the so-called protesters, trying to incite a fight. You can clearly see Tom staying civil, giving them a chance to say their piece, and then countering with calm statements. It only got ugly once someone started throwing the frozen bottles. Anyone see or hear anything different?" asked Nick, looking around the room at his staff.

"Nick, like I said, you are refreshingly naïve for a presidential candidate." Pen's head was smiling and shaking in his corner of the screen. "You saw it on TV. The damage is done. Even when they drop the charges, there won't be any retraction of anything said or implied. Tom won't get his job back. You won't get to change the minds of the millions of ANC and network news viewers who saw a 'riot'. All cleverly cut together by liberal media, with commentary stating your supporters spewed racist hate and attacked a peaceful group of black and brown Anti-Racist League and LGBTQ supporters. Words cannot make anyone unsee those images."

"Nick, he's right. No amount of talking by you or anyone else can undo this," agreed Margie.

He stood up. "Then we need to do the unexpected. Pen, thank you for talking me out of my prior mistake. Chuck, put Tom on the payroll tomorrow. Margie, get me on *Tommy* as soon as you can. They want me to shrink away. To tell my followers to be careful. To stop gathering together and expressing our opinions. Well, they are the ones who are waking a silent majority. One that is trying its damnedest to sleep in. Margie, Chuck," said Nick, turning.

"I want local ARL and LGBTQ chapters invited, *publicly*, to every rally. I want local TV too. And sheriffs. When they don't show, I want it announced they didn't come. I want every rally up on the website in its entirety. I want everyone to know we are transparent and every word we say, every deed we do, is going to be up there for the entire world to see. For the entire world to hear. We will make the vampires terrorizing our society face the light of the sun. Welcome to the team Pen," said Nick, leaning back on camera, and looking into the smiling face of Pen on the big screen.

"I accept," said Pen with a broad smile.

"This will keep our folks in check, too. Knowing everything will be on camera. No more January 6th shenanigans. On either side. Where the FBI are the only ones with the footage exonerating people of wrongdoing, while they hold them indefinitely Soviet style. And my brethren in Congress cherry pick footage only they have access to. Make sure it is all on social media, especially Hibi, where they can't block it or take it down," said Nick, looking at Margie and Jer, sitting next to each other on one side of the conference table.

"You got it, boss," answered Jer and Margie simultaneously, looking at each other with a laugh. Margie's light brown face darkened as Jer quickly looked down at his laptop. Nick smiled at their embarrassment.

"Denise?" asked Nick, waiting for the inevitable rebuke.

"Gonna be expensive. Would help if you would do some more fundraising."

"No reason I shouldn't do this?"

"Come on Nick, would it matter?" asked Denise, in an exasperated tone. "In this case, I believe in your logic, twisted as it is. Fear is their biggest weapon. You bring the crowds together and share the risk amongst them all, and you may be on to something we can replicate. Lexi's minions have limitless resources and will still attack, but at least we will have a rebuttal in every case from our own footage."

Nick turned to the team. They all had smiles on their faces. He turned back to Denise, smiling. Nick raised his hands as if he had just scored a touchdown.

"Screw all of you," commented Denise, now smiling as well.

Nick lowered one arm in time to catch the bran muffin Denise threw at him.

# Chapter 66

"Tommy, you see what I see, right?" asked Nick.

"I think so Senator. But in case our viewers don't, please explain for them. It is important," replied Tommy Charles, as he looked at Nick seated across from him on the set.

"First, I encourage everyone to form their own opinion. Go to our website or Hibi. View all the actual footage of the rally and do *not* rely on the footage from ANC and the others." As Nick finished, he held up his hand, palm down and 'Flipped' it palm up. This was his way of telling his followers the info on the mainstream media outlet he referred to was exactly the opposite of the truth.

"Once you review the actual footage, you'll see both civil discourse and courteous treatment of the attendees. If you watch and listen, you will hear the true instigators are those who showed up wearing black. Many with their faces masked and obscured, and carrying signs. In fact, if you listen to the dialog and the answers from my followers, you will come to the opposite conclusion. The ones who care about minority rights and the rights of the LGBTQ to choose and lead a life, *any* way they chose, are really *my* followers."

"Senator, you are entirely correct. I had time to review the footage. For any honest person, it is clear. Your supporters did nothing wrong. In fact, the idea your local leader, Tom Olsen, is in jail accused of a hate crime is ludicrous. Now jobless, whose children and wife have now had to move out of the state, *in South Dakota*, speaks volumes of the power of the left. Their ability to manipulate public opinion and manufacture outright lies. To destroy common citizens. This is a testament to why and what you are running to stop."

"Tommy, I could not have said it better. As your earlier guest said, the law is clear, there is no hate crime committed. In fact, any physical confrontation resulted from someone throwing a frozen water bottle, hitting Tom. He had an obvious right to self-defense. Even then, as you can see, Tom is wading into the pile trying to pull people apart, not throwing any punches, as they accused him of doing. This is clearly a travesty and another example of political district attorneys going wild."

"Does it not worry you that in a conservative state like South Dakota, this miscarriage of justice can happen?" asked Tommy.

"It does. California, New York, Washington, Oregon, and DC, I would expect this. They would prosecute you for exhaling too much CO2," quipped Nick. Tommy laughed heartily on camera.

"But in the heartland, the home of one of the more reliable conservative states, it is a testament to two things. And I beg your audience, especially those from South Dakota, to pay special attention. I am about to tell you a couple of things you need to look out for," said Nick, turning to stare into the camera.

"*Any* elected official in your state is in an important role. Not just your governor, senator and Congress members. Your Secretary of State makes critical decisions about your elections. How ballots are accessed, counted and how recounts are conducted. Your District Attorney's choose which crimes to prosecute. Where and when to release criminals early or to not even hold them accountable. You may laugh at the antics of the uber liberal DAs in the west coast cities. How that has caused their crime to skyrocket. Pay attention and beware the danger to your way of life from ignoring the elections of these key roles in your state," finished Nick.

"We have said that repeatedly on this show, Senator. There are lots of key decisions about voting, voting rights and access decided by secretaries of state. Ignore who is in these roles at your own peril," agreed Tommy, vigorously.

"Tommy, there is a second point. Perhaps even more important to know. It does not take a lot of money to get people elected to these roles. In fact, I doubt most of your viewers can name their secretary of state and none, their state attorney general."

"I'm sure they can't. I can't," laughed Tommy.

"No surprise. These are background roles. But as I just said, they are key to running and ensuring honest elections and criminal justice. They have enormous power in deciding when balloting starts, if it is all 'mail in' or 'absentee' or 'day of' voting. How many ballot boxes and where they are located. Of whether they bother to purge the eligible voter rolls of people no longer alive and therefore no longer eligible to have a vote cast in their name. These are key roles in our democracy,"

"In fact, in any properly functioning democracy," interrupted Tommy.

"True. It doesn't take much money to win these elections. Typically, only tens of thousands of dollars, compared to the millions spent on congress and governor races. What I would ask all of you is to go look at where the money came from for each of these races in your state. Especially if you have a Party member in these roles. Even more so, if these are Party members in states where your governor, senator, or congress members are majority Opposition," Nick let this register.

"What you will find in almost all cases, as you would in California, Oregon, Washington, and almost every state where we have had any hint of voter irregularity, is one common thread. World Harmony Society backed foundations, think tanks, and PACs have been the primary providers of these campaign funds to these winning candidates."

Tommy broke in. "And who is in charge of these World Harmony Society foundations? Maksim Pavlovich. We have done specials on him in the past on this show, Senator. He is an avowed globalist. He disagrees with the United States' position as the advocate of personal freedom. To him, this freedom is the true barrier to a more unified and happier globalist world."

"Exactly Tommy. Listen, lots of very rich people spend their money on all kinds of causes. But when you see a particular pattern, say no bail laws in states with District Attorneys and Attorney General all supported by these WHS groups. When you see no prosecution of more and more criminal activities and murderers being released earlier and earlier into long sentences. Illegals causing death being deported only to return and cause mayhem again and again. One has to wonder at the recurring pattern."

"The same with defund the police efforts and the ensuing anarchy we see nightly in so many of our Party run urban areas. Fewer police, lax enforcement of laws, no bail, and no prosecution. Look at who the elected officials are in these cities. Check how they got elected. Check who their biggest donors were. Simply put, follow the money and you are bound to find the puppet master," said Nick.

"Senator, you know we agree." Tommy turned to the screen. "Don't take my word for it or the Senator's. This is not a conspiracy theory. Five minutes of research and you can see for yourself on any of these roles. I will give Pavlovich credit. He is not afraid to show exactly where he spends his money and what he advocates for. Unlike many of these dark money outfits. He is transparent in his goal to transform our country and the world. What will you do now Senator," asked Tommy.

"As we said in our press conference. Much like Pavlovich, we will be entirely transparent. Every rally we have of any group sanctioned by my campaign will be open to any who choose to attend. We will publish the date, time, location and invite the local ARL, LGBTQ, or any other Party activist group to join our discussion. I will not tolerate any violence from any of my followers. If they instigate any violence, they will be out of our organization, and I'll cooperate with law enforcement to the fullest extent."

"All we want in return is equality. We want equal consideration and treatment for any who are invited and attend our rallies. If *they* instigate any violence, we'll defend ourselves and seek to detain any who attack us, waiting for law enforcement to arrive to do their job. Also, we will film every aspect of our rallies, all of them, and make sure all of this footage is immediately available for all to see. Not just selectively edited video shown on mainstream media propaganda channels. We will have full transparency."

Tommy was laughing.

"Are you OK?" asked Nick.

Tommy finally stopped laughing.

"Senator, you are a diabolical man. Anyone in the Opposition would be fleeing for the hills after how the media treated you. They would disavow all of their followers at the rally, demanding they apologize for their alleged transgressions. You embrace it. You take care of your accused follower. Paying his legal bills and finding him employment once his woke, castrated company fired him without bothering to wait for the truth. And now you double down. Putting their foot soldiers on notice that they will be filmed. Their dirty deeds exposed for all thinking people to see and judge for themselves. I can only imagine what is happening in the various offices of dirty tricks employed by the Party right now. Brilliant!"

"Tommy, I'm not doing it for me. Personally, I'm not worried. But I want to make sure Americans can stand up and voice an opinion. The Constitution guarantees this. It is what I am fighting to preserve. Against an administration who has made it clear they intend to burn this Constitution on the steps of the Capitol come next January 20th."

"I will fight for that right to voice that opinion whether it is a follower who believes in what I say or one who supports Lexi, ARL, LGBTQ, late term abortion, climate change or any other of our key issues of the day."

"We all have the right to dissent and to voice our pleasure or displeasure for how things are. Without being persecuted, canceled, or locked up for years without charges."

"Amen, Senator," agreed Tommy.

"My goal is simply to give everyone a chance to have civil discourse once again. If only our media would take the same oath. In fact, you hear it here first, but my recommendation would be upon graduating Journalism school, they swear an oath of service as well. Similar to the Hippocratic Oath. The doctor swears to abide by, to 'first do no harm'. Our media and journalists should swear to, 'first tell no lies'."

Tommy laughed again. "Senator, now you are truly delusional. One man's truth is another's lie. Facts are now malleable. With a hot enough forge and a strong enough arm, you can bend even the hardest metal into the shape you want. Today's media does the same with any fact too inconvenient to their narrative. You just saw it in action with your rally."

"Well Tommy, there is a tired and well-worn maxim, 'Hope springs eternal'. All I can do is hope it does not take an eternity to bring integrity back. The people hold the power. If we stopped watching or clicking on news and stations who simply lie, they would have to change or perish. This is the beauty of capitalism. In theory, you give the people what they want or cease to have a business. We have the power to change the channel or turn them off. If enough do this, we also stop their profits. Vote your displeasure with your clicker."

"I love it, Senator. Sounds like a bumper sticker is born. 'Vote with Your Clicker'. Thank you. I'm way over, and no doubt have another room full of pissed off guests whose segments you have talked right through," said Tommy with a smile, reaching across to shake the Nick's hand.

#

As Nick left the studio, he stopped in the green room to grab a water. He looked up into the smiling face of Senator Freddie Garcia.

"I sure hope I didn't step on your segment, Freddie?"

Freddie shook his outstretched hand, smiling.

"Nope, I will still get my two minutes, not your ten," he said ruefully.

"Hey, Tommy can stop me anytime he wants," shrugged Nick.

"You kidding? 'Vote with your Clicker'? You are ratings gold. He should be worried you will take his job after the election."

"You don't think I can win?"

"Nick, no offense, but none of us can win. The Opposition is fragmented, and any support you are getting pulls from us and from Lexi equally, so it is moot. She is a juggernaut," said Freddie, shaking his head.

"Maybe, maybe not."

"I love your solution to the agitators. I agree with Tommy. There are a lot of sphincters puckering at the moment in all these groups getting paid to go start trouble at these rallies. There goes their funding," laughed Freddie.

"Actually, I would still like them to come and to take part. I want to hear them explain why they believe what they believe. If it is all about money, then they should be easy to reason with."

"Are you serious or are you messing with me?" asked Freddie.

Before Nick could answer, a producer came in and led Freddie away. A noted history professor and TV commentator walked up to Nick.

"Senator. Karl Lee Patton," he said, holding out his hand.

"Professor, it is a pleasure to meet you. Please call me Nick. I am a great admirer of your work."

"Thanks Nick. And I of yours."

"What were you discussing tonight?" asked Nick politely.

"The situation in the Middle East. Iran is spreading their influence into Saudi Arabia, Jordan, and now Egypt. Soon Israel will be surrounded by enemies aligned with Iran. Not to mention their influence on Pakistan threatening India. Iran has seen a dangerous resurgence under this administration."

"I agree Professor. Israel is in a very precarious position."

"Please Nick, call me Karl. If Lexi is elected, there will be war in the Middle East, and we may not support Israel. It would be catastrophic, especially if we do not restart our oil and gas production and instead continue down the electrification path. Our supply chains for key parts for this effort are too dependent on our enemies."

"Karl, this is exactly why I love to watch your segments."

"I could say the same about yours. I couldn't help but overhear the last part of your conversation with Senator Garcia. Were you serious?"

"I was and I am. You are a History Professor Emeritus at a top university. You know your Herodotus and Thucydides, Gibbon and De Tocqueville, your Spengler and Shirer, and so many others. People are gullible and easy to sway. Too often it is toward evil and the path of instant gratification or something for nothing. This always ends in societal suicide and the collapse of civilization."

"Without fail, every time," agreed Karl, nodding.

"My feeling is the big thing missing from all this history, was the lack of an attempt by anyone to make a contra argument. Someone who could make that compelling argument for staying the course, for continuing to strive down the path of hardship. Of knowing what you have built will stand the test of time and survive against the popular and facile," paused Nick.

"Nick, that is the challenge. No one has succeeded at it yet," replied Karl.

"It is not the easy path, but if they do not try it, how will we know if there are not indeed many others willing to do this? If they also roused those around them to pull, side by side, maybe it could be stopped. Pulled back from the cliff's edge. Instead of staying silent and becoming victims of dictators, yet again. We must try," declared Nick.

"I think the difference is those who tried, were crushed or killed, Nick. Their resistance movements stopped before they could get enough traction to stop the demise of their society."

"No doubt you are correct. I'm proposing a third way. Not business as usual, which caused the problem and allowed the radical alternative to rise, in this case the Vice President. Instead, a return to true first principles. Reform back to what was intended, a reset, but knowing what we know now to keep from repeating the same mistakes," finished Nick.

"Sounds good to me," agreed Tommy, standing at the entrance to the green room with Senator Garcia.

"Sounds good on paper, but short of implementing your own benevolent dictatorship, it seems unlikely to become reality," doubted Professor Patton.

"Well, you asked, and I answered," shrugged Nick with a laugh.

"Now you see what I have to deal with," moaned Garcia, standing next to Tommy. "This is why I get 2 minutes and he gets 10."

"Technically, he got 12 tonight," laughed Tommy.

Tommy looked around. "There sure is a lot of brain power in this room. I have an unopened bottle of Maker's in my office?"

Everyone smiled.

"Lead the way," said Nick.

# Chapter 67

"Mel, how does he do it?"

"Do what?" responded Mel Arenson.

"Manage to turn every negative into a positive. Take every attack, any of which would paralyze anyone in the Opposition in terror. Instead, he turns it into a rallying cry for his followers?" asked Lexi.

"I am not sure. But we had better figure it out. He doesn't have much money, but every time we dip into the tried-and-true playbook, he defies logic, and turns it around. More free publicity and money."

"Exactly. I thought we told the media to stop covering him," said Lexi in a disgusted tone. "You're my chief of staff. Go put the fear of Lexi in them. When I'm president, make it clear I will not forget who could not do as I asked."

"Lexi, we have done everything we can to stop Tommy. We have threatened his sponsors with boycotts, picketed his house, even threatened his network. None of these are working. Turner is ratings gold. The more we do, the more it becomes a bigger story. We get exactly the opposite of what we are looking for, which is silence. That's why we stopped, especially with the protesters outside Tommy's house. He has little kids with his current wife. It was terrible optics showing our usual protesters harassing her getting the kids in the car to go to daycare. We were losing soccer moms and giving him fresh images of harassment to show every night."

"How about the legal aspects?"

"We continue to use our local law enforcement and government partners to throw red tape in Turner's way. The Homeland ban worked for most of social media, but a few, including Hibi, still host him. That got Martha Summers fully on his side, unfortunately. He uses her store parking lots. Attacks on her and the stores are backfiring, too. Those are lower income stores and a staple in almost every small town in America. We sure don't want to give any of those folks a reason to take advantage of all our mail in voting efforts. We want them fat and comatose on their couches in their trailer homes," said Mel with a clear look on his face, expressing his feelings for people in this demographic.

"I made it clear the last time we talked; her support of Turner was a mistake. She laughed at me."

"Not a wise move for sure," said Mel, feeling sorry for Martha Summers. Lexi never forgot a turncoat.

Lexi sat pondering the answer. Turning in her chair to look across the Potomac at the dome of the Capitol nearby. This was the culmination of her thirty-five plus years in politics. She was mere months from becoming the first female President of the United States. And she was worried. Uncertainty bothered her. It bothered others as well.

#

"Shit man. What the hell happened?" asked Napoleon 'Bone' Bello, as he entered the office of his Anti-Racist League chapter office.

"Bone, man, they did what we asked. Started shouting and insulting them and trying to get them to get into a fight. They wouldn't do it. They kept asking questions. What a bunch of pussies. Who stands there and lets you insult their mother and then asks you if you want to talk about your views on illegal immigration? Those guys are bat shit crazy."

"Bobby, we had better figure this out, or the money is going to dry up. What do you make of Turner's offer?" asked Bone.

"What? You mean his offer to invite ARL and LGBTQ groups to 'peacefully attend and debate issues' at his rallies?"

Bone nodded.

"The guy's a fuckin' loon," said Bobby, laughing and shaking his head as he paced while Bone sat down in a chair.

"Maybe, but what if he means it?"

"You serious? You think he really means it? Fuck him. We will still show up and protest and call out all his racist bullshit. We will make them stand up and fight and then we will bring them down. Just like we did all those white fascist cops in all those towns," said Bobby, talking with his hands. Bone looked at him. Bobby weighed about one-hundred and thirty-five pounds. Bone knew he would run away at the slightest hint of physical violence unless he was there with him. He'd seen it firsthand during the Ferguson riots.

"And his threat to film everything? If it becomes clear, we are the instigators of all the violence and we are the ones spewing all the 'hate'. Then what?" asked Bone, calmly.

"Shit, we got all the networks and the papers. Where are they gonna show the footage? One fucking station and website. Those folks are all racists and homophobes. They are already showing up at Turner's rallies. If we show what is going to happen to them when they do, and it will not stop, they will stop going. This is what they are paying us to do. Don't sweat it, man. You should stop watching EXN." Bobby returned to the desk and sat down.

"What if we took him up on his offer?"

Bobby stared at Bone for a second, not comprehending the question.

Bone stood up. "He wants to give us a platform. Why not take it?"

Bobby, now realizing what he was suggesting, stood again.

"Yo Bone, your old lady put you up to this?"

"Bobby, no, but she might, soon. A friend of hers got car-jacked three blocks from our house. Three fucking blocks away."

"Hey man, I'm sorry. Everybody ok?" asked Bobby, changing his tone.

"Ya. You know who did it?"

Bobby shook his head no.

"Fucking sixteen-year-olds. And you know why?" again Bobby shook his head no.

"Initiation into a fucking MS13 gang. Nadine's friend is lucky the initiation wasn't to put a bullet into her head. Shit, Bobby, what kind of crap is this? At my kid's school they found someone with goddamn Fentanyl pills in their backpack. In elementary school," said Bone, running his hands through his hair.

"Hey man, this shit is happening everywhere. It's why we can't take our foot off the gas. Guys like Turner, and all those Opposition assholes, they want to make sure we never get a chance to get out of this mess they put us in."

"I am not so sure, Bobby. I don't know who is right and who is wrong anymore. But I have kids and a wife, and I don't like the way things are working right now. Something has to change. Keep doing whatever you think we need to in order to keep the money coming in, but let's be careful. Make sure we are part of the solution and not the problem."

Bone got up to leave and Bobby sat back down. After he left, Bobby pulled out his phone.

"Man, we got a problem here…" he said to the voice that answered.

#

"There you have it, Senator Nick Turner, proclaiming he will put a supporter, accused of hate crimes, and instigating a riot on his payroll. Daring other protesters to attend his rallies to receive the same treatment. If this is not an obvious example of fascism and black shirt intimidation, I don't know what else short of replaying Mussolini's rallies is clearer," finished the expert commentator from a liberal think tank and professor of humanism at an Ivy League school.

Maksim Pavlovich raised a bony arm in the air and made a gesture that muted the large holographic display projected in the air in front of his antique desk. He leaned back carefully into the embrace of his leather office chair. Sudden movements were not his friend. His body failing him, kept alive with a cocktail of human growth hormones and other formulas of enzymes, chemicals and experimental serums. His mind was as sharp and close to functioning as a human computer as any on the planet.

He raised his hand again, making a gesture in the air, starting another playback of the interview between Nick Turner and Tommy on his show. Listening to the dialogue, Pavlovich focused on Nick as he made his pronouncement to double down on his followers at their rallies. His plan for surveillance of every aspect of the rallies and his invitation for the agitator to instead join in open debate. Pavlovich made a steeple of his fingers as he rested his forehead against his bony fingers.

It was his enormous fortune, making many of these protests possible. Not just in the US, but against many other regimes in countries throughout the world. Not democracies alone. Pavlovich supported organizations agitating against despotic dictatorships as well. The idea of countries and national sovereignty in any form prevented the formation of global governance.

Through his World Harmony Society foundations and NGOs, he directed billions of dollars of aid to various organizations, all driving toward this outcome. The one major stumbling block to his one world utopia was always the United States. As long as there continued to be an example of the success of individualism and personal freedom, the ability to convince the masses to cede their freedoms in return for one world governance was unattainable.

This one ideal, freedom, had damned billions into poverty and meagre existence. As those with power, driven by a capitalistic orgy of greed, had built vast fortunes off the backs of the less fortunate. Subsuming the wealth and control of entire countries to build their massive personal empires.

Pavlovich had spent his lifetime making up for his father's ruthless deeds and the fortune he built by toppling governments and exploiting natives to amass a fortune in minerals and diamonds in Africa. From the time he succeeded his father, he felt it was his destiny to complete what others had started. The flattening of the curve between those with and those without.

To destroy capitalism and its underlying spoils system. A system rewarding those with the drive and lack of compassion for their fellow man to achieve all at the expense of others. To sacrifice the greater good for their own personal satisfaction. While he had excelled and grown his inherited fortune, beyond the comprehension of most, Pavlovich had devoted these resources to minimizing the ability of the few titans of capitalism to continue destroying the planet.

He believed the elite should rule and decide for the poor and weak minded. Those who, when left to make their own choices, always chose the path of pleasure and destruction over the path of sacrifice and community good. Human nature was such that it would always prioritize pleasure over work. This was the path to certain destruction.

Mankind needed to be taken to the brink of this destruction. To face it and realize at the point of no return, the only way to save itself would be to give up willingly the freedoms that led to this ending. To turn over these decisions to people who could make these painful choices and see them through. People like him. Who had sacrificed all notions of pleasure to lead others to a harmonious existence.

Maksim closed his eyes and contemplated Nick Turner and what to do about him. He did not appear to be going away. The normal measures to silence and neutralize candidates were not working this time. He would have to take a more direct approach.

# Chapter 68

"Gabi is here, Luc," said Annie. "I can leave if you would like? But his desk does not look very comfortable," cautioned Annie, looking at a blushing Inspector Gabrielle Martin.

"I told him to get a couch. It would be much more comfortable," shrugged Annie as she went back to reviewing stacks of reports on the floor in front of her.

Luc appeared in the doorway of his office as Annie finished her inappropriate welcome.

"I don't know Annie, sometimes a hard surface is better," replied Gabi, now enjoying the color coming into Luc's cheeks as the two women continued to banter about sex.

Annie wrinkled up her nose at the thought. "My muscles would be in knots. A couch would be much better," she replied without a look at either Gabi or Luc.

"If you ladies are done," said Luc, "Inspector, so nice of you to return my calls, finally."

Gabi turned to Annie. "Two years? Now I see why."

"Two years, nine months, sixteen days, twelve hours…"

"Enough Annie," responded Luc in a forceful tone.

Annie looked up, startled. Luc never raised his voice. The look of anguish on his face penetrated her autistic persona, causing her to rise quickly and run to Luc, hugging him while sobbing.

"I am so sorry, Luc. Sorry, sorry, sorry."

"Annie, it is ok. I am the one who is sorry," replied Luc in a calming voice he did not feel.

"Annie, what have you found?" he asked, repeating her soothing mantra multiple times. She calmed down, wiping her tears on a sleeve. She turned and returned to her stack of reports, glancing at Gabi as she walked by.

"Still too skinny." She sniffed, sitting down, back to reviewing her material.

Luc glanced at Gabi and motioned with his eyes toward his office.

He closed the door once she entered.

"Inspector, my apologies. I was just playing along with Annie. I did not know it would lead to where it did," said Gabi in an apologetic tone.

"It is fine. Annie takes getting used to. She is hard as steel in some ways and soft as marshmallow in others," answered Luc.

"You summoned me?" asked Gabi, turning formal.

"I would hardly call it a summons. If it were, perhaps you would have answered some of the previous ones before I had to ask Alain and Leon to have you grace my presence."

"Here I am. What are my orders?"

"Gabi, it does not have to be like this. I need your help, and you must understand my task."

"How? You have shared so little and merely used me as your carrier pigeon. I delivered your prior message."

"Yes, I heard. Chaumont said your solution was inspiring."

Gabi was not impressed by Luc suggesting the President of her country found her method of telling law enforcement to be on the lookout for autistic suicide bombers was clever.

When Gabi did not respond, Luc continued. He stood in front of a whiteboard in his office.

"I have kept you in the dark for your own safety."

"I believe I can take care of my safety, thank you very much," replied Gabi, upset at the idea she couldn't.

This was not going as Luc had planned. He stood looking at her.

"I contacted an associate who told me about autism in France. Strides being made or not made. I asked her about the possibility of autistic patients being recruited to do a deed such as a suicide bombing. She said it would be possible as long as the patient did not understand right or wrong."

Gabi was listening carefully and paying attention to Luc's facts.

"She had been involved in a case where I first discovered Annie being used by a criminal syndicate to assist in their money laundering activities. I asked her if she knew of any facilities who might be involved in recruiting autistic candidates for this type of activity," Luc made sure Gabi was following his conversation. She nodded.

"She gave me four names. I visited each, posing as the older brother of a potential patient, looking for a facility to move my brother to."

Gabi broke in at this point. "What did you ask them?"

"Nothing. I tried to understand how patients came to them and how they left. I assumed death being the major reason. It was then I found out that many of these patients, presumably those who showed some propensity for some type of activity, were 'graduated' to facilities where their potential education opportunities could be advanced beyond anything else offered in France."

"Where is that?"

"That is where I am. At one in Lyon, the guide introduced me to the owner, a man name Lauzon. She let slip the idea of this advanced facility. The response of Lauzon, once we mentioned this, told me this was not where they were actually being sent. Rather than raise suspicion, I left at this point."

"You believe these institutions are brokering autistic patients to whom? Terrorists?"

"I am not sure, Gabi. No terrorist is going to take the time to groom an autistic person to where they would wear a suicide vest and stand at a rally, not drawing attention. Trust me, having worked with Annie for years, it is not a simple task to change their behavior or teach them new habits. The autistic mind does not handle change easily. It would take constant effort over a long period. Months, perhaps even years, depending on the level of activity and complexity. This is a very organized effort."

"Who would go to that much trouble?"

"That worries me," answered Luc. "Someone who invests this amount of time and money has much more planned than random assassination or carnage in Christmas markets."

"You think these are related to the Market attacks? Why?" asked Gabi, trying to figure out the connection.

"No hard evidence, but in my gut, I believe two high-profile attacks like this, with this level of planning, have to be connected. With no one claiming success, that is enough proof for me."

"Fine Inspector, but why am I here? You have gotten this far without my help. Why now?"

"Gabi, I have been down this road before. People with this much reach have power and money. Most likely, they also have connections that span borders."

"Again, proof?" asked Gabi.

"I tracked down these so called 'higher' learning institutions the autistic were supposedly sent to for further education. They don't exist. It appears they are sent to Switzerland via Germany and then the trail disappears," said Luc, turning from the whiteboard and walking back to his desk.

Gabi looked at him. "What is the next step?"

"I must be on the right track. I have been under surveillance." He handed Gabi a copy of the picture he had taken from his window after Chaumont's last visit.

"At first, I thought it was Chaumont, but this man was photographing Alain, leaving my apartment after his last visit. I know I have had a tail for the last couple of weeks. By now, they also probably know you have come here as well. Have you told Maximilian you are on a case?"

"Of course not," said Gabi in disgust. "The Minister gave me this case, not the Prefect of Police."

"Then it has to be associated with those behind these deeds. Can you do a search? With no one knowing?" asked Luc, nodding at the photo in her hand.

"It will not be easy. Everything is now catalogued and recorded. But it should not matter. I will do this inspector. What else can I help with?"

"I am not sure yet. I need to contact Dr. Fontaine again and see if she has more information."

At the name, Gabi looked up, startled.

"What?" asked Luc, concerned.

"Dr. Caroline Fontaine?" asked Gabi.

"Yes. What happened?" asked Luc, dreading the response.

"Luc, Mrs. Fontaine and her husband were the victims of a violent home invasion several weeks ago. Her husband is dead. Mrs. Fontaine is in intensive care and not expected to survive. What they did to both of them was extremely barbaric. I started reading the police report and had to stop. The brutality made me sick."

"Where is she?"

"Saint-Louis, I believe."

"I must go. I will contact you. You may be in danger now by working with me. Be watchful, more than ever. Promise me," he said in such an earnest tone, Gabi was taken aback.

"Inspector, I can take care of myself."

Luc grabbed her hand and looked into her eyes. She saw fear there. And something else.

"Gabi, I am serious. These people do nothing by chance. I have put you in danger. As I put Caroline in danger. I led them to her. Please stay with Annie until I return. Be careful. I am sorry," said Luc, deflated, as he let go of her hand and left the office at a run.

"Bye Luc," called out Annie as he left. She looked up at Gabi, standing in the office doorway.

"Why is he running? Did you ask him to marry you first?"

Gabi smiled, looking down at Annie.

"Annie, what do you see?" she said, trying to match Luc's soothing tone. As she sat, Gabi loosened her weapon in her holster, just in case.

#

Luc stood outside the door to Caroline's room in the intensive care wing of the hospital. He looked up as an older gray-haired man in a white doctor's coat arrived.

"Inspector Gauthier?"

"Yes doctor," said Luc.

"You are inquiring after Mrs. Fontaine?"

"I understand she is gravely injured. She has been a colleague. I just found out about the attack."

The doctor took off his glasses and looked around. He grabbed Luc's arm and steered him down the hall toward an empty exam room.

"Inspector, in the almost forty years of practice, I have never seen such a methodical beating designed to inflict maximum pain without killing the victim."

Luc tried to remain impassive as the doctor continued.

"She was barely alive when her neighbors discovered her because of the mail and newspapers. Her husband had been tortured as well, but his death was relatively quick and merciful compared to what she endured. We set the broken limbs, amputated one foot and her right leg, sepsis having already set in. Unfortunately, both hands were also destroyed beyond repair. Every rib was broken and both sides of her jaw. And those were the external injuries. I will not go into the other horrible things they subjected her to. Why would someone do this?"

"Clearly, they believed she had information they wanted."

"Inspector," said the doctor, shaking his head. "No one could endure one thousandth of what she did without telling them everything they wanted to hear. This goes way beyond interrogation. This is a message. The question is for whom. And what kind of monster would deliver a message in this fashion? Worse, who needs to have it delivered at the expense of this poor woman's soul?"

"Is she lucid? Can she speak?"

"In and out. When she is awake, she begs us to kill her."

"Will she survive?"

"Physically, we have done what we can. But without the will to live, it is only a matter of time. She has no desire to continue."

"May I speak to her?"

"You may try."

#

Luc looked down. He barely recognized the figure as a breathing human. Caroline's head was swathed in bandages. A metal halo surrounded her head, holding portions of reconstructed jaws in place. One eye was covered in bandages. All of her limbs were similarly covered. She was resting. Luc was going to leave rather than attempt to wake her, feeling she needed her peace. As he turned to go, her lone eye opened, and she mumbled his name.

Luc approached and held his ear closer to her mouth.

"Luc," she said weakly.

"Yes Caroline, I am here."

"Kill me. Please."

"Rest, just rest."

"No. I must die."

"Don't say that."

"Luc, I have paid,"

Luc paused, confused. "Paid? Caroline, what do you mean?"

"I told them they could do this."

"Do what?"

A tear streamed out of her good eye. "Bomber."

"You told who?"

"Doctor."

"Your doctor?" asked Luc, confused.

She moved her head slightly. "The Doctor."

"A different doctor? Does he have a name?"

She shook her head slightly.

"Caroline, who did this to you?"

Her body shook in response. Luc gently reached out a hand to lightly touch her shoulder.

"I told to use autistic."

Luc nodded.

"Annie."

"I know Caroline, it is alright, Annie is safe."

Her eye widened at Luc's statement. Luc noticed.

"Caroline, did you tell them you spoke to me?"

She closed her eye in response.

"What else Caroline? Help me. What else do you know?"

"Wife."

Luc stiffened. "What?"

"Wife. Snake. Israel," she said weakly as a breath left her body and the monitors surrounding her bed exploded in all manner of warning bells. Within seconds, the doctor was in the room, pushing Luc out of the way. As they started trying to save her life, Luc gently grabbed the doctor by the arm and looked at him. Their eyes met. Luc shook his head. The doctor hesitated, then nodding, spoke to his nurses, reached up, disabling the warning bells.

# Part Three

## Can You Fight Fate?

*"We are our choices."*

Jean-Paul Sartre

# Chapter 69

Dusty Ingram glanced left. The cheap digital clock on the nightstand glowed 5:12am. Turning back, he stared at the old water stains on his apartment ceiling. He'd woken up in a cold sweat. As usual. Reliving *the* patrol in Fallujah.

Each time, he saw the Al-Qaeda insurgent. Watched him aim and pull the trigger. Dusty always got him. A clean shot to the head. But each time, Billy Ray still got shot and still died in his arms, begging and screaming at Dusty to help him. And each time, he woke up still living with the guilt of knowing he didn't react fast enough.

He'd returned to the states, after his fourth tour, a broken man. His post-traumatic stress disorder diagnosed and treated at the VA with a myriad of pills. After two failed attempts at suicide, his doctors concluded the medications *may* have been contributing to, rather than preventing, his depression and suicidal tendencies.

A stint in a VA funded rehab clinic flushed the drugs from his system. They discharged him with as clean a bill of health as any other veteran with lingering PTSD. Abandoned and forgotten by a country who had asked countless young men to run into a hail of bullets. Whose reward was a return to society and a system offering little help for the sacrifices they made.

Dusty had tried to work, to lead a normal life. But he couldn't seem to keep it together enough to hold any job. Some he quit. Some they fired him from. Line cook at a diner, dishwasher at a hotel, handyman at an apartment complex, cashier at a convenience store and various construction jobs. The only job he was ever any good at had been a bouncer at a strip club. He lost that job when he nearly killed a man who fought back while being removed from the club. He'd avoided charges, but they had fired him for being too great a liability.

Dusty currently threw bags into airplanes for a major airline at Denver International. So far, he'd held this job for six months. He drank too much, smoked too much, and drove too fast. Being reckless was the only thing making him feel alive.

He lived in a shabby apartment, once a multi-level motel in a run-down part of Denver, close to the Capitol. His neighbors were hookers, addicts, and drug dealers. He didn't care. They left him alone and he them.

Glancing at the clock again, he leaned over to grab his pack of cigarettes and lighter from the top of his nightstand. They sat next to his loaded Beretta M9 pistol. He lit his cigarette and sat up, leaning against the headboard. He could see the faint light outside around the tightly drawn shades of his lone window, next to the door leading outside onto the balcony breezeway access to all the apartments.

As he smoked in the dark, he noticed multiple shadows quietly crossing back and forth in front of his door. This time of the morning was not one for much traffic outside his apartment. The whores and drug dealers were usually back from their antics, ready to sleep off the night's efforts through the coming daylight hours.

He snuffed out his cigarette, grabbed his pistol and swung his feet to the side, getting out of his bed as his door exploded inward in a shower of cheap wooden splinters. Dusty, whose eyes were adjusted to the darkness, crouched by the side of the bed with his pistol. He could see people filing into his room with rifles and red laser sights sweeping back and forth.

His first shot was dead center in the forehead of the first person in the room, showering those following in blood and brain matter.

Before the first person could even fall, Dusty had moved his aim to the second. This one appeared to have on what looked like body armor and a helmet. His second and third shots hit this person in the throat, sending them down in a gurgling heap. Others followed. Dusty fired twice more into the chest of the next person as the first bullets of return fire hit the surrounding walls. Realizing the third person's vest was preventing his bullets from penetrating, he calmly altered his shot, aiming for the goggles of the shooter, putting two more rounds through that shooter's skull.

Dusty was back in Fallujah, in the cramped hallways of the hovels the local's called homes. Clearing room by room, shooting anything that moved, trying to avoid moving any pieces of furniture or anything that might conceal an IED. The intruders were shouting something. Dusty could not hear or understand. They kept shooting at him. He felt a bee sting as a round hit his right shoulder. The final three intruders were blindly firing their automatic weapons in the room's dark. The red lights of their lasers waving back and forth as they sprayed the room at chest height and into the headboard of his bed. In the dark, they were firing high. Dusty was crouching lower and lower in his corner as the shots continued to fly overhead.

He lowered his aim, shooting the fourth intruder in a knee and then, as they toppled, he finished them with two to the forehead. He moved upward, always seeking unprotected areas of the body. The 9mm round of the Beretta did not have the stopping power for torso shots. They had taught Dusty to seek the exposed weak points.

Those not likely protected. Keeping track of his ammo count in his head, his next shot hit the groin of the fifth shooter. As they crumpled in pain, he fired two more, ripping through their exposed throat sending them to the ground. Five down and three bullets left in his magazine.

The last shooter got lucky. Lowering their aim, two more bullets tore through Dusty's torso. Neither were lethal kill shots. He stared into the eyes of the sixth and final shooter standing in his apartment, looking into their wide brown eyes, the pupils fully opened in the dark, behind the goggles. What he saw was fear. Two more shots to the head and the sixth and final shooter was now on their back. The shooter's reflex shots whizzed past Dusty's ear, one grazing the side of his head.

He crouched in the room. Inhaling, the unmistakable scent of combat surrounding him. The burned toast smell of fired ammunition, blood, and the pungent stink of bowels and urine released by the finality of death. Standing up, he ejected his nearly empty magazine and pulled a fresh one from his nightstand. He grabbed something from the top of the nightstand and stuck it in his right ear. He now heard faint sirens in the distance.

He'd taken one round in the shoulder, one in the hip and one in the upper chest, plus the grazing shot to his head. None appeared to have hit anything vital. He found his pants, calmly pulling them on. The sirens were louder and closer. Their stationary lights flashed blue and red through his lone window. He could also hear faint crying and shouting. The light from the walkway, streaming in through his shattered door, illuminated the writing on the vests of the shooters. Sheriff's Dept.

Dusty's confused mind tried to comprehend. Why would the Sheriff be breaking his door down at 5 am, with no warning? He could hear other heavy footsteps coming and shouts to stand down from outside the door. After dropping his gun on the bed, he stood shirtless with his various Marine Corps tattoos visible on his torso. He put his hands on his head and got down on his knees. Additional deputies entered the room with their guns pointed at him, yelling endless commands. One of them, surveying the carnage, saw the braided ponytail behind the head of the last deputy. He yelled something as he swung the butt of his rifle in Dusty's direction. Dusty did nothing to stop it as it connected with his jaw.

# Chapter 70

"What does it say about a successful country like ours, when you walk around one of its most elegant cities, San Francisco, spending all your time looking down instead of up? Trying not to step on human feces, used needles, or worse, on your walk from breakfast to your hotel? Why is there an app you can use to tell you in real time where the piles of poop are on the sidewalks? Is this the best use of our innovative talent in Silicon Valley?" Nick walked back and forth on the stage.

"When you are looking down on Union Square, an oasis of green in the city's concrete, you instead see a tent city of homeless people? How would you handle trying to give money to a person wearing brown paper bags for shoes when they scream and yell at you, telling you to stop stealing their stuff? How do you explain one of the most walkable cities in the US is now a take your life in your own hands walk through a war zone?" asked Nick, addressing the crowd at the Western Ideas Summit, in the St. Francis hotel in San Francisco.

Lauren Bergamo sat in her chair, listening to Nick give his speech. She was recording it on her phone and taking additional notes in a notebook. Documenting the reaction of the crowd and her own thoughts to Nick's provocative statements. This speech focused on the results of progressive policies in California. He was also commenting on the state of homelessness and how treating symptoms was not helping solve the issues. She raised her head as he appeared to be nearing the end of his tirade against progressive policies.

"It says we are becoming a failed state. When we cannot even provide help for our own citizens and yet we send billions of dollars to Ukraine, Iraq, South Sudan, Syria and other places. Places where most of the money ends up in the pockets of corrupt politicians and heads of states. Why is that? A state like California, the fifth largest economy in the *world*, the

Eden of the United States, has now turned into a progressive hellhole with an outflow of residents so great, you'd think genocide was occurring. More people leave California each year than flee worn torn Sudan," explained Nick, walking back and forth across the stage, giving his speech to a crowd of several thousand business owners, journalists, and influencers from various industries in California.

"Think about that. They are killing each other in the Sudan because of ethnic animosity and fleeing for their life. In the US, they are fleeing confiscatory tax policies, oppressive regulations, and a general desire by the California government to legislate every aspect of your life. This is not healthy, and it is certainly not freedom. What the hell happened here?" asked Nick to cheers from the crowd.

"California has it all. Gorgeous geography, fabulous views, and perfect weather. You have the best minds or did. Why have these Party run states and cities failed so spectacularly? I can explain it. It is called progressivism. I looked it up and here is what good old Wikipedia told me: *a social or political movement that aims to represent the interests of ordinary people through political change and the support of government actions*. That's a pretty open-ended charter. Change through government action. Nice and broad. In short, progressivism is whatever the Party leaders want or need it to be.

"Of course, they'll tell you they mean well, and you need to break a few eggs to make an omelet. The problem is you want your eggs over easy, not scrambled. They'll tell you to give them another chance. We'll eventually get your eggs right. Just give up a few more minor freedoms, a few more choices, for the good of all. Utopian schemes are utopian schemes for a reason. Do you know the origin of the word utopia? Sir Thomas More created the word when he wrote his novel, titled, what else, *Utopia*. He combined the Greek words '*ou*' meaning 'no' and '*topos*' meaning 'place' to define his utopia. Then he explained why this is an unattainable ideal. No place. Nowhere. Not possible."

"The problem with the progressive ideals is they are all rooted in the idea of utopia. They cannot recognize we and our societies are imperfect. They refuse to acknowledge we cannot fix everything. Throwing money at problems or implementing theory as reality is not enough to make bad things go away. This is why the moderates in the Party, like I was, are questioning their loyalty *to* the Party."

The crowd laughed with a few cheering in agreement at this last statement. Lauren looked around at the smiles and nodding heads. This was California, but here was a group of thousands of local business owners and entrepreneurs agreeing the progressive policies of the governor and federal administration were not aligned with their beliefs. She furiously scribbled the response to these statements in her notebook as Nick continued.

"Progressives are hypocrites. Another nice Greek word. One that should really be on the ARL and Antifa banners. Progressives are hypocrites on so many levels. First, they say one thing and do another. They hold you accountable to a rule but break it themselves without consequence. They use their allies in corporations, media and tech to hold you accountable. But these same gatekeepers, snitches and nosey Nellies are never treated with the same disdain when they slip up. Their apologies are *always* accepted. Where is the fairness? Hold everyone accountable to the same rules and laws. Equally. This is one equity position I *can* support. We in the silent majority may be cowed, but we are not blind to this injustice. No more double standards. Lady Justice has a blindfold on for a reason." The crowd roared in agreement.

Once again, Lauren sat bewildered at the response. This was not CST, a conservative convention where Nick's anti-government rhetoric had set off frenzied applause. This was California, where progressive policies had enabled such massive success for so many of those in attendance.

"Here we are, in the Republic of California, the poster child for progressivism. Remember, in my definition, all of this is supposedly being done to help *ordinary people*. Well, ordinary people?" asked Nick, waving his arm to encompass the crowd. "How is that working out for you? Let's do a quick review. Top 5 in taxes. Highest cost of living in the continental US. Most expensive real estate. Highest number of regulations, strictest emissions, highest gas tax. Largest number of illegal aliens, homeless, and unemployed. Highest number of residents on government assistance. Rated in the top five for the *lowest* quality of life. Blackouts are now a daily occurrence in all seasons, combined with top five utility costs. A mandate to stop selling anything but electric cars in less than ten years is only going to make this worse. Even third world countries can keep the lights on. Imagine what will happen when every vehicle in our largest state has to plug in *every night*. It's pretty hard to charge your car if there is a rolling blackout," finished Nick. The crowd once again cheered, agreeing with his litany of results from decades of failed California progressive leadership.

"Progressives hate individuality. They crave, they demand, uniformity. Don't conform. Wake up. Question authority. Think for Yourself and please, please, please reject the progressive agenda. It is evil and it will destroy what the founders built. Oh, yeah, almost forgot, I'm running for president and if you like what you hear, see, or read about me, vote for me. But make sure you vote regardless of who it's for. Use your vote, while you still can. Thank you for the invitation and watch out for the Party poop on the sidewalk on your way out," finished Nick with a smile. The audience gave him a standing ovation as he turned to leave, shaking hands with the host as she took to the podium.

"Thank you, Senator Turner. I think I can speak for the audience. It is refreshing to see honesty from any politician, especially as it pertains to California's policies. Thank you again," she finished as the audience once again clapped while standing and Nick acknowledged them with a nod as he headed off stage.

#

"Senator," asked the AP pool reporter. "You said we are 'a failed state'. Were you referring to California or the US as a whole?"

"Bob, did you listen to my speech? I think I was pretty clear in my litany of bad statistics for which California is a leader. They are not alone. There are other states facing the same issues. The common thread is the implementation of progressive ideas at the state and local level and an unwillingness to stop them and admit when they have failed."

"But you said so yourself Senator, California is the fifth biggest economy in the world. How is that a failed state?" he retorted.

"Bob, you are correct. Statistically it is. Though I believe it is about to fall two more spots in the next GDP ratings as it has been shrinking, not growing. Care to guess who is moving up right behind it in GDP and growing exponentially? Texas. You know what else is happening. In the upcoming census, due to the outmigration of so many citizens, they project California could lose four electoral votes. The population of California is declining precipitously. A majority of those leaving are the top wage earners. Those coming in are primarily low skilled immigrant workers, who are not citizens yet. Hence losing electoral votes. These immigrants will take years to replace the taxes being lost by those high paying earners leaving. This is the definition of a state in decline. It is self-inflicted because of the inability of your governors and politicians to admit their policies are to blame for driving the population away."

Nick called on Ned Wheeler from EXN.

"Senator, you claim it is ok to be homeless as long as they do it somewhere else. Isn't that an elitist's point of view?" he asked.

"Ned, good question. My reasons for claiming the homeless should not be setting up camps in the middle of parks in city centers is not because of the inconvenience to tourists or rich city dwellers. It is because it is illegal to do so. I believe in law and order. Homeless should be in shelters or in hospitals getting the treatment for their addictions and mental issues. Instead of providing more funding to allow them to stay in their tent cities, we need to be funding more beds at the hospitals, more shelters, and more VA treatment options."

"We need to help them find jobs and get them treatment so they can find an apartment and a purpose. There is no shortage of cash. We spend gobs of it with no results as we focus on the symptoms and not the problems. Many of our homeless are returning servicemen and women. They served their country. We should return their sacrifice with some type of guaranteed work training program to help them transition back into civilian life. With eleven million job openings, this should not be hard."

"No, it is not an elitist point of view. We need to do more than simply move them out of sight of the Vice President's brownstone on Nob Hill. I'm suggesting we get them off the street and into locations where they have dignity and a chance to do something with their life instead of being a ward of the failed state."

"Ok, time for one more," said Nick. "Ms. Bergamo, don't want anyone thinking I am avoiding your questions."

Lauren smiled at the sarcasm.

"Senator, you claim the ARL and Antifa protesters should have hypocrisy on their flags. Are you suggesting ARL and Antifa protests are not legitimate?"

"I believe I have answered this before, but here goes again. First, I think racial *equality*, not racial *equity*, is something we should always work to achieve as we have been for these last 160 plus years for those willing to compare actual facts. I also do not subscribe to their mantra of equality of outcome either. All people are different. Some people want to work harder. They should be rewarded commensurate with their willingness to work. The idea others should benefit from those who work harder, while they themselves do not, because they feel they are special or deserve different treatment because race, gender, history, or chosen orientation is simply wrong."

"I believe ARL as it stands today is simply a money laundering operation designed to shake down corporations with the fear of protests and sit-ins and to provide the media with sound bites. The reality, just as it was in the time of other racially motivated violent protest movements, is it is not about racial equality, it is about race baiting, fear, and money. ARL is a perfect army under the progressive hypocrisy doctrine. All of their claims are exactly the opposite of their actions. That is the definition of hypocrisy."

"As for Antifa, they are the black shirts or brown shirts depending on whether you are leaning toward a communist or fascist future under the progressive doctrine. It is funny how Antifa, who claims to be Anti-Fascist, adopts all the tactics of the fascists of old. They must count on no one googling fascism. What I find somewhat hypocritical is the willingness of all of you in the media to ignore the property damage, riots, violence, and the looting perpetrated by these groups. Do you really think we won't see this on social media or other networks, exposing *your own* obvious hypocrisy? Do you think if you, or the ladies on the *Women's Viewpoint*, keep on insisting there is no violence when the buildings behind the reporter are on fire, people will believe what you say versus what they see? People are neither that naïve nor that stupid. Perhaps the media should also google hypocrisy." Before Lauren could retort, Margie appeared at Nick's elbow.

"Thank you all for your time and questions," said Margie, leading Nick back into the green room of the conference hall. Glancing around, always on the lookout for any balloons full of paint, or worse.

"Geez, Nick, does it always have to look like you are ready to kill the reporters asking the questions?" said Chuck, exasperated.

"Chuck, come on, we've been through this before. I was even nice to Bergamo."

"It was one of your more civil exchanges. Looks like she is now ANC's reporter following your campaign. I know Ned is pissed he is not following one of the major party candidates for EXN. You're not likely to get favorable coverage from the one network we talk to," sighed Chuck.

"Hey, I don't need them to be nice. Lexi gets that, and I don't think it helps her. I'd rather have them trying to skewer me. It lets me get my points across when it is a real debate," said Nick, as they all headed back to their rented hotel suite.

Denise met him at the door, hanging up her phone call.

"Nick, can we talk about tactics?" said Denise in a serious tone.

Nick sighed, grabbing a water, sitting in one of the many chairs in the suite. "Fire away."

"I think you're playing into their hands. You keep doing and supporting all the things they say a crazy right winger would say. You are supposed to be the moderate from the middle. Fiscally responsible, socially aware, a caring and compassionate person trying to preserve the Constitution and the Bill of Rights for all. Live and let live. Right?" asked Denise, as the others sat on various couches and chairs.

"Yes," replied Nick carefully.

"Hang on before you 'but' me," said Denise. "Do you go back and listen to what you say? To consider what people really hear from you? You talk as if you are farther right than any Opposition candidate, except maybe Garcia. I want you to spend a bit more time on the things the center left cares about. Equality and women's rights, social issues and compassionate solutions for immigration. Your homeless ideas are good, but then you paint with such a broad brush claiming they are all clueless wards of the state," she finished, trailing off.

"My turn?" asked Nick as Denise nodded.

"I appreciate your concern. Let's consider what *you* are saying. My campaign is really only about three things. Stop listening to anything the media, pundits, politicians and anyone else are saying. Second, use common sense. Everyone has a bullshit meter and they need to *trust* it. Finally, and most importantly, choice. Not choices between Opposition and Party, but choices between right and wrong. We are at a point in our civilization where people will have to choose. A choice to choose freedom for yourself or choose obedience, doing what they say, when. The first is easy, the second should become instinct. The last is the hardest and most important." Nick paused. "You with me so far?" He saw nods.

"I know the warning signs from history. Trust me, they are all flashing a deep red in America. A large majority of the country is exactly where the progressives want them. Docile, confused, scared, and isolated. They know something is wrong, but they are unsure how to register their concern. Cancel culture prevents this." Nick stood.

"I have to awaken them and show them they are strong. Both as individuals and as a group. I have to scare them into action by highlighting all the worst traits of what's been done to *their* society. I'm not talking to the media, because they are the problem. I'm talking to the nobodies. Not to center left or center right or extremes. Those are artificial constructs that are meaningless to each person." Nick became more animated, circling the room, using his hands.

"What they care about are things that directly affect them. The guy driving a truck, painting a house, or fixing your plumbing. I have to rouse the people who in their wildest dreams would never see themselves having any *power* or a *say* in any aspect of how the rules are made. They've been told and shown they *don't* matter. My job is to convince them they do. I don't do that by making promises. I do it by showing them what doing nothing looks like to their family, their community, their future and, ultimately, our country."

"These are the people who will lose what little they have and the future for their children. They need to know this. They need to know this is *not* inevitable. If they stand up *now*, they can be heard and *they* can help stop it. Together as one giant voice in the wilderness. So yes, I sound like a crazy conspiracy nut sometimes, but you know what, the people that really matter, these nobodies, they get it. They know these are not conspiracy theories. They see the reality of all these policies every day."

"Illegals flooding our states and cities, driving down wages, overwhelming small towns services. Crimes not being punished, adult gender issues being forced on ignorant children, out-of-control spending and inflation, and defunded public safety. It's no surprise they're confused and deflated. The one job where none of this should matter, where they should have no meddling, is their children."

"Their most important responsibility is to raise their children and give them a chance at a better life than they have. That used to be called the American Dream. What do they get instead? Children coming home unable to read, write or add, understanding civics or basic biology. But they can recite 42 pronouns, sexual positions none of us have heard of, and a healthy dose of disrespecting anything their parents say. All courtesy of our state run education curriculum. If they dare to stand up to protest this indoctrination, they are denounced and canceled. For these people, *my people*, this is reality today." Nick took a deep breath.

"All of this is courtesy of the *tolerance* one of our parties claims to respect so mightily. We wonder why people are on edge and angry? You may think my ideas seem crack pot, but it is only because you are buying into the media megaphone *saying* they are. Denise, what I'm preaching is not crazy right-wing propaganda. It is a return to debate, to true tolerance. Tolerance for compromise, joint solutions, and common sense. To have faith once again in your neighbor and colleagues and to live in harmony. Knowing we are all not in lockstep on everything, and don't have to be, to thrive mutually."

Nick stopped and looked around the room at his staff.

"Wow, I wish I was recording this," lamented Margie, a surprised look on her face. "That was the best explanation of our campaign goals I have heard."

Nick smiled and held up his phone, showing he had recorded the entire conversation. Greg lifted his as well. Margie's smile was huge.

Denise stood up. She had a strange look on her face as well. "Nick, I've been doing this for a very long time. I've run campaigns for all kinds of less than reputable or insincere candidates. There was always one overarching goal. Win more votes than the other candidate. It was my job. To do it well, I had to turn off all feelings. I was like a lawyer for a mob boss. It was all strategy and tactics. How to take advantage of the other guys' mistakes. How to goad them into making them. It was never about the candidate, their ideals, or the people. It was about winning."

He stood waiting for Denise to make her point.

"Nick, I am sorry. Until just now, I didn't fully get it. I didn't understand what was motivating you to do what you do. What gives you that endless energy and *anger* that comes through in each speech. I figured you were upset at Washington. Now I understand. I guess I'm now 'thinking for myself', as you say. I now, for the first time, see what you mean and why you say what you say. This is not simply more politics as usual. If what you say is true, our country is in deep trouble."

Nick smiled. "Denise, you started this by asking me if I go back and listen to my speeches. Maybe I should ask you the same. Go back and listen yourself. You'll see each one of these is carefully designed to make a key point. They are not random. A point, I might add, not for the media or even my opponents, but to *my* audience. To those who are listening and watching on Hibi. To understand homelessness, government assistance, voting system integrity, what and why the media are controlling our thoughts, or why cancel culture is worse than any weapon they could wield."

"People need to understand the *why* of all these topics. And they need to get angry about it. To understand this is being done *to* them by someone, on purpose. What is happening to our country is not bad luck or even the results of poor decisions. It's intentional, and it's designed to make them obey. Or at a minimum, not resist change. The Constitution is their only shield against these deeds. If we don't get back to first principles and re-institute the rule of law equally to all, then we are doomed. We need to demand our elected officials start acting in *all of our* best interests or lose their job. We need to prevent them from completing the bifurcation of society. Those with Lexi and her masters. And the rest of us, the victims of their policies."

"You make it sound like the next Civil War is coming," observed Earl.

"Isn't it?" answered Nick. "I would even suggest it's already underway. It is not always about armed conflict. Sometimes it's about hearts and minds. Right is on the defensive. We are stronger, but only if we use our strength while we can, to push back."

No one answered as they contemplated this revelation. Nick turned back to everyone.

"Now, if you don't mind, I'd like to enjoy my day off."

"What?" said Chuck and Denise simultaneously. "We thought you were joking."

"I'm not sure that's a good idea, Nick. Your profile is up now. Like it or not, you are pissing off a lot of powerful people. Even more as you get traction. Yes," said Earl, holding up a hand as Nick tried to interrupt. "I know you can take care of yourself, but this is now different. Every crazy in the country, obsessed fans, ninjas, you know, the usual groups."

"Ninjas?" asked Nick, turning with a raised eyebrow.

"Just checking to make sure you are listening."

"Besides, I'm not afraid of ninjas. I studied martial arts."

"Key word is studied. Haven't seen you working out much lately," accused Earl.

"I do it early in the morning while the rest of you slugs are still sleeping. Anyway, I have my phone and if necessary, you can call or track me. I'm going to lie low and walk around this city I used to love. I want to enjoy a free day of obscurity."

"Can't you talk sense into him?" asked Margie in desperation, looking at Chuck. "We need you to work the phones, do some fundraising, and get on some radio shows while we are out here." Chuck shrugged, looking from Nick to Denise.

"Don't look at me, besides he says he knows martial arts," noted Chuck as Nick made an exaggerated chop move with his arms and hands.

"It might do you some good to relax for a day," agreed Denise, surprising everyone.

"All right, see? The task master has given me a weekend pass. I'll see you guys on Sunday morning in time to catch the plane. Where are we off to?"

"Sacramento and then back to Denver. Wait a minute, that is like a day and a half off. I thought you were taking the rest of today?" asked Chuck.

"It's already late afternoon. I want to get up early tomorrow and remember what San Fran was like in the old days. See you on Sunday," said Nick, not pausing for more protests as he left, heading to his room.

As Nick left, his team looked at each other.

Chuck let out a gigantic sigh. "We can work on getting some of the footage from the speech cut into commercials and get it posted on Hibi and our campaign site. We're booked here all weekend. I guess no one expected the boss to actually take a day off."

"I'm more concerned about his ability to keep this up. A simple question and I thought he was going to have a coronary," worried Denise.

"It worked though, didn't it? You're fully converted," added Greg, speaking for the first time.

"True," laughed Denise. "But that kind of passion draws out the same from the opposition. We have to be very careful going forward. What Nick is talking about is not a difference in parties, but one in ideology."

"North and South," interjected Earl. Everyone sat contemplating the statement.

"How much fallout from the speech? He really laid into the progressives and Lexi by proxy," asked Denise.

"Not as much as we need, I'm afraid. Other than appearing on *Tommy*, we aren't getting much coverage on the networks. I really wish he didn't tell everyone to lie to the pollsters. It is hard for us to tell as well if we are making any progress. The fund raising is going well, but I don't know if this is working," questioned Margie.

"We'll know better once we start the summer state fair swings in a month. If he draws sizeable crowds, then we'll know if his message is getting out beyond Tommy's audience," suggested Denise.

"It is. I see it firsthand and I handle the requests for local charters after. It is resonating," said Greg.

"What are you thinking, Earl?" asked Chuck with a look.

"I think this is the last time we should let him out of our sight. I see it and I agree it is resonating and I think his supporters are doing just like he asked. They're hiding in plain sight. Spreading the message and having conversations at every diner and grocery store with their friends and neighbors. It's actually very smart. We can't win in a head-to-head fight against Lexi, but if we can lie low and let the Opposition take all her attention, we can sneak up. Very Sun Tzu," smiled Earl as Denise groaned. "But I think this is a bad idea, letting him roam the city for a day and a half without backup. Especially here. San Francisco is Lexi's territory. It's ground zero for crazy. All it takes is one zealot."

"Can you tail him? You know, from a distance?" asked Denise.

"Not a chance. I'm not exactly inconspicuous. He is no super spy, but he is very aware of his surroundings. At least that's good. Just pray guys. I mean it. This whole movement is about him. Not an idea or even the Constitution. Without him, we are sunk," stressed Earl.

"Amen to that," replied everyone.

# Chapter 71

Nick walked from the Westin St. Francis up Powell Street, turning on Sutter. Changing his sport coat and slacks from earlier in the day. He now wore baggy shorts, a loud Hawaiian shirt, dark blue Crocs on his feet, a Colorado Rockies baseball cap pulled low and dark aviator sunglasses. He was pulling his small suitcase or carrying it depending on the condition of the pavement and the possibility of running into a pile of excrement. The transformation was complete. No one would recognize him in his current disguise. At least he hoped not.

He continued down Sutter, turning on Grant toward Chinatown. Walking up the street in the warm late afternoon sunlight, Nick noticed the Dragon Gate entrance to Chinatown ahead. Just before the gate, he turned into the lobby of the Hotel Triton, an art déco boutique hotel.

He checked in as James Turner and got his room key without being noticed. The lady behind the counter appeared none the wiser. Nick went to the elevator and made his way up to the top floor. The elevator might fit two adults and one piece of luggage. It was not an experience a claustrophobic person would enjoy.

He walked down the hallway to the corner suite on the top floor overlooking the dragon gate. It was small as suites went, a queen bed and desk and a door to the bathroom.But for an old hotel, it was spacious. Nick set his suitcase on the stand and collapsed on the bed. It had been a long time since he could lie down and not have to worry about getting up to make a call, be at a speech, or on a ZOOM chat. He slowed his breathing, as he'd been taught many years prior, and promptly fell asleep.

#

Nick woke to a gentle knocking at his door. The room was dark, and it was dark outside. Turning on the bedside lamp, he went to the door. He must have forgotten to decline the turndown service. As he opened the door, not to find a maid, but to look down into the smiling face of Lauren Bergamo.

Startled, he blurted out. "How the hell did you find me? And, what the hell are you doing here?"

Her smile faded a bit as she seemed to shrink down.

"I wouldn't be much of a reporter if I didn't follow up on my leads."

"And what lead would that be? No one on my staff knows where I went. How did you find me?"

"I was outside the St Francis, waiting for my car to the airport, and I saw you come out incognito. I've been around you enough to see through your poor attempt at a disguise. You can't hide the way you walk and the way you hold yourself. I knew it was you. So, I followed. Figured you weren't going too far, or at least I hoped you weren't since I still had my Jimmy Choo's on," she raised a shapely skirt clad leg, with a black high heel. "No Crocs for me," she smiled. "Do you think I can come in to finish the story before someone calls security?"

Nick stood aside and Lauren walked into the suite, sat down in a chair, and kicked off her heels.

"My aching feet. You have no idea," she groaned.

"Try not taking off combat boots for seven days in a row if you want swollen and sore feet. But I can empathize. If it's any consolation, it works," said Nick, leaning against the doorjamb to the bathroom.

"Why Senator, maybe I should record this, so folks will know you *are* human after all," replied Lauren in a mocking tone.

"I would compliment your legs, but I fear in today's age, it would warrant a slap to the face rather than the intended compliment. Which I assume is the reason you torture yourselves by wearing those?" asked Nick, nodding at the discarded heels.

"Maybe, maybe not. You can be sure we would never admit it to a misogynist like you," grinned Lauren.

"See, my point exactly. I can probably make you a burka out of the sheet if you would feel more comfortable," proposed Nick in a serious tone.

"No, I prefer to see you squirm," smiled Lauren, showing her single dimple. "Anyway, back to my detective work. Thankfully, it wasn't far, and I didn't have to give up. I followed you here and watched from outside as you checked in and went into that insanely small elevator. Watching, I saw you stopped on five."

"I got a room, dumped my luggage, and headed right back to the lobby in case you were leaving fast. After a couple of hours of playing solitaire on my phone, I gave up and went to the desk. By then, the old lady had been replaced by a young guy who had just come on shift. I sweet-talked him into giving me your room number so I could 'surprise my boyfriend' with my earlier flight. Good thing you didn't think to check in under a different last name. And, here I am," finished Lauren.

"Ok Miss Marple, while I am impressed, I think it's time for you to go back to your room or call an Uber to catch your next flight. I'm hungry and I need to eat."

"Miss Marple? How quaint. I think my grandmother read those. Couldn't I have at least been Stephanie Plum? You need to update your reading list. I haven't eaten either. You know your way around San Francisco? I don't," offered Lauren, giving Nick a mischievous look.

"Don't you have to be somewhere? You know, a plane to catch or perhaps another candidate to torment?" questioned Nick.

"Nope. Just heading up to Seattle doing some research. You said you've been here a lot. Show me some sights. What can it hurt? You can consider it the interview I've been trying to get Margie to schedule," proposed Lauren.

"The only way we have dinner is if you promise to turn off the reporter," groaned Nick.

Lauren stood up, holding out her hand.

"Deal."

Nick shook her hand as she once again showed her dimple, smiling. He noticed how much shorter she was without her heels.

"You should change into something warmer if you have it. More comfortable shoes too," he said, as she put her feet back in her discarded very tall heels.

"I have other shoes."

"Good. We'll probably end up walking a bit since I didn't make any reservations. What is your room number?"

"512."

"How long do you need?"

"15 minutes."

 Nick laughed.

"I'll come by in 25. Jeans are fine if you have them. San Francisco is not a formal dining town unless we're going to the Pacific Union Club, which we are not," stated Nick. "See you in 25."

"Don't ghost me," warned Lauren in a firm tone, looking over her shoulder as she left the room.

"I don't even know what that means," laughed Nick.

#

Twenty-five minutes later, Nick knocked at the door of room 512. After a few seconds, Lauren opened the door, telling him to come in as she turned, clearly not yet ready.

"Sorry, almost there," she said, sitting on the bed pulling on a pair of beige suede boots with a short, stacked heel.

"Nice boots. Those ok for walking?" asked Nick.

Lauren tilted her head, thinking.

"Hey, that sounds like a song."

Nick shook his head as Lauren laughed while she pulled on the second boot.

"All right Nancy, don't say I didn't warn you."

"Got it. I've walked a ton in them in the past," replied Lauren. She leaned her head forward and then back to fling her shoulder length reddish brown curls back over her shoulders.

"Warm enough?"

Nick looked at her in her jeans and boots. The boots were form fitting, over the top of her knee in the current style and then at her fluffy white cable-knit sweater. It again surprised Nick at how attractive she was when she wasn't trying to skewer him with a question.

"Should be fine. It can still get chilly at night, even in late May. If you have a light jacket, I'll be happy to carry it for you. As long as the wind stays down, it should be pleasant."

"I have a windbreaker. Where are we headed? Chinatown?"

"We'll walk through. I figure we'll go up to North Beach. There are a couple of places I want to see if they are still there. I'll try to keep the hill climbing to a minimum. Powell is the worst, so we'll walk down Grant," stated Nick, looking at her footwear again.

"Thanks, they are comfortable, but I can't say I have done much uphill walking in DC in them," confided Lauren.

"One other thing, if anyone recognizes us, we need to laugh it off and say we look like *them*. OK? I'd like to avoid the paparazzi experience, if possible."

"Fair enough Senator, I mean *Nick*," she said, smiling.

"Thank you, *Lauren*. Let's go, I'm starving."

Nick led her out of the hotel, heading north on Grant, through the Dragon Gate, towards North Beach. It was still early evening, and the weather was in the upper sixties with no wind, so it was great walking weather. Nick walked on her left, on the street side, as they made their way through the crowds on this busy Friday night. They chatted about the weather and the people, with Lauren asking questions and Nick answering to the best of his knowledge about the history of Chinatown.

As they approached Broadway, they made a right, and Nick led Lauren across the street, grabbing her arm to steady her as they made their way to Columbus. He didn't let go, as they made eye contact. He gently turned her around to look down Columbus at the Transamerica building. The pyramid shaped iconic building was all lit up. Lauren pulled out her phone and took a picture.

"That's an amazing view," admired Lauren. "We close? I'm starving now too."

"Just another block," said Nick, taking her up Columbus. The crowds were larger and louder as they entered the North Beach area, having left Chinatown behind. Nick found the restaurant he was looking for. He was lucky and got a table in a corner where they could watch the people go by outside and still be fairly secluded on the inside.

A waiter promptly arrived to describe some specials and take their drink order.

"Miss?" asked the waiter of Lauren. She ordered a cosmopolitan and Nick ordered a Junipero gin martini, extra dry with blue cheese olives. Lauren stopped the waiter and changed hers to match his.

"Really? Do you like gin or did you change to impress me?"

"I am so tired of drinking tasteless vodka with my girlfriends. With cranberry and orange and chocolate and whatever else they put in it. If I wanted Kool-Aid, I would order it. That's all it ends up being. At home I drink bourbon, scotch, or gin. Tequila makes me sick as a dog, so I avoid that one," revealed Lauren.

"Good to know."

"How about you? Gin your beverage of choice?"

"When I drink, it is gin. Normally I have a beer, but I didn't want you to think I was a hayseed," responded Nick. "It just so happens that Junipero is a local gin and one of the best. I hope you like it."

"I'm sure I will, but we had better order some food to go with it or you'll be carrying me or putting me in the Uber's trunk."

"Then let's order. I chose this without knowing what you like. It has something for everyone. Vegetarian, gluten-free, carnivore, fish, you name it," explained Nick.

"Ah, so this is a test. You make me order and then jump to conclusions?"

"Actually, you order what you like. Just like I will."

The waiter came back with the drinks, and they ordered some appetizers.

"What should we toast?"

"How about my detective skills? If not for them, you'd be eating takeout again," laughed Lauren.

Nick smirked and marveled at her laugh. He raised his glass.

"To Kinsey or Stephanie or whomever you want to be and your *stalking* skills. Sorry, don't know any other female detectives."

"Ha. Here, here," responded Lauren, clinking her martini glass with Nick's.

"That's really smooth, more than I figured."

"It's a good gin, no bite at the end," agreed Nick.

The appetizers arrived. They dug into crispy meatball croquetas, tuna and beet crostini's, and marinated artichoke, goat cheese and olive skewers.

"These are wonderful, especially the meatballs," said Lauren between bites.

"They are. I have surmised you are not gluten-free; or vegan, and you lie to your girlfriends about your love of vodka. What other secrets do you have?"

"Probably less than you, and since I am not a reporter tonight, I will refrain from quizzing you. But if you must know, I grew up in Indiana, on beef and pork, corn, and lots of milk. An all-American childhood."

"Went to Indiana and then Columbia for a Journalism Masters. Got asked to do the weather by a midwestern TV station while at Columbia. I left school and became a weather and traffic girl working my way into roving reporter. The rest is just a series of moves from city to city until I hit the national stage. There you have it in less than 30 seconds," finished Lauren. "Your turn."

As Nick was deciding what to say, the waiter returned for the entrée orders. "Should we get a bottle of wine? I usually limit myself to one mixed drink," explained Nick.

"Sounds good," nodded Lauren.

"Red?"

"Perfect."

Nick ordered the Mourvèdre after consulting with the waiter.

"Mourvèdre? Daring," said Lauren, impressed.

"Actually, I know very little about wine. The only one I recognized was the Cabernet and I try to drink that only with steak. I usually order Pinot Noir, but they didn't have that. What's up with that? It's California and they only have Spanish wines? The nerve. Is Mourvèdre any good?" he asked Lauren in a questioning tone.

"You'll like it. It's like Pinot. A little fruity and not too dry. It'll go well with the tapas we ordered."

"Whew, almost blew that one. Guess I could have choked down a Chardonnay."

"That's another stereotype I hate. Vodka and chardonnay are always assumed to be what women drink. I know very few women who order chardonnay outside of lunch with the girls. I don't know why we all don't just order beers like the guys instead of feeling compelled to sip shitty white wine. Too many *Real Housewives* shows to live up too, I guess."

"They sit around drinking chardonnay? Can't say that is on my viewing list," admitted Nick.

"Yes. Catty gossip about sex, lots of white wine and now smoking pot. And, of course, comparing plastic surgeons and Botox," laughed Lauren.

"And here I am, trying to save the country. If this is popular, it may not be worth saving," commented Nick dryly.

"Hey, I don't watch it either. Though I do admit I watch *The Bachelorette*. I keep hoping all the guys won't turn out to be shits. Usually, it's always the case," admitted Lauren.

"Again, not on my viewing list," replied Nick with a smile.

"What do you watch?"

"Honestly, before I decided to run for president, I watched *NCIS* and *Last Man Standing* reruns and *American Pickers*. I couldn't tell you the last time I watched the network news. I occasionally watched *Tommy*, even before I had him eating out of my palm, as you say."

"*NCIS*? Not sure I ever saw any of those. What was the appeal?" asked Lauren.

"It was excellent writing. The stories were tight, the plots were believable and the characters and their arcs over the course of the 20 years were real. You became invested in them and felt what they felt as they dealt with loss and tragedy. At least the first thirteen seasons, anyway. They just don't do that on TV anymore," declared Nick as Lauren finished sipping her martini.

"Probably because those shallow guys who are on the *Bachelorette*, don't have the attention span to follow a series from episode to episode and season after season. It's a sad situation. No one seems willing to invest the time to learn facts and think for themselves. They take the easy way out and base their opinions on what your network and others tell them to think," observed Nick. Before Lauren could retort, the entrées came along with the wine.

"Your turn," he said to Lauren, holding a glass of wine.

She picked up her glass. "Here's to letting past animosities go by the wayside and new beginnings." Nick clinked his glass with hers and held eye contact until she blushed and broke away.

"Well, what do we have here?" she said, looking at the array of tapas in front of them, changing the subject.

"I think this one is the meat cocadillo, those are the cauliflower bocadillo, that one is obviously the octopus, and the other is the egg one, tortilla espanola. Here we go," said Nick, starting with the octopus.

They dug in with smiles and grimaces and laughed as they compared tasting notes. They both agreed the octopus was different but not bad, but the cauliflower wasn't something they would do again. The meat cocadillo was the favorite of both.

"You forgot a minor item in your rundown," accused Nick.

"Really, what?" asked Lauren, confused, her mouth full of tapas.

"Miss Indiana," noted Nick. "I know how to use the internet and I was curious."

"Oh my god, you Googled *me*?" said Lauren snorting her sip of wine, causing Nick to laugh out loud as well.

"I suppose you didn't return the favor at some point?" countered Nick once she regained her composure.

"Of course, but that is my *job*. You're just a stalker perv," accused Lauren in feigned outrage.

"That is the pot calling the kettle black, Miss 'let me bang on a stranger's hotel room and beg to be fed a meal'," mocked Nick.

"You're hardly a stranger and I don't believe I begged for dinner, although this is much better than room service."

"It was a pretty good meal. You interested in dessert?"

Nick waved for the check when Lauren shook her head about dessert.

"We should vacate the restaurant. These guys like to close early."

"Sounds good."

"You up for walking or would you prefer an Uber? There is a coffee shop across from the hotel that should still be open if we Uber."

"Then Uber it is," agreed Lauren.

Nick requested the Uber on his phone, paid the bill, and left a nice tip. He waved off Lauren when she offered to pay half.

"Not a chance."

She headed to the restroom prior to the Uber arrival. They met at the door as the Uber, a Prius, drove up. He helped her into the back seat and slid in next to her. The Uber headed down Stockton. As they took the left onto Bush, Lauren was pushed against Nick's side,

"Sorry," she said, as she was pushed even harder against him as they turned left onto Grant. She looked up at him, smiling awkwardly. As they got out of the car, the coffeehouse across the way still looked open. They got in just in time.

Lauren had a decaf cappuccino, and Nick ordered a decaf black coffee.

"We can't sit here since they're closing. The lobby is hardly private. My suite has a couple of easy chairs as long as you promise to behave yourself."

Lauren bit her lip, contemplating.

"I guess I can stop stalking long enough to have a cup of coffee."

They entered the lobby and moved into the elevator. as the door was closing, another guest crowded in with a 'sorry, the elevator takes so long'. This caused Nick and Lauren to move to the back, with Lauren pressed against Nick's chest. He wrapped his free arm around her waist to stabilize her, while she held her purse in one and coffee in the other. The other guy got out on three without even a good night or a glance back. The door shut, and the elevator continued up. Nick did not remove his arm. As they arrived at their floor, he turned and backed out the door, helping her as well. They made it to his room and sat down in his chairs. Lauren held her feet out in front of her, stretching.

"Need some help?" asked Nick, glancing at her boots.

"That would be great. I love boots. The season is really pretty much over everywhere but here. Turns out these are not the best for walking after all, but they are the 'in' look this season. I have another pair with more or less flat heels, but I thought these looked better," she smiled as Nick undid the half zips on the suede boots and pulled them off. She sighed in relief. "Thank you," she said, wiggling her toes in her socks.

"No problem," replied Nick. An awkward silence filled the room as they both sipped their coffees.

"Well, thank you for the dinner, even if I sort of blackmailed you into it," said Lauren.

"I have to admit, I enjoyed the dinner and the company. Please don't tell anyone, though. It would hurt both of our reputations."

"Don't worry, I enjoy being the number one 'raving lunatic bitch reporter' attacking that Turner fellow."

"Who said that?" asked Nick with a laugh.

"One of the other EXN opinion ladies, coming to your defense, of course."

"I guess I bring out the best in people."

As they finished their coffee, Lauren asked, "So, where are you off to tomorrow?"

"More detecting, Miss Plum?"

Lauren smiled. "You only said to turn off the reporter for dinner."

"Actually, I am taking tomorrow off as well."

"Really?" Lauren leaned forward in her chair. "That has to be driving them crazy. First, you are wasting a whole day and, frankly, I can't believe they are letting you do anything by yourself at this point."

"They're not happy. One benefit of keeping a low profile and being low in the polls."

"You're not as low in the polls and you know it," responded Lauren in an accusatory tone, leaning back.

"Hey, I only believe what I read in the polls, and we are barely registering," he replied innocently.

"You may fool them, or more likely, they are believing what they want to believe. I get to see the crowds and the reactions. Most of your attendees are not groupies. They're curious and come out to see if you're for real. Each time they leave converted. They tell their friends and relatives. You're way more popular than either you know, think, or will admit," stated Lauren in a serious tone. "Don't forget, I have seen some of your speeches where you tell people to lie to pollsters. You can keep on about low polling, but I'm on to you, Senator."

"We'll see. You off to Seattle in the morning?"

"Unless I get a better offer to see the sights of San Francisco in the daylight, hint hint."

"Ah, the stalker returns. Well, since I didn't have any better offers, I guess I could use some company. We need to get an early start. I was gonna take the ferry to Sausalito for breakfast. There's a nice art gallery there I like to visit. Can you be ready to go at 6:30 am?" asked Nick.

"I'll set an alarm. I promise to wear my other boots, so you won't have to carry me," grinned Lauren.

"You need a wake-up call?" asked Nick with a snicker.

"I think I can handle it," she said, getting up. Nick picked up her boots and handed them to her as he walked her to the door, holding out a hand.

She shook the hand, looked him in the eye, quickly lunged, and gave him a kiss on the cheek before retreating down the hallway to her room. He watched until she got in with a wave.

Getting ready for bed, he stared at his reflection in the mirror and asked, "what in the hell are you doing?"

He checked his alarm and turned off the light.

# Chapter 72

Nick got up at 4:30 am, did his morning Tai Chi routine, then headed out on his run. Running up Powell and down to the wharf, around the Embarcadero, back around to Union Square, finally heading back to his hotel. He dodged piles of both human and dog poop, homeless people sleeping in the doorways, and the occasional street sweeper. He passed a few fellow runners and only toward the end when the sun was rising.

Nick noticed quite a few people wearing hoodies hanging out down some alleys. He was sure he was passing a fair number of drug deals in progress. At the hotel, he showered, then sat down to do some emails while waiting to gather up his charge for the day. Denise sent him an urgent email about a rumor he was in New York City. He responded that no; he was still in San Francisco. Nick told them to enjoy their day off. Only contact him if it was 9-1-1 worthy. Then he paused, deciding to turn his phone off instead.

He put on his Rockies ball cap with his sunglasses on the brim. Wearing a long polo shirt and sweatshirt; jeans and his running shoes. He walked down the hall and gently knocked on Lauren's hotel door, at 6:30 am sharp. The door immediately opened, and he was met with her dazzling smile.

"I'm ready. Surprised? Come on in." He watched as she turned. She was wearing a variation on what she had on last night. Faded jeans, with some rips and black leather boots with flat heels, the boot tops breaking just above her knees, like the other ones. She had on a simple beige sweater and a multicolored scarf she finished tying around her neck. Grabbing a jacket from the bed, she walked to Nick. Her hair pulled back into a ponytail, threaded through the back of a navy-colored ball cap. Her sunglasses were on the brim, like Nick.

"Well, if you're ready, I have an Uber downstairs to take us to the Ferry building."

They headed downstairs into the car and off to the Ferry building. A quick trip this early on a Saturday morning. They had hardly had time to ask each other how they slept before they were exiting the car. In the Ferry building, all the kiosks were still closed. The exception, a coffee stall, going full blast.

They picked up coffees. Nick's black and Lauren's with a single sugar and a shot of cream. Their timing was perfect, boarding the ferry 5 minutes after buying the ticket. They wandered up to the front of the boat as it backed away from the dock and headed out into the bay, generating a cool wind over the bow, and gently rocking in the bay's small waves. They were alone on the prow; the few others having opted to go below in the brisk morning air.

"Here, let me help you," said Nick, helping Lauren put on her jacket. "If you get too cold, we can go inside."

"I should be fine," she said with a shiver, turning to face Nick.

"Is that Alcatraz?" she asked.

"Yes, we are going to go right by it. I went out for a visit years ago when I was in port here."

She looked up at him, with the wind blowing the hair escaping her ponytail into her eyes. "I thought you were in Naval Intelligence? Were you deployed on a ship?" asked Lauren, putting her sunglasses on as the wind picked up.

"I was deployed at sea for a few of the twelve years I spent in the Navy. We came into San Francisco once during Fleet Week. I took a tour to Alcatraz then. It was OK, but hey, just watch *The Rock* and you get the same effect," laughed Nick, bending down to be closer to her ear in the wind.

"You want to go in? The wind is colder than I expected," remarked Nick. Lauren shook her head and leaned against Nick to shield her from the wind. He put his arm around her shoulder, holding her as the ferry rocked more, turning into the tidal flows coming in under the Golden Gate. Putting his sunglasses on as the wind was making his eyes water, he continued turning, trying to shelter Lauren from the direct winds.

They rounded Alcatraz and headed up to the Marin headlands, past Angel Island to Sausalito.

"That's Angel Island. It used to be a military base but is now a state park. Nice hiking there," he said, pointing to the green island off to the right as they went by. Lauren nodded. As they slowed to come into Sausalito, the sun broke through the marine layer and the wind over the bow lessened enough for Lauren to release Nick. As they docked, Nick helped her off the boat onto terra firma. She seemed a bit wobbly, hanging onto his arm to steady herself.

"I'm sorry, I didn't even think to ask if you were alright on a boat. You feeling OK?" asked Nick, in a concerned tone.

"Yeah, I'll be fine once we walk a bit. I'm not very good on the water," groaned Lauren, looking a little green. "I would've sucked in the Navy."

Nick laughed at her joke. "The cafe I like is about a ten-minute walk. Let's go. Let me know if you need to sit?" Lauren nodded in reply.

They walked up Bridgeway Street. The quaint shops were just opening. The crowds were still sparse this early on a Saturday. As the fog lifted and the sun brightened everything, Lauren got her bounce back.

"Don't worry, we'll sit down for the return trip. That should help," assured Nick.

"Promise?" smiled Lauren, looking up at him. He smiled in return.

"There it is, the Lighthouse Cafe," pointed Nick, grabbing a booth in a corner inside. The waitress dropped off menus, coffee with sugar and cream.

"I'm sure you can tell from the menu, pancakes and French toast are the specialties of the house."

"Then I guess I'll order bagels and lox," she replied, looking at him impishly. "Pancakes it is. Actually, I don't like bagels or lox."

"Are you always this sassy in the morning? Or are you delighting in torturing me?" All he got was a smile and a shrug in reply.

Lauren ordered blueberry pancakes and Nick got raspberry with bacon.

"Feeling better?"

"Food will help, and coffee does. Sorry to be such a dud."

"I got seasick the first week every time I deployed. Didn't matter if it was on a carrier or a cruiser, it always took a week to get my sea legs."

"Well, that makes me feel better. What does a Naval Intelligence officer do on a ship? I always assumed you were in an office in the Pentagon?" asked Lauren curiously.

"Without divulging any confidential info. I'd hate to have to kill you just when I am starting to like you."

Lauren gave him a big smile and then stuck her tongue out.

"We gather data, analyze activities of enemy fleets, investigate anything a foreign power can do to damage America. Pretty much the same job we do on land. Try to figure out potential strategies our enemies would use against us and devise strategies and offensives to counter all those activities. Lots of theory and strategizing. Counter terrorism activities, physical and cyber threats, drug interdiction, stuff like that."

"Sounds a bit boring for you. That why you became a pilot?" asked Lauren with a raised eyebrow.

"Been doing your research, I see," he replied with his own raised eyebrow as Lauren broke eye contact, her cheeks now red.

"I am an investigative reporter, after all. You didn't exactly endear yourself to me. Though I admit, you're just mildly irritating now," she said, leaning back, taking another sip of coffee.

Nick laughed, "So you were getting ready to do a hit piece? What did you find?" asked Nick, leaning back himself, putting his hands behind his head.

Lauren hunched forward like she was confiding a secret. "There's this guy, running for president, and you know, other than some press conferences where he picks on the press. In particular, one sharp gorgeous brunette or auburn-haired reporter, depending on her mood, there isn't much out there about him."

Nick leaned in as well.

"Could be, because he has not been a corrupt politician his entire life. Normal people don't have a lot for their Wikipedia page. I wouldn't even have one, if it wasn't for being in the wrong place at the right time in that New York City subway," admitted Nick, tilting his head back and forth, scrutinizing her hair in the light. "Are you brunette or auburn right now?"

"Brunette with a few auburn highlights, you dolt," she said, smiling. "You know, you have an annoying habit of never answering the question."

"I learned how to fly when I was in the Navy. Took lessons on my own and looked at a transfer. Their program was very restrictive. They wanted younger guys, mostly from the academy. At the end of my third tour, I talked to the Navy Reserve about being a Navy Reserve flyer and they said it was not possible without being in the Navy as a pilot. So, I looked at the Air National Guard. They needed pilots. They agreed to let me fly as long as I was willing to redeploy immediately to Iraq and Afghanistan."

"Since I had no commitments, no family, it was fine with me to go fight. I went to flight school, qualified in the A-10, and went back to war. Always volunteering to stay in the combat zone so other guard members with families wouldn't have to deploy. I stayed in country watching as we gave up all the gains we had won, with so much sacrifice, and then through the surge to take it back. I did my part, supporting our guys and gals on the ground." Nick paused as their breakfasts arrived.

"Is that why you left, because of the drawdown?" asked Lauren, spreading lemon curd on her blueberry pancakes.

"Do you even remember the draw down? You must have been in elementary school," smiled Nick.

"Nice try. Nursery school actually, and social services are on their way to get you for cradle robbing, wiseass," said Lauren with a smirk. "Actually, I was starting college when we were reducing our presence in the Middle East after the surge. Seemed like a good plan."

"Yep. Frankly, I agreed. We needed to leave. Both countries. The problem was, we should never have been in Iraq. We didn't have a clue what we were doing. The US is fantastic at taking out armed enemies. But we are horrible at handling domestic rebuilding and understanding tribal relations. Afghanistan was justified but doomed to fail. Did you know Afghans are some of the most conquered people on the planet? Right after the Egyptians. You know what else? They really didn't give a shit who was in charge. I asked them and they shrugged. All I cared about were my brothers and sisters and getting them home in one piece. Sooner made sense to me," observed Nick, eating bites of his pancake, using his fork to make key points.

"In Naval Intelligence, we gathered tons of data and provided millions of scenarios. All of them pointed to the same outcomes. Guerrilla warfare and insurgents *forever*. A permanent force many times what we have in South Korea if we wanted to stop it."

"Getting out was the right move?"

"Absolutely. All the scenarios pointed to endless corruption, regardless of who was in charge. It is the way of the region and it doomed democracy from the beginning. Democracy must start from the bottom up. Our problem is, we always assume everyone wants democracy. To live like us. Pretty arrogant. The people have to want it. The people of Iraq and Afghanistan have no desire to band together and become democratic. You want to know why?"

Lauren shook her head, her mouth full of blueberry pancake.

"Pancakes good?"

"Yummy," she replied finally. "Eat yours while you finish."

"Right," he said, eating a few more bites.

"So why didn't Iraq and Afghanistan take to democracy?"

"Do you know the origin of Iraq?" he asked. Lauren shook her head no. "Must have missed that history lesson."

"Nah. If they don't teach the Revolutionary and Civil Wars, they aren't going to cover the Treaty of Versailles and the British Mandate of Mesopotamia."

"OK, I'll bite. Treaty of Versailles. How does the treaty at the end of World War I impact Iraq?"

"Well, at least you know that much. Ms. Bergamo to the head of the class," praised Nick as Lauren made a slight curtsy.

"At the end of WWI, the British occupied Mesopotamia, which had been part of the Ottoman Empire. Through a series of deals, or mandates, the British created Iraq with no consideration for the ethnic tribes being cobbled together. Sunni Kurds and Christian Assyrians in the north, Sunni Muslim and Shia Muslims all under a Sunni Arabian King. Sounds like a recipe for harmony, right?"

"When you put it that way, why did they do it? Surely somebody must have thought about mixing all these different people together?"

"The League of Nations also created Yugoslavia, a similar mishmash of Serbs, Croats, Slovenes, and Slavic Muslims who also hated each other. Look how well that worked out. But Iraq was really just par for the course for the Brits and their colonial way. They always wanted the benefits without regard for the consequences of the people. It's why they always had so many rebellions in their territories."

"Like ours," nodded Lauren.

"Exactly. Australia is probably the only dominion that never really had a major insurgence against British rule. Iraq was no different." Nick sipped his coffee before continuing.

"From the start, it was nothing but rebellions. Brutally put down under British rule, and then under King Faisal, and every ruler through Saddam. All of them were ethnic parts of Iraq pitted against the other weaker tribes in their country. The entire Iran-Iraq war was Shia Muslim versus Sunni Muslim. It continues today. Saddam gassed the Kurds in the north. We recruited them to help us. Then screwed them afterwards. Again. Just like we did after the first Gulf war." Lauren was paying attention to Nick, in professor mode, fascinated by the history lesson.

"Anyway, democracy can never work when the people hate each other, and it goes back thousands of years. We told the superiors time and time again it would never work in either Afghanistan or Iraq. But look what happened. Too much money being made by the defense contractors, and they fund both political parties. We keep spending money. We leave. It goes to shit. We send troops back in with no plan or end in sight," said Nick, eating some more of his pancakes.

"Hey, we can talk about something else. I didn't mean to dredge up bad memories," said Lauren, reaching out to touch Nick's hand on the table.

"No, it isn't a problem. You asked a question and I owe you the full answer," remarked Nick, continuing his story but not moving his hand from her touch.

"We drew down and gave up all the hard-fought territory. All of us questioned what we risked our lives to accomplish and what our comrades died for? Then, only after this became a political disaster for the prior Party administration, we surged up and destroyed the insurgents, which, as I said, is what we do well."

"Then we leave, and the Taliban comes back again. Except this time, they have US arms, equipment, and technology. Then we go back to droning everything until we recognize them at the UN. Of course, both Afghanistan and Iraq are now in bed with Iran and China. Hosting terrorist camps, shipping tons of opium, and basically back to pre-9/11 status. What was it all for?"

"What should we have done?" asked Lauren quietly, trying to calm Nick, but genuinely interested in his solution.

Nick gave a bitter laugh.

"Well, hindsight is clear. We should have surged the 30,000 troops and stayed. We needed to treat it like a colony. Give it self-rule, but ensure those rules were western. It would take a generation, maybe two, of total occupation. That part I will give the Brits credit for. Bringing education and the rule of law to their colonies. Westernizing them whether they appreciated it or not. It could have been done. We needed to teach the children western values and the value of life in general. We did it in South Korea. Without being vilified as colonizers. It might have worked there too." Nick sighed.

"We don't have the will any longer and the media does not have the patience to allow us to try. Impossible in this day and age. We will only ever react because we don't have the willpower to do what it would take to pre-empt. That is the beauty of democracy. We can't be colonizers. It's not in our DNA," finished Nick.

"You left after the surge worked," asked Lauren, still fishing for why he left the military.

Nick picked at the last of his pancakes and took a sip of coffee, disengaging from her hand on the table.

"More or less. I had done what I could. It was time to move on," answered Nick. "Feeling human again?"

"Yes, the breakfast was wonderful," smiled Lauren.

Nick paid the bill. They took a refill of coffee to go. Leaving the restaurant, they continued walking up the street past the now open gift shops and boutiques. The streets were more crowded as the sun warmed things up. They both needed their sunglasses for the bright sun now.

Nick helped Lauren take off her jacket, tying it around his waist. He started to take off his sweatshirt, pulling it over his head. Lauren snuck a look at his mostly six pack as his polo shirt pulled up in front. She reached out and grabbed the shirt tail as he finished, cradling the coffees against her chest with her other arm.

"Thanks," said Nick, taking back his coffee after tying his sweatshirt around his waist as well.

"How charming," remarked Lauren as Nick twirled for her. "Very fashionable. Who knew the mean ole Senator had a funny side?"

"Hey when you play nice, you get it in return," he said, leading her up the street to an art gallery.

"You OK if we browse a bit?" asked Nick, leading her into the gallery.

"Sure. You been here before?"

"Nicky!" squealed a tall leggy blonde who approached and took Nick into a big hug. "It has been too long," said the woman.

"Lauren, this is Carrie. She owns the gallery. We're out for some breakfast and I wanted to see what's new. It's been a while since I was last in."

"Nice to meet you, Lauren," said Carrie, holding out her hand to shake Lauren's.

"Likewise."

"Have you seen Nano's latest sculptures?" asked Carrie, turning to Nick. "They are so fun." She took Nick's hand and led him further into the gallery. Nick looked over his shoulder at Lauren with a wink, and she responded with a tight smile following.

Lauren watched as Carrie led Nick away. She saw a woman on the wrong side of fifty trying to hold on to youth by dressing too young. With the shiny, line free forehead only Botox provided. As Lauren trailed behind, she hoped she was never in Carrie's position. Carrie led them to a corner of the gallery where several large bronze sculptures were on display.

There was a giraffe that stood almost as tall as Nick, but instead of being lifelike, the sculpture had gears, leaves, acorns, letters, numbers, and all kinds of whimsical pieces embedded in the gold patina. Several other large-scale pieces of cats, a dragon, a dog with a Sherlock Holmes pipe and deerstalker cap and a near life size baby elephant, all with the same unusual embellishments. Nick stood looking at the elephant.

"That is Bobby, beautiful, isn't she, or he? I am not sure if it matters. Look at the mouse on the tail," she said, pointing.

"Carrie, it's a beautiful piece, but you know I already have a small one of Nano's work. Thanks for showing me." Nick smiled at her sales tactics.

"How about you Lauren? I bet it would brighten up your place, or are you two together?" she inquired with a smile.

Nick and Lauren both laughed while shaking their heads and it was Nick's turn to redden slightly.

"We're just friends, Carrie. What is it with women and questions?" asked Nick, walking away to look at the art hanging on the walls.

Lauren took advantage of Nick's absence to quiz Carrie.

"Does he come here often?"

"He used to come in about once a month fifteen years or so ago. He and his girlfriend, Heather. She worked in the city, and they would come over for breakfast and a stroll. He's been in a few times in the last few years," she said, seeing the look on Lauren's face.

"Oh sorry, I have a habit of talking without thinking." Carrie turned and followed after Nick.

"Nicky, we have an entire section of Dr. Seuss art from the Geisel estate, and I just got a wonderful Miro lithograph on consignment."

Lauren browsed through the gallery, looking at the mix of pieces. The variety and style of artwork always amazed her. Some were hideous. Others were strange and still others seemed almost as if they were photos. They were so realistic. She shook her head at the price tag of some pieces.

Lauren stopped in front of a large painting of a leopard crouching down to drink at a stream, looking up at the viewer. The eyes looked alive as the leopard stared back at her. She stifled a shiver and looked closer, seeing the fine lines of the hairs on the leopard. "How does someone paint something so lifelike?" she said to herself in wonder.

"The artist is a Zimbabwean. He used to be a river guide and conservationist on the Zambezi river," said Carrie, coming up behind Lauren silently.

"It's amazing. I can't believe it is a painting and not a photo."

"He never had an art lesson in his life. All self-taught."

"This guy painted this and never studied or took a class? How the hell do you just learn how to do this?" marveled Lauren.

"I don't know, but the result is perfect. This is a signed and numbered giclee, very affordable at only $5000," said Carrie. "I'd be happy to ship it, since you aren't together."

"Excuse me?" replied Lauren, confused, looking at Carrie.

"I meant, if you were together, there would be no need to buy it. Nicky owns the original oil painting."

"He does?" blurted Lauren, startled.

"He does what?" Nick asked, coming up to the two ladies.

"I was explaining to Lauren about the artist's background and the fact you own the original painting of this print."

"Carrie, you are an open book," said Nick, shaking his head. "Yes, I own it and I know Andrew as well. He's a great guy. Marvelous stories and great to hoist a pint with, but not too many. He'll drink anyone under the table."

"You should invite him to come by the gallery. We can have him hand sign the prints we have."

"I'll give you credit, Carrie, you're always thinking. Far as I know, he does not come to the states much," laughed Nick.

Carrie smiled.

"See anything you like?" asked Nick, looking at Lauren.

"I can give you a discount as a friend of Nicky's," chimed in Carrie.

"I think I am a bit out of my league here, but thanks for all the info," replied Lauren.

"Good to see you again, Carrie," said Nick as they turned to go.

"Nicky, you sure I can't interest you in that, Miro? You know how hard those are to find."

"No thanks, Carrie, one is enough. As always, let me know if you come across any of those Jacques Villon aquatints," said Nick, opening the door for Lauren.

They left the gallery and headed back down the street toward the Ferry.

"OK, so let's see, Nicky," said Lauren, looking sideways at him, pulling out an imaginary notebook to read from.

"Naval Intelligence telling the brass how they are doing it wrong. Flyboy committed to helping his brothers and sisters in arms survive the politician's poor decisions. Professor of History, an Art aficionado, and the boyfriend of Heather," said Lauren, this last bit delivered with a bit of drama as Lauren looked up from under the brim of her cap to gauge Nick's reaction.

"Carrie is a chatterbox," said Nick, putting his sunglasses back on. "That's how I met her. Heather and I wandered in here one morning. And no, this is not some vision of me channeling my old girlfriend on you or a move I make with all my dates. An early morning ferry ride, followed by breakfast at the Lighthouse, a stroll through the art gallery and a return to the bat cave where I show you my Batmobile," recited Nick.

Lauren stopped, grabbing his arm and looking at him incredulously. "Oh, my God. You have a Batmobile too!"

Nick made to grab her, but she danced out of the way, laughing. They continued back down the street.

"Any more questions, prosecutor?" prodded Nick.

"I didn't peg you for the art type. How did that happen?" Lauren asked, serious again.

"Heather. She worked in an art gallery in DC when I first met her. She took me to some exhibits, and we went to some shows. I developed my appreciation for art. I continued to enjoy it long after we broke up."

"What happened? If you don't mind me asking," probed Lauren softly as they walked.

"Life happened. It was a long time ago. When I left the Navy and went right back into the Air Guard and an immediate deployment, she gave up. Can't say I blamed her. She felt like I kept choosing to serve my country over her and I guess she would be right. I haven't spoken to her in a very long time. Or thought about her, either. Hey, the Ferry is just pulling in. If we hurry, we can catch this one back." Nick grabbed Lauren by the hand and hurried them both to the dock. They were the last ones on before the Ferry pulled away for the return to San Francisco.

"Do you need to go downstairs?" asked Nick. "It should be smoother because the wind from the ocean will be behind us."

"We can try it outside, might be better with fresh air. Just hang on, please," she said with some concern.

Nick helped her put her jacket back on and stood behind her. He put his hands on her waist as she leaned back into him. They didn't talk, but just stood together. As the Ferry turned inside Alcatraz, Lauren half turned.

"Aren't we going back to the Ferry building?"

Nick shook his head. "Pier 41 down on the wharf."

They docked and walked off the ferry. Lauren grabbed Nick's arm and ran to the rail on the dock.

"Look," she said, pointing at the pile of seals and sea lions laying on the docks below. Some were sleeping, others were 'talking'. They were all piled on top of each other, napping and playing.

Lauren jumped up and down like a little girl. She took out her phone and snapped a couple of pictures. A couple walking by offered to take a picture of the two of them. Nick put his arm around Lauren's waist. Lauren looked at the picture and showed it to Nick. It was a good picture.

"You want a closer look?" asked Nick, as Lauren nodded.

Nick led her around and down to Pier 39, where there were more sea lions sunning on top of each other. Lauren took a few more pictures. They walked among the shops on the pier. Even with the sun, it was a cool and crisp spring day. When Lauren saw a shop dedicated to socks, she grabbed Nick and dragged him in as he groaned in protest.

"Can you believe it? A complete shop devoted to just socks," said Lauren, smiling.

"Oh yeah, unfortunately, I don't have to believe it. I'm in it."

"Sit down while I browse," she said, pushing Nick into a nearby chair.

Nick stared at her as she walked up and down aisles, looking at various socks. Some in bright colors, some long, and others short. Once she turned to see him staring and she showed her single dimple smiling as he held his hand up in front of his eyes. She came and stood in front of him, holding one pair of short lime green socks and two pairs of very long ones.

"Ready?"

"Done already?" asked Nick, in mock concern. She ignored him and held up the socks.

"Aren't these great?"

"The green ones are bright. Not sure where you would wear the others? Around the house to keep your feet warm?" asked Nick, completely serious.

She gave him a look. "Do you ever leave your office at all? Walk around in DC or anywhere? These are boot socks. You wear them to make your boots fit on your legs and to make a fashion statement." Seeing his bewilderment. "Never mind, you're hopeless. Take my word for it, they're fashionable."

"In that case, please let me buy you this wonderful present," said Nick with a flourish, taking the socks and paying for them.

"I can see it now. What was the first thing he bought you?" she said, looking at Nick as he handed the bag to her. "Socks."

Nick smiled.

"Well sock lady, you ready to walk for a bit, or do you need to put them on?"

"Hilarious. Where too?"

Nick pointed up the hill to Coit Tower, overlooking the bay. "It's not as steep as it looks. But the views are the best in the city."

"Let's do it," said Lauren, looking up and answering more cheerfully than her feet felt.

They walked up Stockton chatting about the perfect weather and making small talk.

"So do you like working for ANC?" asked Nick as they walked side by side up the sidewalk.

"Do you like being a senator?" asked Lauren in response.

"No," said Nick, "and for the record, I am not the one redirecting this time."

"You know, I think you're the only senator who would answer 'No'. From what I have seen, once you get to the Senate, a senator spends all their time trying to stay there."

"That's my understanding as well. There sure are a lot of them who've been there for a very long time. There must be something about it I'm not getting, since I'm so eager to leave," answered Nick.

They turned down Lombard and continued walking, arriving at the bottom of Telegraph Hill. Coit Tower now rose high above them.

"Need a rest?"

"Onward," answered Lauren gamely.

They made their way slowly up Telegraph Hill, reaching the top of the hill and the base of the tower. Lauren gave him a look as she caught her breath.

"Gee, that was fun. What else do you have planned to show a girl a good time?"

Nick smiled as he breathed easily.

"Hey, it is all downhill from here."

"This is the best we can do? It's over already?" commented Lauren between deep breaths.

"Haha. I meant the walk. I bought you socks, so maybe you're right, it doesn't get better than that," admitted Nick. "We should get in line for the elevator."

They headed in and got lucky. It was only 10 minutes before they could take the elevator to the top of the tower. The view was breathtaking. They walked around the perimeter, taking in the different angles from the Golden Gate to Alcatraz to the Bay Bridge and Oakland. The tall buildings of downtown and the hills to the west prevented a view of the ocean, but the Golden Gate Bridge was visible in the distance again as they made a full circle.

"Worth the climb?" asked Nick.

"Nick, it's beautiful," she replied, looking out over Alcatraz and the bay in the sun. Nick was looking down at Lauren and not at the view.

"I'm glad you like it," murmured Nick. He reached down with his hand and took hers. She turned. Surprised, and looked up at him. He removed his hat with one hand as he bent down to kiss her. Nick pressed against her lips tentatively until Lauren put her arms around his neck and pressed against him. When they broke the kiss, Lauren was glad she had her sunglasses on.

"And to think I just caught my breath," she said. They continued to hold hands and take in the view. Finally, Nick looked at Lauren again,

"We should go. Plenty more to see."

"Would you like me to take a picture of you two?" asked an older woman, holding her husband's hand.

"Please," said Lauren, handing her phone to the woman and standing with her arms around Nick's waist, leaning into his chest as his arm circled her shoulder. The wind blew her hair out to the side as they both smiled for the photo.

"Thank you so much," said Lauren, looking at the picture. It showed two people, smiling, happy to be in each other's arms. She turned her phone to Nick and airdropped the photo to his phone, along with the one on the pier.

"There, now you have them as well."

"Thanks, now we really should get going," said Nick, smiling, giving her another quick kiss.

"OK," said Lauren, as she reluctantly released his hand. They went back to the line for the elevator down. She leaned back into him and interlaced her fingers on both hands with his. They stood there, not saying anything, just feeling the quicker heartbeats.

When they exited the elevator at the base, Nick once again took her hand and led her down to Greenwich Street.

"What is this?" asked Lauren as Nick led her down steps that looked like they were in the backyards of houses.

"These are the Greenwich steps. They lead from Coit Tower down to the Embarcadero and, yes, they go through people's backyards. Much easier to walk down them than up," laughed Nick.

"This is so cool," remarked Lauren as they continued to walk down hundreds of steps. She was fascinated by the glimpse into the backyards of house after house.

"Would you want one of these houses?" he asked.

"Absolutely not. I don't want strangers walking through my backyard. Lots of times I'm only wearing socks," shared Lauren, squeezing Nick's hand in jest.

"Okay. What else do I need to know?"

"Ha, you ain't getting off that easy. A girl's gotta have her secrets."

"You hungry?" asked Nick.

"I am, after all this mountain climbing."

"Good. Another of San Francisco's famous restaurants is right at the bottom of the steps." Nick led Lauren around the corner from the bottom of the steps and over to the Fog City Diner. It must have been their lucky day. They didn't have to wait to get a booth at the back of the diner. The hats and sunglasses had helped them stay anonymous on Coit Tower. Being in the back of the diner, they scrunched down in the booth to remain unseen.

"I have reservations at Scoma's for dinner tonight, down on Fisherman's Wharf. You should have some type of seafood there. It is all fresh. It's probably *the* iconic restaurant in the city," explained Nick.

"Who are you having dinner with?" asked Lauren slyly.

"Well," said Nick, taking both of her hands in his. "There is this beautiful, brunette reporter with auburn highlights who has a sharp wit, and a sharper tongue I was thinking of asking. Then I found out she has a sock fetish, so not knowing what other habits she might have, maybe I should reconsider? But it is a reservation for two, and she is a pretty amazing kisser. Plus, it is a fabulous seafood dinner, so maybe she might like to go?"

"It is San Francisco, the most romantic city in America, and I did almost throw up on your shoes this morning. Like you said, you bought me socks. How romantic is that? I guess I can make an exception to my 'never date a politician' rule."

"I'm confused. Is that a yes?" asked Nick.

Lauren showed her dimple in reply.

Knowing they were going to have a nice dinner, they opted to split a Margherita pizza, some truffle fries, and a bottle of Pellegrino.

"You still never answered my question about whether you liked ANC or not," pushed Nick as they munched on pizza and fries.

"I enjoy reporting. I like investigating things, digging up facts and exposing lies. Finding the truth. So much of what I have done since joining ANC is not that. I have someone screaming questions to ask in my ear, or producers telling me to do x or y to incite the people I'm questioning. To get a rise out of them for better footage. It is all choreographed. If you're good at sensationalism, you thrive at ANC. If you are looking for facts and true journalism, sadly, and I hate to say it, you are pretty much limited to EXN and lesser outlets."

"Not too surprising," agreed Nick.

"The major networks and papers are definitely in contact with each other, deciding on stories to cover or, more importantly, *not* cover. My producer keeps me from being able to ask about certain topics. They have even threatened us if we don't toe the line. Have you ever wondered why all these people who have had long careers end up on EXN? Trust me, they are not all conservatives. Many of them are concerned about their reputation and they actually like to be watched and appreciated by an audience. They can get that at EXN. So, no, I really don't enjoy working at ANC. But like a professional athlete, I have a contract I need to honor," finished Lauren, ending on a serious note.

"You could be like me and tell them to screw it," said Nick, in a light tone. "Surely you could do something else."

"Like I told you months ago, I tried to quit. I was told in no uncertain terms they would make my life miserable and keep me from working again. I can't not work. Let's talk about something else."

"Sure. Sorry," he said, changing subjects.

They finished their lunch, chatting about the surprise that Lexi had taken so long to clinch the nomination and the strong showing by Senator Klausen from Wisconsin. The absolute mess the Opposition primaries had become with no clear front runner rising to the top.

"Ready for the next stage?"

"As long as it does not involve walking uphill," groaned Lauren with a sigh, thinking of her feet.

"There is a lot more to see and rather than Uber around, I was thinking I would rent a scooter, if you trust me. I can show you more of the city and give your feet a break."

"I trust you."

"Then let's scoot," said Nick, as Lauren groaned at his joke.

#

They found a scooter rental place nearby and got one with enough power to carry both of them up and down the hills. Ten minutes later, they had their helmets on and Nick took off to show Lauren the other side of the Peninsula. She wrapped her arms around his waist and leaned into his back as they got underway.

Nick took her up to the top of Lombard street, down through Union Square to the Moscone Convention Center, then by the baseball park. They rode around the Mission and Castro districts. In many of these areas, they were forced to weave through countless homeless tents set up on the sidewalks and encroaching into the traffic lanes.

He showed her the blocks of Painted Ladies Victorian houses with the bright colors and then into Haight Ashbury, where Nick drove by the house with the giant mannequin legs hanging out of the second story window. Lauren made him stop for photos.

As she got back on the scooter, she commented on all the homeless in the Castro and Mission districts. "I had no idea the homeless problem was so widespread here."

"It's especially bad on the entire west coast. Mild year-round weather, extensive social services, and now no enforcement of any laws, including shoplifting, or all crime short of murder. To be homeless and subsisting on petty crime is pretty easy in San Francisco," explained Nick in a disappointed tone.

"That why you have a gun?" she asked.

"Was wondering if you would say anything. I know you felt it on my back when we took the picture on Coit Tower."

"I was a little startled. First the kiss and then realizing I was hugging Nicky the Kidd," she said, smiling up at him.

"That bother you?" asked Nick as he put his helmet on.

"Nope. And after riding through some of those sketchy neighborhoods, I am glad you have it. I grew up in Indiana. My mother's brothers were all hunters. I never went, but there was plenty of game on the table in the wintertime. Not a big fan of guns, but I can certainly see why folks want and need them now."

"You've seen enough of my speeches to know my feelings on the 2nd Amendment. In our increasingly lawless society, you can protect yourself, or be a victim. I am not into victimhood, so I always carry," finished Nick, as they got back on the scooter.

He pointed out the sights and stopped for Lauren to take more pictures. Coming out of Haight Ashbury, they rode around Golden Gate Park, eventually making it to the Pacific Ocean, where they turned north to Point Lobos and the Seal Rocks. Nick took a picture of her, still wearing her helmet and sunglasses, her long hair blowing in the wind as she stood by the railing taking a picture of the seals.

"Oh Nick, I am having such a good time. Thank you, thank you," she gushed, leaning in to kiss him. It ended up with both of them laughing as they kept banging their helmets. Frustrated, Nick ripped off his helmet, found her lips, and left her breathless.

"Why Senator, I never knew you were so resourceful," she said in her best southern belle drawl. They headed inland. Nick turned into Land's End Park and up to the Legion of Honour building, the art museum in the park. Nick pointed out the large VA hospital in the distance, and the Holocaust memorial.

They exited Land's End Park, onto Lincoln Blvd and Nick pointed out they were driving through the old Presidio army base. They rode through the Presidio, under Highway 101 and up to Fort Mason, where Lauren took another picture of the Golden Gate bridge, this time from below. Back on the scooter and down Mason toward the Marina. Nick stopped the scooter at the Palace of Fine Arts, another of the premier art museums in the city, and one just as famous for the building itself.

The sun was dipping in the distance as they headed up Bay street to Columbus and Grant, finally stopping in front of the Hotel Triton.

"What are you going to do with the scooter?" asked Lauren, taking off her helmet and shaking out her hair before putting her ball cap back on.

"I'll take it back and then walk or Uber back. It's what, almost 3:30 now," said Nick, looking at his watch. "I'll come by at 6:30. Our Reservations are for 7. I am wearing slacks and a sport coat, but you can wear whatever you like. Like I said, it *is* California."

"Don't worry, you won't be disappointed," said Lauren, leaning in and giving Nick a quick kiss.

"See you at 6:30."

She turned and walked into the hotel as Nick watched. He returned the scooter to the rental place and walked back to the Hotel.

# Chapter 73

Nick showered and changed into black slacks, a dark blue dress shirt, and a black sport coat. His one concession to fashion were his handmade Italian dress shoes. Whenever he was in Florence, he went to a local artisan to have his shoes resoled or to purchase new styles.

They were extremely comfortable, having been cut perfectly to match his feet. He'd discovered the cobbler while on leave when posted to Aviano airbase in Italy. Nick spent time wandering around the Italian countryside, even visiting the little town of Nona outside Naples, from where his mother's grandparents had immigrated to the United States.

Nick checked his look in the mirror, took a deep breath, and headed to the door. "Geez, this is not the prom," he said to himself as he headed down the hall to Lauren's room.

He knocked on the door, waiting. The door opened. The woman standing before him was stunning in every sense of the word. Lauren was wearing a black satiny dress, with a soft paisley pattern. Form fitting from slightly below the knee, up past her tapered waist to her bosom with slim shoulder straps. The ensemble was worthy of a Hollywood red carpet. Nick fought desperately to not stare at the impressive cleavage on display at the top of the dress. Her hair falling in lustrous, wavy curls onto her shoulders and her makeup was perfect. He could see how she had won the Miss Indiana title. She wore no other jewelry besides diamond studs in her ears.

"Hey sailor," said Lauren, smiling slightly at the effect of her outfit on Nick.

Nick quickly pulled it together. "My God, you look wonderful. You can't tell me you had that dress in your luggage or if you did, you're missing the red-carpet premiere."

Lauren blushed a deep pink and Nick noticed her dark eyes were now closer to green against the black linen of the dress.

"Let me get my bag," she said, walking into the room. Nick glanced at her stiletto heeled platform pumps of an impressive height. He couldn't help but notice the dark seamed hose disappearing under her dress. As she turned, he glanced up. She caught him staring.

"No, I didn't have this dress," answered Lauren, twirling.

"I'm suddenly feeling severely under dressed. You know I love the dress, but I like the person wearing it more. Did I wipe up the drool?" He wiped his hand across his mouth.

"You're very sweet. You look scrumptious to me. Nice shoes," she said, looking at his feet.

"Hey, I saw *American President*. I'm supposed to compliment *your* shoes. Nice shoes, too."

He offered her an arm and led her to the elevator. As they waited for the elevator to arrive, Lauren turned to him.

"You should never give a girl a couple hours to shop before a big date. Especially not in San Francisco. You're lucky it's my credit card and not yours."

They resisted ravishing each other in the elevator, kissing the entire ride. There was a Black Town car out front waiting.

"I didn't want to take a chance on our Uber being a Prius," laughed Nick as the driver opened the back door and Nick helped Lauren. The driver drove toward the wharf, while Nick grabbed Lauren's hand. They looked at each other, smiling.

"Wait, a sec," said Lauren as they pulled up to Scoma's. She pulled a tissue from her tiny clutch purse and wiped the red lipstick from Nick's mouth, checked her own in a mirror quickly. "All better now".

Nick exited his side and helped Lauren as she carefully exited as the driver held the door.

"Dress make it tough to walk?" asked Nick, noticing how gingerly Lauren was moving.

"Dress, shoes, the complete package. You have no idea, flyboy. This had better be worth the effort," she answered, her white teeth gleaming in stark contrast to her red lipstick.

Nick headed to the door, holding Lauren's hand. As they entered the lobby, a middle-aged Italian man walked up.

"*Signor* Turner, welcome back. We have your room waiting," said the man in accented English. Nick led Lauren forward.

"Giuseppe, let me introduce you to Ms. Lauren Bergamo." It was all Giuseppe could do to not let out a 'Mamma Mia'.

"*Signorina, sei bella mi vuoi sposare*," said Giuseppe in melodious Italian, holding her hand and bending over exaggeratedly to kiss it. She looked confused at Giuseppe, then Nick.

"*Giu ragazzo, che ha preso*," replied Nick, laughing.

"But of course, Senator," said Giuseppe with a smile for Nick. "Please follow me."

Lauren and Nick followed Giuseppe down a hallway, separate from the prying eyes of the main dining room, to a private room near the back of the restaurant. Nick helped Lauren slide into the leather upholstered booth.

"Anything else? Please don't hesitate, *Signor* Turner."

"Thanks Giuseppe."

As Giuseppe left, another waiter entered, who had to be in his seventies.

"Aldo," said Nick, getting up to give him a hug. He turned to Lauren.

"Lauren, this is Aldo, he has been here forever. Aldo, Lauren Bergamo," Aldo too kissed her hand, muttering, "*Sei bellissima*".

"Nicky, what I get you to drink?" asked Aldo in a very thick accent. Decades in the United States had not helped him lose it.

"What do you recommend, Aldo?"

He thought, made a few notes, and announced, "Oysters yes?" Nick looked at Lauren, who nodded.

"Sure."

"*Vegitariano?*" asked Aldo.

"*Nessun problema*," said Nick, answering in Italian.

"*Allergie?*" asked Aldo.

Nick looked at Lauren. "Any allergies, shellfish, nuts?"

"Nope. I pretty much eat everything," laughed Lauren.

"*Fantastico sei così fortuna*," laughed Aldo in return.

"*io sono fortunato*," replied Nick again in Italian.

"Okay, I bring bread and Nicky, *Il tuo italiano è terribile*," said Aldo shaking his head, leaving them alone and sliding the divider closed.

"Okay, spill. You can speak Italian?" asked Lauren in a conspiratorial whisper.

"We can talk normal. That's why I reserved the private room. Not according to Aldo. He said, 'your Italian is terrible'." They both laughed.

"And he's right. I never get to use it, and I'm sure I just butchered it."

"I got the allergies and the vegetarian, but what did he say to you after I said I could eat anything?"

"He said I was a lucky guy," laughed Nick. "And I agreed," Lauren smiled, blushing.

"And what did Giuseppe say? Somehow, I think that was a bit more than 'pleased to meet you'."

"He said you were fantastically beautiful, and would you marry him? I told him to back off. Like a good Italian, I will take care of him later," stated Nick in a mock threatening tone.

"I don't know. He was kinda cute. Are you Italian? Turner is hardly Italian."

"Look at me. Of course, I am Italian. How about Russo, my mother's maiden name? Her grandparents emigrated from Naples. I am half Italian, maybe a bit more counting my dad's side. His side was a mishmash of all kinds. Supposedly his great whatever grandfather came over on the Mayflower. One of my relatives married a full-blooded Cherokee. I have a bit of everything," declared Nick. "How about you? Clearly, you are Italian as well."

"Bergamo is Italian, but according to my dad, his family has been here for generations. My mother's maiden name is Stevens. Also, a hugely anglicized name. Her family were here for generations as well. I never really got to spend much time with many of my grandparents. What I remember was not conversations about where they were from. I guess I'll have to join one of those sites to find out."

"Hey, the way I look at it, we have so intermixed. Heritage is no longer a function other than clever facts used to impress girls," said Nick with a straight face.

"I'm not impressed," replied Lauren, acting aloof, looking at her newly manicured red nails.

"In all fairness, none of those girls looked like you do in that dress. No wonder all the guys were all '*Bella* and *Bellissima*'," said Nick with hand gestures.

"Say it again please," asked Lauren, leaning forward, showing Nick even more cleavage.

"Good God. Please don't do that again," groaned Nick, closing his eyes and holding a hand over them.

"Do what?" asked Lauren, smiling wickedly while leaning forward again when he opened his eyes.

At that moment, the scraping at the door announced the return of Aldo with drinks and appetizers.

"Spritz for the *Bella donna* and a Negroni for *uomo fortunato*. Oysters and Calamari, *buon appetito*," said Aldo, once again leaving and pulling the slider closed.

"Ok, I think yours is a spritz, prosecco, appertivo. Looks like some orange and sparkling water. Mine is a Negroni. Campari, gin, and some sweet vermouth."

"Here's to a wonderful day and an unexpected outcome," glowed Lauren, holding up her glass.

"I second that and add to having dinner with a vision of '*Venere*'," said Nick as they clinked and sipped.

"I hope the last was Venus and not the STD it sounded like," cracked Lauren, causing Nick to choke and spit his drink as he laugh choked on his second sip. It took a second for him to clear his throat.

"You alright?" asked Lauren, concerned, getting ready to get up.

"Fine," croaked Nick.

"Sorry, I make jokes when I am nervous. Bad habit and not very ladylike. I blame the little boy's club I have to work with," noted Lauren as Nick regained his composure and drank from his water glass.

"What do you have to be nervous about?"

"Seriously? Didn't it feel like the Prom to you?"

"Exactly," laughed Nick. "Just like the Prom but without the corsage. You're lucky I didn't turn and run."

"Then you would have gotten the bill for this dress and the shoes and all the rest."

"You bought shoes too? I am flattered. Do I even want to know what all the rest is?" asked Nick carefully.

"Well, much as I would like to say, this is all me, there may be some help here," said Lauren, waving her hand up and down the front of her dress. "Guys have it easy, I bet you already had all of that, didn't you," said Lauren, grabbing an Oyster.

"I did. I figured Chuck or Denise would send me to a dinner tonight with a donor or something, so I brought the jacket," admitted Nick, eating an Oyster and putting Calamari on plates for both.

"Well Senator, explain to me why I should donate to your campaign," said Lauren in a deep voice.

"You shouldn't. I have about as much chance as a snowball in hell. Send your money to St. Jude or Tunnels to Towers. How's you drink?"

"Honestly? A girly drink. You want a taste?" Nick and Lauren swapped drinks and took a sip from each.

"You're right, pretty non-descript. Would you like me to get you something else? I am sure Aldo will bring some Sangiovese with the dinner, but I am happy to get you a different drink."

"Do you like yours?" she asked.

"It's ok, but the vermouth is too sweet. Can't taste the gin."

"Those martinis were pretty good last night," suggested Lauren.

Nick pushed a button on the wall. Aldo knocked and opened the slider. "*Signor* Turner?"

"Aldo, the drinks were fine, but both of us would like something stronger. Do you have Junipero gin?"

Aldo shook his head no. "We have Sipsmith, a very good English gin. *Forte.*"

"Strong? Ok, then we'll have two Sipsmith dry martinis, up with blue cheese olives."

"*Si, Signor* Turner, coming right up. The appetizers good, yes?" asked Aldo.

"*Si,*" answered Lauren with a smile.

Aldo smiled his crooked smile and picked up the other drinks, "*Grazie bella signora,*" as he exited, closing the slider again.

"Do we look like weak drink people?" asked Lauren.

"Honestly, I don't know what we look like," said Nick, eliciting another laugh from Lauren.

Aldo returned with the drinks, and they clinked again.

"To proper drinks," they said together.

"Should I be worried about dinner choices?"

"Na, it's all good. My guess is the Alaskan Halibut and either King Salmon or the seafood of the day. We can share whatever they bring."

On cue, Aldo scratched at the door and opened, delivering two bowls of soup. "Clam Chowder and Sweet Corn Soup," he said, picking up the appetizer plates and leaving two soup spoons.

They each took turns trying the soup. Both were exquisite.

"So why should I support you?" probed Lauren.

"Really, you wanna ruin this dinner by having me convince you to vote for me?"

"I think I already know what you stand for. Remember, I was 'that girl' trying to skewer you."

"Good, because for tonight, I want to forget I am a candidate or a Senator and just be a guy, sitting in front of a girl, asking her," he paused for effect, "to wipe the soup from her lip," smiled Nick.

"Oh my God," she said, picking up her napkin to wipe the little bit of soup on her lip.

"And now you have ruined that line forever. Now it will always be about soup," Lauren pouted.

"Sorry," smiled Nick back.

Sure enough, Aldo scrapped at the door and delivered a platter of Alaskan Halibut and a second of King Salmon, along with a plate of linguini and some Swiss chard with butter. He also set a decanter of Sangiovese on the table after pouring two glasses and retreating.

"This looks wonderful," she said, looking over the meals.

"One more toast. Here is to forgetting about our day jobs and being two normal, single adults having a nice dinner," toasted Nick.

They each tried the fish dishes. Both were melt in your mouth tender and tasty combined with the buttery linguine. They even ate most of the Swiss chard. Finishing the wine, while Aldo cleared the plates.

"Coffee and Tiramisu, Apéritif?"

"A couple of decaf coffees and one Tiramisu Aldo, *grazie*."

The coffee came along with the tiramisu and two forks. "Oh God, that is heavenly," moaned Lauren, tasting the dessert.

"It's pretty good, isn't it?" agreed Nick, sipping his coffee as well. "Do you drink port or cognac?"

"You know what, I have never had either."

"If you are game, let me order one of each for you to try."

"Well, I had another date scheduled for later tonight, but this one is going OK, so I guess I can cancel my safety date."

"I canceled mine the minute I saw you in your dress," laughed Nick. "Guess it took you longer to decide I was OK," said Nick, trying to pout like Lauren.

She laughed. "You need to work on your pout." Lauren slid over on the booth until she was leaning forward seductively next to him and leaned up to kiss him, saying, "I didn't even have a safety date lined up."

At the scratching at the door, they broke their kiss and Lauren sat up in the booth next to Nick.

"*Finis?*" asked Aldo.

"Aldo, how about a 40yr old Tawny port and a Delamain cognac, please?"

"Of course."

Aldo brought the port and the cognac.

Nick pushed the table toward the other side of the booth so Lauren could slide over and snuggle under his arm.

"I've had a wonderful night."

"Me too."

"Take a little taste of the cognac. It's potent," warned Nick.

Lauren tried it and wrinkled up her face.

"Wow, that is strong. Guess I won't be smoking cigars and drinking cognac with the boys anytime soon."

"It's not for everyone, that's for sure," said Nick. "Okay. Let's hope you like the port better."

Lauren took the glass of port, taking a small sip and smiling.

"That's much better. Super smooth. I can see why people drink this to relax at the end of a long day."

"Good," said Nick. He put his feet on the other side of the booth and Lauren curled up against him, kicked off her shoes, and put her feet on his outstretched legs.

They sat like this and drank their after-dinner drinks, Nick listening to Lauren breathing and she his heart with her head on his chest.

"Well, kids, I guess it is time to head back to the ranch," said Nick as Lauren groaned a bit, sat up, and found her shoes with her feet.

Nick pressed the button. Aldo promptly returned with the bill.

He thanked Aldo and Guiseppe as he led them out a side exit, once again avoiding traipsing through the main dining area and risking someone seeing them. He helped Lauren once more into the waiting town car outside the restaurant before climbing in the other side.

Nick slid over to Lauren and she once again put her head on his shoulder as they drove from the wharf to the Hotel.

As the elevator in the hotel closed, thankfully with only the two of them. Nick bent down and kissed her passionately, their hands roaming over each other this time. All too quickly, the elevator signaled the arrival at the 5th floor. Nick held Lauren's hand, walking her to her room. As she opened the door, Nick followed her into the room. They resumed kissing.

She helped Nick remove his jacket, undoing the first few buttons on his shirt, pressing her hands to his bare chest while they continued their kissing. Nick pushed the straps off her shoulders and unzipped the back of her dress, sliding it to her feet. She broke their kiss and finished unbuttoning his shirt, pulling it off. He stopped her and held her at arm's length. She stood before him in a strapless black corset, pushing up her breasts and tapering her waist. A black lace garter belt, low on her waist, held her seamed stockings high on her thighs.

"I assume this is 'the rest' you alluded to at dinner?" asked Nick, admiring her flawless figure in the lingerie and pulling her back into an embrace.

"You like? Actually, I can tell you like it," she said, laughing as they pressed against each other, kissing again.

"You were pretty sure of yourself," said Nick.

Lauren laughed, "Actually, I haven't attached garters to stockings since Prom night and my date never even got to see them. And those stockings," said Lauren, shaking her head. "It took me 15 minutes to get the seams straight. Beats me how they did that way back when. Could you help me out of this corset? I'd like to breathe again. It's crushing me."

"No wonder you were walking so gingerly." Nick undid the clasps down the front of the corset, freeing Lauren's waist and breasts.

"Oh god, thank you. When I bought the dress, the saleslady said I needed the corset for it to fit right," Lauren said, pressing her naked breasts to Nick's chest.

"Has anyone ever said you talk too much?" He asked, his lips against hers, easily picking her up in his arms. She laughed as he set her down on the bed.

"Never," said Lauren as further talking became unnecessary.

#

Much later, Lauren rested her head on Nick's chest, running her fingers through his dark chest hair. She traced her fingers along the scar on the left side of his chest.

"Is that it?"

"Hmm," replied Nick. "Which one?"

Lauren traced a finger lightly down the three inches of scar.

"This one."

"Yep, that's it."

"That must've been horrible, waiting for the bomb to blow up while you have a knife sticking out of your chest. Were you scared?"

"Actually, I had to pee. I spent so much time trying not to wet my pants, it made it easier to forget about the knife," he laughed.

"Or the dead terrorist laying on top of you with an activated suicide vest?"

Lauren shivered, and Nick pulled the sheets higher on her shoulder, pulling her closer.

"It all worked out," he said.

"What are the scars on your back?"

"Wild brunette with traces of auburn," said Nick in a serious tone.

Lauren punched him. "I'm serious," she said with a pretty pout, resting her chin on his chest and staring into his eyes.

"Got those by being stupid. Was riding a horse and didn't cinch the saddle tight. It slipped, I lost my balance, and off I went. My foot got stuck in the stirrup. Horse dragged me through the scrub brush and scraped the shit out of my back. I'm lucky my foot came out or he would have taken me through the rocks. That would not have ended well," said Nick, as he laughed.

Lauren found another scar on his side.

"And this one? This is like a scavenger hunt," she said, laughing.

"Iraq. Bullet penetrated my Warthog, got a purple heart for that one. Scavenger hunt, huh?" said Nick, flipping Lauren over on her back on the bed as she giggled.

"My turn, let's see," as Nick's hands roamed over her body. "We have bumps here and here and what about down here…" Lauren moaned and pulled Nick's mouth down to hers, once again ending any further conversation.

# Chapter 74

Lauren woke up and stretched. Something didn't feel right as she looked down and realized she was still wearing her stockings attached to the garter belt. She burrowed into the covers, smiling.

"Nick," she called out. No answer. She got up and headed for the bathroom. Just as she moved, her door slowly opened. She grabbed the sheet and pulled it up in front of her as Nick entered with coffee and muffins. He saw her standing, holding the sheet, and smiled.

"Sorry, was hoping to get back before you woke." He walked to her, setting down the coffee and muffins. Kissing her tenderly, he pulled the sheet out of her hand.

"I do like those stockings," he said, pushing the hair out of her eyes. Lauren smiled back.

"*Ciao Bellissima,*" he said in his best Italian accent as he bent to kiss her smiling face again. She wrapped her arms around his neck and forgot about the coffee and muffins.

#

Lauren stood in the shower. She was confused by her feelings. Not long ago, Nick Turner was public enemy number one. Now she was sick at the prospect of not being around him. This was just not smart. Not smart for her or for Nick. What had she been thinking? She cried as she washed her hair.

#

Nick stood in the shower in his room as it steamed up. What the hell was he thinking? His team was worried about someone trying to kill him on his weekend alone. What would they say if they knew he was romancing 'that girl'?

Much as he loved how he felt around her, he realized this was just not going to work. No matter how much he wanted it to or how much he loved the way she made him feel. The timing made this an impossibility. He felt horrible about what he knew he had to do.

Deep down inside, he knew this was right. His lot was to keep fighting a fight where he could not afford to have a weakness, a fight most likely not to end well. Lauren would be a weakness to exploit and attack. Lexi would not hesitate to sacrifice her if it helped the campaign and hurt Nick. He was dreading breakfast.

This morning had been even better than the night before. Why did this have to happen now? He was tempted to drop out of the race and drag Lauren back to his cabin in the Rockies. Where they could watch the coming Armageddon in safety. He just couldn't justify his being happy while his country expired.

As the water turned cold, Nick stood and lived with the discomfort.

#

Nick knocked on Lauren's door. She opened the door, once again back in her jeans, sweater, and beige suede boots. She gave him a wan smile. He understood immediately. She had come to the same conclusion. Holding her close, he could feel her starting to cry. She pushed away and wiped her eyes.

"I told myself not to cry," she said, stamping a foot.

"I am so sorry, Lauren. This is my fault."

"Your fault? I'm the one who stalked you. I don't know what made me do it, but I figured I'd just get a chance to learn something no one else knew. Then write a piece about you and scoop everyone."

"If it is any consolation, I felt the same way. When I agreed to dinner, I figured we could solidify our truce, and you could get your interview."

"What do we do now?"

"I can tell you I'll probably never be alone again. At least not between now and election day. Given how this turned out," shrugged Nick, "maybe that is a good thing."

"Hey, at least I wasn't a hooker," retorted Lauren sarcastically, turning away.

Nick walked to her, pushed the hair out of her eyes, red and puffy from crying, and stared down into them.

"My only regret is I can't run away with you. I'll cherish this weekend and this time together. Who knows what the future will bring?" pondered Nick, kissing her tenderly, until she pushed him away, tears welling up again.

"Some Mata Hari I am. Nick, I'm so sorry. This hit me hard. I had no idea this could happen. I never would have come to your room if I knew we'd be doing this on Sunday morning. It sucks."

"I agree with that. Breakfast is a no go?" assumed Nick, quietly.

"Right. All I need now is to go out and cry in public? It'll take me half an hour to fix this," she said, holding her hands up to her eyes.

"All right, so we go back to being a candidate and pain in the ass, but beautiful, reporter," smiled Nick.

"You mean misogynist pain in the ass candidate and stunning intrepid reporter seeking to expose the truth," smiled Lauren back through her teary eyes.

"There it is," responded Nick, smiling big at seeing her dimple.

"Best you go now."

Nick paused, his smile slowly fading. He nodded and turned to the door. He did not look back as he closed the door and Lauren threw herself on the bed, crying into her pillow.

#

Nick walked into the conference room his campaign had rented in the St. Francis Hotel for the Western Ideas Summit. His team was just finishing boxing up and labeling stuff to be sent back to Denver. Chuck looked up.

"Ah, the Prodigal Son returns."

Denise, Margie, Chuck, and Earl all looked up to see Nick standing in the doorway.

"Good timing, we just finished packing everything, of course," groused Denise. "Did you even look at your phone yesterday?"

"Hello to you too, Denise. No, I turned it off."

"You were serious about disappearing. Was it restful? You recharged and ready to go?" asked Denise.

Nick sighed.

"Does it matter? Yes, I am ready to get back in the saddle."

"I hope it worked. No more days off from now until the election," announced Denise. "There is just too much to do and way too risky having you walking around alone."

"I get it. Thanks for letting me take this weekend off," replied Nick in a somewhat dejected tone.

"Did something happen?" asked Earl as Chuck and Denise looked at Nick, concerned.

"Nope, just needed to do some soul searching and make sure I am committed to what we need to do. What *I* need to do. I'm in the right place now and ready. Let's get going. Where to next?" asked Nick, getting back to his old self.

Denise and Chuck both looked at each other, knowing something had indeed changed, but not exactly what.

# Chapter 75

Luc opened the door to his apartment with his left hand, carefully. Standing in the hallway were two of Chaumont's bodyguards. Luc holstered the pistol he held in his right. Chaumont pushed forward into Luc's apartment as he closed the door.

Chaumont spied Luc's scotch. "Luc, pour me one, please."

Luc opened his mouth to remind him of his promise.

"Just pour the fucking drink," said Alain, clearly frazzled. He sat in the lone guest chair.

Luc poured a short scotch, picked up his own, and sat in his chair, staring at his brother-in-law.

"Everything at home, OK?"

Alain looked up, savoring the first sip of alcohol in years. "Yes."

"Why the visit?"

"They found the mother and daughter in the Isar river in Munich. I *am* sorry, Luc."

Luc did not react. He stood and paced in the small apartment. Turning back to Chaumont, the hand holding his scotch quivered.

"You had one task," he said in a dangerous tone. "One task. And you failed. *Again.*" Luc was so angry his entire body was shaking.

"Luc, I did what I could. I could not tell the Chancellor of Germany why I was making the request. He assured me they were under surveillance. I couldn't tell him any more details."

"Please tell me you have better news regarding protection for Annie and the nuns."

"Yes, they are under constant protection, with elite units, at your suggestion. Do you have any more information?" Luc shook his head no.

"What?" asked Luc as his president hesitated.

"They were both brutalized, Luc. The killers left a message. In a waterproof capsule was a note. '*Luc, this is your fault. You know what is coming if you persist*'."

Luc took a big gulp of scotch, the flood of memories from a prior warning ignored, and the consequences, coming back.

"I am truly sorry," said Alain in a small voice.

"Your men are ready when you leave?" asked Luc brusquely.

"Yes, we will take him into custody."

"I want to interrogate him."

"The facial recognition came up empty?" asked Alain.

"Yes. Inspector Martin could not get a match. That tells me he had his facial features altered. That means money and organization."

"Luc, I didn't want to tell you, but Maximilian knows you are working on something for me."

"I am not surprised. He has a web of informants. Who told him?"

"Neither Leon nor I know. When Leon pressed him, he would not reveal his source and told him it was me. I can assure you it was not. He is covering for someone. Leon assures me it could not be Inspector Martin. Do you agree?"

"Yes. Her dislike of du Montfort is genuine. Who else knows?"

"I do not know. Could Annie have told the nuns?"

Luc shrugged. "Unlikely."

"Then someone else knows somewhere. Find them." Chaumont threw back the rest of his drink and got up to leave. "Be careful."

Luc watched from the window as Chaumont left his apartment building with his bodyguards. As they moved toward his car, a group of men in black converged on the man standing in the doorway down the street with a camera taking pictures. He did not resist, as Chaumont's men arrested him. Luc could not wait to get his chance to interrogate his shadow.

# Chapter 76

"How'd it go?" asked Chuck as Nick got in the car.

"Better than expected, she's in and she's going to provide warehousing support, food, and other staples to any groups we assemble. I think this is the last piece."

"That's great. Jesus, the hell with being President. If you can really make this work, maybe you should be a community organizer," suggested Chuck. He pulled out of the hotel in Los Angeles, where Nick had finished his meeting with Martha Summers.

"Chuck isn't being president the same as being a community organizer?" asked Nick with a sideways look at Chuck.

He glanced back, his forehead wrinkling up as he contemplated Nick's statement. "You know, I guess I never considered that angle. Maybe if the President were treated more like that and less like a king, things might work out better."

"Exactly. I think we're ready. With Summers on board, that gives us support and potentially lots of job openings. We have Spalding's property and temp units to help with the housing. We've got Jeremy already to help with the logistics and computers. Manetti, the pharma guy, to help with any medical supplies. Coach to help with the people management. Throw in Patterson for financial management and overall organization, and finally Williamson for transportation and I think we have put together a dream team to pull this off," remarked Nick.

Chuck shook his head. "It is a great idea, Nick, but we need to be really careful. Folks are going to call it a sham to help raise your visibility. We have to be really careful about anyone you hire getting any free stuff from the org or people will say it is in-kind donations. Jenny is looking into all the legal stuff."

"I don't want it bogged down in minutiae. If we can't make it work to have them help our campaign, nix that, it is more important Blue Morpho succeeds."

"Got it, but man, you should get a Nobel prize for pulling this together," said Chuck.

"I haven't done anything yet. Who do you think I am? The last community organizer candidate?" said Nick with a smile. "Let's wait for the results before we declare victory. Besides, I would refuse it on principle alone."

"Ya? The prize also has like a million and a half dollars."

"Really? I didn't know they came with money?" mused Nick, looking at his phone while Chuck drove.

"You're pretty excited about this, aren't you?" grinned Chuck.

"You weren't with us when we walked through that tent city. At first, I felt sorry for them, lost humanity. Then I got angry. I visited other urban cities and even walked around DC. There is homelessness and hopelessness all around these super affluent neighborhoods. Here we are, the greatest and richest country in the world, and how do we help? We buy them more fucking tents," said Nick with clear disgust in his tone.

"When I talked to people like Trapper and others in all these cities, the story is the same. These were just people who had bad luck. They will work; they want to contribute, and they are not looking to be wards of the state forever. When Trapper told me about the vicious cycle of trying to find a job but being unable to get to the interview, or of the interviewer's inability to see beyond the fact they were homeless, it hit me. All they needed was a matchmaker. They are not without skills. They are not worthless, which is what the media implies. Capitalism can be tough, no doubt, but nothing says it has to keep people down. I want to lend a hand and give them a chance to get back in the game," said Nick.

"It's a wonderful solution to the problem. No one can argue politics on this one," replied Chuck.

Nick laughed, "Now who is being Pollyanna? This is all about politics and everyone will make it that way. They'll ignore the fact most of the funders are former and current Party mega donors and focus on me being the organizer. According to them is all about publicity. They'll scrutinize our efforts, highlighting any setback and minimizing any improvement. Count on it."

"You're forgetting one key item. Most of the tents are gone from Venice Beach already. When the tents start disappearing from the other beaches of LA and the streets of San Francisco, it is going to be because of you. Not because of Lexi or the Governor of California or the mayors of San Fran or LA. All Party by the way. And the Opposition has been no better at solving this. This is also a left hook to all the policies Lexi is proposing. They'll try to say it was their policies, but the reality is it'll be because of Blue Morpho, not government help. You are offering hope and purpose. They are offering handouts and dependency."

"Oooh, that last bit is great. You mind if I steal it for my speech?" asked Nick, looking at Chuck while scribbling in his notebook.

"Be my guest. You are a strange politician. You won't let me write speeches for you, and you won't use a teleprompter."

"One less thing to break. Besides, I am doing alright, aren't I?"

"Better than OK. You are authentic. People get it and love it," agreed Chuck. "Jenny should be ready to review the launch plans."

"Ok, here we go."

# Chapter 77

"Are we ready?" asked Nick.

"I think so," said Jenny. She handed Nick a t-shirt with the image of a giant blue butterfly on the front.

"This is really cool," admired Nick, smiling while holding up the t-shirt. On the back it read 'The Blue Morpho Redemption Project. Where everyone has value and no one is a statistic', with an image of the Blue Morpho butterfly, wings spread flying.

Jenny smiled. "We are handing them out to everyone."

"Screw that," said Nick, taking off his sport coat and pulling the t-shirt on over his dress shirt before putting his jacket back on. "How do I look?"

"Great," replied Jenny, laughing and smiling at her boss.

"Back to my original question."

"All the legal stuff is long since completed. We have officially created the non-profit org, Blue Morpho Redemption 'for the purpose of helping the less fortunate find work and purpose. To get off the streets and into meaningful work and once again become self-sufficient'. It is front and center on the organization's website."

"I like it. Funding in place?"

"It's too bad you can't get that kind of money in your campaign," said Jenny. "We have close to four billion dollars pledged from your billionaires to start, including the additional two every year from Spalding. We are filming the ad campaigns with Coach Sampson. We still need to get you in the launch one with him. How did you ever convince him to join this effort? After he retired from coaching the Raiders, he did some motivational speaking and then just disappeared," asked Jenny.

"I know a guy who played for him and asked him to make a call. We had a conversation; I explained the plan, and he agreed to come on board. He said he was bored anyway," deadpanned Nick.

"Well, he won't be bored from now on. However it happened, it is great. Some advisors donated property in various locations: LA, San Fran, Seattle, Chicago, Atlanta, Austin, Denver, DC. We are working on transferring all of it to Blue Morpho and then we will use those as the base camps for the first groups from each city to move into."

"We also already have several businesses lined up to do interviews. Volunteer clinics in each of the cities to do medical exams and help anyone with issues. With Summers now on board, we can work with her volunteers to stock the properties. She's also pledged to interview anyone interested in working in any of her stores near the Blue Morpho villages. Williamson is pledging to provide transportation to run shuttles back and forth from the villages to Summer's stores."

Nick nodded as Jenny continued.

"Next, we'll work with Trapper. Get him to be the spokesperson to enter each tent city. He's had success in Venice and Huntington Beach so far. He can find the leaders and work with them to convince them it is not a trick. Then to get them to help build a list of skills for each person so they can be matched to the proper job opportunities," Jenny paused.

"You alright Jenny?" asked Nick, seeing Jenny was on the verge of tears.

"No," she said, reaching for her purse. "Oh crap, I'm sorry Nick, but this is just so unbelievable. What you're doing in the middle of a presidential campaign? Taking the time and effort to build this out. To get others on your team and to pull all this together in a couple of months. It is incredible," she said through sniffles.

"OK," said Nick slowly. "What's really getting to you?"

She burst into tears. Nick got up and went to her as she stood. He gave her a hug. Once she stopped sobbing, she dabbed her eyes and her nose. "Shit," she said as she sat back down. Nick handed her a glass of water.

"Spill," ordered Nick.

"Oh Nick, I wish this could have happened years ago. I had an older brother who lost everything in some shady business dealings his partners had tried. He lost his wife and family and his house. He got addicted to heroin. We tried to help, for years, but he eventually ended up homeless on the streets of LA. They found him one night under a bypass. He'd overdosed and his 'friends' had stripped his body of everything."

"To end in a state like that was just criminal. Kurt had skills; he had integrity and so much to give, but society chewed him up and spit him out. No one stopped to help. He was just like a wreck on the road. People driving by and gawking, but no one thinking *they* could help. What you are doing is going to make such a difference. I can't tell you how proud I am. How proud all of us are to be working with you," said Jenny, pulling herself back together. "Sorry, sorry," she said.

"Jenny, you know how I feel about apologies."

Jenny laughed through her tears. "Right, Gibb's rules again."

"Number six. OK, let's go solve the world's problems, starting with our homeless," stated Nick.

They headed out to the waiting press conference.

# **Chapter 78**

"Do you know America gives more than $500 billion a year in charitable donations? Over 75% of that comes from individuals. Think about that, $375 billion, about $1000 per citizen each year. That is a lot of compassion for your fellow humans."

"Americans are far and away the most generous of anyone on the planet. Today, we are gathered to bring together this same compassion and caring, the same generosity, to ensure our homeless benefit as well," announced Nick, standing at a podium with a group of finished and under construction buildings behind him.

"Today we announce the Blue Morpho Redemption Project, BMRP or simply Blue Morpho. The charter is to provide those less fortunate not with charity, but a path, through work, to get back on their feet. Back to becoming contributing members of society. People who will one day be among those who'll provide their own help to those less fortunate."

"We chose the Blue Morpho butterfly as the name and symbol of our organization. To the Greeks, the Blue Morpho was a symbol of good luck. Delivering news of the future, of one's destiny. Our Blue Morpho is all about helping people shape their futures and achieve their destinies."

"Today, we have many who are homeless, leading lives of quiet desperation. Forgotten by society. They camp out in tents and under overpasses. Sleep in doorways and struggle for food, medicine, warmth, and companionship. We pass them every day on our morning commute. The unpersons. Well, guess what? But for the grace of God, you could easily be in their place. Many are veterans, people who put their lives in danger so we can order our lattes and our drive-thru sandwiches. They gave their livelihood so we could enjoy ours. Do we not owe them help in return?" Nick paused, looking out over several hundred invited guests and media.

"Indeed, we do. I have talked to some of these folks on Venice Beach in California, in Seattle, Denver, DC, New York, Chicago and other places. The story is the same. Whether laid low by injury or mental health. By lack of access to medical care or simply bad luck in business, many are just unlucky. They can contribute to society. For most, they are no less talented or willing than you or me. For these, it is not only our civic duty, it is our moral duty to ensure we do all we can to help those in need to get the care they need. The opportunity to once again practice self-reliance. Most of all, to reacquire the dignity of what it means to be a contributing member of society." There was polite applause at the end of this statement as Nick paused.

"I am pleased to announce we have assembled a group of civic-minded citizens from all walks of life, who have come together to form this organization. We have the funds and the knowhow to make this a success. To help those willing to be helped, and to ensure those unable to, get the help they need to heal. This is not charity. We are not simply throwing money at the problem. To make our own consciences feel better. No, we are doing. *Doing* is what is most important. As someone once said, you give someone a fish, they eat well for a meal. If you instead teach them how to fish, you have enabled them to eat for life."

"Blue Morpho intends to do just that. We intend to help people up. To provide them with housing and work. A temporary stop on the road to recovery and self-reliance. We are not building permanent housing, nor are our benefits given without stipulation. As I said earlier, we are here to help those who *want* to help themselves. Mostly we are here to get people off the addiction to government assistance and back onto their own feet. Toward a future with prospects and a path to a life of freedom. Freedom to choose their own path without BMRP or the state, local, or federal government involved in telling them how to lead their life." There were more cheers at this statement as Nick's followers in the crowd agreed with his words.

"Today we have gathered here, where one of our first Blue Morpho Villages is under construction. This land was donated. Just as it was in other cities where we're building these villages. Oakland, Portland, Seattle, Chicago, Austin, Houston, New Orleans, and others all have activities similar to what you see behind me. Within this village are temporary housing, medical facilities, schools, a general store, and other necessities, all operated by the community with oversight from volunteers and paid staffers."

"Any who move into the housing understand it is for short term. They pay minimal rent and sign contracts to keep up the grounds and the inside of their house. They pledge to stay off drugs and to meet voluntary standards. In return, they are getting housing, access to subsidized food and clothing. They're being offered access to classes to help them identify their skills, their goals and to match them with perspective employers both locally and around the country." Nick could see many in the audience digesting his words. Journalists were writing and others were now paying attention, no longer looking at phones.

"What I discovered talking with these folks is there is an untapped wealth of knowledge and skill, totally underutilized. What I also discovered was one of the biggest hurdles to getting out of the homeless life was lack of access to transportation. And computers and other tools necessary to get access to the job openings where their skills could be used. We chartered BMRP to provide that helping hand. To match the skills of those in our program with companies in need of their skills. To graduate them from these villages to good-paying jobs. Get them back out on their own as soon as possible. We're already seeing success with our first members. In fact, many of them would be here today, except they are now already at their new jobs," said Nick as the assembled crowd clapped.

"This *can* work. No one involved in this program wants anything from it, other than the success of its members. The land is donated. Same with the construction materials and temporary housing. Much of the food and medical care in each village is stocked through direct donations. We have paid medical personnel in each village. We have also arranged with local hospitals to fund additional beds to treat people in need of mental health evaluation and care. The matchmaking services, the computers and networks, the staff to run these and build the databases of employers and to arrange the interviews and transportation to these interviews are all funded by donations. It is working," Nick paused.

"The beauty of all of this is our footprint, as much as possible, is both green and carbon neutral. Using sustainable building methods and energy as much as possible. Our entire endeavor is self-funded. We have neither asked for, nor would we, accept a single dollar of federal, state or local assistance for our program. Arguably, the results of our efforts will far exceed those of traditional federal programs. Simply throwing money at the symptoms without addressing the root causes of homelessness. The hope is over time, our efforts will allow state and local governments to reallocate funding for homeless symptom management to other worthwhile causes."

"The board of directors are well-known and successful people who, while not trying to hide their involvement, prefer to remain behind the scenes of the activities. However, I would like to introduce two people who have been and will continue to ensure the program is successful. In case you didn't know, I'm running for President and my involvement with BMRP ceases as of right now given my previous engagement," said Nick to laughter from the crowd.

First, I would like to introduce former Army Medic, Sergeant Ryan Erikson. He is also known as Trapper to his former co-habitants at the now nearly empty Venice Beach homeless encampment.

Trapper stood up and walked to Nick, shaking his hand and then giving him a hug before going to the podium. He was now clean shaven and did not resemble the homeless man Nick had met on Venice beach just a few months ago.

"Thank you. I will keep this brief. Public speaking is not my thing. When Nick came down to Venice Beach, I was using my Army medical training to help my fellow homeless camped out there. Nick was the first politician who truly came to see the issues firsthand. He wasn't looking for a photo op or to make any promises. No cameras, no reporters, and no security. He wanted to understand our problem and our reasons for being there. He didn't tell me to get a job or anything like we had heard from so many others. Nor did he promise to give us funding, more toilets, tents, free needles or any of the other government programs just masking the genuine problems we faced."

"He listened. And he asked a lot of questions. Trying to understand. What he heard was most of us were the victims of circumstances beyond our control. What he heard was we were lost and didn't know how to find our way back to normal. He realized the 'help'," said Trapper, raising his hands in air quotes, "was in fact no help at all, but a way to ensure the status quo. Even if they meant well, there was no path to resolution. During this conversation, Nick and I talked about the skills we possessed on that beach. I told him of folks who got interviews but couldn't get to them. Or if they did, the clothes and appearance would immediately make a poor impression. It was a vicious cycle. He heard how it depressed those who wanted to break out and made them unable or unwilling to try any more for fear of continued rejection and, worse, pity from those outside the camp."

"It was Nick who came up with the idea for matching the skills to the jobs. For setting up the BMRP villages and getting the funding and buy in from all these people to enable this to be a reality. It was Nick who pulled it all together, who made it possible for us to get cleaned up, to get medical care, to get roofs over our heads, to start once again working for ourselves. We left the beach and built the village behind you. Many are here today, working in the village or in jobs nearby, contributing to the community. Many have moved on, as Nick said, having found jobs in other cities, where these jobs enabled them to move out of this village and into mainstream society once again. All because of this program. Because of Nick and his faith in all of us. This has given us back our self-esteem and our confidence, making us once again believe we can contribute as members of society."

"Personally, it has given me a purpose. Once I came back from Afghanistan, I lost my way. Lost my family and my job and came to Venice because, frankly, I didn't give a shit anymore. What I had seen in the war ate at me every day. The carnage, the utter disregard for life. Then I came back and found a country obsessed with lattes and TV shows, celebrity idiots and athletes arguing over frivolous things while others half a world away wondered if they would survive the night. I was angry, and I took it out on my family. They couldn't understand why I couldn't just fit back into this society."

"Now I know why. I didn't have the purpose here I had in the army. I had my buddies to protect and help. Here, I had responsibility, but no real reason I was doing *anything*. I found that purpose on the beach when a senator and presidential candidate came by and stopped long enough to listen to my problem and those around me. Then instead of walking away or promising to help, he did something."

Trapper paused for a second before continuing.

"He has done more to solve homelessness than our state and federal governments have ever done. He is not treating the symptom, ensuring a comfortable existence with this cancer. No, he is cutting it out and working to make sure we are cancer free. For this, I cannot say enough how happy I am that day happened. I have even seen my daughter again, something I never thought would happen. Thank you, Nick," said Trapper, breaking down and putting his hand in front of his face. Nick got up and embraced him as the crowd cheered. Trapper went back to take his seat, smiling through his tears.

Nick, too, had blurry eyes as he stepped to the microphone once more. "Thank you, Trapper. Folks, Ryan is a real-life example of the goodness to be found in every homeless encampment. We are the richest, most powerful, and most compassionate country on the planet. There is no reason we cannot help everyone who wants to be helped. I spoke of two people. The second person I would like to introduce really needs no introduction."

"Through much cajoling and arm twisting, I have convinced him he is the right person to lead the Blue Morpho Redemption Project and to ensure our vision is a reality across this great nation. Without further comment, I would like to introduce the former Super Bowl Champion coach of the then Oakland Raiders, Coach Alfred Sampson."

A large and rotund older black man with mostly gray hair stood up and gave Nick a big bear hug before approaching the podium to loud and lengthy applause. He held up his hands.

"First, you should applaud Nick and all the donors who have supported and made these villages and the entire program a reality," said Coach, as the crowd responded accordingly.

"I want to follow on what Ryan had to say. It is both an honor and a challenge to accept this role in leading BMRP. We have a mighty task ahead of us. Not unlike turning a bunch of misfit underachievers into a super bowl winning team. I accept the challenge. I will make it my life's goal to continue this effort, to assist all who will put in the work and the effort to build our winning team. Finally, I pledge to help every member of my team achieve all they can. To help them return to society in a meaningful and fulfilling way."

He paused for a moment. "I am a private person. When I retired from coaching, I wanted to disappear. I did a pretty good job of it. One thing you may not know is how this organization and its goals have touched me personally. I had a son, Dion. He got involved in drugs, ended up homeless and died on the street from an overdose. I know both the anguish and the pain of watching someone go through this. But also know how important it is to give them a path back to dignity and humanity and to not assume they are irredeemable."

"I ignored my son and wrote him off after many attempts at rehab and the best therapy money could buy. He continued to relapse and fail. To where I could do no more for him. It is only now, after he has been gone for so long," he said, pausing, emotional. "As I listened to Ryan, and then to Nick. When he asked me to join and to literally hundreds of others in our program, that I now know what I did not then." Coach wiped his own eyes again.

"I did not understand how he could keep relapsing. He lacked nothing. At least from my point of view. What he lacked was purpose. He had no reason to continue. He had no mission, no path to follow other than the one of least resistance. Into drug induced oblivion and a life of petty theft on the street. I know now, my answer should have been to help him find that purpose, but I too was blind to this need."

"No longer," said Coach with conviction, his hand smacking the podium audibly. "It is *my* mission, *my* path, to see that everyone has a purpose. To help them discover it and to ensure, again, no one who has the will to live, the will to overcome their demons, is ever left to fight them alone. Never without help, guidance, and support available to help them return to normalcy. Nick, board members and every individual who has or will donate. Please know, I will give this my all. Just as I did to get our Super Bowl championship. We will persevere and overcome adversity and we will do it together. Thank You." The crowd stood and clapped as Coach finished his impassioned speech.

Coach turned and walked to Nick, who shook his hand and hugged him again. Nick returned to the podium once more.

"I now invite you to take a tour of the Blue Morpho village behind us. We will meet at the picnic area outside the general store where we have some food and drinks available, and I'll take a few questions. Thank you all for coming out."

The group of invitees and press made their way from the stage down the main street of the Pasadena Blue Morpho Village and folks looked into one of the newly finished houses and several of the temporary units Everett Spalding had donated. They were spartan, but a far cry from sleeping in a tent on the beach. They also looked at several construction sites where other buildings were being worked on, including one for non-denominational church services. Finally, they all sat on various picnic benches under a large outdoor area covered with a canopy. Once there, Nick sat on a stool and iced tea in hand, ready to answer questions from the press.

"Senator, first I commend you for the idea of what you have described. However, there are over 750,000 homeless according to the latest statistics from the White House. That is the equivalent of a city roughly the size of Seattle or San Francisco. Looking around at this village, I don't see this having much of an impact, frankly," said Meghan from *Radio Broadcast Systems*, RBS, one of the oldest of the major TV networks.

"Meghan, thank you for the question. First, I agree it is a big problem to tackle. Of those 750,000, more than half are in California. New York City has 20%. It is not as simple as just building Blue Morpho villages. We are not claiming to solve it, but to offer alternatives and ways for those inclined to have an opportunity. With what we have underway and planned so far, we expect space for 10,000 around the country to be in place in the next 4-6 weeks. The goal is to start graduating people out of the communities and into meaningful work to allow them to rent their own apartments in the communities where they work. Every project starts with one. New York is tough to crack, for instance." Nick sipped from his tea while folks finished scribbling.

"We are fighting state regulations and frankly we are fighting a general malaise of folks who are so beaten down, the idea of leaving the homelessness in their urban setting to go to New Jersey or off Manhattan is not an easy sell. But, we will continue in our efforts, and we'll grow as demand for our services grows. Hopefully, the number will decline as our capacity expands and we'll have a lasting impact," said Nick, pointing to another reporter from AP.

"Senator, there has been speculation this is all about raising your profile in an election year since you are polling so low?"

"Well, it is true I am polling low," laughed Nick. "But I would answer with 'who cares'? This is much bigger than any presidential election. These are people's lives. Trust me, my staff, some of whom are here today, would be the first to agree with you. Why am I spending my precious campaign time building an anti-homeless program?"

"I think the answer to that is exactly what we saw from Ryan and Coach today. This problem and this solution are more worthy of my time and frankly *your* time, than any presidential campaign. This will have a long-lasting impact well beyond the current election cycle," predicted Nick. He scanned the crowd, seeing a beautiful smiling face.

"Miss Bergamo?"

"Thank you, Senator. If I may, as you have said, there are many wealthy businessmen and women on the board of governors and who have donated large sums, in both cash and land, supplies, etc. as your own data sheet on the project explains," said Lauren holding up the press packet. "For the record, how would you explain how this can be done with none of them making a profit?"

Nick paused for a second, choosing his words, not wanting to go easy on Lauren for fear others would wonder why they were being nice to each other. "Depends on your definition of profit. I fully expect some of these folks to profit from our efforts. I expect to profit from this as well," said

Nick, pausing for effect as everyone sat up straighter, figuring Lauren had backed him into a corner.

"It is my hope, as one of the largest employers in the country, Mrs. Summers' stores will end up hiring many of these fine individuals. The same with several others. My campaign is planning on hiring these folks to work on my campaigns as *paid* staffers. I feel people who have lived as they have. Who have seen the horrors some of them have seen in life. They know and appreciate what life and this country offer to those willing to work to earn a living. I would think the other campaigns would benefit from hiring folks like this as well."

"These are exactly the kinds of people I want working for me and I assume others would want them too. These are the people for whom I am running to be their president. The working man and woman. So, in terms of profit for individuals, I can assure you, Ms. Bergamo, none of the board members is taking a salary or expects any form of recompense. In fact, Coach has refused any salary as well, but we will cover his operating expenses. Many non-profits pay their leaders handsomely, so Coach is certainly entitled to it, just as a CEO of a corporation."

"In fact, we would be happy to show our books. They are on our website. You can see what they donated. We are not trying to hide assets or put any into dummy corporations or offshore accounts. Plus, none of the donated goods are being written off by their donors, though they may legally do so. Would that all organizations have this same level of transparency?" Lauren was looking down, making notes.

"If I may, please make sure you ask the same of the World Harmony Society or ARL. Or perhaps some of the ex-presidential foundations claiming to do so much good. It only seems fair they too should be subject to the same level of scrutiny," finished Nick. Lauren kept her head down. She did not want to look up and have anyone see her smiling when she should be scowling.

"I think that about does it. I thank you for your time," said Nick as the assembled folks clapped. He stayed talking to folks, shaking hands and taking pictures with the attendees.

As he and Earl, Chuck, Denise, Margie, Jenny, and Greg piled into the suburban for the trip back to LA, he asked them what they thought.

"Well, I think you got one bit right. How crazy your staff think you are spending so much time on this instead of raising money or talking to folks," carped Denise.

"Come on Denise, surely you can see this trumps what we can do in the campaign. If we do this right, it will live well beyond this election and many others," stated Nick.

"True, but that is not my job. Are you done with this now? Can we get back to winning an election?"

"Aye, aye Captain," saluted Nick from the front seat.

"We got some great footage today," said Greg.

"We can also use a lot of the sound bites, so we have plenty we can repurpose into stuff for Hibi and the website," said Margie.

"Good, be careful. This was not a campaign event, so I don't want to lay it on too thick about using it for sympathy votes or anything," said Nick.

"Nick, we just wasted a whole day and now some of the best feel good footage we have, and you want to limit exposure too?" fumed Denise.

"Sorry, you said it yourself. This is separate."

"Changing subjects," interjected Earl, playing peacemaker as he drove. "Did you see them?"

"See who?" said Chuck and Denise at the same time.

"The FBI and probably some of Lexi's goons, as well. They were in the back, watching and listening," said Earl.

"Yeah, I noticed. Not too surprised. I hope they leave the donors out of this. That's why I answered Bergamo the way I did and threw in the bit about the books and having her ask some of those other groups with convoluted and hidden funding the same questions. If they come after us, we can point to doing the same for others," said Nick.

"What was up with that? You and Bergamo kiss and make up?" asked Denise, as Nick choked on his water in the front seat. Chuck leaned over and started thumping him on the back.

"Geez, I'm OK. Stop pummeling me," complained Nick finally. "What do you mean? I thought I gave her what for. You told me to be nicer. I thought I was pretty good with all of them today."

"I didn't expect you to actually do it," said Denise in a sarcastic tone.

"OK, next time I will rip their heads off again," smiled Nick, as Denise looked at him.

# Chapter 79

Maksim Pavlovich finished watching the press conference on the holographic screen projected in front of his desk. He pressed a button on his desk. His aide, Petr Saickow, entered through a side door. He approached and stood in front of the desk, to the side of the projected screen.

"Sir?"

"Petr, I want you to research all you can on this organization Turner is starting. I want to know who the donors are, who the employees are and where they are building their 'villages'. If they are being as transparent as Turner claims, this should be a simple task. I want you to contact our assets in all these states. Any permits they apply for, I want them delayed. If they can't be stopped, slow them down."

"Yes, sir."

"I want protesters in front of the major donor's stores or places of business. How they are scamming the homeless or exploiting them for slave wages. Something like that. This needs to be discredited. I want articles in our newspapers highlighting how this is a scam by Turner to curry favor and get more attention for his nascent campaign. I want the same on our TV stations." Petr nodded in response, taking notes.

"See if we can find some of the homeless in these camps who are unbalanced and get them drugs or encourage them to rape or steal or set fire to a building and claim mental imbalance in defense. We must ensure this is not a success. We cannot have Turner solve a problem, so many of our own organizations have ensured stays relevant."

"Sir, should we be putting pressure on the Governors of these states where the homeless encampments are being emptied into these villages?"

"Petr, most of them are so pathetic. If they were to attack Turner, he would use it to his advantage. We will stick to media attacks on Turner and attack the weaker allies, the donors and the homeless themselves. This should be enough to stop this from gaining traction. Find the employers who hire them. Anonymously contact them with allegations of rape or child abuse, or something similar in their new hires backgrounds. Get them back on the street and disillusioned with Turner. Then interview the employer saying they trusted Turner's org to provide them with honest citizens. How they were just trying to help, and this is what they got."

"Of course, sir, this should be easy enough to accomplish. American corporations appear to be easily cowed into submission at the slightest hint of scandal."

Pavlovich nodded. "If that doesn't work, we will escalate to more drastic measures."

"Understood sir. Is it not strange that he is spending his time on this instead of on his campaign? Is he setting this up, so he has something to do when he drops out?" asked Petr.

"Petr, our friend Mr. Turner, is becoming a worthy adversary. He understands human nature and understands what works with the common working man. He utterly rejects the traditional path of promises and groveling. This makes him dangerous because he is righteous. He is doing nothing for himself."

"Sir, so this is not an act to win votes."

"Oh no Petr, spend more time studying America. It is narcissistic and indolent. Its people are spoiled, fat and lazy. They have become soft, like Rome, before the barbarians sacked it. They cannot be roused to save themselves from themselves. Or at least I felt that was true. We have worked long and hard to ensure America became weak and soft. We needed them to be unable to resist when we implement our globalization plans with Ms. Smythe-Thomas at the helm."

"Turner's arrival was unexpected. His words are making people think. Thankfully, he is not getting enough traction to upset our plans, but we need to make sure he is in no position to rouse resistance when we do."

"We will solve the homeless problem once we have power. They do not need compassion. They are simply parasites on the body. Once we are able, we will eradicate them, like the infection they are. They do not need salvation, just resolution. That is all Petr. Let me know your progress in two days."

Petr gave a slight bow, turned, and left. Once he was gone, Pavlovich pressed another button, causing various security measures to engage turning his office into a secure communications center. He tapped on a keyboard. His holographic screen changed into a visual representation of a Chinese Dragon.

Soon, a mechanical voice responded.

"Hello," came an answer from the holographic Dragon.

"What is he up to?" asked Pavlovich, his own voice also masked by technology. His voice was being broadcast from a Chinese Rat hologram displayed on the other end of the conversation.

"Turner? Beats me. He is wasting his precious time building a giant homeless shelter instead of building up support for his campaign," replied Dragon.

"I disagree. You must be careful. This can gather momentum,"

"We have been too successful ensuring our homeless problem is not solved easily. What he is proposing is only going to scratch the surface. As fast as he helps a few, there will be more to replace them as we continue to cancel any who dare stand against our progressive policies. Do not worry," paused Dragon.

"In fact, per his own statement, there are 750,000 homeless Americans. What he did not say is we have an endless supply of equally indigent and homeless illegals. Millions, in fact, who continue to strain the social services of all these states and their programs. Even were he to get all 750,000 into jobs, we have tens of millions ready to replace them. This problem will not disappear or be solved by Turner," he finished with conviction.

"You, of course, are closer, but the optics are good, and he is appealing to the poorer working classes. All revolutions start by uniting these people against the rulers. Trust me," answered Pavlovich skeptically.

"We will keep an eye on it. If it gets traction, we will throw obstacles in its path. He is getting two minutes on the networks and it is not even for his campaign. Most of it is for the football coach coming out of retirement.

And the story about his son. That's what people will remember. Trust *me*," said Dragon.

"I will monitor, too. It is too important. I am tired of waiting for success. This is our time, and nothing will stop us, including Turner," said Rat.

"Agreed, but he continues to poll in the very low single digits. His fund raising is nowhere near where it needs to be and he is irrelevant, speaking at VFWs and State Fairs. He has almost zero time on the networks and cable. We are not making the same mistake we made before. Without media exposure, his message is simply not getting to enough people to make a difference. The media has orders to starve him of coverage. He is simply out of sight," finished Dragon.

"Let's keep it that way," finished Pavlovich, ending the call.

# Chapter 80

Lexi looked up in her office in the Eisenhower Executive Office Building across from the West Wing of the White House. She had a ceremonial office in the West Wing and another in the Capitol when the Senate was in session. But she preferred to use her actual office in the Eisenhower building.

"What are your agents saying about this butterfly thing Turner is doing?" asked Lexi.

"Lexi, officially, my agency does nothing domestically. You know this," said CIA Director Rhett Chadwick.

"Uh, huh? And unofficially?"

"Well, as you know, since Claude passed, the FBI is officially leaderless. Karen is the acting director, but there is some confusion about existing operations since Claude's death. My aides are telling me Turner's speeches are getting more and more provocative and seditious. His crowds are also getting more enthusiastic, but still no reports of any widespread violence. At least not at rallies where he is speaking. He is successful at keeping his followers non-violent, but the protesters are still showing up and agitating. No more incidents like South Dakota, yet," said Rhett.

"But he is still under 4% in the polls. Some of them only show 2%. The only place he is drawing sizeable crowds is a couple of state fairs, and those people are there to see the bands. He is not the one drawing the crowds."

Rhett simply shrugged. As he was getting ready to respond, someone knocked at the door.

"Enter," said Lexi loudly.

Karen Coleman and Mel Arenson walked into the office and took two seats.

"Karen, how are you holding up?" asked Lexi.

"I'm doing fine, still trying to get over the idea Claude is gone. Thank you for asking and thank you for the wonderful eulogy you gave at his funeral."

"The least I could do. Claude was a friend too."

Karen nodded.

"We were discussing our friend Mr. Turner and his new crusade to solve the homeless problems of America," said Lexi, smiling while shaking her head. "You have agents shadowing his speeches?"

Karen seemed a bit startled. These were now *her* agents as the acting director.

"We have. He is pretty provocative, and his message resonates with his crowds. The crowds are still relatively small. He is not advocating any violence, mostly he is telling people to vote and to think for themselves. He paints a bleak picture of progressive policies and life under your future administration," smiled Karen.

"I'm a big girl. I can take it. He needs to be careful, because when I win, he had better be prepared to shut his mouth. There will be a new sheriff in town and I won't have to put up with him preaching sedition. I am sure we can bring charges against him, right?" she finished looking at her two senior intelligence agency directors. They dutifully smiled and nodded.

"Mel, I'll ask you what I asked Rhett. Is this butterfly thing just a photo op?" asked Lexi.

"I believe he really thinks he can make a difference. He has certainly lined up a ton of resources and donations of property to make it a reality. I'm not sure how he convinces these Party mega donors to give all this money for this cause, but doesn't get any donations to his own presidential campaign? Very strange."

"Is there anything we can do to punish these folks for funding this effort? Karen?"

"We can look into it, but it all seems to be on the up and up from our perspective. He posted their books and is being transparent. I'd suggest Javier look into it with Justice, or some of the state AGs."

Mel shrugged. "Or the IRS? If they want to waste their money trying to solve an unsolvable problem, why should we care? If Turner wants to waste his campaign time trying to set up non-profits to fight homelessness? It tells me he's resigned, that he'll never get out of the low single digits. The story on the networks is about Coach Sampson coming out of retirement. This is not worth our time."

"Alright. Karen, watch it. And keep monitoring his speeches. If he advocates for violence, I want his ass in jail."

"Lexi, I think that is an overreaction and something the media would have to cover. Plus, he would get his chance to denounce his treatment in front of a courthouse. Let's keep ignoring him. He can pick on Progressives all day long, but in the end, his speeches have very little substance. He is not offering any solutions or how he is going to help solve any problems. More and more, he sounds like an Opposition candidate. He gets up there, says progressives suck, and you are the devil incarnate. People like it when they hear it, but at the end of the talk, they walk away realizing he is not promising to help them do anything to solve any problems. It just won't hunt," cautioned Mel.

"Devil incarnate, huh?" smiled Lexi.

"You should take it as a compliment. He's lecturing all his crowds, like a college professor, trying to educate them on why your policies are bad. Most of these folks have never been to college and don't need a candidate lecturing them. Stay focused and then we will crush whomever the Opposition put up as the sacrificial lamb."

"OK, I won't worry about Turner. Rhett, you are pretty quiet. Any update on the Christmas tragedies? Things seem to be moving so slowly," observed Lexi.

"We are helping Interpol as much as possible. They're a bit baffled. There is no connection between any of the terrorists. It's not religious fanatics. They can't find any common threads. Plus, no one is taking credit. We are woefully short on clues."

"That's unfortunate. It would be nice to give people closure on how and why this happened and who was responsible," sighed Lexi.

"I agree. Interpol has not given up, but most of the resources have moved on to other issues. Human trafficking, cyber threats, other known terrorist organizations and various immigration issues in the European countries," explained Rhett.

"Speaking of which, how is France's new president doing?"

"They elected Chaumont after Christmas. He put his commission together to figure out how to grant full citizenship to the Muslim immigrants in the *banlieues*. The result is now strikes and riots of the working-class French who stand to lose the most. They face competition for jobs and wage pressures if they grant the immigrants full citizenship. He can't win. He has his hands full," admitted Rhett.

"Well, as always, we are here to help. Mel, let's make sure we get an update from Susanna at the next cabinet meeting." Mel nodded, making some notes.

"Alright folks, I need to head out. Where am I headed, Mel?"

"Fund raiser in Manhattan."

"Ha. Right. How much?"

"$50,000 a plate. 200 attendees."

"How many of these has Turner managed to do?"

Mel laughed. "None. Probably because he knows no one wants to pay $1000, let alone $10000, to be lectured to by a college professor."

"Good point," said Lexi, laughing as well.

# Chapter 81

"That settles it. The Opposition does not have a nominee for the first time since 1976. The disunity then allowed an unknown Governor, Jimmy Carter, to take advantage of the divided Opposition party. This time around, Lexi Smythe-Thomas is the prohibitive favorite and has already clinched the Party nomination after stiff competition from Senator Klausen," said Adam Mullen, the stately veteran newscaster leading the EXN prime time news program.

On the screen, a graph showed the four primary candidates in the Republican race. "As we can see from the graph, Governor Blackbird has a good sized lead, but nowhere near the number necessary to clinch the nomination. In second place is Senator Garcia of Texas and then Governor Kacey Carson of South Carolina and Governor Wilson of Florida in third and fourth, respectively."

"It seems none of them could gain a plurality of support, and each approached their campaign differently. We now bring in EXN contributor Rory Kane, former presidential chief of staff and a founder of the Opposition Center PAC. Rory, what happened?" asked Adam.

"Adam, none of them would compromise on any of the issues. They all thought they were representing a majority of the Opposition voters. Take Garcia, for instance. He is the most conservative, and he figured all the Opposition voters worried about open borders, out-of-control spending and abortion would flock to him. Blackbird is a centrist and a compromiser. He has some squishiness on abortion, on the border, on the spending, on the military, on the courts, and so on."

"Right, he seems to run on getting along with the Party to get things done," pointed out Adam.

"While he makes nobody, except maybe the evangelicals, totally mad, he also seems to be very wishy-washy on how he would solve the problems or stop the Party. But he is the less scary version of Garcia. Carson and Wilson never really defined themselves nationally. Especially Wilson, who thought his handling of Florida in times of crisis would make him the natural choice to lead the nation."

"If there was a surprise this primary season, it was the failure of Wilson, once a favorite, to get any traction. He stunned everyone by failing to excite the Opposition," agreed Adam.

"Carson was counting on being female and being in the right time and place to seize the momentum for different candidates. She is likable, runs her state well, and has moderate views on abortion, but she is not seen as a leader. She is my candidate for the VP slot."

"Would that give Blackbird enough if he picked Carson?" asked Adam.

"Possibly. Blackbird needs all of Carson's and some of Wilson's or Garcia's to get over the top. Garcia can't get there unless he compromises with Blackbird, and we all know they hate each other, personally and ideologically, so that ain't happening. Unless one of them really screws up in the next month before the convention, I don't see this being resolved until the convention. Carson and Wilson want to keep their votes and leverage them into positions in most likely a Blackbird administration. But whomever the Opposition chooses, they will be a severe underdog to the Vice President," finished Rory.

"What about Turner?" asked Adam. "Is he a serious contender, or is he this cycle's independent, there, but ignored?"

"Honestly, I don't know, Adam," said Rory in an exasperated tone, a frown showing on his round face.

"What?" said Adam with a smile and a mock show of surprise. "You don't know? Who does?"

"That's just it, nobody knows. It is very strange. As you know, we have gotten pretty sophisticated in our polling capabilities and while many polls aren't worth the digital paper they are printed on, there are a few legitimate polling companies who strive to get it right every time, not just the last poll before the election. I have talked to some of these groups, specifically the Victory group, and they tell me something's going on."

"Like what?"

"Look, Turner is drawing bigger and bigger crowds everywhere he goes. Much bigger than any opposition candidate. Hell, they are bigger than the Party crowds too. He has been running a stealth campaign, staying off cable except here and then primarily only *Tommy*. He stays away from the traditional talk shows. The other candidates show up on them like flies on you know what. He talks to anyone who will stand still and listen *in person*. And you know he is an extremely compelling speaker. Did you see his speech at the Louisiana spring state fair?" asked Rory.

"Eventually. I saw it on Hibi, because the app I was watching took it down in the middle of my watching it," laughed Adam. "Have only used Hibi since, but that is another story. It was quite effective, and the crowd was enthusiastic."

"Me too," smiled Rory. "Hibi may have finally solved the uncensored free speech social media app conundrum. Back to the question. Adam, he took the stage between two of the most popular bands in the world. He was talking politics. His five minutes turned into thirty. They ate it up and cheered and asked for an encore. Now, just for a second, imagine the President or the Vice President got on stage and tried to talk politics? They would have lasted 30 seconds. We saw it years ago when they practically booed the Party Speaker of House off the stage before a mid-term. And that was a friendly audience." Rory shook his head.

"Anyone who can pull this feat off is not polling at 5%. I am sorry, but there is no way any of these polls showing him at 2% or 4% are correct. I would stake my career on it," said Rory.

"Who are his supporters?" asked Adam.

"This is where it gets tricky. He seems to focus on the middle class and working-class voters. Those most affected by the economic issues and those most directly affected by the flood of illegal immigrants. Because of his lack of coverage, his policy positions haven't been scrutinized or challenged. They're posted on this website and seem very middle of the road and pragmatic. But who knows until he faces an angry candidate or crowd if he will stick to them or cave? Eventually, he has to make more detailed defense of his stances. Right now, there is no one to ask him because the media won't cover him."

"I'll tell you one thing. His homeless stance, and his ability to offer a solution, pulling together significant funding from Party mega donors, is impressive. This is showing specific traits a president needs. The fact he did this while simultaneously running for president is impressive. He's eating into Lexi's base a bit and peeling off some moderate Opposition, but I don't think Lexi has much to worry about from Turner or the Opposition frankly," finished Rory.

"Rory, thanks for your insight, as always. We have a month until the conventions at the end of July to dissect this situation ten ways to Sunday. Anything to finish?" asked Adam.

"Just one more. Turner is supposed to be publishing a book in the next few weeks. We'll see if we can tell more about him and his stance on key issues from the book. My sources tell me he actually wrote it himself, from that purple notebook we always see him carrying. No ghost writer, so we'll see if it is a fluffy biography or a serious book about what he thinks we should do to solve our problems," ended Rory.

"Indeed, we will. Thank you, Rory," said Adam.

# **Chapter 82**

Throughout the rest of June, Nick continued barnstorming the country attending state fairs and holding rallies in every town with one of Martha's stores. His crowds continued to grow and his grassroots orgs kept expanding.  He was still only showing mid single digit support in the polls. Causing many pundits to question why he was staying in the race, despite excellent fundraising amounts. This too set off the pundits. They questioned who was donating and why were they throwing money at such a lost cause? Whenever pressed on these facts, Nick smiled.

After the fourth of July break, Nick sat sipping his second cup of coffee of the morning. As was usually the case, Nick had been the first to arrive, well before the sun was fully up. Since it was a ninety-minute drive from his home in Ft. Collins, Nick kept an apartment in a high-rise apartment building next door to the office building his campaign headquarters occupied a floor of in downtown Denver. Every morning he woke at 4:30 for his Tai Chi, a long treadmill run, and a workout in the gym downstairs.

He was reviewing the final draft of his upcoming book. He was pretty happy with the edits his team had made. They'd clarified his thoughts into logical positions and a coherent set of messages they were calling the Turner Doctrine.

Denise knocked and entered through his open door.

"*The Turner Doctrine*? Really?" asked Nick, as Denise took a chair, smiling.

"I know, but it sounded kind of catchy. Plus, we can publish the chapter headings and stances as a reference card. We want to distribute them at the state fairs."

"I'm not James Monroe," laughed Nick.

"But you know one. Pretty well, if what Chuck says is true."

"Dolly? She is only a Monroe by marriage. Good to know Chuck is spreading gossip. I may have to take him out back," threatened Nick.

"Don't hurt him. We need him. Everyone in Washington knows how you and Dolly hit it off at her party."

"Two parties. That is the totality of our interaction."

"Maybe you should call her. Women like that won't wait to be courted forever."

"Gee, Mom, glad you stopped by. Did you bring my clean laundry as well?" asked Nick in a sarcastic tone.

Denise smiled, knowingly. "Just saying. Are you ready for the latest bit of strangeness?"

"It's early, but fire away."

"Governor Blackbird wants to meet with you," said Denise.

"About?"

"I'm guessing about being his Vice President."

"Pretty presumptuous, since he doesn't even have the nomination," remarked Nick. "Besides, he is probably gonna need to give it to one of the others in order to clinch the nomination."

Denise shrugged. "Regardless, there is a plane waiting for you at Centennial to fly you up to Pierre. We know he is serious."

"It's a waste of my time and his. I'm a pilot…,"

"Not a co-pilot, I know," finished Denise. "Let's take the meeting and see what he has to say. You can do email on the flight there and back, so we're not losing a day," offered Denise.

"OK. Tell them I'm on my way. I'll get Earl to drive me out."

#

"Did you enjoy the flight?" asked George Blackbird, the Governor of South Dakota, and lead primary vote recipient for the Opposition party. He was a rather unremarkable, almost 6 foot tall, almost handsome, almost impressive, and almost commanding in his presence. He was extraordinarily unextraordinary. Nick felt it the first time he met him in the green room at EXN. It was no different on his home turf of the Governor's mansion.

"Yes, it was a pleasant flight. Thanks for not making me fly commercial," answered Nick with a smile as he sat down, setting his purple notebook and phone on a side table.

"Well Senator, as I think you can tell by landing outside town and driving you here to an underground entrance, I can't exactly let it out that I am having this conversation with you. I think folks would think it is pretty presumptuous," said the Governor.

"Please call me Nick. I figured as much. Why am I here Governor?"

"Nick, as you know, I am a pretty moderate Opposition member and many of my positions are not those of many of Senator Garcia's core supporters. I need to appeal to moderates in both parties and independents. Then hope I pick up Garcia's supporters, who are certainly not going to vote for Lexi," he said in all seriousness.

"And how do you plan to do that, Governor?"

The Governor seemed caught off guard by the question.

"I'm not sure I understand, Nick. By campaigning the way, I have so far. Taking positions of moderation and compromise. We need to work together to solve our problems. Being divisive is not allowing us to make any progress. This is how I have gotten the support I have in South Dakota," he said again, in a serious tone.

Nick paused, choosing his words carefully.

"Governor, no offence, but I have been on the inside of the Party. If there is one thing they are, it is unified in the determination to not compromise with anyone. They are not interested in working across the aisle, they are only interested in destroying the other side. Destroying any in opposition to their stances. They'll do whatever it takes to achieve the power where they no longer need to convince anyone to help them."

"I don't agree. With all due respect, Senator, you have only been in Washington for less than two years. I have been in politics for over forty and I understand the give and take. The grandstanding in the press and the deal making in the back room. I think you are mistaking these as the reality. It is my experience the deals can be done; you just have to find the right combination of give and take," proposed the Governor.

Nick noticed he was now the Senator again, rather than Nick.

"Governor, did you ever meet Senator Wilhelm?" asked Nick.

The Governor stiffened a bit at the question.

"Yes, I had the pleasure of meeting him several times."

"I wish I had known him better. I can tell you, the antics of the Majority Leader and my presidential opponent, and potentially yours, are not grandstanding alone. It was deadly for Senator Wilhelm. It was a no holds barred, take no prisoners move, to end the filibuster. That is not the actions of a Party or leadership seeking compromise," stated Nick.

"Maybe, but I have to believe we can find a way to work together, to find common ground. Our enemies abroad are becoming emboldened by our focus on domestic issues. We need to project a united front, or our enemies are going to move, and we are not going to stop them. I can't believe the VP or Garcia or anyone else would support this happening rather than working together," mused Blackbird.

"Governor, I applaud your faith that patriotism would trump politics. But I believe it is misplaced. The Party, and therefore Lexi, are worried about the foreign issues, true. But they are laser focused on consolidating power and getting control first. Then they will worry about what other countries are doing."

"Them I am afraid I have wasted half a day of your time, because it appears there is little we have in common, other than a desire to lead this country," declared the Governor rising.

"I know you don't want it," said Nick rising, "but I will offer it, anyway. If you do not treat Lexi as the most dangerous and vicious wild animal you can imagine, she will chew you up and spit you out. She is in it to win. She won't hesitate to use any information, sacrifice anyone, and call in any favors she has anywhere on the planet to win."

Nick continued as Blackbird stiffened at the idea Lexi would be ruthless.

"She has a vision of what the US should look like. You and I can at least agree on this one. Her vision is not anything near what we hold dear. You need to move to your right, your strength, and your only hope of winning is in the Opposition conservatives. I know you hate Garcia, but without his support and his people, you don't have a chance. You need him more than you need me. It is impossible to please everyone. You have to stand for *something*," said Nick, realizing he may have gone too far with the last statement, seeing the look on Governor's face.

"Son, you have a long way to go to understand politics and how this game is played," said the Governor, dismissively.

"Governor, you could not have paid me a better compliment. I am not a politician and saving our country from destruction is certainly not a game to me." Nick picked up his notebook and phone.

"I think if you can have someone drive me to the airport, I'll make my own way back to Denver," said Nick walking out to meet an aide who would drive him to the airport as the Governor was already responding to email on his phone, ignoring Nick.

#

"Where the hell are you?" asked Denise's voice from the speakerphone on Nick's mobile phone.

"According to the phone GPS, I am about 30 minutes west of North Platte, Nebraska," answered Nick.

"WHAT? Are you driving back from Pierre? What the hell happened?" asked Denise, concerned.

"Well… Let's just say Governor Blackbird and I didn't see eye to eye on pretty much anything," laughed Nick, watching the road as he drove his rental slightly above the speed limit.

"Jesus, did he refuse to fly you back?"

"No, nothing like that. I decided I would fly back commercial. When I got to the airport, the next flight to Denver wasn't for six hours, so I figured I could drive it in the same time as the flight. I just rented a car. I'll call Earl when I am thirty minutes from the airport, so he can pick me up at the rental car center," said Nick. "I'm actually enjoying the drive. Good way to clear the mind."

"OK. What did you do to piss him off?"

"Denise, he is an idiot. Now that I've had an actual conversation with him, I can see why Garcia can't stand him. He is *so* wishy-washy. He really believes he can pull a coalition of moderate Party, Opposition, and independents to him by saying he will work with the Party to work out compromises. Thinks he can negotiate with Lexi," explained Nick.

"That's why he couldn't get a plurality of the opposition votes. Many of the opposition think, as you do, that Lexi is a menace. There's still a wing of them that wants to be left alone. Those are Blackbird's voters. You're doing better with them than he is," laughed Denise.

"Maybe, but I'll never win over Garcia's far right faction just like Blackbird can't," said Nick.

"Like hell you can't. A decorated war hero. Someone who stood up to terrorists. Who is pro second amendment and pro constitution."

"And pro women's choice," said Nick.

"Right, sort of forgot about that one."

"Denise, the Opposition have a legacy of losing. They're only on the field to put up a fight and a show. Then to lose, maybe closely, but in the end to be the noble losers. I don't want to be an Opposition candidate. I only care about preserving the Constitution. Everyone is welcome in our tent. We aren't part of either party."

"OK. I'll let Earl know you will call when you are close. Nick, I am sorry. I encouraged you to talk to him," apologized Denise.

"It was worth it, Denise. He is vulnerable. If we keep up our efforts, I think we will get a bunch of his supporters who know he can't win. After Lexi spends three months beating him up, a lot of his supporters are going to be looking for alternatives. Can you imagine how Lexi will slaughter him in the debates? It is going to be brutal."

Nick could hear Denise laughing in the background.

"You are correct. Lexi is a great debater."

"No worries. Now we know how wimpy he is. That is good for us, because if he ends up being the candidate, we are going to be the natural place for Garcia's voters to go, if they bother to vote. We may need to court Garcia to throw his support to us. Boy, that would frost Blackbird," laughed Nick as he drove.

"You got that right. It would cause a civil war in the Opposition party. The only one that really helps is Lexi," said Denise, with a sigh.

"We'll see. The times they are a changing."

# Chapter 83

Lauren was in the green room of the *ANC Tonight* prime time news show. The producer came in and told her ten minutes to air time and seven to the break. She nodded, looking at her phone. A wave of nausea hit suddenly. She rushed down the hall to the women's room and into a stall just as her stomach heaved the contents of her dinner. After heaving for a few seconds more, another wave of nausea washed over her, covering her forehead in perspiration.

"Fuck." She quickly dabbed her forehead and wiped her mouth, while checking her smile in the mirror. A frantic producer was looking for her when she hurried back out to the green room.

"Geez, Lauren, get a move on. We need you in the chair."

She followed him to the stage and quickly got mic'd up. The makeup artist came by to touch up her look. From the makeup artist's look, she could tell that she had messed up her hair and makeup. She quickly dabbed her forehead, made a couple of quick flicks to pull her hair farther forward.

"You OK?" asked Marty Nash, a look of concern on his gray headed and perfect, distinguished newsman looking face, with his deep baritone voice.

"Might have been something I ate or maybe I am catching a cold. Don't lean in too close," she replied with a smile.

The producer counted down out of the commercial.

"Welcome back. Tonight, I am joined by our White House correspondent, Lauren Bergamo. Welcome Lauren."

"Thank you, Marty, it's good to be in the studio for a change," she replied, practicing her breathing to calm down, knowing her face was probably flushed.

"Lauren, it is our understanding, you have some breaking news for our viewers tonight?" asked Marty.

"That's right Marty, I have sources that say Senator Nick Turner visited Governor Blackbird at the governor's mansion in Pierre, South Dakota, today. Now I don't have any knowledge of what their conversations were about, but speculation and common sense would say they were talking about the vice-presidential spot on a potential Blackbird-Turner ticket," said Lauren.

"Wow. That is an interesting proposal, Lauren. Don't you think Blackbird is going to need to offer that role to one of the other primary candidates to get over the top?" asked Marty.

Lauren laughed.

"I didn't say it was a good decision. Marty, I'm reporting what happened. I agree with you, it seems to make more sense to talk to the other primary opponents. They're the ones with the pledged delegates he needs to secure the nomination. However, Turner brings support from the Party, Opposition, and independents to the ticket. That is my guess why he is talking to him."

"Care to share your source?"

"Marty, you know I can't do that."

"Do you have any other info on how the delegates are going to break? Surely Blackbird is trying to get his support lined up before the convention. I can't imagine he wants to go to their and risk a floor vote," suggested Marty.

"You would think not. It's well known that Garcia and Blackbird dislike each other. I don't envision them ever agreeing to support each other. I also can't see Garcia ever accepting a VP slot from Blackbird, so that pairing is out," guessed Lauren.

"Dislike? I would say the only person Blackbird and Garcia hate more than each other is the VP," agreed Marty with a hearty, deep laugh.

Lauren laughed as well. "I have to cover these people daily, so I give them the benefit of the doubt, and it is Washington, DC, Marty."

"That's true."

"Anyway, the problem facing Garcia is he needs both Carson and Wilson to come to his side and then he needs a few of Blackbird's delegates to defect to him even then. I just don't see that happening. His dogged conservative stance on *everything* means he is unwilling or unable to risk compromise for fear of losing his conservative supporters. I would say it goes to the convention and there are a couple of votes to prove to Blackbird how much he needs Carson and then see what he offers her," stated Lauren.

"Do you think there is a chance Turner could accept?"

"No. From my interactions with Turner, I can't see him wanting to play second fiddle to anyone. He believes he is on a mission, and he cannot do that from the number two position."

"Very interesting. Lauren, feel free to come back when you learn more. We're certainly seeing an interesting presidential race this year."

"Thanks Marty," finished Lauren, smiling.

"Well, be right back," said Marty as they broke for commercial. Lauren stood to remove her microphone and vacate the stage for the next guest. She picked up her bag from the locker and grabbed a ginger ale from the beverage fridge.

As she headed out the door, her phone rang.

"Jeff, what's up?" she answered.

She listened to her producer, even holding the phone away from her ear as a loud and upset voice projected.

"It just happened. I heard from a source and put a call into Marty to see if he wanted me to appear."

She was listening again.

"Yes, I told Marty what I wanted to talk about."

Listening, she cradled the phone while opening the ginger ale.

"Hey, I can't help it if they don't talk. No, I can't divulge my sources. I can't predict when I get scoops and last time I checked, we are a breaking news channel, right?" argued Lauren, listening again. "You have a good night too, Jeff."

# Chapter 84

Lauren sat at her desk, reviewing her emails and browsing the web for news highlights of the day. She checked her phone, opened an app, and glanced at its contents. Jeff stood at the entrance to her cube, leaning against the partition. She closed the app before looking up.

"Hey," said Lauren.

"Hey yourself," said Jeff in a hurtful tone.

"Oh, come on, you can't still be upset I went on Marty's show with my tip?" asked Lauren.

"The guys upstairs were upset we didn't give notice so they could hype your story," accused Jeff, shaking his head.

"That's what they're mad about? They couldn't do a teaser? Geez. What do you need, Jeff? I'm busy."

"What are you working on?"

"A piece about the lack of press conferences by the President. And trips on Air Force One."

"Sounds pretty boring."

"It is. That's the point. We have all kinds of shit going down all around the world and the President is basically MIA. Hell, the press doesn't even bother to challenge the press secretary any more about the next presidential press conference. We get daily briefings about all the stuff going on and the phone calls and the occasional press conference from Lexi, but other than a few waves on his way to Marine One. Or his monthly breakfast coffee and muffin at 6:30 in the morning with select reporters. The President hasn't been speaking to the public what, maybe half a dozen times this year?"

Jeff shrugged. "Maybe they finally tired of managing all his gaffes? Out of sight is one way to keep his foot out of his mouth."

"Jeff, it makes little sense. It is an election year. And it is July. He hasn't even come out to endorse Lexi, not that it will matter or help much. I'm worried we are in a *Wag the Dog* sequel," said Lauren.

"Got any proof to go with this rumor?"

"Is that the issue? You don't want me reporting on unsubstantiated rumors? Come on," she said in a disgusted tone. "Have you watched Wayne's show lately? It is all made up lies about the Opposition and innuendo about hidden agendas, dark money, and shadow organizations pulling the strings of the candidates. That is conspiracy theory stuff," said Lauren defiantly.

"I'm not Wayne's producer. He is trying to get his ratings to a quarter of Tommy's," said Jeff.

"Good luck. First, he might try to cut back to, I don't know, maybe only half a dozen lies a night," said Lauren, grimacing in mock pain.

"Lauren, what brought this on? Wayne is an open book. What he does shouldn't surprise anyone."

"Alright, you didn't come here to debate our opinion show lineup. Obviously, you are on a mission and it is…?"

"Boss wants to know if your source is reliable. He questions the veracity of your claim that Blackbird would meet with Turner. He thinks you are being played," said Jeff, looking at his phone.

"I guess time will tell. As he has made clear, I am under contract. He can fire me anytime, if he thinks I am making shit up."

"Hey, whoa, no need to get upset. It was just a question. It might help if you could identify your source," said Jeff carefully.

Lauren laughed. "You'd make a lousy spy. I'm not going to reveal my source. You can tell whoever the 'boss' really is, I'm confident in my story. Blackbird met with Turner. I did some further checking this morning and found flight manifests. It confirmed a flight yesterday from Denver to Pierre on a jet leased to Blackbird's campaign. The only passenger was Nick Turner. Now what would he be doing going to Pierre South Dakota on a Blackbird campaign plane?" she finished tapping a finger to her chin while gazing at the ceiling.

Jeff smiled at this confirmation.

"Now get outta here. I have work to do," said Lauren, putting her earbuds back in her ears and turning back to her laptop.

Jeff straightened up and headed out of the cube. He texted as he walked, 'no source and she verified NT was in SD so the rumor was true'.

Lauren watched out of the corner of her eye as Jeff walked away. She smiled to herself, and then another wave of nausea overcame her. She knew what was coming and headed to the restroom.

Touching up her face in the mirror, she felt her forehead. She could have a temperature. She felt a little achy. Maybe she should get a quick COVID test. There was a variant from Kashmir going around DC. It had arrived with a diplomatic delegation who had left a few weeks ago, leaving a host of vaccinated people sick with mild COVID symptoms. She had attended one of those events.

# Chapter 85

Nick walked into the campaign office in Arlington, followed by Chuck, and sat down at his desk while Chuck took a seat as well.

"How are we doing?" Chuck asked.

"Me? Fine. Living the dream," replied Nick, picking through the piles of mail, staring at a tall stack of unread bills before the Senate.

"Looking for something specific?" asked Chuck.

"No, looking to see what kind of crap is going on here while I am on the road."

"Boss, we got this under control. You need to focus on the campaign. Nothing consequential gets done in an election year. You are not abandoning your constituents," assured Chuck.

Nick leaned back in his chair and stared at the ceiling.

"I see they're going with Guerrero for the Senate, huh?"

Chuck nodded. "He breezed through the primaries. He's an excellent candidate for the Party in Colorado. Hispanic, married to a black woman, adopted kids, one of whom is gay. He has marched with ARL and supports defunding the police. If he were a vet missing a leg, he'd check all the boxes. As usual, the Opposition beat each other up and ended up picking someone who can't possibly win, a rancher from the Western Slope. Your seat will be safely back in Party hands come January. Lexi and Fontana will be happy."

"Did I make a mistake, Chuck? Should I have run for a full Senate term?"

"As what? The Party would have primaried you after the filibuster vote. As Opposition? They would scream fake from the rooftops. Once you cast that vote, you made your choice, independent or bust. You're a man without a party. You know what? That's OK in this climate. The parties bring a lot of baggage," noted Chuck, looking through notes while he talked.

"I feel like we are teetering on the edge of going over the cliff and I don't know if I am doing enough or doing it the right way. As I tell people in my speeches, if you had the chance to meet Hitler in 1930, would you have the courage to shoot him, knowing only you know what you prevent? It seems to me we are at that point and the more I do this, the more I talk, the reactions I see and get to my ideas, the more I know this is right and necessary. It can't be too little or too late, or I am needlessly exposing people to cancellation. I feel the need to go faster is all. Does that make any sense?" finished Nick as he stood up to pace the room.

"What brought this on?"

"Something Blackbird said."

"Oh, I see. Nick, you're a threat. Of course, he would try to throw you off your game. You are both going for the same voters."

"Ya, but he may be right."

"What did he say? Nick, you gotta let this shit roll off your back," said Chuck, setting down his work. "You're the toughest man I have ever met. The shit you have been through and yet you are willing to take more abuse to save the country. Don't let a few words get to you."

Chuck watched Nick pace back and forth.

"Spill it."

"He pulled rank. He said I've only been in Washington for a year and implied I cannot see through the grandstanding to the actual deal making in the background. I answered him I was not a politician, and that was worth far more than his 40 years of political experience. I gave him some advice not to underestimate Lexi, told him he needed Garcia's conservatives, and that he needed to stand for something. That last bit got me booted," laughed Nick.

"You told him all that?" asked Chuck, standing and laughing. "In the first five minutes?"

"In the only five minutes. That's how long the meeting lasted."

"Jesus Nick. Have you told Denise?"

"No, what is the problem? We didn't see eye to eye, no biggee," said Nick, shrugging.

"Nick, you really don't understand the game. There is no greater insult than to tell a career politician he or she needs to stand for something. He would have been pissed if Lexi had told him that, but you? A neophyte who has never been through a single election. Who has never had to compromise their principles to win support or had to smile at a corporate mogul to get a big donation when what you want to do is punch out his face?"

Chuck shook his head as he paced.

"You have never had to play the game. The back and forth negotiating and compromise, the give and take and knowing when you have gotten as much as you can get without torpedoing the whole deal. There is an art to it, and while an outsider, *like you*, thinks it is corrupt, low down, slimy and not a little bit unethical, a lotta bit immoral and probably, flat out illegal, this is how things get done in Washington," said Chuck walking to the bar.

"You know what, Chuck, and please don't take this the wrong way, but that is exactly how Blackbird sounded when he told me he was experienced and I was not."

"I am not offended, because you see Nick, I too have been playing that game. I don't have what it takes to be the talent. But I am damn good at the number two spot. I like it down in the trenches. Where the real negotiating happens. It is not always pens and paper, emails and texts, sometimes it's knives, reputations, and careers."

"And here I only thought you were confirming my windmills, Sancho," said Nick with a smile.

Chuck drank his water, nodding. "That is how the sausage is made. You need to understand, as a single person, you cannot change the way Washington works. Besides, humans are ultimately corrupt. We think, therefore, we are corrupt. The hell with the water, I need a drink," said Chuck, setting down the bottle of water and pulling out the scotch.

Nick stood in silence, digesting Chuck's words as he handed him a glass of scotch. "Chuck, why?"

"Why what?" he asked, sitting on the sofa in the office.

"Why would you say that? And Blackbird? Why is Lexi the way she is? Chuck, I don't believe all humans are corrupt. I think you have sold your soul so many times in the course of your time here, you don't recognize it can be different," declared Nick, holding up a hand as Chuck tried to reply.

"I don't mean that as a criticism. It is just an observation. Believe me, I appreciate the sacrifices you have made to be that number two. Working behind the scenes for me and for Richard's all these years. But I must disagree. If we cannot hope for more than status quo from our public servants, from our president, from our government, we do not deserve this exercise in self-rule."

"If I, or someone else, cannot rouse the sleeping giant, to see how corrupt we have allowed our government to become, then we deserve to be the next Rome and bring on the barbarians. Chuck, if what you say is true, and it is unchangeable, then we are irredeemable and we deserve whatever fate Lexi has in store for us. For the meek submit to slaughter, the brave fight to live another day or die trying, knowing they did not go quietly or willingly into bondage," concluded Nick.

Chuck got up from his seat on the couch, walking over to Nick. Nick was unsure if he had gone too far with Chuck as he had with Blackbird. He prepared to let Chuck slug him, when instead Chuck broke out in a smile and held out his hand, which Nick took.

"Congratulations, you have graduated. You have looked the enemy in the eye, and you have resisted the temptation to join the Dark Side, to put on the One Ring and rule them all, to use the Elder Wand for your own gratification," said Chuck.

"Gee, *Lord of the Rings*, *Star Wars*, and *Harry Potter* all in one sentence. You forgot the Infinity Stones," remarked Nick.

"Sorry, I never read comic books as a kid," said Chuck, smiling.

"You're not sore? For a minute there, I thought you were going to slug me."

"Ya right, you forget how much I know about you. I don't want to end up in the hospital when you pull some of those ninja moves on me," laughed Chuck, going back to the bar for a refill.

"Besides, there wasn't anything you said that wasn't true. Some of us, maybe more than I think, who work in Washington *have* been waiting for the other shoe to drop. To reform or to collapse. Everyone knows it is coming."

"I hope it's here. Now we have to see if we can push it to the proper outcome," prompted Nick.

"Are you sure which outcome is the correct one?"

Nick stood thinking about Chuck's question. He was not sure he had the answer to it. There was a knock on the door before he could answer.

"Come in," yelled Nick.

Denise entered the room, saw the drinks in their hands.

"Can I get one of those?"

"Just kidding" said Denise, seeing the worried look on their faces. "But I sure could use one."

Nick fixed Denise a club soda with a lime.

Chuck looked at Denise and took his seat back on the couch. Nick handed Denise her drink as she sat at the opposite end from Chuck. He sat in a chair facing them.

"What's up?"

Denise took a long sip of her soda, closed her eyes.

"Did you tell anyone about your meeting with Blackbird?"

Nick looked at Denise.

"No. Obviously his staff knew, and they took me to the airport, but no one said anything when I got my car. My only conversations about Blackbird have been with you."

"Let me have your phone," asked Denise. Nick handed her the phone. She put it in what looked like a foil bag. "I'll have Earl and our techs check it for malware or tracking devices. I got a call from Blackbird's campaign manager. He ripped me a new one. He claims we leaked the meeting to that Bergamo bitch. She went on ANC and blabbed out that Blackbird was vetting you for VP. He said he didn't appreciate the lack of confidentiality being displayed, but understood you are low in the polls. Desperate to do anything to get attention."

"Really, what could I have to gain by being seen or even contemplated for a role in the Opposition administration for vice president?" asked Nick.

"In the minds of Washington insiders, that is exactly how the game is played. Chuck can vouch for that," she said, looking at Chuck, who nodded.

"They think you have no chance, so you build your brand. Take a VP slot, raise your status as you campaign. Toil for 4 or 8 years as the heir apparent, or run against Lexi in 4 years as the Opposition candidate if she wins. This is how it is played. He figures you leaked it as part of the game," finished Denise.

"Well, that would be all well and good," answered Nick, laughing. "Except I told him to his face I am not playing this game. His game or Lexi's. If I don't win, I have no intention of making politics a career. Not sure what I will do, but I won't be a talking head or a pundit. Of that, I can assure you."

"So how did Bergamo figure out you were meeting? The only folks who knew were in this room and Earl. I can't imagine he is the leak."

"Me neither. It must be on Blackbird's side. After all, as you say, those campaigns are full of operatives, could be one of them is feeding Bergamo, or maybe someone recognized the name on the rental?" offered Nick, hesitating slightly as he almost called her Lauren. He had to be careful talking about her.

"That must be it. I told his campaign manager to look closer to home. He insists very few knew on his side as well. I guess it could have been the pilot or the driver?" guessed Denise. "Anyway, he is not thrilled with you right now."

"I can live with that. Any time he mentions me, it legitimizes us that much more. We win if he says nothing, and we win if he complains. Come to think of it, I wish I had orchestrated this because it really was a pretty good plan," Nick remarked with a rueful smile. When Denise looked at him, he held up his hands in defense. "I swear I really had nothing to do with this."

"Good. If you did something like that without telling me…," she finished with a fierce look.

"Got it. Warning sent and received," he continued to hold up his hand defensively.

"Now I really need that drink," she said, looking into her club soda. "You ready for the next revelation in a night of strange ones?"

"What now?"

"Do you know Mel Arenson?"

"No, but I know who he is."

"He called me today, kibbitzing about the Blackbird meeting and how you can't trust anyone in this town, blah, blah, blah. Mel doesn't call you unless he needs or wants something, and I know Mel very well."

Nick noticed she was flustered. It was the first time he had ever seen her unsure of herself.

"OK, I'll bite. What did he want?"

"He says Lexi wants to talk."

"About what?" said Nick, looking her way. Then the realization hit him. "No fucking way. You can't be serious. After what I did to them." Nick was now standing.

"Hey, remember what I said about the game?" voiced Chuck. "Enemies one day, friends the next, if that's what it takes to make the deal work. She doesn't have to give the VP spot to anyone for payback. Certainly not to Klausen. She is looking to see who brings the most to her ticket. You have a hold on the moderates she is losing because of her progressive platform. Adding you could help bring some of them back into the fold. She is thinking you would moderate some of her, shall we say, more radical ideas. It makes perfect political sense. Hell, maybe she even thinks you might think of joining up with Blackbird. Though you and Garcia would make a much better ticket," said Chuck.

"No. I won't talk to her. It's like a dalmatian going to lunch with Cruella de Vil. I am not going to do it," said Nick with finality.

"Can you please stop with the movie references," pleaded Denise, holding her hands on her temples. "You're hurting my head."

"Ok, it's like Joan of Arc meeting the French Bishop for lunch at the stake in the square. Is that better?"

"Smartass. They made a movie about that too, Audrey Hepburn if I remember right," retorted Denise, giving him a look and the finger, before easing it with a smile.

"What do we do?" asked Chuck.

"I already told you, I am not meeting with her."

"Let's think about it. How can we turn this into a positive for us?" she asked.

"The only way this works for us is if it gets out like the meeting with Blackbird did," stated Chuck.

"Well, we are hardly about to do that, especially after being accused of it before," said Nick.

"Pretty hard to keep anything secret in this town. Even if you go, it will probably get out anyway, regardless," shrugged Denise.

"What do I have to gain by talking to her? We all know I'm not going to accept. She has to know this as well. Why even bother? How does it help her to meet with me?"

"Maybe she really thinks you want to win bad enough to support her. Maybe she figures it helps her to look magnanimous in talking to someone who thwarted the administration's plans," pondered Chuck.

"I know her. She is extremely confident; most would say arrogant. I think she honestly believes she can offer Nick much more than he can get on his own. She believes the polls and thinks you really *are* in single digits. Thinks you'll jump at the chance to help shape policy. That you care about power and your future in politics. This is where she is miscalculating," suggested Denise.

"Right, but what is in it for me?"

"It will leak. She is making a huge miscalculation by meeting with you. She is not considering the result of you rebuffing her advances. Trust me, Lexi is used to getting what she wants, when she wants it, on her terms. In every aspect of life. I have seen it and I have lived it," Denise said, grimacing.

"That sounds ominous." Denise stared back at Nick without a reply.

"When it leaks, it will show two things. First, it shows deep down inside she is afraid of you. Second, it will show to the world that you are not a joke. It will show you matter, and your candidacy is legitimate. This will drive more moderates from her to you. When you turn her down, she is likely to find ways to derail our campaign. It will put a target on our backs we didn't have before," pointed out Denise, with a glance from Nick to Chuck.

"Is it worth it?" asked Chuck.

"We have been intentionally lying low. Staying low in the polls to avoid having the full ire of Lexi on us. Does this change if I meet with her and say no?" asked Nick, once again pacing the room.

"I would say it is not worth it, *if* it were after the conventions. But since it is mid-July and the conventions start next week, the attention of the world and of both campaigns are going to be on each other. I think she'll be pissed but she'll have to turn to attacking Blackbird or whomever the Opposition chooses, as the primary focus of her attacks. You'll go back to being an annoyance. She's like a spider, very patient. She figures she'll get her revenge on you after she is president. You are fucked either way," Denise scowled as she finished.

"Have I told you two how much I love politics?" asked Nick with a laugh of his own. "Give me some Taliban or Al Qaeda any day of the week. At least I know they are trying to kill me, not asking me to sit down and have tea. And I could shoot back. It was kill or be killed and no quarter was given or expected. Here it is a kabuki dance of whirling blades. Watch everywhere all the time."

"I tried to tell you. Calling it a game is a very poor choice of words. The people who win this game have control of the largest economy, the world's biggest arsenal of destruction, and the best trained army in the world. It is quite the prize," explained Chuck.

"Well, that's not why I want it, but I get it. That scares me even more to think of the tools Lexi would have at her disposal to *enforce* her changes."

"Do I set up the meet? asked Denise.

"Yes. But I'm not looking forward to this."

"You shouldn't. Watch her like a hawk, listen to every word, watch every move she makes, and choose your own words carefully. Treat her like a snake looking for an opening to strike," warned Denise with such passion and concern, both Chuck and Nick stopped and looked at her. She noticed their looks of concern.

"Don't worry, boys. I have been bitten by that snake before and it was not pleasant. Just giving you fair warning," shrugged Denise in answer to their looks.

"Sounds like a story for another time," observed Nick.

"And a lot more scotch," confirmed Denise. She was not smiling as she said it.

# Chapter 86

Lauren sat in the office of a clinic near the Washington Bureau of ANC. She'd just had the indignity of having a swab stuffed up her nose to the back of her throat. Now she was waiting for the results of the newly enhanced COVID test. She browsed the texts and emails, checking her news feeds and apps for updates. While looking at one, she noticed something. She quickly opened a browser window and typed in some text. Glancing at the results put a smile on her face. She held her phone to her ear.

"Hello Marty? Lauren. You ready to make some more news tonight?" she asked, listening. "OK, be ready."

Lauren went up to the desk and provided her cell number and asked them to text her the results when they came in. Hurrying to her car, she looked at her phone again.

Now armed with a large cup of chai with skim milk from a local drive through coffee house, she drove to her stakeout. She found an unmetered parking space, sipped her chai, and put the camera with its zoom lens on her lap. She'd occasionally pick up the camera to scan the entrance and exits of an office building as people went in and out.

The contents of her stomach did a few rumbles but remained in place. "Damn COVID," she said to herself. She picked up a plastic bag from the center console, just in case. There would be no running to a restroom if she lost the battle with her stomach. She wondered if the chai was the best thing for it, but it was that or a month-old protein bar from the glove box. The chai won.

#

Nick walked into Lexi's campaign office in Arlington. She was making no attempt to keep his arrival a secret. He stopped at the reception area where a professionally dressed young woman met him. She recognized Nick and led him through what seemed like a football field of cubicles.

These were filled with volunteers working the phones and filling envelopes with mailers.

It looked like Santa's workshop on Christmas Eve. The aide took Nick through the center of the operation and to a conference room in the corner. She knocked and opened the door, motioning Nick to enter. Lexi rose from her seat, youthful and elegant as always.

"Senator Turner, thank you for coming over to our office. Have you met Mel?" asked Lexi, her long blonde hair forward over one shoulder, her smile wide, and icy blue eyes piercing as always.

Nick looked from Lexi to Mel. While Lexi looked like a queen in residence, Mel did not even resemble the court jester. He looked more like someone who would bring the bedpan to the queen. He reminded Nick of the sad sack from the World War two comic strip. Small, emaciated, bald with wire-rim glasses and a poorly tailored suit.

"Nice to meet you, Mel," offered Nick as they shook hands.

"Pleased to meet you, Senator."

"I'll leave you two to your conversation," finished Mel as he left the conference room.

Lexi walked to the door and flipped the switch, bringing the light curtain in the glass down and then flipping it back on to obscure the glass. She also flipped a second switch and Nick heard a whirring noise.

"It's a SCIF, just like the situation room, keeps people from eavesdropping on conversations," noted Lexi. "Coffee, water?"

"I'm happy to get myself some coffee. Where is it?" asked Nick, looking around.

"I believe there is a carafe on the counter in the corner," pointed Lexi.

Nick went over to the counter and poured a cup.

"Would you like one as well?"

"Why, yes I would, thank you. One sweetener and one cream, please."

Nick doctored up Lexi's coffee and handed the cup to her.

"What should we toast?" asked Nick playfully.

"I would say Senator Wilhelm, but you might find that in poor taste," stated Lexi, setting the tone for their conversation.

"So much for pleasantries," nodded Nick. "Why am I here?"

"Are you going to join Blackbird's ticket?"

"What part of 'there is no way I would betray the ideals of the Opposition party by even considering Senator Turner as my running mate', from his press conference, did you miss?" asked Nick, laughing.

Lexi smiled. "You may fool others with your 'aw shucks' persona and your 'Mr. Smith' speeches. I think you are enjoying your role in this election. I can see someone who is hungry for power. The power to implement what you feel is right. Think about it. You and I are no different in that respect."

Lexi paced at the end of the room.

"I have invested a lifetime of decisions and sacrifices to get to where I am. You show up on the scene with your high ideals and holier than thou speeches. Expecting to skip all the preliminaries. The pain and suffering, compromise and, frankly, the learning experiences of what works and what does not," noted Lexi, sitting down in a chair at the end of the conference table, now facing Nick. She crossed her shapely legs, displaying her signature red soled heels.

Nick, still standing, did not respond, sensing the lecture would continue. "You see Nick, you don't mind if I call you Nick?" asked Lexi, as he nodded, sipping his coffee.

"Governing is about trying things. It is about pushing the status quo aside. It is about taking risks. Doing things others would shrink away from out of fear of failure. But if you don't do this, you don't know what will work and make a difference and what falls short. It is this approach that has allowed me to achieve what I have."

"Most of these senators and congressmen are scared shitless of doing the wrong thing or getting dinged in an opinion poll. I subscribe to 'the any press is good press rule'. If you are trying and failing, you are getting known. When you keep trying and eventually succeed, they remember you failed, but then they realize you did not give up and kept trying until you got it right. That is my secret, or maybe not so secret. I know what I want, and I do what it takes to get it. That means not being afraid to take risks and never settling. And here I am, Vice President, and soon to be the first female president," finished Lexi, smiling at Nick over her coffee.

"I'm sure there is a point, but I seem to be too dense to pick up on it," queried Nick, leaning against a windowsill.

"I like you. Before you wasted your career on that vote, I should have spent more time with you. With my help, the sky could have been the limit. I can't stay president forever," noted Lexi.

"From what I hear, I am sure the 22nd amendment will not be a limiting factor for your plans," suggested Nick, pointedly.

"Probably right, but I won't live forever and there will come a time when we need to figure out a succession. That is a conversation for another day. I know we don't see eye to eye on a lot of things, but you have to face reality. To stand up to the challenges the rest of the world is throwing our way, we need to be united. We need to be led by someone strong and forceful."

Nick sipped his coffee, preferring to hear her full message before responding.

"We may have been founded on the ideas of individual liberty and freedom and a desire to be left alone. We did fine that way. But it led to an outcome and success beyond anything our founders could have imagined. Frankly, our affluent society has become too large and complex to continue to be managed by our agrarian, decentralized Constitution. We needed to modernize and build ways to manage the colossal scale we have achieved."

"We have been working toward this for over 100 years. Roosevelt, Teddy that is, and Wilson were both progressives, as you have reminded folks in your speeches. They both agreed our country had achieved a size where it was unreasonable to assume congressmen elected to serve temporarily would have the skills to dive into every topic and understand it to a depth to make informed decisions."

"The administrative state was born. I know you think this is the problem. But look at the alternative. You have been in congress for almost two years. Do you honestly think any of them can read a bill or write one? Truly understand the complex economics, the limitations of pharmaceutical ethics, what the FDA should and should not do to approve cancer drugs, meat packing, AI, or bitcoin regulations? It goes on and on."

Nick stared at her, remaining silent.

"Do we honestly want a bunch of transient amateur power mad megalomaniacs in charge of something as important as when it is safe to drink the water or when the epi-pen you rely on to save your life is still effective? I know I don't. Neither did Roosevelt nor Wilson. Sure, we have to give some of our freedoms to the state. To manage and regulate, especially when it is being done for the good of the people," lectured Lexi, gauging Nick's reaction.

"Madame Vice President," said Nick.

"Hold on," ordered Lexi. "When it is the two of us, call me Lexi, please."

"I'm sorry, I can't do that," he responded, shaking his head. "I will agree with you that progressivism did good things in the beginning. Busting up monopolies, ending child labor, focusing on safety in food, the workplace, drugs, cars, etc. It is the unintended consequences of good deeds which have proliferated and are causing more harm than good. The problem is when a pendulum swings, it will keep swinging past center and continue until it hits the end of its arc. I want to push it back to the center and stop it. Progressivism wants to lock it in place at the extreme left of the arc."

Lexi's icy gaze remained fixed on Nick as he continued.

"My concern is the administrative state has no accountability. When we don't like those amateurs in congress or the presidency, we can vote them out and replace them with other amateurs. Without that threat, what stops them from going crazy and redoing everything? It is the same with the administrative state. They aren't beholden to anyone. If you try to dismantle them or hold them accountable, they simply dig in, hunker down, and wait for the next set of amateurs to arrive who are distracted by something else. It is these unaccountable permanent state bureaucrats who are the ones preventing progress."

"When the amateurs in charge are dangerous, aren't we glad these bureaucrats can 'dig in' and prevent them from laying waste to everything?" asked Lexi.

"Who decides on what is right or wrong? The idea of our country was one of checks and balances. They intentionally built us to prevent widespread change based on passionate argument. The administrative state has no check and no balance. They tilt the scales to their control and their way, with no check. We have given up our freedoms and our ability to impact the laws a little at a time continuously for over 100 years," Nick spoke, using his hands to make his points as Lexi looked on from her seat.

"It has taken away our freedoms and our desire to keep these, to exercise our own free will. The administrative state has made us dependent on them for direction and support. It has bred out of us our individual spirit, the spirit that allowed us to send our sons to Europe in 1917 to fight for an ideal, rather than our soil. Then to storm the beaches of Normandy to preserve Western Civilization from another totalitarian state, bent on taking away freedom," said Nick, passionately.

"Perhaps it is time for Western Civilization to adjust to modern times, Senator," retorted Lexi coyly.

"By removing individual freedom? Is that modernization? Freedom is difficult to get and to preserve. And it is even harder to get back once lost. When you have it, you get to choose your direction and, as you said, when we make a mistake, we get to fix it. The administrative state never has to answer for any mistakes. It simply doubles down and replaces one set of regulations with other regulations. Instead of stopping the bad, they add more regulations to fix the ones that didn't work. That is how we end up with 1000+ page bills. Bills that do not tell you what they pass and then leave the details to guess who, the administrative state, to figure out how to dictate to the citizens. This is not freedom, this is servitude. I, for one, am not yet ready to trade free thought and action for the yoke of the ox," finished Nick with feeling.

Lexi sat through Nick's response, appearing to pay attention and smiling throughout.

"Nick, your solution to this 'problem'," she said, raising her hands for emphasis, "would create chaos. No matter how much you want to enable people to be responsible for their own actions, a clear majority of them do not want to make all the decisions in their lives."

"Are you certain?" asked Nick calmly.

"I am. They look at those of us who have a lifetime of experience. To our pools of experts and leading minds in all fields available to the administrative state to help us understand the issues. Then, to determine the proper steps to achieve the outcomes in the best interests of everyone. They trust us to be the stewards of our government and their lives. In fact, perhaps, they used their freedom of choice to put this 'administrative state' in place to do just what it is doing," suggested Lexi.

"Do you believe that, or do you believe they are ignorant of the decisions being made until it is too late to change them?" asked Nick.

"If they did not agree, they would not keep electing the Party. We have reached a point where the Opposition minority no longer have the best interests of the people at heart. The continued ability of this minority to throw a wrench in the works. To prevent policies the majority supports, is not checks and balances, it is obstruction."

"As you say, we have been on this path for over 100 years. This is a steady alteration of the way we look at our freedom and our choices and what we expect our government to provide. We are not the same citizens of 1776 or even 1900. Just like the administrative state, our citizens have progressed as well. They support the idea of the social safety nets, social justice, equality and equity regardless of class, race, color, or socio-economic status. This is progress." Lexi stood and walked around the conference room as she continued.

"The capitalism experiment has been fine for those that succeed, but for those who do not or who have no opportunity to succeed, capitalism is grossly unfair. Dooming these unfortunates to squalor and poverty and no hope. Progressivism gives hope to all by flattening the curve. It takes away the competitive disadvantage and provides greater opportunity to all," explained Lexi, filling a glass with water and leaning back against a wall, looking at Nick as she continued.

"I think my nomination ensures we will continue to improve our government and progress to where the minority can no longer prevent the plans of the majority. The founders clearly ensconced the idea of majority rule by making us a democracy. They never envisioned a small minority of voters being able to stop the majority from implementing *anything*. The filibuster was there to ensure a minority voice, not to enable a few to block all progress. We'll work to make sure majority rule, as the founders wanted, becomes the law of the land," asserted Lexi.

Nick contemplated the persuasiveness of the Vice President.

"Madame Vice President, I appreciate the opportunity to talk and to better understand your position. Clearly, we do not agree as to the founders' intentions. The argument you are making is both persuasive and compelling. Anytime you are promising something for nothing. Less work for giving up something intangible, like freedom. Especially when keeping that freedom means hard work, toil, and no guaranteed outcome. It is bound to appeal to many as the path of least resistance."

Lexi shrugged. "We shall see who is the better judge of the character of America's citizens."

"As you have pointed out, you have achieved the nomination for president and from what I see out there on the Opposition side, I don't think you are going to get much of a fight in the national election."

"And in your own campaign, what are you hoping to achieve by agitating?" asked Lexi, now sipping water.

"Mine is simply a desire to ensure people think about the consequences of their votes. It is the History professor in me. I'm merely trying to tell people to make an informed decision. To understand what they give up if they choose to give up their freedoms to your administrative state. We do still have a democracy. People should be allowed to express their thoughts on this, by their vote. It is my reasoning for being in the race. I am sure your aide's tour of your campaign apparatus was to show me what a real campaign looks like. It is truly impressive."

Lexi smiled. "If you can't win and the Opposition can't win, why would you not consider joining our campaign? You don't strike me as the kind of person who is used to losing. You can help define these policies and ensure we are not implementing things the minority does not approve of in the administrative state. Seems like a much better use of your time and talent than wasting it on a Quixotic crusade," finished Lexi, lounging provocatively against the windowsill, fixing Nick in her icy gaze.

Nick contemplated Lexi, her pose, and the offer it entailed. Even he was surprised at his primal response to her beauty and the carnal temptation. He only now began to realize just how dangerous she was and would continue to be. Any thought he could retreat to the obscurity of college professor vanished in this instance at her look. For the first time in years, Nick had a knot of fear in his stomach as he made his choice.

"I appreciate the offer. I really do. All of it. But we have fundamentally different views of what the people really want. You are correct, there may indeed be a plurality of citizens who are perfectly happy looking to the government for purpose and direction. I don't *want* to believe this is the case. I need to find out for myself. If I'm wrong and our experiment in Constitutional rule is no longer what a majority want, I will go quietly back to my teaching," said Nick, holding out his hand to Lexi, who remained standing by the window.

"Fair warning Senator. After all the dust settles, the offer to include you in my administration will no longer be available. I need people who support and believe in our point of view. I need them with us in the trenches. After the victory, there will be no carpetbaggers showing up to profit off our risk and labor. I should also point out; I have the memory of an elephant. You are making some pretty provocative accusations on the campaign trail. As Vice President, I cannot do much, especially as a competing candidate, but as President there will be appropriate steps to punish those who have showed they are enemies of progress and enemies of *our* state," threatened Lexi in a firm tone ignoring Nick's outstretched hand.

"Madame Vice President," stated Nick, lowering his hand and walking toward the door to the conference room.

"I have no desire to serve in your administration. I thank you for the consideration," Nick paused. "And the warning." Lexi continued to stand motionless, her icy blue eyes intensely following him as he walked. Nick picked up his notebook and phone and headed out the door. An aide stood outside to walk Nick to the exit with a smile on her face and a 'have a nice day' to him as the elevator door closed.

As Nick exited the building, a camera snapped pictures of him leaving and walking back to his campaign office.

#

Mel watched as Nick left the conference room. Once he was sure he was gone, he entered the conference room. Lexi was still standing against the wall, sipping her water.

"Well?"

"You were right. He is a patriot and incorruptible. Once this election is over, our young Mr. Turner should have an unfortunate accident. He is dangerous Mel."

"Turned you down, did he?" commented Mel as he took a chair.

Lexi reddened at Mel's remark before she realized he was talking about the Vice-Presidential slot. Mel noticed her reaction as well.

"Yes. We both made our arguments, equally well articulated and concluded we are incompatible."

"I see. Well, it was certainly a long shot. Do you think he really talked to Blackbird? What about Garcia?" asked Mel.

"I believe he talked to Blackbird. Gauging his laughter when I asked him, he simply parroted back Blackbird's public line about never even considering Nick, let alone talking to him. Me thinks Blackbird protested too vigorously for it not to have happened. As for Garcia, he and Turner are too alike. Neither would want to be second. No, he is committed to his crusade. He truly believes he can 'wake up' the silent majority."

Mel shook his head. "Too bad. He would have been a great asset on our side."

Lexi looked at Mel. "I made the offer, and he turned it down. No second chances."

Mel suspected Lexi was more upset about the unspoken offer, than the VP slot. Hell hath no fury like a woman scorned. And when that woman was Alexis Smythe-Thomas, all Mel could do was feel sorry for Nick Turner.

# Chapter 87

Lauren was once again in the green room at ANC, waiting to appear on Marty's *ANC Tonight* show with her latest scoop.

The producer came in to tell her it was just five minutes. As a courtesy this time, she sent a text to her producer Jeff and told him she was about to appear on Marty's program. She also remarked she had proof this time of her scoop.

"This is becoming a regular occurrence. Once again, we're joined by ANC White House correspondent Lauren Bergamo. She has more breaking news about the ongoing saga of the presidential primaries. Lauren, what do you have for us tonight?"

"Well Marty, once again, Senator Turner is a popular guy. I had a tip he was meeting with another candidate. Of course, what they talked about is unknown to me or anyone, but I think it will surprise us by whom," said Lauren, pausing for effect.

"Garcia?" asked Marty.

"Nope. Show the pictures, please," requested Lauren.

"Up on the screen you see a series of pictures taken earlier this afternoon of Senator Turner leaving the Campaign Headquarters of Vice President Smythe-Thomas," said Lauren. "Now who knows, maybe they were discussing the upcoming foreign aid bill, or maybe she was worried he might throw his hat in the ring with an Opposition candidate," said Lauren with a triumphant smile.

"Wow, now that is a bombshell. Who would have guessed it? Only eight months ago, Mr. Turner was committing career suicide and now he is being courted by the leading candidates of both parties?" whistled Marty.

"It sure looks that way," confirmed Lauren.

"Did your sources provide any further info? How long they talked? Anything else?"

"Near as they could figure out, it was probably close to an hour."

"Interesting. Doubt they were going over a bill, given their history," said Marty with a laugh.

"Probably a fair assumption."

"And since Blackbird is on record saying he would never offer the VP slot to Turner, I'm guessing that didn't go well or," said Marty, pausing, "this could all be posturing. We all know how they play the game in this town. Profess hate one minute and then they are all buddy-buddy to pass a bill. Who knows," he shrugged.

"You are definitely right, Marty. Like you said, Turner has gone from pariah to the most popular guy at the dance," said Lauren with a smile.

"Well, she doesn't need to give Klausen the VP to get his supporters, so she can pick a candidate who helps her the most. Turner is an intriguing pick, but they seem to have diametrically opposed views on government. The VP makes it very clear she thinks progressivism is the future, and the Constitution is the impediment. Turner is the opposite. He is all about the Constitution and dismantling the administrative state. On the surface, it seems like there is no way they could come to an agreement. But boy, if they could, Lexi would be even more unstoppable," remarked Marty.

"My thought as well. The moderates Lexi lost to Klausen are going to go somewhere. Both Turner and Blackbird are angling for those voters and Turner probably has the inside track to pick up the Party ones, more than Blackbird. Lexi probably doesn't need all of them and if Turner and Blackbird, again presuming he gets the nomination, split those votes, even better for her."

"Again, very perceptive."

"You angling to get back in the field, Marty?" asked Lauren with a laugh.

"Lauren, I did my time standing outside the White House in the rain waiting for tidbits of info. Enjoy it while you can. From what I hear, the food on Air Force One is much better than in my day."

"I wouldn't know. Marty, there hasn't been a trip on Air Force One for over seven months," said Lauren in a questioning tone. "And they invite no press on Air Force Two when the Vice President travels on official business. Only on campaign swings."

"That is a conversation for another day. I have one question. The meeting with Blackbird was pretty clandestine. The meeting with the Vice President does not seem to be cloaked in as much secrecy," noted Marty.

"What does she have to hide? She already has the nomination and, as you say, now it is all about helping the ticket. Having her talk to Turner doesn't hurt her or make anyone mad. She doesn't care, and in fact, if she is trying to send a message to Garcia, Wilson, or Carson, she has more to offer than any of the Opposition," said Lauren.

"We only have 30 seconds. I asked the same question the other night. Will he take it?" he asked.

"I don't think so. Same reason as before. He doesn't want to be number two. He's on a crusade to get people to research and think for themselves, or so he says," said Lauren, quickly catching herself falling out of her public 'I hate Turner,' persona. "I don't think he thinks he can win, but as you know, he claims he just wants people to be more engaged and stop believing all of us blindly," said Lauren, with a convincing sneer, swinging her arm wide to imply all media was lying.

"Thank you, Lauren. Keep us posted on your next scoop," said Marty.

"Thanks Marty, will do," Lauren struggled to smile, her stomach suddenly rebelling as they exited the spot. As soon as the camera was off and went to commercial, Lauren practically tore off her mic and exited the stage almost at a run. Marty called out after her if she was alright.

This time she did not make it to a stall and had to throw up in a sink. She crouched over it, heaving. As her stomach settled, she washed the debris in the sink down the drain, grimacing the whole time as her cramps continued. She turned her phone back on and texts started coming in.

Several from Jeff, and one she went to immediately from the clinic. Her COVID test was negative. It had to be the flu. Shit, nobody wanted to get sick in the summer. She left the bathroom and headed to her company provided Washington apartment.

#

Lauren woke up in the middle of the night, soaked in sweat as a wave of nausea flooded over her. Cramps in her stomach had her doubling over in pain as she sat on the edge of the bed. After they died down, she got up and dashed to the bathroom, where she once again hung her head over the toilet bowl with dry heaves, having been uninterested in any dinner. She sat down, leaning against the vanity cabinet, and took a big swig of Pepto.

She would have to go to the doctor tomorrow and get something for this. As she sat on her bathroom floor in her old T-shirt, another thought crossed her mind. In a terror, she leaped to her feet, grabbed her phone, opened her browser, and typed in some words. Scanning the results, she clicked on a site, reading. She collapsed on the floor, leaning against the bed, crying. She was simply suffering from acute morning sickness.

"Oh fuck," she said out loud, "what am I supposed to do now?" She crawled back into bed and cried herself to sleep. Again.

# Chapter 88

"Lexi, we need to decide on the VP. The convention is coming up and we should announce it now, so we can get the coverage leading up," said Mel.

"I know. I don't like any of the options. Jackson is too pretty, McDonnell is too bitchy, and Zimmer wants my job. She is too ambitious and too likely to kill me," laughed Lexi.

"Too much like you," smiled Mel.

Lexi gave Mel an icy glance.

"I need someone to be seen and not heard, like elder Bush was for Reagan. Everybody wants to be a star now."

"Do you blame them? Does it have to be a woman of color, or can we pick a man?" asked Mel.

"I never really thought about it. I always assumed we would be the first all-woman ticket. But we are much more ruthless than men and I frankly can't count on any of these women to follow my lead."

"Maybe a black man, say an elder statesman type," said Mel.

"Who?"

"Jimmy Jefferson," said Mel.

Lexi sat in her chair and put her fingers together, contemplating what Mel suggested.

"It could work. He was a senator and a governor and that will help with Pennsylvania too," said Lexi.

"Plus, he was an ambassador and worked in the CIA, too," added Mel.

"Do you think he would take it?"

"If you call him and ask him, I believe he will. His politics are not as progressive as ours, but he was a big Civil Rights guy. Supported John Lewis. I think we can count on him to follow our lead."

"How old is he now? 70?" asked Lexi.

"He just turned 72, but he is very spry," responded Mel.

"Sounds like you had this prepped and ready."

"That's my job," he smiled in reply.

"Okay, set up a meeting so I can see for myself."

"Already did," said Mel, continuing to smile as Lexi scowled at being handled.

#

"That's a surprise," said Denise. "And a mistake, I think. She should have picked a black woman, or even better, a Hispanic woman."

Nick and his senior staff all stood in the conference room crowded around the TV where Lexi was announcing a tall, distinguished looking, older black man with gray hair as her Vice President.

"I don't know. JJ is a solid, if not spectacular, choice. He is safe, experienced and *is* black. He won't challenge Lexi on her policy positions," explained Chuck.

"Do you know him?" asked Nick.

"Yes," Denise and Chuck replied at the same time. They looked at each other and laughed.

"You first," said Chuck.

"I crossed his path a few times when I was working on various re-election campaigns when he was both governor and a senator. He seems pretty shrewd. No dummy for sure," remarked Denise.

"I agree. He was just going out as a senator to run for governor of Pennsylvania when I started working with Senator Richards. They were on a couple of committees, and I got to see how his mind works. He has a blind spot for race. A bit of a radical for that cause, no surprise. I know he was out marching with ARL back in the George Floyd days. Lexi will use him to solidify the black vote. He is a bit too old and represents the John Lewis style black activist. The modern ARL movement knows nothing of the Civil Rights struggle and frankly they don't care about equality like Lewis and MLK. They want blood. And money," finished Chuck.

"I agree. But he can solidify the black voters who vote. We know the black youth has next to no voter participation. I think this means she is scared. He is someone who won't challenge her. No ambition at his age, so this is a safety pick. He may help her in Pennsylvania. Very peculiar," said

Denise, thinking aloud. "My guess is she did not want anyone threatening her position as Queen Bee. Another ambitious and capable woman as a number two would only lead to competition. Our Lexi hates competition."

"You seem to know her awfully well?" commented Nick in a questioning tone.

Denise looked at Chuck.

"Surely, he knows, right?" Chuck nodded. Denise looked back at Nick.

"Speaking of which," said Chuck, changing the subject. "We should probably get serious about choosing our running mate, too."

"I know, I know," said Nick, still thinking through Denise's answer. "I need someone who believes in our cause."

"And someone who has nothing to lose because this is probably a career ender. You need to lean toward someone at the end of their career," frowned Denise.

"Or someone out of politics who does not care about a political career any longer," added Chuck.

"Hello. I am standing right here," waved Nick, raising his hand. "Geez, that is good advice. Should they commit hari-kari before or after the election results are in?"

Denise and Chuck both glared back at Nick, who turned his palms up in surrender.

"There are some good former congressmen who think like we do," continued Denise. "I can give you a list to peruse."

"Normally I would suggest we pick someone who could help us in a key swing state, but in our case, we need help in every state," said Chuck with a snort.

"I'll decide soon, right after the conventions," agreed Nick. "Let's see who the Opposition nominates."

"The Party has a woman and a black man. The Opposition will probably end up with Blackbird and who knows? Maybe Carson?" guessed Denise.

"I can tell you the person I pick is not going to check a box."

Denise shook her head, her face showing her anger. "You really don't understand this. It is about votes. Making decisions that get us votes. There is nothing else that matters. Saying things that get us votes. Votes. Every decision should be about votes."

"Hey everyone, now Denise thinks we can win," announced Nick, smiling, breaking some of the tension.

"My job is to help you win. In order to win, you need more votes than the other guys. Simple as that. You need to make decisions and say things that win us votes. Not ones that lose them. If you don't do that, the rest of the team and the fans lose faith. Keep that in mind as you pick your running mate," growled Denise.

"Tom Brady is our best pick?" asked Nick.

"I'd support that," smiled Margie, looking up.

"Geez Margie, he is practically old enough to be your dad," said Greg from a corner of the room.

"Not much older than Nick," said Jenny with a smile, which she quickly hid when Nick looked at her. "I'd be happy with Tom; he is not too old for me."

"Good luck. While that might not be a bad pick, there can only be one quarterback, so you can't pick someone to compete with. They need to support you and be committed to doing that," stated Chuck.

"Besides, Tom likes to win," said Denise in a deadpan tone.

"Ouch," groaned Nick, feigning being stabbed in the back. "I'm going to have to fire all of you. From now on, let's at least act like we can win. With you guys on my team, why do I need opponents?"

"What's the name of the team the Globetrotters always beat?" asked Greg.

"Maybe you guys can all get jobs at Comedy Club's soon," responded Nick. "Real soon."

"Or we could go on with Dr. Phil to discuss the trauma of working on your presidential campaign," suggested Chuck.

"Alright back to work. Go get some more of those votes Denise is obsessed with," ordered Nick. "Enough daydreaming about Tom Brady."

"Nick, I got a strange message from EXN," said Margie looking at her phone. "I have a private number from Tommy. They would like you to call."

"Is that weird?" asked Nick, looking around the room.

Denise shrugged. "In this campaign, nothing surprises me. Call him."

"Alright, I'll be right back," he said, walking out of the conference room.

They all turned back to the TV and watched Jimmy, 'JJ' Jefferson, giving a speech about what an honor it was to be selected by the Vice President to join the Party Presidential ticket.

Nick returned to the conference room.

"That was quick," commented Greg. "Wrong number?"

Nick laughed and shook his head.

"What did you say about this being a strange campaign?"

"What did Tommy want?" asked Denise. "Does *he* want to be your VP?"

Nick laughed, "Now that would have been news. No, they invited me to join their convention prime time news team in their booth to provide commentary and insight for both conventions."

"What? This could be huge." remarked Denise, in a disbelieving tone.

"I know. Is there any reason I can't or shouldn't do it?" asked Nick.

"Jenny?" asked Denise, already thinking how to leverage this additional exposure.

"I don't think so. You are free to do whatever you want. It is not a campaign contribution and since you are now a registered Independent, there is nothing wrong with you offering comment on the conventions. As long as you don't disclose any senate business, which applies any time you talk to the media, I think it is fine. Sounds like a great opportunity to get more folks a chance to know you. Their ratings are always the highest for conventions. Be lots of folks who don't normally watch EXN tuning in," said Jenny.

"Chuck, Denise, Margie?" asked Nick.

"Do it," nodded Chuck.

"I agree," smiled Margie. "This could be a godsend of free coverage and then the rebuttal coverage you'll get on the other networks. You'll get exposed to many people who don't know you well, just like Jenny said. Convention demographics skew much older and these are folks you are not getting to as much with your appearances."

"Call him back and accept. We don't have you booked at any state fairs during the conventions, so you can be there all four nights if they want you," stated Denise.

"OK, this should be interesting. Another first for a presidential campaign," observed Nick.

# Chapter 89

Nick looked up at the knock on his door in their Denver campaign office. He saw Earl, Jenny, and Denise standing in his doorway.

"What's up guys?"

"Nick, do you watch the news?" asked Jenny.

Nick laughed. "Is that a trick question?" He stopped, seeing they were not smiling in return. "No, why? What happened? Come on in."

They all filed in and took seats.

"Nick, there was a shooting back in May. The sheriff's department was following up on a Red Flag warning about someone who'd been accused of domestic abuse previously. The complaint said he was a menace to himself and an ex-girlfriend," explained Denise.

"It was in one of those run-down converted motel apartment complexes off East Colfax," added Earl. "Six deputies showed up just in case. Because of the prior complaint, they also got a no-knock warrant signed off by a local judge. They didn't want to take any chances."

"Uh oh. I am sensing it didn't go well," guessed Nick, getting up.

"That is an understatement. They entered the complex around 5 am, knocked down the guy's door, start yelling sheriff's department and the shots start flying," stated Earl.

"How bad?" asked Nick.

"Bad. The guy shot and killed all six deputies, including a female deputy," answered Denise.

"Really? Who was this guy, Mitch Rapp?" asked Nick incredulously.

"Nick, it gets worse. They kicked in the door to the wrong apartment. The resident was a former Marine sergeant. Four tours, silver star, couple of bronze stars with valor, couple more purple hearts. He responded like he was trained, and killed all of them," explained Earl.

"Shit. Didn't he hear them yelling?"

"Turns out he is deaf in one ear and mostly in the other. It was one reason he got discharged. Claims he did not put his hearing aid in until after the firefight. He said they were shouting, but he couldn't understand them. Plus, it was dark. He has a spotless record, so he had no reason to assume it was legitimate. He figured it was a home invasion and defended himself. He got shot three times and grazed a fourth. Claims he didn't realize they were sheriff's deputies until after it was all done," finished Earl, shaking his head.

"He was also suffering with PTSD and tried suicide twice before the VA stopped pumping him full of psychotic drugs, supposedly to help him 'treat' it," added Jenny, in disgust.

Nick sat on the edge of his desk, thinking. Then he looked up.

"How do you know all this, and the treatment? Isn't that confidential? HIPAA and all that."

"Nick, his lawyer is a friend of mine and called me. He wants to talk to you. He says the media and the Sheriffs are all trying his client in the public square and are not owning up to their mistakes. His client just defended himself," finished Jenny.

"Nick, I would counsel you to be very careful with this one. It has stink all over it. No matter what you say, you will end up pissing off your following. Right now, the cops love your law-and-order stance. But if you come out in favor of the Marine, after he kills six of their comrades, including a young woman, you are going to alienate a lot of folks. Give both parties plenty to attack you with," warned Denise.

"Earl, tell him the rest," pushed Jenny as Denise scowled.

"There is more?" asked Nick.

Earl and Jenny nodded as Denise looked away.

"When the sheriff's started returning fire, they were firing indiscriminately at where they thought the marine was in the room. The marine, Dusty Ingram is his name, was down low by then and in a corner. A majority of their rifle rounds were hitting the wall behind his bed, where they expected he was. He saw their shadows outside his window and was just out of bed with his pistol when they broke down his door." Earl paused before continuing, reluctantly.

"You know what those buildings are like, thin walls. Forty-seven bullets penetrated the wall and entered the apartment on the other side. A father and child were killed, and the mother was injured as well. The Sheriffs are trying to blame Dusty for their deaths as well, saying if he had listened to them and not started defending himself, they would not have returned fire and those innocents in the other apartment would not have been killed and injured. The child was nine months old."

"This is a horrible tragedy," sighed Nick, sitting.

"I'm not done," added Earl.

"You've got to be kidding."

"The guy who was the intended target of the raid and whose weapon they intended to seize, heard the commotion. In the confusion, he got in his car and sped away, chased by deputies who saw him. He died after a high-speed chase where two *other* people died when he caused them to wreck their car. He had no gun. Didn't even own one. Apparently, the Ex was trying to get him back for dumping her, so she 'Swatted him'."

"Swatted?" asked Nick.

Jenny and Denise looked at him. "Do you ever turn on the TV? Swatting is a real problem. Besides trolling people online, the pajama-razzi are also now calling in domestic violence and gun shots 'heard' types of calls into 911. Typically, for celebrities and politicians they dislike. Usually of the Opposition variety. The cops show up, along with the TV cameras, conveniently tipped off as well. They make it look like someone is doing something wrong. As they say, a picture is worth a thousand words. No matter how many times the person gets on TV to say they were swatted, the pictures of the cops rummaging through their house looking for drugs, or guns or a beat-up teenager make the point. The images are there forever. That is 'Swatting'," finished Jenny.

"What happens to the folks who call it in? Please tell me they are punished," remarked Nick.

"Never," answered Earl. "It was starting to happen in Colorado when you mercifully called me to your service. Lots of time, the calls are on disposable phones. Any name they give is false. The problem is law enforcement has to respond, or they get called out if the one they ignore is real. Here, it was swatting, combined with utilizing the Red Flag laws, as a reason to seize the guy's gun. You know how much our governor loves his Red Flag laws," noted Earl sarcastically, referring to Governor Morris.

Nick sat down, leaning forward with his head hanging down. When he raised his head, Denise shook her head at the look on his face.

"No. Don't do it. Please, Nick. We don't need this. There is no win here. Only bad everything. Earl, tell him what will happen," ordered Denise, looking over at Earl.

"Nick, she is right. I *know* the facts and can review them objectively. But if I was the Sheriff and lost my deputies, and you came out against me, I'd be pissed to high heaven," said Earl.

"Denise, this is exactly what I have been preaching. Actions have consequences. People have to take responsibility for their actions. These deaths were preventable. The highway deaths, the people in the apartment, the sheriff's deputies. Breaking down the wrong apartment door. They all started because of one problem. Red Flag laws. I am telling you, if we don't use this to stop it, this is only the first of many more innocent lives this will ruin or end. Not just here, but across the country as these are implemented federally," Nick paused.

"This is not the first time this has happened in Colorado. It is another example of the unintended consequences of trying to legislate 'good'. A seemingly reasonable idea on paper, taking guns away from potential suicides and mass murderers based on the word of conscientious family or neighbors. What could go wrong with that? Everyone is honest and forthright and interested in the good of all, right?" Denise had an angry look on her face as Nick continued.

"Instead, we get vindictive colleagues, exes, neighbors and strangers 'swatting' folks, knowing this will cause mayhem and destruction to the target's livelihoods. Worst case, it is leading to the deaths of innocent civilians and sheriffs. We have taken 'your word against mine' and weaponized it, with little to no risk for the accuser and a world of hurt for the target, whether legitimate or not. This has to stop," finished Nick, looking at his team.

"If Margie were here, you know she'd disagree," begged Denise.

"Her argument would be a good one, just like Earl's. The benefits of taking guns out of the hands of potential suicides is far outweighed by the reality of human nature using this tool for harm against anyone. We'll have to find better ways to stop suicides. Ways that don't require sheriff's breaking down doors to seize guns," stated Nick.

"Nick, as a former sheriff, who had to enforce this law, I can tell you, we hated them. We were hyper-alert when we did. Knowing someone has a gun and you are there to take it forces people into irrational thinking. A criminal is already there, and we are prepared for that. An honest, upstanding citizen has a hard time comprehending why we would take their guns and it sends them into defensive mode immediately," said Earl, pausing for effect. They are not trained, and the adrenalin makes them do stupid things.

"This is their means of protection from all things bad and we are there to take it, for no reason, in their mind. I have witnessed it firsthand. I will tell you one thing, it underscores the reason the 2nd amendment even exists and the fourth I believe. This is exactly the argument why the common man should have guns. We validate it every time we try to enforce these laws. It IS the Government coming for your guns and your right to self-defense, primarily from that same government. It is exactly the result the Party wants everywhere."

"I agree Earl," replied Nick firmly. "Jenny, I want to meet with the lawyer. After the conventions."

"Will do. I'll tell him to come by then," answered Jenny, smiling, while Denise sat scowling and shaking her head in disapproval.

# Chapter 90

The Party convention in Philadelphia got underway on Monday in late July. As is usually the case, the first day was an exercise in supporters from various groups standing on stage. They delivered speeches to groups of paid staffers and hard-core supporters who occupied the well of the convention floor. Only political junkies and party zealots enjoyed the early days of conventions. It was payback time. The fifteen minutes of fame for everyday people supporting a myriad of causes relevant to the Party platform tent. It was a big tent.

They had speech after speech from marginalized groups in American society. Each gave a heartfelt picture of what it was like to be a minority in America. Whether it was blacks from Nigeria or a Vietnamese Hmong, Puerto Rican, or American Samoa, from the Philippines to Guatemala, Somalia, Ecuador and, of course, Mexico. They all told the same story. Systemic discrimination, corporate greed using their cheap labor, and an unfair system where there were little to no protections for them. Many were not citizens, but they all sang the praises of the Party's progressive social safety net. Thanking America for giving them haven.

Many told tales of illness and disease for themselves or their children, most of whom received care because of government Medicaid or volunteer organizations. They heralded the reuniting of family members through chain migration and lenient border policies. Most also explained how they could not have survived without the Party championed SNAP and various welfare benefits.

The theme of the day was the consistent blocking of the expansion of these social services to help underserved and underprivileged immigrants. Their sole crime was they were not born in America. There was also the implication they suffered more because they were also not white. The crowd cheered enthusiastically. The stories were heartfelt and honest. Sometimes gut wrenching, terrifying, and many ended with family members who lost their lives attempting to get to America to lead the American Dream.

The networks, made up of mostly white executives, minimized the actual broadcasting of these speeches, and instead showed bits and pieces, mostly from the Congressmen and women, and former candidates. The talking heads on the liberal networks made the most of the stories.

Cherry picking the most heart wrenching to highlight the injustice, discrimination, and outright meanness of the Opposition party. None of this was unexpected in a party consisting primarily of one issue voters. The Party's coalition had expanded exponentially with the inclusion of the new sexual orientations and gender fluidity they had helped champion in the schools and society.

The ratings for the convention's first night were abysmal. Some of the worst in a trend of ever decreasing interest by the citizenry in the overall political process.

Nick was scheduled to join the EXN prime time election coverage team on the second, third, and fourth nights. During the second day, the Party adopted the platform by unanimous acclamation of the now more crowded convention floor.

"Well Senator, your thoughts on the Convention so far and on the Party platform specifically," asked silver haired Adam Mullen, EXN's lead election anchor.

"Adam, I think they are so confident they no longer need to hide their progressive agenda. Did I hear you say this is your 11th convention?"

"My fourteenth presidential election cycle and eleventh set of conventions as a reporter. It is actually the 12th convention set if you count the ones I attended as a boy with my father," he answered, smiling.

"In all your time, you probably more than most have seen the battle for relevancy of the progressives. Especially in getting their desires included on the party platform. This year it is front and center for all to see. In this document," commented Nick, holding up a moderately thick set of papers. "They are coming out, guns blazing, metaphorically speaking, since it is the progressives," said Nick with a smile. Adam chuckled as well.

"Not surprising when you combine this with the removal of the filibuster and the attempt to pass the four bills earlier this year to limit guns, pack the Supreme Court, expand the states, and provide amnesty to illegals. These are designed to create party majorities which theoretically could never be overturned. You now see in their platform the way they intend America to look going forward."

"If you bother to read the entire manifesto, you'll find blanket amnesty, single payer health care, free college, wiping out college debt, universal guaranteed wages, gun bans to be followed soon by voluntary buy backs and eventually confiscation through the adoption and enforcement of Red Flag laws. Shall I go on?" asked Nick, unsure of how long he should talk.

"Please do, Senator. It's why we have you up here. For your analysis of both parties, platforms, and candidates," said Adam.

Nick nodded, "More states, an expanded Supreme Court, defunded police, mandatory diversity training, diversity quotas in the military and in all Federal jobs, and importantly, what amounts to a true Ministry of Truth with the ability to censor everything published on any medium," Nick paused shaking his head.

"Finally, there is ninety-page addenda explaining all the climate change measures to reduce and remove fossil fuels from our country. Requiring mandatory solar and wind retrofitting to all businesses and private residencies and a complete phaseout of all nuclear, coal, *and* natural gas power plants in the next 10 years. This is besides the already in progress phase out of internal combustion cars in the next seven years. Essentially, taking California state laws and making them Federal, applying to all the states."

"I suspect we will hear much of the same in the Vice President's speech on Thursday. Lenin and Marx dreamed of a worker's paradise. This is their wildest dream codified in a series of promises and guarantees if the Party are elected," finished Nick.

"That is quite the summation, Senator, and quite the interpretation," said Billy McCall, the morning news anchor for EXN. "What do you think the reaction will be in the polls?"

"Billy, the polls are biased and typically help the Party with that bias, showing the readers and viewers the perception they want to show. Which of course is a much wider acceptance of their policies than the populace truly has." before Nick could continue, he was interrupted.

"Do you really believe that, Senator? Or do you say that because you are not polling well?" asked Diane Paxton, the lone woman in the booth. With fiery red hair and a red dress to match, she was Billy's co-anchor on the morning news program.

"It is true I am not polling well Diane," laughed Nick. "But I am not putting much stock in any of the polls; mine or anyone else's. As has been shown time and time again, the only polls that matter are the ones the day of or the day before elections. It is always amazing how 12- or 15-point Party leads shrink to 1 or no lead in that final poll, when one can no longer be influenced," said Nick in a confident voice.

"Polls are like the late-night infomercials highlighting massive weight loss in only five days. Buyer beware. To answer Billy's question, I think there will be the usual convention bounce for the VP. I think today's platform will be reported very little and published nowhere the voting public is likely to review it. Admittedly, most of them couldn't care less what is in the Party platform. In fact, I would hazard a guess I am the only one in this booth who read the entire thing. Probably holds true for this entire convention center, and possibly the candidate herself." His booth mates laughed at the last statement, and it was clear from their grins he was correct. None of them had read it.

"We have succeeded in dumbing down our electorate to a point where we probably deserve everything that happens to us. We now have the results of generations of progressive led school indoctrination. None of the VP's voters will be much inclined to look at the platform, but they will heartily endorse all the free stuff," said Nick.

"One could say the same for the Opposition platform," retorted Diane accusingly, her green eyes flashing ire at Nick as he stared back.

"You are correct Diane, nobody on the Opposition side reads theirs either. I will be equally harsh when I read their platform, but it will not be as radical as this," finished Nick, dropping the hundreds of pages onto the dais with a clear thump.

"This is an exercise in wasting time and making people, particular staffers, feel they are contributing something monumental to the cause. They will pay more attention on Thursday night when Lexi gives her speech. That is the one time when the other networks can no longer hide the radical nature of the platform. They'll be forced to show her progressive agenda in all its glory. But again, who will watch who is not already a Lexi acolyte?"

"Rory, do you agree with the Senator on the demographics and polling" asked Adam, turning to the last member of the broadcast booth. Rory Kane was an analyst and number cruncher. He was known for his extensive use of chalkboards to make his points.

"I agree with the Senator on the inaccuracy of the polls in the last few election cycles. After the debacle with the exit polling in the last half dozen presidential elections, we lost another tool in our arsenal to gauge voter sentiment. With all the mail in voting now, it is really difficult to predict outcomes accurately. Especially the day of election voter turnout. We have more data than ever. Yet our accuracy of predictions is getting worse each cycle, not better," said Rory.

"Why is that, Rory?" asked Billy.

"Billy, we have no way to forecast the mail in and absentee ballot returns. Nor the breakdown of votes being cast since we have no tracking of where they are coming from, in different parts of the state, or a particular county. You combine this with day of voting that may or may not be high turnout depending on how many of the mail in votes came from what parts. Add to this the ability to vote a week to two or even three weeks before the election. It throws a wrench into the whole predictive modeling we have relied on for decades," said Rory, exasperated by the polling situation.

#

Denise sat watching the coverage with Chuck in the conference room in Denver.

"Don't do it," she pleaded. "I knew we should have had him sit on a sensor so we could push it right now," she said. They held their breath as the camera panned out to the entire group. Nick had opened his mouth to speak.

"NO!" Denise shouted at the screen, standing.

#

"Senator, did you have something to add?" asked Adam.

"No, Adam, I was just going to agree with Rory's assessment. The nature of the vote now leads to speculation about what, when and how many votes are being counted and where. It makes guesses about actual turnout moot until they count the ballots. Polling is even less valuable now that voting starts so early in so many states. Heck, there is even a debate scheduled after 17 states have already started voting," noted Nick.

#

Denise raised her hands to the ceiling, saying a silent prayer of thanks that Nick had not mentioned cheating or fraud. It was the one thing they had made him promise to not discuss during his time on TV.

# Chapter 91

As the convention rolled into day three, Lexi's name was put forth for the nomination. They easily confirmed her as the winner, with her home state of California putting her over the top. As they headed to prime-time speeches, Tommy joined them in the booth as the Vice Presidential nominee, Jim Jefferson, delivered his Vice-Presidential nomination speech.

"That seemed like a safety speech," stated Billy.

"I imagine they want to leave all the meat to Lexi's acceptance speech. This was more of a reminder of the Vice-Presidential nominee's extensive experience and his ties to the Civil Rights movement, which *are* very impressive," commented Nick.

"I agree," added Adam. "This was the 'I am just the warm-up act and heaven help me if I steal any of the candidate's thunder' kind of speech."

"Tommy, you have any thoughts on this?" asked Billy.

"I do. What does he bring to the ticket?" The look on Tommy's face revealed his bewilderment at the choice.

"I sit here scratching my head, trying to do the calculus. He is old and not ambitious. He is not a woman, so there won't be any comparisons or cat fights between the two of them. Sure, he may help her in Pennsylvania, but she should win that with or without his help. The VP is one of the most powerful tools you have to leverage. This pick should shore up where you are weakest. Now Nick, you would have put her into the 400 electoral vote range minimum if she had asked you to be her VP. By the way, did that actually happen?" asked Tommy, out of the blue, as everyone turned to Nick.

Nick simply smiled.

"Did you ask a question, Tommy?"

"There were pictures of you leaving her campaign headquarters and Lauren Bergamo over at ANC said that was why you were there," said Diane in an accusatory tone.

"I was out for a walk, and nature called. That building happened to be the closest with a public restroom," said Nick with a shrug.

"You took your time with nature. Bergamo said you were in there for an hour according to her sources," said Tommy, laughing.

"Hey, I came on as a guest, not to be grilled," said Nick, holding up his hands. "JJ is her VP. He is a solid and respectable choice from what I know about him. There is also a saying, once you have been a pilot, you never want to be a co-pilot again."

"Well put, Senator, but I still think Lexi is more concerned about being challenged within her own party. She did not pick anyone else who she might feel threatened by. I think that is a mistake on her part," said Tommy.

#

As day four drew to a close, the audience waited for Lexi to make her way to the stage to give her acceptance speech. As the band played, she came out in an azure blue dress with matching high heels, a simple silver belt highlighting her slim figure and legs, and a single strand of pearls around her neck. She looked the epitome of the former fashion model she had been as a teenager and collegiate. She did not look like the ruthless politician she had become.

Lexi talked for 45 minutes, forcefully expressing her support for the need to advance the progressive agenda. To counter the hate and antiquated restrictions of the Opposition. Who were obstructionist and want to keep poor people poor, college students indebted, races segregated, sexes suppressed, and foreign wars inflamed. She used soaring rhetoric to highlight the improvements she had accomplished and would continue to champion to free the people from their servitude to corrupt corporations, idle rich, racist police, feckless criminal justice systems and Opposition who only favored more of the same.

By the time she finished, she'd worked the crowd into a thrashing frenzy of 'LST' and 'Lexi' screaming minions. As they released the balloons from the ceiling, her husband, Pete, joined her on stage, and her Vice President,

Jimmy Jefferson and his wife Jackie. They waved and waved as the ovations went on for five minutes. The band played various campaign oriented rock and pop songs. All willingly provided to the campaign by their artists, who wholeheartedly supported her. The party was just beginning and would continue into the wee hours as several Hollywood and pop stars had agreed to put on an impromptu concert for her supporters.

In the booth above, as the pandemonium on the floor continued, the panel discussed the speech.

"I thought the speech was very effective," said Adam. "Just as you said days ago Senator, she highlighted the platform but juxtaposed it against some opposition, prior administration restriction, or inactions she would correct with each new implemented progressive item."

"It was a wonderful speech. She knows how to work the crowd and play to the strengths of her message. When to throw red meat to each of her one issue constituencies in the crowd below," agreed Nick.

"One issue?" asked Diane questioningly.

"Yes Diane, my gut feeling is most in the Party are under the tent because they have one significant issue that trumps all their other issues or feelings. Even if the Party is against all the other things the person is for, it is this one issue that makes them stay in the tent."

"I am not sure I am following your logic," continued Diane.

"Abortion, climate change, universal healthcare, gay and trans rights, ARL, equity, etc. They are voting against their best interests on all the other issues. Economy, funding police and personal safety, open borders, inflation, foreign policy issues, education, terrorism. All things most voters are concerned about. However, these concerns get thrown out the window because the American *Pravda* media swears the Opposition wants to keep *Roe* overturned and all other reasonable abortion legislation from being enacted, for example. Or the need to reduce man-made climate change or there will be no planet for their children. These voters all have their issue which they are adamantly against. They let it overwhelm their common sense and their overall wellbeing. Gender reassignment surgery without parental consent, chain migration or birthright citizenship, ensure pre-existing condition healthcare or canceling student loan debt. The list goes on," Nick was told to keep going by the producer talking in his earpiece, despite Diane's reddening face.

"Lexi has a broad coalition of voters the Party has cultivated for decades to vote faithfully against a majority of their own best interests, primarily because of the duplicity of media. That is why I call it the American *Pravda*. All media outlets have an approval of less than 10% in your own surveys. *You* tarnished your brand and role to where everyone believes it is pure propaganda. Mostly for the left. Hence *Pravda*, for those old enough to remember the old Soviet communist paper of record," concluded Nick.

Diane was clearly going to take exception to Nick's characterization, but Tommy jumped in first.

"Senator, do you think anyone listening to Lexi understands the full implications of her agenda and what would really happen to America if they were successful in implementing these changes?"

"Tommy, some yes. Most of those undulating masses on the floor do not know the consequences of these actions. Like so many peoples who have lived through these socialist experiments in other countries, if she is successful, we will add our name to the history books along with the others," said Nick.

"My entire candidacy is predicated on trying to educate those masses of the possibilities of what could happen to them," said Nick, point a finger off camera at the cheering and celebration mass of people on the convention floor.

"If they are not self-aware and if they do not consider what the outcome could look like if even a portion of what she advocates is implemented. She did a masterful job today in triggering her followers without disclosing to the rest of the viewers the truly radical results they can expect."

"I believe you are correct, Senator," said Tommy.

"All the other networks, the rest of social media, the papers of record are all busy putting on the red *Pravda* berets, hammering out copy in praise of the 'New Dawn' speech. Highlighting how removing the obstacles of obstruction, mainly the Bill of Rights and the Supreme Court, just as they did the filibuster, will enable the new dawn in America," continued Nick, using his hands now as he evangelized to the broader audience of

TV viewers. Many watching had never seen him or heard his message of common sense.

"No, their media and cultural allies are all busy preparing for an all-out blitz to highlight the *humanity* of all this change. This is what I am fighting to balance. This is the goal of my campaign, to enlighten each of these groups on both sides of the aisle. To peel them away once they realize we have more in common than we differ. We can probably solve their one issue as well, through compromise, not coercion."

Nick paused again, listening in his earpiece for a cue to stop. When he got none, he continued to his last point.

"Only through education can this truly be stopped. This is not about money, endorsements, or flashy commercials. It is about looking folks in the eyes and helping them open their own to the possibilities. For good or simply to recognize the danger of sitting on the sidelines or believing the BS," revealed Nick.

The others in the booth sat enthralled by what Nick was saying. Even Diane appeared mesmerized by Nick. When he finished, he had to break them out of their trance.

"Tommy, surely you have some retort to my answer," said Nick with a smile.

"Senator, I couldn't have said it better myself. As always, and as we always say, every election, this is the most important election of our lifetime," said Tommy.

"Senator, how did you know it would be called the 'New Dawn' speech? I am hearing in my ear this is how it is being referred to by the other networks," asked Billy, surprised.

"Billy, she said it three times in her speech. It is what she wanted people to remember. Not all the radical changes but a theme of her helping America achieve a 'New Dawn'. Free from racism and bigotry, sexism, homophobia, corruption, economic malaise, gridlock in congress, etc. You don't use a catch phrase like that three times unless you want it to be remembered. That's how I guessed it. I didn't think 'Authoritarian Socialism in America' was likely to be the *Times* headline tomorrow, even though that was really what the body of the speech was about." Tommy guffawed off camera.

"What does Blackbird do to counter? What do you do?" asked Billy.

"Blackbird still has to win the nomination and then pick a running mate. He won't have much say on the platform because it'll be proposed and accepted before there is even a nominee. Whoever it is will have to support it wholeheartedly even if they don't agree with all the content. That is not a good start."

Tommy, off camera, said, "That is an understatement." Nick smiled on camera before continuing.

"Then they'll have to focus on where they differ from Lexi. I am independent for a reason; it means I'm not loaded down with the hundreds of years of collective baggage from these two parties. No mandate to accept all the positions of either. Instead, I'm free to cherry pick the best from both sides and find that sweet spot where most of the middle agrees with me over Blackbird or Smythe-Thomas. That's what I have to keep doing. Find the middle ground and the path of common sense. This is the third way," finished Nick.

"Well Senator, good luck with your path. From what I've seen tonight, it is going to be both uphill and steep," ended Diane.

# Chapter 92

"Well folks, welcome to week two of the greatest spectacles on earth. Last week we saw a unified Party convention where the Vice President sailed to the nomination, enthralled her followers and the nation with her vision of the future. This week, we are at the Opposition national convention and it is exactly opposite," announced EXN's Adam Mullen.

"Typically, this evening is where we would feature the speech by the vice president nominee and report on the nomination of the presidential candidate. However, we're not prepared for either at this point on day three. The Opposition cannot agree on a candidate and that candidate cannot pick a Vice President until they decide," continued Adam.

"If we can pan the camera down to the floor, please, you can see it is wall to wall with delegates from all the states. They've been gathered like this all day, with a quick break for lunch."

"Let me bring in our convention expert Chris Teller, to explain for us exactly what's happening on the floor today."

"Thank you, Adam. It's been quite a day. We haven't seen a convention like this since 1952, when it took several votes before Adlai Stevenson was nominated," stated Chris.

"What exactly is the process?" asked Billy McCall from the other side of Diane Paxton who was sitting next to Chris.

"Earlier today, we had a roll call of the states for nomination of a candidate for President. The Opposition convention rules state the delegates must vote the way the rules of each of their states demand. Some states are winner take all like Colorado. Most are proportional, like Texas, where your number of delegates is apportioned based on the number of primary votes. As you know, no one entered the convention with enough pledged delegates to reach the 50% threshold."

"Now, between the primaries and today, my sources tell me there were many conversations between Governor Blackbird, other candidates, and even others. Some of whom may be in this booth if rumors are true," said Chris with a grin, looking at Nick. The camera quickly cut to Nick, who was sitting on the other side of Adam, but kept his smile fixed as others looked at him as well. Chris continued.

"Anyway, Blackbird was trying to convince Governor Carson to pledge her delegates to put him over the top. My sources tell me Blackbird didn't contact Senator Garcia for his. Garcia, Carson, and Wilson were all also talking to each other to see if they could come together to challenge Blackbird. Bottom line, we had the first vote where the delegates voted the way the primary voters voted and, just as in the primary, no one got the majority."

"So that means what?" asked Adam, raising one gray-haired eyebrow in question.

"That means all bets are off now. After the first votes, the delegates can vote anyway they would like. So that is the reason you see all this activity on the floor. Each of the major candidates' floor leaders are working the state delegate leaders. Trying to convince them to vote for their candidate. Deals are being discussed for various favors. Positions in the administration and other patronage jobs. This is reminiscent of the backroom deal making common in the first half of the 20th century. In fact, all the way through the sixties. Each delegate in each state is now up for grabs," said Chris in an excited voice.

"So, what has happened since that first vote?" asked Diane, joining the conversation for the first time.

"It has been interesting. We have had four more votes. Blackbird actually lost a few of his pledged delegates, but picked up a few of Garcia's and a couple of Wilson's, but there was still no majority. What we are seeing now is the next round of votes and deal making and offers. This will go on until someone is offered a deal they can't refuse. It will only happen when someone has enough leverage to put a candidate over the top," said Chris.

"How many times will it take, do you think?" asked Billy.

"Well, you may not want to hear this, but they did not nominate Warren Harding until the 10th vote. The record was Thomas Davis, the Democrat nominee, in 1924. It took 103 votes before they settled on him," laughed Chris.

Adam could be heard groaning in the background.

"103?" said Billy. "Good lord, we'll be here until September."

"I don't think it will take that long," laughed Chris. "My sources are telling me all four of the candidates are standing firm. The three of them cannot come together and win without Blackbird. Blackbird cannot win without Carson's delegates and, of course, he needs to keep his from defecting to them. Right now, any of them could still win."

"Chris, I believe they have finished the sixth vote on the floor," commented Nick, thankfully giving the cameras and anchors something else to talk about.

"It appears you're right, Senator. Let's go to the convention floor and check in with Ned. What is the status?" asked Adam. The camera showed a picture of Ned Wheeler standing amongst the South Dakota delegation on the floor. It was loud, and Ned had one hand on his earpiece, trying to hear Adam.

"Adam, they just finished the latest vote and there was little change. Blackbird is still in the lead. Garcia's and Carson's blocks stayed with their candidate and Wilson's split about 60/40 for Blackbird and Garcia. The next vote will happen shortly once the latest round of deal making is over. Stay tuned."

"Thank you, Ned. Billy here, are you hearing anything else? Any rumors of deals?"

"Garcia's handlers have been running around on the floor after the vote. I don't know what is going on or what he is trying to get accomplished, but it seems like something may be happening. Maybe he and Blackbird have a deal. I have no confirmation," said Ned.

"No way Garcia compromises," offered Nick.

"Senator, you have been silent during the conversation. Do you have some thoughts on this?" asked Diane, looking at Nick.

"I have a lot of thoughts, Diane. My main one is a concern. The primary opponent party to a progressive takeover of our country is hopelessly fragmented. I know Senator Garcia a little. He is very principled, and he isn't going to budge from his conservative issues stance. His delegates are also very loyal, being conservative as well. I don't see them going anywhere. So next, you now need a sizeable chunk of Blackbird's moderates to defect, and move to Garcia, perhaps with Wilson's, in return for Wilson being offered the VP slot with Garcia."

"But Blackbird's delegates are also very loyal. You have an impasse. Wilson cannot be kingmaker, but Carson can, at least with Blackbird. But clearly Blackbird does not want to give Carson what she wants, which must be the VP slot. So, until someone gives in, this will continue. Blackbird still has a slight advantage as long as he can hold his delegates. But the bigger question is when this is done, can they unify around the candidate and give the Vice President a run for her money? I fear they cannot," said Nick seriously.

"But doesn't that help you Senator," asked Diane.

"Diane, all I care about is defeating the Vice President and her progressive agenda. More specifically, the platform the Party adopted. Whether it is me or the Opposition is irrelevant," stated Nick.

"Really Senator?" asked Billy. "That is a pretty magnanimous position."

"Billy, I am an American. I dislike the direction our country is going. The hollowing out of the Constitution and the attacks on the Bill of Rights. To be honest, I think the Opposition party cannot stop her. This is why I entered the race. To offer an alternative, a campaign for the common man, for moderates in both parties, appealing to common sense."

"You mean common people, correct Senator?" asked Diane, archly.

Nick stared at her, angry at what he was seeing on the convention floor below. He threw caution to the wind. "Diane, I meant what I said. If our citizens are too ignorant, or too sensitive to understand when a term is inclusive, then it is their problem, not mine. We are not, despite our media's obsession with pronouns, a complete nation of snowflakes who get hysterical over guys, chairman, fireman, police chief and many other euphemistic phrases most understand to be non-gender specific.

Nor do I endorse the latest fad of removing white, black and brown from every description in the misunderstood belief that speaking or writing the name of a color is racist. We have way more important things to worry about and fix."

Diane sat back, fuming, as the rest of the panel attempted to hide smiles. Nick kept going when no one responded.

"Diane, most people know right from wrong. We know when we are being manipulated. And now, many know enough to know when the media spouts the administration's propaganda. But as is always the case, the Progressives and their allies push it too far. Now people are on to the 'man behind the curtain' pulling the levers. We have a big problem and frankly our media, our American *Pravda*, is straying from facts to outright advocating for only one side."

"From COVID disinformation and lockdowns based on what turned out to be very *unsettled* science. To cancel culture, and ignoring the violence, murder and mayhem being covered up as peaceful protests. Crime is not worse according to American *Pravda* when gangs of thugs invade stores, carjack folks on the street to steal their dogs, and follow folks' home to rob them. People are wising up to the blatant lies and manipulation. The real question is whether enough of them will wake up to this and band together to do something about it? Or will they remain lazy and controlled getting their daily fix of lies and propaganda from the Progressive's official communications arms in our American *Pravda* media outlets?" asked Nick with passion, shaking his head.

"Senator, I let you get away with the comparison of the American Media to the Soviet propaganda news arm *Pravda* last week because I thought you were making a joke. Your continued comparison of American journalism to Soviet propaganda is an unacceptable statement. If you would please refrain from doing it while a guest on our program, we would appreciate it," ordered Diane, her face red with indignation.

None of the men on the panel jumped in to agree or disagree. Nick looked Diane in the face.

"Ms. Paxton, was that your opinion or was your producer speaking in your ear asking you to make that request of me?" asked Nick. The tension on the panel made everyone sit up straight. Adam looked like he was about to speak, to play peacemaker, when Diane, who was at first taken aback by Nick's question, responded before him.

"It was our producers," she said. "Your implications go beyond the pale and paint all journalists with a broad brush accusing all of us, including this network, of being tools for the progressives. As a guest, perhaps you should consider not insulting your hosts."

"Really? Adam, are your earpieces and Billy's tied into the same frequency as Diane's? Please understand this is a seminal moment for EXN." Nick pointed to a large screen TV on the convention floor that was showing EXN in one corner. A large group of delegates were standing around, quietly watching it, the closed caption showing the dialogue of the commentators on the screen. On it, Nick could be seen pointing down toward them. Many looked up at the booth high above the floor. It was a surreal moment.

"Either you are going to make my point for me, or the truth is going to be clear," noted Nick. There was a pause on the set.

Nick spoke after a few seconds. "Actually, let me help you. There is a lot of yelling in my ear, the same as yours I believe from the very producers who are now claiming they did not tell Ms. Paxton to berate me," said Nick bending and taking an earpiece out of his own ear, for all to see.

He looked at Diane. "You forgot they needed to give me cues as well, Ms. Paxton. But I thank you for confirming both your own position and that of the rest of the American *Pravda*, with a few exceptions," said Nick, nodding at Adam and Billy.

"Most media outlets are indeed simply parroting the words and deeds the administration tells them to. So no, Ms. Paxton, I won't stop referring to the consortium of network news, cable news, social media, and most print news as the American *Pravda*. Until they prove to me and to my fellow citizens, they aren't just the propaganda arm of the Party and this administration. They no longer deserve the benefit of the doubt. For reasons we have just experienced."

Diane's face was beet red, and she had a terrified look in her eyes, knowing she was cornered. No one spoke and the producers were yelling at Billy and Adam to jump in and do something. They did not, so Nick continued.

"I certainly hope this changes. My fear is shortly they they you will all morph into the Ministry of Truth from Orwell's *1984*. Silencing every voice who dissents, who calls out their lies or seeks to open other eyes to their manipulation. Like banning me from social media and now your attempt to cancel me on cable news as well," suggested Nick. The tension in the room was palpable.

While Nick was speaking, there was a commotion off screen. When he finished, the camera returned to Adam and Billy, who were trying to draw attention to the upcoming seventh vote, hoping it would begin quickly. Finally, Billy turned toward Diane's chair.

"We're happy to be joined by Tommy in the booth now, just back from the floor." The camera turned to show Tommy putting an earpiece in and straightening his tie as he took Diane's seat. Diane was nowhere to be seen.

"Sorry guys just ran up from the floor after the last vote," announced Tommy with a smirk, looking at Nick.

"Anything to report?" asked Billy.

"Frankly, it is chaos. No one knows how this is going to end. Carson and Garcia are digging in and Wilson has so few delegates they barely register, Florida and a few others. I don't know who is going to give, but Blackbird is still in the pole position," said Tommy, as Billy let out a burst of laughter.

"Sorry, sorry, the producers were yelling in my ear. Apparently, the other networks are going crazy about Nick's American *Pravda* media speech. They have forgotten about the convention and are focusing on Nick, sorry I mean Senator Turner," said Billy.

"Oh, and they think we should not have you in here getting free campaign time and are working on lawsuits against EXN for campaign finance violations."

"I'm happy to leave. Don't want to cause you guys *more* issues," announced Nick, smiling, starting to get up.

"Oh no, you are not about to leave over telling the truth. When they react like this, you are on to something. You hit the bullseye by telling the truth about them. Predictably, they are circling the wagons," commented Tommy.

"Ok, looks like the next vote is starting already. Let's listen in. Alabama is the first. Garcia won all those delegates," said Billy.

"The Great State of Alabama, home of the Crimson Tide, casts 50 delegates," said the portly gentleman, wearing a straw hat with Alabama across the brim.

"For Senator Nick Turner."

Nick stood up abruptly, shaking his head.

"No, no, no," shouted Nick, turning to Tommy with an angry look. "Did you do this?"

Tommy held up his hand, the smile exiting his face, as he saw Nick was clearly pissed. The camera panned from Nick to Tommy, to the pandemonium on the convention floor.

Nick turned to the camera as he sat. "Senator Garcia, I hope you or your team are watching. If this is your idea of a solution, while I appreciate the sentiment and the faith, I am NOT interested in the Opposition nomination. Please stop this before your divide your party even more."

"Unbelievable," said Adam, listening to the states being called out on the floor.

"Holy moly," said Billy out loud. "The other networks are having a cow. They hated you before, now they are coming unglued. Chris, has there been anything like this before?"

"Honestly, no. There have been dark horse candidates like Harding in 1920 and Dewey in 1948 and even Jimmy Carter in 76, but he was just an unknown in the primaries. He won enough delegates to win on the first convention vote. To have something like this where they pick someone of a different party, or I guess no party really, for a major party nomination, is unprecedented."

Nick was looking at texts coming in on his phone. So were Tommy and even Adam.

"Sorry folks, we are getting up to the second updates on our phones and in our ears. As you see from the tote board, states are coming in and it appears all of Garcia's are going for Nick. What is surprising is all of

Carson's delegates are deferring their votes," said Billy. "This is getting interesting for sure. What is that?" asked Billy, holding his hand to his ear.

"OK, amidst all the noise in the booth and on the floor. It looks like Wilson has thrown his delegates to Nick, ah, Senator Turner that is," said Billy as he saw Nick shaking his head.

"Senator, if you get the nomination, accept it for the good of the country," begged Tommy.

"Tommy, if you have any pull down there, get them to stop. I am not part of the Opposition party. I cannot beat the Vice President as an Opposition candidate," replied Nick, pleading.

"Are you sure?" asked Tommy earnestly, as the rest of the booth watched them.

"Senator, Colorado just changed its delegates from Blackbird to you. If he loses a few more, you are on your way," said Adam.

Nick looked at his phone. Amongst the texts flying in was one from Blackbird.

"Is this your doing?"

Nick texted back. "No. I did not know."

"Getting a lot of texts?" asked Adam innocently.

"Yep," said Nick laughing "what's the count?"

Nick looked down as Blackbird replied. 'I dont believe you.'

"Looks like you are slightly ahead at this point. If Blackbird doesn't lose any more and Carson's stay with her, it will be no majority again."

Nick looked down at his phone, again. This time it was buzzing on silent ring, a number he did not recognize. He let it go to voice mail. Next, a text came in. From Denise, 'Carson wants to talk.'

Nick closed his eyes. Adam, Billy, and Tommy were all watching.

"Anything you care to share, Senator?" asked Tommy pointedly.

Nick opened his eyes and smiled.

"Nope."

He texted Denise back. 'Tell her I appreciate it, but I can't accept.'

Chris was working on some paper, "Senator, you are at 48% and Blackbird is at 40%. Carson's delegates amount to about 12% It all comes down to which way she goes. I am sure if you offered her the VP she would make you the candidate," said Chris in an excited voice.

Nick said nothing and shook his head no.

"Hang on," said Adam. "Carson is coming to the delegation from South Carolina on the floor."

A pretty, petite woman with a blond bob hairdo and a sweet southern drawl addressed the crowd.

"My fellow Opposition delegates, I appreciate your faith in me. I have instructed all of my delegates to cast their vote for…" she paused for effect. "Governor Blackbird of South Dakota as our next President of the United States." The South Carolina delegation cheered, as did North Carolina, another state where she held most of the delegates. There were a considerable number of boos from the audience as well at the announcement.

"The Palmetto State casts its votes for Governor Blackbird." The rest of the outstanding Carson delegates in the various states followed South Carolina, announcing support for Blackbird, putting him over the 50% threshold and making him the next Opposition presidential nominee, by a very slight majority.

"Well, that was certainly exciting," remarked Billy. "Disappointed Senator?"

"Hardly. I'm flattered. Honestly, I am. But the Opposition needs to nominate someone from their own party. My beliefs are not the beliefs of the Opposition platform. Nor are they aligned with the Progressive platform of the Vice President. If they had given me the nomination, I would have reluctantly declined it for that reason. I appreciate the faith so many of the delegates have in my policies, enough to put me forth as a compromise candidate." Nick made a fist and said, "I either owe Senator Garcia a nice bottle of Scotch or a knuckle sandwich. I'll continue my candidacy as an independent. I look forward to hearing Blackbird's speech tomorrow to see how well he pulls the Opposition together."

Adam broke in, "It's official. Blackbird just announced Governor Kacey Carson of South Carolina is his Vice-Presidential nominee. She will give a speech before him tomorrow, during closing night."

"And that closes the circle. What a day," commented Billy. "Tommy, you're awfully quiet."

Tommy had been sitting in Diane's old chair, deflated once Carson agreed to support Blackbird, instead of Nick.

"You know, Billy, I really had hope for a minute. Like Nick, I want the Vice President to keep from advancing the Progressive agenda. I am here to offer opinions, not news, so I can say, I really think Nick has a better platform. Better ideas than the Opposition nominee, and this opportunity to make Nick the Opposition candidate gave me hope. I have to say, I feel like Garcia's supporters tonight, like I have no party," admitted Tommy.

Nick turned to look at Tommy. "Tommy, you're allowed to vote for someone besides the Opposition. So can Garcia's followers and Blackbirds and Lexi's. In fact, maybe it is time for people to break out of their blind faith in political parties and think for themselves, voting for the person and not the party?"

"Good point Senator," agreed Adam.

"We'll see what tomorrow brings. Maybe Blackbird will offer an olive branch to Garcia and his wing and unify the Opposition behind him," offered Adam.

"Final thoughts, Chris?" asked Billy.

"The candidate who emerges from a brokered convention on the opposition side, has only won about 40% of the time. The odds do not favor Blackbird."

"That wraps up our coverage from the Opposition Convention tonight. Please join us tomorrow for the speeches from the Opposition candidates," said Adam.

Nick looked at his phone. He had 214 unread texts. It was going to be a long night.

# Chapter 93

"Boss, you should have taken Carson's call," said Denise's face on Nick's laptop the next morning. Denise, Chuck, Greg, and Margie were doing a ZOOM conference call with Nick.

"Why? I wasn't going to accept her offer. In return, making her my VP for putting me over the top?"

"Do you think that is what she wanted?" asked Greg.

"Oh yeah, it definitely was," said Denise with a laugh. "She is an ambitious little minx. She would much prefer to be a VP to Nick than to Blackbird, but he left her no choice."

"I asked Tommy the same thing, Denise. Did *you* put a bug in Garcia's ear to do this? You two know each other," accused Nick.

"Honestly, I wish I could claim credit. What did Tommy say?"

"He claimed it wasn't him, but he talked to Garcia and he told Tommy what he was going to do. Tommy got into the booth just as the vote was starting, so he really didn't have time to warn me."

"That was pretty clear boss," laughed Margie. "Your reaction was priceless. You should watch it. If you knew, then you should get an Oscar. You jumped up and started shouting 'No, no, no'. It was authentic as hell. There is already a meme on the internet."

"Do I even want to know?" asked Nick.

Margie laughed as Nick continued.

"I can tell you; it surprised the shit out of me and I was sincere. I was terrified I would win and then have to decline it. That would have cost me a ton of voters, looking ungrateful. Instead, I think I just picked up 40% of the Opposition vote," said Nick.

"40 percent?" asked Chuck. "I don't know about that many, but Blackbird is toast. He will try to unify them tonight, but his problem is in his own party way more than the Party."

"We'll see. He is going to trash me, if only out of spite for my showing. He knows I could have won. I don't know if he knows Carson offered to come to my side, but he probably suspects. He knows he didn't get to the top on his own merits. He's going to come after me and, of course, Garcia. When he really needs to focus on Lexi. But he won't. We are an easier target. Lexi will let him spend his money picking on us and let him campaign himself right out of the race," stated Nick.

"The headlines are interesting," shared Margie. "Some are highlighting your nomination and highlighting the split in the Opposition party. 'They had to nominate a former Party member to save them'. Others are fixating on your treatment of Diane Paxton as sexist, misogynistic and an example of mansplaining and bullying. There are only a few stories about the fact she lied."

"Are we surprised? Makes my point," shrugged Nick.

"There are more favorable opinion print pieces being published by right leaning folks. Some are pointing out the hypocrisy of the press crowing over how Diane's true colors came out when you told the truth about the American Media. Good news is American *Pravda* is trending on social media, so your phrase is sticking. Social media are banning posters as fast as they can for forwarding stories or mentioning it. Hibi is full of mentions and EXN has stories on their website. Billy is covering it on the morning news program from the convention. Diane is nowhere to be seen. They have that pretty blonde on this morning," finished Margie.

Chuck spit up his coffee, stifling a laugh.

"Something I said" asked Margie, with a sarcastic tone.

"Margie, which one?" asked Chuck, trying to recover from his snorted coffee.

"Excuse me? Which one what?" growled Margie.

"Pretty blonde. EXN is nothing but pretty blondes. Diane was about the only one who *wasn't* blonde," said Chuck.

Margie flipped him off.

"Now children, play nice," laughed Nick. "Any word about what they are doing with her?"

"Nothing official," answered Greg. "Denise, have you heard anything?"

"I hear she won't be there tonight either. I suspect Tommy will start the night up there with you in the booth. They probably won't announce anything until Monday. You can't have a bleeding-heart anchoring news on a right leaning channel. She blew it. My guess is she will either end up on a network being your biggest critic or on ANC or FLNC, where she can complain about you," said Denise.

Nick shrugged. "What else? Anything important?"

"You need to think about what you will say when folks ask why you wouldn't have accepted the nomination if you had won."

"That one is easy," laughed Nick. "I'm not Opposition. They need an Opposition candidate."

"Thought any more about your VP?" asked Denise.

"I am thinking about it, promise. We can make some calls next week."

"Have you thought about Garcia?" asked Chuck.

"I have, but I don't think it would be a good move."

"You need to fly down to Texas soon and talk to him. If you can get him to endorse you, that will go a long way to elevating our brand and public status. His voters are up for grabs, and I think you are going to be the most conservative candidate in the race, as strange as that sounds," said Chuck.

"Except for the two inconvenient truths. First, I am not a conservative and second, abortion," said Nick.

"You really haven't gone on record with your abortion stance, other than being pro-choice," observed Margie.

"He will next week. He addresses the Women's Right to Choose conference," said Denise. "After that everyone will know the details."

"Did you get me a spot at the Evangelical World Congress gathering?" asked Nick.

"I did. They were hesitant, but I assured them they would want to hear what you have to say. The largest pro-life conference is not usually a place pro-choice speakers get invited," noted Denise.

"I hope my message works for both, and we can find a common ground. If *that* is well received, then we can go to Garcia to see if he thinks Opposition conservatives can live with my view," said Nick.

"And that stance is?" asked Margie looking up from her tablet.

"You'll just have to wait until next week," said Nick with a wink.

"It wasn't in the book draft we reviewed," remarked Margie.

"That's because it is not policy. It is personal. It has to be spoken, it can't be explained, it has to be heard," said Nick. "I have reviewed it with Chuck and Denise. They approve. You have to trust me."

"And I don't suppose either of you will share?" asked Margie, staring at her colleagues.

Chuck and Denise smiled.

"You know, you make it really hard to be your communications director. Especially when I don't know what's going to come out of your mouth. Like last night, for instance. I did not know I'd have to work on comments for," she said, holding up her hand and counting off fingers. "Your ruining an EXN news anchor's career, turning down a chance to be the Opposition nominee, and calling all the press the second generation of Russian Propaganda," remarked Margie, throwing her hands up in frustration.

"Margie, welcome to Denise's daily world. I'm sorry I'm not more organized and structured and following the tried-and-true candidate playbook or what people think it should be. But I don't work that way. Even if we did, I would just be going off script, anyway. It would piss all of you off at all the work you did, that I then ignored. Think of it this way, I am preventing you from spending a ton of work I would ignore," finished Nick, smiling.

"Gee thanks," said Margie sarcastically, softening it with a smile.

"Got that right," remarked Denise. "Screwed up reverse psychology and rationalization if I have ever heard one. Just roll with it Margie, think of it as job security. We follow behind Nick with the shovels."

Nick laughed. "That makes it sound like I'm incontinent or something."

"Or something, for sure," said Denise, shrugging in her little screen on Nick's laptop.

"OK, I can see this conversation is quickly going downhill. Anything else? I was up until 3 am last night and believe it or not, I am going to hit the gym and then take a nap before tonight's events."

"Try not to get anyone *we like* fired from EXN tonight," suggested Chuck.

"Hilarious. I didn't get her fired. She did it herself. Let's not imply anything different. I don't want anyone saying this is my fault. I'm serious on this one, folks. Like I was when Bergamo lied. What she got was exactly what they all need to get when they lie so outrageously. If we don't push back, they'll think they can continue to get away with it," ordered Nick.

"No more jokes about it then," said Chuck with a tone of finality. "But please don't go ballistic on every reporter who asks you about it, OK?"

"Alright, I will dial it down when I correct them. Fair enough."

"We'll see," said Chuck. "Go get some rest and we'll be watching tonight."

# Chapter 94

Nick walked into the Charlotte Arena and Convention Center and took the elevator up to the EXN broadcast booth. The producer and Adam greeted him. Adam was being mic'd up, while having his makeup and hair touched up.

"Welcome Nick. You ready for another eventful night?" asked Adam with his crooked smile. He was old school and had resisted the urge to have his teeth capped and bleached to the unnatural state so many TV personalities favored. An early habit of smoking and continued consumption of gallons of coffee gave them the typical yellowed appearance of a lifetime of use. Nick had found this was the easiest way to tell the real journalists from the fake ones.

"Can't top last night," declared Nick.

"Probably not. You were right. We have advanced copies of Governor Blackbird's and Carson's speeches. He is not making any attempt to win back Garcia's conservatives. He is relying on Carson to extend the olive branch," revealed Adam.

"It won't be enough. She is a conservative of convenience," stated Nick. "Like I said, the only way they get back in his court is if he promises to put Constitutional Judges on the bench. To make sure *Roe* does not get codified by Congress, to lock down the border and commit to significant budget cuts to many of the social safety nets. He's not going to commit to do any of those. Blackbird wants to be seen as the unifier, the great negotiator, the compromiser in chief. He wants to juxtapose his compromise and 'working together' views with Lexi's 'my way or the highway' progressive agenda. It ain't gonna fly."

"I am afraid I have to agree. We're not sure how best to make this race competitive," said Adam. "A non-competitive race is bad for our business."

"I know how," said Tommy, arriving to get mic'd up.

"No doubt," laughed Adam, as Nick answered instead.

"It really is simple. You focus on facts. And hypocrisy. You relentlessly point out their lies. On all sides. Keep forcing the people to open their eyes and understand a) they are lying, b) they have been doing this for a very long time and c) they are not lying to help you, but to help themselves get money, power, and control. If you talk long enough, and to enough people, your message will get through," finished Nick, counting the points on his fingers, as the tech started attaching his lapel mic as well. Tommy replied before Nick could continue.

"Then the question becomes, do they want to take the red pill or are they happy living their blue pill life of ignorance and leisure? Oblivious to the fact their life is a mirage, and they are being used to 'power' the corrupt elitest machine," said Tommy.

"*The Matrix* was many decades ago. Do you really think any of these millennials and GenZ'ers even know what you're talking about?" asked Nick.

"You obviously don't even watch your own advertising," responded Tommy, laughing.

"What are you talking about?"

Tommy looked down at his phone and handed it to Nick. On the screen was a scene, similar to the movie, but not scenes from it. The voice over continued, 'You have a choice in America. Today, many are leading a life of leisure. Blissfully going about their business, playing video games, trolling on social media, and living off unemployment.' Images of video games, texts shouting in all caps and young people using an EBT card to buy chips, dips and beer flashed on the screen.

These images were followed by more of businesses with signs in windows begging for workers. Offering ever increasing wages as the commentary resumed. 'Perfectly willing to depend on government assistance and living in mom and dad's basement. Uninterested in leading their own life and making their own decisions. This is the Progressive agenda. To keep you happy and dependent on everyone but yourself. Doing their bidding to continue this lifeless existence. This is the blue pill. Here is what they have in store for you, if you keep taking the blue pill of dependency.'

The images then showed the scene where all the humans were wearing Virtual Reality goggles, hooked up to the machine providing power while the mind-altering drugs made them believe they were living the life shown in their virtual realities.

'This is not life, it is not the utopia they make it out to be. It is slavery.' The images showed the Soviets and Chinese peasants working in the field. Sanding in long lines for bread in Russia. Newspaper headlines detailing famine and mass starvation in socialist and communist countries. Finally, lines of people exiting train cars at concentration camps. These images spun in and out of the frame as the voice over continued. 'They use you up and then discard you.' Scenes of bodies being bulldozed into trenches 'Don't fall for it. Don't take the blue pill. Wake up, disconnect from their virtual reality utopia. Take the red pill, start thinking for yourself and support Nick Turner for President.'

The voice over finished with a scene of someone taking the Red Pill, tearing off their VR goggles, pulling the cords loose from machines labeled 'Free Stuff', 'CRT', 'Social Media', 'Propaganda', 'Power', 'Control'.

They then look each way in a building with thousands of people standing as far as the eye can see in either direction. All wearing their VR goggles. Mindless drones. The person punches a hole in a wall, allowing sunlight into the dark room, until they have a hole big enough to exit.

The person walks out into a field of flowers, toward the sun, preparing to lead their own life free from the building behind them labeled Citizen Biological Renewable Energy Plant Number #12,450.

"Good ad. I'll have to let Denise and Margie know," said Nick, handing the phone back to Tommy.

"Good ad? It is fucking brilliant, and it is resonating. You have 150 million views and the *movie* has had a resurgence of downloads. Even though you are not using footage from it, the producers have got to love the additional revenue thanks to your use of similar concepts," remarked Tommy.

"Fantasy land is intoxicating. So is the promise of free stuff. Just ask all those Russian revolutionaries who ended up chopping trees in Siberia or the Jacobins who supported Robespierre when he marched Louis and Marie

Antoinette to the Guillotine. Robespierre's friends and supporters found out in a hurry his promises were empty, as he marched them to that same guillotine shortly thereafter," explained Nick.

"Professor, I love your history lessons. We get insights into the fact we have seen all this before. Everyone needs to know how this picture ends, preferably before it happens," laughed Tommy.

"We do? Which picture is that?" asked Billy, arriving in the booth. He was already mic'd up and perfectly groomed, as always.

"The fall of Rome, the sequel," said Tommy, "America."

"Oh," responded Billy, not getting the analogy at all. "We should probably take our seats."

"Just the four of us tonight?" asked Nick.

Adam laughed, and Billy gave him a strange look. Tommy tried to stifle a laugh, and it came out as a snort.

"Something I said?" smiled Nick, as they took their seats.

"Perhaps." said Adam, trailing off. "Rory will join us later to give his thoughts on the initial polling. Looks like Lexi is sitting in the high 50s, Blackbird is in the low 30s and you are hanging around 9-10%.

"Polls are useless," added Nick.

"OK, here we go gents," said a producer off camera.

"Welcome to our final night coverage of the Opposition Presidential Convention. Tonight, I am once again joined by...," droned Adam.

#

The night was much less eventful than the nomination night, and it seemed to be anti-climactic. Governor Carson looked tiny on stage as she gave her speech, accepting the Vice-Presidential Nomination. She talked about her efforts to overcome discrimination as a female politician in the south. Fighting for recognition and to be taken seriously. They had given her the unenviable task of trying to take the ticket further to the right.

She spoke of the importance of unity. Of the sanctity of life, the need to ensure *Roe* was not re-instituted in Congress. Instead replaced with sensible legislation *voted* on by the people in each of the states. The cheering in the arena was tepid at what should have been one of the largest applause lines for the Opposition.

She further tried to appeal to Garcia's supporters by admitting the need to shut the border down. Reducing the number of illegal immigrants and to ensure asylum seekers are truly fleeing political oppression. Rather than just coming to get better wages, only to send their earnings back to their native country. She finished her speech and got applause, but nothing like the enthusiasm Jim Jefferson had seen from his VP acceptance speech the week prior.

The guys in the booth all commented on the unfortunate scenario of having to be the first speech after last night. And being given the task of winning back the conservatives. They commented on the hope that Carson's speech would not be the limit to their efforts to woo back Garcia's backers. Nick's prediction to the group was we had seen the last mention of Garcia's conservative concerns. He was correct.

Governor Blackbird came out to accept the nomination and launched into one of the most wishy-washy centrist speeches of all time. There was nothing he was for, nothing he was against. He positioned himself to the world as the man to bring all sides together to negotiate.

To reach agreement on race relations, Middle East peace, social media monopolies, corporate profits, gay rights, universal healthcare, sensible gun control, and Chinese and Russian de-escalation. Blackbird hit all the major topics. In each case, he claimed he had the ability and experience to pull these groups together in a room and hammer out deals for mutual benefit.

At the end of his speech, his supporters applauded and cheered appropriately, but the crowd on the floor seemed diminished. In fact, many of the state delegations supporting Garcia had already left the convention and gone home a day early. Nick made the most telling comment of the evening, summing up Blackbird's speech.

"Adam, he is appearing to be the marriage counselor, handed a hard case. The two participants have already put each other in the hospital. Sawed cars in half and burned down the family house. His solution is to put them in a room together to talk it out?" said Nick as Tommy laughed off camera, while Adam and Billy grinned.

"It just isn't going to work. The time for reconciliation is long past. On so many of the topics he mentioned, the time for negotiation is past as well. Now is the time for action and consequence. Negotiation is going to be seen as yet another attempt to avoid the actual problem. It will be more concessions by the US or the West in exchange for promises from our enemies."

"They will gladly agree, take their plunder, and then promptly ignore their promises to change, as always. These regimes, and I see the Party as a regime, see negotiation as appeasement. They do not respect it and it has no impact on getting them to change their strategy. Nor to mitigate their actions. It is commendable on paper, but when your enemies have no desire to reach a new negotiated position, it is useless and, frankly, dangerously naïve," suggested Nick.

"You don't think this is effective?" asked Billy.

"Billy, and I am saying this as a commentator, asked an opinion and not as a Presidential Candidate trying to win votes. No, I don't think it is effective. Blackbird's job one is not to fix the country, it is to beat the Vice President. What he said tonight won't win back a key part of his constituency. Without these folks in his camp, he really has no chance. He thinks he is going to win moderates from Lexi to make up for this." Tommy, Adam, and Billy all nodded in agreement.

"He is not countering Lexi at all. She fully understands this is a war for hearts and minds. Negotiated positions and stances of moderation will win over no one. They only had to do two things tonight. They did neither. He did not extend the olive branch to Garcia and his people and promise to support things they care about. Second, he did not counter any of Lexi's proposed hard line changes with his own plans," pointed out Nick.

"That pretty much sums it up, Senator. Blackbird has a lot of work to do, but it is not hopeless. He has a couple months to build up momentum and attack the VP's positions," remarked Tommy.

"At least we now have our official candidates. Senator, thank you for joining us in the booth for both conventions. It has been excellent having your opinions from the point of view of an actual candidate. Good luck with your own campaign and we'll be watching," finished Adam.

They closed out the coverage as the Opposition delegates continued to celebrate and cheer to blaring music. As the cameras turned off, the guys took off their microphones and shook hands, heading out. Nick walked out with Tommy.

"That certainly was interesting. I think it is the first time a presidential candidate has been present to critique the competition's speeches and convention," offered Tommy.

"It is an unorthodox campaign cycle for sure," agreed Nick as they made their way out to the private entrance where cars were waiting to take them to their hotels. Nick and Tommy shared a car, since they were both staying at the same hotel. As the car pulled away, Tommy turned to Nick.

"It certainly worked for us. We had the biggest convention audiences ever, including the networks on the last two days of both conventions. I think it helped you as well. Introducing you to many people who may have only heard your name because of the filibuster vote or New York."

"I appreciate the opportunity."

"Promise me you'll talk to Garcia. Please. Get him to support you," begged Tommy.

"Tommy, your true colors are showing," said Nick with a smile.

"Hey, I am an opinion guy. I have made no apologies for my disdain for the current administration, and Lexi is not just a continuation. She is an accelerated version on steroids. I'm not going to sit by idly and watch everything we have built get torn down by the progressives," threatened Tommy.

"Don't let the FBI hear you say that. Or the FCC."

"At some point, we all have to take some risk to change things," shrugged Tommy.

"I agree, and I'll do my part. The Garcia thing will have to wait. When the time is right and if I think conservatives will accept my stance on certain issues, we'll talk. If not, they can stay home or vote for Blackbird. But I'm not going to moderate my stance just to win votes. That is not what I am about. Ultimately, it is not about you or me, it is about them."

Tommy looked at him, thinking. Nick continued.

"We may be too far gone, with the free stuff, the promise of more. They may willingly choose to keep taking the blue pill and lead the life of dependency *and* obedience, rather than the much harder road of independence and free will. America is not easy. You have to fight for it, every day. If you don't, there are always forces tearing at it from the edges. All I can do, all we can do, is to warn them about the hazards. They decide whether to succumb and give in or whether to keep fighting for freedom to choose," stated Nick.

Tommy didn't reply as they pulled into the hotel.

"Drink?" Tommy.

"Not tonight. I have an early flight tomorrow. I am sure Margie has me booked on your show soon. My book is about to publish, so I will want to come on to discuss its content."

"Anytime. You are always welcome."

"Thanks Tommy, I mean it. I know it was you. This has your not so subtle fingerprints all over it. Freddie would have called me directly to ask if I would accept, before doing this. Nice try," said Nick, gripping his hand tighter.

"I gotta do what I think is right. We almost pulled it off. You should have taken Kacey Carson's call. There were others, not just me and Freddie. Remember our conversations in my office? That started it. And many others you have converted these last seven months. From both parties. All working behind the scenes. They are as disappointed *and* worried as I am."

"It would never have worked. I need to win or lose as an independent."

"Independent is a good word to describe you. Maybe you should start the Independence Party," suggested Tommy.

"I think George Wallace beat me to it," laughed Nick. "Don't think I want to name my party after a right-wing racist."

"Good point. Glad one of us is a historian," agreed Tommy, with a startled laugh.

"We'll see how well I do. A party name is the last of my worries. First, I need to get a few votes and see if anyone wants to follow my ideas."

"Oh, I think you'll be surprised. You almost won the Opposition nomination without even trying. That says something, right?" asked Tommy.

"Considering who I was up against, does it?" asked Nick, turning to look at Tommy as he headed to the elevator. Being the compromise nominee among a bunch of poor options is not a wholehearted endorsement.

Tommy merely shrugged and laughed.

"Goodnight, Senator," he said as Nick entered the elevator.

# The End

# Our Choice: Freedom or Obedience

# Connect with the Author

- Author website: www.ejriceauthor.com
- Facebook author site: https://www.facebook.com/ejriceauthor
- Substack Blog site: https://ejriceauthor.substack.com/
- Twitter/X account: https://twitter.com/EJRiceauthor
- Instagram: https://www.instagram.com/ericriceauthor.
- TikTok: https://www.tiktok.com/eric.rice.author